PRAISE FOR THE INCOMPARABLE BESTSELLERS OF

JUDITH M^cNAUGHT

NIGHT WHISPERS

"Never miss a McNaught! *Night Whispers* heads like the *Titanic* toward its iceberg of a climax—with shocking revelations. . . . Judith McNaught has written her most stunning work of fiction to date. Sexy, smart, and page-turning, this is a must-read."

—Barnesandnoble.com

"Fans of romantic suspense will shout that the great Judith McNaught has written something wonderful with her perfect novel, *Night Whispers*. . . . A tender triumph that will leave readers awed. . . . The characters are warm and charming, and will long be remembered."

—BookBrowser.com

"Fiery passion, taut suspense, and unforgettable characters. . . . McNaught has truly outdone herself with *Night Whispers*. It is a testimony to her impressive talent. . . . Equal parts romance and suspense, this is a must-read for mystery and romance fans alike. . . . You'll find yourself delighted with this excellent book."

—*Rendezvous*

REMEMBER WHEN

"[A] clever take on the ultra-affluent, ultra-cynical social scene of McNaught's hometown of Houston. . . . McNaught has a lot of fun with a marriage of convenience that turns out to be anything but."

—*Chicago Tribune*

"Excellent. . . . [A] charming and sparkling tale."

—*Romantic Times*

"Romantic, witty, and entertaining. . . ."

—*San Antonio Express-News*

UNTIL YOU

"Delicious. . . . A perfectly wonderful story, with lively, funny, well-rounded characters. *Until You* is a laughing, loving book, a page-turner and a delight."

—*The Advocate* (Baton Rouge, LA)

"Brilliantly done and completely entertaining . . . a surefire hit."

—*Ocala Star-Banner* (FL)

WHITNEY, MY LOVE

"The ultimate love story, one you can dream about forever."

—*Romantic Times*

"A wonderful love story . . . fast-paced and exciting . . . great dialogue!"

—Jude Deveraux, *New York Times* bestselling author of *The Summerhouse*

Books by Judith McNaught

Whitney, My Love
Almost Heaven
Double Standards
A Kingdom of Dreams
Once and Always
Paradise
Perfect
Something Wonderful
Tender Triumph
Until You
Remember When
Night Whispers
Water's Edge

Published by POCKET BOOKS

For orders other than by individual consumers, Pocket Books grants a discount on the purchase of **10 or more** copies of single titles for special markets or premium use. For further details, please write to the Vice President of Special Markets, Pocket Books, 1230 Avenue of the Americas, 9th Floor, New York, NY 10020-1586.

For information on how individual consumers can place orders, please write to Mail Order Department, Simon & Schuster, Inc., 100 Front Street, Riverside, NJ 08075.

Judith McNaught

Paradise

Tender Triumph

POCKET BOOKS

New York London Toronto Sydney Singapore

This book is a work of fiction. Names, characters, places and incidents are products of the author's imagination or are used fictitiously. Any resemblance to actual events or locales or persons living or dead is entirely coincidental.

Grateful acknowledgment is made for permission to reprint the following:

"Nobody Loves Me Like You Do" by Pamela Phillips and James P. Dunne. Copyright © 1983, 1984 by Ensign Music Corporation. All rights reserved. Used by permission of The Famous Music Publishing Companies.

"Long Ago and Far Away" by Ira Gershwin and Jerome Kern. Copyright © 1944 by Polygram International Publishing, Inc. Copyright Renewed. All rights reserved. Used by permission of Polygram International Publishing, Inc.

"What Are You Doing the Rest of Your Life" by Michael Legrand, Alan Bergman and Marilyn Bergman. Copyright © 1969 by EMI UNART CATALOG INC. All rights reserved. International Copyright Secured. Used by permission of CCP/Belwin, Inc.

An *Original* Publication of POCKET BOOKS

POCKET BOOKS, a division of Simon & Schuster, Inc.
1230 Avenue of the Americas, New York, NY 10020

Paradise copyright © 1991 by Eagle Syndication, Inc.
Tender Triumph copyright © 1983 by Judith McNaught

McNaught, Judith.
  Paradise ; Tender triumph / Judith McNaught.
    p. cm.
  ISBN 0-7434-2833-1
    I. Consolidation and merger of corporations—Fiction. 2. Department stores—Fiction. 3. Women executives—Fiction. 4. Indiana—Fiction. I. Title: Paradise ; Tender triumph. II. McNaught, Judith. Tender triumph. III. Title: Tender triumph. IV. Title.

PS3563.C3884 P37 2001
813'.54—dc21   2001034030

First Pocket Books trade paperback printing August 2001

10 9 8 7 6 5 4 3 2 I

POCKET and colophon are registered trademarks of Simon & Schuster, Inc.

Cover art by Lisa Litwack; photo credits: Index Stock Imagery, Tony Stone Images

Printed in the U.S.A.

These titles were previously published individually by Pocket Books.

Contents

Paradise

Anyone who is closely involved with me when I'm working on a novel could tell you that it requires certain things to maintain any sort of relationship—including incredible patience, extraordinary tolerance, and the ability to believe I'm actually working when I'm staring off into space.

This novel is dedicated to my family and friends who possess those traits in abundance and who have enriched my life beyond measure:

To my son, Clayton, and my daughter, Whitney, whose pride in me has been a tremendous source of pleasure. And relief.

And to those very special people who offered their friendship and then had to bear more than their fair share of the burden of that friendship—especially Phyllis and Richard Ashley, Debbie and Craig Kiefer, Kathy and Lloyd Stansberry, and Cathy and Paul Waldner. I couldn't ask for a better "cheering section" than all of you.

Acknowledgments

To Robert Hyland, for a lifetime of enormous favors.

To attorney Lloyd Stansberry, for providing me with countless answers on the legal technicalities involved in this novel.

To the extraordinary department store executives across the nation who shared their time and expertise with me, and without whose assistance this novel could never have been written.

With her scrapbook opened beside her on her canopied bed, Meredith Bancroft carefully cut out the picture from the *Chicago Tribune*. The caption read *Children of Chicago socialites, dressed as elves, participate in charity Christmas pageant at Oakland Memorial Hospital*, then it listed their names. Beneath the caption was a large picture of the "elves"—five boys and five girls, including Meredith—who were handing out presents to the kids in the children's ward. Standing off to the left, supervising the proceedings, was a handsome young man of eighteen, whom the caption referred to as "Parker Reynolds III, son of Mr. and Mrs. Parker Reynolds of Kenilworth."

Impartially, Meredith compared herself to the other girls in the elf costumes, wondering how they could manage to look leggy and curvy while she looked . . . "Dumpy!" she pronounced with a pained grimace. "I look like a troll, not an elf!"

It did not seem at all fair that the other girls who were fourteen, just a few small weeks older than she was, should look so wonderful while she looked like a flat-chested troll with braces. Her gaze shifted to her picture and she regretted again the streak of vanity that had caused her to take off her glasses for the photograph; without them she had a tendency to squint—just like she was doing in that awful picture. "Contact lenses would definitely help," she concluded. Her gaze switched to Parker's picture, and a dreamy smile drifted across her face as she clasped the newspaper clipping to what would have been her breasts if she *had* breasts, which she didn't. Not yet. At this rate, not ever.

The door to her bedroom opened and Meredith hastily yanked the picture from her chest as the stout, sixty-year-old housekeeper came in to take her dinner tray away. "You didn't eat your dessert," Mrs. Ellis chided.

"I'm fat, Mrs. Ellis," Meredith said. To prove it, she scrambled off the antique bed and marched over to the mirror above her dressing table. "Look at me," she said, pointing an accusing finger at her reflection. "I have no waistline!"

"You have some baby fat there, that's all."

"I don't have hips either. I look like a walking two-by-four. No wonder I have no friends—"

Mrs. Ellis, who'd worked for the Bancrofts for less than a year, looked amazed. "You have no friends? Why not?"

Desperately in need of someone to confide in, Meredith said, "I've only pretended that everything is fine at school. The truth is, it's terrible. I'm a . . . a complete misfit. I've always been a misfit."

"Well, I never! There must be something wrong with the children in your school. . . ."

"It isn't them, it's *me*, but I'm going to change," Meredith announced. "I've gone on a diet, and I want to do something with my hair. It's awful."

"It's *not* awful!" Mrs. Ellis argued, looking at Meredith's shoulder-length pale blond hair and then her turquoise eyes. "You have striking eyes and very nice hair. Nice and thick and—"

"Colorless."

"Blond."

Meredith stared stubbornly at the mirror, her mind magnifying the flaws that existed. "I'm almost five feet seven inches tall. It's a lucky thing I finally stopped growing before I became a giant! But I'm not hopeless, I realized that on Saturday."

Mrs. Ellis's brows drew together in confusion. "What happened on Saturday to change your mind about yourself?"

"Nothing earth-shattering," Meredith said. *Something earth-shattering*, she thought. *Parker smiled at me at the Christmas pageant. He brought me a Coke without being asked. He told me to be sure and save a dance for him Saturday at the Eppingham party.* Seventy-five years before, Parker's family had founded the large Chicago bank where Bancroft & Company's funds were deposited, and the friendship between the Bancrofts and Reynoldses had endured for generations. "Everything is going to change now, not just the way I look," Meredith continued happily as she turned away from the mirror. "I'm going to have a friend too! There's a new girl at school, and *she* doesn't know that no one else likes me. She's smart, like I am, and she called me tonight to ask me a homework question. She *called* me, and we talked about all sorts of things."

"I did notice you never brought friends home from school," Mrs. Ellis said, wringing her hands in nervous dismay, "but I thought it was because you lived so far away."

"No, it isn't that," Meredith said, flopping down onto the bed and staring self-consciously at her serviceable slippers that looked just like small replicas of the ones her father wore. Despite their wealth, Meredith's father

had the liveliest respect for money; all of her clothing was of excellent quality and was purchased only when necessary, always with a stern eye toward
durability. "I don't fit in, you see."

"When I was a girl," Mrs. Ellis said with a sudden look of comprehension, "we were always a little leery of children who got good grades."

"It's not just that," Meredith said wryly. "It's something besides the way
I look and the grades I get that makes me a misfit. It's—all this," she said,
and made a sweeping gesture that encompassed the large, rather austere
room with its antique furniture, a room whose character resembled all the
other forty-five rooms in the Bancroft estate. "Everyone thinks I'm completely weird because Father insists that Fenwick drive me to school."

"What's wrong with that, may I ask?"

"The other children walk or ride the school bus."

"So?"

"So they do *not* arrive in a chauffeur-driven Rolls!" Almost wistfully,
Meredith added, "Their fathers are plumbers and accountants. One of
them works for us at the store."

Unable to argue with the logic of that, and unwilling to admit it was
true, Mrs. Ellis said, "But this new girl in school—she doesn't find it odd
that Fenwick drives you?"

"No," Meredith said with a guilty chuckle that made her eyes glow with
sudden liveliness behind her glasses, "because she thinks Fenwick *is* my
father! I told her my father works for some rich people who own a big
store."

"You didn't!"

"Yes, I did, and I—I'm not sorry. I should have spread that around
school years ago, only I didn't want to lie."

"But now you don't mind lying?" Mrs. Ellis said with a censorious look.

"It *isn't* a lie, not entirely," Meredith said in an imploring voice. "Father
explained it to me a long time ago. You see, Bancroft & Company is a corporation, and a corporation is actually owned by the stockholders. So you
see, as president of Bancroft & Company, Father is—technically—
employed by the stockholders. Do you understand?"

"Probably not," she said flatly. "Who owns the stock?"

Meredith sent her a guilty look. "We do, mostly."

Mrs. Ellis found the whole notion of the operation of Bancroft &
Company, a famous downtown Chicago department store, absolutely baffling, but Meredith frequently displayed an uncanny understanding of the
business. Although, Mrs. Ellis thought with helpless ire at Meredith's
father, it wasn't so uncanny—not when the man had no interest in his

daughter *except* when he was lecturing her about that store. In fact, Mrs. Ellis thought Philip Bancroft was probably to blame for his daughter's inability to fit in with the other girls her age. He treated his daughter like an adult, and he insisted that she speak and act like one at all times. On the rare occasions when he entertained friends, Meredith even acted as his hostess. As a result, Meredith was very much at ease with adults and obviously at a complete loss with her peers.

"You're right about one thing though," Meredith said. "I can't go on tricking Lisa Pontini about Fenwick being my father. I just thought that if she had a chance to know me first, it might not matter when I tell her Fenwick is actually our chauffeur. The only reason she hasn't found out already is that she doesn't know anyone else in our class, and she always has to go straight home after school. She has seven brothers and sisters, and she has to help out at home."

Mrs. Ellis reached out and awkwardly patted Meredith's arm, trying to think of something encouraging to say. "Things always look brighter in the morning," she announced, resorting, as she often did, to one of the cozy clichés she herself found so comforting. She picked up the dinner tray, then paused in the doorway, struck with another inspiring platitude. "And remember this," she instructed Meredith in the rising tones of one who is about to impart a very satisfying thought, "every *dog* has its *day!*"

Meredith didn't know whether to laugh or cry. "Thank you, Mrs. Ellis," she said, "that is *very* encouraging." In mortified silence she watched the door close behind the housekeeper, then she slowly picked up the scrapbook. When the *Tribune* clipping had been safely taped to the page, she stared at it for a long moment, then reached out and lightly touched Parker's smiling mouth. The thought of actually dancing with him made her shiver with a mixture of terror and anticipation. This was Thursday, and the Eppingham dance was the day after tomorrow. It seemed like years to wait.

Sighing, she flipped backward through the pages of the big scrapbook. At the front were some very old clippings, yellowed now with age, the pictures faded. The scrapbook had originally belonged to her mother, Caroline, and it contained the only tangible proof in the house that Caroline Edwards Bancroft had ever existed. Everything else connected with her had been removed at Philip Bancroft's instructions.

Caroline Edwards had been an actress—not an especially good one, according to her reviews—but an unquestionably glamorous one. Meredith studied the faded pictures, but she didn't read what the columnists had written because she knew every word by heart. She knew that Cary Grant had escorted her mother to the Academy Awards in 1955, and that David Niven had said she was the most beautiful woman he'd ever seen, and that David Selznick had wanted her in one of his pictures. She knew that her mother had roles in three Broadway musicals and that the critics had panned her acting but praised her shapely legs. The gossip columnists had hinted at serious romances between Caroline and nearly all her leading men. There were clippings of her, draped in furs, attending a party in Rome; wrapped in a strapless black evening gown, playing roulette in Monte Carlo. In one photograph she was clad in a skimpy bikini on the beach in Monaco, in another, skiing in Gstaad with a Swiss Olympic Gold Medalist. It was obvious to Meredith that wherever she went, Caroline had been surrounded by handsome men.

The last clipping her mother had saved was dated six months after the one in Gstaad. She was wearing a magnificent white wedding gown—laughing and running down the cathedral steps on Philip Bancroft's arm beneath a shower of rice. The society columnists had outdone themselves with extravagant descriptions of the wedding. The reception at the Palmer House Hotel had been closed to the press, but the columnists faithfully reported all the famous guests who were present, from the Vanderbilts and Whitneys, to a Supreme Court justice and four U.S. senators.

The marriage lasted two years—long enough for Caroline to get pregnant, have her baby, have a sleazy affair with a horse trainer, and then go running off to Europe with a phony Italian prince who'd been a guest in this very house. Beyond that, Meredith knew little, except that her mother had never bothered to send her so much as a note or a birthday card. Meredith's father, who placed great emphasis on dignity and old-fashioned values, said her mother was a self-centered slut without the slightest conception of marital fidelity or maternal responsibility. When Meredith was a year old, he had filed for divorce and for custody of Meredith, fully prepared to exert all the Bancroft family's considerable political and social influence to assure that he won his suit. In the end he hadn't needed to resort to that. According to what he'd told Meredith, her mother hadn't bothered to wait around for the court hearing, let alone try to oppose him.

Once he was granted custody of Meredith, her father had set out to ensure that she would never follow her mother's example. Instead, he was determined that Meredith would take her place in a long line of dignified Bancroft women who'd led exemplary lives dedicated to charitable good works that befitted their station, and to which not a single breath of scandal had ever been attached.

When it came time for her to start school, Philip had discovered to his annoyance that standards of conduct were relaxing, even among his own social class. Many of his acquaintances were taking a more liberal view of child behavior and sending their children to "progressive" schools like Bently and Ridgeview. When he inspected these schools, he heard phrases like "unstructured classes" and "self-expression." Progressive education sounded undisciplined to him; it foretold lower standards of education and deportment. After rejecting both those schools, he took Meredith with him to see St. Stephen's—a private Catholic school run by the Benedictine nuns, the same school his aunt and his mother had attended.

Her father had approved of all he saw the day they visited St. Stephen's: Thirty-four first-grade girls in demure gray-and-blue-plaid jumpers, and ten boys in white shirts and blue ties, had come instantly and respectfully to their feet when the nun had shown him the classroom. Forty-four young voices had chorused, *"Good morning, Sister."* Furthermore, St. Stephen's still taught academics in the good old-fashioned way—unlike Bently, where he'd seen some children finger-painting while the other students, who *chose* to learn, worked on math. As an added benefit, Meredith would receive strict moral training here as well.

Her father was not oblivious to the fact that the neighborhood surrounding St. Stephen's had deteriorated, but he was obsessed with the idea that Meredith be raised in the same manner as the other upstanding, upright Bancroft women who had attended St. Stephen's for three generations. He solved the matter of the neighborhood by having the family chauffeur drive Meredith to and from school.

The one thing he didn't realize was that the girls and boys who attended St. Stephen's were not the virtuous little beings they'd seemed to be that day. They were ordinary kids from lower-middle-class families and even some poor families; they played together and walked to school together, and they shared a common suspicion of anyone from an entirely different and far more prosperous background.

Meredith hadn't known about that when she arrived at St. Stephen's to start first grade. Clad in her neat gray-and-blue-plaid uniform jumper and carrying her new lunch pail, she'd quaked with the nervous excitement of any six-year-old confronting a class filled with strangers, but she'd felt little actual fear. After spending her whole life in relative loneliness, with only her father and the servants as companions, she was happily anticipating the prospect of finally having friends her own age.

The first day at school went well enough, but it took a sudden turn for the worse when classes were dismissed and the students poured out the school doors into the playground and parking lot. Fenwick had been waiting in the playground, standing beside the Rolls in his black chauffeur's uniform. The older children had stopped and stared—and then identified her as being rich, ergo "different."

That alone was enough to make them wary and distant, but by the end of the week, they'd also discovered other things about "the rich girl" that set her apart: For one thing, Meredith Bancroft spoke more like an adult than a child; in addition, she didn't know how to play any of the games they played at recess, and when she did play them, her unfamiliarity made her seem clumsy. Worst of all, within days, she was teacher's pet because she was smart.

Within a month, Meredith had been judged by all her peers and branded as an outsider, an alien being from another world, to be ostracized by all. Perhaps if she'd been pretty enough to inspire admiration, it would have helped in time, but she wasn't. When she was nine she arrived at school wearing glasses. At twelve she had braces; at thirteen, she was the tallest girl in her class.

A week ago, years after Meredith had despaired of ever having a real friend, everything had changed. Lisa Pontini had enrolled in the eighth grade at St. Stephen's. An inch taller than Meredith, Lisa moved like a model and answered complicated algebra questions like a bored scholar. At noon that same day, Meredith had been sitting on a low stone wall on the perimeter of the school grounds, eating her lunch, exactly as she did every day, with a book open in her lap. Originally, she'd started bringing a book to read because it dulled the feeling of being isolated and conspicuous. By fifth grade she'd become an avid reader.

She'd been about to turn a page when a pair of scuffed oxfords entered her line of vision, and there was Lisa Pontini, looking curiously at her. With Lisa's vivid coloring and mass of auburn hair, she was Meredith's complete opposite; moreover, there was an indefinable air of daring confidence about Lisa that gave her what *Seventeen* magazine called panache. Instead of wearing her gray school sweater with its school emblem demurely over her shoulders as Meredith did, Lisa had tied the sleeves in a loose knot over her breasts.

"God, what a dump!" Lisa announced, sitting down beside Meredith and looking around at the school grounds. "I've never seen so many short boys in my life. They must put something in the drinking fountains here that stunts their growth! What's your average?"

Grades at St. Stephen's were expressed in percentiles carried out to a precise decimal point. "It's 97.8," Meredith said, a little dazed by Lisa's rapid remarks and unexpected sociability.

"Mine's 98.1," Lisa countered, and Meredith noticed that Lisa's ears were pierced. Earrings and lipstick were forbidden on the school grounds.

While Meredith was noting all that, Lisa was looking her over too. With a puzzled smile, she demanded bluntly, "Are you a loner by choice or are you some sort of outcast?"

"I never thought about it," Meredith lied.

"How long do you have to wear those braces?"

"Another year," Meredith said, deciding she didn't like Lisa Pontini at all. She closed her book and stood up, glad the bell was about to ring.

That afternoon, as was the custom on the last Friday of every month, the students lined up in church to confess their sins to St. Stephen's priests. Feeling, as always, like a disgraceful sinner, Meredith knelt in the confessional, and told her misdemeanors to Father Vickers, including such sins as disliking Sister Mary Lawrence and spending too much time thinking about her appearance. Finished, she held the door open for the next person, then she knelt in a pew and said her assigned prayers of penance.

Since students were allowed to leave for the day after that, Meredith went outside to wait for Fenwick. A few minutes later, Lisa walked down the church steps, putting on her jacket. Still flinching from Lisa's comments about her being a loner and having to wear braces, Meredith watched warily as the other girl looked around and then sauntered over to her.

"Would you believe," Lisa announced, "Vickers told me to say a whole rosary tonight for penance for a little necking? I'd hate to think what penance he hands out for French kissing!" she added with an impudent grin, sitting down on the ledge beside Meredith.

Meredith hadn't known that one's nationality determined the way a person kissed, but she assumed from Lisa's remark that however the French did it, the priests definitely didn't want St. Stephen's students doing it. Trying to look worldly, she said, "For kissing that way, Father Vickers makes you clean the church."

Lisa giggled, studying Meredith with curiosity. "Does your boyfriend wear braces too?"

Meredith thought of Parker and shook her head.

"That's good," Lisa said with an infectious grin. "I always wondered how two people with braces could possibly kiss and not get stuck together. My boyfriend's name is Mario Campano. He's tall, dark, and handsome. What's your boyfriend's name? What's he like?"

Meredith glanced at the street, hoping Fenwick wouldn't remember that school got out early today. Although she was uneasy with the topic of conversation, Lisa Pontini fascinated her, and Meredith sensed that for some reason the other girl truly wanted to be friends. "He's eighteen and he looks," Meredith said honestly, "like Robert Redford. His name is Parker."

"What's his first name?"

"That is his first name. His last name is Reynolds."

"Parker Reynolds," Lisa repeated, wrinkling her nose. "Sounds like a society snob. Is he good at it?"

"At what?"

"Kissing, of course."

"Oh. Well—yes. Absolutely fantastic."

Lisa sent her a mocking look. "He's never kissed you. Your face turns pink when you lie."

Meredith stood up abruptly. "Now, look," she began angrily. "I didn't ask you to come over here, and I—"

"Hey, don't get into a sweat over it. Kissing isn't all that wonderful. I mean, the first time Mario kissed me, it was the most embarrassing moment of my entire life."

Meredith's anger evaporated now that Lisa was about to confess something about herself, and she sat back down. "It was embarrassing because he kissed you?"

"No, it was embarrassing because I leaned against the front door when he did it, and my shoulder hit the doorbell. My father pulled the door open, and I went crashing backwards into his arms with Mario still holding on to me for dear life. It took *ages* to untangle all three of us on the floor."

Meredith's shriek of laughter was abruptly terminated by the sight of the Rolls turning the corner. "There's my—my ride," she hedged, sobering.

Lisa glanced sideways and gaped. "Jesus, is that a Rolls?"

Nodding uncomfortably, Meredith said with a shrug as she picked up her books, "I live a long way from here, and my father doesn't want me to take the bus."

"Your dad's a chauffeur, huh?" Lisa said, walking with Meredith toward the car. "It must be great to be able to ride around in a car like that, pretending you're rich." Without waiting for Meredith to answer, she said, "My dad's a pipe fitter. His union's on strike right now, so we moved here where the rent's even cheaper. You know how that goes."

Meredith had no idea "how that goes" from any personal experience, but she knew from her father's angry tirades what effect unions and strikes had on business owners like the Bancrofts. Even so, she nodded in sympathetic reaction to Lisa's grim sigh. "It must be tough," she said, and then impulsively added, "Do you want a ride home?"

"Do I! No, wait—can I do it next week? I've got seven brothers and sisters, and my ma will have twenty chores for me to do. I'd rather hang around here a little while, and then get home at the normal time."

That had been a week ago, and the tentative friendship that began that day had blossomed and grown, nourished by more exchanged confidences and laughing admissions. Now, as Meredith sat gazing at Parker's picture in the scrapbook and thinking about the dance Saturday night, she decided to ask Lisa for advice at school tomorrow. Lisa knew a lot about hairstyles and things. Perhaps she could suggest something that would make Meredith more attractive to Parker.

She followed through with that plan as they sat outside, eating their lunch the next day. "What do you think?" she asked Lisa. "Other than having plastic surgery, is there anything I could do to myself that would really make a difference by tomorrow night—anything at all that would make Parker see me as older and pretty?"

Before replying, Lisa subjected her to a long, thorough scrutiny. "Those glasses and braces aren't exactly inspirations to passion, you know," she joked. "Take off your glasses and stand up."

Meredith complied, then waited in amused chagrin as Lisa strolled around her, looking her over. "You really go out of your way to look plain," Lisa concluded. "You have great eyes and hair. If you'd use a little makeup, take off your glasses, and do something different with your hair, ol' Parker might just give you a second look tomorrow night."

"Do you really think he would?" Meredith asked, her heart in her eyes as she thought of him.

"I said he *might*." Lisa corrected Meredith with ruthless honesty. "He's an older man, so your age is a drawback. What answer did you get for that last problem on the math test this morning?"

In the week they'd been friends, Meredith had become accustomed to Lisa's rapid-fire changes of topic. It was as if she were too bright to concentrate on only one topic at a time. Meredith told her the answer she'd gotten, and Lisa said, "That's the same one I got. With two brains like ours," she teased, "it's obvious that's the right answer. Did you know everyone in this dumpy school thinks that Rolls belongs to your dad?"

"I never told them it didn't," Meredith said truthfully.

Lisa bit into her apple and nodded. "Why should you? If they're so dumb they think a rich kid would go to school here, I'd probably let them think the same thing."

That afternoon after school, Lisa was again willing to have Meredith's "father" drive her home as Fenwick had reluctantly agreed to do all week. When the Rolls pulled up in front of the brown brick bungalow where the

Pontinis lived, Meredith took in the usual tangle of kids and toys in the front yard. Lisa's mother was standing on the front porch, wrapped in her ever-present apron. "Lisa," she called, her voice heavily accented with Italian, "Mario's on the phone. He wants to talk to you. Hiya, Meredith," she added with a wave. "You stay for supper soon. You stay the night too, so your papa don't have to drive out here late to bring you home."

"Thank you, Mrs. Pontini," Meredith called, waving back from the car. "I will." It was the way Meredith had always dreamed it would be—having a friend to confide in, being invited to stay overnight, and she was euphoric.

Lisa shut the car door and leaned in the window.

"Your mother said Mario is on the phone," Meredith reminded her.

"It's good to keep a guy waiting," Lisa said, "it keeps him guessing. Now, don't forget to call me Sunday and tell me everything that happens with Parker tomorrow night. I wish I could do your hair before you leave for the dance."

"I wish you could too," Meredith said, although she knew she'd never be able to prevent Lisa from discovering that Fenwick wasn't her father if she came to the house. Each day she'd intended to confess the truth, and each day she stalled, telling herself that the longer Lisa knew the real her, the less difference it would make to Lisa whether Meredith's father was rich or poor. Wistfully, she continued, "If you came over tomorrow, you could spend the night. While I was at the dance, you could do homework, then when I got back home, I could tell you how it went."

"But I can't. I have a date with Mario tomorrow night," Lisa remarked unnecessarily. Meredith had been stunned that Lisa's parents permitted her to go out with boys at fourteen, but Lisa had only laughed and said Mario wouldn't dare get out of line because he knew her father and uncles would come after him if he did. Shoving away from the car, Lisa said, "Just remember what I told you, okay? Flirt with Parker and look into his eyes. And wear your hair up, so you look more sophisticated."

All the way home, Meredith tried to imagine actually flirting with Parker. His birthday was the day after tomorrow—she'd memorized that fact a year ago, when she first realized she was falling in love with him. Last week she'd spent an hour in the drugstore looking for the right card to give him tomorrow night, but the cards that said what she *really* felt would have been much, much too gushy. Naive though she was, she figured Parker wouldn't appreciate a card that said on the front "To my one and only love . . ." So she'd regretfully had to settle for one that said "Happy Birthday to a Special Friend."

Leaning her head back, Meredith closed her eyes, smiling dreamily as she pictured herself looking like a gorgeous model, saying witty, clever things while Parker hung on to her every word.

With a sinking heart Meredith stared at herself in the mirror while Mrs. Ellis stood back, nodding approval. When Mrs. Ellis and she had gone shopping last week, the velvet dress had seemed to be a glowing topaz. Tonight it looked like metallic brown velvet, and her shoes that had been dyed to match had a matronly look with their short, stocky heels. Mrs. Ellis's taste ran to the matronly, Meredith knew; moreover, she and Meredith had both been under her father's strictures to choose a dress that was "suitable for a young girl of Meredith's age and upbringing." They'd brought three dresses home for Meredith's father's approval, and this was the only one that he hadn't felt was entirely too "bare" or too "flimsy."

The only thing about her appearance that didn't fill Meredith with dismay was her hair. Normally she wore her straight shoulder-length hair parted on the side with one barrette above the ear, but Lisa's remarks had convinced her she did need a new, more sophisticated style. Tonight she'd persuaded Mrs. Ellis to do it up in a cluster of thick curls at the crown with little tendrils at the ears, and Meredith thought it looked very nice.

"Meredith," her father said, walking into her room, leafing through a handful of opera tickets, "Park Reynolds needed two extra tickets to *Rigoletto*, and I told him he could use ours. Would you give these to young Parker tonight, when you—" He looked up, his eyes riveting on her, and scowled. "What have you done to your hair?" he snapped.

"I thought I'd wear it up tonight."

"I prefer your hair the way you usually wear it, Meredith." Bending a look of dark displeasure on Mrs. Ellis, he said, "When you came into my employ, madam, I thought we agreed that in addition to your supervisory duties as housekeeper, you would also advise my daughter on feminine matters when necessary. Is that hairdo your idea of—"

"I specifically asked Mrs. Ellis to help me do my hair this way, Father," Meredith intervened as Mrs. Ellis turned pale and began to tremble.

"In that case, you should have asked her advice," Philip said, "instead of *telling* her what you wanted her to do."

"Yes, of course," Meredith said. She hated to disappoint her father or annoy him. He made her feel as if she were singularly responsible for the success or failure of his entire day or night if she spoiled his mood.

"Well, no harm done," he conceded, seeing that Meredith was properly contrite. "Mrs. Ellis can fix up your hair before you leave. I brought you something, my dear. A necklace," he added, withdrawing a flat, dark green velvet case from his pocket. "You may wear it tonight—it will look very well with your gown." Meredith waited while he fidgeted with the clasp, imagining a gold locket perhaps or—"These are your grandmother Bancroft's pearls," he announced, and it took an effort for her to hide her dismay while he withdrew the long strand of fat pearls. "Turn around and I'll fasten them."

Twenty minutes later, Meredith stood before the mirror, trying valiantly to convince herself she looked nice. Her hair was restyled in the same straight, girlish fashion she always wore, but the pearls were the last straw. Her grandmother had worn them nearly every day of her life; she'd *died* wearing them, and now they felt like leaden weights against Meredith's nonexistent bosom. "Excuse me, miss." The family butler's voice outside her door brought her whirling around. "There's a Miss Pontini downstairs who claims to be a school friend of yours."

Trapped, Meredith sank down on the side of her bed, thinking madly for some way out of this, but there was none and she knew it. "Would you bring her here, please."

A minute later Lisa walked in and looked around the room as if she'd suddenly found herself on a strange planet. "I tried to call," she said, "but your telephone was busy for an hour, so I decided to take a chance and come over." Pausing, she turned in a half circle, studying everything. "Who owns this pile of rocks anyway?"

At any other time, that irreverent description of this house would have made Meredith giggle. Now she could only say in a small, strained voice, "My father does."

Lisa's expression hardened. "I pretty much figured that out when the man who answered the front door called you Miss Meredith in the same voice Father Vickers says 'Holy Virgin Mary.' " Turning on her heel, Lisa started for the door.

"Lisa, wait!" Meredith pleaded.

"You've had your little joke. This has really been a great day," Lisa added sarcastically, whirling back around. "First Mario takes me out for a ride and tries to get my clothes off—and when I go over to my 'friend's' house, I find out she's been making a fool of me."

"No, I haven't!" Meredith cried. "I let you think Fenwick—our chauffeur—was my father because I was afraid the truth would come between us."

"Oh, sure. Right," Lisa countered with scornful disbelief. "Rich little you desperately wanted to be friends with poor little me. I'll bet you and all your rich friends have been laughing about my ma begging you to have spaghetti with us and—"

"Stop it!" Meredith burst out. "You don't understand! I like your mother and father, and I wanted you for a friend. You have brothers and sisters and aunts and uncles and all the things I've always wished *I* had. What makes you think that because I live in this stupid house, everything is automatically wonderful? Look how it's affected you! One look and you don't want anything to do with me, and that's how it's been at school for as long as I can remember. And for your information," she finished, "I *love* spaghetti. I *love* houses like yours, where people laugh and shout!"

She broke off as the anger on Lisa's face was replaced by a sarcastic smile. "You love noise, is that it?"

Meredith smiled wanly. "I guess I do."

"What about your rich friends?"

"I don't really have any. I mean, I know other people my age, and I see them now and then, but they all go to the same schools, and they've been friends for years. I'm an outsider to them—an oddity."

"Why does your father send you to St. Stephen's?"

"He thinks it's, well, character building. My grandmother and her sister went there."

"Your father sounds weird."

"I guess he does, but his intentions are good."

Lisa shrugged, her voice deliberately offhand. "In that case, he sounds pretty much like most fathers." It was a tiny concession, a tentative suggestion of commonality, and silence fell in the room. Separated by a canopied Louis XIV bed and a gigantic social chasm, two extraordinarily bright teenagers recognized all the differences between them and regarded each other with a mixture of dying hope and wariness. "I guess I'd better be going," Lisa said.

Meredith looked bleakly at the nylon duffel Lisa had brought, obviously intending to spend the night if it was all right. She lifted her hand in a tiny gesture of mute appeal, then dropped it, knowing it was useless. "I have to leave pretty soon too," she said instead.

"Have a—a good time."

"Fenwick can take you home after he drops me off at the hotel."

"I can ride the bus," Lisa began, but for the first time she actually noticed Meredith's dress, and she broke off in horror. "Who picks out your clothes—Helen Keller? That's not what you're really wearing tonight, is it?"

"Yes. Do you hate it?"

"Do you really want to know?"

"I don't think so."

"Well, how would *you* describe that dress?"

Meredith shrugged, her expression chagrined. "Does the word *frumpy* mean anything to you?"

Biting her lip to hide her laughter, Lisa raised her brows. "If you knew it was ugly, why did you buy it?"

"My father liked it."

"Your father has lousy taste."

"You shouldn't say words like *lousy*," Meredith said quietly, knowing Lisa was right about the ugliness of the dress. "Words like that make you sound tough and hard, and you aren't—not really. I don't know how to dress or wear my hair, but I know I'm right about how to talk."

Lisa stared at her open-mouthed, and then something began to happen—the gentle bonding of two entirely dissimilar spirits who suddenly realize that they each have something very special to offer the other. A slow smile lit Lisa's hazel eyes, and she tipped her head to the side, thoughtfully scrutinizing Meredith's dress. "Pull the shoulders down a little onto your arms, let's see if that helps," she instructed suddenly.

Meredith grinned back and dutifully tugged them down.

"Your hair looks like hell—lous—*awful,*" Lisa amended, then she glanced around, her gaze lighting on a bouquet of silk flowers on the dresser. "A flower in your hair or tucked into that sash might help."

With the true instincts of her Bancroft forebears, Meredith sensed that victory was within her grasp and that it was time to press her advantage. "Will you spend the night? I'll be back by midnight, and no one will care how late we stay up."

Lisa hesitated and then she grinned. "Okay." Redirecting her attention to the problem of Meredith's appearance, she said, "Why did you pick shoes with such stubby little heels?"

"They don't make me look as tall."

"Tall is *in,* dopey. Do you have to wear those pearls?"

"My father wanted me to."

"You could take them off in the car, couldn't you?"

"He'd feel awful if he knew it."

"Well, *I* won't tell him. I'll lend you my lipstick," she added, already rummaging in her purse for her makeup. "What about your glasses? Do you absolutely have to wear them?"

Meredith stifled a giggle. "Only if I need to see."

Forty-five minutes later, Meredith left. Lisa had said she had a talent for decorating everything—from people to rooms—and Meredith believed her now. The silk flower pinned into her hair behind her ear made Meredith feel more elegant and less dowdy. The slight touch of blusher on her cheeks made her look more lively, and the lipstick, though Lisa said it was a little too bright for her pale coloring, made Meredith feel older and more sophisticated. Her confidence at an all-time high, Meredith turned in the doorway to her room and waved good-bye to Lisa and Mrs. Ellis, then she smiled at Lisa. "Feel free to redecorate my room while I'm gone, if you want."

Lisa gave her a jaunty thumbs-up sign. "Don't keep Parker waiting."

December 1973

The bells ringing in Matt Farrell's brain were overwhelmed by the increasing thunder of his heart as he buried himself full-length into Laura's eager, demanding body, driving into her as she rode him hard, her hips forcing him deeper. She was wild . . . close to the edge. . . . Bells began to clang rhythmically. Not the melodious bells from church steeples in the center of town, or the echoing bells of the fire station across the street.

"Hey, Farrell, you in there?" *Bells.*

He was definitely "in there." In her, close to exploding. *Bells.*

"Dammit, Farrell . . ." *Bells.* "Where the hell"—*bells*—"are you?" It seeped through his mind then: Outside by the gas pumps, someone was jumping on the hose that rang inside the service station and shouting his name.

Laura froze, a low scream in her throat. "Oh my God, there's someone out there." Too late. He couldn't stop, wouldn't stop. He hadn't wanted to start this here, but she'd insisted and enticed, and now his body wouldn't heed the threat of intrusion. Clasping her rounded buttocks, he yanked her down, drove up into her, and finished. A pulse beat of rest, and then he rolled to a sitting position, gently but hurriedly pushing her off. Laura was already tugging her skirt down and adjusting her sweater. He shoved her behind a stack of retreads and stood up just as the door opened and Owen Keenan strode into the gas station service bay, scowling and suspicious. "What the hell is goin' on in here, Matt? I been hollerin' the place down."

"I was taking a break," Matt replied, combing his hands through his dark hair which was ruffled from Laura's eager caresses. "What do you want?"

"Yer pa's drunk down at Maxine's. Sheriff's on his way. If you don't want him spending the night in the drunk tank, you better get to him first."

When Owen left, Matt picked up Laura's coat from the floor, where they'd lain on it, then dusted it off and held it while she put her arms into the sleeves. She'd had a friend drop her off there, he knew, which meant she'd need a ride. "Where did you leave your car?" he asked.

She told him and he nodded. "I'll take you to your car before I go rescue my father."

Christmas lights were strung across the intersections as Matt drove down Main Street, their colors blurring in the falling snow; at the north end of town, a red plastic wreath hung above the sign that said WELCOME TO EDMUNTON, INDIANA. POP. 38,124. From a loudspeaker provided by the Elks Club, "Silent Night" blared out its tune colliding with the notes of "Jingle Bells" pouring out of a plastic sleigh on the roof of Horton's Hardware.

The softly falling snow and Christmas lights did wonders for Edmunton, lending a Norman Rockwell aura to what was, in harsh daylight, a small town perched above a shallow valley where clusters of stacks rose from the steel mills and spewed perpetual geysers of smoke and steam into the air. Darkness cloaked all that; it hid the south end of town, where neat houses gave way to shacks and taverns and pawnshops, and then to farmland, barren in the winter.

Matt pulled his pickup truck into a dark corner of the parking lot beside Jackson's Dry Goods Store, where she'd left her car, and Laura slid next to him. "Don't forget," she said, wrapping her arms around his neck. "Pick me up tonight at seven, at the bottom of the hill, and we'll finish what we started an hour ago. And Matt, stay out of sight. Daddy saw your truck down there the last time and started asking questions."

Matt looked at her, suddenly disgusted with his sexual attraction to her. She was beautiful, rich, spoiled, and selfish, and he knew it. He'd let himself be used as her stud, let himself be conned into clandestine meetings and furtive gropings, let himself descend to lurking around at the bottom of the hill instead of going up to the front door, as her other—acceptable—dates undoubtedly did.

Other than sexual attraction, they had absolutely nothing in common. Laura Frederickson's daddy was Edmunton's richest citizen, and she was in her freshman year at an expensive eastern college. Matt worked in a steel mill during the day, moonlighted as a mechanic on weekends, and went to night school at the local branch of Indiana State University.

Leaning across her lap, he opened the truck door, his voice hard and implacable. "Either I pick you up at your front door tonight, or you'd better make other plans for the evening."

"But what will I tell Daddy when he sees your pickup in the drive?"

Coldly impervious to her stricken look, Matt said sardonically, "Tell him my limousine is in the shop for repairs."

December 1973

*T*he long procession of limousines inched forward toward the canopied entrance of Chicago's Drake Hotel, where they stopped to allow their youthful occupants to alight.

Doormen moved back and forth, escorting each new group of young arrivals from their cars to the lobby. Not by word or expression did any of the Drake doormen exhibit the slightest amusement or condescension toward the young guests arriving in custom-tailored tuxedos and formal gowns, for these were not ordinary children dressed up for a prom or a wedding reception, overawed by their surroundings and uncertain of how to behave. These were the children of Chicago's most prominent families; they were poised, confident, and the only evidence of their youth was perhaps in their ebullient enthusiasm for the night that lay ahead.

Toward the rear of the procession of chauffeur-driven automobiles, Meredith watched the other young people alight. Like herself, they were here to attend Miss Eppingham's annual dinner and dance. This evening, Miss Eppingham's students, who were all between the ages of twelve and fourteen, would be expected to demonstrate the social skills they'd acquired and polished during her six-month course—skills that they would need in order to move gracefully in the rarefied social stratum it was automatically assumed they would inhabit as adults. For that reason, all fifty of the students, properly attired in formal clothing, would pass through a receiving line tonight, be seated for a twelve-course dinner of state, and then attend the dance.

Through the windows of her car Meredith watched the cheerful, confident faces of the others as they gathered inside the lobby. She was the only one who'd arrived alone, she noted, watching as the other girls emerged in groups or arrived with "escorts"—often older brothers or cousins who'd already graduated from Miss Eppingham's course. With a sinking heart she noted the beautiful gowns the other girls were wearing, saw the sophisticated ways their hair had been swept into elaborate curls entwined with velvet ribbon or held back with jeweled barrettes.

Miss Eppingham had reserved the Grand Ballroom for tonight, and Meredith walked up the staircase from the marble lobby, her stomach twisting with nerves, her knees shaking with apprehension. At the landing, she spotted the ladies' lounge and headed straight toward it. Once inside, she went over to the mirror, hoping to reassure herself about her appearance. Actually, given what Lisa had had to work with, Meredith decided she didn't look that bad. Her blond hair was parted on the right side and held back with a silk flower, then it fell straight as a stick to just above her shoulders. The flower gave her a mysterious, worldly look, she decided with more hope than conviction. Reaching into her handbag, she took out Lisa's peach lipstick and applied a bit of it. Satisfied, she reached up, unclasped the pearls, and put them into her purse, then she took off her glasses and tucked them in with the pearls. "Much better," she decided with soaring spirits. If she didn't squint, and if the lights were dim, there was a chance Parker might think she looked very nice.

Outside the Grand Ballroom the Eppingham students were waving to one another and gathering into groups, but no one waved to her or called out her name and said, "I hope we're sitting together, don't you?" It wasn't their fault, she knew. In the first place, most of the others had known each other since babyhood; their parents were friends; they'd attended one another's birthday parties. Chicago society was a large, exclusive clique, and the adult members naturally felt it incumbent upon themselves to preserve the exclusivity of the clique at the same time they ensured their children's admission to it. Meredith's father was the only dissenter to that philosophy;

on the one hand, he wanted Meredith to take her rightful place in society, on the other, he did not want her corrupted by children whose parents were more lenient than he.

Meredith made it through the receiving line without difficulty, then she proceeded to the banquet tables. Since seating was indicated by engraved place cards, she surreptitiously removed her glasses from her purse and peered at each card. When she located her name at the third table, she discovered she was seated at a table with Kimberly Gerrold and Stacey Fitzhugh, two of the girls who'd been "elves" with her in the Christmas pageant. "Hello, Meredith," they chorused, looking at her with the sort of amused condescension that always made her feel clumsy and self-conscious, then they turned their attention to the boys seated between them. The third girl was Parker's younger sister, Rosemary, who nodded a disinterested greeting in Meredith's general direction and then whispered something to the boy beside her that made him laugh, his gaze darting in Meredith's direction.

Sternly repressing the uneasy conviction that Rosemary was talking about *her*, Meredith looked brightly around *her*, pretending that she was fascinated with the red and white Christmas decorations. The chair on her right was left vacant, she later discovered, due to the fact that its designated occupant had the flu, which left Meredith in the awkward position of having no dinner partner.

The meal progressed, course after course, and Meredith automatically selected the right piece of sterling flatware from the eleven pieces arrayed around her plates. Dining with this formality was routine at home, as it was for many of the other Eppingham students, so she didn't even have indecision to distract her from the awkward isolation she felt as she listened to a discussion about current movies.

"Did you see that one, Meredith?" Steven Mormont asked, belatedly adhering to Miss Eppingham's stricture about including *everyone* at the table in conversation.

"No—I'm afraid not." She was spared the need to say more because just then the orchestra began to play, and the dividing wall was opened up, indicating that the diners were now expected to gracefully conclude their table conversations and make their stately way into the ballroom.

Parker had promised to drop in on the dancing, and with his sister there, Meredith knew he would. Besides, his college fraternity was having a party in one of the other ballrooms, so he was in the hotel. Standing up, she smoothed her hair, made certain her tummy was tucked in, and headed for the ballroom.

For the next two hours Miss Eppingham did her duty as hostess by circulating among her guests and making certain each one had someone to talk to and dance with. Time after time, Meredith watched her dispatch some reluctant boy in Meredith's direction with orders to ask her to dance.

By eleven o'clock, most of the Eppingham crowd had broken up into small groups and the dance floor was all but deserted—owing no doubt to the outdated dance music being played by the orchestra. Meredith was one of four couples still dancing, and her partner, Stuart Whitmore, was carrying on an animated discussion about his goal of joining his father's law firm. Like Meredith, he was serious and smart, and she liked him better than any of the other boys she knew from this crowd, particularly because he'd *wanted* to dance with her. She was listening to Stuart, her eyes glued on the entrance to the ballroom, when Parker suddenly materialized in the doorway with three of his college friends. Her heart leapt into her throat when she saw how gorgeous he looked in his black tuxedo with his thick, sun-streaked blond hair and tanned face. Beside him, every other male in the ballroom, even the two who'd accompanied him, looked insignificant.

Noticing that Meredith had suddenly stiffened, Stuart broke off his discourse on law school requirements and glanced in the direction she was staring. "Oh—Rosemary's brother is here," he said.

"Yes, I know," Meredith replied, unaware of the dreamy tone of her voice.

Stuart heard it and grimaced. "What is it about Parker Reynolds that makes girls get all breathless and fluttery?" he demanded with wry humor. "I mean, just because he's taller, older, and six times smoother than me, why would you prefer him?"

"You shouldn't belittle yourself," Meredith said with absentminded sincerity, watching Parker stride across the ballroom for his duty dance with his sister. "You're very intelligent, and very nice."

"So are you."

"You're going to be a brilliant lawyer, just like your father."

"Would you like to go out next Saturday night?"

"What?" Meredith gasped, her gaze snapping to his face. "I mean," she hastily said, "it's nice of you to ask, but my father won't let me date until I'm sixteen."

"Thanks for letting me down easily."

"I wasn't!" Meredith replied, but then she forgot everything because one of Rosemary Reynolds's boyfriends had just cut in on Parker, and he was turning toward the ballroom doors to leave. "Excuse me, Stuart," she said a little desperately, "but I have something to give to Parker!" Unaware that she was attracting the amused notice of a great many pairs of eyes, Meredith rushed across the deserted dance floor and caught up with Parker just as he was about to leave with his friends. They gave her a curious look, as if she were a clumsy bug that had skittered into their midst, but Parker's smile was warm and real. "Hello, Meredith. Enjoying your evening?"

Meredith nodded, hoping he would remember his promise to dance with her, her spirits sinking to a new, unparalleled low when he continued to wait for her to say whatever she'd rushed over there to say. A hot flush of embarrassment stained her cheeks bright pink when she belatedly realized she was gazing at him in worshipful silence. "I—I have something to give you," she said in a shaky, horrified voice, rummaging in her purse. "I mean, my father wanted me to give you this." She pulled out the envelope with the opera tickets and birthday card, but the pearl necklace came out too and spilled on the floor. Hastily, she bent down to pick it up at the same instant Parker did and her forehead banged hard against his. "Sorry!" she burst out as he said, "Ouch!" When she lurched upright, Lisa's lipstick fell out of her open purse and Jonathan Sommers, one of Parker's friends, bent down to pick that up. "Why don't you just turn your purse upside down so we can pick everything up at once," Jonathan joked, his breath reeking of liquor.

Horribly aware of the titters of laughter from the Eppingham students who were watching, Meredith thrust the envelope at Parker, shoved the pearls and lipstick into her purse, and turned, blinking back tears, intending to beat an ignominious retreat. Behind her, Parker finally remembered their dance. "What about the dance you promised me?" he said good-naturedly.

Meredith whirled around, her face lighting up, "Oh, that. I'd—forgotten. Do you want to? Dance, I mean?"

"It's the best offer I've had all evening," he gallantly replied, and as the musicians began to play "Bewitched, Bothered, and Bewildered," Meredith walked into Parker's arms and felt her dream become reality. Beneath her fingertips she could feel the smooth fabric of his black tuxedo jacket and the solid hardness of his back. His cologne smelled spicy and wonderful, and he was a superb dancer. Meredith was so hopelessly overwhelmed that she spoke her thoughts aloud. "You're a wonderful dancer," she said.

"Thank you."

"And you look very nice tonight in your tuxedo."

He chuckled softly and Meredith tipped her head way back, basking in the warmth of his smile as he said, "You look very nice too."

Feeling a fierce blush heat her cheeks, she hastily looked at his shoulder. Unfortunately all the standing up and down and tipping her head back and forth had loosened the pin holding the flower in her hair, and it slid unnoticed to hang drunkenly from its wired stem. Thinking madly for something sophisticated and witty to say, she tipped her head back and said brightly, "Are you enjoying your Christmas break?"

"Very much," he said, his gaze dipping to the vicinity of her shoulder and the fallen blossom. "And you?"

"Yes, very much," she answered, feeling incredibly gauche.

Parker's arms dropped away the instant the music ended, and with a smile, he said good-bye. Knowing she couldn't stand and stare at him while he walked away, Meredith hastily turned around and caught her reflection in a mirrored wall. She saw the silk flower hanging crazily from her hair and snatched it out, hoping that it had just that very second fallen.

Waiting in line at the coat check, she stared morosely at the flower in her fingers, horribly afraid it had been dangling on her shoulder the entire time she danced with Parker. She glanced at the girl standing beside her, and as if the other girl read her thoughts, she nodded. "Yep. It was hanging down while you danced with him."

"I was afraid of that."

The other girl grinned sympathetically, and Meredith remembered her name—Brooke. Brooke Morrison. Meredith had always thought she seemed nice. "Where are you going to school next year?" Brooke asked.

"Bensonhurst, in Vermont," Meredith told her.

"Bensonhurst?" Brooke repeated, wrinkling her nose. "It's in the middle of nowhere and it's as regimented as a prison. My grandmother went to Bensonhurst."

"So did mine," Meredith replied with a depressed sigh, wishing her father weren't so insistent on sending her there.

Lisa and Mrs. Ellis were slumped in chairs in Meredith's room when Meredith opened the door. "Well?" Lisa asked, jumping up. "How was it?"

"Wonderful," Meredith said with a grimace, "if you don't count the fact that everything fell out of my purse when I gave Parker the birthday card. Or that I babbled to him about how terrific he looked and danced." She flopped down in the chair Lisa had just vacated and it belatedly struck her that the chair she was sitting in had been moved. In fact, her entire bedroom had been rearranged.

"Well, what do you think?" Lisa asked with a sassy grin as Meredith slowly looked around, her face reflecting surprise and pleasure. Besides rearranging the furniture, Lisa had dismantled the vase of silk flowers and now bunches of those flowers were pinned to the tie-backs on Meredith's canopied bed. Green plants had been purloined from other parts of the house and the austere room had acquired a feminine, garden atmosphere. "Lisa, you're amazing!"

"True." She grinned. "Mrs. Ellis helped."

"I," Mrs. Ellis disagreed, "only provided the plants. Lisa did everything else. I hope your father doesn't object," she added uneasily, standing up to leave.

When she was gone, Lisa said, "I was sort of hoping your father would look in here. I mean, I had this great little speech all prepared. Want to hear it?"

Meredith returned her grin and nodded.

Positively oozing good breeding and impeccable diction, Lisa made her speech: "Good evening, Mr. Bancroft. I'm Meredith's friend, Lisa Pontini. I plan to become an interior designer, and I was practicing up here. I do hope you don't object, sir?"

She did it so perfectly that Meredith laughed, then she said, "I didn't know you plan to be an interior designer."

Lisa sent her a derisive look. "I'll be lucky if I get to finish high school, let alone go to college and study interior design. We don't have the money for college." In an awed voice she added, "Mrs. Ellis told me your father is *the* Bancroft of Bancroft & Company. Is he away on a trip or something?"

"No, he's at a dinner meeting with the board of directors," Meredith answered, and because she assumed Lisa would be as fascinated with the corporate functioning of Bancroft & Company as she was, she continued, "The agenda is really exciting. Two of the directors think Bancroft's ought to expand into other cities. The controller says it's fiscally irresponsible, but the merchandising executives all insist that the added buying power we'd have would increase our overall profits."

"That's all mumbo-jumbo to me," Lisa said, her attention on a big schefflera in the corner of the room. She moved it a few feet forward, and the effect of the simple change was quite startling.

"Where are you going to high school?" Meredith asked, admiring her transformed bedroom and thinking how unjust it was that Lisa couldn't go to college and make the most of her talents.

"Kemmerling," Lisa answered.

Meredith winced. She passed Kemmerling on her way to St. Stephen's. St. Stephen's was old, but immaculately well-kept, Kemmerling was a big, ugly, sprawling public school and the students looked very shabby and tough. Her father had repeatedly stressed the idea that excellent educations were obtained at *excellent* schools. Long after Lisa had fallen asleep, an idea was taking shape in Meredith's mind, and she planned her strategy more carefully than she'd ever planned anything, with the exception of her imaginary dates with Parker.

5

*E*arly the next morning, Fenwick drove Lisa home, and Meredith went down to the dining room, where her father was reading the newspaper, waiting to have breakfast with her. Normally she'd have been curious about the outcome of his meeting last night, but now she had something more pressing on her mind. Sliding into her chair, she said good morning, then she launched her campaign while his attention was still on the article he was reading. "Haven't you always said that a good education is vital?" she began. When he nodded absently, she continued. "And haven't you also said that some of the public high schools are very understaffed and inadequate?"

"Yes," he replied, nodding again.

"And didn't you tell me the Bancroft family trust has endowed Bensonhurst for decades?"

"Mmmm," he murmured, turning to the next page.

"Well," Meredith said, trying to control her mounting excitement, "there's a student at St. Stephen's—a wonderful girl, from a very devout family. She's very smart, and she's talented too. She wants to be an interior designer, but she'll have to go to Kemmerling High because her parents can't afford to send her to a better school. Isn't that sad?"

"Mmmm," he said again, frowning at an article about Richard Daley. Democrats were not among his favorite people.

"Wouldn't you say it's *tragic* that so much talent and intelligence and, and *ambition* will go to waste?"

Her father raised his gaze from the newspaper and regarded her with sudden intensity. At forty-two he was an attractive, elegant man with a brusque manner, piercing blue eyes, and brown hair turning silver at the temples. "Just what are you suggesting, Meredith?"

"A scholarship. If Bensonhurst doesn't offer one, then you could ask them to use some of the money the trust has donated for one."

"And I could also specify that this scholarship is to be awarded to the girl you've been talking about, is that it?" He made it sound as if what Meredith was asking was unethical, but she already knew that her father believed in using his power and connections whenever, and wherever, they would benefit his purpose. That's what power was for, he'd told her hundreds of time.

She nodded slowly, her eyes smiling. "Yes."

"I see."

"You'd never find anyone more deserving," she prodded eagerly. "And," she added, seized by inspiration, "if we don't do something for Lisa, she'll probably end up on *welfare* someday!" Welfare was a subject guaranteed to evoke a strong negative response in her father. Meredith wanted desperately to tell her father more about Lisa, and about how much their friendship mattered to her, but some sixth sense warned her not to do it. In the past, her father had been so overprotective of her that no child had ever met his standards for a suitable companion for her. He'd be much more likely to think Lisa deserved a scholarship than that she deserved to be Meredith's friend.

"You remind me of your grandmother Bancroft," he said after a thoughtful pause. "She often took a personal interest in some deserving but less fortunate soul."

Guilt stabbed at her, for her interest in having Lisa at Bensonhurst was every bit as selfish as it was noble, but his next words made her forget all that: "Call my secretary tomorrow. Give her whatever information you have about this girl, and ask her to remind me to call Bensonhurst."

For the next three weeks Meredith waited in an agony of suspense, afraid to tell Lisa what she was trying to accomplish because she didn't want her to be disappointed, yet unable to believe Bensonhurst would refuse her father's request. American girls were being sent to school in Switzerland and France now, not to Vermont, and not to Bensonhurst with its drafty stone dormitories and rigid curriculum and rules. Surely, the school wasn't filled to capacity as it once had been; therefore they wouldn't want to risk offending her father.

The following week a letter from Bensonhurst arrived and Meredith hovered anxiously by her father's chair while he read it. "It says," he finally told her, "they're awarding Miss Pontini the school's one scholarship based on her outstanding scholastic achievements and the Bancroft family's recommendation as to her desirability as a student." Meredith let out an unladylike whoop of glee that earned her a chilly look from her father before he continued: "The scholarship will cover her tuition and room and board. She'll have to get herself to Vermont and provide her own spending money while she's in school."

Meredith bit her lip; she hadn't considered the cost of a flight to Vermont or spending money, but having succeeded this far, she was almost cer-

tain she could think of something else. Perhaps she could convince her
father that they should drive; then Lisa could ride to Vermont with them.

The next day Meredith took all the brochures about Bensonhurst, along
with the letter about the scholarship, to school. The day seemed to last a
week, but finally she was sitting at the Pontinis' kitchen table while Lisa's
mother bustled about, laying out Italian cookies as light as air, and offering
her homemade cannoli. "You're getting too skinny, like Lisa," Mrs. Pontini
said, and Meredith obediently nibbled on a cookie while she opened her
schoolbag and laid out the Bensonhurst brochures.

A little awkward in her role of philanthropist, she talked excitedly
about Bensonhurst and Vermont and the excitement of traveling, then she
announced that Lisa had been granted a scholarship to go there. For a
moment there was dead silence while Mrs. Pontini and Lisa both seemed
unable to absorb the last part of that, then Lisa slowly stood up. "What am
I," she burst out furiously, "your newest *charity!* Who the hell do you think
you are!"

She stormed out the back door and Meredith followed her. "Lisa, I was
only trying to help!"

"Help?" Lisa snapped, rounding on her. "What makes you think I'd
want to go to school with a bunch of rich snobs like you who'd look at me
like a charity case? I can just see it, a school full of spoiled bitches who
complain about having to get by on the thousand dollars a month allowance
their daddies send them—"

"No one would know you're there on a scholarship unless you tell
them—" Meredith began, then she paled with angry hurt. "I didn't know
you think of me as a 'rich snob' or a 'spoiled . . . spoiled bitch.' "

"Listen to you—you can't even say the word *bitch* without choking on it.
You're so damned prissy and superior!"

"You're the snob, Lisa, not me," Meredith interrupted in a quiet,
defeated voice. "You see everything in terms of money. And you didn't need
to worry about fitting in at Bensonhurst. I'm the one who doesn't seem to
fit in anywhere, not you." She said that with a calm dignity that would have
pleased her father immensely, then she turned and left.

Fenwick was waiting in front of the Pontini house. Meredith slid into
the backseat of the car. There was something wrong with her, she realized—something about her that prevented people from feeling comfortable
with her, no matter their social class. It did not occur to her that perhaps
there was something special—a fineness and sensitivity—about her that
made other kids want to put her down or stay away from her. It occurred to
Lisa, who was watching the car pull away, hating Meredith Bancroft for

being able to play teenage fairy godmother, and despising herself for the ugliness, the unfairness of her feelings.

At lunch the next day Meredith was sitting in her usual place, outside, huddled in her coat, eating an apple and reading a book. From the corner of her eye she saw Lisa walking toward her, and she concentrated harder on her book.

"Meredith," Lisa said, "I'm sorry about yesterday."

"That's okay," Meredith replied without looking up. "Forget it."

"It's pretty hard to forget that I was lousy to the nicest, kindest person I've ever met."

Meredith glanced at her and then back at her book, but her voice was softer, though final. "It doesn't matter anymore."

Sitting down beside her on the stone ledge, Lisa continued doggedly, "I was a witch yesterday for a lot of selfish, stupid reasons. I felt sorry for myself because you were offering me this fantastic chance to go away to a special school, to *feel* like someone special, and I knew I'd never be able to go. I mean, my ma needs help with the kids and the house, and even if she didn't, I'd need money for the trip to Vermont and other stuff once I got there."

Meredith had never considered that Lisa's mother couldn't or wouldn't spare her, and she thought it seemed horribly unfair that Mrs. Pontini's having had eight children meant *Lisa* had to be a part-time mother too. "I didn't think about your mother and father not letting you go," she admitted, looking at Lisa for the first time. "I sort of thought, well, that parents always *wanted* their children to get a good education if they possibly could."

"You were half right," Lisa said, and Meredith noticed for the first time that Lisa looked as if she were bursting with news. "My *ma* does. She had a big fight with Pa over it after you left. He said a girl doesn't need to go to fancy schools, just to get married and have babies. Ma started waving this big spoon at him and yelling that *I* could do better than that, and then everything started happening. Ma called my gramma and *she* called my aunts and uncles, and they all came over to the house, and pretty soon everybody was chipping in money for me. It's only a loan. I figure if I work hard at Bensonhurst, I ought to be able to get a scholarship to some college after that. Later, I'll get a great job and repay everybody."

Her eyes were shining as she reached out impulsively and squeezed Meredith's hand. "How does it feel," she asked softly, "to know you're responsible for changing someone's entire life? To know that you've made dreams come true for me and Ma and my aunts—"

Unexpectedly, Meredith felt the hot sting of tears behind her eyes. "It feels," she said, "pretty nice."

"Do you think we could be roommates?"

Meredith nodded, her face beginning to shine.

Several yards away, a group of girls who were eating their lunches together looked up and stared: Lisa Pontini—the new girl in school—and Meredith Bancroft—the weirdest girl in school—had suddenly stood up, and they were crying and laughing and hugging each other, jumping up and down.

6

June 1978

The room Meredith had shared with Lisa at Bensonhurst for four years was cluttered with packing boxes and half-filled suitcases. Hanging on the closet door were the blue caps and gowns they'd worn at the commencement ceremony the previous night along with the gold tassels that indicated they'd both graduated with highest honors. In the closet, Lisa was putting sweaters into a box; beyond the open door of their room, the hall was filled with the unfamiliar sound of male conversation as fathers, brothers, and boyfriends of departing students carried suitcases and boxes downstairs. Meredith's father had spent the night at a local inn and was due in an hour, but Meredith had lost track of time. Overcome with nostalgia, she was flipping through a thick stack of photographs she'd taken from her desk, smiling at the memories each one evoked.

The years Lisa and she had spent in Vermont had been wonderful ones for both of them. Contrary to Lisa's original fear that she would be an outcast at Bensonhurst, she'd soon established herself as a trendsetter among the other girls, who regarded her as daring and unique. In their freshman year, it was Lisa who organized and led a successful raid on the boys at Litchfield Prep in retaliation for their attempted panty raid on Bensonhurst. In their sophomore year, Lisa designed a stage setting for Bensonhurst's annual school play that was so spectacular, pictures of it made the newspapers in several cities. In their junior year, it was Lisa who Bill Fletcher asked to Litchfield's spring dance. Besides being the captain of Litchfield's soccer team, Bill Fletcher was also fantastically good-looking and very smart. On the day before the dance, he scored twice on the field and once again in a nearby motel, where Lisa gave him her virginity. After that momentous event, Lisa returned to the room she shared with Meredith and cheerfully revealed the news to the four girls who had gathered there. Flopping onto her bed, she had grinned and announced, "I am no longer a virgin. You may feel completely free to ask me for advice and information from now on!"

The other girls obviously regarded that as yet another example of Lisa's intrepid independence and sophistication, because they laughed and cheered, but Meredith had been worried and even a little appalled. That night, when their friends left, Meredith and Lisa had their first real quarrel since coming to Bensonhurst. "I can't believe you *did* that!" Meredith had exploded. "What if you got pregnant? What if the other girls spread it around? What if your parents find out?"

Lisa had reacted with matching force. "You're not my keeper and you're not responsible for me, so stop acting like my mother! If you want to wait around for Parker Reynolds or some other mythical white knight to sweep you off your feet and into bed, then do it, but don't expect everyone else to be like you! I didn't buy all that purity crap the nuns fed us at St. Stephen's," Lisa continued, flinging her blazer into the closet. "If you were stupid enough to swallow it, then be the eternal virgin, but don't expect me to be one too! And I'm not careless enough to get pregnant—Bill used a condom. Furthermore, the other girls aren't going to say a word about what I did, because *they've* already done it! The only shocked little virgin in our room tonight was you!"

"That's enough," Meredith interrupted stonily, starting over to her desk. Despite the surface calm in her voice, she was squirming with guilt and embarrassment. She did feel responsible for Lisa because she was the one who'd brought her to Bensonhurst. Moreover, Meredith already knew she was morally archaic, and that she had no right to inflict restrictions on Lisa simply because they'd somehow been inflicted on herself. "I didn't mean to judge you, Lisa, I was worried about you, that's all."

After a moment of tense silence, Lisa turned to her and said, "Mer, I'm sorry."

"Forget it," Meredith replied. "You were right."

"No, I wasn't," she said, looking at Meredith with pleading and desperation. "It's just that I'm not like you, and I can't be. Not that I haven't tried now and then."

That admission wrung a grim laugh from Meredith. "Why would you want to be like me?"

"Because," Lisa said with a wry smile, then she mimicked Humphrey Bogart and said, "you've got class, baby. Class with a capital K."

Their first real confrontation ended with a truce that was declared that same night over a milk shake at Paulson's Ice Cream Shoppe.

Meredith thought about that night as she looked through the photographs, but her reminiscences came to an abrupt halt as Lynn McLaughlin poked her head into the room and said, "Nick Tierney called on the pay phone out in the hall early this morning. He said your phone in here is already disconnected, and that he's going to stop by in a little while."

"Which one of us did he call to talk to?" Lisa said. Lynn replied that he'd called for Meredith, and when she left, Lisa plunked her hands on her hips and turned to Meredith with a mock glower. "I knew it! He couldn't take his eyes off you last night even though I practically stood on my head to make him notice me. I should never have taught you how to wear makeup and pick out your clothes!"

"There you go again," Meredith shot back, grinning, "taking all the credit for my meager popularity with a few boys." Nick Tierney was a junior at Yale who'd dutifully come here to watch his sister graduate yesterday, and had dazzled all the girls with his handsome face and great build. Within minutes of setting eyes on Meredith, he'd become the one who was dazzled, and he made no secret of it.

"*Meager* popularity with a *few* boys?" Lisa repeated, looking fantastic even with her red hair pinned into a haphazard knot atop her head. "If you went out with half the guys who've asked you in the last two years, you'd break my own record for dedicated dating!"

She was about to say more, when Nick Tierney's sister tapped on the open door. "Meredith," she said with a helpless smile, "Nick is downstairs with a couple of his friends who drove up from New Haven this morning. He says he's determined to help you pack, proposition you, or propose to you—whichever you prefer."

"Send the poor, lovesick man and his friends up here," Lisa said, laughing. When Trish Tierney left, Lisa and Meredith regarded each other in silent amusement, opposites in every way. Completely in accord.

The past four years had wrought many changes in them, but it was in Meredith that those changes had been the most dramatic. Lisa had always been striking; she'd never been hampered with the need for eyeglasses or cursed with baby fat. The contact lenses Meredith bought with her allowance two years before had eliminated her need for glasses and allowed her eyes to come into prominence. Nature and time had taken care of all the rest by giving an emphasis to her delicately carved features, thickening her pale blond hair, and rounding and narrowing her figure in all the right places.

Lisa, with her flaming curly hair and flamboyant attitude, was earthy and glamorous at eighteen. Meredith, in contrast, was quietly poised and serenely beautiful. Lisa's vivaciousness beckoned to men; Meredith's smiling reserve challenged them. Whenever the two girls went places together, males turned to stare. Lisa enjoyed the attention; she loved the thrill of dating and the excitement of a new romance. Meredith found her recent popularity with the opposite sex curiously flat. Although she enjoyed being with the boys who took her skiing and dancing and to their parties, once the newness of being sought after wore off, dating boys for whom she felt no more than friendship was pleasant, but not as wildly exciting as she'd expected it to be. She felt that way about being kissed too. Lisa attributed all that to the fact that Meredith had wrongly idealized Parker and now continued to compare every male she met to him. That undoubtedly accounted for part of Meredith's lack of enthusiasm, but the majority of it was probably caused by the simple fact that she had been raised in an adult household which was, moreover, dominated by a forceful, dynamic businessman. And although the boys she dated from Litchfield Prep were nice to be with, she invariably felt much older than they.

Meredith had known since childhood that she wanted to get her college degree and take her rightful place at Bancroft & Company someday. The Litchfield boys, and even their older college-age brothers whom she'd met, didn't seem to have any goals or interests other than sex, sports, and drinking. To Meredith, the idea of surrendering her virginity to some boy whose primary aim was to add her name to the list of Bensonhurst virgins deflowered by Litchfield men—a list that purportedly hung in Crown Hall at Litchfield—was not only nonsensical, it was humiliating and sordid.

When she did become intimate with someone, she wanted it to be someone she admired and trusted; she wanted tenderness and understanding, and she wanted romance too. Whenever she thought of having a sexual relationship, she envisioned more than making love; she envisioned long walks on the beach, holding hands and talking; long nights in front of a fireplace, watching the flames—and talking. After trying unsuccessfully for years to truly communicate with, and be close to, her father, Meredith was determined that her eventual lover would be someone she could talk to and who would share his thoughts with her. And whenever she envisioned that ideal lover, he was always Parker.

During the years she'd been at Bensonhurst, Meredith had managed to see Parker fairly often when she was home on vacations—an endeavor that was made easier by the fact that both Parker's family and hers belonged to the Glenmoor Country Club. At Glenmoor, it was traditional for the membership to appear en masse at the club's major dances and sports events. Until a few months before, when she'd turned eighteen, Meredith had been prohibited from attending the club's adult functions, but she'd managed to avail herself of those opportunities Glenmoor did offer. Each summer she'd invited Parker to be her partner in the junior-senior tennis matches. His acceptance had always been gracious; their matches had always been dismal defeats, owing mostly to Meredith's extreme nervousness at playing with him.

She'd used other ruses too, over the years, like convincing her father to give several dinner parties each summer, one of which always included Parker and his family. Since Parker's family owned the bank in which all of Bancroft & Company's funds were deposited, and since Parker was already an officer of that bank, he was practically obliged to come to dinner both for business reasons and to act as Meredith's dinner partner.

At Christmastime, Meredith had twice managed to be standing under the mistletoe, which she'd hung in the foyer, when Parker and his family came to pay their annual holiday call on the Bancrofts, and she always went with her father when it was time to return the visit to the Reynoldses.

As a result of the mistletoe trick during her freshman year, Parker was the one who gave Meredith her first kiss; she'd lived on the memory of that until the next Christmas, dreamed about the way he felt and smelled and smiled at her before he kissed her.

Whenever he came to dinner, she loved listening to him talk about business at the bank, and she especially loved the walks they began taking afterward, while their parents lingered over brandy. It was during their walk last summer that Meredith made the mortifying discovery that Parker had always known she had a crush on him. He'd begun by asking her how the skiing had been the past winter in Vermont, and Meredith had regaled him with a funny story about going skiing with the captain of Litchfield's ski team. When Parker stopped laughing at the fact that her date had to chase her ski down the face of the mountain, which he'd done with style and flair, he said with smiling solemnity, "Every time I see you, you're more beautiful than the time before. I guess I've always known that someone was going to eventually take my place in your heart, but I never thought it would be usurped by some jock who rescued your ski. Actually," he teased, "I was getting used to being your favorite romantic hero."

Pride and common sense kept Meredith from blurting out that he'd misunderstood and that *no one* had taken his place; maturity stopped her from pretending he'd never had a place in her heart. Since he obviously wasn't destroyed by her imagined defection, she did the only thing she could do, which was to try to salvage their friendship and simultaneously treat her crush on him as if she, too, regarded it as an amusing thing of her youthful past. "You knew how I felt?" she asked, managing to smile.

"I knew," he averred, returning her smile. "I used to wonder if your father would notice and come looking for me with a gun. He's very protective of you."

"I've noticed that too," Meredith joked, although that particular issue was far from a laughing matter then or now.

Parker had chuckled at her quip, and then he'd sobered and said, "Even though your heart belongs to a skier, I hope this doesn't mean our walks and dinners and tennis games are over. I've always enjoyed them, I mean that."

They'd ended up talking about Meredith's college plans and her intention to follow in her ancestors' footsteps, all the way to the president's office at Bancroft & Company. He alone seemed to understand how she felt about taking her rightful place at Bancroft's, and he sincerely believed she could do it if she wanted it badly enough.

Now, as Meredith stood in the dorm room, thinking about seeing him again after an entire year had passed, she was already trying to prepare herself for the possibility that all Parker would ever be was a friend. The prospect was disheartening, but she felt certain of his friendship, and that meant a great deal to her too.

Behind Meredith, Lisa walked out of the closet with her last armload of clothes and dumped them on the bed beside an open suitcase. "You're thinking of Parker," she teased. "You always get that dreamy look on your—" She broke off as Nick Tierney arrived in the doorway, his two friends blocked from view behind him.

"I've told both these guys," he announced, tipping his head toward his unseen friends, "that they're about to see more beauty in one room than they've seen in the entire state of Connecticut, but that since I was here first, I have first choice, and my choice is Meredith." Winking at Lisa, he stepped aside. "Gentlemen," he said with a sweeping gesture of his hand, "allow me to introduce you to my 'second choice.'" The other two walked in looking bored, cocky, and collegiate, a matched pair of Ivy League models. They took one look at Lisa and stopped dead.

The muscular blond in the lead recovered first. "You must be Meredith," he said to Lisa, his wry expression making it clear that he thought Nick had stolen the best for himself. "I'm Craig Huxford and this is Chase Vauthier." He nodded to the dark-haired twenty-one-year-old beside him who was looking Lisa over like a man who has finally beheld perfection.

Lisa folded her arms across her chest and regarded them both with amusement. "I'm not Meredith."

Their heads turned in unison to the opposite corner of the room, where Meredith was standing.

"*God*—" Craig Huxford whispered reverently.

"God—" Chase Vauthier echoed as they looked from one girl to the other and back again.

Meredith bit her lip to keep from laughing at their absurd reaction. Lisa raised her brows and dryly said, "Whenever you boys are through with your prayers, we'll offer you a Coke in return for your help stacking these packing boxes for the movers."

They started forward, grinning. Behind them, Philip Bancroft walked in a half hour early and came to a halt, his face darkening with fury as he looked at the three young men. "What the hell is going on in here?"

The five occupants of the room froze, then Meredith stepped in and tried to smooth matters over by hastily introducing the boys to her father. Ignoring her effort, he jerked his head at the door. "Out!" he snapped, and when they'd left, he turned on the girls. "I thought the rules of this school prohibited men other than fathers from entering this goddamned building."

He didn't "think" that, he knew it. Two years ago, he'd paid a surprise visit on Meredith, and when he arrived at the dorm at four o'clock on a Sunday afternoon, he'd seen boys sitting around downstairs in the dorm's lounge area, just inside the main doors. Before that weekend, male visitors had been allowed into the lounge on weekend afternoons. After that day, males were banned from entering the building at all times. Philip had gotten the rules changed himself by storming into the administrator's office and accusing her of everything from gross negligence to contributing to the delinquency of minors, then he threatened to notify all the parents of those facts and to cancel the large annual endowment the Bancroft family gave to Bensonhurst.

Now Meredith fought down her fury and humiliation over his behavior to the three boys who'd done nothing to warrant his wrath. "In the first place," she said, "the school year ended yesterday, so the rules don't apply. Secondly, they were only trying to help us stack these boxes for shipping so we can leave—"

"I was under the impression," he interrupted, "that *I* was coming here this morning to do all that. I believe that was why I got out of bed at—" He broke off his tirade at the sound of the administrator's voice.

"Excuse me, Mr. Bancroft," she said. "You have an urgent phone call downstairs."

When he left to take his call, Meredith sank down on the bed and Lisa slammed her Coke onto the desk. "I cannot understand that man!" she said furiously. "He's impossible! He won't let you date anyone he hasn't known since babyhood, and he scares off everyone else who tries. He gave you a car for your sixteenth birthday, and he won't let you drive it. I have four brothers who are *Italian*, dammit, and combined they're not as overbearingly protective as your father is!" Unaware that she was only adding to Meredith's angry frustration, she walked over and sat down beside her. "Mer, you have to do something about him, or this summer is going to be worse than the last one for you. I'm going to be gone for half of it, so you won't even have me to hang around with." The staff at Bensonhurst had been so impressed with Lisa's grades and her artistic talent that they'd gotten her a six-week European scholarship, where the chosen student was allowed to select whatever city best suited her future career plans. Lisa had decided on Rome and enrolled in a course on interior design there.

Meredith slumped back against the wall. "I'm not as worried about this summer as I am about three months from now."

Lisa knew she was referring to the battle she was having with her father over which college to attend. Several universities had offered Lisa full scholarships, and she'd chosen Northwestern University because Meredith was planning to go there. Meredith's father, however, had insisted she apply to Maryville College, which was little more than an exclusive finishing school in a Chicago suburb. Meredith had compromised by applying to both, and she'd been accepted by both. Now she and her father were in a complete standoff on the issue. "Do you honestly think you're going to be able to talk him out of sending you to Maryville?"

"I am not going there!"

"You know that and I know that, but your father is the one who has to agree to pay the tuition."

Sighing, Meredith said, "He'll give in. He's impossibly overprotective of me, but he wants the best for me, he really does, and Northwestern's business school is the best. A degree from Maryville isn't worth the paper it's written on."

Lisa's anger gave way to bafflement as she considered Philip Bancroft, a man she'd come to know and yet could not understand. "I realize he wants the best for you," she said. "And I admit he's not like most of the parents who send their kids to school here. At least he gives a damn about you. He calls you every week and he's been here for every single major school event." Lisa had been shocked their first year at Bensonhurst when she realized most of the other girls' parents seemed to live wholly apart from their children, and that expensive gifts that arrived in the mail were usually a substitute for parental visits, phone calls, and letters. "Maybe I should talk to him privately and try to convince him to let you go to Northwestern."

Meredith shot her a wry look. "What do you think that would accomplish?"

Bending over, Lisa gave a frustrated yank on her left sock and retied her shoe. "The same thing it accomplished the last time I stood up to him and took your side—he'd start thinking I'm a bad influence on you." In order to prevent Philip from thinking exactly that, Lisa had, except once, treated Philip Bancroft like a beloved, respected benefactor who'd gotten her admitted to Bensonhurst. Around him she was the personification of deferential courtesy and feminine decorum, a role that was so opposite to her blunt, outspoken personality that it chafed on her terribly and usually made Meredith laugh.

At first Philip seemed to regard Lisa as some sort of foundling he'd sponsored and who was surprising him by acquitting herself well at Bensonhurst. As time passed, however, he showed in his own gruff, undemonstrative way that he was proud of her and perhaps felt a modicum of affection for her. Lisa's parents couldn't afford to come to Bensonhurst for any school functions, so Philip had assumed their role, taking her out to dinner when he took Meredith out, and generally showing an interest in her school activities. In the spring of the girls' freshman year Philip had even gone so far as to have his secretary call Mrs. Pontini and ask if there was anything she wanted him to take to Lisa when he flew to Vermont for Parents' Weekend. Mrs. Pontini had eagerly accepted his offer and arranged to meet him at the airport. There, she presented him with a white bakery box filled with cannoli and other Italian pastries, and a brown paper bag containing long, pungent rolls of salami. Irritated at having to board his flight looking—he later told Meredith—like a damned hobo boarding a Greyhound bus with his lunch in his arms, Philip nevertheless delivered his parcels into Lisa's hands, and he continued to act as surrogate parent to her at Bensonhurst.

Last night, in honor of graduation, he presented Meredith with a rose topaz pendant on a heavy gold chain from Tiffany's. To Lisa, he gave a much less expensive, but unquestionably lovely, gold bracelet with her initials and the date artfully engraved among the swirls on its surface. It, too, had been purchased at Tiffany's.

In the beginning, Lisa had been completely uncertain of how to respond to him, for although he was unfailingly courteous to her, he was always aloof and undemonstrative—much as he behaved to Meredith. Later, upon weighing his actions and discarding his surface attitude, Lisa cheerfully announced to Meredith that she'd decided Philip was actually a soft-hearted teddy bear who was all bluff and no bite! That wholly erroneous conclusion led her to try to intercede for Meredith during the summer after their sophomore year. On that occasion Lisa had told Philip, *very* courteously and with her sweetest smile, that she truly thought Meredith deserved a little more freedom during the summer. Philip's response to what he called Lisa's "ingratitude" and "meddling" had been explosive, and only her abject and instantaneous apology prevented him from carrying out his threat to put an end to Meredith's association with her and to suggest to Bensonhurst that her scholarship there be given to someone "more deserving." The confrontation had left Lisa staggered by more than just his incredibly volatile reaction. From what he said to her, she finally realized that Philip had not merely suggested that the scholarship be given to her, but that the scholarship came from the Bancroft family's private endowment to the school. The discovery made her feel like a complete ingrate, while his explosive reaction left her in a state of angry frustration.

Now Lisa felt again that same impotent anger and bewilderment at the rigid restrictions he imposed on Meredith. "Do you really, honestly believe," she said, "that the reason he acts like your watchdog is because your mother cheated on him?"

"She didn't cheat on him just once, she was a total slut who slept with everyone from horse trainers to truck drivers after they were married. She purposely made a laughingstock out of my father by having flagrant affairs with sleazy nobodies. Parker told me last year, when I asked him, what his parents knew about her. Evidently, everybody knew what she was like."

"You told me all that, but what I don't understand," Lisa continued bitterly, "is why your father acts like lack of morals is some kind of genetic flaw you might have inherited."

"He acts that way," Meredith replied, "because he partially *believes* it."

They both looked up guiltily as Philip Bancroft walked back into the room. One look at his grim face and Meredith forgot her own problems. "What's wrong?"

"Your grandfather died this morning," he said in a dazed, gruff voice. "A heart attack. I'll go and check out of the motel and get my things. I've arranged for both of us to get on a flight that leaves in an hour." He turned to Lisa. "I'll rely on you to drive my car back home." Meredith had talked him into driving instead of flying so that Lisa could ride back with them.

"Of course I will, Mr. Bancroft," Lisa said quickly. "And I'm very sorry about your father."

When he left, Lisa looked at Meredith, who was staring blankly at the empty doorway. "Mer? Are you okay?"

"I guess so," Meredith said in an odd voice.

"Is this grandfather the guy who married his secretary years ago?"

Meredith nodded. "He and my father didn't get along very well. I haven't seen him since I was eleven. He called though, to talk to my father about things at the store, and to me. He was—he was—I liked him," she finished helplessly. "He liked me too." She looked up at Lisa, her eyes glazed with sorrow. "Besides my father, he was my only close relative. All I have left are a few fifth or sixth cousins who I don't even know."

🌿 7

*I*n the foyer of Philip Bancroft's house, Jonathan Sommers hesitated uneasily, searching through the crowds of people who, like himself, had come to pay the obligatory condolence visit on the day of Cyril Bancroft's funeral. He stopped one of the caterer's staff who was carrying a tray of drinks and helped himself to two that had been destined for other guests. After tossing down the vodka and tonic, Jonathan deposited the empty glass in a large potted fern, then he took a swallow of the scotch in the second glass and wrinkled his nose because it wasn't Chivas Regal. The vodka, combined with gin he'd drunk from a flask in the car outside, made him feel slightly better fortified to face the funeral amenities. Beside him, a tiny elderly woman was leaning on a cane, studying him with curiosity. Since good manners seemed to require that he speak to her, Jon cast about for some sort of polite conversation pertinent to the occasion. "I hate funerals, don't you?" he said.

"I rather like them," she said smugly. "At my age, I regard each funeral I attend as a personal triumph, because *I* was not the guest of honor."

He swallowed a bark of laughter, because loud laughter on this austere occasion would be a severe breach of the etiquette he'd been taught to observe. Excusing himself, he put the unfinished scotch down on a small table beside him and went off in search of a better drink. Behind him, the elderly lady picked up the glass and took a dainty sip. "Cheap scotch!" she said in disgust, and put it back where he'd left it.

A few minutes later Jon spotted Parker Reynolds standing in an alcove off the living room with two young women and another man. After stopping at the buffet table to get another drink, he walked over to join his friends. "Great party, isn't it," he remarked with a sarcastic smile.

"I thought you hated funerals and never went to them," Parker said when the chorus of greetings was over.

"I do hate them. I'm not here to mourn Cyril Bancroft, I'm here today to protect my inheritance." Jon took a swallow of his drink, trying to wash away the bitterness he felt over what he was about to say. "My father is threatening to disinherit me again, only I think the old bastard really means it this time."

Leigh Ackerman, a pretty brunette with a lovely figure, looked at him in amused disbelief. "Your father is going to disinherit you if you don't attend funerals?"

"No, my lovely, my father is threatening to disinherit me if I don't 'straighten up' and make something of myself immediately. Translated, that means I am to appear at funerals of old family friends such as this one, and I am to participate in our family's newest business venture. Or else I'm cut off from all that lovely money my family has."

"Sounds dire," Parker said with an unsympathetic grin. "What new business venture have you been assigned to?"

"Oil wells," he said. "More oil wells. This time my old man has cut a deal with the Venezuelan government to carry out exploration operations over there."

Shelly Fillmore glanced at the small gilt-framed mirror over Jon's shoulder and touched a finger to the corner of her mouth, smoothing a tiny smudge of vermilion lipstick. "Don't tell me he's sending you to South America?"

"Nothing as essential as that," Jon scoffed bitterly. "My father is turning me into a glorified personnel interviewer. He put me in charge of hiring the crews to go over there. And then you know what the old bastard did?"

His friends were as accustomed to Jon's tirades against his father as they were to his drunkenness, but they waited to hear his newest complaints, anyway. "What did he do?" Doug Chalfont asked.

"He checked up on me. After I picked out the first fifteen able-bodied, experienced men, my old man insisted on meeting everyone I'd interviewed personally so that he could rate my ability to choose men. He rejected half of my choices. The only one he really liked was this guy named Farrell, who's a steelworker and who I wasn't going to hire. The closest Farrell's ever been to an oil rig was two years ago, when he worked on a few little ones in some damned cornfield in Indiana. He's never been near a big rig like we'll have in South America. Furthermore, Farrell doesn't give a damn about oil drilling. His only interest is the one-hundred-fifty-thousand-dollar bonus he'll get if he sticks it out for two years over there. He told my father that right to his face."

"So why did your father hire him?"

"He said he liked Farrell's style," Jon sneered, tossing down the rest of his drink. "He liked Farrell's ideas about what he planned to do with the bonus when he gets it. Shit, I half expected my father to change his mind about sending Farrell to Venezuela and offer him my office instead. As it is, I have been ordered to bring Farrell in next month and 'acquaint him with our operation and introduce him around.' "

"Jon," Leigh said calmly, "You're getting drunk and your voice is getting loud."

"Sorry," he said, "but I've had to listen to my father singing this guy's praises for two damned days. I'm telling you, Farrell is an arrogant, ambitious son of a bitch. He has no class, no money, no nothing!"

"He sounds divine," Leigh joked.

When the other three remained silent, Jon said defensively, "If you think I'm exaggerating, I'll bring him to the Fourth of July dance at the club and you can all see for yourself what sort of man my father thinks I ought to be."

"Don't be an idiot," Shelly warned him. "Your father may like him as an employee, but he'll castrate you if you bring someone like that to Glenmoor."

"I know," Jon said with a tight smile, "but it would be worth it."

"Just don't dump him on us if you bring him there," she warned after exchanging glances with Leigh. "We aren't going to spend the evening trying to make small talk with some steelworker just so you can spite your father."

"No problem. I'll leave Farrell all by himself and let him flounder while my father looks on, watching him try to figure out what fork to use. My old man won't be able to say a word to me either. After all, he's the one who told me to 'show Farrell the ropes' and 'look after him' while he's in Chicago."

Parker chuckled at Jon's ferocious expression. "There must be an easier way to solve your problem."

"There is," Jon said. "I can find myself a wealthy wife who can support me in my accustomed style, and then I can tell my old man to go fuck himself." He glanced over his shoulder and signaled a pretty girl in a maid's uniform who was passing a tray of drinks. She hurried over and he grinned at her. "You're not only pretty," he told her as he put his empty glass on her tray and took a fresh one, "You're a life saver!" From the flustered way she smiled at him and then blushed, it was obvious to Jon, and to the rest of the group, that she was not immune to his six-foot-one muscular body and attractive features. Leaning close to her, Jon said in a stage whisper, "Is it possible that you're only working for a caterer as a lark, but that your father actually owns a bank or a seat on the exchange?"

"What? I mean, no," she said, charmingly flustered.

Jon's smile turned teasing and sexy. "No seat on the exchange? How about some factories or some oil wells?"

"He's—he's a plumber," she blurted out.

Jonathan's grin faded, and he sighed. "Marriage is out of the question, then. There are certain financial and social requirements that the winning candidate for my wife will have to be able to meet. However, we could still have an affair. Why don't you meet me in my car in a half hour. It's the red Ferrari out in front."

The girl left, looking both miffed and intrigued.

"That was completely obnoxious of you," Shelly said, but Doug Chalfont nudged him and chuckled. "I'll bet you fifty bucks that girl is waiting in your car when you leave."

Jon turned his head and started to reply, but his attention was suddenly diverted by the sight of a breathtaking blonde wearing a black sheath with a high collar and short sleeves, who was walking down the stairs and into the living room. He stared at her with slackened jaw as she paused to talk to an elderly couple, and when a group of people shifted and blocked her from his view, he leaned sideways, trying to see her. "Who are you looking at?" Doug asked, following his gaze.

"I don't know who she is, but I'd like to find out."

"Where is she?" Shelly asked, and everyone looked in the direction he was staring.

"There!" Jon said, pointing with his glass as the crowd around the blond moved and he saw her again.

Parker recognized her and grinned. "You've all known her for years, you just haven't seen her in a while." Four blank faces turned to him, and his grin widened. "That, my friends, is Meredith Bancroft."

"You're out of your mind!" Jon said. He stared hard at her but could find little resemblance between the gauche, rather plain girl he remembered and the poised young beauty he beheld: Gone was the baby fat, the glasses, the braces, and the ever-present barrette that used to hold back her straight hair. Now that pale golden hair was caught up in a simple chignon with tendrils at her ears framing a face of classic, sculpted beauty. She looked up then, somewhere to the right of Jon's group and nodded politely at someone, and he saw her eyes. Halfway across the room, he saw those large aquamarine eyes, and he suddenly remembered those same startling eyes peering up at him long ago.

Strangely exhausted, Meredith stood quietly, listening to people who spoke to her, smiling when they smiled, but she couldn't seem to absorb the reality that her grandfather was dead, and that the hundreds of people who seemed to be drifting from room to room were here because of that. The fact that she hadn't known him very well had reduced the grief she'd felt for the last few days to a dull ache.

She'd caught a glimpse of Parker at the graveside service, and she knew he could very well be somewhere in the house, but in view of the melancholy circumstances, it seemed wrong and disrespectful to go looking for him in hopes of furthering a romantic relationship at that time. Furthermore, she was growing just a little bit weary of always being the one who sought him out; it seemed to her that it was his turn to make some sort of move toward her. As if thinking of him had suddenly summoned him to her side, she heard an achingly familiar masculine voice say in her ear, "There's a man over in that alcove who's threatened my life if I don't bring you over so that he can say hello."

Already smiling, Meredith turned and put her hands into Parker's outstretched palms, then felt her knees go weak as he pulled her forward and kissed her cheek. "You look beautiful," he whispered, "and very tired. How about going for one of our walks after we get the social amenities over with?"

"All right," she said, surprised and relieved that her voice sounded steady.

When they reached the alcove, Meredith found herself in the ludicrous position of being reintroduced to four people she already knew, four people who had acted as if she were invisible when she'd last seen them several years earlier, and who now seemed gratifyingly eager to befriend her and include her in their activities. Shelly invited her to a party the following week and Leigh urged her to sit with them at Glenmoor's Fourth of July dance.

Parker deliberately "introduced" her to Jon last. "I can't believe it's you," he said, but the alcohol was making his words a little slurred. "Miss Bancroft," he continued with his most winning grin. "I was just explaining to these people that I'm in urgent need of a suitably rich and gorgeous wife. Would you marry me next weekend?"

Meredith's father had mentioned Jonathan's frequent rifts with his disappointed parents to her; Meredith assumed Jon's "urgent need" to marry a "rich" woman was probably the result of one of those, and his entire attitude struck her as funny. "Next weekend will be perfect," she said, smiling brightly. "My father will disown me for marrying before I finish college, though, so we'll have to live with *your* parents."

"God forbid!" Jonathan shuddered, and everyone laughed, including Jonathan.

Putting his hand on Meredith's elbow, Parker rescued her from further nonsense by saying, "Meredith needs some fresh air. We're going for a walk."

Outside, they strolled across the front lawn and wandered down the drive. "How are you bearing up?" he asked.

"I'm fine, really—just a little tired." In the ensuing silence, Meredith tried to think of some sort of witty and sophisticated repartee, then she settled for simplicity and said with sincere interest, "A lot must have happened to you in the last year. . . ."

He nodded and said the last thing Meredith wanted to hear. "You can be one of the first to congratulate me. Sarah Ross and I are getting married. We're going to announce our engagement officially at a party Saturday night."

The world tilted sickeningly. Sarah Ross! Meredith knew who Sarah was and she didn't like her. Although she was extremely pretty and very vivacious, she'd always struck Meredith as being shallow and vain. "I hope you'll be very happy," she said, carefully hiding her doubt and disappointment.

"I hope so too."

For a half hour they strolled about the grounds, talking about his plans for his future and then about her plans for her own. He was wonderful to talk to, Meredith thought with a feeling of poignant loss—encouraging and understanding, and he completely supported her desire to attend Northwestern instead of Maryville.

They were heading toward the front of the house when a limousine pulled up in the drive and a striking brunette got out of it followed by two young men in their early twenties. "I see the grieving widow has finally decided to put in an appearance," Parker said with uncharacteristic sarcasm as he looked at Charlotte Bancroft. Large diamond earrings glittered at her ears, and despite the simple gray suit she was wearing, she looked alluring and curvaceous. "Did you notice that she didn't shed a tear at the funeral? There's something about that woman that reminds me of Lucretia Borgia."

Privately Meredith agreed with the analogy. "She isn't here to accept condolences. She wants the will read this afternoon, as soon as the house clears out, so that she can go back to Palm Beach tonight."

"Speaking of 'clearing out,' " Parker said, glancing at his watch, "I have an appointment in an hour." Leaning forward, he pressed a brotherly kiss to her cheek. "Tell your father I said good-bye."

Meredith watched him as he walked away, taking all her romantic girlhood dreams with him. The summer breeze ruffled his sun-streaked hair, and his strides were long and sure. He opened his car door, stripped off the jacket of his dark suit, and put it over the back of the passenger seat. Then he looked up and waved good-bye to her.

Trying desperately not to dwell on her loss, she forced herself to walk forward to greet Charlotte. Not once during the service had Charlotte spoken to either Meredith or her father; she had simply stood between her sons, her expression blank. "How are you feeling?" Meredith asked politely.

"I'm feeling impatient to go home," the woman retorted icily. "How soon can we get down to business?"

"The house is still full of people," Meredith said, mentally recoiling from Charlotte's attitude. "You'll have to ask my father about the reading of the will."

Charlotte turned on the steps, her face glacial. "I haven't spoken to your father since that day in Palm Beach. The next time I speak to him, it will be when *I'm* calling all the shots and he's begging me to talk to him. Until then you'll have to act as interpreter, Meredith." She walked into the house with a son on each side of her like an honor guard.

Meredith stared at her back, chilled by the hatred emanating from her. The day in Palm Beach Charlotte had referred to was still vividly clear in Meredith's memory. Seven years earlier, she and her father had flown to Florida at the invitation of her grandfather, who'd moved there after his heart attack. When they arrived they discovered that they had not been invited merely for the Easter holidays, but rather to attend a wedding— Cyril Bancroft's wedding to Charlotte, who had been his secretary for two decades. At thirty-eight, she was thirty years younger than he, a widow with two teenage sons only a few years older than Meredith.

Meredith never knew why Philip and Charlotte detested each other, but from what little she heard of the explosive argument between her father and grandfather that day, the animosity had started long before, when Cyril still lived in Chicago. With Charlotte within hearing, Philip had called the woman a scheming, ambitious slut, and he'd called his father a silly, aging fool who was being duped into marrying her so that her sons would get a piece of Cyril's money.

That trip to Palm Beach had been the last time Meredith had seen her grandfather. From there, he had continued to control his business investments, but he left the operation of Bancroft & Company entirely to Meredith's father, as he had done from the day he moved to Palm Beach. Although the department store represented less than one fourth of the family's net worth, by its very nature its operation required her father's complete attention. Unlike the family's other vast holdings, Bancroft's was far more than a mere stock transaction that yielded dividends; it was the foundation of the family's original wealth and a source of great pride.

"This is the last will and testament of Cyril Bancroft," her grandfather's attorney began when Meredith and her father were seated in the library along with Charlotte and her sons. The first bequests were for large sums that went to various charities, and after that four more bequests were made to Cyril Bancroft's servants—$15,000 each to his chauffeur, housekeeper, gardener, and caretaker.

Since the attorney had specifically requested that Meredith be present, she had already assumed that she was probably the recipient of some small bequest. Despite that, she jumped when Wilson Riley spoke her name: "To my granddaughter, Meredith Bancroft, I bequeath the sum of four million dollars." Meredith's mouth fell open in shocked disbelief at the enormous sum, and she had to concentrate on listening while Riley continued: "Although distance and circumstances have prevented me from getting to know Meredith well, it was apparent to me when I last saw her that she is a warm and intelligent girl who will use this money wisely. To help ensure that she does, I make this bequest with the stipulation that the funds are to be held in trust for her, along with any interest, dividends, etc., until she attains the age of thirty. I further appoint my son, Philip Edward Bancroft, to act as her trustee and to maintain full guardianship over said funds."

Pausing to clear his throat, Riley looked from Philip to Charlotte to her sons, Jason and Joel, and then he began to read Cyril's words again: "In the interest of fairness, I have divided the rest of my estate as evenly as possible between my remaining heirs. To my son, Philip Edward Bancroft, I bequeath all my stock, and my entire interest in, Bancroft & Company, a department store which constitutes approximately one fourth of my entire estate." Meredith heard it, but she couldn't make sense of it. "In the interest of fairness" he'd left his only child one fourth of his estate? Surely, if he meant to divide everything evenly, his wife was entitled to no more than one half, not three fourths. And then, as if from a distance, she heard the attorney finish, "To my wife, Charlotte, and my legally adopted sons, Jason and Joel, I leave equal shares in the remaining three-fourths of my estate. I further stipulate that Charlotte Bancroft is to act as trustee over Jason and Joel's portion until such time as they have both attained the age of thirty."

The words *legally adopted* tore at Meredith's heart as she saw the look of betrayal flash across her father's ashen face. Slowly, he turned his head and looked at Charlotte; she returned his stare unflinchingly while a smile of malicious triumph spread across her face. "You conniving bitch!" he said between his teeth. "You said you'd get him to adopt them, and you did."

"I warned you years ago that I would. I'm warning you now that our score still isn't settled," she added, her smile widening as if she was thriving on his fury. "Think about that, Philip. Lie awake at night, wondering where I'll strike you next and what I'll take away from you. Lie awake, wondering and worrying, just like you made me lie awake eighteen years ago."

The bones of his face stood out as he clamped his jaws to stop himself from dignifying that with a reply. Meredith tore her gaze from the two of them and looked at Charlotte's sons. Jason's face was a replica of his mother's—triumphant and malicious. Joel was frowning at his shoes. *Joel is soft*, Meredith's father had said years ago. *Charlotte and Jason are like greedy barracudas, but at least you know what to expect of them. The younger boy, Joel, makes my skin crawl—there's something strange about him.*

As if he sensed that Meredith was looking at him, Joel glanced up, his expression carefully noncommittal. He didn't look strange to Meredith or at all threatening. In fact, when she'd last seen him on the occasion of the wedding, Joel had gone out of his way to be nice to her. At the time, Meredith had felt sorry for him because his mother openly preferred Jason, and Jason, who was two years older, seemed to feel nothing for his brother but contempt.

Suddenly Meredith couldn't stand the oppressive atmosphere in the room any longer. "If you'll excuse me," she said to the lawyer, who was spreading some papers out on the desk, "I'll wait outside until you're finished."

"You'll need to sign these papers, Miss Bancroft."

"I'll sign them before you leave, after my father has read them."

Instead of going upstairs, Meredith decided to go outside. It was getting dark and she wandered down the steps, letting the evening breeze cool her face. Behind her, the front door opened, and she turned, thinking it was the lawyer calling her back inside. Joel stood there, arrested in midstep, as startled as she by their confrontation. He hesitated as if he wanted to remain but wasn't certain he was welcome.

It had been hammered into her head that one was always gracious to anyone who was one's guest, so Meredith tried to smile. "It's nice out here, isn't it?"

Joel nodded, accepting the unspoken invitation to join her if he wished, and he walked down the steps. At twenty-three, he was shorter by several inches than his older brother, and not as attractive as Jason. He stood, looking at her, as if unable to think what to say. "You've changed," he finally said.

"I imagine I have. I was eleven years old the last time I saw you."

"After what just happened in there, you must wish to God you'd never laid eyes on any of us."

Still a little dazed by the terms of her grandfather's will and unable to assimilate what it all meant in terms of the future, Meredith shrugged. "Tomorrow I may feel that way. Right now I just feel—numb."

"I'd like you to know—" he said haltingly, "that I didn't plot to steal your grandfather's affection or his money from your father."

Unable to either hate him or forgive him for cheating her father of his rightful inheritance, Meredith sighed and looked up at the sky. "What did your mother mean in there—about settling a score with my father?"

"All I know is that they've hated each other for as long as I can remember. I have no idea what started it, but I do know my mother won't stop until she's satisfied with her revenge."

"God, what a mess!"

"Lady," he replied with deadly certainty, "it's only just *begun*."

A chill raced up Meredith's spine at that grim prophecy, and she snapped her gaze from the sky to his face, but he merely lifted his brows and refused to elaborate.

8

*M*eredith yanked a dress out of her closet to wear to the Fourth of July party, tossed it across the bed, and pulled off her bathrobe. This summer, which had begun with a funeral, had degenerated into a five-week battle with her father over which college she would attend—a battle that had escalated into a full-fledged war the previous day. In the past, Meredith had always bent over backward to please him; when he was needlessly strict, she told herself it was only because he loved her and was afraid for her; when he was brusque, she rationalized that he had responsibilities that tired him, but now, now that she'd belatedly discovered that his plans for her were on a collision course with her own, she was not willing to give up her dreams to pacify him.

From the time she was a young girl, she'd assumed that someday she would have the chance to follow in the footsteps of all her forebears and take her rightful place at Bancroft & Company. Each successive generation of Bancroft men had proudly worked their way up through the store's hierarchy, starting there as a department manager, then moving up through the ranks to vice president, and later, president and chief executive officer. Finally, when they were ready to turn the direction of the store over to their sons, they became chairman of the board. Not once in nearly one hundred years had a Bancroft failed to do that, and not once in all that time had any Bancroft ever been ridiculed by the press or by the store's employees for being incompetent or undeserving of the titles they eventually held. Meredith believed, she *knew*, she could prove herself worthy too, if she were just given the chance. All she wanted or expected was that *chance*. And the only reason her father didn't want to give it to her was that she hadn't had the foresight to be his son instead of his daughter!

Frustrated to the point of tears, she stepped into the dress and pulled it up. Reaching behind her back, she struggled with the zipper as she walked over to the dressing table and looked in the mirror above it. With complete disinterest she surveyed the strapless cocktail dress that she'd bought weeks before for that night's occasion. The bodice was sheared at the sides so that it crisscrossed her breasts, sarong-style, in a multicolored rainbow of pale pastel silk chiffon, then it nipped in at the waist before falling in a graceful swirl to her knees. Picking up a hairbrush, she ran it through her long hair. Rather than expend the effort of doing anything special with it, she brushed it back off her face, twisted it up into a chignon, and pulled a few tendrils loose at her ears to soften the effect. The rose topaz pendant would have been the perfect accent for her dress, but her father was also going to Glenmoor tonight, and she refused to give him the satisfaction of seeing her wear it. Instead, she clipped on a pair of ornate gold earrings inset with pink stones that sparkled and danced in the light, and left her shoulders and neck bare. The hairstyle gave her a more sophisticated look and the golden tan she'd acquired looked lovely against the strapless bodice of the dress; if it hadn't, Meredith wouldn't have cared, nor would she have changed into something different. How she looked was a matter of complete indifference to her; the only reason she was going was that she couldn't stand the thought of staying home and letting frustration drive her insane, and that she'd promised Shelly Fillmore and the rest of Jonathan's friends that she'd join them there.

Sitting down at the dressing table, she slipped on a pair of pink silk moiré heels she'd bought to wear with the dress. When she straightened, her gaze fell on the framed copy of an old issue of *Business Week* that was hanging on the wall. On the cover of the magazine was a picture of Bancroft's stately downtown store, with its uniformed doormen standing at the main entrance. The fourteen-story building was a Chicago landmark, the doormen a historic symbol of Bancroft's continuing insistence on excellence and service to its customers. Inside the magazine was a long, glowing article about the store, which said that a Bancroft label on an item was a status symbol; the ornate B on its shopping bags the emblem of a discriminating shopper. The article also commented about the remarkable competence of Bancroft heirs when it came to running their business. It said that a talent for—and love of—retailing seemed to have been passed along in Bancroft genes from its founder, James D. Bancroft.

When the writer had interviewed Meredith's grandfather and asked him about that, Cyril had reportedly laughed and said it was possible. He'd added, however, that James Bancroft had begun a tradition that had been handed down from father to son—a tradition of grooming and training the heir from the time he was old enough to leave the nursery and dine with his parents. There, at the dining table, each father began to speak to their sons about whatever was happening at the store. For the child, these daily vignettes about the store's operation constituted the equivalent of ongoing bedtime stories. Excitement and suspense were generated; knowledge was subtly imparted. And absorbed. Later, simplified problems were casually brought up and discussed with the teenager. Solutions were asked for—and listened to, though rarely found. But then, finding solutions wasn't the real goal anyway; the goal was to teach and stimulate and encourage.

At the end of the article, the writer had asked Cyril about his successors and, as Meredith thought about her grandfather's reply, she felt a lump in her throat: "My son has already succeeded me to the presidency," Cyril had said. "He has one child, and when the time comes for her to take over the presidency of Bancroft & Company, I have every faith Meredith will carry on admirably. I only wish I could be alive to see it." Meredith knew that if her father had his way, she would never assume the presidency of Bancroft's. Although he'd always discussed the operation of the store with her, just as his father had done with him, he was adamantly opposed to her ever working there. She made that discovery while they were having dinner soon after her grandfather's funeral. In the past, she'd repeatedly mentioned her intention of following tradition and taking her place at Bancroft's, but either he hadn't listened or he hadn't believed her. That night he did take her seriously, and he informed her with brutal frankness that he did not expect her to succeed him, nor did he *want* her to. That was a privilege he planned to reserve for a future grandson. Then he coldly acquainted Meredith with an entirely different tradition and one he intended she follow: Bancroft women did not work at the store, or anywhere else, for that matter. Their duty was to be exemplary wives and mothers, and to donate whatever additional talents and time they had to charitable and civic endeavors.

Meredith wasn't willing to accept that; she couldn't, not now. It was too late. Long before she'd fallen in love with Parker—or thought she had—she had fallen in love with "her" store. By the time she was six, she was already on a first-name basis with all of the doormen and security clerks. At twelve she knew the names of every vice president and what his responsibilities were. At thirteen she'd asked to accompany her father to New York, where she'd spent an afternoon at Bloomingdale's, being shown around the store, while her father attended a meeting in the auditorium. When they left New York, she'd already formed her own opinions—not all of them correct—about why Bancroft's was superior to "Bloomie's."

Now, at eighteen, she already had a general knowledge of things like workers compensation problems, profit margins, merchandising techniques, and product liability problems. Those were the things that fascinated her, the things she *wanted* to study, and she was *not* going to spend the next four years of her life taking classes in romance languages and Renaissance art!

When she told him that, he had slammed his hand down on the table with a crash that made the dishes jump. "You are going to Maryville, where both your grandmothers have gone, and you will continue to live at home! At *home!*" he reiterated. "Is that clear? The subject is closed!" Then he'd shoved his chair back and left.

As a child, Meredith had done everything to please him, and please him she had—with her grades, her manners, and her deportment. In fact, she'd been a model daughter. Now, however, she was finally realizing that the price of pleasing her father and maintaining the peace was becoming much higher: It required subjugating her individuality and surrendering all her dreams for her own future, not to mention sacrificing a social life!

His absurd attitude toward her dating or going to parties wasn't her main problem right now, but it had become a sharp point of contention and embarrassment for her this summer. Now that she was eighteen, he appeared to be tightening restrictions instead of loosening them. If Meredith had a date, he personally met the young man at the door and subjected him to a lengthy cross-examination while treating him with an insulting contempt that was intended to intimidate him into never asking her out again. Then he set a ridiculously early curfew of midnight. If she spent the night at Lisa's, he invented a reason to call her and make certain she was there. If she went out for a drive in the evening, he wanted an itinerary of where she was going; when she came back home he wanted an accounting of every minute she'd been gone. After all those years in private schools with the strictest possible rules, she wanted a taste of complete freedom. She'd earned it. She *deserved* it. The idea of living at home for the next four years, under her father's increasingly watchful eye, was unbearable and unnecessary.

Until now she'd never openly rebelled, for rebellion only ignited his temper. He hated being opposed by anyone and, once riled, he could remain frigidly angry for weeks. But it wasn't only fear of his anger that had made her acquiesce to him in the past. In the first place, part of her longed for his approval. In the second place, she could understand how humiliated he must have been by her mother's behavior and the scandal that had followed. When Parker had told her about all that, he'd said her father's overprotective attitude toward Meredith was probably due to the fear of losing her—for she was all he had—and partly to the fear that she might inadvertently do something to reawaken the talk about the scandal her mother had created. Meredith didn't particularly like that last idea, but she'd accepted it, and so she'd spent five weeks of the summer trying to reason with him; when that failed, she'd resorted to arguing. Yesterday, however, the hostilities between them had erupted into their first raging battle. The bill for her tuition deposit had come from Northwestern University, and Meredith had taken it to him in his study. Calmly and quietly, she had said, "I am not going to go to Maryville. I'm going to Northwestern and getting a degree that's worth something."

When she handed him the bill, he tossed it aside and regarded her with an expression that made her stomach cramp. "Really?" he jeered. "And just how do you plan to pay your tuition? I've told you I won't pay it, and you can't touch a cent of your inheritance until you're thirty. It's too late to try for a scholarship now, and you'll never qualify for a student loan, so you can forget about it. You will live here at home and go to Maryville. Do you understand me, Meredith?"

Years of suppressed resentment came spilling out, bursting past Meredith's dam of control. "You're completely irrational!" she cried. "Why can't you understand—"

He stood up slowly, deliberately, his gaze slicing over her with savage contempt. "I understand perfectly!" he sneered furiously. "I understand there are things you want to do—and people you want to do them with—that you know damned well I wouldn't approve of. *That's* why you want to go to a big university and live on campus! What appeals to you most, Meredith? Is it the opportunity to live in coed dorms with boys swarming through the halls and crawling into your bed? Or is it—"

"You are *sick!*"

"And you are just like your mother! You've had the best of everything and all you want is the chance to crawl into bed with the scum of the world—"

"Damn you!" Meredith had blazed, stunned by the force of her own uncontrollable rage. "I'll never forgive you for that. Never." Pivoting on her heel, she had headed for the door.

Behind her, his voice boomed like a thunderclap. "Where do you think you're going!"

"Out!" she had flung over her shoulder. "And another thing, I won't be home by midnight. I'm through with curfews!"

"Come back here!" he shouted. Meredith ignored him and walked down the hall and out the front door. Her fury only intensified as she flung herself into the white Porsche he'd given her on her sixteenth birthday. Her father was demented. He was sick! She spent the evening with Lisa and deliberately stayed out until almost three A.M. Her father was waiting up for her when she returned, pacing in the foyer. He roared and called her names that tore at her heart, but for the first time in her life Meredith wasn't intimidated by his wrath. She endured his vicious verbal attack, and with every cruel word he said, her resolve to defy him increased.

Protected from interlopers and sightseers by a tall iron fence and a guard at the gatehouse, the Glenmoor Country Club sprawled across acres of majestic lawns dotted with flowering shrubs and flower beds. A long, curving drive lit by ornamental gas lamps meandered through stately oak and maple trees to the front door of the club, then curved back again to the main road. The club itself, a rambling three-story white-brick structure with wide pillars marching across its stately façade, was surrounded by two championship golf courses and rows of tennis courts off to the side. At the back, French doors opened onto wide terraces covered with umbrella tables and potted trees. Flagstone steps descended from the lowest terrace to the two Olympic-size pools below. The pools were closed to swimmers tonight, but thick, bright yellow cushions had been left on the chaise longues for those members who might desire to watch the fireworks display from a prone position, or recline between dances when the orchestra came outside to play after that.

Dusk was just beginning to fall as Meredith drove past the main doors where attendants were busy helping members out of their cars. She pulled into the crowded parking lot on the side of the building and parked her car between a gleaming new Rolls belonging to the wealthy founder of a textile mill and an eight-year-old Chevrolet sedan belonging to a much wealthier financier. Normally there was something about dusk that lifted her spirits, but as she got out of her car, she was thoroughly depressed and preoccupied. Other than her clothes, she owned nothing she could sell to raise the money she needed to pay her own college expenses. Her car was in her father's name and her inheritance was under his control. She had exactly $700 in her bank account, $700 to her name. Racking her brain for some way to pay her own tuition, she walked slowly toward the club's main doors.

On special nights like this the club's lifeguards did double duty as parking attendants. One of them hurried up the front steps to hold the door open for her. "Good evening, Miss Bancroft," he said, flashing her a killer smile. He was muscular and good-looking, a med student at the University of Illinois. Meredith knew all that because he'd told her last week when she was trying to sunbathe. "Hello, Chris," she said absently.

In addition to being Independence Day, the Fourth of July also marked the founding of Glenmoor, and the club was alive with laughter and conversation as members with cocktails in their hands wandered from room to room, clad in the tuxedos and evening dresses that were mandatory attire for tonight's dual celebration. The interior of Glenmoor was far less imposing and elegant than some of the newer country clubs around Chicago. The Oriental carpets that covered the polished wood floors were fading, and the sturdy antique furniture in the various rooms created an aura of stuffy complacency rather than glamour. In that respect, Glenmoor was like most of the other premier country clubs in the nation. Old and intensely exclusive, its prestige and desirability came not from its furnishings or even its facilities, but from the social standing of its membership. Wealth alone could not gain one a coveted membership at Glenmoor unless it was also accompanied by sufficient social prominence. On those rare occasions when an applicant for membership met those two standards, he was still required to have the unanimous approval of all fourteen men on Glenmoor's membership committee before submission for comments to the general membership. Those rigid requirements had, in the last few years, scotched the membership aspirations of several newly successful entrepreneurs, countless physicians, innumerable congressmen, a number of players for the White Sox and Bears, and a state supreme court justice.

Meredith, however, was impressed by neither the club's exclusivity nor by its members. They were simply familiar faces, some of whom she knew fairly well, others not well at all. As she walked down the hallway, she nodded and smiled automatically at those people she knew, while she looked into the various rooms for the people she was supposed to meet. One of the dining rooms had been turned into a mock casino for the evening; the other two had been set up for a lavish buffet. All of them were crowded. Below, on the ground floor, an orchestra was tuning up in the club's main banquet room and, judging from the volume of noise coming up the stairwell as she passed it, Meredith assumed there was a crowd down there as well. As she passed the card room, she glanced warily in it. Her father was an inveterate cardplayer, as were most of the other people in the room, but he wasn't there and neither was Jon's group. Having checked out all the rooms on this floor except the club's main lounge, Meredith went there next.

Despite its large size, the decor of the lounge had been intended to create an atmosphere of coziness. Overstuffed sofas and wing chairs were grouped around low tables, and the brass wall sconces were always dimmed so that they cast a warm glow against the mellow oak paneling. Normally the heavy velvet draperies were drawn across the French doors at the back of the lounge; tonight they'd been opened so that guests could stroll out onto the narrow terrace off the lounge, where a band was playing soft music. A bar stretched the entire length of the room on the left, and bartenders moved back and forth from the guests seated at the bar to the mirrored wall behind, where hundreds of liquor bottles were stacked on shelves beneath subdued spotlights.

Tonight the lounge was crowded too, and Meredith was about to turn around and head downstairs when she spotted Shelly Fillmore and Leigh Ackerman, who'd both phoned to remind her she was expected to join them tonight. They were standing at the far end of the bar along with several more of Jonathan's friends and an older couple who Meredith finally identified as Mr. and Mrs. Russell Sommers—Jonathan's aunt and uncle. Pinning a smile on her face, Meredith walked up to them, and then froze as she noticed her father standing with another group of people just to their left. "Meredith," Mrs. Sommers said when Meredith had said hello to everyone, "I love your dress. Where on earth did you find that?"

Meredith had to glance down to see what she was wearing. "It came from Bancroft's."

"Where else!" Leigh Ackerman teased.

Mr. and Mrs. Sommers turned aside to speak to other friends, and Meredith kept one eye on her father, hoping he would stay completely away from her. She'd been standing still for several moments, letting his presence completely unsettle her, when it suddenly struck her that he was even managing to ruin this evening for her! That made her angrily decide to show him he couldn't do it and that, furthermore, she wasn't beaten yet. She turned and ordered a champagne cocktail from one of the bartenders, then she beamed her brightest smile on Doug Chalfont and gave an excellent imitation of being fascinated with whatever he was telling her.

Outside, twilight deepened into night; inside, conversations escalated in volume in direct proportion to the liquor being consumed, while Meredith sipped her second champagne cocktail and wondered if she ought to try to get a job and, in so doing, present her father with further proof of her resolve to go to a good college. She glanced at the mirror behind the bar and caught him watching her, his eyes narrowed with cool displeasure. Idly she wondered what he disapproved of now. Possibly it was her strapless dress, or, more likely, it was the attention Doug Chalfont was paying to her. It couldn't have been the glass of champagne she was holding, however. Just as Meredith had been required to speak like an adult as soon as she learned to talk, she had also been expected to conduct herself as an adult. When she was twelve, her father had started permitting her to stay at the table when he had a few guests in for dinner. By the time she was sixteen, she was learning to act as his hostess, and she sipped wine with dinner guests—in moderation, of course.

Beside her, Shelly Fillmore said it was probably time to go into the dining room or else risk losing their reserved table, and Meredith gave herself a mental shake, belatedly remembering her vow to have a good time tonight. "Jonathan said he'd join us in here before dinner," Shelly added. "Has anybody seen him?" Craning her neck, Shelly looked around the thinning crowd in the lounge, many of whom were also starting to proceed to the dining rooms. "My God!" she burst out, staring at the entrance of the lounge. "Who is that? He's absolutely gorgeous!" That remark, made in a louder tone than she'd intended, caused a ripple of interest, not only among the entire group Meredith was with, but with several other people who'd overheard her exclamation and were turning around.

"Who are you talking about?" Leigh Ackerman asked, peering about the room. Meredith, who was facing the entrance, glanced up and knew instantly *exactly* who had caused that awed, avaricious expression on Shelly's face! Standing in the doorway, with his right hand thrust into his pants pocket, was a man who was at least six feet two, with hair almost as dark as the tuxedo that clung to his wide shoulders and long legs. His face was sun-bronzed, his eyes light, and as he stood there, idly studying the elegantly dressed members of Glenmoor, Meredith wondered how Shelly could ever have described him as "gorgeous." His features looked as if they had been chiseled out of granite by some sculptor who had been intent on portraying brute strength and raw virility—not male beauty. His chin was square, his nose straight, his jaw hard with iron determination. All in all, Meredith thought he looked arrogant, proud, and tough. But then, she'd never been very attracted to dark, overly macho men.

"Look at those shoulders," Shelly rhapsodized, "look at that face. Now, that, Douglas," she teased, turning to Doug Chalfont, "is pure, undiluted sex appeal!"

Doug considered the man and shrugged, grinning. "He doesn't do a thing for me." Turning to one of the other men in their party whom Meredith had met for the first time tonight, he asked, "How about you, Rick? Does he turn you on?"

"I won't know until I see his legs," Rick joked. "I'm a leg man, which is why *Meredith* turns me on."

At that moment, Jonathan appeared in the doorway, looking a little unsteady on his feet, and looped his arm around the newcomer's shoulders while glancing about the room. Meredith saw the triumphant little smile he fired at his friends when he spotted all of them at the end of the bar, and she realized instantly that he appeared to be semi-drunk, but she was completely baffled by the groaning laugh that issued from both Leigh and Shelly. "Oh, no!" Leigh said, looking from Shelly to Meredith with comic dismay. "Please don't tell me that magnificent male specimen is the laborer who Jonathan hired to work on one of their oil rigs!"

Doug Chalfont's burst of laughter had drowned out most of Leigh's words, and Meredith leaned closer to Leigh. "I'm sorry—what did you say?"

Speaking quickly so that she could finish before the two men reached them, Leigh explained, "The man with Jonathan is actually a steelworker from Indiana! Jon's father made him hire the guy to work on their oil rig in Venezuela."

Puzzled not only by the laughing looks being exchanged among Jonathan's other friends, but Leigh's explanation as well, Meredith said, "Why is he bringing him here?"

"It's a joke, Meredith! Jon's angry with his father for forcing him to hire the guy, and then holding him up to Jon as the latest example of what *he* ought to be. Jon brought the guy here to spite his father—you know, to force his father to meet him socially. And you know what's really funny about all this," she whispered just as the two men arrived. "Jon's aunt just told us that his father and mother decided at the last minute to spend the weekend at their summer place instead of coming here—"

Jonathan's overloud, slurred greeting made everyone within hearing turn and stare, including his aunt and uncle and Meredith's father. "Hi, everyone," he boomed, waving an expansive arm to include all of them. "Hi, Aunt Harriet and Uncle Russell!" He waited until he had everyone's attention. "I'd like all of you to meet my buddy, Matt Terrell—no, F-Farrell," he hiccuped. "Aunt Harriet, Uncle Russell," he continued, grinning widely, "say hello to Matt, here. He's my father's latest example of what I ought to be when I grow up!"

"How do you do?" Jonathan's aunt said civilly. Tearing her icy glance from her drunken nephew, she made a halfhearted effort to be courteous to the man he'd brought with him. "Where are you from, Mr. Farrell?"

"Indiana," he replied in a calm matter-of-fact voice.

"Indianapolis?" Jonathan's aunt said, frowning. "I don't believe we know any Farrells from Indianapolis."

"I'm not from Indianapolis. And I'm certain you don't know my family."

"Exactly where are you from?" Meredith's father snapped, ready to interrogate and intimidate any male who went near Meredith.

Matt Farrell turned and Meredith watched in secret admiration as he met her father's withering glance unflinchingly. "Edmunton—south of Gary."

"What do you do?" he demanded rudely.

"I work in a steel mill," he retorted, managing to look and sound just as hard and cold as her father had.

Stunned silence followed his revelation. Several middle-aged couples who'd been hanging back, waiting for Jonathan's aunt and uncle, looked uneasily at each other and moved away. Mrs. Sommers obviously decided to make an equally hasty exit. "Have a pleasant evening, Mr. Farrell," she said stiffly, and headed off to the dining rooms beside her husband.

Suddenly everyone was in motion. "Well!" Leigh Ackerman said brightly, looking around at all the people in their group *except* Matt Farrell, who was standing back and slightly to the side. "Let's go eat!" She tucked her hand in Jon's arm and turned him toward the door as she pointedly added, "I reserved a table for nine people."

Meredith did a fast count; there were nine people in their group— excluding Matt Farrell. Paralyzed with disgust for Jonathan and all his friends, she remained where she was for the moment. Her father saw her standing in the general proximity of Farrell and stopped on his way to the dining room with his own friends, his hand clamping her elbow. "Get rid of him!" he spat out loudly enough for Farrell to hear, and then he stalked off. In a state of angry, defiant rebellion, Meredith watched him leave, then she glanced at Matt Farrell, not certain what to do next. He'd turned toward the French doors and was gazing out at the people on the terrace with the aloof indifference of someone who knows he is an unwanted outsider, and who therefore intends to look as if he prefers it that way.

Even if he hadn't said he was a steelworker from Indiana, Meredith would have known within moments of meeting him that he didn't belong. For one thing, his tuxedo didn't fit his broad shoulders as if it had been custom made for him, which meant it was probably rented, nor did he speak with the ingrained assurance of a socialite who fully expects to be welcomed and liked wherever he is. Moreover, there was an indefinable lack of polish to his mannerisms—a subtle harshness and roughness that intrigued and repelled her at one and the same time.

Given all of that, it was astonishing that he should suddenly remind Meredith of herself. But he did. She looked at him standing completely alone, as if he didn't care about being ostracized—and she saw herself when she was at St. Stephen's school, spending every recess with a book in her lap trying to pretend *she* didn't care either. "Mr. Farrell," she asked as casually as she could, "would you like something to drink?"

He turned in surprise, hesitated a moment, and then nodded. "Scotch and water."

Meredith signaled a waiter who hurried to her side. "Jimmy, Mr. Farrell would like a Scotch and water."

When she turned back, she found Matt Farrell studying her with a slight frown, his gaze drifting over her face, her breasts and waist, then lifting again to her eyes, as if he were suspicious of her overture and trying to figure out why she'd bothered making it. "Who was the man who told you to get rid of me?" he asked abruptly.

She hated to alarm him with the truth. "My father."

"You have my deepest and most sincere sympathy," he mocked gravely, and Meredith burst out laughing because no one had ever dared criticize her father, even indirectly, and because she suddenly sensed that Matt Farrell was a "rebel," just as she'd decided to be. That made him a kindred spirit, and instead of pitying him or being repelled by him, she suddenly thought of him as a brave mongrel who'd been unfairly thrust into a group of haughty pedigrees. She decided to rescue him. "Would you like to dance?" she asked, smiling at him as if he were an old friend.

He gave her an amused look. "What makes you think a steelworker from Edmunton, Indiana, knows how to dance, princess?"

"Do you?"

"I think I can manage."

That was a rather unfair assessment of his ability, Meredith decided a few minutes later as they danced outside on the terrace to the slow tune the little band was playing. He was actually quite competent, but he wasn't very relaxed and his style was conservative.

"How am I doing?"

Blissfully unaware of the double meaning that could be read into her light-hearted evaluation, she said, "So far, all I've been able to tell is that you have good rhythm and you move well. That's all that really matters anyway." Smiling into his eyes to take away any taint of criticism he might mistakenly read into her next words, she confided, "All you actually need is some practice."

"How much practice do you recommend?"

"Not much. One night would be enough to learn some new moves."

"I didn't know there are any 'new' moves."

"There are," Meredith said, "but you have to learn to relax first."

"First?" he repeated. "All this time, I've been under the impression that you were supposed to relax *afterward.*"

It hit her suddenly, what he was thinking and saying. Giving him a level look, she said, "Are we talking about dancing, Mr. Farrell?"

There was an unmistakable reprimand in her voice, and it registered on him. For a moment he studied her with heightened interest, reassessing, reevaluating. His eyes weren't light blue as she'd originally thought, but a striking metallic gray, and his hair was dark brown, not black. When he spoke, his quiet voice had an apology in it. "We are now." Belatedly explaining the reason for the constraint she'd sensed in his movements, he said, "I tore a ligament in my right leg a few weeks ago."

"I'm sorry," Meredith said, apologizing for asking him to come out here. "Does it hurt?"

A startling white smile swept across his tanned face. "Only when I dance."

Meredith laughed at the joke and felt her own worries begin to fade into the background. They stayed outside for another dance, talking about nothing more meaningful than the bad music and the good weather. When they returned to the lounge, Jimmy brought their drinks. Goaded by mischief and resentment for Jonathan, Meredith said, "Please charge these drinks to Jonathan Sommers, Jimmy." She glanced at Matt and saw the surprise on his face.

"Aren't you a member here?"

"Yes," Meredith said with a rueful smile. "That was petty revenge on my part."

"For what?"

"For—" Belatedly realizing that anything she said now would sound like pity or embarrass him, she shrugged. "I don't like Jonathan Sommers very much."

He looked at her oddly, picked up his drink, and tossed down part of it. "You must be hungry. I'll let you go and join your friends."

It was a polite gesture intended to excuse her, but Meredith had no desire to join Jon's group now, and as she looked around the room, it was obvious that if she did leave Matt Farrell there, no one else was going to make the slightest effort to befriend him. In fact, every one in the lounge was giving both of them a wide berth. "Actually," she said, "the food here isn't all that wonderful."

He glanced at the occupants of the lounge and put his glass down with a finality that told her he intended to leave. "Neither are the people."

"They aren't staying away out of meanness or arrogance," she assured him. "Not really."

Slanting her a dubious, disinterested look, he said, "Why do *you* think they're doing it?"

Meredith saw several middle-aged couples who were friends of her father's—nice people, all of them. "Well, for one thing, they're embarrassed about the way Jonathan acted. And because of what they know about you— where you live and what you do for a living, I mean—most of them simply concluded that they don't have anything in common with you."

He obviously thought she was patronizing him because he smiled politely and said, "It's time for me to go."

Suddenly the idea of having him leave with nothing but humiliation to remember the evening didn't seem fair at all. In fact, it seemed unnecessary and . . . and unthinkable! "You can't leave yet," she announced with a determined smile. "Come with me, and bring your drink."

His eyes narrowed. "Why?"

"Because," Meredith declared with stubborn mischief, "it helps to have a drink in your hand to do this."

"Do what?" he persisted.

"Mingle," she declared. "We are going to mingle!"

"Absolutely not!" Matt caught her wrist to draw her back, but it was too late. Meredith was suddenly bent on ramming him down everyone's throat and making them like it.

"Please humor me," she said softly, her gaze beseeching.

A reluctant grin tugged at his lips. "You have the most amazing eyes—"

"Actually, I'm terribly nearsighted," she teased with her most melting smile. "I've been known to walk into walls. It's a pitiful thing to watch. Why don't you give me your arm and guide me out into the hall so I don't stumble?"

He wasn't proof against her humor or that smile. "You are also very single-minded," he replied, but he chuckled and reluctantly offered her his arm, prepared to humor her.

A few steps down the hall Meredith saw an elderly couple she knew. "Hello, Mr. and Mrs. Foster." She greeted them cheerfully as they started to stroll past without seeing her.

They stopped at once. "Why, hello, Meredith," Mrs. Foster said, then she and her husband smiled at Matt with polite inquiry.

"I'd like you to meet a friend of my father's," Meredith announced, swallowing her laughter at Matt's incredulous glance. "This is Matt Farrell. Matt is from Indiana, and he's in the steel business."

"A pleasure," Mr. Foster said genially, shaking Matt's hand. "I know Meredith and her father don't play golf, but I hope they told you we have two championship courses here at Glenmoor. Are you going to be here long enough to play a few rounds?"

"I'm not certain I'm going to be here long enough to finish this drink," Matt said, obviously expecting to be forcibly evicted when Meredith's father discovered she was introducing Matt as his friend.

Mr. Foster nodded in complete misunderstanding. "Business always seems to get in the way of pleasure. But at least you'll see the fireworks tonight—we have the best show in town."

"You're going to tonight," Matt predicted, his narrowed gaze focused warningly on Meredith's guileless expression.

Mr. Foster returned to his favorite subject of golf, while Meredith struggled unsuccessfully to keep her face straight. "What's your handicap?" he inquired of Matt.

"I think *I'm* Matt's handicap tonight," Meredith interceded, slanting Matt a provocative, laughing look.

"What?" Mr. Foster blinked.

But Matt didn't answer and Meredith couldn't, because his gaze had fixed on her smiling lips, and when his gray eyes lifted to hers, there was something different in their depths.

"Come along, dear," Mrs. Foster said, observing the distracted expressions on Matt and Meredith's faces. "These young people don't want to spend their evening discussing golf." Belatedly recovering her composure, Meredith told herself sternly she'd had too much champagne, then she tucked her hand through the crook of Matt's arm. "Come with me," she said, already walking down the staircase to the banquet room where the orchestra was playing.

For nearly an hour she guided him from one group to another, her eyes twinkling at Matt with shared laughter while she smoothly told outrageous half-truths about who he was and what he did for a living. And Matt stood beside her, not actively helping her, but observing her ingenuity with frank amusement.

"There, you see," she announced gaily as they finally left the noise and music behind and walked out the front doors, strolling across the lawn. "It isn't *what* you say that counts, it's what you *don't* say."

"That's an interesting theory," he teased. "Do you have any more of them?"

Meredith shook her head, distracted by something she'd subconsciously noted all evening. "You don't talk at all like a man who works in a steel mill."

"How many of them do you know?"

"Just one," she admitted.

His tone abruptly shifted to a serious one. "Do you come here often?"

They'd spent the first part of the evening playing a kind of silly game, but she sensed that he didn't want any more games. Neither did she, and that moment marked a distinct change in the atmosphere between them. As they wandered past rose beds and flower gardens, he started asking her about herself. Meredith told him she'd been away at school and that she'd just graduated. When his next question was about her career plans, she realized that he'd erroneously assumed she meant she'd graduated from college. Rather than correcting him and risking some sort of appalled reaction when he discovered she was eighteen, not twenty-two, she sidestepped the problem by quickly asking him about himself.

He told her he was leaving in six weeks for Venezuela and what he was going to be doing while he was gone. From there, their conversation shifted with astonishing ease from one subject to another, until they finally stopped walking so that they could concentrate better on whatever was being said. Standing beneath an ancient elm on the lawn, oblivious to the rough bark against her bare back, Meredith listened to him, completely entranced. Matt was twenty-six, she'd discovered, and besides being witty and extremely well-spoken, he had a way of listening intently to what she said as if nothing else in the world mattered. It was disconcerting, and it was very flattering. It also created a false mood of complete intimacy and solitude. She'd just finished laughing at a joke he'd told her, when a fat bug dived past her face and buzzed around her ear. She jumped, grimacing and trying to see where it had gone. "Is it in my hair?" she asked uneasily, tipping her head down.

He put his hands on her shoulders and inspected her hair. "No," he promised. "It was just a little June bug."

"June bugs are disgusting, and that one was the size of a large hummingbird!" When he chuckled, she gave him a deliberately smug smile. "You won't be laughing six weeks from now, when *you* can't walk outside without tripping over snakes."

"Is that right?" he murmured, but his attention had shifted to her mouth, and his hands were sliding up the sides of her neck to tenderly cradle her face.

"What are you doing?" Meredith whispered inanely as he began slowly rubbing his thumb over her lower lip.

"I'm trying to decide if I should let myself enjoy the fireworks."

"The fireworks won't start for another half hour," she said shakily, knowing perfectly well she was going to be kissed.

"I have a feeling," he whispered, slowly lowering his head, "they're going to start right now."

And they did. His mouth covered hers in an electrifyingly seductive kiss that sent sparks exploding through Meredith's entire body. At first the kiss was light, coaxing; his mouth shaped itself to hers, delicately exploring the contours of her lips. Meredith had been kissed before, but always by relatively inexperienced, overeager boys; no one had ever kissed her with Matthew Farrell's unhurried thoroughness. His hands shifted, one of them drifting down her spine to draw her closer, while the other slid behind her nape, and his mouth slowly opened on hers. Lost in the kiss, she moved her hands inside his tuxedo jacket, up his chest, over his broad shoulders, and then she wrapped her arms around his neck.

The minute she molded herself against him, his mouth opened farther, his tongue tracing hotly across her lips, urging them to part, and then demanding it. The moment that they did, his tongue plunged into her mouth, and the kiss exploded. His hand covered her breast, caressing it through her bodice, then restlessly swept behind her, cupping her bottom and pulling her tightly against him, making her vibrantly aware of his aroused body. Meredith stiffened slightly at the forced intimacy, and then for no explainable reason on earth, she laced her fingers through his hair and crushed her parted lips to his.

It seemed like hours later when he finally dragged his mouth from hers. Her heart racing like a trip-hammer, she stood in the circle of his arms, her forehead resting on his chest, while she tried to cope with the turbulent sensations she'd felt. Somewhere in her drugged mind it began to occur to her that he was going to think she was behaving very oddly about what had, in reality, been only a simple kiss. That embarrassing possibility finally made her force her head up. Fully expecting to see him watching her with puzzled amusement, she raised her gaze to his chiseled features, but what she saw there wasn't derision. His gray eyes were smoldering, his face was harsh and dark with passion, and his arms tightened automatically, as if unwilling to let her go. Belatedly, she realized his body was still rigidly aroused, and she felt a peculiar sense of pleasure and pride that he had been, and was still, as affected by the kiss as she was. Without thinking what she was doing, her gaze dropped to his mouth. There was bold sensuality in the mold of those firm lips, and yet some of his kisses had been so exquisitely gentle. Tormentingly gentle . . . Longing to feel that mouth on hers again, Meredith lifted her gaze to his, an unconscious request in her eyes.

Matt understood the request, and a sound that was half groan, half laugh tore from his chest, his arms already tightening. "Yes," he answered hoarsely, and seized her lips in a ravenous, devouring kiss that stole her breath, and drove her mad with pleasure.

Some time later, laughter rang out, and Meredith jerked awkwardly out of his arms, whirling around in alarm. Dozens of couples were strolling out of the club to watch the fireworks—and well ahead of them was her father who was stalking toward her with rage in every long, ground-covering stride. "Oh, my God," she whispered. "Matt, you have to leave. Turn around and walk away! Now."

"No."

"Please!" she almost cried. "I'll be fine, he won't say anything to me here, he'll wait until we're alone, but I don't know what he'll do to you." A moment later Meredith knew the answer to that.

"There are two men on their way out here to escort you off the grounds, Farrell," her father hissed, his face contorted with fury. He turned on Meredith and caught her arm in a viselike grip. "You're coming with me." Two of the club's waiters were already walking across the driveway. As her father gave her arm a jerk, Meredith appealed once more to Matt over her shoulder. "Please, please go—don't make a scene."

Her father pulled her two steps forward, and Meredith, who had no choice but to walk or be dragged, was relieved almost to tears when both waiters who had been coming toward Matt slowed and then stopped. Matt had apparently started walking toward the road, Meredith realized with relief. Her father evidently reached the same conclusion, for when the waiters looked uncertainly to him for further instructions, he said, "Let the bastard go, but call the gate and make sure he doesn't come back."

As they approached the front doors, he turned to Meredith, his expression livid. "Your mother made herself the talk of this club, and I'll be damned if you're going to do it too. Do you hear me!" He flung her arm down as if her skin were contaminated by Matt's touch, but he kept his voice low. Because a Bancroft, no matter how great the provocation, never aired family grievances in public. "Go home and stay there. It will take you twenty minutes to get to the house; in twenty-five minutes I'm going to call you, and God help you if you aren't there!"

With that he turned on his heel and stalked into the clubhouse. In a state of sick humiliation, Meredith watched him go, then she went inside and got her purse. On the way to the parking lot, she saw three couples standing out in the shadows of the trees, all of them kissing.

Her vision blurred by tears of futile rage, Meredith had already driven past the solitary figure who was walking with a tuxedo jacket hooked over his right shoulder before she realized it was Matt. She braked to a stop, so consumed with guilt for the humiliation she'd caused him that she couldn't immediately look at him.

He walked up to her side of the car and bent slightly, looking at her through the open window. "Are you all right?"

"I'm fine." With a halfhearted attempt at flippancy, she glanced at him. "My father is a Bancroft, and the Bancrofts never quarrel in public."

He saw the unshed tears shimmering in her eyes. Reaching through the open window, he laid his callused fingertips against her smooth cheek. "And they don't cry in front of other people either, do they?"

"Nope," Meredith admitted, trying to absorb some of his wonderful indifference to her father. "I—I'm going home now. Can I drop you somewhere on the way?"

His gaze shifted from her face to the death grip she had on the steering wheel. "Yes, but only if you'll let me drive this thing." He spoke as if he merely wanted a chance to drive her car, but his next words made it obvious he was concerned about her ability to drive in her state of mind. "Why don't I drive you home, and I'll call a cab from there."

"Be my guest," Meredith said brightly, determined to salvage what little pride she had left. She got out and walked around to the passenger side.

Matt had no trouble mastering the gearshift, and a minute later the car glided smoothly out of the country club drive and shot out onto the main road. Headlights flew past in the dark and the breeze blew through the windows as they drove in silence. Far off to the left some other fireworks display came to a grand finale in a spectacular cascade of red, white, and blue. Meredith watched the brilliant sparks glitter and then slowly fade as they drifted downward. Belatedly recalling her manners, she said, "I want to apologize for what happened tonight—for my father, I mean."

Matt shot her an amused sideways look. "He's the one who should apologize. It hurt my pride when he sent those two flabby, middle-aged waiters to throw me out. At least he could have sent four of them—just to spare my ego."

Meredith gaped at him, amazed because he obviously wasn't the least bit intimidated by her father's wrath, and then she smiled, because it felt wonderful to be with someone who wasn't. With a jaunty look at his powerful shoulders, she said, "If he really wanted to get you out of there against your will, he'd have been wiser to send six."

"My ego and I *both* thank you," he said with a lazy grin, and Meredith, who would have sworn a few minutes ago that she'd never smile again, burst out laughing.

"You have a wonderful laugh," he said quietly.

"Thank you," she said, startled and pleased beyond proportion to the compliment. In the pale light from the dashboard she studied his shadowy profile, watching the wind ruffle his hair, wondering what it was about him that could make a few simple, quiet words seem like a physical caress. Shelly Fillmore's words floated through her mind, providing the probable answer . . . "pure, undiluted sex appeal." A few hours earlier she hadn't thought Matt was extraordinarily, attractive. She did now. In fact, she was certain women drooled over him. No doubt they were also the reason he knew how to kiss as well as he did. He had sex appeal, all right—and a whole lot of experience kissing. "Turn in here," she said a quarter of an hour later when they approached a pair of huge wrought-iron gates. Reaching forward, she pressed a button on the dashboard and the gates swung open into her driveway.

9

"This is home," Meredith said as he pulled to a stop in front of the house.

He looked up at the imposing stone structure with its leaded glass windows while Meredith unlocked the front door. "It looks like a museum."

"At least you didn't say mausoleum," she said, smiling over her shoulder.

"No, but I thought it."

Meredith was still smiling at his blunt quip as she showed him into the darkened library at the back of the house and turned on a lamp, but when he went directly to the phone on the desk and picked it up, her heart sank. She wanted him to stay, she wanted to talk, she wanted to do *anything* to fend off the despair that she knew would overwhelm her again when she was alone. "There's no reason for you to leave so soon. My father will play cards until the club closes at two A.M."

He turned at the note of desperation in her voice. "Meredith, I'm not a bit worried about your father for my own sake, but you have to live with him. If he comes home and finds me here—"

"He won't," Meredith promised. "My father wouldn't let death interrupt his card games; he's an obsessive cardplayer."

"He's damned obsessive about you too," Matt said flatly, and Meredith held her breath while he hesitated before finally hanging up the phone. This was probably going to be the last pleasant evening she would have for months, and she was determined to make it last. "Would you like a brandy? I'm afraid I can't offer you anything to eat because the servants are already in bed."

"Brandy will be fine."

Meredith went over to the liquor cabinet and took out the brandy decanter. Behind her, he said, "Do the servants lock the refrigerator at night?" She paused, a brandy snifter in her hand. "Something like that," she evaded.

But Matt wasn't fooled—she realized it the moment she brought his glass over to the sofa and saw the amusement gleaming in his eyes. "You can't cook, can you, princess?"

"I'm sure I could," she joked, "if someone showed me where the kitchen is, and then pointed out the stove and refrigerator."

The corners of his mouth deepened into an answering smile, but he leaned forward and purposefully put his glass on the table. She knew exactly what he intended to do even before he caught her wrists and firmly pulled her toward him. "I know you can cook," he said, tipping her chin up.

"What makes you so sure?"

"Because," he whispered, "less than an hour ago you set me on fire."

His mouth was a fraction of an inch from hers when the shrill ring of the telephone made her lurch out of his arms. When she answered it, her father's voice was like an arctic blast. "I'm glad to see that you had sense enough to do as I told you. And Meredith," he added, "I was on the verge of permitting you to go to Northwestern, but you can forget about that now. Your behavior tonight is living proof that you can't be trusted." He hung up on her.

With shaking fingers, Meredith replaced the receiver. Her arms began to tremble and then her knees, until her whole body was quaking with futility and rage, and she braced her palms on the desk to steady herself.

Matt came up behind her and put his hands on her shoulders. "Meredith?" he said, his voice deep with concern. "Who was that? Is anything wrong?"

Even her voice shook. "That was my father checking to make certain that I came home as ordered."

He was silent for a moment, and then he said quietly, "What have you done to make him distrust you like this?"

Matt's thinly veiled accusation tore at her heart, hacking away at her rapidly disintegrating control. "What have I done?" she repeated, her voice rising with hysteria. "What have I *done?*"

"You must have given him some reason to think he has to guard you like this."

Savage resentment boiled up inside of Meredith, erupting into a mass of churning rage. Her eyes bright with tears and some half-formed purpose, she swung around on him and slid her hands up his hard chest. "My mother was promiscuous. She couldn't keep her hands off other men. My father guards me because he knows I'm like her."

Matt's eyes narrowed as she wrapped her arms fiercely around his neck. "What the hell do you think you're doing?"

"You know what I'm doing," she whispered, and before he could answer, she pressed herself against his full length and kissed him long and lingeringly.

He wanted her—Meredith knew it the moment his arms encircled her, pulling her tightly against his hardening body. He wanted her. His mouth seized hers in a hungry, consuming kiss, and she tried to do her best to make certain he didn't change his mind—and that she couldn't change hers. Her fingers clumsy and urgent, she tugged the studs loose from his shirt-front and opened his shirt, sliding her hands up his chest, spreading the white cloth wide apart, baring what looked to be an acre of bronzed muscle with springy dark hairs, then she closed her eyes tightly, reached behind her back and started tugging on the zipper of her dress. She wanted this, she'd *earned* it, she told herself fiercely.

"Meredith?"

His quiet voice made her head jerk up, but she didn't have the courage to lift her gaze above his chest.

"I'm flattered as hell, but I've never actually seen a woman rip off her clothes in the throes of passion, particularly after only one kiss."

Defeated before she'd begun, Meredith leaned her forehead against his chest. His hand slid over her shoulder, long fingers curving around her nape, his thumb stroking, while his other hand slid around her waist and moved her closer. Then his fingers moved down her bare back to the zipper of her dress. The bodice of a very expensive chiffon gown came loose.

Swallowing audibly, she started to lift her arms to shield herself from view, and hesitated. "I'm . . . not very good at this," she said, raising her eyes to his.

His lids drifted down, his gaze shifting to the tops of her breasts. "Aren't you?" he whispered huskily as he bent his head.

Meredith wanted to find nirvana; she sought it in that next kiss. And she found it. Her fingers flexing against the corded muscles in his back, she kissed him with blind need, and when his parted lips moved insistently against hers, she welcomed the suggestive invasion of his tongue. She returned it, and made him gasp and clench her tighter. And then, suddenly, she wasn't in control anymore; she wasn't aware of anything except sensations. His mouth seized hers in stormy desire, her clothes came loose and a cold draft hit her. Her hair tumbled down over her shoulders, freed by his hands, and the room tilted as she was brought down onto the sofa beside a hard, demanding, naked male body.

And then it stopped, and Meredith surfaced a little from a dark, sweet world where she felt only his mouth and the stirring stroking of his hands over her flesh. She opened her eyes and saw him leaning up on his forearm, studying her face in the mellow glow of the desk lamp. "What are you doing?" she whispered, but the thin, wispy voice didn't sound like hers.

"Looking at you." As he said it, his gaze moved down along the sides of her breasts past her waist, then down her thighs and legs. Embarrassed, Meredith stopped him from what he was doing by touching her lips to his chest. His muscles flinched reflexively as she brushed her lips over his skin, and his hand sank slowly into the hair at her nape, lifting her forward. This time when she raised her gaze to his, he bent his head. His mouth captured hers almost roughly, his tongue parting her lips and driving into her mouth in a fiercely erotic kiss that sent flames shooting through her entire body. Leaning over her, he kissed her until she heard herself moaning softly, and then his mouth was at her breasts, making them ache while his fingers explored and tormented and made her back arch against his hand. He moved, his body shifting on top of her, his hips insistent, his lips rough and tender against the curve of her neck and cheek. His mouth returned to hers again, parting her lips; his legs wedged between hers, parting her thighs, and all the while his tongue was tangling with hers, withdrawing and plunging deep. And then he stopped.

Cradling her face between his palms, he ordered hoarsely, "Look at me." Somehow Meredith managed to surface from her sensual daze; she forced her lids open and looked into his scorching gray eyes. The moment she did, Matt drove into her with a force that tore a low cry from her throat and made her body arch like a bow. In that split second he recognized he'd just taken her virginity, and his reaction was more violent than hers. He froze, his eyes clenched shut. His shoulders and arms taut, he stayed there inside her, unmoving. "Why?" he demanded in a raw whisper.

She shivered at the accusation she thought she heard and misunderstood his question. "Because I haven't done it before."

That answer made his eyes open and what she saw wasn't disappointment or accusation, it was tenderness and regret. "Why didn't you tell me? I could have made this much easier for you."

Spreading her fingers over his cheek, Meredith said with a soft, reassuring smile, "You did make it easy. And perfect."

That accomplished what nothing else had. It made him groan. He covered her lips with his and, with infinite gentleness, began to move inside her, withdrawing almost all the way and slowly plunging deep, steadily increasing the tempo of his driving strokes, giving and giving and giving until Meredith was wild beneath him. Her fingernails bit into his back and hips, clutching him to her, while the passion raging inside her built into a holocaust, and still it went on and on, until it finally exploded in long soul-destroying bursts of extravagant pleasure. Gathering her into his arms, Matt shoved his fingers into her hair, kissing her with fiery urgency, and drove into her one more time. The deep raw hunger of his kiss, the sudden surge of liquid from his body into hers, made Meredith clasp him tighter and moan with the exquisite sensation.

Her heart beating frantically, she moved onto her side with him, her face pressed against his chest, his arms tight around her. "Do you have any idea," he whispered in a shaken, hoarse voice, his lips brushing her cheek, "how exciting you are, and how responsive?"

Meredith didn't answer, because the reality of what he'd done was beginning to seep through her, and she didn't want to let it. Not now, not yet. She didn't want anything to spoil this. She closed her eyes and listened to the lovely things he continued to say to her while he laid his hand against her cheek, idly brushing his thumb over her skin.

And then he asked something that did need a response and the magic faded, receding beyond her reach. "Why?" he asked her quietly. "Why did you do this tonight? With me?"

She tensed at the difficult, probing question, sighed with a feeling of loss, and pulled out of his arms, wrapping herself in the afghan lying over the end of the sofa. She'd known about the physical intimacy of sex, but no one had warned her about this strange, uneasy aftermath. She felt stripped bare emotionally; exposed, defenseless, awkward. "I think we'd both better get dressed," she said nervously, "and then I'll tell you whatever you want to know. I'll be right back."

In her room, Meredith put on a navy and white robe, tied the belt around her waist, and went back downstairs, still barefoot. As she passed the clock in the hall, she glanced at it. Her father would be home in an hour.

Matt was on the phone in the study, fully dressed with the exception of his tie, which he'd shoved into his pocket. "What's the address here?" he asked. She told him and he relayed it to the cab company he had called. "I told them to be here in a half hour," he said. Walking over to the coffee table in front of the sofa, he picked up his abandoned brandy glass.

"Can I get you anything else?" Meredith asked, because that question seemed like something a good hostess normally asked a guest when the evening neared its end. Or was that what a waitress asked, she wondered a little hysterically.

"I'd like an answer to my question," he said. "What made you decide to do this tonight?"

She thought she heard a tautness in his voice, but his face was completely expressionless. She sighed and looked away, self-consciously tracing an inlaid square on the desk. "For years my father has treated me like a . . . a closet nymphomaniac, and I've never done anything to deserve it. Tonight when you insisted he must have some reason for 'guarding me,' something just snapped inside of me. I think I decided that if I was going to be treated like a tramp, I might as well have the experience of sleeping with a man. And at the same time, I had some insane idea of punishing you—and him. I wanted to show you that you were wrong."

After several moments of ominous silence, Matt said curtly, "You could have convinced me I was wrong by simply telling me that your father is a tyrannical, suspicious bastard. I would have believed you."

In her heart, Meredith knew that was true, and she glanced uneasily at him, wondering if anger had been her only reason for instigating what had just happened, or if she'd simply used anger as an excuse to experience intimately that sexual magnetism she'd felt from him all night. *Used.* That was the operative word. In a strange sort of way she felt guilty for using a man she had liked enormously to retaliate against her father.

In the lengthening silence, he seemed to evaluate what she'd said, and what she hadn't said, and to guess what she was thinking. Whatever conclusions he drew from all that obviously didn't please him very much, because he abruptly put down his glass and glanced at his watch. "I'll walk down to the end of the drive."

"I'll show you out." Polite sentences spoken between two strangers who'd been doing the most intimate possible things together less than one hour ago. That incongruity registered on her as she straightened from the desk. At the same moment his gaze riveted on her bare feet, shot back to her face, and then ricocheted to her hair tumbling loose about her shoulders. Barefoot, hair down, and in a long robe, Meredith did not look quite the way she did in a strapless evening dress with her hair in a sophisticated chignon. She knew before he asked the question what it was going to be.

"How old are you?"

"Not . . . quite as old as you think."

"How old?" he persisted.

"Eighteen."

She expected some sort of reaction to that. Instead, he looked at her for a long, hard moment, and then he did something that made no sense to her. Turning, he went over to the desk and wrote something on a slip of paper. "This is my phone number in Edmunton," he said calmly, handing it to her. "You can reach me there for the next six weeks. After that, Sommers will know how to get in touch with me somehow."

When he left, she walked upstairs, frowning at the scrap of paper in her hand. If this was Matt's way of suggesting she give him a call sometime, it was arrogant, rude, and completely obnoxious. And a little humiliating.

For most of the following week, Meredith jumped every time the phone rang, afraid that it was going to be Matt. Just the recollection of the things they'd done made her face burn with embarrassment, and she wanted to forget it and him.

By the following week she didn't want to forget it at all. Once the guilt and fear of discovery had receded, she found herself thinking about him constantly, reliving the same moments she'd wanted to forget. Lying in bed at night, with her face pressed into the pillow, she felt his lips on her cheek and neck, and she recalled each sexy, tender word he'd whispered to her with a tiny thrill. She thought about other things too, like the pleasure of being with him while they talked on the lawn at Glenmoor, and the way he'd laughed at the things she said. She wondered if he was thinking about her, and if he was, *why* didn't he call . . .

When he didn't phone the week after that, Meredith realized she was obviously very forgettable and that he hadn't thought her "exciting" or "responsive" at all. She went over and over the things she'd said to Matt just before he left, wondering if something she'd said was the reason for his silence now. She considered the possibility that she might have hurt his pride when she told him the truth about why she'd decided to sleep with him, but she found that very hard to believe. Matthew Farrell wasn't the least bit insecure about his sexual attraction—he'd carried on that sexual banter with her within minutes of meeting her, when they first danced. It was more likely he hadn't called because he'd decided she was too young to bother with.

By the end of the following week, Meredith no longer wanted to hear from him. Her period was two weeks overdue, and she wished to God she'd never *met* Matthew Farrell at all. As one day drifted into the next, she couldn't think about anything except the terrifying possibility that she'd gotten pregnant. Lisa was in Europe, so there was no one to turn to or help make the time go faster. She waited and she prayed and she promised fervently that if she wasn't pregnant, she'd never have intercourse again until she was married.

But either God wasn't listening to her prayers or He was immune to bribery. In fact, the only one who seemed to notice and care that she was in a silent agony was her father. "What's wrong, Meredith?" he asked repeatedly. Not long ago the biggest problem in her life was not being able to go to the college she wanted to attend. Now that problem seemed infinitesimal. "Nothing is wrong," she told him. She'd been too worried to argue with him over what happened with Matt at Glenmoor, and too distracted to engage in any more battles with him thereafter.

Six weeks after she met Matt, Meredith's second period did not occur on its usual date, and her fear escalated to terror. Trying to console herself with the fact that she didn't feel sick in the mornings or any other time, she made an appointment for a pregnancy examination and test.

Five minutes after she hung up the phone, her father knocked on her bedroom door. When she called to him to come in, he walked over to her and held out a large envelope. The return address read Northwestern University. "You win," he said shortly. "I can't stand any more of this mood you've been in. Go to Northwestern if it's that damned important to you. I'll expect you home on weekends, however, and that is *not* negotiable!"

She opened the envelope that contained the notice that she was officially enrolled for the fall semester, and she managed a weak smile.

Meredith didn't go to her own doctor because he was one of her father's cronies. Instead, she went to a dingy family planning clinic near Chicago's South Side where she was certain no one would know her. The harassed physician there confirmed her worst fears: She was pregnant.

Meredith heard that with a peculiar dead calm, but by the time she got home, her numbness had given way to mindless, gripping panic. She could not face an abortion, she didn't think she could face giving the baby up for adoption, and she could not face her father with the news that she was about to become an unwed mother and the newest scandal in the Bancroft family. There was only one other alternative, and Meredith took it: She called the number Matt had given her. When no one answered the phone she called Jonathan Sommers and lied that she'd found something of Matt's and needed to send it to him. Jonathan provided her with Matt's address and the information that Matt hadn't yet left for Venezuela. Her father was out of town, so she packed a small suitcase, left him a note saying that she'd gone to visit friends, got into her car, and drove to Indiana.

In her despondent state of mind, she saw Edmunton as a bleak town of smokestacks, factories, and steel mills. Matt's address was in a distant rural area that, to her, was just as bleak. After a half hour of driving up one county highway and then another, Meredith gave up trying to locate the road he'd written down and pulled into a run-down gas station to ask directions.

A fat, middle-aged mechanic came out, his eyes sweeping over Meredith's Porsche, and then her, in a way that made her skin crawl. She showed him the address she was trying to find, but instead of telling her where it was, he turned and yelled over his shoulder, "Hey, Matt, isn't this your road?"

Meredith's eyes widened as the man who'd had his head beneath the hood of an old truck in the service station slowly straightened and turned. It was Matt; his hands were covered with grease, his jeans were old and faded, and he looked exactly like a mechanic in some godforsaken little town. She was so stunned by how different he looked, and so panicked about her pregnancy, she couldn't hide her reaction as he walked up to the car. He saw it, and it doused the surprised smile from his chiseled features; his face hardened, and when he spoke, his voice was devoid of emotion. "Meredith," he said, acknowledging her with a curt nod. "What brings you here?"

Instead of looking at her, he was concentrating on wiping his hands on the rag he'd pulled out of his back pocket, and Meredith had the clutching feeling that he'd just guessed why she was there, and *that* accounted for the sudden chill in his attitude. She wished, very devoutly, that she were dead— and with equal fervency that she hadn't gone there. He obviously wasn't going to want to help, and any grudging help he could offer, she didn't want. "Nothing, really," she lied with a hollow laugh, her hand already hovering over the gearshift. "I just decided to take a drive and found myself heading this way. I guess I'd better be going though, and—"

He lifted his gaze from the rag to hers then, and her voice suffocated as a pair of piercing gray eyes locked onto hers . . . cold, probing, speculative eyes. *Knowing* eyes. Reaching down, he opened the door. "I'll drive," he clipped, and in her state of wild tension, Meredith obeyed automatically, getting out of the car and walking around it. Over his shoulder, Matt glanced at the fat man who was hovering at the hood of the car, watching the scenario with disgustingly ill-bred fascination. "I'll be back in an hour."

"Hell, Matt, it's already three-thirty," the other mechanic said, his face splitting into a grin that displayed a missing front tooth. "Knock off for the day. A classy piece like this one deserves more than just an hour with you."

Meredith's humiliation was complete, and to add to her misery, Matt looked absolutely incensed as he rammed the Porsche into gear and shot out onto the winding county road, gravel spraying from the tires. "Do you mind slowing down a little?" she asked shakily, surprised and relieved when he immediately eased off the accelerator. Feeling that some sort of conversation was demanded, she said the only thing she could think of at the moment. "I thought you worked in a mill."

"I work there five days a week. I moonlight here the other two as a mechanic."

"Oh," she said uneasily. A few minutes later, they rounded a curve and he flipped on the turn indicator, then he pulled into a small clearing in a grove of trees with an old, weathered picnic table in the middle of it. Lying in the grass beside a crumbling brick barbecue was a wooden sign with faded letters carved into it that said MOTORISTS PICNIC GROUNDS. COURTESY, EDMUNTON LIONS CLUB.

He turned off the ignition and in the silence Meredith could hear her blood pounding frantically in her ears as she stared straight ahead, trying to adjust to the fact that the inscrutable stranger beside her was the same man she'd laughed with and made love with six weeks before. The dilemma that had sent her there hung over her like a stifling pall, indecision raged at her, and tears she refused to shed ached in her eyes. He moved and she jumped, her head jerking toward him—but all he was doing was getting out of the car. He came around to her side and opened her door, and Meredith got out. Looking around with feigned interest, she said, "It's pretty here," but her voice sounded strained and taut to her own ears. "I really have to be getting back though."

Instead of answering, he leaned his hip on the picnic table, his weight braced on the opposite foot, and quirked an expectant brow at her—waiting, she supposed, for some sort of additional explanation about her visit. His prolonged silence and unwavering scrutiny were tearing away at the control she was fighting to maintain. The thoughts that had screamed through her mind all day began their terrifying chanting again: She was pregnant, and about to become an unwed mother, and her father was going to be demented with rage and pain. She was pregnant! She was *pregnant!* She was pregnant—and the man who was semi-responsible for her heartbreak was sitting there watching her squirm with the detached interest of a scientist observing a bug wriggling under a microscope. Suddenly and irrationally furious, Meredith rounded on him. "Are you angry about something, or are you just being perverse by refusing to say anything?"

"Actually," he replied evenly, "I'm waiting for you to begin."

"Oh." Meredith's burst of fury gave way to misery and uncertainty as she searched his composed features. She'd ask him for advice, she decided, reversing her decision of a few minutes ago. Just advice, that's all. God knew, she had to talk to someone! Crossing her arms over her chest as if to protect herself from Matt's reaction, she tipped her head back, swallowing painfully as she pretended to study the leafy canopy above. "As a matter of fact, I did have a specific reason for coming here today."

"I assumed you did."

She glanced at him, trying to guess if he'd assumed anything else, but his expression was unreadable. She returned her gaze to the leaves, watching them blur as scalding tears stung her eyes. "I'm here because—" She couldn't say the words, the ugly, shameful words.

"Because you're pregnant," he finished for her in a flat voice.

"How did you guess?" she choked bitterly.

"Only two things could have brought you here. That was one of them."

Drowning in isolated misery, she said, "What was the other one?"

"My superb dancing?"

He was joking, and the wholly unexpected reaction was Meredith's undoing. The dam of tears broke; she covered her face with her hands and her body shook with wrenching sobs. She felt his hands close on her shoulders, and she let him pull her forward between his thighs and into his arms. "How can you j-joke at a time like this?" she wept against his chest, but she was painfully glad for the silent comfort he was offering with his embrace. He pressed a handkerchief into her hand, and Meredith shuddered, struggling desperately for control. "Go ahead and say it," she told him, wiping her eyes. "I was stupid to let this happen."

"You won't get any argument from me on that."

"Thank you," she said sarcastically, dabbing at her nose. "Now I feel much better." It dawned on her then that he was reacting with amazing and admirable calm and that her attitude was only making matters worse.

"Are you absolutely certain you're pregnant?"

Meredith nodded. "I went to a clinic this morning, and they said I'm six weeks pregnant. I'm also certain the baby's yours, in case you're wondering and you're too polite to ask."

"I'm not *that* polite," he said sardonically. Her teary aquamarine eyes snapped to his, blazing with affront at what she mistook for his challenge, and he shook his head to silence her outburst. "It isn't courtesy that stopped me from asking, it's a knowledge of basic biology. I don't doubt that I'm responsible." She'd half expected recriminations, shock, and disgust from him; the fact that he was reacting with quiet, unemotional logic was incredibly reassuring and utterly baffling. Staring at the button on his blue shirt, she brushed away a tear and heard him calmly ask the question that had been torturing her for hours: "What do you want to do?"

"Kill myself!" she admitted dismally.

"What's your second choice?"

Her head jerked up at the reluctant smile she heard in his voice. Her brows drawing together in confusion, Meredith looked at him, struck by the indomitable strength in that rugged face, comforted by the surprising understanding she saw in his steady gaze. She pulled back slightly, needing to think, and felt a twinge of disappointment when he dropped his arms immediately. Even so, his calm acceptance of the facts had communicated itself to her, and she felt considerably more rational than she had all day. "All my choices are horrible. The people at the clinic thought an abortion was a logical choice. . . ." She waited, fully expecting him to urge her to do exactly that. If she hadn't caught the imperceptible tightening of his jaw, she'd have thought him either indifferent to the idea or even in agreement with it. As it was, she still wasn't completely certain. She looked away and her voice broke. "But I——I don't think I can face it, not alone. Even if I did, I don't know if I could live with myself afterward." She drew a long, quavering breath, trying to steady her voice. "I could have the baby and give it up for adoption, but, oh, God, that wouldn't solve things. Not for me. I'd still have to tell my father I'm an unwed mother, and that's going to break his heart. He'll never forgive me. I know he won't! And——and I keep thinking of how my baby would feel, later on, wondering why I gave it away. And I know I'd spend the rest of *my* life looking at children, wondering if that one was mine, and if it's wondering about me and looking for *me*." She brushed away another tear. "I don't think I could live with the doubt or the guilt."

She glanced at his inscrutable features. "Could you possibly comment on some of this?" she demanded.

"As soon as you say something I disagree with," he informed her in a tone of authority he'd never used on her before, "I'll let you know."

Daunted by his tone, but comforted by his words, she said, "Oh." Nervously rubbing her palms on the legs of her tan slacks, Meredith continued, "My father divorced my mother because she slept around. If I go home and tell him I'm pregnant, I think he'll throw me out. I don't have any money, but I'll inherit some when I'm thirty. I can try to raise my baby myself, somehow, until then. . . ."

He finally spoke. Two words—terse and final. "*Our* baby."

Meredith nodded shakily, relieved to the point of tears that he felt that way. "The last alternative is one you—you aren't going to like. I don't like it either. It's obscene. . . ." She trailed off in humiliated anguish, then she summoned all her courage and began again, her words rushing out. "Matt, would you be willing to help me convince my father we fell in love, and decided to get . . . get married right away? Then we could tell him a few weeks from now that I'm pregnant? Naturally, after the baby is born, we'll get a divorce. Would you agree to an arrangement like that?"

"With great reluctance," he snapped after a prolonged pause.

Drowning in humiliation at his long hesitation and ungracious acceptance, Meredith turned her face away. "Thank you for being so gallant," she replied sarcastically. "I'll be happy to put it in writing that I don't want anything from you for the baby, and that I promise to give you a divorce. I have a pen in my purse," she added, starting for the car with some half-formed, angry idea of writing out an agreement there and then.

His hand locked on her arm as she stalked past him, pulling her to an abrupt halt and turning her around. "How the hell do you expect me to react?" he bit out. "Don't you think it's just a little unromantic on *your* part to begin by telling me you find the idea of marrying me 'obscene' and to start talking about a divorce in the same breath you mentioned marriage?"

"Unromantic?" Meredith repeated, gaping at his harsh features, torn between hysterical laughter at his monumental understatement and alarm at his anger. But then the rest of what he'd said hit her, banishing her mirth and making her feel like a thoughtless child. "I'm sorry," she said, looking directly into enigmatic silver eyes. "I truly am. I didn't mean that marrying you is obscene to me. I meant that getting married because I'm already pregnant is an obscene reason for doing something that's—that's supposed to happen only because two people are in love."

Limp with relief, she watched his expression soften. "If we can make it to the courthouse before five o'clock," he said, straightening and taking charge, "we can get the license out of the way today and get married on Saturday."

Getting a marriage license struck Meredith as being appallingly easy and sickeningly meaningless. She stood beside Matt, producing the necessary documents to prove her age and identity, watching him sign his name and signing hers beneath it. Then they walked out of the old courthouse in the center of town while the janitor waited impatiently to lock the doors behind them. Engaged to be married. As simply and unemotionally as that. "We made it just in time," she said, her smile bright and brittle, her stomach churning. "Where are we going now?" she added as she slid into the car, automatically letting him drive because she didn't want to bother.

"I'm going to take you home."

"Home?" she repeated tautly, noticing he didn't look one bit more pleased about what they'd just done than she felt. "I can't go home, not until we're married."

"I wasn't referring to that stone fortress in Chicago," he corrected her, sliding into the seat beside her. "I was talking about my home." As tired and bemused as she felt, his disdainful description of her house still made her smile a little. She was beginning to realize that Matthew Farrell wasn't awed or intimidated by anything, or anyone. Turning, he rested his arm across the back of her seat, and her smile faded at his implacable tone. "I agreed to get a license, but before we take the final step, we're going to have to come to an agreement on some things."

"What things?"

"I don't know yet. We'll talk more at home."

Forty-five minutes later, Matt turned off a county road lined with neatly tended cornfields into a rutted driveway. The car rattled and pounded over the wooden planks of a little bridge that spanned a creek, rounded a curve, and Meredith had her first glimpse of the place he called home. In sharp contrast to the well-kept fields in the distance, the quaint frame farmhouse looked forlorn and badly in need of paint. In the yard, weeds were winning the battle for space with grass, and the door on the barn to the left of the house was hanging drunkenly on one hinge. Despite all that, there was evidence that someone had once loved and enjoyed the place; pink roses were blooming riotously on a trellis beside the porch and there was an old wooden porch swing hanging from the limb of a giant oak tree in the front yard.

On the way there, Matt had told her that his mother had died seven years before, after a long bout with cancer, and that he lived there with his father and his sixteen-year-old sister. Overwhelmed with nervousness at the thought of meeting his family, Meredith tipped her head toward the right, where a farmer was driving a tractor through a field. "Is that your father?"

Matt paused as he leaned down to open her door, glanced in the direction she indicated, and shook his head. "That's a neighbor. We sold most of our land years ago, and we lease the rest to him. My father lost what little interest he had in farming when my mother died." He saw the tension in her face as they started up the porch steps, and he put his hand on her arm. "What's wrong?"

"I'm scared to death about facing your family."

"There's nothing to be afraid of. My sister will think you're exciting and sophisticated because you're from the big city." After a hesitant pause, he added, "My father drinks, Meredith. He started when they told him my mother's illness was terminal. He holds down a regular job and he's never abusive. I'm telling you this so you'll understand him and be able to make allowances. He's been completely sober for a couple of months, but that can end at any time." It wasn't an apology, it was a statement of fact, spoken in a calm, nonjudgmental voice.

"I understand," she said, though she'd never had any close association with an alcoholic in her life and she didn't understand at all.

She was spared the need to worry about it further because at that moment the screen door banged open and a slim girl with Matt's dark hair and gray eyes raced onto the porch, her gaze glued to the car in the yard. "Omigod, Matt, a Porsche!" Her hair was cut almost as short as his, and it made her pretty features even more vivid. She turned to Meredith, her face alive with reverent wonder. "Is it yours?"

Meredith nodded, taken aback by the surge of instantaneous liking she felt for the girl who resembled Matt so much, and yet had none of his reserve. "You must be incredibly rich," she continued ingenuously. "I mean, Laura Frederickson is *very* rich, but she's never had a Porsche."

Meredith was stunned by the mention of money and curious about Laura Frederickson; Matt looked extremely annoyed by the mention of both. "Knock it off, Julie!" he warned.

"Oh, sorry," she said, grinning at him. To Meredith she said, "Hi. I am Matt's incredibly bad-mannered sister, Julie. Are you guys coming inside?" She opened the screen door. "Dad got up a little while ago," she added to Matt. "He's working the eleven o'clock shift this week, so dinner will be at seven-thirty. Is that okay?"

"Fine," Matt said, putting his hand on Meredith's back, ushering her inside. Meredith glanced about her, her heart beating a frantic tattoo as she braced herself to meet Matt's father. The interior of the house looked much like the exterior—quaint, with signs of neglect and wear that overshadowed its early-American charm. The wooden plank floors were scarred and scuffed, and the braided rugs that were scattered about were worn and faded. At right angles to a brick fireplace with bookshelves built into the wall, a pair of nubby green armchairs faced a sofa upholstered in a patterned cloth that long ago had resembled autumn leaves. Beyond the living room was a dining room with maple furniture, and beyond that an open door revealed a kitchen with a sink that stood on legs. A stairway on the right led from the dining room to the second floor, and a very tall, thin man with graying hair and a deeply grooved face was walking down it, a folded newspaper in one hand, a glass filled with dark amber liquid in the other. Unfortunately, Meredith hadn't seen him until that moment, and the uneasiness she felt as she looked around the house was still written across her face when her eyes riveted on the glass in his hand.

"What's going on?" he asked as he walked into the living room, glancing from Meredith to Matt to Julie, who was hovering near the fireplace, surreptitiously admiring Meredith's pleated slacks, Italian sandals, and khaki safari shirt.

In answer, Matt introduced Meredith to him and to Julie. "Meredith and I met when I was in Chicago last month," he added. "We're getting married on Saturday."

"You're *whaaat?*" his father uttered.

"Fantastic!" Julie cried, diverting everyone. "I always wanted a big sister, but I never imagined she'd come with her very own Porsche!"

"Her very own what?" Patrick Farrell demanded of his irrepressible daughter.

"Porsche," Julie repeated ecstatically, racing over to the window and drawing the curtain back to show him. Meredith's car glinted in the sunlight—sleek, white, and expensive. As completely out of place as she was. Patrick evidently thought so too, because when he looked from the car to Meredith, his shaggy brows jerked together until the creases between his faded blue eyes deepened to furrows. "Chicago?" he said. "You were in Chicago for only a few days!"

"Love at first sight!" Julie declared, leaping into the breach of taut silence. "How romantic!"

Patrick Farrell, who'd seen the uneasy expression on Meredith's face when she glanced around the house a moment earlier, attributed her reaction to disdain for his home and for him, not to her own frighteningly uncertain future. Now he glanced out the window at her car, then turned and looked at her frozen face. "Love at first sight," he repeated, studying her with unconcealed doubt. "Is that what it was?"

"Obviously," Matt said in a tone that warned him to drop the subject, then he rescued Meredith by the expedient means of asking her if she'd like to rest before dinner. Meredith would have eagerly grabbed at barbed wire to haul herself out of this. Next to telling Matt she was pregnant, this was the second most humiliating confrontation of her life. She nodded at Matt while Julie insisted that Meredith use her room, and Matt went out to the car for Meredith's overnight bag.

Upstairs, Meredith sank morosely onto Julie's four-poster, and Matt put her single piece of luggage on a chair. "The worst is over with," he told her quietly.

Without looking up, she shook her head, twisting her fingers in her lap. "I don't think so. I think it's only beginning." Seizing on the smallest of her looming problems, she said, "Your father hated me on sight."

Laughter tinged his voice. "It might have helped if you hadn't looked at the glass of iced tea he was holding like it was a coiled snake."

Flopping back on the bed, she stared at the ceiling and swallowed, ashamed and bewildered. "Did I do that?" she asked hoarsely, closing her eyes as if to shut out the image.

Matt looked down at the forlorn beauty draped across the bed like a drooping flower, and in his mind he saw her as she'd been at the country club six weeks ago, filled with laughing mischief and doing her effective damnedest to ensure that he enjoyed himself. He noted the changes in her while something strange and unfamiliar tugged heavily at his heart, and his mind pointed out the absurdities of their dilemma:

They didn't know each other at all; they knew each other intimately.

In comparison to every other female he'd had sex with, Meredith was a complete innocent; she was pregnant with his child.

There was a social gulf between them a thousand miles wide; they were going to bridge that gulf with marriage. And then widen it with divorce.

They had absolutely nothing in common; nothing except one astonishing night of lovemaking—sweet, hot lovemaking, where the seductive, insistent temptress in his arms had become a panicky virgin, and then a tormenting delight. An unforgettable night of lovemaking that had haunted him for weeks afterward, a night when he had been willingly seduced, only to become the insistent seducer who was more desperate than ever in his life to give them both a climax they'd never forget.

And he certainly had.

Thanks to his unsurpassed diligence and determination in that endeavor, he'd made himself a father.

A wife and child were definitely not a part of Matt's master plan right now; on the other hand, he'd known when he devised the plan and followed it for ten long years, that sooner or later something was going to happen and he was going to have to adapt it to suit new requirements. The responsibility for Meredith and the baby was coming at a very inopportune time, but Matt was used to shouldering enormous responsibilities. No, the responsibility didn't bother him as much as other things did—the most immediate of which was the absence of hope and laughter on Meredith Bancroft's face. The possibility that because of what happened six weeks ago, those two things might never brighten that entrancing face of hers bothered him more than he would have believed possible. Which was why he leaned over her, braced his fists on either side of her shoulders, and in a voice he'd meant to be teasing, he ordered sharply, "Cheer up, sleeping beauty!"

Her eyes snapped open, narrowed, dropped to the smile on his lips, then lifted to his eyes again in confused misery. "I can't," she whispered hoarsely. "This whole idea is insane, I see that now. We'll only be making things worse for each other, and the baby, by getting married."

"Why do you say that?"

"Why?" she repeated, flushing with humiliation. "How can you ask me why? My God, you didn't even want to take me out again after that night. You haven't even *phoned*. How can—"

"I intended to call you," he interrupted. She rolled her eyes at that unbelievable claim, and he went on. "In a year or two—as soon as I got back from South America." If she weren't so miserable, Meredith would have laughed in his face at that one, but his next words, spoken with quiet force, stunned her and doused the impulse. "If I'd thought for one minute you actually *wanted* to hear from me, I'd have called you long before this."

Torn between disbelief and painful hope, Meredith closed her eyes, trying unsuccessfully to deal with her bewildering, uncontrollable reactions. Everything was extremes—extremes of despair, of relief, of hope, of joy.

"Cheer up!" Matt ordered again, inordinately pleased that she'd apparently wanted to see him again. Among other things, he'd assumed six weeks ago that in the harsh light of day, she'd reevaluate things and decide his combined lack of money and social standing were impossible obstacles to any further relationship. Evidently she hadn't felt that way. She drew a ragged breath, and not until she spoke did Matt realize that she was trying valiantly to respond to his urging to cheer up. With a tremulous smile she said darkly, "Are you planning to be a nag?"

"I think that's supposed to be my line."

"Really?"

"Mmm," he confirmed. "Wives nag."

"What do husbands do?"

He gave her a look of deliberate superiority. "Husbands command."

In contrast to her next words, her smile and voice were angelically sweet. "Would you like to bet on that?"

Matt tore his gaze from her inviting lips and looked into jewel-bright eyes. Mesmerized, he answered with blunt honesty. "No."

And then the last thing that he expected occurred. Instead of cheering her up, he realized she was crying, and just when he was blaming himself for making her do that, Meredith put her arms around him and pulled him down to her. Burying her face in the curve of his neck and shoulder, she turned into his arms as he stretched out beside her on the bed, her slim shoulders shaking. When she finally spoke, several moments later, her words were rendered almost indistinguishable by tears. "Does a farmer's fiancée have to can and pickle things?"

Matt muffled a stunned laugh, stroking her luxuriant hair. "No."

"Good, because I don't know how."

"I'm not a farmer," he reassured her. "You know that."

The real cause of her misery came pouring out in a sob of deep, pure grief. "I was supposed to start college next month. I *have* to go to college. I p-planned to be president someday, Matt."

Astonished, Matt tipped his chin down, trying to see her face. "That's a hell of a goal," he said before he could stop himself. "President of the United States . . ."

That last, perfectly serious remark, startled a shriek of teary laughter from the unpredictable young woman in his arms. "Not of the United States, of a store!" she corrected him, and the gorgeous eyes she raised to his were suddenly swimming with tears of laughter now instead of despair.

"Thank God for that," he teased, so eager to keep her smiling that he paid no attention to the implications of what he was saying. "I expect to be a reasonably rich man in the next few years, but buying you the presidency of the United States might be beyond my means even then."

"Thank you," she whispered.

"For what?"

"For making me laugh. I haven't cried this much since I was a child. Now I can't seem to stop."

"I hope you weren't laughing at what I said about being rich."

Despite his light tone, Meredith sensed that he was extremely serious about that, and she sobered. She saw the determination in that square jaw, the intelligence and hard-bitten experience in those gray eyes. His life had not given him any of the advantages that it offered men of her own class, but she sensed instinctively that Matt Farrell had a rare kind of strength coupled with an indomitable will to succeed. She sensed something else about him too—that despite his arbitrary attitude and the mild cynicism she'd glimpsed, there was a core of gentleness within him. His behavior today was proof of that. She had initiated their lovemaking six weeks ago, and this pregnancy and hasty marriage was undoubtedly as disastrous to his life as it was to hers. Yet, not once had he torn into her for her stupidity or carelessness, nor had he told her to go to hell when she asked him if he would marry her—which she'd half expected him to do.

Watching her study him, Matt knew she was rating his chances to succeed and make good his claim; he also knew how incongruous that claim would seem to her, particularly now. The night he'd met her, he'd at least *looked* successful. Now, however, she knew what sort of place he came from; she'd seen him with his head under the hood of a truck and grease all over his hands, and he remembered that momentary flash of shock and repugnance on her face. And so, as he looked down at that beautiful face of hers, he waited for her to laugh at his pretension—no, not laugh—she was much too well-bred to laugh in his face; she'd say something condescending, and he'd know it in an instant, because those expressive eyes of hers would give away her real thoughts.

She finally spoke, her voice quiet, thoughtful, smiling. "Planning to set the world on fire, are you?"

"With a torch," he averred.

To his complete shock, Meredith Bancroft lifted her hand and shyly laid it against his tense jaw, her fingers spreading over his cheek. The smile on her lips transferred to her eyes, making them glow. Softly, but with absolute conviction, she whispered, "I'm sure you will, Matt."

Matt opened his mouth to say something, and he couldn't speak; the touch of her fingers, the proximity of her body, and the look in her eyes suddenly drugged his mind. Six weeks ago, he'd been wildly attracted to her; in the space of a moment, that latent attraction erupted with a force that made him lean down and seize her mouth with hard, demanding hunger. He devoured its sweetness, stunned by his own urgency, astonished when he had to slow down and coax her lips apart, because he knew instinctively she was feeling a little of what he was feeling. And when her lips did part and begin to move with his, he was shocked by the surge of triumph he felt. Common sense fled; Matt leaned up and over her, his body already rigid with desire, and almost groaned a few minutes later when she tore her mouth from his and held her hands against his chest to keep him away. "Your family," she gasped desperately. "They're downstairs . . ."

Matt reluctantly dragged his hand from her bared breast. His family. He'd forgotten about all that. Downstairs it had been obvious that his father had leapt to the correct conclusion as to the reason for their sudden marriage—and the wrong conclusions about the sort of woman Meredith was. He needed to go downstairs and straighten that out, he did not need to reinforce his father's opinion that Meredith was a rich slut by staying up in this bedroom with her right now. He was amazed he'd forgotten that; he was more amazed by his unparalleled lack of control where she was concerned. Slow, gorgeous lovemaking hadn't been what he'd intended just then—swift, total possession had been his goal, and that had never happened to him before.

Tipping his head back, Matt drew a steadying breath and got off the bed, removing himself from the proximity of temptation. Leaning a shoulder against the bedpost, he watched her scoot up into a sitting position. She glanced uneasily at him, hastily straightening her clothes, and he grinned as she modestly covered the breasts he'd been kissing and caressing a moment before. "At the risk of sounding outrageously impulsive," he remarked casually, "I'm beginning to find the notion of a marriage in name only not only gothic, but impractical. It's obvious we have a strong sexual attraction to each other. We've also made a baby together. Maybe we ought to consider taking a shot at living like married people. Who knows," he added, lifting his broad shoulders in a shrug, a smile tugging at his lips, "we might like it."

Meredith wouldn't have been more surprised if he'd grown wings and started flying around the room, then she realized he was merely tossing the idea around as a possibility, not making a suggestion. Torn between resentment at his offhand attitude and an odd kind of pleasure and gratitude that he'd even brought the idea up, she said nothing.

"There's no hurry," he added with a roguish grin as he straightened. "We have a few days to make up our minds."

When he left, Meredith stared at the closed door in exhausted disbelief, completely dazed by the speed with which he reached conclusions, gave orders, and switched directions. There were very distinct and startlingly different sides to Matthew Farrell, and she wasn't at all certain who he really was. The night she met him, she'd seen a chilling harshness in him; yet, that same night, he had smiled at her jokes, quietly talked to her about himself, kissed her into insensibility, and made love to her with demanding passion and exquisite tenderness. Even so, she had a feeling that the gentleness he nearly always showed her wasn't necessarily his norm, and that he wasn't to be underestimated. She had an even stronger feeling that whatever Matthew Farrell chose to do with the rest of his life, someday he was going to be a force to be reckoned with. She fell asleep thinking he already *was* a force to be reckoned with.

Whatever Matt had said to his father before Meredith came down to dinner was evidently effective, because Patrick Farrell seemed to accept without further challenge the fact that they were getting married. Even so, it was Julie's determined chatter that kept the meal from being a nerve-racking ordeal for Meredith. Matt was generally silent and thoughtful during most of it. At the same time, he seemed to dominate the room and even the conversation, simply by being present and listening to what was being said.

Patrick Farrell, who should have been the head of the household, had clearly abdicated that role to Matt. A slender, brooding man with a face that bore traces of dissipation and tragedy, he deferred to Matt whenever a question came up about who ought to do what. Meredith thought him both pitiful and somehow frightening, and she continued to feel that he didn't particularly like her either.

Julie, who seemed to have willingly accepted the role of cook and housekeeper to the two men, was like a Fourth of July sparkler; every thought she had burst from her lips in a torrent of enthusiastic words. Her devotion to Matt was obvious and total; she jumped up to get him coffee, asked his advice, and listened to whatever he said as if God Himself were rendering an opinion. Meredith, who was trying desperately not to think about her own problems, wondered how Julie had kept her enthusiasm and optimism here; she wondered how any girl who seemed as bright as Julie could willingly forsake some sort of career for a future of looking after her father, which Meredith assumed was what she planned to do. Immersed in her thoughts, it took Meredith a moment to realize Julie was talking to her.

"There's a department store in Chicago called Bancroft's," Julie told her. "I see their ads in *Seventeen* sometimes, but mostly in *Vogue*. They have fantastic stuff. Matt brought me a silk scarf from there once. Do you ever shop there?"

Meredith nodded, her smile unconsciously warming at the mention of the store, but she didn't elaborate. There hadn't been time to tell Matt of her connection to Bancroft's, and Patrick had already reacted so negatively to her car that she didn't want to do it there. Unfortunately, Julie gave her no choice.

"Are you any relation to those Bancrofts—the people who own the department store, I mean?"

"Yes."

"A close relation?"

"Pretty close," she said, helplessly amused by the excited glee in Julie's big gray eyes.

"How close?" Julie asked, putting her fork down, peering at her. Matt paused, his coffee cup halfway to his mouth, staring at her. Patrick Farrell leaned back in his chair, frowning at her.

With a silent sigh of defeat, Meredith admitted, "My great-great-grandfather founded the store."

"That's fantastic! Do you know what my great-great-*great* grandfather did?"

"No, what?" Meredith asked, so drawn into Julie's contagious enthusiasm that she forgot to look at Matt to see how he'd reacted.

"He immigrated to this country from Ireland and started a horse ranch," Julie told her, standing up and beginning to clear the table.

Meredith smiled and got up to help her. "Mine was a horse thief!" Behind her, both men picked up their coffee cups and took them into the living room.

"Was he really a horse thief?" Julie asked as she filled the sink with soapy water. "Are you sure?"

"Positive," Meredith averred, adamantly refusing to turn to watch Matt walk away. "They hanged him for it."

They worked in companionable silence for a few moments, then Julie said, "Dad's working double shifts for the next few days. I'm going to spend tonight with a girlfriend, studying. I'll be back in the morning in time to make breakfast though."

Distracted by Julie's remark about studying, Meredith overlooked the fact that she was evidently going to be alone with Matt tonight. "Studying? Aren't you on summer vacation?"

"I'm going to summer school. That way, I'll be able to graduate in December—two days after I turn seventeen."

"That's young to graduate."

"Matt was sixteen."

"Oh," Meredith said, wondering about the quality of a rural school system that let everyone graduate so early. "What will you do after you graduate?"

"Go to college. I'm going to major in one of the sciences, but I haven't decided which one yet. Biology, probably."

"Really?"

Julie nodded and said with pride, "I have a full scholarship. Matt's waited until now to go away because he wanted to be certain I'd be okay on my own. It's just as well, though, because it gave him a chance to get his M.B.A. while he was waiting around for me to grow up. Although he'd have had to stay in Edmunton and keep working anyway, just to finish paying off Mom's medical bills."

Meredith whirled around and gaped at her. "Matt had a chance to get his what?"

"His M.B.A.—you know, master's degree—business administration. That's what comes after you get your bachelor's degree," she prompted help-fully. "Matt had a dual major for his undergraduate degree—economics and finance. Brains run in our family," she added, then she saw Meredith's blank shock and stopped. Hesitantly, she said, "You—you don't know any-thing at all about Matt, do you?"

Only how he kisses and makes love, Meredith thought with shame. "Not much," she admitted in a small voice.

"Well, you shouldn't blame yourself. Most people think Matt's hard to get to know, and you two have known each other for only two days." That sounded so sordid that Meredith turned away, unable to face her. She picked up a mug and started wiping it. "Meredith," Julie said, looking wor-riedly at her averted face, "it's nothing to be ashamed of—I mean it's no big deal to me that you're pregnant." Meredith dropped the mug and it rolled across the linoleum under the sink. "Well, it isn't!" Julie persisted, bending down and scooping it up.

"Did Matt tell you I'm pregnant?" Meredith managed. "Or did you fig-ure it out for yourself?"

"Matt told my dad privately, and I eavesdropped, although I'd already figured it out myself, actually."

"Wonderful," Meredith said, drowning in mortification.

"I thought it was pretty neat," Julie agreed. "I mean, until Matt told Dad all about you, I was starting to feel like *I* was the only virgin alive over the age of sixteen!"

Meredith closed her eyes, feeling a little faint from the wild leaps of intensely revealing conversation and angry that Matt had discussed her with his father. "That must have been quite a little gossip session they were having," she said bitterly.

"Matt wasn't gossiping about you! He was straightening out my dad about what sort of girl you are." That made Meredith feel immeasurably better, and when Julie saw it, she continued in a slightly different vein. "Thirty-eight of the two hundred girls in my high school class this year are pregnant. Actually," she confided a little dispiritedly, "I've never had to worry about it. Most guys are afraid to kiss me."

Feeling that some reply was in order, Meredith cleared her throat and said, "Why?"

"Because of Matt," Julie said succinctly. "Every guy in Edmunton knows Matt Farrell is my brother. They know what Matt would do to them if he found out they tried anything with me. When it comes to guarding a woman's 'virtue,'" she added with a laughing sigh, "having Matt around is like wearing a chastity belt."

"Somehow," Meredith said before she could stop herself, "I didn't find that to be exactly true."

Julie laughed, and Meredith suddenly found herself laughing with her.

When they joined the men in the living room, Meredith braced herself for an awkward couple of hours of watching television, but Julie again took matters into her own hands. "What shall we do?" she asked, looking expectantly from Matt to Meredith. "I know, how about a game or something? Cards? No, wait, how about something really silly—" She turned to the bookshelves, running her finger past several games. "Monopoly!" she said, looking over her shoulder.

"Not me," Patrick said. "I'd rather watch this movie."

Matt had no desire whatsoever to play any game, particularly that one, and he was on the verge of suggesting that Meredith go for a walk with him, when he realized that what she probably needed was some relief from anything intense, which their conversation outside would undoubtedly become. Moreover, she'd established a rapport with Julie and seemed to feel comfortable with her. He nodded, trying to appear as if he enjoyed the prospect, then he glanced to Meredith for a decision. She didn't look any more enthusiastic than he felt, but she smiled and nodded too.

Two hours later he admitted to himself that the Monopoly game had been an unexpected and unqualified success that even he'd enjoyed. With Julie as instigator, the game had immediately become a kind of farce, with both girls trying their damnedest to beat him and, failing that, to cheat him. Twice he'd caught Julie stealing the money he'd already won, and now Meredith was coming up with outrageous reasons for refusing to pay him his due. "No excuses this time," he warned Meredith as her token landed on a property he owned. "You owe me fourteen hundred for that."

"No, I don't," she said with a smug grin. She pointed to the little plastic hotels he'd put on his property, one of which she'd nudged with her finger. "That hotel is encroaching on my easement. You built on my land, therefore you owe me."

"I'll 'encroach on your easement' but good," he threatened, chuckling, "if you don't hand over my money."

Laughing, Meredith turned to Julie. "I have only one thousand. Can you lend me some?"

"Sure thing," Julie said, even though she'd already lost all her money. Reaching out, she snatched several $500 bills from Matt's pile and handed them to Meredith. A few minutes later, Meredith admitted defeat. Julie went to get her books and Meredith finished putting the game away, then she got up to return it to the bookshelf. Behind her, Patrick Farrell stood up. "I'd better get going," he said to Matt. "Did you leave the truck at the garage?" When Matt said he had, and that he'd get a ride into town in the morning to pick it up, Patrick turned to Meredith. Throughout their rowdy Monopoly game, she'd felt his eyes on her. Now he smiled—a grim, uncertain smile. "Good night, Meredith."

Matt stood up too, and asked her if she felt like going for a walk.

Glad for any reprieve that would keep her from lying in bed, worrying, Meredith said, "That sounds nice."

Outside, the night air was balmy, and the moon painted a wide path across the yard. They'd just walked down the porch steps when Julie came out behind them, a sweater over her shoulders and schoolbooks in her arms. "See you in the morning. Joelle's picking me up at the end of the drive. I'm going over to her house to study."

Matt turned, brows pulling together. "At ten at night?"

She paused, her hand on the railing, an exasperated smile on her pretty face. "Matt!" she said, rolling her eyes at his obtuseness.

He caught on then. "Tell Joelle I said hello." She left, hurrying toward the car lights at the end of the gravel drive, and Matt turned to Meredith, asking her something that had obviously been puzzling him. "How do you know about encroaching on easements and zoning violations?"

Tipping her head back Meredith gazed at the harvest moon hovering overhead like a huge golden disk. "My father has always talked to me about business. There was a zoning problem when we built our branch store in the suburbs, and a problem with an easement when the developer paved the parking lot." Since he'd already asked a question, Meredith asked him one that had been plaguing her for hours. Pausing, she reached up and pulled a leaf from a low branch overhead while she made an unsuccessful effort to keep the accusation out of her voice. "Julie told me you have an M.B.A. Why did you let me think you were an ordinary steelworker who was heading off to Venezuela to chase your luck in the oil fields?"

"What makes you think steelworkers are ordinary and people with M.B.A.'s are special?"

Meredith heard the mild reprimand in those words and she flinched inwardly. Leaning her shoulders against the tree trunk behind her, she said, "Did I sound like a snob?"

"Are you one?" he asked, shoving his hands into his pockets, studying her.

"I—" She hesitated, searching his shadowy features, strangely tempted to say whatever she thought he wanted to hear, and, just as firmly, she resisted the temptation. "I probably am."

She didn't hear the disgust in her voice, but Matt did and the glamour of his sudden, lazy grin made her pulse leap. "I doubt it."

The three words made her feel inordinately pleased. "Why?"

"Because snobs don't worry about whether they are or not. However, to answer your question, part of the reason I didn't say anything about the degree is that it doesn't mean anything unless, and until, I can put it to use. Right now all I have are a bunch of ideas and plans that may not work out the way I think they should."

Julie had said most people found him difficult to get to know, and Meredith could easily believe that. And yet, there were many times, like now, when she felt an odd sense of being so attuned to him that she could almost read his mind. Quietly she said, "I think the other reason you let me go on thinking you're a steelworker was that you wanted to see if it would matter to me. It was a—a test, wasn't it?"

That startled a chuckle from him. "I suppose it was. Who knows—that's all I may ever be."

"And now you've switched from steel mills to oil rigs," she teased, her eyes laughing, "because you wanted a job with more glamour, is that it?"

With an effort, Matt resisted the temptation to snatch her into his arms and muffle his laughter against her lips. She was young and pampered and he was going to a foreign country where many common necessities would be luxuries. This sudden, insane impulse to take her with him that kept prodding at him was just that—insane. On the other hand, she was also brave, sweet, and pregnant with his child. *His* child. Their child. Perhaps the idea wasn't so insane. Tipping his head back, he looked up at the moon, trying to ignore the notion, and even while he was doing it, he found himself suggesting something that would help him decide. "Meredith," he said, "most couples take months learning about each other before they get married. You and I have only a few days before we get married, and less than a week before I have to leave for South America. Do you think we could try to cram a few months into a few days?"

"I guess so," she said, puzzled by the sudden intensity in his voice.

"Okay, fine," Matt said, strangely at a loss as to how to begin now that she'd agreed. "What would you like to know about me?"

Gulping back a surge of startled, self-conscious laughter, Meredith looked at him, stupefied, and then she wondered if he was referring to genetic questions she might have about him as the father of her baby. Peering at him, she asked hesitantly, "Do you mean that I should ask you things like—like is there any history of insanity in your family, and do you have a police record?"

Matt bit back a shout of laughter at her choice of questions, and said with sham gravity, "No—to both those things. How about you?"

Solemnly, she shook her head. "No insanity, no police record either."

He saw it then—the answering laughter glowing in her yes, and for the second time in moments he had to restrain the urge to clasp her to him.

"Now it's your turn to ask me something," she offered lamely. "What do you want to know?"

"Just one thing," he said with blunt honesty as he placed his hand high on the tree trunk behind her. "Are you half as sweet as I think you are?"

"Probably not."

He straightened and smiled because he was almost certain she was wrong. "Let's walk, before I forget what we're supposed to be doing out here. In the interest of complete honesty," he added as they turned and strolled down the lane that curved toward the main road, "I've just remembered that I *do* have a police record." Meredith stopped short, and he turned and said, "I was busted twice when I was nineteen."

"What were you doing at the time?"

"Fighting. *Brawling* would be a better word. Before my mother died, I'd managed to convince myself that if she had the best doctors and stayed in the best hospitals—only the best—then she wouldn't die. We got her the best, my father and I. When the insurance ran out, we sold the farm equipment and everything else we could liquidate to keep paying the medical bills. She died anyway," Matt said in a carefully unemotional voice. "My father hit the bottle, and I went looking for something of my own to hit. For months afterward I was spoiling for a fight, and since I couldn't get my hands on the God my mother had such faith in, I settled for any mortal who wanted to take me on. In Edmunton it's not hard to find a fight," he added with a wry smile, and not until that moment did Matt realize he was confiding things to an eighteen-year-old girl that he'd never admitted to anyone else, even himself. And the eighteen-year-old girl was looking at him with a quiet understanding that completely belied her years. "The cops broke up two of the fights," he finished, "and they busted all of us. It's no big deal. There's no record of it anywhere except Edmunton."

Touched by his confidence, Meredith said softly, "You must have loved her very much." Aware that she was treading on shaky ground, she said, "I never knew my own mother. She went to Italy after my parents' divorce. I guess I was lucky, don't you, not to have known her and loved her all those years, and then lost her?"

Matt realized exactly what point she was trying to make, and he didn't deride her efforts. "Very nice," he said with quiet gravity, then he shook off the mood and wryly announced, "I have amazingly excellent taste in women."

Meredith burst out laughing, then felt a jolt of delight when his hand slid across her back, curving around her waist to draw her tightly against his side as they walked. A few steps later, she thought of something that brought her up short. "Have you ever been married before?"

"No. Have you?" he added, teasing.

"You know perfectly well I haven't—hadn't done—" She stopped, uneasy with the topic.

"Yes, I do know," he confirmed. "What I can't understand is how anyone who looks like you could have reached the age of eighteen without losing your virginity to some rich, smooth-talking preppy boy along the way."

"I don't like preppy boys," Meredith replied, then she glanced at him, bemused. "I never actually realized that before."

That pleased Matt immensely because she sure as hell wasn't marrying one. He waited for her to say more. When she didn't, he prompted her disbelievingly. "That's it? That's the answer?"

"That's part of it. The whole truth is that I was so homely until I was sixteen that boys stayed completely away from me. By the time I wasn't homely anymore, I was so mad at them for ignoring me all those years that I didn't have a very high opinion of them on the whole."

Matt looked at her beautiful face, her tempting mouth, and radiant eyes, and he grinned. "Were you really homely?"

"Let me put it this way," she said dryly, "if we have a little girl, she'll be better off if she looks like *you* when she's young!"

Matt's sharp crack of laughter exploded into the soft night silence and he yanked her into his arms. Laughing, he buried his face in her fragrant hair, surprised by his feelings of tenderness because she'd apparently been homely, touched that she had confided it to him, and elated because . . . because . . . He refused to think of why. All that mattered was that she was laughing too, and that her arms had slid around his waist. With a solemn smile, he rubbed his jaw against her head and whispered, "I have *exquisite* taste in women."

"Well, you wouldn't have thought that a couple of years ago," she said, laughing and leaning back in his arms.

"I'm a man of vision," he assured her quietly. "I would have thought it even then."

An hour later they were sitting on the porch steps facing each other, their backs propped against the railing. Matt was one step higher, his long legs stretched out in front of him. A step below him, Meredith was sitting with her knees drawn up against her chest, her arms wrapped around them. They were no longer making a conscious effort to get to know each other because Meredith was pregnant and they were getting married. They were simply a couple sitting outside on a late summer night, enjoying one another's company.

Leaning her head back, Meredith listened to a cricket chirping, her eyes half closed.

"What are you thinking about?" he asked quietly.

"I'm thinking that it will be autumn soon," she said, lifting her gaze to his. "Autumn is my absolute favorite season. Spring is overrated. It's soggy and the trees are still bare from winter. Winter drags on and on, and summer is nice, but it's all the same. Autumn is different. I mean, is there any perfume in the world that can compare with the smell of burning leaves?" she asked with an engaging smile. Matt thought she smelled a hell of a lot better than burning leaves, but he let her continue. "Autumn is exciting— things are changing. It's like dusk."

"Dusk?"

"Dusk is my favorite time of day, for the same reason. When I was young, I used to walk down our driveway at dusk in the summer and stand at the fence, watching all the cars going by with their headlights on. Everyone had a place to go, something to do. The night was just beginning . . ." She trailed off in embarrassment. "That must sound incredibly silly."

"It sounds incredibly lonely."

"I wasn't lonely, not really. Just daydreaming. I know you got an awful impression of my father at Glenmoor that night, but he's not the ogre you imagine. He loves me, and all he's ever tried to do is to protect me and give me the best." Without warning, Meredith's lovely mood dissolved, and reality came crashing over her with sickening force. "And in return I'm going to go home in a few days, pregnant and—"

"We agreed not to worry about any of that tonight," he interrupted.

Meredith nodded and tried to smile, but she couldn't control her thoughts as easily as he apparently could. Suddenly she saw her child standing at the end of some driveway in Chicago, alone, watching the cars going by on the road. No family, no brothers and sisters, no father. Just her. And she wasn't sure she could be enough.

"If autumn is your favorite thing, what's your least favorite?" Matt asked, trying to divert her.

She thought a moment. "Christmas tree lots on the day after Christmas. There's something sad about those beautiful trees that no one picked out. They're like orphans no one want—" She broke off, realizing what she was saying and quickly looked away.

"It's after midnight," Matt said, rolling to his feet, knowing her mood was beyond salvaging. "Why don't we go to bed?"

It sounded as if he was taking it for granted they would, or should, go to bed together, and Meredith suddenly felt a sick lurch of panic at that. She was pregnant and he was going to marry her because he had to; the whole situation was already so sordid, it made her feel cheap and humiliated as it was.

In silence they turned off the living room lights and walked up the stairs. The door to Matt's room was immediately off the landing, while Julie's was to the left, at the end of the hall, with a bathroom in between. When they approached his door, Meredith took matters into her own hands. "Good night, Matt," she said shakily. Stepping around him, she tossed a fixed smile over her shoulder, and left him standing in his doorway. When he made no attempt to stop her, her emotions veered crazily from relief to chagrin. Apparently, she decided as she stepped into Julie's room, pregnant women had no sex appeal whatsoever, not even to the same man who'd gone crazy in bed with you a few weeks prior. She opened the door and walked into Julie's room.

Behind her, Matt spoke in a flat, calm voice. "Meredith?"

She turned and saw him still standing in the doorway of his room, his shoulder propped against the door frame, his arms crossed loosely over his chest. "Yes?"

"Do you know what my least favorite thing is?"

His implacable tone told her the question wasn't casual, and she shook her head, wary at whatever he was getting at. He didn't keep her in doubt. "It's sleeping alone when there's someone down the hall who I know damned well should be sleeping with me." Matt had meant that to be more an invitation than a curt observation, and his lack of tact with her surprised him. A dozen expressions chased themselves across her lovely face—embarrassment, unease, doubt, uncertainty—and then she gave him a small smile, hesitated, and said firmly, "Good night."

Matt watched her walk into Julie's room and close the door behind her, and he stood for a long moment, knowing perfectly well that if he went after her and tried tender persuasion he could very likely convince her to come to bed with him. And yet, for some reason, he was suddenly, adamantly, unwilling to do it. Turning, he went into his room, but he left his door open, still convinced that she wanted to be with him, and that if she did, she'd come back here when she had gotten ready for bed.

Clad in pajama bottoms that he'd had to search through his drawers to find, he stood at the window, looking out at the moonlit lawn. He heard Meredith leave the bathroom after her shower, and he tensed, listening to her footsteps. They retreated down the hall into Julie's room and then a door closed. She'd made her decision, he realized with equal parts of surprise, annoyance, and disappointment. And yet, none of those three emotions had as much to do with unrequited sexual desire as they did with something deeper and more general. He had wanted some sign from her that she was ready for an actual relationship with him; as much as he hoped for that, he wasn't willing to do anything to try to persuade her that she was. It had to be her decision, her choice, freely made. She'd made that choice when she walked away from him and down the hall. If she'd had any doubts about what he wanted her to do, what he'd said to her in the hall would have removed them.

Turning away from the window, he breathed a sigh of frustrated irritation, and faced the fact that he was probably expecting far too much from an eighteen-year-old. The thing was, it was damned hard to remember how young Meredith actually was. Pulling back the sheet, he got into bed and linked his hands behind his head, staring at the ceiling, thinking about her. Tonight she'd told him about Lisa Pontini and how they'd become friends, and he'd realized from what she said that Meredith was not only at ease in country clubs and mansions, she was also totally at home with the Pontini family as well. She was utterly without artifice or affectation, Matt thought, and yet there was an unmistakable gentility in her, an inherent elegance that was as appealing to him as her intoxicating face and entrancing smile.

Weariness finally nudged him and he closed his eyes. Unfortunately, none of those attributes were going to help her or make the idea of going off to South America with him seem the slightest bit enticing, unless she *felt* something for him. And she obviously didn't, or she'd have been with him now. The idea of trying to persuade a reluctant, pampered eighteen-year-old to go to Venezuela with him when she didn't have the courage or the conviction to walk down a hall to him was not only repugnant, it was futile.

With her head bent, Meredith stood beside Julie's bed, torn apart with yearnings and misgivings she couldn't seem to control or predict. Her pregnancy wasn't having any physical effects yet, but it was evidently playing havoc with her emotions. Less than an hour ago she hadn't wanted to be in bed with Matt, and now she did. Common sense warned her that her future was already terrifyingly uncertain, and that giving in to her growing attraction to him would only make things more complicated. At twenty-six he was much older than she and far more experienced in every facet of life—a life that was completely alien to her. Six weeks ago, when he was wearing a tuxedo and she was in familiar surroundings, he'd seemed almost like other men she'd known. But here, clad in jeans and a shirt, there was an earthiness about him that both attracted her and alarmed her. He'd wanted her to come to bed tonight, and he'd made that emphatically clear. When it pertained to women and sex, Matt was obviously so sure of himself that he could stand there and baldly tell her what he wanted her to do. Not *ask* her or try to persuade her, but tell her! No doubt he was considered quite a stud around Edmunton, and why not— the night she'd met him, he'd been able to make her writhe with passion even though she was scared sick. He knew just where to touch and how to move to make her lose her mind, and all that sexual expertise hadn't been gotten from books! He'd probably made love hundreds of times in hundreds of ways with hundreds of women.

And even while she thought it, her mind rebelled at believing Matt had no feeling for her other than sexual. True, he hadn't called her in the six weeks since he'd left Chicago; equally true, she'd been so upset that night, she couldn't have given him the idea she wanted him to call her. His claim that he'd intended to call her when he got back from South America in two years had seemed ludicrous when he said it. Now, in the silent darkness, after listening to him talk tonight about his plans for the future, she had the feeling he'd wanted to *be* somebody when he called her the next time. She thought of what he'd told her about his mother's death; surely that boy who'd grieved and raged couldn't have grown into a shallow, irresponsible man whose only real interest in women was—Meredith brought herself up short. Matt was far from being irresponsible. Not once since she'd gotten there had he tried to evade any responsibility for the baby. Furthermore, based on things he'd said and some remarks of Julie's, Matt had been shouldering much of the responsibility for the entire family for years.

If sex was all he had on his mind tonight, why hadn't he tried to persuade her to come to bed with him, when he'd made it eloquently clear he wanted her there? She remembered the tender look in his eyes when he'd asked if she was as sweet as he thought she was. That same look had warmed those gray eyes repeatedly while they sat on the porch.

Why hadn't he tried to talk her into going to bed with him?

The answer hit her, and it made her feel weak with relief and strangely terrified. He'd definitely wanted to make love, and he certainly knew how to convince her they should, but he'd refused to do that. He wanted something even more tonight from her than her body. She knew it without knowing how she did.

Or, perhaps, she was just being as overemotional now as she'd been for days.

Meredith straightened, shaking with uncertainty, her hand unconsciously splaying over her flat belly. She was scared and confused and wildly attracted to a man she didn't know or understand. Her heart thundering, she silently opened the door to Julie's room. He'd left his door open—she'd seen that when she came out of the bathroom after her shower. If he was already asleep, she decided, she'd come back and go to bed. She'd leave this up to fate.

He was asleep, she realized as she stood in his doorway, watching him in the moonlight that spilled through the sheer curtains on the window. Her heart slowed to a normal tempo, and still she stood there, marveling at this fierce tug on her emotions that had sent her to him in the first place. Awkwardly aware that she was standing in his doorway, watching him sleeping, she turned silently.

Matt had no idea what woke him, or how long she'd been standing in that doorway, but when he opened his eyes, she was leaving. He stopped her with the first careless words that came to mind. "Don't do that, Meredith!"

The harsh order brought Meredith whirling around, her hair spilling over her left shoulder. Not certain what he'd meant or what he was thinking, she tried to see his expression through the darkness, and when she couldn't, she started forward.

Matt watched her moving toward him. She was wearing a short silk nightshirt that barely covered the tops of her shapely thighs. He shifted sideways and moved the covers back for her. She hesitated, and instead sat down beside him, her hip against his, her eyes wide with confusion as they searched his. When she spoke, her voice was low and shaky. "I don't know why, but I'm more scared this time than I was the last."

Matt smiled somberly as his hand lifted to her cheek, then curved around her nape. "So am I." In the lengthening silence, they remained perfectly still, the only movement the slow stroking of Matt's thumb against her neck, as both of them sensed that they were about to take the first step down a new uncharted path. Meredith sensed it subconsciously; Matt recognized it with complete clarity and, even so, there was something infinitely right about what they were going to do. No longer was she an heiress from another world; she was the woman he had wanted to possess the moment he saw her, and she was sitting beside him, her hair cascading over his arm like a thick satin waterfall. "I think it's only fair to warn you," he whispered as his hand tightened on her nape, beginning to exert pressure to draw her mouth down to his, "that this could turn out to be an even bigger risk than the one you took six weeks ago." Meredith looked into his smoldering eyes and knew that he was warning her about some sort of deep emotional involvement. "Make up your mind," he whispered huskily.

She hesitated, and then her gaze dropped from his compelling eyes to that mobile mouth. Her heart stopped, she stiffened and lurched back, and his hand fell away, "I—" she said, starting to shake her head and stand up, and then something stopped her. With a smothered moan, Meredith leaned down and kissed him, crushing her mouth against his, and Matt's arms swept around, holding her close, then tightening like a vise as he rolled her onto her back, his mouth fierce and insistent.

The magic began again as it had six weeks ago, only different this time, because it was hotter, sweeter, more turbulent.

And a thousand times more meaningful.

When it was finished, Meredith turned onto her side, limp and damp and sated, feeling his legs and thighs pressing against the backs of hers. She drifted toward sleep, his hand still moving lazily over her arm, then coming to rest against her breast in a way that was both possessive and deliberately provocative. Her last waking thought was that he wanted her to know he was there; that he was claiming another kind of right that he hadn't asked for and she hadn't granted. It was just like him to do that. She fell asleep smiling.

"Did you sleep well?" Julie asked the next morning as she stood at the kitchen counter, buttering toast.

"Very well," Meredith said, trying desperately not to look as if she'd spent the night making love with Julie's brother. "Can I do anything to help with breakfast?"

"Not a thing. Dad's working double shifts for the next week, from three in the afternoon to seven in the morning. When he gets home all he'll want to do is eat and go to sleep. I've already got his breakfast ready. Matt doesn't eat breakfast. Do you want to bring him his coffee? I usually bring it up to him just before his alarm goes off, which is"—she glanced up at the kitchen clock, a plastic thing shaped like a teakettle—"in ten minutes."

Pleased with the idea of doing something as domestic as waking him up with coffee, Meredith nodded and poured some into a mug, then she looked at the sugar bowl and hesitated uncertainly.

"He drinks it black," Julie said, smiling at Meredith's confusion. "And, by the way, he's a bear in the morning, so don't expect cheerful conversation."

"Is he, really?" Meredith considered that new tidbit of information.

"He isn't mean, he's just silent."

Julie was partially right. When Meredith knocked on his door and went inside, Matt rolled over onto his back, looking completely disoriented. His only greeting was a slight grateful smile as he levered himself into a sitting position, reaching out for the mug of coffee. Meredith hovered uncertainly by the bed, watching him drink it as if he needed it to survive the next few minutes, then she turned to go, feeling unnecessary and intrusive. He caught her wrist to stop her, and she obediently sat down beside him. "Why am I the only one who's exhausted this morning?" he finally asked, his voice still a little husky with sleep.

"I'm a morning person," Meredith told him. "I'll probably be drooping this afternoon."

His eyes moved over Julie's plaid shirt which she'd tied in a knot at the midriff, then it slid over Julie's white shorts. "On you, that outfit looks like it belongs on a billboard."

It was the first compliment he had ever paid her, except for the things he murmured to her when they were making love. Meredith, who normally didn't think much of compliments, memorized that one. Not because of what he said, but the tender way he'd said it.

Patrick came home, ate breakfast, and went to bed. Julie left at 8:30 with a cheery wave and the announcement that she was going to her girl-friend's house after school and intended to stay the night there again. At 9:30, Meredith decided to call home and leave a message for her father with the butler. Albert answered the phone and gave her a message from her father instead. Her father said that she was to come home immediately, and that she'd better damned well have a good explanation for vanishing like this. Meredith asked Albert to tell her father that she had a wonderful reason for staying away, and that she'd see him Sunday.

After that, time seemed to drag. Careful not to wake up Patrick, she went into the living room, looking for something to read. The bookshelves offered several possibilities, but she was too restless to concentrate on a long novel. Among the copies of magazines and periodicals on the top shelf, Meredith found an old pamphlet on crocheting. She studied it with mounting interest while fanciful and artistic baby booties took shape in her mind.

With no other diversions available, she decided to give crocheting a try, and she drove into town. At Jackson's Dry Goods, she purchased a magazine dedicated to crocheting, a half-dozen skeins of thick yarn and a fat wooden crochet hook as big around as her finger, which the sales clerk assured her was best for a beginner to use. She was unlocking her car, which she'd parked in front of the Tru Value Hardware store, when it occurred to her that the responsibility for dinner tonight might fall to her. Tossing the bag with the yarn into the car, she recrossed the street and went into the grocery store. For several minutes she wandered the aisles, assailed by justifiable doubts about her cooking ability. At the meat counter, she scanned the packages, biting her lip. Julie's meat loaf had been wonderful last night; whatever Meredith made was going to have to be simple. Her gaze drifted past the steaks, pork chops, and calf's liver, then riveted on the packages of hot dogs as inspiration struck her. With luck, she might be able to turn dinner into an adventure in nostalgia tonight instead of a culinary catastrophe. Smiling, she bought the hot dogs, a package of buns, and a huge bag of fat marshmallows.

Back at the house, Meredith put away the groceries and sat down with her crochet hook and the magazine with the illustrated crocheting instructions. According to the introduction, the chain stitch was the basis for all crochet stitches and beginners were not to proceed to the next step until they were able to make at least a hundred perfectly uniform chain stitches. Meredith obediently began to make chain stitches, each one of which was about a half inch around due to the enormous crochet hook and thick yarn she was using.

As morning wore into afternoon, the worries she'd been hiding from came back to plague her, so she crocheted harder to keep them away. She would *not* think about pediatricians . . . or what labor felt like . . . whether Matt would want visiting rights for their baby . . . nursery school . . . whether Matt really meant what he'd said about their having a real marriage . . .

Chain stitches cascaded from her crochet hook, fat and uniform, landing in a large pool of soft cream rope at her feet. She looked down, knowing perfectly well it was long past time to stop and to proceed to step two, but she didn't feel up to the challenge, and besides, there was a certain grim satisfaction, a sense of badly needed control, that came from the repetitive task. At two o'clock, the pregnancy that did not yet seem real made itself known with sudden demands for sleep, and Meredith put the crochet hook down. Curling up almost thankfully on the sofa, she glanced at the clock. She could grab a quick nap and still be up in time to put her yarn away and be ready when Matt came home. When Matt came home . . . The thought of him returning to her after a hard day at work filled her with delight. As she laid her cheek against her hand, she remembered the way he had made love to her, and she had to make herself think of something else, because the memory was so powerful and stirring that she ached for him. She was in serious danger of falling in love with the father of her baby. Serious danger? she thought with a smile. What could possibly be lovelier—as long as Matt felt the same way. And she rather thought he did.

The sound of gravel crunching beneath tires drifted in through the open window, and her eyes snapped open, her gaze flying to the clock. It was 4:30. She lurched to a sitting position and combed her fingers through her hair, shoving it off her forehead. As she reached out to pick up the yarn and put it away, the front door swung open and her heart responded with a leap of joy to the sight of him. "Hi," she said, and she had a sudden vision of other evenings just like this one, when Matt would come home to her. She wondered if he'd thought about her at all, and then chided herself for being foolish. She was the one with too much time on her hands; he had been busy and undoubtedly preoccupied. "How was your day?"

Matt looked at her standing near the sofa, while visions of more days like this paraded across his mind, months and years of days when he'd come home to a golden-haired goddess with a smile that always made him feel as if he'd just single-handedly slain a dragon, cured the common cold, and found a means to world peace. "My day was fine," he said, smiling. "What did you do with yours?"

She'd spent part of it worrying and the rest thinking and dreaming of him. Since she couldn't very well tell him that, she said, "I decided to take up crocheting." She held up the skein of yarn to prove her claim.

"Very domestic," Matt teased, then his gaze slid down the rope of chain stitches that descended from the skein and ended beneath the coffee table. His eyes widened. "What are you making?"

Meredith stifled an embarrassed giggle because she didn't have the remotest idea. "Guess," she said, trying to save face, hoping he'd think of something.

Walking over, Matt bent down, picked up the end of the stitches, and began backing up until he'd stretched the chain out twelve feet to the end of the room. "A carpet?" he ventured gravely.

Somehow she managed to control her features and look wounded. "Of course it's not a carpet."

He sobered at once and started toward her, instantly contrite. "Give me a hint," he said gently.

"You shouldn't really need a hint. It's obvious what it's going to be." Fighting to keep her face straight, she announced, "I'm planning to add a few more rows to what I've already crocheted—so it will be wider—then I'm going to starch the whole thing, and you can use it to fence your property!"

His shoulders shaking with laughter, Matt hauled her into his arms, oblivious to the crochet hook jabbing in his chest.

"I bought some things for dinner tonight," she told him, leaning back in his arms.

Matt had intended to take her out. He tipped his chin down, smiling with surprise. "I thought you said you don't know how to cook."

"You'll understand when you see what I bought," she said, and he put his arm around her shoulders and walked into the kitchen. She took out the hot dogs and his gaze shot to the marshmallows.

"Very clever," he said with a grin. "You figured out a way to make *me* do the cooking."

"Believe me," she said gravely, "it's safer this way."

He'd been home for less than ten minutes and it was the second time Matt had felt as if life was suddenly filled with joy and laughter.

She brought out a blanket and the food, and Matt eventually built a campfire. They spent the evening outside, happily eating hot dogs that were overcooked, buns that were undercooked, and marshmallows that dripped into the fire; they talked about everything from the terrain of South America, to Meredith's unusual lack of troublesome pregnancy symptoms, to the proper degree of doneness for marshmallows. At twilight, they'd finished eating and Meredith cleared away the plates, then she went into the kitchen to wash the dishes. With his knee drawn up, Matt waited for her to return, his gaze drifting idly from the darkening sky above to the leaves he'd just gathered up and heaped on the fire to surprise her.

When Meredith came back out, the air was pungent with the delicious aroma of autumn, and Matt was sitting on the blanket, trying to look as if there was nothing whatsoever strange about the smell of burning leaves in August. She knelt down on the blanket across from him, looked at the fire, then she raised her face to his, and even in the darkness Matt could see her eyes shining. "Thank you," she said simply.

"You're welcome," he replied, his voice strangely husky to his own ears. He held out his hand to her, then had to fight down a wave of desire when she misunderstood his invitation to sit beside him and, instead, moved between his legs so that she could sit with her back against his chest and watch the fire. Desire was followed by exquisite delight a moment later when she softly confessed, "This is the nicest night I've ever had, Matt."

He slid his arm around her waist from behind, his fingers splaying protectively across her flat stomach, and tried not to sound as touched as he felt. With his free hand he brushed her hair aside and kissed her nape. "What about last night?"

She bent her head forward, offering his mouth better access, and promptly amended, "This is the *second* nicest night I've ever had."

Matt smiled against her skin and nipped her ear, but passion was already erupting through his body, raging through his veins like wildfire, refusing to be delayed or denied. Shaken by the force of it, he turned her face up to his and captured her mouth. Her lips moved against his, sweetly, softly at first, then deliberately provocative as her tongue slipped between his lips. Matt lost control. He forced his hand inside her shirt, his fingers closing over her breast, and her moan of pleasure broke the last fragile thread of his restraint. Turning her in his arms, he laid her down on the blanket, his body half covering hers, and shoved his fingers into her hair, holding her captive for a plundering kiss. He was so attuned to her that he sensed her momentary hesitation as the ferocity of his ardor stunned her into immobility. It stunned him too, this desperate, demanding need to possess her completely, this necessity to make a conscious effort to slow himself down. It consumed him so completely that he never realized her hesitation came not from fear of his stormy passion, but from her inexperience and uncertainty about how to return and stimulate it. Even if he had realized it, he'd have hesitated about showing her how to do it right then, because pacing himself so that he could prolong their lovemaking was already incredibly difficult. And so he undressed her slowly, with fingers made awkward because they trembled, and he kissed her until she was writhing beneath him, her hands rushing over his heated skin. The touch of her hands and mouth set him on fire, and each soft sound she made sent his blood roaring as he led her from one plateau to the next higher one, whispering hoarse, heated words of pleasure to her. She followed him, joining him, until he finally made her cry out, her body racked with tremors, and then he poured himself into her.

Afterward, he wrapped the blanket around them, and lay beside her, gazing up at a sky quilted with stars, inhaling the nostalgic fragrance of an early autumn. In the past, making love had always been an act of mutual pleasure; with Meredith it was an act of spellbinding beauty. Exquisite, tormenting, magical beauty. For the first time in his life, Matt felt utterly contented, completely at peace. The future was more complicated than it had ever been, and yet he had never felt more confident that he could shape it to suit them—if only she gave him the chance and the time. Time.

He desperately needed more time with her to strengthen this strange, fragile bond that was drawing them closer together with each hour they spent together. If he could get her to agree to go to South America with him, he'd have time to strengthen that bond and she'd stay married to him. He believed that. Tomorrow he was going to call Jonathan Sommers and without telling him why, he would try to find out what sort of housing and medical facilities were available in the area. For himself, he hadn't given a damn. Meredith and his baby were another story.

If he couldn't take her with him . . . That was the problem. He couldn't change his mind about going to South America. For one thing, he'd signed a contract; for another, he needed the $150,000 bonus for staying over there so that he could use it to capitalize his next investment. Like the foundation of a skyscraper, that $150,000 was the foundation for his entire grand plan. It wasn't as much money as he'd have liked it to be, but it would suffice.

As he lay there beside her, he considered forgetting about the whole damned plan and staying in the States with her, but he couldn't do that either. Meredith was accustomed to the best. She was entitled to it, and he wanted her to have it. And the only way he could hope to give it to her was by going to South America.

The thought of leaving her behind and then losing her because she got tired of waiting for him, or she lost faith in his ability to succeed, would normally have been driving him crazy. But he had one more thing in his favor: She was pregnant with his child. Their baby would give her a strong reason to wait for him and trust him.

The same pregnancy that Meredith had regarded as a calamity, Matt now regarded as an unexpected gift from fate. When he left her in Chicago, he'd thought it would be at least two years before he could come back and try to court her in style—assuming he hadn't already lost her to someone else. She was beautiful and captivating and hundreds of men would have been after her while he was gone. One of them would have probably caught her, and he'd known that the night he left her.

But now fate had stepped in and handed him the world. The fact that fate had never been very kind to the Farrell family was something that Matt refused to let dampen his spirits. He was now prepared to believe in God, fate, and universal goodness all because of Meredith and the baby.

The only thing he actually found a little hard to believe was that the sophisticated young heiress he'd met at the country club, the bewitching blonde who drank champagne cocktails and handled herself with smiling poise, was actually curled up beside him, asleep in his arms, his baby sheltered inside her.

His baby.

Matt spread his fingers over her abdomen, and smiled against her neck because Meredith had no idea how he actually felt about their child. Or how he felt about her because she hadn't tried to get rid of it—and him. That first day when she'd itemized her options, the mention of the word *abortion* had made him feel like throwing up.

He wanted to talk about the baby with her and tell her exactly how he felt about all this, but for one thing, he felt like a selfish bastard for being so happy about something that distressed her so much. For another thing, she was dreading the confrontation with her father, and any mention of her pregnancy seemed to remind her of what was ahead.

The confrontation with her father . . . Matt's smile faded. The man was a son of a bitch, but somehow he'd raised the most amazing woman Matt had ever met, and for that Matt was profoundly grateful to him. He was so grateful that he was willing to do whatever he could to ease things between Meredith and her father when he took her to Chicago on Sunday. Somehow he was going to keep remembering that Meredith was Philip Bancroft's only child, and that for reasons that could be clear only to Meredith, she loved that arrogant bastard.

 10

W here's Meredith?" Matt asked Julie when he came home from work the next afternoon.

She looked up from the dining room table, where she was doing her homework. "She went riding. She said she'd be back before you got home, but you're two hours early." With a grin, she added, "I wonder what the attraction could be here?"

"Brat," Matt said, rumpling her dark hair as he headed for the back door.

Meredith had told Matt yesterday that she enjoyed riding, so Matt had called their neighbor that morning and arranged for Meredith to ride one of Dale's horses.

Outside, he walked across the yard, past the overgrown patch that had been his mother's vegetable garden, while he searched the fields off to the right for a sign of her. He was halfway to the fence when he saw Meredith coming, and the sight sent fear curling up his spine. The chestnut horse was at a smooth, ground-eating gallop, running along the fence line, and Meredith was leaning low over its neck, her hair tossing wildly about her shoulders. As she came nearer, he realized she was going to turn and head the horse toward their barn. Matt changed direction, heading there too, watching her while his pulse rate slowed to a more even tempo and his fear receded. Meredith Bancroft rode like the aristocrat she was—light and lovely in the saddle and in complete control.

"Hi!" she called, her face flushed and glowing as she brought the horse to a stop in the barnyard beside a bale of rotted hay. "I'll have to cool him down," she said as Matt reached for the horse's bridle, and then everything happened at once: Matt's heel clipped the tines of an old rake left lying on the ground just as Meredith started to swing her leg over the horse's back, and the handle of the rake flew up and hit the horse in the nose. With an outraged snort, the horse lurched and reared. Matt let go of the bridle and made a futile grab for Meredith, and she slid backward, landing on her rump on the hay, then sliding to the ground.

"Goddammit!" he burst out, crouching down and clutching her shoulders. "Are you hurt?"

The bale of hay had broken Meredith's short fall, and she wasn't hurt, she was just mortified and confused about what had happened. "Am I *hurt?*" she repeated with a look of comic shock as she pushed herself to her feet. "My pride is worse than hurt. It's demolished—destroyed—"

He watched her, his eyes narrowed with concern. "What about the baby?"

Meredith paused in the act of brushing hay and dirt off the seat of Julie's borrowed jeans. "Matt," she informed him with a wry, superior look, letting her hands rest on the seat of her pants, *"this* is *not* where the baby is."

He finally realized where her hands were and where she'd fallen. Amusement and relief washed through him, and he feigned a perplexed look. "It isn't?"

For several minutes Meredith sat contentedly, watching him cool the horse, then she remembered something and grinned. "I finished crocheting your sweater today," she called.

He stopped short and stared at her, his expression dubious. "You . . . made that long ropy thing into a sweater? For me?"

"Of course not," Meredith said, managing to look hurt. "That long ropy thing was only a practice project. I made the actual sweater today. It's a vest, though, not a sweater. Want to see it?"

He said he did, but he looked so uneasy that Meredith had to bite down on her lip to stop from laughing. When she emerged from the house several minutes later, she was carrying a bulky-knit beige vest with her crochet hook stuck into it, and the skein of beige yarn from yesterday.

Matt was just walking out of the barn, and they converged near the bale of hay. "Here it is," she said, producing everything from behind her back. "What do you think?"

His eyes shifted with unconcealed dread to her hands, riveted on the sweater, then rose to her innocent face. He was stunned, and he was impressed. He was also visibly touched that she'd made it for him. Meredith hadn't expected that, and she felt a little uneasy about her joke. "That's amazing," he said. "Do you think it will fit?"

Meredith was certain it would. She'd checked the sweaters in his drawers to make sure she bought the right size. When she brought this one home, she'd carefully removed the labels. "I think so."

"Let me try it on."

"Right here?" she asked, and when he nodded, she tugged the crochet hook loose, fighting down her increasing guilt. Slowly and with infinite care, he lifted it from her hands and put it on, smoothing it over his striped shirt, tugging his collar into the right position. "How do I look?" he asked, posing with his hands on his hips and his feet planted slightly apart.

He looked absolutely wonderful—broad-shouldered, narrow-hipped, ruggedly handsome, and lethally sexy, even in faded jeans and an inexpensive sweater.

"I like it, especially because you made it for me yourself."

"Matt," she said uneasily, prepared to confess.

"Yes?"

"About the sweater . . ."

"No, sweetheart," he interrupted, "don't apologize because you didn't have time to make more of them for me. You can do that tomorrow."

Meredith was still reeling from the heady thrill of hearing his deep voice call her "sweetheart" when his words registered, and she saw the amusement gleaming in his eyes. In a deliberately threatening gesture, he bent down and grabbed a stick from the ground, then he started toward her and Meredith started backing up, laughing helplessly. "Don't you dare!" she giggled, scooting around the hay bales and backing toward the barn. Her shoulders collided with the side of the building and she made a wild sideways lunge, but Matt caught her wrist, jerking her up short and pressing his body against the full length of hers.

Cheeks flushed, eyes sparkling with laughter, she looked up at his grinning face. "Now that you've caught me," she teased, "what are you going to do with me?"

"Now, there's a question," he said in a husky voice. His gaze fixed on her lips, and he bent his head, kissing her with deliberate, lazy sensuality until Meredith was responding, then he deepened the kiss, parting her lips with his own, his tongue probing. And Meredith forgot they were standing in plain sight of the house in broad daylight. She curved her hand around his nape, holding him close, and fed his hunger with her own, welcoming the deliberately suggestive rhythm of his tongue. By the time he finally lifted his head, they were both breathing fast and hard and his aroused body had left an invisible imprint on hers.

Matt drew a long breath and tipped his head back, sensing instinctively that now was an ideal moment to urge her to come to South America with him. He debated about how to do it and, because he was so damned afraid she'd refuse, he decided to tip the scales in his favor with a form of coercion. "I think the time has come for our talk," he stated as he straightened and looked at her. "I told you when I agreed to get married that I was probably going to have some stipulations. I wasn't certain then what they were going to be. Now I am."

"What are they?"

"I want you to join me in South America." Having made that pronouncement, Matt waited.

Torn between shock at his stipulation, extreme pleasure at what that stipulation was, and exasperation at the dictatorial tone he'd used, she said, "I'd like to understand something. Are you telling me that the marriage is off if I don't agree to what you're asking?"

"I'd rather you answer my question before I answer yours."

It took several moments before Meredith finally realized that after pressuring her by implying he might refuse to marry her, Matt was now trying to see if she'd agree without his use of an actual threat. With an inner smile at the unnecessary and arbitrary way he was going about achieving his goal, Meredith appeared to consider the matter very carefully. "You want me to go off to South America with you?"

He nodded. "I talked to Sommers today. He said the housing and medical facilities are adequate. I need to see them for myself and make sure of it. If they're acceptable, I want you to join me there."

"I don't think it's a very fair offer," she said, straightfaced, shoving away from the barn and deliberately repaying him for his methods by making him wait for her answer.

He stiffened a little. "Right now it's the best I can do."

"I don't think you're doing very well," Meredith said, strolling toward the house to hide her smile. "I get a husband, a baby, and a house of my very own, plus the excitement of going off to South America. You get a wife who will probably cook your shirts, starch your food, and misplace your—"

She yelped in laughing surprise as his hand landed on her backside, and when she spun around she collided with his body, but Matt wasn't smiling. He was looking down at her with an indescribable expression on his face, pulling her tightly against his chest.

In the kitchen, Julie stood at the window and watched Matt kiss Meredith and then reluctantly let go of her. When she walked away, he stood with his hands on his hips, watching her and grinning. "Dad," she said, tossing an awed, beaming grin over her shoulder at her father, "Matt's falling in love!"

"God help him if he is."

She turned in surprise. "Don't you like Meredith?"

"I saw the way she looked at this house the first time she walked into it. She was looking down her nose at it and everything in it."

Julie's face fell, then she shook her head. "She was scared that day. I could tell she was."

"Matt's the one who ought to be scared. If he doesn't make it as big as he plans to, she'll dump him on his ass for some rich bastard and he won't end up with anything, not even visiting rights with my grandchild."

"I don't believe that."

"He hasn't got a chance in a million of being happy with her," Patrick said harshly. "Do you know what it does to a man to be married to a woman he loves, and to want to give her the best of everything—or at least better than what she had before she married him, and then not to be able to do it? Can you imagine how it feels to look in a mirror every day and know you're failing and, because you are, that you're a failure?"

"You're thinking about Mom," Julie said, searching his haggard face. "Mom never thought you were a failure. She told Matt and me both a hundred times how happy you made her."

"Too bad I didn't make her less happy and keep her more alive," he said bitterly, turning to walk away. The faulty logic and signs of depression weren't lost on Julie. Working double shifts this week was wearing him down, she knew. She knew it as surely as she knew that soon, maybe tomorrow, he was going to drink himself into a stupor. "Mom lived five years longer than the doctors said she could," Julie reminded him. "And if Matt wants Meredith to stay with him, he'll find a way to make it happen. He's like Mom. He's a fighter."

Patrick Farrell turned and looked at her, his smile grim. "Was that a pointed reminder to me to fight temptation?"

"No," she said, "it's my way of begging you to stop blaming yourself because you couldn't do more. Mom fought hard and you and Matt fought right along with her. You two finally paid off the last of her hospital bills this summer. don't you honestly think it's time to forget?"

Patrick Farrell reached out and tipped her chin up. "Some people feel love in their hearts, Julie. Some of us feel it all the way into our souls. We're the ones who can't forget." He took his hand away and glanced out the window, and his face took on a harsh look. "For Matt's sake, I hope to God he isn't like that. He's got big plans for the future, but it's going to mean sacrifices, and that girl has never made a sacrifice in her life. She won't have the courage to stick by him, and she'll bolt on him the minute the going gets rough."

Meredith stood in the doorway, shocked into immobility by what she'd heard him say. He turned to walk out and they came face-to-face. Patrick had the grace to look slightly embarrassed, but he stood his ground. "You heard that, and I'm sorry, Meredith. It's still the way I feel."

She was hurt and he could see it, but she looked him straight in the eye. With quiet dignity she said, "I hope you'll be just as eager to say you were wrong about me when you realize you are, Mr. Farrell."

She turned and headed up the stairs, leaving Patrick staring after her in stunned silence. Behind him, Julie said smugly, "You sure scared her to death, Dad. I see what you mean about Meredith having no courage."

Patrick frowned at her, but as he headed off to work he stopped and looked up the stairway. Meredith was on her way down with a sweater, but she hesitated on the top step. Without a great deal of hope that she would, he said, "If you prove me wrong, Meredith, you'll make me a very happy man."

It was a tentative offer of a truce, and she accepted it with a nod.

"You're carrying my grandchild," he added. "I'd like to see him grow up with two parents who are still married to each other when he finishes college."

"So would I, Mr. Farrell."

That almost startled a smile from him.

11

*S*unlight slanted through the windshield, and Meredith watched it gleaming on the gold wedding band that Matt had slid onto her finger the previous day during a simple civil ceremony performed by a local judge and witnessed only by Julie and Patrick. In comparison to the lavish formal church weddings she'd attended, her own had been brief and businesslike; the "honeymoon" that followed it in Matt's bed had been anything but that. With the house to themselves, he had kept her awake until dawn, making love to her again and again—trying to atone, she suspected, for not being able to take her on a proper honeymoon.

Meredith thought about that as she idly rubbed her ring against the sundress she'd borrowed from Julie. In bed, Matt always gave, and he gave, and he gave—yet he seemed not to want or need her to do anything to please him in return. Sometimes when he was making love to her, she longed to give him the same soul-destroying pleasure that he was lavishing on her, but she was hesitant to take the initiative without some form of encouragement from him first. It bothered her that he seemed to give more than he received—but when he shifted on top of her and drove deeply into her melting body, Meredith forgot about it. She forgot the world.

This morning, when she was still half asleep, he had put a breakfast tray on the nightstand and sat down beside her. For as long as she lived, Meredith knew she would remember the boyish glamour of his white smile as he leaned over her and whispered, "Wake up, sleeping beauty, and give this frog a kiss."

She looked at him now, and there was nothing boyish about that square jaw and tough chin, but there were other times—times when he laughed, or when he was sleeping and his dark hair was tousled, that his features were absolutely endearing, rather than rugged. And those eyelashes! The other morning she'd noticed those thick, spiked eyelashes lying against his cheek while he slept, and she'd had an absurd impulse to lean down and tuck him in because he looked like a little boy.

He caught her studying him and teased, "Did I forget to shave this morning?"

That startled a laugh from her because it was in such conflict with the direction of her thoughts. "Actually, I was thinking that you have eyelashes that a girl would kill for."

"You'd better watch it," he warned, shooting her a mock scowl. "I beat up a kid in the sixth grade for saying I had eyelashes like a girl's."

Meredith laughed, but as they neared her house and the confrontation with her father, the lighthearted mood they'd both tried to preserve began to disintegrate. Matt had to leave for Venezuela in two days, so their time together was quickly running out. And although he'd agreed not to tell her father about her pregnancy yet, he was personally opposed to the idea.

Meredith didn't like it either. It added to her feeling of being a child bride, and she hated that feeling. While she waited to join Matt in South America, she intended to learn to cook. In the past few days, the idea of being a real wife, with a husband and a place of their own, had taken on an enormous appeal despite the daunting description he'd given her of what that place of their own would probably be like.

"Here we are," Meredith said a few minutes later as they turned into the drive. "Home sweet home."

"If your father loves you as much as you think he does," Matt told her with quiet reassurance, helping her out of the car, "he'll try to make the best of this once he gets over the shock." Meredith hoped he was right, because, if he wasn't, it meant she would have to live at the farm while Matt was gone, and that she didn't want to do—not with Patrick Farrell feeling about her the way he did.

"Here goes," she said, drawing a deep breath as they walked up the steps to the front door. Since she'd called this morning and asked Albert to tell her father she'd be home in the early afternoon, Meredith assumed her father would be waiting.

She was right. The moment she opened the door, he stalked out of the living room, looking like he hadn't slept in a week. "Where in the hell have you been?" he thundered, looking ready to shake her. Unaware of Matt, who was standing a few steps behind her, he raged, "Are you trying to drive me out of my goddamned mind, Meredith?"

"Just be calm for a minute, and I'll explain," Meredith said, lifting her hand in Matt's direction.

He glanced to the left and saw who Meredith had been with. "Son of a bitch!"

"It's not what you're thinking," Meredith cried. "We're married!"

"You're what?"

Matt answered the question in a calm, implacable voice. "Married."

In the space of three seconds Philip Bancroft arrived at the only possible reason that Meredith would marry someone she didn't know. She was pregnant. "Oh, *Christ!*" The ravaged look on his face, the anguished fury in his voice, hurt Meredith more than anything he could have done or said to her. And just when she knew it couldn't get worse, she discovered it was only beginning. Rage had replaced his shock and sorrow. Turning on his heel, Philip ordered them both into his study, then he slammed the door behind them with a crash that shook the walls.

Ignoring Meredith completely, he prowled back and forth across the study like a maddened panther, and every time he looked at Matt, his eyes flashed with murder and hatred. For what seemed like hours, he swore at Matt, he accused him of everything from rape to assault, and he grew more incensed when Matt endured his vicious tirade in an impassive, tight-lipped silence that resembled indifference.

Shaking with nerves and drowning in shame, Meredith sat beside Matt on the sofa where they'd made love. She was so overwrought that it took several minutes before she finally realized that her father was less infuriated by her pregnancy than he was by her marriage to an "ambitious, low-class degenerate." When he finally ran out of words, he flung himself into the chair behind his desk and sat there in ominous silence, his gaze riveted on Matt, tapping the end of a letter opener on the desk.

Her throat aching with unshed tears, Meredith realized that Matt had been wrong. This was not something her father would adjust to or get over. She was going to be cast out of his life, just as her mother had been, and despite all their disagreements, she was utterly shattered. Matt was still a virtual stranger, and from this day forward her father would be a stranger too. There was no point trying to explain or defend Matt, because whenever she'd interrupted her father's tirade to do that, he'd either ignored her or gotten angrier.

Standing up, she said with as much dignity as she could, "I was going to stay here until I go to South America. Obviously, that's impossible. I'll go upstairs and pack a few things." She turned to Matt to suggest he wait for her in the car, but her father interrupted her, his voice taut with strain. "This is your house, Meredith, and where you belong. Farrell and I need to have a private talk, however."

Meredith didn't like the sound of that, but Matt nodded curtly for her to go.

When the door closed behind her, Matt waited for another tirade to begin, but Bancroft seemed to get himself under control. He sat at his desk, his fingers steepled, staring at Matt for several long, hard moments—mentally calculating, Matt suspected, the best way to ram home whatever he planned to say next. His fury hadn't gotten him anywhere, so Matt knew he would try another tack. He did not, however, expect Philip Bancroft to stumble onto Matt's only vulnerable place where Meredith was concerned: Guilt. Nor did he expect him to be as eloquently lethal.

"Congratulations, Farrell," Bancroft sneered in a bitter, sarcastic voice. "You've gotten an innocent eighteen-year-old girl pregnant, a girl with her whole life in front of her—a life that would have given her a college education, traveling, the best of everything." Raking Matt with a contemptuous stare, he said, "Do you know why there are clubs like Glenmoor?" Matt remained silent, and Philip told him the answer. "They're to protect our families, our *daughters*, from smooth-talking filth like you."

Bancroft seemed to sense he'd drawn blood with those remarks, and with the instincts of a vampire, he went for more. "Meredith is eighteen and you've stolen her youth by getting her pregnant and getting her married. Now you want to drag her all the way down with you—you want to take her to South America to live like a laborer's drudge. I've been to South America, and I know Bradley Sommers. I know *exactly* what sort of drilling operation he's planning in Venezuela, where it is, and what it's really like. You'll have to hack out paths through the jungle in order to get from what passes for civilization down there to the drilling site. When the next rain comes, the paths will be gone. Supplies are airlifted in and out by helicopter, there's no phone, no air-conditioning, no nothing! And that humid hellhole is where you intend to take my daughter?"

Matt had known when he took the job that the $150,000 bonus drilling companies paid was to compensate for certain deprivations, but he was fairly confident he could work things out for Meredith. Despite his loathing for Philip Bancroft, Matt knew the man was entitled to some form of assurance about Meredith's future well-being. For the first time since he arrived, he spoke. "There's a large village sixty miles away," he began in a flat, resolute voice.

"Bullshit! Sixty miles is eight hours by jeep, assuming the path you hacked out last time hasn't already been reclaimed by the jungle! Is that the village where you're planning to ditch my daughter for a year and a half? When do you plan to see her? You'll be working twelve-hour shifts, as I understand it."

"There are also cottages on site," Matt pointed out even though he suspected, and he'd told Meredith, they might not be adequate by his standards, regardless of what Sommers claimed. He also knew Bancroft was right about the terrain and the inconveniences. He was gambling that

Meredith might find Venezuela beautiful and their brief time there something of an adventure.

"That's a great life you're offering her," Philip shot back with cutting scorn. "A shack on site or a hovel in some godforsaken village in the middle of nowhere!" Abruptly, he changed the angle for the next verbal knife. "You've got a tough hide, Farrell, I'll give you that. You took everything I could hand out without so much as a flinch. Do you also have a conscience, I wonder? You've sold my daughter your dreams in return for her whole life. Well, she had dreams too, you bastard. She wanted to go to college. She's been in love with the same man since childhood too— A banker's son who could have given her the world. She doesn't think I know about that, but I do. Did you?"

Matt's jaw tightened, but he said nothing.

"Tell me something, where did she get the clothes she has on?" Without waiting for an answer, Philip jeered. "She's been with you for a few days and she doesn't even look the same! She looks like she's been dressed by Kmart. Now, then," Philip said, his voice turning businesslike, "that brings us to the next issue which I'm sure is vital to you: Money. You are not going to see one *cent* of Meredith's money! Am I making myself clear?" he snapped, leaning forward in his chair. "You've already robbed her of her youth and her dreams, but you aren't ever going to see one cent of her money. I have control of it for twelve more years. If, by some chance she's still with you in twelve years, before I turn it over to her, I'll invest every goddamned cent of it in things she can't sell or trade for twenty-five years."

When Matt remained icily silent, he continued. "If you're thinking I'll take pity on the way she's living with you and start doling out money to make things better for her—ergo, for you—you don't know me very well. You think you're tough, Farrell, but you don't know what tough is yet. I'll stop at nothing to get Meredith free of you, and if that means letting her walk around in rags, barefoot and pregnant, I'll let it happen! Have I made myself clear so far?" he snapped, his control slipping a notch at Matt's lack of reaction.

"Perfectly," Matt bit out. "And now let me remind you of something," he continued with an inured expression that belied the battering he'd taken from guilt as Bancroft had hammered away. "There is a child involved here. Meredith is already pregnant, so most of what you've said is already immaterial."

"She was supposed to go to college," Philip countered. "Everybody knew that. I'll send her away, and she can have the baby. Also there is still time to consider another alternative—"

Fury ignited in Matt's eyes. "Nothing happens to that baby!" he warned in a low, savage voice.

"Fine. You want it, you take it."

In all the chaos of the past week that was one alternative neither of them had discussed. Because as things had turned out it hadn't been necessary. With a great deal more conviction than he felt at that moment, Matt said, "This is completely irrelevant. Meredith wants to stay with me."

"Of course she does!" Philip flung back. "Sex is a new experience for her." Casting a knowing, contemptuous look over Matt, he added, "Not for you though, is it?" Like two duelists, they circled mentally, but Philip had the sharpest rapier and Matt was on the defensive. "When you're gone, and sex isn't part of your allure, Meredith will think more clearly," Philip stated with absolute conviction. "She'll want her dreams, not yours. She'll want to go to college and go out with her friends. And so," he concluded, "I'm asking you for a concession, and I'm willing to pay handsomely for it. If Meredith is like her mother, her pregnancy won't really be apparent until she's past six months. So that she'll have time to reconsider, I want you to talk her into keeping this revolting marriage and the pregnancy secret—"

Rather than let Philip think he'd gotten Matt to agree, Matt said shortly, "She's already decided to do that until after she joins me in South America." The look of pleasure on Bancroft's face made Matt grit his teeth.

"Good, if no one knows you're married, that makes everything neater and cleaner when you get divorced. Here is what I'm offering you, Farrell: In return for you letting go of my daughter, I'll contribute a sizable chunk of money to finance whatever wild-assed scheme she mentioned you have in mind after you leave South America."

In frigid silence Matt watched Philip Bancroft take a large checkbook from his desk. Out of petty vengeance, Matt sat there and let Bancroft write out a check because he wanted to put him to the trouble before he refused it. It was small retribution for the inner torment he'd managed to cause Matt.

Finished, Bancroft threw his pen down and stalked across the room while Matt slowly stood up. "Five minutes after you walk out of this room, I'll have a stop-payment order put on this check at my bank," Bancroft warned. "As soon as you convince Meredith to give up on this travesty of a marriage and let you raise the child, I'll instruct the bank to let the check clear. This money is your reward—one hundred and fifty thousand dollars—for not destroying the life of an eighteen-year-old girl. Take it," he ordered, holding out his hand.

Matt ignored it.

"Take the check, because it's the last cent of my money you'll ever see."

"I'm not interested in your goddamned money!"

"I'm warning you, Farrell," he said, his face darkening with rage again, "take this check."

With icy calm Matt said, "Shove it up your—"

Bancroft's fist slammed forward with surprising force. Matt dodged the blow, grabbed Bancroft's arm in mid-swing, then he yanked him forward, spun him around, and jerked his arm up high behind his back. In a soft snarl, he said, "Listen to me very carefully, Bancroft. In a few years I'll have enough money to buy and sell you, but if you interfere in my marriage, I'll *bury* you! Do we understand each other?"

"Let go of my arm, you son of a bitch."

Matt shoved him forward and stalked toward the door.

Behind him, Bancroft recovered his composure with amazing speed. "We have Sunday dinner at three," he snapped. "I'd prefer you not upset Meredith by telling her what transpired in here. As you pointed out, she is pregnant." Pausing with his hand on the door knob, Matt turned, his silence a tacit consent, but Bancroft wasn't finished. Surprisingly, he seemed to have spent his fury and was now reluctantly accepting that he couldn't put an end to the marriage, and that further attempts to try might very well cause a permanent estrangement between Meredith and himself. "I don't want to lose my daughter, Farrell," he said stonily. "It's obvious you and I are never going to like each other, however, for her sake, we can at least try to get along."

Matt studied the other man's angry, set face, but there was no sign of duplicity in his expression. Furthermore, what he was suggesting was logical, sensible, and in his own and his daughter's best interests. After a moment, Matt nodded curtly and accepted the offer at face value. "We can try."

Philip Bancroft watched him walk out and close the door, then he slowly tore the check into pieces, a tight smile on his face. "Farrell," he said derisively, "You've just made two enormous mistakes—you refused this check, and you underestimated your adversary."

Lying beside Matt, Meredith stared at the shadowy canopy above her bed, alarmed by the change she'd sensed in him ever since he'd spoken with her father. When she'd asked him what took place in the library, all Matt would tell her was, "He tried to talk me into getting out of your life." Since the two men had treated each other civilly ever since their private meeting, Meredith assumed they'd declared a truce, and she'd teasingly asked, "Did he succeed?" Matt had said no, and she'd believed him, but tonight he'd made love to her with a grim determination that was completely unlike him. It was as if he wanted to brand her with his body—or else he were saying good-bye . . .

She stole a sideways glance at him; he was wide awake, his jaw tight, lost in thought, but she couldn't tell whether he was angry, sad, or simply preoccupied. They'd known each other for only six days, and now more than ever she realized what a handicap that was, because she couldn't gauge his mood at all.

"What are you thinking about?" he asked abruptly.

Startled by his sudden willingness to talk, she said, "I was thinking we've known each other for only six days."

A mocking smile twisted his handsome mouth, as if he'd expected her to say something like that. "That's an excellent reason to give up the idea of staying married, isn't it?"

Meredith's uneasiness escalated to sick panic at his words, and with sudden clarity, she understood the reason for her violent reaction: She was in love with him. Helplessly in love and painfully vulnerable because of it. Hoping to affect a casual attitude, she rolled over onto her stomach and braced herself on her forearms, not certain whether he'd been making a statement or trying to second-guess her thoughts. Her first impulse was to assume that he'd just stated his opinion and to try to salvage her pride by agreeing with him or pretending indifference. But if she did that, she'd never know for certain, and uncertainty was something that drove her crazy. Furthermore, it didn't seem very mature to go leaping to conclusions, especially right now, when there was so much at stake. She decided to follow her second impulse and to find out what he'd meant. Scrupulously avoiding his gaze she traced a circle on her pillow and, summoning all her courage, she said, "Were you asking me for my opinion just now, or were you telling me yours?"

"I was *asking* if that's what you were thinking."

Relief surged through her, and Meredith smiled as she shook her head and explained, "I was thinking it's hard for me to understand you tonight because we've only known each other for such a short time." When he didn't reply to that, she looked at him and saw that he still looked grim and preoccupied. "It's your turn now," she said with a nervous, determined smile. "What have *you* been thinking about?"

His silence tonight had unnerved her; now that he was talking, his words chilled her. "I was thinking that the reason we got married was because you wanted the baby legitimized, and because you didn't want to tell your father you were pregnant. The baby's legitimized. Your father already knows you're pregnant. Instead of trying to make this marriage work, there's another solution, one we didn't consider before, but we should now: I can take the baby and raise it."

Her resolve to react with calm maturity collapsed, and she leapt straight to an obvious conclusion. "That would relieve you of the burden of an unwanted wife, wouldn't it."

"I didn't suggest it for that reason."

"Didn't you?" she said scornfully.

"No." He shifted onto his side and touched her arm, sliding his hand caressingly over her skin.

Meredith's temper exploded. "Don't you dare try to make love to me again!" she burst out, jerking her arm away. "I may be young but I still have a right to know what's going on, and not be used all night like a—a—body with no mind! If you want out of this marriage, just say so!"

His reaction was nearly as volatile as hers. "Dammit, I'm not trying to get out of anything! I am drowning in guilt, Meredith. *Guilt*, not cowardice! I got you pregnant and you came to me in a panic, so I got you married too. As your father eloquently phrased it," he added with bitter self-contempt, "I have stolen your youth. I've stolen your dreams and sold you mine."

Overjoyed that guilt, not regret, was causing his mood, Meredith expelled her breath in a rush of relief and started to say something, but Matt was now intent on proving to her that he was truly guilty of stealing her youth and that her expectations for the future were probably unrealistic. "You said you didn't want to stay at the farm while I'm gone," he pointed out. "Has it occurred to you that the farm is one hell of a lot nicer than where you're going? Or are you under some infantile impression that you'll live like this in Venezuela, or after we come back? Because if you are, you're in for a shock. Even if things work out exactly like I think they should, it will be years before I can afford to support you in the manner to which you're accustomed. Hell, I may *never* be able to afford a house like this—"

"A house like this—" Meredith interrupted, gaping at him in laughing horror, then she flopped face down on the pillow and dissolved into gales of muffled mirth.

Above her, his voice was taut with angry bewilderment. "This is not a damned bit funny!"

"Yes it is," she said, laughing into the pillow. "Th-this is an awful house! It's unwelcoming and I've *never* liked it." When he didn't respond, Meredith got herself under partial control and shoved back up onto her forearms, then she pushed her hair aside and stole a laughing peek at his inscrutable face. "Want to know something else?" she teased, thinking of his confession that he'd stolen her youth.

Determined to make her understand the sacrifices he was causing her to make, Matt restrained the urge to run his hand over the shimmering mass of waving hair that spilled over her back, but he couldn't keep the answering smile from his voice. "What is it?" he whispered tenderly.

Meredith's shoulders trembled with fresh merriment. "I didn't like my youth, either!" She'd hoped for a favorable response to that announcement, and she got one. He seized her mouth in a hard kiss that robbed her of breath and the ability to think. While she was still trying to recover from the effects of it, he said harshly, "Promise me one thing, Meredith. If you change your mind about anything while I'm gone, promise me you won't get rid of the baby. No abortion. I'll arrange to raise it myself."

"I'm not going to change my—"

"Promise me you won't get rid of the baby!"

Realizing it was senseless to argue, she nodded, looking deeply into those ominous gray eyes. "I promise," she said with a soft smile.

Her reward for that promise was another hour of lovemaking, but this time he was the man she knew.

Meredith stood in the driveway and kissed Matt good-bye for the third time that morning. The day had not started off very well. At breakfast, her father had asked if anyone else knew about their marriage, and that reminded Meredith that she'd called Jonathan Sommers last week when no one answered the phone at the Edmunton house.

To save face, she'd told Jonathan she'd found a credit card of Matt's in her car after she gave him a ride home from Glenmoor, and that she didn't know where to send it. Jonathan had provided the information that Matt was still in Edmunton. As her father pointed out, it made the idea of announcing their marriage just two days after that phone call to Jonathan ridiculous. He suggested that Meredith go to Venezuela and let everyone think they'd gotten married there. Meredith knew he was right, but she wasn't good at deception, and she was angry because she'd inadvertently created the need for more of it.

Now Matt's departure was hanging over her like a cloud. "I'll call you from the airport," he promised. "Once I get to Venezuela and check out the facilities, I'll call you from there, but it won't be on a phone. We'll have radio communications with a base station that has an actual telephone. The connection won't be very good, and I'm not going to have access to it except in emergencies. I'll convince them this time that calling you to tell you I arrived safely constitutes an emergency," he added. "I won't be able to pull off something like that again though."

"Write to me," she said, trying to smile.

"I will. The mail service will probably be lousy, so don't be surprised if days go by with no letters and then they arrive in a group."

She stayed there in the drive, watching him leave, then walked slowly back into the house, concentrating on thinking of a few weeks from now when, with luck, they'd be together. Her father was standing in the hall, and he gave her a pitying look. "Farrell is the sort of man who needs new women, new places, new challenges all the time. He'll break your heart if you let yourself count on him."

"Stop it," Meredith warned, refusing to let what he said bother her. "You're wrong. You'll see."

Matt kept his promise to call her from the airport, and Meredith spent the next two days finding things in the house to keep her occupied while she waited for him to call from Venezuela. The call came on the third day, but Meredith wasn't there; she was waiting nervously to see her obstetrician because she was afraid she was miscarrying.

"Spotting during the first three months isn't that unusual an occurrence," Dr. Arledge said when she was dressed and sitting in his office. "It may not mean anything. However, most miscarriages occur during the first three months." He said it as if he half expected her to be relieved. Dr. Arledge was a friend of her father's. She'd known him for years, and Meredith had no doubt that he'd already done what her father had—assumed she'd gotten married because she was pregnant. "At this point," he added, "there's no reason to presume you're in jeopardy of miscarrying."

When she asked him about going to Venezuela, he frowned a little. "I can't advise it unless you're absolutely certain about the quality of available medical facilities."

Meredith had spent nearly a month hoping fiercely that if she was pregnant, she'd miscarry; now she was incredibly relieved that she wasn't going to lose Matt's baby. . . . Their baby.

The thought kept her smiling all the way home.

"Farrell called," her father said with the same disdainful voice he used whenever he spoke of Matt. "He said he'd try to call you again tonight."

Meredith was sitting by the phone when it rang, and Matt hadn't exaggerated when he said the phone connection would be bad. "Sommers's idea of adequate is a joke," he told her. "There's no way you can come down here right away. It's mostly barracks housing. The good news is that one of the cottages should be vacant in a few months."

"Okay," she said, trying to sound cheerful, because she didn't want to tell him why she'd gone to the doctor.

"You don't sound very disappointed."

"I am disappointed!" she said emphatically. "But the doctor said miscarriages occur in the first three months, so it's probably better if I stay here 'til then."

"Is there a particular reason you've started worrying about miscarrying?" he asked during the next pause in the static and racket.

Meredith assured him she was feeling just fine. When he'd originally told her he wouldn't be able to call her after the first time, she'd been disappointed, but it was so hard to hear him above the static and shouting voices all around him, she didn't mind so much. Letters, she decided when she hung up, would be almost as good.

Lisa came back from Europe to start college when Matt had been gone two weeks, and her reaction to Meredith's story about meeting and marrying Matt was almost comic—once she realized Meredith wasn't at all unhappy about anything that had happened. "I can't believe this!" she said over and over again as she gaped at Meredith, who was sitting on her bed. "There is something wrong with this picture," she teased. "*I* was the reckless one and you were Bensonhurst's own Mary Poppins, not to mention the *most* cautious person alive! If anyone fell for a guy on first sight, got pregnant, and had to get married, it was supposed to be me!"

Meredith grinned at her infectious merriment. "It's about time I got to be first doing something."

Lisa sobered a little. "Is he wonderful, Mer? I mean, if he isn't really, really wonderful, then he isn't good enough for you."

Talking about Matt and her feelings for him was a new and complicated experience, particularly because Meredith knew how odd it would seem if she said she loved him after knowing him for six days. Instead, she nodded and smiled and said feelingly, "He's pretty wonderful." Once she started, however, she found it a little difficult to stop talking about him. Curling her legs beneath her, she tried to explain. "Lisa, have you ever met anyone and then known within minutes that he's the most special person you're ever going to meet in your life?"

"I generally feel that way about everybody I date at first—I'm kidding!" She laughed when Meredith threw a pillow at her.

"Matt *is* special, I mean that. I think he's brilliant—I mean literally brilliant. He's incredibly strong and a little dictatorial at times, but inside him there's something else, something fine and gentle and—"

"Do we by any chance happen to have a picture of this paragon?" Lisa interrupted, as fascinated by the glowing look on Meredith's face as the words she said.

Meredith promptly produced a picture. "I found it in a family photo album his sister showed me, and Julie said I could have it. It was taken a year ago, and even though it's just a snapshot and not very good, it reminds me of more than just his face—there's some of his personality too." She handed Lisa the snapshot of Matt; he was squinting a little in the sunlight, his hands shoved into the back pockets of his jeans, grinning at Julie, who was taking the picture.

"Oh, my *God!*" Lisa said, wide-eyed. "Talk about animal magnetism! Talk about male charisma . . . sex appeal . . ."

Laughing, Meredith snatched the picture away. "That is my husband you are drooling over."

Lisa gaped at her. "You always liked clean-cut, blond, all-American types."

"Actually, I didn't think Matt was especially good-looking when I first saw him. My taste has improved since then though."

Sobering, Lisa said, "Mer, do you think you're in love with him?"

"I love being with him."

"Isn't that the same thing?"

Meredith smiled helplessly and said, "Yes, but it sounds less foolish than saying you're in love with somebody you've known only a few days."

Satisfied, Lisa shot to her feet. "Let's go out and celebrate! Dinner's on you."

"You're on," Meredith laughed, already walking toward her closet to change clothes.

The mail service from Venezuela was much worse than Matt had said it would be. In the following eight weeks, Meredith wrote Matt three or four times a week, but she got only five letters—a fact her father regularly remarked upon with more gravity than satisfaction. Meredith invariably reminded him that the letters she did get were very long—ten or twelve pages. Furthermore, Matt was working twelve-hour days doing hard physical labor, and he couldn't be expected to write as often as she did. Meredith pointed that out to him too. What she never mentioned was that the last two letters had been much less personal than the preceding ones. Where at first Matt had written about missing her and making plans, he began to write more about the scene at the oil rig and the Venezuelan countryside. But whatever he wrote about, he made it come vividly alive for her. She told herself he was writing about these things not because he was losing interest in her, but because he wanted to keep her own interest in her, but because he wanted to keep her own interest piqued in the country she'd be visiting.

Trying to keep busy to help the days pass, Meredith read books on pregnancy and child rearing, shopped for baby things, and planned and dreamed. The baby that had not seemed real at first was now making its presence known by causing the periodic bouts of nausea and fatigue that should have occurred earlier, combined with some ferocious headaches that sent Meredith to bed in a dark room. Even so, she bore it with good humor and the absolute conviction that this was a special experience. As the days wore on, she fell into the habit of talking to the baby as if, by placing her hand on her still-flat stomach, it could hear her. "I hope you are having a good time in there," she teased one day as she lay on her bed, her headache finally fading, "because you are making me sick as a dog, young lady." In the interest of impartiality, she varied "Young man" with "Young lady," since she didn't have the slightest preference.

By the end of October, Meredith's four-month pregnancy was thickening her waist, and her father's regular comments about Matt wanting out of the marriage were beginning to ring with truth. "It's a damned good thing you didn't tell anyone but Lisa you married him," he remarked a few days before Halloween. "You still have options, Meredith, don't forget that," he added with rare gentleness. "When this pregnancy starts to show, we'll tell everyone you've gone away to college for the winter semester."

"Stop talking like that, dammit!" Meredith exploded, and marched up to her room. She'd decided to make a point to Matt about his lack of writing by cutting way back on her own letters to him. Besides, she was beginning to feel like a lovelorn idiot, writing to him all the time when he couldn't be bothered to send a postcard.

Lisa called late that afternoon. In two minutes she sensed Meredith's strained nerves and assessed the cause. "No letter from Matt today?" she guessed. "And your father is playing his favorite tune, right?"

"Right," Meredith said. "It's been two weeks since letter number five arrived."

"Let's go out," Lisa announced. "We'll get all dressed up—that always makes you feel better, and we'll go somewhere nice."

"How about going to Glenmoor for dinner?" Meredith said, executing a plan she'd been toying with for weeks. "And maybe," she confessed a little grimly, "Jon Sommers will be there. He usually is. You could ask him all about oil drilling, and maybe he'll bring up Matt."

"Okay, fine," Lisa said, but Meredith knew that Lisa's opinion of Matt was sinking with each day that no letter arrived.

Jonathan was in the lounge with several other men, talking and drinking. When Meredith and Lisa walked in, they caused quite a stir, and it was absurdly easy to wangle an invitation to join the men at their table. For nearly an hour, Meredith sat only a few feet from where she had stood with Matt near the bar four months before, watching as Lisa gave an Academy Award–winning performance that fooled Jonathan into believing she was thinking about switching her major to geology and specializing in oil exploration. Meredith learned more about drilling than she wanted to know, and virtually nothing about Matt.

Two weeks later Meredith's doctor wasn't smiling and confident when he talked to her. She was spotting again, seriously. When she left, she was under instructions to restrict all activities. Meredith wished more than ever before that Matt were there. When she got home, she called Julie just to talk to someone close to him. She'd called Matt's sister twice before for the same reason, and each time, Julie and her father had heard from Matt that week.

In bed that night, Meredith lay awake, willing the baby to be all right, and willing Matt to write to her. It had been a month since his last letter. In it, he'd said he was extremely busy and very tired at night. She could understand that, but she couldn't understand why Matt had time to write to his family and not to her. Meredith laid her hand protectively over her abdomen. "Your daddy," she whispered to the baby, "is going to get a very stern letter from me about this."

She assumed that worked, because Matt drove eight hours to get to a telephone and called her. She was so glad to hear from him, she almost left handprints on the receiver, but he sounded a little abrupt and a little cool. "The cottage on the site isn't available yet," he told her. "I've found another place here, in a small village. I'll be able to get there only on weekends though."

Meredith couldn't go, not now, when the doctor wanted to see her every week, and she wasn't supposed to walk around more than a little. She couldn't go and she didn't want to scare Matt by telling him the doctor thought she might be on the verge of losing the baby. On the other hand, she was so angry with him for not writing, and so frightened for the baby, she decided to scare him anyway. "I can't come down," she said. "The doctor wants me to stay home and not move around very much."

"How odd," he shot back. "Sommers was down here last week and he told me you and your friend, Lisa, were at Glenmoor dazzling all the men in the lounge."

"That was *before* the doctor told me to stay home."

"I see."

"What do you expect me to do," Meredith shot back with rare sarcasm, "hang around here day after day and wait for your occasional letters?"

"You might give that a try," he snapped. "By the way, you're not much of a correspondent."

Meredith took that to be a criticism of her letter-writing style, and she was so furious that she almost hung up.

"I gather you don't have anything else to say?"

"Not much."

When they hung up, Matt leaned his hand against the wall beside the phone and closed his eyes, trying to block out the phone call and the agony of what was happening. He'd been gone three months, and Meredith no longer wanted to come to South America. She hadn't written him in weeks; she was already resuming her old social life and then lying to him about being home in bed. She was only eighteen, he reminded himself bitterly. Why *wouldn't* she want a social life? "Shit!" he whispered in helpless futility, but after a few minutes he straightened with resolve. In a few months things at the drilling site would be under better control, and he'd insist that they give him four days off so that he could fly home and see her. Meredith wanted him and she wanted to be married to him; no matter how few letters she wrote or what she did, he knew in his heart that was still true. He'd fly home, and when they were together, he'd be able to talk her into coming back with him.

Meredith hung up the phone, flung herself across the bed, and cried her eyes out. When he'd told her about the house he'd found, he certainly hadn't tried to make it sound nice, and he hadn't acted like he particularly cared whether she came or not. When she finished, she dried her eyes and wrote him a long letter apologizing for being a "bad correspondent." She apologized for losing her temper and, surrendering all her pride, she told him how much his letters meant to her. She explained in great detail what the doctor had told her.

When she finished, she carried the letter downstairs and left it for Albert to mail. She'd already given up hovering by the mailbox out at the road, waiting for letters from Matt that never came. Albert, who served as butler-chauffeur and maintenance man, walked in right then with a dust-cloth in his hand. Mrs. Ellis had taken three months off for her first vacation in years, and he'd reluctantly assumed some of her tasks too. "Would you please mail this for me, Albert?" she asked.

"Of course," he said. When she left, Albert took the letter down the hall to Mr. Bancroft's study, unlocked an antique secretary, and tossed that letter on top of all the others, half of which were postmarked from Venezuela.

Meredith went upstairs to her bedroom and was halfway to the chair at her desk when the hemorrhaging started.

She spent two days in the Bancroft wing of Cedar Hills Hospital, a wing named after her family in honor of their huge endowments, praying the bleeding wouldn't start again and that Matt would miraculously decide to come home. She wanted her baby and she wanted her husband, and she had a terrible feeling she was losing both.

When Dr. Arledge released her from the hospital, it was on condition that she remain in bed for the duration of her pregnancy. As soon as she came home, Meredith wrote Matt a letter that not only informed him she was in danger of losing their baby, but that was, moreover, *meant* to scare him into worrying about her. She was ready to do almost anything to stay on his mind.

Complete bedrest seemed to solve the problem of impending miscarriage, but with nothing to do but read or watch television or worry, Meredith had ample time to reflect on painful reality: Matt had obviously found her a convenient bed partner, and now that they were apart, he had found her completely forgettable. She started thinking about the best ways to raise her baby alone.

That was one problem she had worried about needlessly. At the end of her fifth month, in the middle of the night, Meredith hemorrhaged. This time none of the skills known to medical science were able to save the baby girl whom Meredith named Elizabeth in honor of Matt's mother. They nearly failed to save Meredith, who remained in critical condition for three days.

For a week after that she lay in bed with tubes running into her veins, listening anxiously for the sound of Matt's long, quick strides in the corridor. Her father had tried to call him, and when he couldn't get through, he'd sent him a telegram.

Matt didn't come. He didn't call.

During her second week in the hospital, however, he answered her telegram with one of his own. It was short, direct and lethal:

A DIVORCE IS AN EXCELLENT IDEA. GET ONE.

Meredith was so emotionally battered by those eight words that she refused to believe he was capable of sending a telegram like that—not when she was in the hospital. "Lisa," she'd wept hysterically, "he'd have to *hate* me before he'd do this to me, and I haven't done anything to make Matt hate me! He didn't send that telegram—he didn't! He *couldn't!*" She talked Lisa into putting on another performance for the benefit of the staff at Western Union in order to find out who sent it. Western Union reluctantly provided the information that the telegram had indeed been sent by Matthew Farrell from Venezuela and charged to his credit card.

On a cold December day Meredith emerged from the hospital with Lisa walking on one side of her and her father on the other. She looked up at the bright blue sky, and it looked different, alien. The whole world seemed alien.

At her father's insistence, she enrolled for the winter semester at Northwestern and arranged to share a room with Lisa. She did it because they seemed to want her to, but in time, she remembered why it had once meant so much to her. She remembered other things too—like how to smile, and then how to laugh. Her doctor warned her that any future pregnancy would carry an even greater risk to her baby and herself. The thought of being childless had hurt terribly, but somehow she coped with that too.

Life had dealt her several major blows, but she had survived them and, in doing so, she found in herself an inner strength she didn't know she possessed.

Her father hired an attorney who handled the divorce. From Matt she heard nothing, but she finally reached the point where she could think of him without pain or animosity. He had obviously married her because she was pregnant and because he was greedy. When he realized that her father had complete control of her money, he simply had no further use for her. In time, she stopped blaming him. Her reasons for marrying him had not been unselfish either; she had gotten pregnant and been afraid to face the consequences alone. And even though she had thought she loved him, he had never deceived her by claiming to love her—she had deceived *herself* into believing he did. They had married each other for all the wrong reasons, and the marriage had been doomed from the start.

During her junior year she saw Jonathan Sommers at Glenmoor. He told her his father had liked an idea of Matt's so well that he'd formed a limited partnership with him and put up the additional capital for the venture.

That venture paid off. In the eleven years that followed, a great many more of Matt's ventures also paid off. Articles about him and pictures of him appeared frequently in magazines and newspapers. Meredith saw them, but she was busy with her own career, and it no longer mattered what he did. It mattered to the press though. As year faded into year, the press became increasingly obsessed with his flamboyant corporate successes and his glamorous bedroom playmates, who included several movie stars. To the common man, Matt apparently represented the American Dream of a poor boy making good. To Meredith, he was simply a stranger with whom she had once been intimate. Since she never used his name and only her father and Lisa knew that she had ever been married to him, his widely publicized romances with other women never caused her any personal embarrassment.

12

Wind whipped up whitecaps and sent them tumbling, frothing onto the sand twenty feet below the rocky ledge where Barbara Walters strolled beside Matthew Farrell. A camera tracked their progress, its dark glass eye observing the pair, framing them against a background of Farrell's palatial Carmel, California, estate on the right, and the turbulent Pacific Ocean on the left.

Fog was rolling in like a thick, undulating blanket, propelled forward by the same wild gusts that were playing havoc with Barbara Walters's hair and spitting sand at the camera's lens. At the prearranged spot, Walters stopped, turned her back to the ocean, and started to address another question to Farrell. The camera swiveled too, but now it saw only the couple framed against a dismal backdrop of gray fog while wind blew Walters's hair across her face.

"Cut!" she called out, irritably shoving hair out of her eyes, trying to free the strands sticking to her lipstick. Turning to the woman who was in charge of makeup, she said, "Tracy, do you have anything that will hold my hair down in this wind?"

"Elmer's Glue?" Tracy suggested with a lame attempt at humor, and motioned to the van parked beneath the cypress trees on the west lawn of the Farrell estate. After excusing herself to Farrell, Walters and the makeup girl headed toward the van.

"I *hate* fog!" the cameraman announced bitterly as he glowered at the thick gray mist shrouding the coastline, obliterating the panoramic view of Half Moon Bay that he'd envisioned using as cinematic background for this interview. "I *hate* fog," he repeated, turning his scowling face up to the sky. "And I hate wind, goddammit!"

He had addressed his complaint directly to the Almighty, and, as if in answer, a fistful of sand blew up like a miniature whirlwind at the cameraman's feet and hurtled itself into his chest and face.

The assistant cameraman chuckled. "Apparently, God isn't very fond of *you* either," he observed, watching the irate man dust sand off his eyebrows. He held out a cup of steaming coffee. "How do you feel about coffee?"

"I hate that too," the cameraman muttered, but he took the cup.

The assistant nodded in the direction of the tall man standing a few yards away, gazing out at the ocean. "Why don't you ask Farrell to stop the wind and clear the fog? From what I hear, God probably takes His orders from Farrell."

"If you ask me," Alice Champion chuckled, joining the pair and sipping her own coffee, "Matthew Farrell *is* God." Both men shot an ironic look at the script girl, but they said nothing, and Alice knew their silence represented their own reluctant awe of the man.

Over the rim of her coffee cup, she studied Farrell as he stood looking out across the ocean—a solitary, somewhat secretive ruler of a financial empire called Intercorp, an empire he had created out of his own sweat and daring. A tall, urbane monarch who sprang from the steel mills of Indiana, Matthew Farrell had somehow purged himself of any of the characteristics that might have been identified with his lowly origins.

Now, as he stood on the ridge, waiting for the interview to continue, Alice thought he absolutely radiated success, confidence, and virility. And power. Most of all, Matthew Farrell emanated raw, harsh power. He was tanned, suave, and impeccably groomed, yet there was something about him that even his tailor-made clothes and polite smile couldn't conceal—a danger, a ruthlessness that made others try to amuse, rather than annoy him. It was as if his entire being gave off a silent warning not to cross him.

"Mr. Farrell?" Barbara Walters stepped down from the van, clamping her blowing hair down against her temples with both hands. "This weather's impossible. We'll have to set up inside the house. It will take us about thirty minutes. Can we use the living room?"

"Fine," Matt said, his annoyance at this delay concealed behind a brief smile. He did not like reporters of any kind, from any medium. The only reason he'd agreed to allow Barbara Walters to interview him was that there'd been a long rash of publicity about his private life and amorous affairs, and it was beneficial to Intercorp's image for its chief executive officer to be seen in his corporate persona for a change. When it came to Intercorp, Matt made whatever sacrifices were necessary. Nine years ago, after he finished working in Venezuela, he'd used his bonus and the additional money Sommers put up, to buy a small automotive parts manufacturing company that was teetering on bankruptcy. A year later, he sold it for twice what it had cost. Using his share of the profits and additional money he borrowed from banks and private investors, he formed Intercorp and, for the next several years, he continued to buy up companies that were teetering on bankruptcy—not because they were poorly managed, but only because they were undercapitalized—then he shored them up with Intercorp's capital and waited for a buyer.

Later, instead of selling the companies off, he began a carefully planned acquisition program. As a result, in one decade, he'd built Intercorp into the financial empire he'd imagined during those grim days and nights he labored in the steel mills and sweated on the oil rig. Today, Intercorp was a massive conglomerate headquartered in Los Angeles that controlled businesses as diverse as pharmaceutical research laboratories and textile mills.

Until recently, Matt had made it a practice to purchase only selected companies that were for sale. A year ago, however, he had entered into negotiations to buy a multibillion-dollar electronics manufacturer headquartered in Chicago. Originally, the company had approached him, asking if Intercorp would be interested in acquiring them.

Matt had liked the idea, but after spending a great deal of revenue and many months finalizing the agreement, the officers of Haskell Electronics had suddenly refused to accept the previously agreed-upon terms. Angry at the waste of Intercorp's time and money, Matt decided to acquire Haskell with or without their consent. As a result of that decision, a fierce and well-publicized battle ensued. At the end of it, Haskell's officers and directors were left lying crippled on the financial battlefield, and Intercorp had gained a very profitable electronics manufacturer. Along with victory, however, Matt also acquired a reputation as a ruthless corporate raider. That didn't particularly faze him; it was no more irksome than his reputation as an international playboy which the press had bestowed upon him. Adverse publicity and the loss of his personal privacy were the costs of success, and he accepted them with the same philosophical indifference that he felt for the fawning hypocrisy he encountered socially, and the treachery he faced from business adversaries. Sycophants and enemies came with extraordinary success, and if dealing with them had made him extremely cynical and wary, that, too, was the price he'd had to pay.

None of that bothered him; what did bother him was that he no longer derived much gratification from his successes. The exhilaration he used to feel when he faced a difficult business deal had been missing for years, probably, he'd decided, because success was virtually a foregone conclusion now. There was nothing left to challenge him—at least there hadn't been until he'd decided to take over Haskell Electronics. Now, for the first time in years, he was feeling some of the old adrenaline and anticipation. Haskell was a challenge; the huge corporation needed to be completely restructured. It was top-heavy with management; its manufacturing facilities were antiquated, its marketing strategies outdated. All of that would have to change before it could begin to realize its full profit potential, and Matt was eager to get to Chicago and get started. In the past whenever he acquired a new company, he'd sent in the six men who *Business Week* magazine had dubbed his "takeover team" to evaluate the organization and make recommendations. They'd been at Haskell for two weeks already, working in the sixty-story high-rise that Haskell owned and occupied, waiting for Matt to join them. Since he expected to be in Chicago off and on for the better part of a year, he'd bought a penthouse apartment there. Everything was in readiness, and he was eager to leave and get started.

Late last night he'd returned from Greece, where negotiations to acquire a shipping fleet had taken four long, frustrating weeks, instead of two, to bring to fruition. Now the only thing that was holding him up was this damned interview. Silently cursing the delay, Matt turned toward the house. On the east lawn, his helicopter was already waiting to take him to the airport, where the Lear he'd bought was ready to take off for Chicago.

The helicopter pilot returned Matt's brief wave, then gave the thumbs-up sign that the chopper was fueled and ready to fly, but he glanced worriedly toward the wall of fog closing in on them, and Matt knew his pilot was as eager as he to be airborne. Crossing the flagstone terrace, he entered the house through the French doors that opened into his private study. He was reaching for the telephone, intending to call his Los Angeles office, when the door across the room banged open. "Hey, Matt—" Joe O'Hara poked his head into the opening, his gruff, uncultured voice and unkempt appearance a jarring contrast to the almost antiseptic grandeur of the marble-floored study with its thick cream carpet and glass-topped desk. Officially, O'Hara was Matt's chauffeur; unofficially, he was his bodyguard, and far better suited to that role than the role of chauffeur—for when O'Hara slid behind the wheel of an automobile, he drove as if he were jockeying for first place in the Grand Prix.

"When're we leavin' for Chicago?" O'Hara demanded.

"As soon as I get this damned interview over with."

"Okay. I phoned ahead and the limo will be waitin' for us on the runway at Midway. But that's not what I came in here to tell you," O'Hara continued, walking over to the window and parting the draperies. Gesturing for Matt to join him, he pointed toward the wide, curving drive that wound through the cypress trees at the front of the house. His weathered face softened and his voice became low, lustful. "Take a look at that sleek sweetheart out there," he said as Matt walked over to the window. Someone else would have expected the sweetheart to be a woman, but Matt knew better. After O'Hara's wife died, cars became his only remaining love. "She belongs to one of the cameramen who came out here with the Walters broad."

The sweetheart was a 1959 red Cadillac convertible in mint condition.

"Will you look at them globes," O'Hara said, referring to the car's headlights in the awed, lascivious voice of an adolescent looking at a *Playboy* centerfold. "And those curves! Sleek, Matt, real sleek. Makes you want to run yer hands across 'em, don't it?" He nudged the silent man beside him with an elbow. "Have you ever seen anything prettier than that?"

Matt was spared the need to reply by the arrival of the script girl, who politely said they were finished setting up in the living room.

The interview had been proceeding along predictable lines for nearly an hour, when the door suddenly opened and a woman hurried into the room, her lovely, unsuspecting face wreathed in a smile. "Matt, darling, you're back! I—" Every head in the room swiveled, the ABC crew gaped, the taping session forgotten as Meryl Saunders rushed forward wearing a red negligee so transparent, so suggestive, that it would have made the lingerie buyer at Frederick's of Hollywood blush.

But it was not Meryl's body the ABC group was staring at, it was her face—a face that graced movie and television screens all over the world; a face whose girlish sweetness and outspoken religious beliefs had made her America's darling. Adolescents liked her because she was so pretty and looked so young; parents liked her because she set a wholesome image for their teenagers; and producers liked her because she was one hell of an actress and because any movie she was in was guaranteed to gross in the mega-millions. Never mind that she was twenty-three years old with a strong sexual appetite—in the pulse beat of shocked silence that greeted Meryl's arrival, Matt felt as if he'd been caught in the act of seducing Alice in Wonderland.

Like the valiant little trooper she was on the movie set, Meryl smiled politely at the speechless group, made a pretty apology to Matt for interrupting him, then turned and walked out with all the modest dignity of a pinafore-clad student in a girls' convent school—which was a true tribute to her acting skills, since the little red G-string and the cheeks of her fanny were clearly visible beneath the fiery red negligee draping her lithesome body.

Barbara Walters's face was a mirror of conflicting reactions, and Matt braced himself for the inevitable barrage of prying questions about Meryl, sorry that her carefully constructed public image was about to be demolished. But Ms. Walters merely asked if Meryl Saunders was a frequent houseguest of his. Matt replied that she enjoyed staying at his house whenever it was unoccupied, as it often was.

To his surprise, the journalist accepted his evasive answer and returned to the topic she'd been discussing before Meryl's arrival. Leaning slightly forward in her chair, she asked, "How do you feel about the growing number of hostile corporate takeovers?"

"I think it's a trend that's bound to continue until such time as guidelines are set up to control it," Matt replied.

"Is Intercorp planning to swallow up any more?"

A leading question, but not unexpected, and he sidestepped it smoothly. "Intercorp is always interested in acquiring good companies in order to further our own growth and theirs."

"Even if the company doesn't *wish* to be acquired?"

"It's a risk we all run, even Intercorp," he replied, smiling politely.

"But it would take another giant the size of Intercorp to swallow you up. Is anyone immune to a forced merger with you—friends, and so forth? I mean," she teased, "is it possible our very own ABC could find itself your next prey?"

"The object of a takeover attempt is called the target," he said dryly, "not the prey. However," he joked, "if it will set your mind at rest, I can assure you that Intercorp does not have an acquisitive eye on ABC at this time."

She laughed and then gave him her best professional media journalist smile. "Can we talk a little about your private life now?"

Carefully concealing his irritation behind a bland smile, he asked, "Could I prevent you?"

Her smile widening, she shook her head and began. "During the past few years you've reportedly had torrid love affairs with several movie stars, a princess, and most recently with Maria Calvaris, the Greek shipping heiress. Were these widely publicized love affairs real, or were they invented by the gossip columnists?"

"Yes," Matt replied unanswerably.

Barbara Walters laughed at his deliberate evasion, then she sobered. "What about your marriage? Can we talk about that?"

Matt was taken so off guard that he was momentarily speechless. "My what?" he said, unable to believe he'd heard her correctly. *Unwilling* to believe it. No one had ever discovered his brief, misbegotten marriage to Meredith Bancroft eleven years ago.

"You've never married," she clarified, "and I was wondering if you have any plans to marry in the future."

Matt relaxed and uninformatively replied, "It's not out of the question."

13

November 1989

Crowds of Chicagoans strolled along Michigan Avenue, their unhurried pace due partly to the unseasonably mild November day and partly to the jam of shoppers gathered at the windows of Bancroft & Company, which were already spectacularly decked out for Christmas.

In the years since the store's opening in 1891, Bancroft's had evolved from a quaint two-story brick building with dome-shaped yellow awnings at its windows into a fourteen-story glass-and-marble structure that covered an entire city block. But regardless of the many alterations that Bancroft's had undergone, one thing had not changed: A pair of doormen attired in maroon and gold livery still stood formal sentinel at the store's main entrance. This small touch of stately elegance remained—a visible statement of Bancroft's continued insistence on dignity and graciousness.

The two elderly doormen, who were so fiercely competitive that they'd rarely spoken to each other in the thirty years they'd worked together, surreptitiously watched the arrival of a black BMW, and each doorman silently willed the driver to draw up on his side of the doors.

The car pulled up to the curb, and Leon, on one side of the doors, held his breath, then expelled it in an irritated sigh as the car glided past him and halted directly in front of his adversary's territory. "Miserable old coot!" Leon muttered at his counterpart as Ernest hurried forward. "Good morning, Miss Bancroft," Ernest said as he opened Meredith's door with a flourish. Twenty-five years ago, he'd opened the door of her father's car, taken his first look at Meredith, and said exactly the same thing in exactly the same reverent tone.

"Good morning, Ernest," Meredith replied, smiling and handing him her keys as she got out of the car. "Will you ask Carl to park my car for me? I had a lot to carry this morning, and I didn't want to have to bring it all the way from the parking garage." Valet parking was another elegant convenience that Bancroft's offered to its customers.

"Certainly, Miss Bancroft."

"Tell Amelia I said hello," she added, referring to his wife. Meredith was on familiar terms with many of the store's longtime employees; they were like family to her now, and this store—the main store of a growing chain that today had seven stores in various cities—was as much a home to her as the mansion she'd grown up in or her own apartment.

Pausing on the sidewalk, she watched the crowds gathered in front of the store windows. A smile touched her lips and her heart swelled with pleasure. It was a feeling she experienced nearly every time she gazed up at Bancroft's elegant façade, a feeling of pride and enthusiasm and fierce protectiveness. Today, however, her happiness was boundless because last night Parker had taken her in his arms and said with tender solemnity, "I love you, Meredith. Will you marry me, darling?" Afterward he had slid an engagement ring on her finger.

"The windows are better than ever this year," she said to Ernest as the crowd shifted and she glimpsed the stunning result of Lisa's talent and skill. Lisa Pontini had already earned widespread industry acclaim for her work at Bancroft's. In another year, when her boss retired, Lisa was slated to take his place as director of visual presentation.

Eager to find Lisa and tell her the news about Parker, Meredith opened the passenger door of her car, gathered up two briefcases and several stacks of files, and headed for the main doors. As soon as she entered the store, a security agent spotted her and came forward. "May I help you with those, Miss Bancroft?"

Meredith started to decline, but her arms were already aching, and besides, she felt an irresistible urge to stroll around before she went to see Lisa, and to luxuriate in what looked to be another record sales day based on the crowds of shoppers already thronging the aisles and counters. "Thank you, Dan, I'd appreciate that," she said, shifting the load of heavy files into his arms and handing him both briefcases.

When he headed off toward the elevators, Meredith absently straightened the blue silk scarf she'd looped through the lapels of her white coat and, tucking her hands into her pockets, she strolled past the cosmetic aisles. Shoppers jostled her as they hurried toward the banks of escalators in the center of the store, but the bustle only added to her pleasure.

With her head tipped back, she gazed up at the thirty-foot-high white Christmas trees that soared above the aisles, their branches trimmed with twinkling red lights, huge red velvet bows, and enormous red glass ornaments. Festive wreaths decorated with sleighs and bells were hanging on the mirrored square pillars that dotted the store, and "Deck the Halls" was playing gaily on the speaker system. A woman who was looking at handbags saw Meredith and nudged her friend. "Isn't that Meredith Bancroft?" she exclaimed.

"That is definitely Meredith Bancroft!" one of the women pronounced. "And that writer who said she looks like a young Grace Kelly was right!"

Meredith heard them, but she scarcely registered what they said. In the last few years, she'd grown accustomed to people staring at her and talking about her. *Women's Wear Daily* had called her "the embodiment of cool elegance"; *Cosmopolitan* called her "total chic." *The Wall Street Journal* called her "Bancroft's reigning princess." Behind the doors of Bancroft's boardroom, the directors called her "a pain in the ass."

Only the last description mattered to Meredith; she didn't care what the newspapers and magazines wrote about her—except for whatever value their articles had for adding to the store's prestige. But the board of directors mattered to her immensely, for they had the power to thwart her, to block her dreams for Bancroft's continued expansion into other cities. The president of Bancroft's treated her with no more affection or enthusiasm than the directors did. And he was her father.

Today, however, not even her ongoing battle with her father and the board over expansion plans could dampen Meredith's spirits. She felt so completely happy that she had to restrain the urge to hum along with the Christmas carol. Instead, she indulged her high spirits by doing something she used to do as a little girl: She walked over to one of the mirrored pillars, leaned close to it, peering into the mirror and pretending to poke a strand of hair into place, then she grinned and winked at the security agent she knew would be sitting inside the pillar, watching for shoplifters.

Turning, she headed for the escalator. It had been Lisa's idea to decorate every floor in a different color, and to key the hues according to the merchandise on the particular floor. Meredith thought it was very effective—particularly when she stepped off the escalator on the second floor, which contained the fur salon and designer gowns. Here, all the white trees were trimmed in a soft mauve with shimmering gold bows. Directly in front of the escalators, seated in front of his "house," was a Santa Claus clad in white and gold. On his knee was a mannequin—a beautiful woman wrapped in a magnificent french lace peignoir who was pointing prettily to a $25,000 mink coat lined in mauve.

The smile that had been lurking in Meredith's heart dawned across her face as she recognized that the aura of extravagant luxury created by the display was a subtle and effective invitation to shoppers who ventured onto this floor to indulge themselves with similar extravagance. Judging by the large number of men looking at the furs and the many women trying on the designer gowns, the invitation was being accepted. On this floor, each of the designers were given their own salon, where their collections were displayed. Meredith walked down the main aisle, nodding occasionally to those employees whom she knew. In the Geoffrey Beene salon, two stout women in mink coats were admiring a slinky blue-beaded gown with a $7,000 price tag. "You'll look like a sack of potatoes in that, Margaret," one of them warned the other. Ignoring her, the woman turned to the salesclerk. "I don't suppose," she said, "you have this in a size twenty?"

In the next salon, a woman was urging her daughter, a girl of about eighteen, to try on a velvet Valentino gown, while a salesclerk hovered discreetly in the background, waiting to assist. "If you like it," the daughter replied, flinging herself down onto the silk sofa, "then *you* wear it. I'm not going to your stupid party. I told you I wanted to spend Christmas in Switzerland."

"I know, darling," her mother replied, looking guilty and apologetic as she spoke to the sulking teenager, "but just this once we thought it would be nice to spend Christmas at home together."

Meredith glanced at her watch, realized it was already one o'clock, and headed for the bank of elevators so that she could find Lisa and share her news. She'd spent the morning at the architect's office going over the plans for the Houston store, and she had a busy afternoon ahead of her.

The design room was in actuality an enormous storeroom located in the basement, beneath the street level, that was crammed with design tables, dismembered mannequins, giant bolts of cloth, and every conceivable prop that had been used in the display windows during the last decade. Meredith wended her way through the chaos with all the familiar expertise of a former inhabitant—which she was. As part of her early training, she'd worked in every department in the store. "Lisa?" she called out, and a dozen heads of helpers who worked for Lisa glanced up. "Lisa?"

"Over here!" a muffled voice shouted, then the skirt around the table was thrust aside and Lisa's head of curly red hair poked out. "Now what?" the voice demanded irritably, the hazel eyes peering at Meredith's legs. "How can I get anything done with all these interruptions?"

"Beats me," Meredith cheerfully replied, perching her hip on the top of the table and grinning at Lisa's startled face. "I've never figured out how you find anything back here at all, let alone *create* it."

"Hi," Lisa replied, looking sheepish as she crawled out from beneath the table on all fours. "I've been trying to rig some wires under there so we can have the table tipped for the Christmas dinner treatment we're doing in the furniture department. How was your date with Parker last night?"

"Oh, fine," Meredith answered. "The usual, more or less," she lied, making a great show of fiddling with the lapel of her coat with her left hand which now bore a sapphire engagement ring. She'd told Lisa yesterday that she had a hunch Parker was going to propose.

Lisa plunked her fists on her hips. "The usual! God, Mer, he was divorced two years ago, and you've been going out with him for over nine months. You spend almost as much time with his daughters as he does. You're beautiful and intelligent—men fall over themselves when they get one look at you, but Parker has been 'looking you over' for months now—at very close range—and I think you're wasting your time on him. If the idiot was going to propose, he would have done it already—"

"He has," Meredith said with smiling triumph, but Lisa had launched into her favorite diatribe and it took a moment for Meredith's words to register. "He's all wrong for you anyway. You need somebody to pull you out of your conservative shell and make you do crazy, impulsive things—like voting for a Democrat just once, or going to the opera on Friday instead of Saturday. Parker is too much like you, he's too methodical, too steady, too cautious too—you're kidding! He proposed?"

Meredith nodded, and Lisa's gaze finally dropped to the dark sapphire in its antique setting. "Your engagement ring?" she asked, snatching Meredith's hand, but as she examined the ring, her smile vanished behind a puzzled frown. "What is this?"

"It's a sapphire," Meredith replied, unperturbed by Lisa's visible lack of enthusiasm for the antique piece. For one thing, she'd always liked Lisa's bluntness. Secondly, not even Meredith, who loved Parker, could convince herself the ring was dazzlingly beautiful. It was fine, and old, and a family heirloom; she was perfectly content with that.

"I figured it's a sapphire, but what are those smaller stones? They don't sparkle like good diamonds."

"They're an old-fashioned cut—not so many facets. The ring is old. It belonged to Parker's grandmother."

"He couldn't afford a new one, hmm?" she teased. "You know," she continued, "until I met you, I used to think people with money bought gorgeous things and price was no object. . . ."

"Only new money does that," Meredith chided. "Old money is *quiet* money."

"Yeah, well, old money could learn something from new money. You people keep things until they're worn out. If I ever get engaged and the guy tries to foist off his grandmother's worn-out ring on me, it's all over right then. And what," she continued outrageously, "is the setting made of? It isn't very shiny."

"It's platinum," Meredith replied on a suffocated laugh.

"I *knew* it—I suppose it will never wear out, which is why whoever bought this thing two hundred years ago had it made out of that."

"Exactly," Meredith answered, her shoulders shaking with laughter.

"Honestly, Mer," Lisa answered, laughing with her, but there were tears in her eyes. "If you didn't feel you have to be a walking advertisement for Bancroft & Company chic, you'd still be wearing clothes from college."

"Only if they were very *sturdy* clothes."

Without further pretense Lisa wrapped her in a fierce hug. "He's not half good, enough for you. No one is."

"He's *perfect* for me," Meredith argued, laughing and returning Lisa's hug. "The opera benefit ball is tomorrow night. I'll get a pair of tickets for you and Phil," Meredith said, referring to the commercial photographer Lisa was dating. "We're giving an engagement party afterward."

"Phil's in New York," Lisa said, "but I'll be there. After all, if Parker's going to be a member of our family, I have to learn to love him." With an irrepressible grin, she added, "Even though he *does* foreclose on widows for grins—"

"Lisa," Meredith said more seriously, "Parker hates your banker jokes, and you know it. Now that we're engaged, couldn't you please stop bickering with him?"

"I'll try," she promised. "No more bickering and no more banker jokes."

"And no more calling him Mr. Drysdale?"

"I'll stop watching *Beverly Hillbillies* reruns altogether," Lisa swore.

"Thanks," Meredith answered, standing up. Lisa turned away abruptly and became strangely preoccupied with forcing the wrinkles out of a bolt of red felt. "Is anything wrong?"

"Wrong?" Lisa asked, turning back, her smile overbright. "What could be wrong? My best friend has just gotten engaged to the man of her dreams. What are you going to wear tomorrow night?" she asked, hastily changing the subject.

"I haven't decided. I'll stop on the second floor tomorrow and pick something smashing out. In fact, while I'm there I'll take a look at the bridal gowns too. Parker is determined to have a big, splashy wedding with all the trimmings and formalities. He doesn't want me to be cheated merely because he already had a big formal wedding."

"Does he know about—about that other thing, your other 'wedding'?"

"He knows," Meredith said, her voice turning somber. "Parker was very kind and very understanding," she began, then abruptly broke off as a series of bells began chiming insistently on the store's loudspeaker system. Shoppers were used to hearing them and ignored them, but each division head had an assigned code, and they responded as quickly as possible. Meredith paused, listening: Two short bells, a pause, then one more. "That's my page number," she said with a sigh, standing up. "I have to run anyway. There's a staff meeting in an hour, and I still have some notes to read."

"Give 'em hell!" Lisa said, and abruptly crawled back beneath the table, reminding Meredith of a tousled redheaded child playing in a makeshift tent she'd erected in the family dining room. Meredith went to the phone on the wall near the door and called the store operator. "This is Meredith Bancroft," she said when the operator answered. "You just paged me."

"Yes, Miss Bancroft," the operator said. "Mr. Braden in security asked if you could come to his office as soon as possible. He said to tell you it's important."

14

*T*he security offices were on the sixth floor, behind the toy department, discreetly concealed from view by a false wall. As vice president of operations, the security division fell under Meredith's supervision, and as she walked past an aisle where shoppers were examining elaborate electric trains and Victorian dollhouses, she wondered grimly whom security had caught stealing that required her to be there. It couldn't be an ordinary shoplifter, because they'd handle that without her, which meant it was probably an employee. Store employees, from executives to salesclerks, were closely watched by the security division. Although shoplifters accounted for eighty percent of the number of thefts from the store, it was employee theft that did the most monetary damage. Unlike shoplifters, who could steal only what they could hide and carry, employees had dozens of opportunities and dozens of methods to steal every day. Last month the security division had caught a salesclerk who'd been issuing bogus credits to friends for false merchandise returns, and the month before a jewelry buyer had been fired for taking $10,000 worth of bribes to buy inferior merchandise from three different suppliers. Meredith always felt as if there was something extraordinarily sordid and sickening about a thief who was also an employee; it was difficult not to feel almost betrayed. Bracing herself, she stopped at a door that said MARK BRADEN, DIRECTOR OF SECURITY AND LOSS PREVENTION and went into the large waiting room that adjoined Mark's office.

Two shoplifters, a woman in her twenties and another in her seventies, were seated in the vinyl and aluminum chairs against the wall, under the watchful eye of a uniformed security agent. The younger woman was huddled in her chair with her arms wrapped around her stomach and traces of tears on her cheeks; she looked bedraggled, poor, and terrified. In sharp contrast, the older shoplifter was a picture of cheerful, elegant propriety— an elderly porcelain doll clad in a red and black Chanel suit, sitting erectly in her chair with her handbag propped primly on her knees. "Good morning, my dear," she chirped in her reedy voice when she saw Meredith. "How are you today?"

"I'm fine, Mrs. Fiorenza," Meredith said, stifling her angry frustration as she recognized the elderly lady. Agnes Fiorenza's husband was not only a respected pillar of the community and the father of a state senator, he was also a member of Bancroft's board of directors, which made the entire situation touchy, which in turn was undoubtedly why Meredith had been summoned to security. "How are you?" Meredith asked before she thought better of it.

"I'm very unhappy, Meredith. I've been waiting out here for a half hour, and as I explained to Mr. Braden, I really can't linger. I have to attend a luncheon in honor of Senator Fiorenza in a half hour, and he'll be dreadfully upset if I'm not present. After that, I'm speaking to the Junior League. Do you think you could hasten matters up a bit for me with Mr. Braden?"

"I'll see what I can do," Meredith said, keeping her expression noncommittal as she opened the door to Mark's office. Mark Braden was leaning against the edge of his desk, sipping a cup of steaming coffee and talking to the security agent who'd seen the younger woman actually purloin the items she'd taken.

An attractive, well-built man of forty-five with sandy hair and brown eyes, Braden had been a security specialist in the air force and he took his job at Bancroft's every bit as seriously as he had taken his responsibilities to maintain national security. Meredith not only trusted and respected him, she liked him and that was evident in her wry smile as she said, "I saw Agnes Fiorenza in the waiting room. She wants me to tell you that you're keeping her from an important luncheon."

Braden held up his free hand in a gesture of helpless disgust and let it fall. "My instructions are to let you deal with the old bat."

"What did she filch this time?"

"A Lieber belt, a Givenchy handbag, and these." He held out a pair of huge, gaudy blue crystal earrings from the costume jewelry section that would have looked bizarre on the diminutive elderly lady.

"How much unused credit does she still have?" Meredith asked, referring to the account her harassed husband had set up with the store to cover his wife's thefts in advance.

"Four hundred dollars. It won't cover it."

"I'll talk to her, but first, could I have a cup of that coffee?" Privately, Meredith was fed up with coddling the old lady while others, like the young woman out there beside her, were prosecuted to the full extent of the law. "I'm going to have the doormen ban Mrs. Fiorenza from the store after this," Meredith decided aloud, knowing full well such an action might incur the wrath of her husband. "What did the younger woman take?"

"An infant's snowsuit, mittens, and a couple of sweaters. She denies it," he said with a fatalistic shrug, handing Meredith her cup of coffee. "We've got her on videotape. Total value of the goods is about two hundred dollars."

Meredith nodded, sipping, wishing to God the bedraggled mother out there had admitted the theft. By denying it, she was forcing the store to prove it—and to prosecute her—in order to protect itself from some future lawsuit for fraudulently detaining her. "Does she have a police record?"

"My contact at the police department says no."

"Would you be willing to drop the charge if she signs a statement admitting the theft?"

"Why the hell should we?"

"For one thing, it's costly to prosecute and she has no prior record. For another, I find it highly distasteful to let Mrs. Fiorenza go away with a scold for stealing designer things she can easily pay for, and at the same time prosecute that woman for stealing warm clothes for her child."

"I'll make you a deal—you ban Fiorenza from the store and I'll let the other one off, provided she'll admit to the theft. Deal?"

"Deal," Meredith said emphatically.

"Bring in the old lady," Mark instructed the security agent.

Mrs. Fiorenza entered the room in a cloud of Joy perfume, all smiles but looking rushed. "Goodness, you took long enough, Mr. Braden."

"Mrs. Fiorenza," Meredith said, taking charge, "you've repeatedly put us all to a great deal of trouble because you insist on taking things from the counters without paying for them first."

"I know I'm troublesome at times, Meredith, but that certainly doesn't justify your using that censorious tone on me."

"*Mrs. Fiorenza!*" Meredith said, further irritated at being spoken to like an ill-bred child. "People go to jail—for years—for stealing things valued at less than the amount of these—" She gestured to the belt, the handbag, and the earrings. "There's a woman out there in that waiting room who took warm clothes for her baby, and *she's* in danger of going to jail. But you—you take trifles that you don't need."

"Good heavens, Meredith," Mrs. Fiorenza interrupted, looking appalled. "You can't think I took those earrings for myself! I'm not completely selfish, you know. I do charitable things for people too."

Confused, Meredith hesitated. "You mean you donate things you steal—like those earrings—to charity?"

"Gracious me!" she replied, her china-doll face pulled into a scandalized expression. "What worthwhile charity would accept *those* earrings? They're atrocious. No, indeed. I took them to give to my maid. *She* has awful taste. She'll love them. Although, I do think you ought to mention to whoever purchased those earrings for the store that they do nothing to enhance the image of Bancroft's! Goldblatt's, I think, might find them suitable stock, but I can't see why Bancroft's—"

"Mrs. Fiorenza," Meredith interrupted, ignoring the absurd direction the discussion had taken, "I warned you last month that if you were caught shoplifting again, I'd have to tell the doormen to bar you from the store."

"You aren't serious!"

"I am completely serious."

"I am barred from shopping at Bancroft's?"

"Yes."

"This is an outrage."

"I'm sorry."

"My husband is going to hear about this!" she said, but her voice had taken on a timid, pathetic tone.

"He'll hear about it only if you choose to tell him," Meredith said, sensing that the elderly lady's intended threat was filled with more alarm than anger.

Her head lifted proudly, but there was a catch in her voice as she said, "I have no desire to ever shop in this store again. I shall take my business to I. Magnin's. *They* wouldn't dream of giving an inch of counter space to those awful earrings!"

She picked up the handbag she'd put on the desk a few moments before, patted her soft white hair into place, and departed. Sagging against the wall, Meredith looked at the two men in the room and took a sip of coffee, feeling sad and uneasy—as if she'd just slapped an old woman. After all, her husband *did* ultimately pay for whatever she was caught stealing, so it wasn't as if Bancroft's lost money—at least, not when they caught her.

After a moment she said to Mark, "Did you notice that she seemed, well, pathetic, somehow?"

"No."

"I suppose it's for her own good," Meredith continued, studying the odd expression on his face. "Who knows, we may have taught her a lesson by handing out a punishment instead of ignoring what she does. Right?"

Braden smiled slowly, as if deeply amused, then, without replying, he picked up the phone and pressed four buttons. "Dan," he said to one of his security agents on the main floor, "Mrs. Fiorenza is on her way down. Stop her and insist that she give you the Lieber belt she has in her purse. Right," he said into the phone, grinning at Meredith's stricken expression, "the same belt you caught her stealing earlier. She just stole it from my desk."

When he hung up, Meredith shook off her stunned chagrin and glanced at her watch, her mind turning to the meeting that was scheduled for that afternoon. "I'll see you in the staff meeting later. Is your status report ready?"

"Yep. My department looks good. Losses are down by an estimated eight percent over last year."

"That's wonderful," she said, and she meant it.

Now, more than ever, Meredith wanted her entire division to shine. Her father's cardiologist was insisting that he either retire from Bancroft's presidency, or, at the very least, take a six-month leave of absence. He'd decided to take a leave of absence, and yesterday he'd met with the board of directors to discuss who should be named interim president while he was on leave. Beyond that, all she knew was that she desperately wanted a chance to fill in for him while he was away. So did at least four of the other executive vice presidents. She'd worked as hard for it—harder—than any of them; not as *long* as two of them, but with ferocious diligence and indisputable success. Moreover, there had always been a Bancroft in the president's chair, and if she hadn't been born female, Meredith knew the interim presidency would belong to her automatically. Her grandfather had been younger than she when he took over, but he hadn't been hampered by his father's bias against his sex or by a board of directors who had such awesome control over decisions. That last was partly Meredith's fault. She'd been the one who campaigned and fought for Bancroft's expansion into other cities. To do that had required raising enormous amounts of capital, which could be accomplished only by taking Bancroft & Company public—selling shares of its stock on the exchange. Now anyone could buy a share of its stock and each share carried one vote. As a result, the board members were accountable to, and elected by, the public shareholders instead of merely being puppets chosen—or dismissed—by her father. Worse for Meredith, all the board members held large blocks of stock themselves, which they could vote and which gave them even more power. On the good side, many of them were the same twelve men who'd been on Bancroft's board for years; they were friends and business acquaintances of her father's or grandfather's, so they still tended to do as her father suggested.

Meredith needed the six-month term as interim president to prove to her father and to the board that when her father did eventually retire, she could handle the responsibilities of the presidency.

If her father recommended that Meredith be appointed to succeed him while he was on leave of absence, then the directors would surely give their approval. Her father, however, had been infuriatingly noncommittal about his meeting with the board and even about when the board would announce its decision.

Putting her coffee cup down on Mark's desk, Meredith glanced at the tiny snowsuit that had been stolen by the woman in the waiting room, and she felt the same ache of sadness that gripped her whenever she faced the fact that she'd never have a baby of her own. Long ago, however, she'd learned how to hide her emotions from coworkers, and her smile was untroubled as she said, "I'll talk to the other woman on my way out. What's her name?"

Mark told her, and Meredith went into the waiting room. "Mrs. Jordan," she said to the pale young mother who'd stolen the children's garments, "I'm Meredith Bancroft."

"I've seen your picture in the papers," Sandra Jordan retorted. "I know who you are. So what?"

"So, if you continue to deny that you stole those things, the store will have to prosecute you."

So hostile was her expression that if Meredith hadn't known what the woman had taken, and she hadn't seen the glint of frightened tears in her eyes, she might well have abandoned her attempted charity. "Listen to me carefully, Mrs. Jordan, because I'm telling you this out of compassion. Take my advice or take the consequences: If you deny taking those things, and we let you go without prosecuting you and *proving* you did, you could turn around and sue us for unjustly accusing and detaining you. The store cannot risk such a lawsuit; therefore, if you deny it, we *have* to go through the entire legal ordeal now that we've detained you. Do you understand me so far? There is a videotape of you stealing children's garments that was filmed by one of the cameras in the ceiling in that department. We can and will produce the tape in court in order to prove not only that you are guilty, but that we are *innocent* of wrongly accusing you. Are you following me?"

Meredith paused and stared at the young woman's rigid face, unable to tell if she was grasping the lifeline Meredith was offering her.

"Am I supposed to believe that you let shoplifters go so long as they admit they took stuff?" she said, looking dubious and disdainful.

"Are you a shoplifter, Mrs. Jordan?" Meredith countered. "Is that what you are—a common, habitual shoplifter?" Before the woman could strike back verbally, Meredith softened her voice. "Female shoplifters of your age ordinarily take clothes for themselves, or perfume or jewelry. You took winter clothes for a child. The police have no record of any prior arrest on you. I prefer to think you're a mother who acted out of desperation and a need to keep her baby warm."

The young woman, who evidently was more familiar with confronting adversity than compassion, seemed to crumple before Meredith's eyes. Tears rose in her eyes and began to trace down her cheeks. "I seen on TV that you shouldn't ever admit to doing anything unless your lawyer is present."

"Do you have a lawyer?"

"No."

"If you don't admit you stole those things, you're going to *need* one."

She swallowed audibly. "Before I admit it, would you put it in writing—legal like—that you won't set the police after me if I do admit it?"

That was a first for Meredith. Without consulting with the store's attorneys, she couldn't be certain that doing so might not later be construed as some sort of written "bribe," or cause some other sort of ramifications. She shook her head. "You're complicating this needlessly, Mrs. Jordan."

The young mother shuddered with fear and doubt, and then she drew a long, shaky breath. "Well, if I was to admit what I did, would you give me your word not to set the police after me?"

"Would you take my word?" Meredith quietly asked.

For a long moment the other woman searched Meredith's face. "Should I?" she asked finally, her voice shaky with terror.

Meredith nodded, her expression soft. "Yes."

Another hesitation, a long, strangled breath, and then a nod that she accepted Meredith's word. "Okay—I—did steal those things."

Glancing over her shoulder at Mark Braden, who had silently opened the door and was watching the scenario, Meredith said, "Mrs. Jordan admits to taking the clothing."

"Fine," he said tonelessly. In his hand was the statement of admission she'd have to sign and he handed it to the forlorn woman, along with a pen.

"You didn't say," she told Meredith, "I'd have to *sign* a confession."

"When you've signed it, you may leave," Meredith replied with quiet reassurance, and was subjected to another long, searching look by the young woman. Her hand shook, but she signed it and shoved it back at Mark.

"You can leave, Mrs. Jordan," he said.

She grasped the back of her chair, looking on the verge of relieved collapse, her gaze riveted on Meredith. "Thank you, Miss Bancroft."

"You're welcome." Meredith was already walking down the hall and into the toy department when Sandra Jordan came rushing up behind her. "Miss Bancroft?" When Meredith stopped and turned, she blurted out, "I seen—I mean, I *saw* you on television news a few times—at fancy places, wearing furs and gowns, and I wanted to say you're a lot prettier even than you look on TV."

"Thank you," Meredith said with a slight, self-conscious smile.

"And I—I wanted you to know, I've never tried to steal anything before either," she added, her eyes pleading with Meredith to believe her. "Here, look," she said, pulling her wallet out of her purse and removing a photograph from it. A baby's tiny face with enormous blue eyes and an enchanting toothless smile gazed back at Meredith. "That's my Jenny," Sandra said, her voice turning somber and tender. "She got real sick last week. The doctor said I have to keep her warmer, but I can't afford the electric bill now. So I figured if she just had warmer clothes—" Tears sprang to her eyes and she blinked fiercely. "Jenny's father took off when I got pregnant, but that's okay because me and Jenny—we got each other, and that's all we need. But I couldn't bear it if I—if I lost my Jenny." She opened her mouth as if to say more, then she turned on her heel and fled. Meredith watched her rush down an aisle filled with hundreds of teddy bears, but what she saw was the baby in the photograph, a tiny pink bow in her hair and a cherub's smile on her face.

Minutes later Sandra Jordan was stopped by the security guard at the main door when she tried to leave the store. "Mr. Braden is coming down, Mrs. Jordan," he informed her, and Sandra's whole body began to quake at the horrible realization that she'd undoubtedly been tricked into signing a confession so they could turn her over to the police. She was sure of it when Braden walked up to her carrying a large Bancroft's shopping bag, which she instantly realized contained the pink snowsuit, along with all the other evidence of her attempted theft—including a large teddy bear which she hadn't even touched. "You lied," she cried in a strangled voice as Braden held the bag out to her.

"These things are for you to take home, Mrs. Jordan," he interrupted, his smile brief and impersonal, his tone that of one who was making a speech he'd been told to make. In a daze of gratitude and disbelief, Sandra took the bag with Jenny's warm clothes and a teddy bear in it and clutched it protectively to her chest. "Merry Christmas from all of us at Bancroft & Company," he said flatly, but Sandra knew the gifts weren't from him or a donation from the store either. Lifting her eyes to the mezzanine above, she searched through a blur of tears for a sign of the beautiful young woman who'd looked at Jenny's picture with such poignant gentleness in her smile. She thought she saw her then—Meredith Bancroft standing in her white coat on the mezzanine, smiling down at her. She thought so, but she wasn't sure because scalding tears were flooding her eyes and spilling down her cheeks. "Tell her," she whispered chokily to Braden, "Jenny and I said thank you."

The offices of the senior executives were on the fourteenth floor, situated on both sides of a long, wide, carpeted corridor that fanned out in opposite directions from the circular reception area. Portraits of all the Bancroft presidents hung in ornate gilt frames on the walls of the reception area above the Queen Anne sofas and chairs that were provided for visitors. To the left of the receptionist's desk was the office and private conference room that had historically belonged to Bancroft's president. To the right were the executive offices with secretaries seated outside them separated by functional as well as ornamental partitions of carved mahogany.

Meredith stepped off the elevator and glanced at the portrait of James Bancroft, the founder of Bancroft & Company, her great-grandfather, twice removed. *Good afternoon, Great-grandfather,* she said silently. She'd been saying hello to him every day forever, and she knew it was silly, but there was something about the man with his thick blond hair, full beard, and stiff collar that filled her with affection. It was his eyes. Despite his pose of extreme dignity, there was daring and devilment in those bright blue eyes.

And he had been daring—that and innovative as well. In 1891 James Bancroft had decided to break with tradition and offer the same price to all customers. Until that time, local customers everywhere paid lower prices than strangers, regardless of whether they came to a feed store or to Bancroft & Company. James Bancroft, however, had daringly placed a discreet sign in the window of his store for passers-by to see: ONE PRICE FOR EVERYONE. Sometime later, James Cash Penney, another enterprising storekeeper in Wyoming, had made the policy his own, and in the ensuing decades, it was J. C. Penney who got the credit for it. Nevertheless, Meredith knew, because she'd found it in an old diary, that James Bancroft's decision to charge one price to all had predated J. C. Penney's.

Portraits of her other ancestors hung in identical frames along the walls, but Meredith paid them scarcely a glance. Her thoughts were already switching to the weekly executive staff meeting that lay ahead.

The conference room was unusually silent when Meredith entered it, and the tension in the air was almost tangible. Like Meredith, everyone was hoping Philip Bancroft might give some clue today as to who his temporary successor was likely to be. Sliding into a chair near the end of the long table, she nodded to the nine men and one woman who, like her, were all vice presidents, and who comprised Bancroft's executive staff. Bancroft's hierarchy was simply arranged and efficient. In addition to the controller who headed the financial division, and the store's chief counsel who headed the legal division, there were five more vice presidents who were also general merchandise managers. Combined, those five men were responsible for buying all the merchandise within the giant department store and all its branch stores. Separately, they were each responsible for a large, preestablished group of merchandise. Although each of them had managers who reported to them, and buyers and clerks who, in turn, reported to the managers, the ultimate responsibility for the success or the failure of their individual merchandise groups fell on their shoulders.

Two more of the vice presidents at the conference table were in charge of activities that helped to move the merchandise *out* of the stores—the vice president of advertising and sales promotion whose group planned the store's sales campaigns and bought the radio, television, and newspaper space to advertise them; and the vice president of visual presentation, for whom Lisa worked, whose staff was responsible for displaying all the merchandise within the stores.

Meredith's position as senior vice president of operations put her in charge of everything else that involved the running of the stores, from security and personnel to expansion and forward planning. It was in this latter area that Meredith had found her niche and made her mark in the retailing community. In addition to the five new stores that had been opened under her direction, the sites for five more stores had been selected, and construction was already under way at two of them.

The only other woman at the conference table was in charge of creative merchandising. It was her responsibility to predict fashion trends in advance, and to make recommendations to the general merchandising managers. Theresa Bishop, who held that position, was seated across the table from Meredith, talking quietly with the controller.

"Good morning." Her father's voice sounded strong and brisk as he strode into the conference room and took his place at the head of the table. His next words jarred everyone into a state of electrified expectation. "If you're wondering if any decision has been reached as to an interim president, the answer is no. When it is, you will all be duly advised. Can we now dispense with that topic and get down to the business of department stores. Ted"—his narrowed gaze swerved to Ted Rothman, the vice president who was in charge of purchasing cosmetics, intimate apparel, shoes, and coats—"according to last night's reports from all our stores, sales of coats are down by eleven percent compared to this same week last year. What's your answer for that?"

"My answer," Rothman replied with a smile, "is that it's unseasonably warm, Philip, and customers aren't concentrating on outer clothing as much as they normally would at this time of the year. It's to be expected." As he spoke, he stood up and walked over to one of the computer screens built into a wall cabinet, and quickly pressed a series of keys on the keyboard. The store's computer systems had long ago been updated at Meredith's urgings—and at considerable expense—so that at any given instant, sales figures were available from every department in every one of their stores, along with comparisons based on this time last week, or last month, or last year. "Sales of coats in Boston, where the temperature this weekend dropped to a more normal seasonal level are"—he paused, watching the screen—"*up* by ten percent over last week."

"I'm not interested in last week! I want to know why our coat sales are down from last year."

Meredith, who'd been on the phone with a friend at *Women's Wear Daily* last night, looked at her glowering father. "According to *WWD*," she said, "coat sales are down in all the chains. They're printing a story on it in the next issue."

"I don't want excuses, I want explanations," her father bit out. Inwardly, Meredith winced a little—but not much. From the day she'd forced him to acknowledge her value as a Bancroft executive, her father had gone out of his way to prove to her, and to everyone else, that his daughter got no favoritism from him. Quite the opposite, in fact. "The *explanation*," she said calmly, "is jackets. Winter jackets sales are up by twelve percent, nationwide. They're taking up the slack in coat sales."

Philip heard her, but he did not give her the small courtesy of acknowledging the worth of her input by so much as a nod. Instead, he turned on Rothman, his voice clipped. "What are we supposed to do with all the coats we'll have left?"

"We cut back on our orders for coats, Philip," Rothman said patiently. "We don't expect to have any surplus." When he didn't add that Theresa Bishop had been the one to advise him to buy jackets heavily and cut back on coats, Gordon Mitchell, the vice president who was responsible for dresses, accessories, and children's wear, was quick to point out Rothman's omission. "As I recall," he said, "the jackets were purchased instead of coats because Theresa told us the trend toward shorter skirts would cause women to look toward jackets this year rather than coats." Mitchell had spoken up, Meredith knew, not because he gave a damn whether Theresa got credit, but because he didn't want Rothman to get the credit. Mitchell never missed an opportunity to try to make the other merchandising vice presidents look less competent than himself. He was a petty, malicious man who had always repelled Meredith despite his good looks.

"I'm sure we're all well aware and appreciative of Theresa's fashion clairvoyance," Philip said with stinging derision. He did not like women among his vice presidents, and everyone knew it. Theresa rolled her eyes, but she did not look to Meredith for empathy; to do so would have showed a kind of mutual dependency, ergo, weakness, and they both knew better than to show any sign of that to their formidable president. "What about the new perfume that rock star is going to introduce—" Philip demanded, glancing at his notes and then at Ted Rothman.

"Charisma." Rothman provided the name of the perfume and the celebrity. "Her name is Cheryl Aderly—she's a rock star/sex symbol who—"

"I know who she is!" Philip said shortly. "Will Bancroft's get to debut her perfume or not?"

"We don't know yet," Rothman replied uneasily. Perfumes were one of the highest profit items in a department store, and being given the exclusive right in a city to introduce an important new scent was a coup. It meant free advertising from the perfume company, free publicity when the star came to the store to promote it, and a huge influx of women shoppers who flocked to the counters to try it and buy it.

"What do you mean, you don't know?" Philip snapped. "You said it was virtually in the bag."

"Aderly is hedging," he admitted. "As I understand it, she's eager to shed her rock-star image and do some serious acting, but—"

Philip threw down his pen in disgust. "For Christ's sake! I don't give a damn about her career goals! What I want to know is whether Bancroft's is going to snag the debut of her perfume, and if not, *why* not!"

"I'm trying to answer you, Philip," he said in a cautious, placating voice. "Aderly wanted to debut her perfume at a classy store to lend her a classy new image."

"What could be classier than Bancroft's?" Philip demanded, scowling, and without waiting for a reply to that rhetorical question, he said, "Did you find out who else she's considering?"

"Marshall Field's."

"That's a crock! Field's doesn't begin to outclass us and they can't do the job for her that we can!"

"At the moment, our 'class' seems to be the problem." Ted Rothman held up his hand when Philip's face turned an angry red. "You see, when we began negotiating the deal, Aderly wanted that class image, but now her agent and her advisers have half convinced her that it's a mistake for her to try to ditch the sexpot/rock star image that's won her so many teenage fans. For that reason, they're talking to Field's—looking at them as a sort of compromise image."

"I want that debut, Ted," Philip stated in a flat tone. "I mean that. Offer them a bigger cut of the profits if necessary, or tell them we'll share some of their local advertising costs. don't offer more than what it will take, but get that debut."

"I'll do my best."

"Haven't you been doing that all along?" Philip challenged. Without waiting for a reply, he turned to the vice president sitting beside Rothman, then one at a time he worked his way around the table, subjecting each VP to the same curt cross-examination that Rothman had received. Sales were excellent and each vice president was more than capable; Philip knew it, but as his health had worsened, so had his disposition. Gordon Mitchell was the last to come under Philip's fire: "The Dominic Avanti gowns look like hell—they look like last year's leftovers, and they aren't selling."

"One of the reasons they aren't selling," Mitchell announced with a bitter, accusing glance at Lisa's boss, "is because your people went out of their way to make the Avanti items look ridiculous! What was the idea of putting sequined hats and gloves on those mannequins?"

Lisa's boss, Neil Nordstrom, regarded the angry VP down the length of his nose, his expression placid. "At least," he commented, "Lisa Pontini and her crew managed to make that stuff look interesting, which it wasn't."

"Enough, gentlemen," Philip snapped a little wearily. "Sam," he said, turning to speak to Sam Green, the store's chief legal counsel, who was seated on his immediate left, "what about that lawsuit that woman filed against us—the one who claimed she tripped in the furniture department and hurt her back?"

"She's a fraud," Sam Green replied. "Our insurance carrier just discovered she's filed four other lawsuits against other retailers for the same thing. They aren't going to settle with her. She'll have to take us to court first, and she'll lose if she does."

Philip nodded and directed a cool glance at Meredith. "What about the real estate contracts on the land in Houston you're so determined to buy?"

"Sam and I are working out the final details. The seller has agreed to divide the property, and we're ready to draw up a contract."

He acknowledged her response with another curt nod and turned in his chair to address the controller, who was seated on his right. "Allen, what do you have to report?"

The controller glanced at the lined yellow pad in front of him. As chief financial officer of the Bancroft Corporation, Allen Stanley was responsible for all things financial, including the store's credit department. His twenty years of stressful, intellectual combat with Philip Bancroft had, in Meredith's opinion, probably caused Allen to lose much of his hair as well as making him look sixty-five rather than the fifty-five he was. Controllers and their staffs did not generate income for the store. Neither did the legal or the personnel divisions. As far as Philip was concerned, those three divisions had to be tolerated like a necessary evil, but he regarded them as little more than leeches. Moreover, he despised the fact that the heads of those three divisions were forever giving him reasons why he couldn't do something instead of telling him how he could do it. Allen Stanley still had five years to go until he could take early retirement, and there were times when Meredith wondered how he was going to make it. When Allen spoke, his voice was carefully precise and noticeably hesitant. "We had a record number of new applications for credit cards last month—almost eight thousand of them."

"How many did you approve?"

"Roughly sixty-five percent."

"How in the hell," Philip spat out furiously, tapping the end of his Waterman pen on the table to emphasize each word, "can you justify rejecting three thousand out of eight thousand applications? We're trying to attract new cardholders, and you're rejecting them as fast as the applications come in! I shouldn't have to tell you how profitable interest on those cards is

to our operation. And I'm not even *counting* the loss of revenue from purchases those three thousand people will *not* make at Bancroft's because they
can't shop here on credit!" As if he suddenly recalled his bad heart, Meredith watched him make a visible effort to calm himself.

"The applications we rejected were from people who aren't credit worthy,
Philip," Allen stated in a firm, reasonable tone. "Deadbeats, as you well know,
do not *pay* for what they purchase *or* the interest on their accounts. You may
think rejecting those applications cost us money, but the way I see it, my staff
has *saved* Bancroft's a fortune in uncollectible debts. I've established basic
requirements that must be met before we issue anyone a Bancroft's card, and
the fact is that three thousand people could not meet those requirements."

"Because the requirements are too damned high," Gordon Mitchell put
in smoothly.

"What makes you say that?" Philip demanded eagerly, always prepared
to find fault with the controller.

"I say that," Mitchell replied with malicious satisfaction, "because my
niece told me that Bancroft's just rejected *her* application for a credit card."

"Then she wasn't credit worthy," retorted the controller.

"Really?" he drawled. "Then why did Field's and Macy's just issue her
new cards? According to my niece, who's a junior in college, her rejection
letter said that she had an inadequate credit history. I presume that means
you couldn't find out anything about her, either bad or good."

The controller nodded, his pale, lined face creased into a glower.
"Obviously, if that's what our letter said, that's what happened."

"What about Field's and Macy's?" Philip demanded, leaning forward.
"They obviously have access to more information than you and your people do."

"No, they don't. We all use the same credit bureau for reports. It's obvious their credit requirements are more lenient than mine."

"They aren't *yours*, dammit, this store is not *yours*—"

Meredith interceded, knowing that while the controller would
adamantly defend his own actions, and his staff's, he rarely had the spine to
point out Philip's own mistakes to him, including this particular error in
judgment, which happened to be Philip's own. Motivated by an unselfish
desire to defend Allen Stanley and a very selfish desire to avoid another
lengthy wrangle that the rest of the executives, including herself, would all
have to sit through, Meredith interrupted her father's tirade. "The last time
this topic came up," she told him, managing to sound both courteous and
objective, "you felt that history had shown us that college students are often
bad credit risks. You instructed Allen to deny credit cards to all college students except in rare instances."

Silence descended on the conference room—the eerie, watchful silence that often ensued whenever Meredith opposed her father, but today it was heavier than ever, because everyone was watching for any sign of leniency in Philip's rigid attitude toward his daughter—a sign that would indicate that she was his choice to succeed him. In truth, her father was no more exacting than his counterparts at Saks or Macy's or any other large retailer, and Meredith knew it. It was his brusque, autocratic style that she objected to, not the demands he made. The executives gathered around the conference table had chosen retailing as a career, knowing beforehand that it was a frenetic, demanding business where sixty-hour weeks were the norm, not the exception, for anyone who wanted to make it to the top—and stay there. Meredith, like the others, had known that, just as she had known that in her case she would have to work harder, longer, and more effectively than all the others if she was to claim the presidency that would have automatically been hers had she had the foresight to be born a male.

Now she entered into the topic under debate, knowing full well that while she might earn her father's respect, she would incur a disproportionate amount of his resentment. He sent a disdainful glance her way. "What would *you* suggest, Meredith?" he asked, neither admitting nor denying that the rule had been his.

"The same thing I suggested last time—that college students with no bad credit information be granted credit cards, but with a low limit—say five hundred dollars—for the first year. At the end of the year, if Allen's people are satisfied with the payment records, then the cardholder's maximum can be increased."

For a moment he simply looked at her, then he turned away and without appearing to have heard her, he continued the meeting. An hour later he closed the deerskin folder with his meeting notes in it and glanced at the executives at the conference table. "I have an inordinately heavy schedule of meetings today, gentlemen—and ladies—" he added in a condescending tone that always made Meredith long to take a poke at him. "We'll have to omit going over the best sellers for the week. Thank you for coming. The meeting is adjourned. Allen," he said in an offhand voice, "go ahead and offer charge accounts with a five-hundred-dollar limit to college students so long as they don't have bad credit."

That was it. He didn't give Meredith recognition for the idea, or acknowledge her in any way. He behaved as he most often did when his talented daughter showed excellent judgment: He reluctantly took her suggestions without ever admitting their value, or hers, to the store. But they were valuable, and everyone knew it. Including Philip Bancroft.

Meredith gathered up her notes and left the conference room beside Gordon Mitchell. Of all the candidates for the role of interim president, Mitchell and Meredith were the two most likely to be given the job; Mitchell knew it, and so did Meredith. At thirty-seven, he had more years in retailing than Meredith, and that gave him a slight edge over her, but he'd joined Bancroft's only three years before. Meredith had been with Bancroft's seven years, and, more important, she had successfully spearheaded Bancroft's expansion into other states; she had argued and cajoled and ultimately persuaded her father and then the store's bankers to finance that expansion. She herself had chosen the locations for the new stores, and she herself remained deeply involved in all the endless details of building and stocking those stores. Because of all that, as well as her prior experience in Bancroft's other divisions, she had one thing to offer the board of directors that no other candidate for president had, including Gordon Mitchell, and that was versatility. Versatility, and a broader range of understanding of store operations. She stole a sideways glance at Gordon, and saw the calculating expression in his eyes as he looked at her. "Philip told me he's taking a cruise at the doctor's orders, when he goes on leave," Gordon began as they walked down the carpeted hallway past the secretaries posted in cubicles outside the vice presidents' offices. "Where is he planning—" He broke off as his secretary stood up at her desk and, raising her voice slightly, said, "Mr. Mitchell, you have a call on your private line from Mr. Bender. His secretary says it's rather urgent."

"I told you not to answer my private line, Debbie," he snapped. Excusing himself to Meredith, Mitchell stalked past his secretary into his office, and closed the door. Outside his office, Debbie Novotny bit her lip, watching Meredith Bancroft walk away. Whenever "Mr. Bender's secretary" called, Gordon got tense and excited, and he always closed the door when they talked. For nearly a year, he'd been promising to divorce his wife so that he could marry Debbie, and now she was suddenly terrified that the reason he'd been stalling was because "Mr. Bender's secretary" was actually a phony name for a new lover. He'd made other promises he hadn't kept too, like saying he would promote Debbie to a buyer and give her a raise. Her heart hammering in her throat, Debbie gingerly picked up her phone. Gordon's voice was low, alarmed: "I told you to stop calling me at the office!"

"Calm down, this won't take long," Bender said. "I've still got a shitload of those silk blouses you bought left over, and a mountain of that costume jewelry. I'll give you twice your usual cut if you'll take the stuff off my hands." It was a man's voice, and Debbie was so relieved that she started to hang up when it struck her that what Bender was talking about sounded like bribery.

"I can't," Gordon snapped. "I've seen that last batch of blouses and the jewelry you shipped in here, and it's mediocre crap! We've gotten away with our arrangement this long only because your stuff had some quality. If someone around here gets a close look at that last batch of stuff, they're going to demand to know who bought it and why. When they do, my merchandise managers are going to point the finger straight at me and say I *told* them to buy from you."

"If you're worried about it," Bender said, "fire both of them, then they won't be around to point the finger."

"I'll have to, but that doesn't change anything. Look, Bender," Gordon said with cold finality, "our relationship has been profitable for both of us, but it's over. It's too risky. Secondly, I think I'm going to be offered the interim presidency here. When that happens, I'll be completely out of the merchandising end of things."

Bender's voice turned menacing. "Listen to me very closely, you schmuck, because I'm only going to lay this out for you one time: You and I have had a very good thing going, and your ambitions are no concern of mine. I paid you a hundred thousand bucks last year—"

"I said the deal's over."

"It's not over until I say it is, and it's a long way from over. Cross me, and I'll make a phone call to old man Bancroft—"

"And tell him what?" Gordon jeered. "That I refused your bribe to buy your crap?"

"No, I'll tell him about how I'm an honest businessman, and you've been bleeding me for kickbacks before you'll let your people buy my excellent merchandise. That's not bribery, that's extortion." He paused a minute to let that sink in, then he added, "And there's always the IRS to worry about, isn't there? If they were to get an anonymous phone call and start checking you out, I'll bet they'd find out that you've got an extra hundred thousand bucks somewhere that you didn't declare. Income tax evasion is fraud, sweetheart. Extortion and fraud."

In the midst of Gordon's growing panic, he heard a sound on the telephone—a strange, muffled sound of a file cabinet being closed. "Hold on a minute," he said quickly, "I need to get something out of my briefcase." Ignoring his briefcase which was lying on his desk where he'd left it, he put the phone down, then he walked over to his office door and silently turned the knob, opening it a crack: His secretary was seated at her desk, a telephone receiver to her ear, her hand over the mouthpiece—and only one phone line was lit up on her telephone. White-faced with fury and panic, he closed the door and returned to his desk. "We'll have to finish our discussion tonight," he snapped. "Call me at home."

"I'm warning you—"

"All right, all right! Call me at home. We'll work something out."

Somewhat appeased, Bender said, "That's better. I'm not completely unreasonable. Since you have to turn down Bancroft's job, I'll raise your cut."

Gordon hung up the phone and punched the button on the intercom. "Debbie, will you come in here?" he said, then he released the button and added, "Stupid, meddling bitch!"

A moment later Debbie opened the door, her stomach in knots, her illusions about him all but shattered, terrified that her face would betray her guilty knowledge.

"Close the door and lock it," Gordon said, forcing a husky note into his voice as he came around his desk and walked over to the sofa. "Come here," he added.

Confused by the sensual note in his voice and the contrasting coldness in his eyes, Debbie approached him warily, then stifled a cry of panicked surprise when he yanked her into his arms. "I know you were listening in on my phone call," Gordon said, forcing himself to ignore the impulse to put his hands around her throat. "I'm doing it for us, Debbie. When my wife is finished with me after the divorce, I'll be cleaned out. I need money for us—to give you the things you should have. You understand, don't you, sweetheart?"

Debbie looked up at his handsome face and saw the endearing pleading in his eyes, and she understood. She believed. His hands were unzipping her dress, pulling it down, and when his fingers shoved into her bra and bikini pants, she pressed against him, offering him her body. Her love. Her silence.

Meredith was just picking up the telephone when her secretary passed her office door. "I was at the copy machine," Phyllis explained, walking into the office. At twenty-seven, Phyllis Tilsher was intelligent, intuitive, and completely sensible in every way except one: She was irresistibly attracted to irresponsible, unreliable men. It was a weakness that she had laughingly discussed with Meredith during the years that they had worked together. "Jerry Keaton in personnel called while you were gone," Phyllis continued, and with her usual smiling efficiency she began to report the calls she'd taken for Meredith. "He said there's a possibility one of our clerks is going to file a discrimination suit."

"Has he talked to the legal department?"

"Yes, but he wants to talk to you too."

"I have to go back to the architect's office to finish looking over the plans for the Houston store," Meredith said. "Tell Jerry I can see him first thing Monday morning."

"Okay. Mr. Savage also called." She broke off as Sam Green knocked politely on the door frame. "Excuse me," he said to them both, and then he added, "Meredith, can you spare me a few minutes?"

Meredith nodded. "What's up?"

"I just got off the phone with Ivan Thorp," he said, frowning as he walked up to her desk. "There may be a hitch in the deal for the Houston land."

Meredith had spent more than a month in Houston looking for suitable sites on which Bancroft's could build not only a new store, but an entire shopping center. She'd finally located an absolutely ideal spot within sight of The Galleria, and they'd been negotiating with Thorp Development, who owned the property, for months. "What sort of a hitch?"

"When I told him we're ready to write a contract, he said he may already have a buyer for all their properties, including that one."

Thorp Development was a Houston holding company that owned several office buildings and shopping centers as well as undeveloped land, and it was no secret that the Thorp brothers wanted to sell the entire company; that had been in the *Wall Street Journal*. "Do you believe they really have a buyer? Or is he trying to get us to make a higher opening offer for the land?"

"The latter probably, but I wanted you to know there could be some competition we didn't anticipate."

"Then we'll have to work it out, Sam. I want to build our next store on that piece of property more than I've ever wanted to build any other store anywhere else. The site is perfect. Houston is starting to recover from its slump, but building prices are still nice and low. By the time we're ready to open, their economy will be booming."

Meredith glanced at her watch and stood up. It was three o'clock on a Friday afternoon which meant traffic would already be getting heavy. "I have to run," she said with an apologetic smile. "See if your friend in Houston can find out anything about Thorp having another buyer."

"I've already called him. He's checking around."

16

*M*att's limousine barged through the Friday afternoon downtown traffic, bullying its way swiftly toward the sixty-story high-rise that was Haskell Electronics' national headquarters. In the backseat, Matt glanced up from the report he was reading just as Joe O'Hara swung the limo around a cab, ran a red light, and, hammering repeatedly on the car's horn, bluffed a group of intrepid Chicago pedestrians into getting out of his way. Less than ten feet from Haskell's underground parking garage, Joe slammed on the brakes and swung the car into the entrance. "Sorry, Matt," he said with a wry grin, glancing up and noticing Matt's scowl in the rearview mirror.

"One of these days," Matt replied shortly, exasperated, "I'd like you to explain what makes you want to turn pedestrians into hood ornaments." His voice was drowned out as the nose of the long car dipped down, tires screeching endlessly as they wound around and around, descending to the parking level reserved for chief executives, avoiding the wall beside them by scant inches. No matter how elegant or expensive the car was, O'Hara still drove it like a fearless teenager in a souped-up Chevy with a blonde in his lap and a six-pack of beer on the seat. If his reflexes weren't still as quick as any teenager's, he'd have lost his driver's license and probably his life years before.

He was also as loyal as he was daring and, ten years ago in South America, those traits had caused him to risk his life dragging Matt to safety when the truck Matt was driving lost its brakes, plunged down an embankment, and caught fire. For his efforts, Joe had received a case of his favorite whiskey along with Matt's unending gratitude.

Strapped over Joe's shoulder, beneath his jacket, was a .45 automatic that he'd bought years ago when he first drove Matt across the Teamsters' picket lines at a trucking company he'd just bought. Matt privately thought the gun was unnecessary. Although only five feet ten, Joe was 225 pounds of solid muscle with a pugnacious face that verged on ugly, and a scowl that was distinctly menacing. He was better suited to the job of bodyguard than chauffeur: He looked like a sumo wrestler. He drove like a maniac.

"Here we are," Joe called, managing to brake the car to a smooth stop near the private elevator beneath the building. "Home sweet home."

"For a year or less," Matt said, closing his briefcase. Normally when Matt bought a company, he remained on the premises for only a month or two—long enough to meet with his own men while they evaluated the management staff and to make recommendations. In the past, however, he'd bought only well-managed companies that were in trouble because they were short of operating capital for one reason or another. The changes he instituted at those companies were mostly minor and done simply to tune up their operation and make it fit in with Intercorp's. Haskell was different. Old methods and procedures would have to be discarded in favor of new; benefits redetermined, salaries adjusted, loyalties altered, a vast new manufacturing facility constructed in suburban Southville, where he'd already bought land. Haskell needed a major overhaul. Between the shipping company he'd just bought and Haskell's reorganization, Matt was going to be working long, arduous days and nights, but he'd been doing that for years. In the beginning, he'd done it out of some desperate compulsive desire to succeed, to prove he could. Even now, when he'd succeeded beyond his wildest imaginings, he kept up his exhausting pace—not because he enjoyed it or the success anymore, but because it was habit. And because nothing else gave him any more satisfaction either. He worked hard, and when he took the time to play, he played hard. Neither was particularly meaningful or gratifying. But streamlining Haskell, making it into all the things it should be, was a challenging goal. Maybe that's where he'd gone wrong, Matt decided as he put his key into the lock of the private express elevator that went to the executive floors of the building. He'd created a huge conglomerate by buying desirable, well-run companies that needed Intercorp's financial backing. Maybe he should have bought a few that needed more than that. His takeover team had been here for two weeks, making their evaluations. They were upstairs, waiting to meet with him, and he was eager to get started.

On the sixtieth floor the receptionist answered her telephone and listened to the information being imparted to her by the uniformed guard who also acted as a receptionist in Haskell's lobby on the ground floor. When she hung up, Valerie went over to the secretary seated to her right. "Pete Duncan said a silver stretch limo just turned into the garage," she whispered. "He thinks it's Farrell."

"Silver must be his favorite color," Joanna replied with a meaningful glance at the new six-foot-square silver plaque with the Intercorp insignia which had been hung on the rosewood wall behind her desk.

Two weeks after the Intercorp takeover, a band of carpenters had arrived, supervised by a man who identified himself as Intercorp's interior design manager. When he departed two weeks later, the entire reception area on the one hundredth floor, as well as the conference room and Matt Farrell's future office, had been completely redecorated. Where once there had been time-worn Oriental carpets and dark wood furniture gently scarred with age, there were acres of silvery carpet covering every inch of floor and modern burgundy leather sofas arranged in groups with Lucite coffee tables in front and beside them. It was a well-publicized idiosyncrasy of Matt Farrell's that every division and acquisition of Intercorp's was immediately redecorated to look like all his other holdings.

Valerie and Joanna, along with several of the other secretaries on this floor, were now very familiar, not only with Matthew Farrell's reputation and quirks, but with his ruthlessness. Within days after Intercorp acquired Haskell, the president—Mr. Vern Haskell—had been forced to take an early retirement. So were two of the senior vice presidents, one of whom had been Vern Haskell's son, the other his son-in-law. Another VP refused to resign and was fired. The offices of those loyal VPs—which were situated on this floor, but on the opposite side of the building—were now occupied by three of Farrell's henchmen. Three more of his men were stationed elsewhere in the building—spying on everyone, according to rumor, asking prying questions, and making out lists, undoubtedly of whom to fire next.

To make matters worse, it wasn't just the senior executives who'd been squeezed out of their jobs; Mr. Haskell's secretary had been given her "choice" of either working for some minor executive or leaving with her boss, because Matthew Farrell insisted on sending his *own* secretary in from California. That had caused a fresh furor of fear and resentment among the remaining executive secretaries, but that was nothing compared to how they felt about Farrell's secretary when she actually arrived: Eleanor Stern was a stick-straight, skinny, wire-haired tyrant/busybody who watched them like a hawk and who still used words like "impertinence" and "propriety." She arrived at the office before anyone else, left after everyone else, and when the door to her office was open, which it wasn't now, she could hear the quietest feminine laugh or word of casual gossip. When she did, she would get up and come to stand in her doorway like an irate master sergeant until the recreational chat came to its inevitable and awkward end. For that reason Valerie resisted the impulse to call several of the secretaries and tell them Farrell was about to arrive, so they could come over on some invented excuse and at least have a look at him.

The movie magazines and tabloids made him sound like a handsome, sophisticated hunk who dated movie stars and European royalty. The *Wall Street Journal* said he was "a corporate genius with a Midas touch." Mr. Haskell said on the day he left that Matthew Farrell was "an arrogant, inhuman bastard with the instincts of a shark and the morals of a marauding wolf." As Joanna and Valerie waited for a glimpse of him, they were already predisposed to despise him on sight. And they did.

The soft ding of the elevator bell struck the reception area like a hammer on a gong. Matthew Farrell strode out, and the very air suddenly seemed to crackle with the suppressed energy of his presence. Deeply tanned and athletically built, he stalked swiftly toward them, reading a report and carrying a briefcase, a beige cashmere topcoat looped over his forearm. Valerie stood up uncertainly. "Good afternoon, Mr. Farrell." For her courtesy, she received a daunting glance from cool gray eyes, a curt nod, and then he swept past like the wind—powerful, unsettling, and completely indifferent to mere mortals like Valerie and Joanna.

Matt had been here once before to attend an evening meeting, and he walked with unerring certainty into the private suite of offices that had belonged to Haskell's president and his secretary. Not until he closed the door of the secretary's office did he tear his attention from the report he'd been reading in the elevator, and then it was only to glance perfunctorily at his own secretary, who'd worked closely with him for nine long years. They did not greet each other or indulge in small talk; they never had. "How is everything going?"

"Quite well," Eleanor Stern replied.

"Is the agenda ready for the meeting?" he added, already starting toward the tall rosewood double doors that opened into his private office.

"Of course," she replied, matching his brisk manner perfectly. They'd been an ideal match from the very first day she'd arrived at his office along with twenty other women, most of them young and attractive, who'd been sent over to Matt by an employment agency. Earlier that same day, he'd seen a picture of Meredith in a copy of *Town and Country* magazine that someone had left in the cafeteria. She was lying on a Jamaican beach with a collegiate polo player. The caption said she was vacationing with school friends. More bitterly determined to succeed than ever as a result of that picture, he had begun interviewing the applicants. Most of them were airheads, or openly flirtatious, and he was in no mood to tolerate either stupidity or women's wiles. What he wanted, needed, was someone smart and reliable, someone who would keep pace with his newly reinforced drive to make it to the top. He'd just tossed the last applicant's résumé in the wastebasket, when he looked up and saw Eleanor Stern marching toward him in her stout-heeled shoes, plain black suit, her gray hair in a prim bun. She thrust her résumé into his hand and waited in stoic silence while Matt read the pertinent facts which included the information that she was fifty years old, unmarried, and that she could type 120 words per minute and take shorthand at 160 words per minute. Matt had glanced up at her, intending to question her, only to have her announce in a frosty, defensive voice, "I am not unaware that I'm twenty years older than those other applicants out there, and twenty times less attractive. However, because I have never been a beautiful woman, I've had to develop and rely upon my other qualities."

Taken aback, Matt had asked, "What are those qualities?"

"My mind and my skills," she'd replied. "In addition to my typing and shorthand skills, I am also a paralegal and a full-charge bookkeeper. Furthermore, I can do something that very few twenty-year-olds can do anymore—"

"And that is?"

"I can *spell!*" The remark with all its prim superiority and implied disdain for anything less than perfection appealed to him. She had a certain aloof pride that Matt admired, and he sensed in her the same rigid determination to get the job done that he felt. Based on that instinctive belief that she was right for the position, he said bluntly, "The hours are long and the salary isn't great now. I'm just getting started. If I make it to the top, I'll take you with me. Your salary will go up according to your contribution."

"Agreed."

"I'll be traveling a great deal. Later, there may be times when you'll have to accompany me."

Amazingly, her pale eyes had narrowed. "Perhaps you ought to be more specific about my duties, Mr. Farrell. Women undoubtedly find you an extremely attractive man; however—"

Dumbfounded that she apparently thought he was planning to make a pass at her, and angered by her censorious, unsolicited opinion of his appeal to other women, Matt had replied in a voice even colder than hers, "Your duties would be purely secretarial, and no more. I'm not interested in an affair or a flirtation; I don't want cake on my birthday, or coddling, *or* your opinions on personal matters that pertain to me alone. All I want is your time and your skills."

He'd been much harsher than he'd ordinarily have been, which owed itself more to that picture of Meredith than to Eleanor Stern's attitude, but she didn't mind in the least. In fact she seemed to prefer the sort of working arrangement he'd described. "I find that completely agreeable," she announced.

"When can you start?"

"Now."

He'd never regretted his decision. Within a week, he'd realized that like him, Eleanor Stern could work at a ceaseless, killing pace without ever wearing out or wearing down. The more responsibility he gave her, the more she accomplished. They never bridged the barrier that had been erected between them when she expressed alarm over his intentions. At first they had simply been too absorbed in their mutual work to give it thought. Later it didn't seem to matter; they had fallen into a routine, and it worked magnificently for both of them. Matt had made it all the way to the top, and she had worked day and night beside him, without complaint. In fact, she was a nearly indispensable asset to his business life, and, true to his word, he had rewarded her loyalty and efforts liberally: Miss Stern's salary was $65,000 a year—more than many of Intercorp's mid-level executives were paid.

Now, she followed him into his office and waited as he laid his briefcase on the polished rosewood desk that had been delivered recently. Normally he handed her at least one microcassette filled with instructions and dictation for her to transcribe. "There's no dictation," Matt explained, unlatching his briefcase and handing her a stack of files. "And I didn't have a chance to go over the Simpson contract on the plane. The Lear had an engine problem, so I had to take a commercial flight here. The baby in front of me was evidently having problems with his ears, and he screamed for the entire flight."

Because he'd opened the conversation, Miss Stern evidently felt required to participate. "Someone should have done something for him."

"The man beside me volunteered to smother him," Matt said, "but the baby's mother was no more amenable to that solution than she'd been to mine."

"What was your solution?"

"A shot of vodka with a brandy chaser." Closing his briefcase, he said, "How good is the clerical staff up here?"

"Some of them are very conscientious. However, Joanna Simons, whom you passed on your way in here, is barely adequate. Rumor has it that she was more than a secretary to Mr. Morrissey, which I am inclined to believe. Since her skills are nonexistent, it stands to reason her talents lie in some other area."

Matt barely noticed her sniff of prim disapproval. Tipping his head toward the conference room that adjoined his office, he said, "Is everybody in there?"

"Of course."

"Do they all have copies of the agenda?"

"Of course."

"I'm expecting a call from Brussels sometime during the next hour," Matt said, already starting for the conference room. "Put that one through to me right away, but hold any others."

Six of Intercorp's most talented vice presidents were seated on a pair of long burgundy suede sofas that faced each other across a large glass and marble coffee table in the conference room. The men stood up as Matt came forward, each of them shaking his hand, each of them studying his features for some indication of the outcome of his trip to Greece. "It's good to have you back, Matt," the last man said as Matt shook his hand. "Well, don't keep us in suspense," Tom Anderson added. "How was Athens?"

"Extremely pleasant," Matt replied as they all moved over to the conference table. "Intercorp now owns a fleet of tankers."

Triumph, full-bodied and sweet, swept through the room, and then voices rose as everyone began discussing plans to utilize Intercorp's newest "family branch."

Leaning back in his chair, Matt observed the six high-powered executives who were seated before him. All of them were dynamic, dedicated men, the best in their individual fields. Five of them had come from Harvard, Princeton, and Yale; from UCLA and MIT, with degrees in fields ranging from international banking to marketing. Five of them were wearing $800 custom-tailored business suits, discreetly monogrammed Egyptian cotton shirts, and carefully chosen silk ties. Grouped together, as they were now, they looked like a four-color ad for Brooks Brothers—something headed: When you've reached the pinnacle, only the best is good enough. In contrast to them, the sixth man, Tom Anderson, was a jarringly discordant figure in his green-and-brown-plaid jacket, green trousers, and paisley tie. Anderson's passion for loud clothes was a source of great amusement among the other impeccably dressed men on the takeover team, but they rarely jibed him about it. For one thing, it was difficult to sneer at a man who stood six feet four and weighed 245 pounds.

Anderson had a high school equivalency degree, no college at all, and he was aggressively proud of it. "My degree is from the school of life," he would announce whenever he was asked about his education. What he left unsaid was that he possessed an uncanny talent no school could provide: He was instinctively, intuitively sensitive to the nuances of human nature. He knew within minutes of talking to a man what motivated him and made him tick, whether it was vanity, greed, ambition, or something much different.

On the surface he was a plain-spoken, giant bear of a man who liked to work in his shirt-sleeves. Beneath that unpolished surface, Tom Anderson had a gift for negotiating—and a knack for getting to the crux of a problem that was invaluable, especially when he was dealing with the unions on Intercorp's behalf.

But of all his attributes, Matt prized one the most: Anderson was loyal. He was, in fact, the only man in the room whose talents were not for sale to the highest bidder. He'd worked for the first company that Matt had bought. When he sold it, Tom elected to take his chances with Matt rather than the new owners who'd offered him an excellent position and a better salary.

Matt paid the other men on the acquisition team enough to ensure they would not be tempted to sell out to a rival corporation; he paid Anderson even more because he was completely dedicated to Matt and to Intercorp. He never regretted what they cost him because, as a team, they were the best—but it was Matt himself who channeled their energies in the right direction. The master plan for Intercorp's growth was his alone, and he altered it as he saw fit. "Gentlemen," he said, interrupting their discussion about the tankers. "We'll talk about the tankers another time. Let's talk about Haskell's problems."

Matt's post-acquisition methods were unique and effective. Rather than wasting months trying to sort out the company's problems, find the causes and cures, and weed out the executives who weren't performing to Intercorp's standards, Matt did something much different: He sent in the group of men gathered in the conference room to work side by side with the existing vice presidents of the acquired company. Each of the six men was an expert in a particular corporate area, and in a matter of weeks they could familiarize themselves completely with their individual division, assess the talents of the vice president of that division, and locate the weaknesses and strong points of that division.

"Elliott," Matt said to Elliott Jamison, "let's start with you. Overall, how does Haskell's marketing division look?"

"Not bad, but not great either. They have too many managers here, as well as in the regional offices, and too few sales reps out in the field selling the products. Their existing customers get lavished with attention, but the reps don't have time to open up new accounts. Considering the high quality of Haskell's products, Haskell should have three or four times the number of customers they have now. At this point I'd tentatively suggest adding fifty reps to their sales force. Once you have the Southville plant constructed and operating, I'd suggest adding fifty more."

Matt jotted a note on the yellow legal pad on the table in front of him and returned his attention to Jamison. "What else?"

"Paul Cranshaw, the marketing vice president, will have to go, Matt. He's been with Haskell for twenty-eight years and his marketing philosophy is antiquated and foolish. He's also inflexible and unwilling to change his ways."

"How old is he?"

"His file says fifty-six."

"Will he take an early retirement if we offer it to him?"

"Possibly. He's not going to quit on his own, that's for sure. He's an arrogant son of a bitch and openly hostile about Intercorp's takeover."

Tom Anderson lifted his gaze from an admiring study of his paisley tie. "That's not surprising. He's a distant cousin of old Haskell's."

Elliott looked at him in surprise. "Really?" he said, reluctantly fascinated with Tom's ability to ferret out information without ever seeming to try. "That fact wasn't in his personnel file. How did you find it out?"

"I had a delightful conversation with a charming old gal down in the records section. She's been here longer than anyone else, and she's a walking diary of information."

"No wonder Cranshaw was so damned abrasive. He'll definitely have to go—he's a tremendous morale problem, among other things. That's it for generalities, Matt. I'll meet with you next week and we can go over specifics."

Matt turned to John Lambert for financial information.

Taking his cue, Lambert glanced at his notes and said, "Their profits are good, we knew that before, but there's plenty of room for streamlining and cutting down on expenses. Also, they do a lousy job of collecting their own receivables. Half their accounts take six months to pay, and it's because Haskell hasn't made it a policy to be more aggressive with their collections."

"Are we going to have to replace the controller, then?"

Lambert hesitated. "That's a tough call to make. The controller claims that Haskell was the one who didn't want the customers urged to pay up any quicker. He says he's tried for years to implement a more aggressive procedure, but old man Haskell wouldn't hear of it. Putting that aside, he runs a pretty tight ship. Morale is very high in his division and he's a good delegator. He has just enough supervisors to get the job done, and they do it well. His department is lean."

"How did he react to your invading his realm? Did he seem willing to adapt to change?"

"He's a follower, not a leader, but he's conscientious. Tell him what you want done, and it'll be done. On the other hand, if you want innovations and aggressive accounting procedures, he's not likely to come up with them on his own."

"Get him straightened out and on the right track," Matt said after a moment's hesitation. "When we name a president here, he can keep an eye on him. Finance is a big division; it seems to be in good shape. If morale is high there, I'd like to keep it that way."

"I agree. By next month I'll be ready to discuss a new budget and pricing structure with you."

"Fine." Matt turned to the short blond man who specialized in all matters pertaining to personnel and personnel policies. "David, what's the story in human resources?"

"It's not bad. Pretty good, actually. The percentage of minority employees is a little low, but not low enough to get us in the headlines or lose us government contracts," David Talbot replied. "Human resources has done a good job of establishing and maintaining sound hiring and promotion practices, and so forth. Lloyd Waldrup, the vice president who heads that division, is sharp and well qualified for his job."

"He's a closet bigot," Tom Anderson argued, leaning forward to pour himself a cup of coffee from the sterling silver coffee service in the center of the table.

"That's a ridiculous allegation," Talbot said irritably. "Lloyd Waldrup gave me the reports showing the number of women and minorities within the various job categories, and there's a fair percentage of them with management titles."

"I don't believe the reports."

"Jesus, what *is* it with you, Tom!" he snapped, turning in his chair to glower at Tom's imperturbable features. "Every time we acquire a company, you start in on the human resources managers. What is it, specifically, that makes you nearly always dislike them?"

"I guess it's that they are *nearly always* power-hungry ass kissers."

"Including Waldrup?"

"*Especially* Waldrup."

"And which of your acclaimed instincts leads you to believe that of him?"

"He complimented my clothes two days in a row. I never trust anyone who compliments my clothes, particularly if he's wearing a conservative gray suit."

Muted chuckles broke the tension building in the room, and even David relaxed. "Is there any other reason to believe he's a liar about his hiring and promotion practices?"

"Yep, there is," Tom said, carefully keeping the plaid sleeve of his jacket out of his coffee as he reached for the sugar bowl. "I've been wandering around this building for a couple of weeks now, while you've been busy doing your job down in human resources, and I couldn't help noticing one little thing." He paused to stir the sugar in his coffee, which annoyed everyone in the room except Matt, who continued to regard him with calm interest, then Tom leaned back and propped his ankle atop his opposite knee, the coffee cup in his hand.

"Tom!" David said testily. "Will you get to the point so we can go on with the meeting! What did you notice while you were walking around this building?"

Completely unperturbed, Tom lifted his shaggy brows and said, "I saw men sitting in private offices."

"So what?"

"What I didn't see were any women sitting in them, except in the accounting division, where there've historically been women managers. And only a couple of the women who did have offices had secretaries sitting outside of them. Which made me wonder if your buddy Waldrup isn't handing out some fancy titles to keep the ladies happy and make himself look good on his employment reports. If these women actually have management-level jobs, where are their secretaries? Where are their offices?"

"I'll check it out," David said with an irritated sigh. "I'd have discovered it sooner or later, but it's better to know it now." Turning to Matt, he continued. "At some point in the future we're going to have to bring Haskell's vacation policy and salary scales into some sort of alignment with Intercorp's. Haskell gives their people three weeks vacation after three years employment and four weeks after eight years. That policy is costing the company a fortune in lost time and the constant need to hire additional temporary help."

"How do their wage scales compare?" Matt asked.

"They're lower than ours. Haskell's philosophy was to give employees more time off but pay them less. I'll meet with you and go over this in more detail when I've had a chance to work up some figures and recommendations."

For the next two hours Matt listened while the remaining men reported on their individual areas and debated solutions. When they were finished discussing Haskell, Matt brought them up-to-date on developments in other divisions of Intercorp that might concern them now or later, developments that ranged from a threatened union strike at Intercorp's textile mill in Georgia to the design and capabilities of the new manufacturing facility he intended to build for Haskell on the large parcel of land he'd purchased in Southville.

Throughout the entire meeting, one man, Peter Vanderwild, remained silent and attentive, like a brilliant, slightly awed graduate student who understood all the basics—but who was learning the finer points from a group of experts. At twenty-eight, Peter was a former Harvard "whiz kid" with a genius I.Q., who specialized in reviewing companies for Intercorp to acquire, analyzing their potential for profit, and then making his recommendations to Matt. Haskell Electronics had been one of Vanderwild's choices, and it was going to be his third winner in a row. Matt had sent him here to Chicago with the rest of the team because he wanted Peter to experience firsthand what happened *after* a company was acquired. He wanted him to observe what could *not* be seen on the financial statements that Peter relied on so heavily when he made his recommendations to buy a company—like controllers who were lax about collecting money, and human resources directors who were closet bigots.

Matt had brought him there to observe and to be observed. Despite Peter's outstanding success thus far, Matt knew he still needed guidance. Moreover, he was cocky and hypersensitive, brash and timid, depending upon the situation, and that was something Matt intended to curb. He had a tremendous amount of raw talent; it needed channeling.

"Peter?" Matt said. "Any new developments in your area that we ought to hear about?"

"I have several possible companies in mind that would be excellent acquisitions," Peter announced. "They're not as big as Haskell but they're profitable. One of them is a nice little computer software company in silicon valley—"

"No software companies, Peter," Matt said firmly.

"But JLH is—"

"No software companies!" Matt interrupted. "They're too damned risky right now." He saw the embarrassed flush creep up Vanderwild's neck. Reminding himself that his goal was to direct the younger man's enormous talents, not to crush his enthusiasm, Matt curbed his impatience and added, "It's no reflection on you, Peter. I've never told you my feelings about software companies. What else do you want to recommend?"

"You mentioned you wanted to expand our commercial property division," Peter said hesitantly. "There is a company in Atlanta, another here in Chicago, and a third one down in Houston. All three are looking for someone to buy them out. The first two own mostly high- and mid-rise office buildings. The third one, in Houston, is predominantly invested in commercial land. It's a family-owned company, and the two Thorp brothers, who've run it since their father died a few years ago, reportedly can't stand each other." Still flinching from Matt's swift rejection of his last recommendation, Peter hastened to point out the drawbacks of this one. "Houston has been in a long slump, and I suppose there's no reason to assume its recent recovery will continue. Also, since the Thorp brothers can't agree on anything, the deal would probably cause us more trouble than it's worth—"

"Are you trying to convince me it's a good idea or a bad one?" Matt asked with a smile to atone for his earlier curtness. "You make the choices based on your best judgment, and I'll shoot them down for you. That's my job, and if you start doing my job plus your own, I won't have anything to do. I'll feel useless."

Chuckles greeted that joking remark and, getting up, Peter handed him a folder labeled RECOMMENDED ACQUISITIONS/COMMERCIAL PROPERTY COMPANIES. In it were data sheets on the three companies he'd mentioned, and a dozen other, less appealing ones. More relaxed now, he sat back down.

Matt opened the file and saw that the dossiers were long and Peter's analyses were very complex. Rather than detain the other men needlessly, he said, "Peter has been his usual thorough self, gentlemen, and this file is going to take considerable time to go over. I think we've covered everything that needs to be discussed for now. I'll meet with each of you next week. Let Miss Stern know when you're ready to go over your individual divisions in more detail." To Peter he said, "Let's go over this in my office."

He'd just sat down at his desk when his intercom buzzed, and Miss Stern told him that his Brussels call was coming through. With the phone cradled between his shoulder and jaw, Matt began looking over the financial statement of the Atlanta company Peter had recommended.

"Matt," Josef Hendrik said, his delighted voice rising above the static on the line, "we have a bad connection, my friend, but my excellent news cannot wait for a better one. My people here are in full accord with the limited partnership I proposed to you last month. They offered no opposition to any of the stipulations you made."

"That's fine, Josef," Matt replied, but his enthusiasm was somewhat dampened by jet lag and the realization that it was much later than he'd thought. Beyond the broad expanse of windows at the outer wall of his office, the sky was shrouded in darkness and lights were twinkling in the adjoining skyscrapers. Far below on Michigan Avenue, he could hear car horns honking as commuters sat in snarled rush hour traffic, trying to fight their way home. Reaching toward the lamp on his desk, Matt switched it on, then he glanced at Peter, who got up and turned the overhead lights up as well. "It's later than I thought, Peter, and I still have several phone calls to make. I'll take this file home and look through it over the weekend. We'll discuss it Monday morning at ten o'clock."

17

*R*efreshed from a sauna and shower, Matt wrapped a towel around his waist and reached for the wristwatch lying on the black marble vanity that swept around his circular bathroom. The telephone rang, and he picked it up.

"Are you naked?" Alicia Avery's sultry voice asked before he'd said a word.

"What number are you calling?" he said with feigned confusion.

"Yours, darling. *Are* you naked?"

"Semi-naked," Matt said, "and running late."

"I'm so glad you're finally in Chicago. When did you get in?"

"Yesterday."

"I have you in my clutches at last!" She laughed, an enticing, contagious laugh. "You can't believe the fantasies I've been having, thinking about tonight when we get back from the opera's benefit ball. I've missed you, Matt," she added, blunt and direct as always.

"We're going to see each other in an hour," Matt promised, "if you let me get off the phone, that is."

"All right. Actually, Daddy made me call. He was afraid you'd forget about the opera benefit tonight. He's almost as eager to see you as I am—for very different reasons, of course."

"Of course," Matt joked.

"Oh, and I may as well warn you that he intends to put you up for membership at the Glenmoor Country Club. The ball is the perfect spot to introduce you to some of the members and get their vote, so he'll try to drag you all over if you let him get by with it. Not that he needs to bother," she added. "You'll be a shoo-in. Oh, and the press will be there en masse, so prepare to be mobbed when they see you. It's very humiliating, Mr. Farrell," she teased, "to know my date is going to cause more of a sensation tonight than I am. . . ."

The mention of the Glenmoor Country Club, where he'd met Meredith that long-ago Fourth of July, made Matt's jaw tighten with grim irony, and he hardly heard the rest of what Alicia said. He already held memberships in two country clubs, both of them as exclusive as Glenmoor. He rarely used the clubs he belonged to, and if he joined one in Chicago, which he had no desire to do, it sure as hell wouldn't be Glenmoor. "Tell your father I appreciate the thought, but I'd rather he didn't." Before he could say more, Stanton Avery picked up an extension. "Matt," he said in his bluff, hearty voice. "You haven't forgotten the opera benefit shindig tonight, have you?"

"I remembered it, Stanton."

"Good, good. I thought we'd pick you up at nine, stop at the Yacht Club for drinks, and then go on to the hotel. That way, we won't have to sit through *La Traviata* before the serious drinking and partying begins. Or are you especially fond of *La Traviata?*"

"Operas make me comatose," Matt joked, and Stanton chuckled in agreement. In the past several years Matt had attended dozens of operas and symphonies because he moved in a social stratum where sponsorship of, and attendance at, cultural functions was necessary from a business standpoint. Now that he was unwillingly familiar with most famous symphonies and operas, his original opinion of them hadn't changed: He found most of them boring as hell and all of them overlong. "Nine is fine," he added.

Despite his dislike of operatic music and of being mobbed by the press, Matt was generally looking forward to the evening as he buckled on his wristwatch and picked up his shaver. He had met Stanton Avery in Los Angeles four years before, and whenever Matt was in Chicago or Stanton was in California, they tried to get together. Unlike many of the dilettante socialites Matt had met, Stanton was a tough, blunt, down-to-earth businessman, and Matt liked him immensely. In fact, if he could choose a father-in-law, Stanton would have been his choice. Alicia was much like her father—sophisticated and polished but direct as hell when it came to getting what she wanted. They had both wanted him to accompany them to the opera benefit tonight, and they wouldn't take no for an answer. He'd ended up not only agreeing to attend, but agreeing to contribute $5,000 as well.

Two months ago, when Alicia was with him in California and blatantly hinting that they ought to get married, Matt had briefly entertained the idea, but the impulse had passed very quickly. He enjoyed Alicia in bed and out of it, and he liked her style, but he'd already had one disastrous marriage to a spoiled, rich Chicago socialite, and he had no intention of repeating the experience. Conversely, he'd never seriously considered remarrying because he'd never been *able* to duplicate the feelings he'd had for Meredith—that violent, possessive, insane need to see and touch and laugh with her; that volcanic passion that controlled him and couldn't be sated. No other woman had looked up at him and made him feel humbled and powerful at the same time—or ignited that same desperate desire to prove that he could be more and better than he was. To marry someone who didn't do that to him was settling for second-best, and second-best in anything wasn't good enough. At the same time, he had absolutely no desire to ever again experience those tormenting, stormy, crushing emotions again. They'd been as painful as they were pleasant, and when his misbegotten marriage was over, the mere memory of them—and of the traitorous young wife he'd adored—had made his life a hell for years afterward.

The truth was that if Alicia *had* been able to get under his skin as Meredith had, he'd have broken off with her as soon as he felt it happening. He didn't want, would never permit himself, to be that vulnerable to anyone, ever again. Now that he was in Chicago, Alicia wasn't likely to let the issue of marriage drop. If she didn't, he was either going to have to make it clear that was permanently out of the question, or he would have to put an end to their very delightful relationship.

Shrugging into his black tuxedo jacket, Matt strolled out of the bedroom and into the living room. He still had fifteen minutes before Stanton and Alicia were due to arrive, so he walked over to the far corner of the apartment and up to the raised platform that contained a bar and several sofas comfortably arranged for conversation. He'd chosen this building, and this apartment, because all the outer walls were broad expanses of curved glass that offered a breathtaking view of Lake Shore Drive and the Chicago skyline. For a moment, he stood looking out, then he walked over to the bar, intending to have a brandy. As he did so, his jacket brushed against the newspaper that his housekeeper had left neatly folded on an end table, and the newspaper flipped onto the floor, the sections spilling out.

And he saw Meredith.

Her photograph leapt out at him from the last page of the front section—her smile perfect, her hair perfect, her expression perfect. Typical Meredith—he thought with icy revulsion as he picked up the paper and looked at her picture—posed and packaged for effect and appearances. She'd been a beautiful teenager, but whoever did her media photos was going overboard to make her look like Grace Kelly as a young woman.

His gaze shifted from her picture to the article below it, and for a split second he tensed with surprise: According to the columnist, Sally Mansfield, Meredith had just become engaged to her "childhood sweetheart," Parker Reynolds III, and Bancroft & Company intended to celebrate her February wedding with a national sale in all their stores.

A smirk of ironic amusement twisted Matt's lips as he tossed the paper aside and walked over to the window. He'd been married to the treacherous little bitch, and he didn't even *know* she'd had a "childhood sweetheart." But then, he hadn't really known her at all, Matt reminded himself. What he did know of her, he despised.

In the midst of that thought, Matt suddenly realized that what he was thinking didn't match what he was feeling. Evidently he was reacting out of old habit, because he didn't actually despise her anymore. All he truly felt for her was cold distaste. What had happened between them was so long ago, time had eroded every strong emotion he'd felt for her, even loathing. In its place there was nothing . . . nothing except disgust and pity. Meredith had been too spineless to be treacherous; spineless and completely dominated by her father. When she was nearly six months pregnant, she'd aborted their baby and sent Matt a telegram afterward, telling him what she'd done and that she was divorcing him. And despite what she'd done to his baby, he'd been so insane about her that he'd flown back with some demented intention of trying to talk her out of an immediate divorce. When he got to the hospital, he was informed at the lobby desk in the Bancroft wing that Meredith did not want to see him, and a security guard accompanied him back out the doors. Thinking those instructions might have been issued by Philip Bancroft, not Meredith, Matt had gone back the next day, only to be met by a cop at the front door who slapped an injunction into his hand, an injunction Meredith herself had obtained that made it illegal for him to go near her.

For years Matt had pushed those memories, along with the anguish he'd felt over the baby, into some dark, safe recess of his mind, because he couldn't stand to think of it. Putting Meredith out of his mind had become an art he'd practiced and perfected. At first he did it out of self-preservation. Later, out of habit.

Now, as he gazed at the twinkling headlights far below on Lake Shore Drive, he realized he didn't need to do that anymore. She had ceased to exist for him.

He'd known when he made the decision to spend the next year in Chicago that Meredith and he would be bound to encounter each other, but he'd refused to let it affect his plans. Now he realized he needn't have bothered to consider it, because it didn't matter. They were both adults; the past was over. Meredith was nothing if not well-bred. They'd both be able to carry off their meeting with the polite courtesy that was expected of adults in these situations.

Matt climbed into Stanton's stretch Mercedes and shook his friend's hand, then his gaze shifted to Alicia, who was swathed in an ankle-length sable coat the same color as her dark glossy hair. She reached out and put her hand in his, smiling into his eyes—seductive, direct, and appealing. "It's been a long time," she said in that rich, soft voice of hers.

"Too long," he replied, and he meant that.

"Five months," she reminded him. "Do you intend to shake my hand or are you going to kiss me properly?"

Matt tossed a helpless, amused glance at her father—an explanation of intent. Stanton answered with an indulgent, paternal smile of permission, and Matt tugged Alicia's hand, pulling her unceremoniously onto his lap. "How properly did you have in mind?" he asked.

She smiled and said, "I'll show you."

Only Alicia would have dared to kiss a man the way she did in front of her father. But then, not many fathers would have smiled and politely diverted their gaze to the side window while their daughters kissed a man with a lingering sensuality designed to be sexually arousing. Alicia did and Matt was. They both knew it. "I think you've really missed me," she said.

"And I think," he told her, "one of us should have the grace to blush."

"That's very provincial of you, darling," she informed him, laughing as she reluctantly took her hands from his shoulders. "Very middle class."

"There was a time," he reminded her pointedly, "when being middle class would have been an improvement."

"You're proud of that, aren't you?" she teased.

"I suppose I am."

She slid off his lap, crossed her long legs, and her coat parted to reveal a thigh-high slash in the side of her black sheath gown. "What do you think?" she asked.

"You can find out later what he thinks," Stanton said, suddenly impatient with his daughter's monopoly of his friend. "Matt, what do you know about the rumors that Edmund Mining is going to merge with Ryerson Consolidated? Before you answer that," he said, "how is your father? Does he still insist on staying at the farm?"

"He's fine," Matt said, and it was true. Patrick Farrell had been sober for eleven years. "I finally convinced him to sell the farm and move to the city. He'll be staying with me for a few weeks, then he's going to visit my sister. I have to go out to the farm later this month and pack up family mementos. He doesn't have the heart to do it."

The vast ballroom of the hotel with its soaring marble columns, glittering crystal chandeliers, and magnificent vaulted ceiling was always splendid, but tonight Meredith thought it was especially wonderful. The decorations committee had turned it into a gorgeous winter fairyland, with white gazebos blanketed in artificial snow and filled with red roses and holly. Near the center of the room, a larger gazebo with roses trailing up its columns and "snowbanks" at its sides was occupied by an orchestra playing a salute to Rodgers and Hart. Fountains bearded with glittering artificial icicles spouted geysers of sparkling champagne while waiters circulated among the guests, offering hors d'oeuvres to those who didn't wish to help themselves from the giant silver-plated tiers laden with food.

Tonight, the lavishness of the decorations were enhanced by the glitter of jeweled silks and brocaded velvets, as the patrons of the opera, who'd turned out en masse, paused in their laughing conversations to pose for photographers from the media or strolled about, greeting friends. Near the center of the room, Meredith stood beside Parker, his hand possessively at her waist, accepting good wishes from friends and acquaintances who'd read about their engagement. When the last group drifted away, Meredith looked at Parker, her face lit up with sudden laughter.

"What's so funny?" he asked with a tender smile.

"The song the orchestra is playing," she explained. "It's the same one we danced to when I was thirteen." When he looked puzzled, she added, "At Miss Eppingham's party at the Drake Hotel."

Parker's expression cleared and he grinned at the memory. "Ah, yes— Miss Eppingham's mandatory night of misery."

"It was miserable," Meredith agreed. "I dropped my purse, and bumped your head, and stepped all over your feet while we danced."

"You dropped your purse, and we bumped heads," he said with the same gentle sensitivity to her feelings that she'd come to love, "but you did not step on my feet. You were adorable that night. In fact, that was the first night I actually noticed what amazing eyes you have," he continued with a reminiscent smile. "You looked up at me with the oddest, most intent expression—"

Meredith burst out laughing. "I was probably considering the best way to propose to you!"

He grinned, his arm tightening around her. "Really?"

"Absolutely." Her smile wavered when she noticed a gossip columnist bearing down on them. "Parker," she said quickly, "I'm going up to the lounge for a few minutes. Sally Mansfield is headed this way, and I don't want to talk to her until I find out on Monday who at Bancroft's told her that nonsense about Bancroft's celebrating our wedding with a national sale.

"The person who did it will have to ask her to print a retraction,"

Meredith said with finality as she reluctantly pulled away from his encompassing arm, "because there isn't going to be any such sale. Please watch for Lisa," she added as she started toward the grand staircase that led up to the mezzanine. "She should have been here long ago."

"We timed it perfectly, Matt," Stanton said as Matt lifted the fur coat off Alicia's shoulders and handed it to the coat-check girl stationed off the ballroom. Matt heard him, but his attention was momentarily diverted by the daring expanse of creamy flesh exposed by the wide, plunging neckline of Alicia's black velvet sheath. "That's quite a gown," he told her, his expression warm with amusement and frank desire.

She held his gaze, her head tipped back, a knowing smile curving her vermilion lips. "You are the only man," she softly told him, "who can make 'that's quite a gown' sound like an irresistible invitation to join you in bed for at least a week."

Matt chuckled at that as they started toward the dazzling lights and noisy clamor of the party. Ahead, he saw two photographers snapping pictures and a television crew roaming through the crowd, and he braced himself for the inevitable descent of the press.

"Was it?" Alicia asked as soon as her father stopped to talk to friends.

"Was it what?" Matt said, pausing to take two glasses of champagne from the tray of a passing waiter.

"An invitation for a week of glorious fucking like the one we had two months ago?"

"Alicia," Matt admonished her mildly, nodding politely to two men he knew, "behave yourself." He would have started forward, but Alicia remained stubbornly where she was, studying him with deepening intensity. "Why haven't you ever married?"

"Let's discuss that some other time."

"I tried the last two times we were together, but you evaded it."

Annoyed with her obstinacy, her topic, and her timing, Matt put his hand beneath her black-gloved arm and guided her off to the side. "I gather," he told her, "that you intend to discuss it here and now."

"I do," she said, meeting his gaze, chin proudly high.

"What's on your mind?"

"Marriage."

He paused and Alicia saw the sudden chill in his eyes, but what he said was even more cutting than his expression: "To whom?"

Stung by his deliberate insult and furious with her tactical blunder in trying to force his hand, she glared at his implacable expression, and then the tension drained from her. "I suppose I deserved that," she admitted.

"No," Matt said shortly, angry with his own excessive tactlessness, "You didn't."

Alicia stared at him, confused, wary, and then she smiled a little. "At least we know where we stand—for now."

His answering smile was brief, cool, and distinctly unencouraging. With a sigh Alicia tucked her hand in the crook of his arm. "You are," she told him bluntly as he led her forward, "the *hardest* man I've ever met!" Trying to inject some levity into the moment, she sent him a seductive sideways glance and added truthfully, "Physically, as well as emotionally, of course."

Lisa shoved her engraved invitation at the doorman stationed outside the ballroom. Stopping just long enough to pull off her coat and check it, she scanned the milling throng, looking for Parker or Meredith. Spotting Parker's blond head near the bandstand, she headed toward him, brushing past Alicia Avery, who was strolling slowly beside a very tall, dark-haired, broad-shouldered man whose profile seemed vaguely familiar. As Lisa wended her way through the crowd, men turned to gaze appreciatively at the figure she presented—a willowy redhead clad in billowing red satin lounge pants and a black velvet jacket, with a beaded black band tied around her forehead—an utterly incongruous and inappropriate ensemble that some-how—on Lisa—looked exactly right.

Other men thought that, but not Parker. "Hi," she said, coming up beside him as he filled his glass from one of the champagne fountains.

He turned, his gaze narrowing with disapproval on her clothes, and Lisa bridled at his unvoiced criticism. "Oh, no!" she speculated dramatically, looking at his handsome, glowering face with sham alarm. "Has the prime rate gone up again?"

His irate gaze jerked from the cleavage exposed by her jacket to her taunting expression. "Why don't you dress like other women?" he demanded.

"I don't know," Lisa said, pausing as if to think it over, then with a bright smile, she announced, "It's probably the same stroke of perversity that makes you enjoy foreclosing on widows and orphans. Where's Meredith?"

"In the ladies' lounge."

Having thus indulged in the sort of uncharacteristic rudeness that had festered between both of them for years, they both stoically sought to avoid looking at each other by focusing their attention on the crowd. Simultane-ously, a subdued commotion erupted off to their right, and they both looked in that direction, watching as television crews and newspaper reporters, who'd been wandering among the guests or standing on the sidelines, suddenly galvanized into action, rushing toward their prey. Flashes from cameras started going off, and Lisa leaned farther to the right, catching a glimpse of the press mobbing the dark-haired man she'd noticed with Alicia Avery. Television cameras were aiming at his face as he escorted her forward through the explosion of flashbulbs and the throng of reporters waving microphones at him. "Who is that?" she asked, glancing uncertainly at Parker.

"I can't see—" Parker began, watching the uproar with mild interest, but when the crowd parted, he tensed. "It's Farrell."

The last name, combined with the full view of Farrell's tanned face, was enough to tell Lisa that the man with Alicia was Meredith's faithless, heartless former husband. Hostility exploded inside her as she watched him stop to answer questions being called out to him by reporters, while Alicia Avery hung on his arm, smiling for the photographers. For a long moment Lisa stood there, remembering the anguish he'd caused Meredith and contemplating the wholly satisfying idea of marching up to him in front of the fawning media and calling him a son of a bitch right to his face! Meredith wouldn't like that, she knew; Meredith hated scenes and, besides, no one but Parker and Lisa knew that Meredith and he had ever been involved in any way. Meredith! The thought hit her at the same instant it struck Parker, wiping the bland, civilized expression from his own face as he watched Farrell. "Did Meredith know he was going to be here?" she gasped at the same instant Parker clasped her arm and ordered, "Find Meredith and warn her that Farrell's here."

As Lisa sidled and shoved her way into the crowd, Matthew Farrell's name was already passing through them like a whispered chant. He'd broken away from the press, except for Sally Mansfield, who was standing behind him as he spoke with Stanton Avery near the foot of the grand staircase. Keeping one eye on Farrell so she could warn Meredith where he was, and her other eye on the balcony, Lisa plunged forward, then stopped in helpless dismay as Meredith suddenly appeared and started down the staircase.

Since she couldn't get to her before she reached the bottom step and passed by Farrell, Lisa stood still, taking grim satisfaction in the fact that Meredith had never looked more stunning than she did right now—when her lousy ex-husband was about to see her for the first time in eleven years! In complete defiance of the current slinky fashions, Meredith was wearing a full-skirted strapless gown of shimmering white satin with a tightly fitted bodice sewn with seed pearls and strewn with white sequins and tiny crystals. At her throat was a magnificent ruby and diamond necklace that was either a gift from Parker, which Lisa was inclined to doubt, or on loan from the estate jewelry department of Bancroft's, which Lisa figured was more likely.

Partway down the staircase, Meredith stopped to speak to an elderly couple, and Lisa held her breath. Parker stepped up beside her, his gaze shifting restlessly from Farrell to Sally Mansfield to Meredith.

His attention on what Stanton was saying to him, Matt looked around for Alicia, who'd gone to the powder room, and someone called his name— or what sounded like his name. Turning his head, he looked for the source of the voice, looked higher, toward the staircase. . . . And he froze. With his champagne glass arrested halfway to his mouth, Matt stared at the woman on the staircase who had been a girl, and his wife, the last time he saw her. And at that moment he understood why the media loved to compare her to a young Grace Kelly. With her blond hair caught up in an elegant cluster at the nape, entwined with small white roses, Meredith Bancroft was a breathtakingly beautiful image of breeding and serenity. In the years since he'd last seen her, her figure had ripened, and her delicately boned face had acquired a radiance that was mesmerizing. Matt's shock vanished as quickly as it had hit him, and he managed to drink his champagne and nod at whatever Stanton was saying to him, but he continued to study the lush beauty on the staircase—only now it was with the detached interest of an expert examining a piece of art he already knows is flawed and a fake.

Except that even he could not entirely harden his heart against her as she stood there, listening to an older couple who were stopping her from descending the stairs. She had always gotten along well with people much older than she was, Matt remembered, thinking of the night she had taken him under her wing at her country club, and his heart softened yet more. He searched for signs of the brittle woman executive in her, but what he saw was an entrancing smile, shining turquoise eyes, and an unexpected aura of being—he searched his mind for the word and all he could think of was *untouched*. Perhaps it was the virginal white she wore, or the fact that while most of the other women were wearing seductive gowns that were slashed down to the navel and up to the thigh, Meredith had bared only her shoulders, and she *still* managed to look more provocative than they. Provocative and regal and unattainable.

Within him he felt the last vestiges of bitterness subside. More than beauty, there was a gentleness about her that he'd forgotten—a gentleness that had to have been overridden by nothing less than stark terror in order for her to have gone through with that abortion. She had been so young when she was forced to marry him, Matt thought now, and she hadn't really known him at all. No doubt she expected to end up living in some dirty town like Edmunton, married to a drunk—as Matt's father had been—and trying to raise their child. Her father would have damned sure tried to convince her that was going to happen; he'd have done anything to put an end to her alliance with a nobody—including convincing her to have an abortion and divorce him. Matt had realized all that shortly after their divorce. Unlike her father, Meredith had never been a snob, not really. Well-bred and carefully raised, yes, but never actually such a complete snob that she'd have done those things to Matt and their child. Fear and youth and pressure from her domineering father had done that. He realized that now. After eleven years it had taken seeing her again to realize what she had been. And what she still was.

"Beautiful, isn't she?" Stanton said, nudging Matt.

"Very."

"Come with me, I'll introduce you to her and her fiancé. I need to speak to her fiancé anyway. By the way, you should get to know Parker—he controls one of the biggest banks in Chicago."

Matt hesitated, and then he nodded. Meredith and he were bound to see each other at all sorts of social functions; it seemed best to get past the hurdle of the first confrontation now rather than later. At least this time, when he was introduced to her, he wouldn't have need to feel like a social leper.

Scanning the crowd for Parker, Meredith descended the last step, then stopped at the sound of Stanton Avery's bluff, jovial voice beside her. "Meredith," he said, putting a detaining hand on her arm, "I'd like to introduce you to someone."

She was already smiling, already beginning to extend her hand as she shifted her gaze from Stanton's grin to a very tall man's tanned throat and then to his face. *Matthew Farrell's face.* Mind reeling, stomach churning, she heard Avery's voice as if in a tunnel, saying, "This is my friend, Matt Farrell. . . ." And she saw the man who had let her lie alone in the hospital when she lost his baby, then sent her a telegram telling her to get a divorce. Now he was smiling down at her—that same, unforgettable, intimate, charming, *loathsome* smile, while he reached out to take her hand, and something inside of Meredith burst. She jerked her hand out of Matt's reach, looked him over with freezing contempt, and turned to Stanton Avery. "You really ought to be more selective about your friends, Mr. Avery," she said with cool hauteur. "Excuse me." Turning her back, Meredith walked away, leaving behind her a fascinated Sally Mansfield, a stunned Stanton Avery, and an infuriated Matthew Farrell.

It was three A.M. before the last of Meredith and Parker's guests left Meredith's apartment, leaving only the two of them with her father. "You shouldn't be up so late," Meredith told him as she sank down on a chintz-covered Queen Anne chair. Even now, hours after confronting Matthew Farrell, she still shook inside when she thought of it, only now it was anger with herself that haunted her—that, and the savage fury in his eyes when she left him standing there with his hand outstretched to her, looking like a fool.

"You know perfectly well why I'm still here," Philip said, pouring himself a glass of sherry. He hadn't learned of Meredith's meeting with Farrell until an hour ago when Parker told him, and he obviously intended to hear the details.

"Don't drink that. The doctors said you shouldn't."

"Damn the doctors, I want to know what Farrell said to you. Parker tells me you cut Farrell dead."

"He didn't have a chance to say a word to me," Meredith replied, and she told him exactly what had transpired. When she was finished, she watched in frustrated silence as he swallowed down the forbidden sherry— an aging, impressive, silver-haired man in a custom-tailored tuxedo. He had dominated and manipulated her for most of her life, until she had finally found the courage and fortitude to withstand the force of his iron will and volcanic temper. And despite all that, she loved him and worried about him. He was all the family she had, and his face was drawn from illness and fatigue. As soon as his leave of absence was arranged he was taking an extended cruise, and his doctor had made him promise that he'd neither worry about Bancroft & Company, world affairs, or anything whatsoever. For the six weeks he was away, he wasn't to watch the news, read the paper, or do anything that wasn't completely frivolous and restful. Tearing her gaze from her father, she looked at Parker and said, "I wish you hadn't told my father what happened tonight. It wasn't necessary."

Sighing, Parker leaned back in his chair and reluctantly told her of something she hadn't known. "Meredith, Sally Mansfield saw—and probably heard—the whole confrontation. We'll be lucky if everyone doesn't read about it in her column tomorrow."

"I hope she prints it," Philip said.

"I don't," Parker countered, ignoring Philip's glower with his usual unruffled calm. "I don't want people asking questions about *why* Meredith snubbed him."

Leaning her head back, Meredith let out a ragged sigh and closed her eyes. "If I'd had time to think, I wouldn't have done it—not so openly, anyway."

"Several of our friends were asking about it already tonight," Parker said. "We'll have to think of some explanation," he began, but Meredith interrupted him.

"Please," she said wearily, "not tonight. I, for one, would like to go to bed."

"You're right," Parker said, and stood up, giving Philip little choice except to leave with him.

18

*I*t was nearly noon by the time Meredith got out of the shower. Clad in burgundy wool slacks and a sweater, with her hair pulled up into a ponytail, she wandered into the living room and looked with renewed dismay at the Sunday *Tribune* she'd flung onto the sofa after seeing Sally Mansfield's column. The very first item Sally had written was about last night's fiasco:

> Women all over the world seem to be falling prey to Matthew Farrell's legendary charm, but our own Meredith Bancroft is certainly immune to him. At the opera benefit ball Saturday night, she gave him what would have been called in olden days the "cut direct." Our lovely Meredith, who is reputedly gracious to one and all, refused to shake Matthew Farrell's hand. One wonders why.

Too tense to work and too weary to go out, Meredith stood in the center of the lovely room, looking at the antique tables and chairs as if they were as unfamiliar to her as her own inner turmoil. The Persian carpet beneath her feet was patterned in pale green and rose on a cream background. Everything was exactly as she'd wanted it, from the chintz draperies pulled back from the wide windows to the ornate French desk she'd found at an auction in New York. This apartment, with its view of the city, had been her only real extravagance—this and the BMW she'd bought five years earlier. Today the room seemed jumbled and unfamiliar, exactly as her thoughts were.

Abandoning the notion of working for a while, she walked into the kitchen and poured a cup of coffee. With her back against the counter, she sipped her coffee, waiting for the feeling of unreality to vanish, avoiding thinking about last night until her head cleared. With a fingernail she idly traced the vines that wound through the ceramic tiles on the countertop. Plants hung from the ceiling over the breakfast nook, basking in the sunlight coming through the windows. Today the sky was overcast. So was she. The hot, fresh coffee was doing more to erase the numbness in her mind than the shower had, and as full awareness returned, she could hardly bear the angry shame she felt for her behavior last night. Unlike Parker and her father, Meredith didn't regret what she had done because of a fear about the repercussions of Sally Mansfield's column. What hammered at her was the fact that she had lost control—no, that she had lost her mind! Years ago she had forced herself to stop blaming Matthew Farrell, not so much for his sake but for her own, because the fury and pain she'd felt at his betrayal had been more than she could endure. A year after her miscarriage, she had made herself think over, objectively, all that had happened between them; she had struggled and worked for that objectivity, and when she'd found it, she'd clung to it until it was a part of her.

Objectivity—and a psychologist she'd talked to in college—had enabled her to understand that what had happened to them had been inevitable. They'd been forced to marry each other, and except for the child they'd conceived together, they did not have one single other reason to stay married. They'd had nothing in common, nor would they ever have had. Matt had been callous in the way he'd ignored her plea to come home from South America when she miscarried, and more callous in his immediate demand for a divorce. But beneath his surface charm, he'd *always* been invulnerable and uncompromising. How could he be otherwise, given his background? He'd had to fight his way through life, coping with a drunken father, a young sister, a job in the steel mills, and all the rest. If he weren't tough, and hard, and consumed with self-purpose, he'd never have made it out of there. When he treated Meredith with such painful indifference eleven years ago, he was simply being what he was: hard and cold and tough. He'd done his duty and married her, prompted perhaps partially by greed. He'd soon realized Meredith had no money of her own and, when she lost the baby, he had no further reason to remain married to her. He had none of her values, and if they'd stayed married, he'd have broken her heart. She'd come to understand all that—or at least she'd thought she had. And yet, last night, for one horrible, turbulent moment she'd lost her objectivity and her composure. That should never have happened, *wouldn't* have happened if she'd had just a few minutes warning before she had to confront him—or if he hadn't smiled at her in that warm, familiar, intimate way! Her hand had actually itched to slap that phony smile off his face.

What she'd said to Stanton had been what she felt; what dismayed her most were the uncontrollable, wrenching feelings that had made her say it. And what she feared was that it might happen again. But even as the thought occurred to her, she realized there was no possibility of that. Except for resenting the fact that Matt had become more handsome, and had acquired more superficial charm than any man with his utter lack of scruples had a right to, she felt nothing now. Evidently, the explosion of emotions she'd felt last night had been the last feeble eruption from a dead volcano.

Now that she'd reasoned her way through it, Meredith felt considerably better. Pouring another cup of coffee, she carried it into the living room and sat down at her desk to work. Her beautiful apartment once again felt orderly and familiar and serene—just like her mind. She glanced at the telephone on her desk, and for one absurd instant she felt an impulse to call Matt Farrell and do what good breeding dictated: apologize for making a scene. She dismissed that nonsensical impulse with a light shrug as she opened her briefcase and took out the financial data for the Houston store. Matthew Farrell hadn't given a damn about what she thought or what she did when they were married. Therefore, he certainly wouldn't care what she did last night. Besides, he was so egotistical and so inured, nothing could hurt or offend him.

19

At exactly ten o'clock on Monday morning, Peter Vanderwild presented himself to Miss Stern, whom he'd privately nicknamed "The Sphinx," then he waited like an irritated supplicant for her to acknowledge him. Not until she was damned good and ready did she stop typing and aim her basilisk gaze at him. "I have an appointment to see Mr. Farrell at ten o'clock," he informed her.

"Mr. Farrell is in a meeting. He will see you in fifteen minutes."

"Do you think I should wait?"

"Only if you have nothing whatsoever to do for the next fifteen minutes," she replied frostily.

Dismissed like a recalcitrant schoolboy, Peter strode stiffly to the elevator and returned to his office. That seemed infinitely wiser than remaining on the sixtieth floor and thus proving to her he had nothing to do for fifteen minutes. At 10:15 Miss Stern motioned him into the inner sanctum while three of Haskell's vice presidents were still filing out of it, but before Peter could open his mouth, the phone on Matt Farrell's desk rang.

"Sit down, Peter," Matt said. "I'll be with you in a minute." With the phone at his ear, Matt opened the file on potential acquisitions that Peter had left with him. All of them were corporations that owned large blocks of commercial real estate, and Matt had reviewed each one over the weekend. He was pleased with several of Peter's choices, impressed by the extraordinary thoroughness of his research, and slightly stunned by some of his recommendations. When he hung up the phone, he leaned back in his chair and concentrated all his attention on Peter. "What do you particularly like about the Atlanta company?"

"Several things," Peter replied, startled by the abruptness of the question. "Their properties are mostly new commercial mid-rise buildings with a high percentage of occupancy. Nearly all their tenants are established corporations with long-term leases, and all the buildings are extremely well maintained and managed. I saw that myself when I flew to Atlanta to look them over."

"What about the Chicago company?"

"They're into high-rent residential buildings in prime locations here and their profits are excellent."

Matt's gaze narrowed on the younger man as he bluntly pointed out, "From what I could see in this file, many of their buildings are over thirty years old. The cost of renovating and repairs will begin eating into those excellent profits in seven to ten years."

"I took that into account when I prepared that profit forecast in the file," Peter said. "Also, the land those buildings are sitting on will always be worth a fortune."

Satisfied, Matt nodded and opened the next file. It was this recommendation that had made him wonder if Peter's acclaimed genius might not have been overrated, along with his common sense. Frowning at Vanderwild over the top of the folder, he said, "What made you consider this Houston company?"

"If Houston continues its economic recovery, property values are going to soar and—"

"I realize that," Matt interrupted impatiently. "What I want to know is why you would recommend we consider acquiring Thorp Development.

Everybody who reads *The Wall Street Journal* knows that company has been for sale for two years, and they know *why* it hasn't sold: It's ridiculously over-priced and it's badly managed."

Feeling as if the chair he was sitting in had suddenly become electrified, Peter cleared his throat and doggedly persevered. "You're right, but if you'll bear with me a moment, you might change your opinion about its desirability." When Farrell nodded curtly, Peter plowed ahead: "Thorp Development is owned by two brothers who inherited it ten years ago when their father died. Since they got control of the company, they've made a lot of poor investments, and to do that, they've mortgaged most of the properties their father had acquired over the years. As a result, they're in debt up to their corporate ears to Continental City Trust in Houston. The two brothers can't stand each other, and they can't agree on anything. For the past two years one brother has been trying to sell off the entire company with all its assets in a single bloc, while the other brother wanted to split up the assets and sell them off in pieces to anyone who'll buy one. Now, however, they don't have any choice except to do the latter, and do it quick, because Continental is about to start foreclosing."

"How do you know all this?" Matt asked.

"When I flew to Houston in October to visit my sister, I decided to look Thorp over and check out some of their properties while I was there. I got the name of their banker, Charles Collins, from Max Thorp, and I called him when I got back here. Collins was desperately eager to 'help' Thorp find a buyer, and he talked his head off. In the course of our conversation, I began to suspect that the reason for his eagerness might be that he needs to get Thorp's loans off his books. He called me last Thursday and told me Thorp was eager to work a deal with us and that they'd sell out very cheap. He urged me to reconsider and make them an offer. If we move quickly, I figure we can pick up any of Thorp's properties for the amount of the mortgages on them, rather than their actual value, because Collins is about to foreclose and Thorp obviously knows it."

"What makes you think he's about to foreclose?"

Peter smiled a little. "I called a banker friend of mine in Dallas and asked if he knew Collins at Continental City Trust. He said he did, and he made a friendly phone call to Collins, ostensibly to commiserate about the sad state of banking in Texas. Collins told *him* the bank examiners were pressuring him to foreclose on several large, delinquent loans—including the ones to Thorp." Peter paused in silent triumph, waiting for some sort of compliment from his dispassionate boss for the thoroughness and outcome of his research; what he got was a brief smile and an almost imperceptible nod of approval. It felt as if God had just blessed him. Buoyed up beyond all bounds of reason by that, Peter leaned forward in his chair. "Are you interested in hearing about some of the properties Thorp owns? A couple of them are *prime* parcels that could be developed and sold for a fortune."

"I'm listening," Matt said, though he wasn't nearly as interested in buying and developing raw land as he was in buying commercial buildings.

"The best of Thorp's properties is a very desirable fifteen-acre parcel of land two blocks from The Galleria which is an enormous and deluxe shopping center with its own hotels. Neiman-Marcus is in the Galleria complex; Saks Fifth Avenue and a lot of exclusive designer boutiques are close by, and the expressway is within sight. Thorp's property is between the two shopping complexes, and it's the perfect site for another top-quality department store and mall."

"I've seen the area when I was there on business," Matt put in.

"Then you surely know what a bargain it would be if we could buy that piece of land for the twenty million Thorp owes on it. We could either develop it ourselves or hold on to the land and sell it later for a nice profit. Five years ago, it was worth $40 million. If Houston continues its economic recovery, it'll be worth that soon."

Matt was jotting notes in the Thorp file and waiting for a break in Peter's recitation so that he could explain that he preferred that Intercorp invest in commercial buildings, when Peter added, "If you're interested, we'd have to move quickly because both Thorp and Collins indicated they're expecting an offer for that property at any hour. I thought they were trying to hustle me until they named names. Evidently Bancroft & Company, here in Chicago, is hot for the land, and no wonder! There's nowhere else in Houston like it. Hell, we could grab it for twenty million and turn around in a few months and sell it to Bancroft's for twenty-five to thirty million, which is what it's actually worth." Peter's voice trailed off, because Matthew Farrell's head had snapped up and he was staring at Peter with a very strange expression on his face.

"What did you say?" he demanded.

"I said that Bancroft & Company plans to buy the land," Peter said, wary of that cold, calculating, ominous look in Farrell's eyes. Thinking Farrell wanted more information, he added quickly, "Bancroft's is like Bloomingdale's or Neiman-Marcus—old, dignified stores with a predominantly upper-class clientele. They've begun expanding into—"

"I'm familiar with Bancroft's," Matt said tightly. His gaze shifted to the file on Thorp and he studied the appraisal on the Houston land with heightened interest. He saw the figures on the appraisal documents, and he realized the land was a bargain with a huge potential for profit. But profit wasn't on his mind right now. With renewed anger, he was thinking of Meredith's actions Saturday night.

"Buy it," he said softly.

"But don't you want to hear about some of the other properties?"

"I'm not interested in anything except the piece of property that Bancroft's wants. Tell legal to draw up an offer, contingent on our own appraiser agreeing with Thorp's appraiser on the value of the land. Take it to Houston tomorrow and present it to Thorp yourself."

"An offer?" Peter almost stammered. "For how much?"

"Offer fifteen million, and give them twenty-four hours to sign the contract or we'll walk. They'll counter immediately with twenty-five. Settle at twenty, and tell them we want ownership of the property within three weeks or the deal is off."

"I really don't think—"

"There's another contingency. If Thorp accepts our offer, they are to keep the entire transaction completely confidential. No one is to know we're buying that land until after the sale is consummated. Tell legal to include all that in the contract, along with the other usual contingencies."

Suddenly Peter felt uneasy. In the past, when Farrell had invested in or bought companies Peter had recommended, he hadn't done it on Peter's recommendations alone. Far from it. He'd checked things out himself and taken precautions. This time, however, if something went wrong, Peter would be solely and entirely held to blame. "Mr. Farrell, I really don't think—"

"Peter," Matt interrupted with silky finality. "Buy the goddamned property."

Nodding, Peter stood up, but his unease was growing by the moment.

"Phone Art Simpson in our legal department in California, give him the contingencies, and tell him I want the contracts here tomorrow. When they arrive, bring them in and we'll discuss the next steps."

When Vanderwild left, Matt turned in his chair and looked out the windows. Obviously, Meredith still thought of him as an inferior lowlife, beneath her contempt, which was her right to do. It was also her right to make her feelings clear to everyone who read the Chicago newspapers, which was what she'd done. However, exercising those rights was going to cost her about ten million dollars—the additional price she was going to have to pay Intercorp for the land she wanted in Houston.

20

*M*r. Farrell said I was to bring these contracts to him as soon as they arrived," Peter informed Miss Stern in an assertive tone, late the following afternoon.

"In that case," she replied with thin gray brows raised, "I would suggest you do exactly that."

Irritated at having lost yet another skirmish with her, Peter swung on his heel, knocked on the rosewood door of Matt Farrell's office, and opened it. In Peter's desperation to dissuade Farrell from acting precipitously on the Houston land, he failed to notice that Tom Anderson was at the far end of the large office, studying a painting that had just been hung on the wall. "Mr. Farrell," Peter began, "I have to tell you that I'm extremely uneasy about this Thorp deal."

"Do you have the contracts?"

"Yes, I do." Reluctantly, Peter handed the contracts to him. "But will you at least listen to what I have to say?"

Farrell nodded to one of the burgundy suede chairs that made a semi-circle in front of his desk. "Sit down, while I look these over, and then you can have your say."

In nervous silence, Peter watched him reading the long, complex documents that committed Intercorp to a cash outlay of millions of dollars without a trace of expression on his face. Suddenly, Peter wondered if the man was ever susceptible to such human weaknesses as doubt or fear or regret or any other strong emotion.

In the year since Peter had joined Intercorp, he'd seen Matt Farrell decide he wanted to accomplish something; when he did, he could untangle complications that had kept his staff running in circles, override any remaining obstacles, and have the deal closed in a matter of a week or two. When motivated to achieve an objective, he plowed through any obstacles in his path, human or corporate, like a deadly tornado—with awesome force and complete lack of emotion.

The other men who worked closely with Farrell as part of his "reorganization team" were better at hiding their awe and uncertainty about their employer than Peter was, but Peter sensed they felt as he did. Two nights ago they'd all worked until ten o'clock, and they'd invited Peter to join them for a late dinner. Tom Anderson had decided at the last minute to continue working. During that dinner it became obvious to Peter for the first time that not one of those four men knew Farrell much better than he himself did. Only Tom Anderson seemed to be privileged with Farrell's trust and friendship, though no one knew how he'd earned it.

His speculations came to an abrupt end as Farrell made two changes to the contracts, initialed them, signed his name at the bottom, and slid the documents across his desk to Peter. "These are all right as amended. What's your problem with the deal?"

"There are a couple of them, Mr. Farrell," Peter replied, straightening in his chair and trying to recover his earlier assertive attitude. "In the first place, I have the feeling you're going ahead with this deal because I led you to believe that we could make a quick, easy profit by reselling the land to Bancroft & Company. Yesterday, I thought that was a virtual sure thing, but I've spent the last day and a half researching Bancroft's operation, going over their financial statements, and I've also made some phone calls to some friends of mine on Wall Street. Last I talked to someone who knows Philip and Meredith Bancroft personally—"

"And?" Farrell demanded impassively.

"And now I'm not completely confident Bancroft & Company will be financially able to buy the Houston land. Based on everything I found out, I think they're heading for big trouble."

"What sort of trouble?"

"It's rather a long explanation, and I can only speculate, based on the facts and on a hunch I have."

Instead of berating him for not getting directly to the point, which Peter half expected, Farrell said, "Go on."

The two small words of encouragement banished Peter's nervous uncertainty, and he became the confident, capable investment brain they'd written up in the business magazines when he was still at Harvard. "All right, here's the overall picture: Until a few years ago, Bancroft's had a couple of stores in the Chicago area, and the company was virtually stagnant. Their marketing techniques were antiquated, their management team relied too much on the 'prestige' of their name, and they, like the dinosaur, were on the road to extinction. Philip Bancroft, who's still president, ran the stores as his father had run them—like a family dynasty that didn't need to respond to economic trends. Then along came his daughter, Meredith. Instead of going to some finishing school and devoting herself to showing off for the society pages, she decides that she wants to take her rightful place in Bancroft's hierarchy. She goes to college, majors in retailing, graduates summa cum laude, and gets her master's degree—none of which thrills her father, who tries to turn her off on the idea of working for Bancroft's by making her start at the store as a clerk in the lingerie department."

Pausing for a moment, Peter explained, "I'm giving you all this background so that you'll have a handle on who's running the store—literally."

"Go on," Farrell said, but he sounded bored, and he picked up a report on his desk and began reading it.

"During the next few years," Peter continued doggedly, "Miss Bancroft works her way up through the ranks and along the way she acquires a hell of a good firsthand grasp of everything involved in retailing. When she's promoted into merchandising, she starts pushing for Bancroft's to market its own private-label brands—a highly profitable move which they should have made long before. When that idea yields big profits, Papa shifts her into furniture merchandising which had been a losing proposition for the store. Instead of failing there, she pushes for a special 'museum antique' section, which gets written up in all the newspapers and brings shoppers into the store to ogle the antiques, which are on loan from museums. While they're there, the shoppers naturally wander over to the regular furniture department, and suddenly they're spending their furniture money at Bancroft's instead of at the suburban furniture stores.

"Papa then makes her manager of public relations, which had been a meaningless position that involved little more than approving an occasional donation to some charity and supervising the annual Christmas pageant in the auditorium. Miss Bancroft promptly set about conceiving more annual special events to bring shoppers into the store—but not just the ordinary ones like fashion shows. She also used the family's social connections with the symphony, the opera, the art museum, etc. For example, she got the Chicago Art Museum to move an exhibit to the store, and she talked the ballet into performing the *Nutcracker* during the Christmas season in the store's auditorium. Naturally, all that caused an explosion of media coverage, which, in turn, created an escalated awareness of Bancroft & Company with Chicagoans and gave the store an even more elite image. Shoppers began coming to the store in record numbers, and her father switched her over to fashion merchandising, which was the next place she excelled. There, her success probably owed itself as much to her appearance as to any particular fashion talent. I've seen newspaper clippings of her and she's not only classy, she's stunning. Some of the European designers evidently thought so too, when she went over there to talk to them about letting Bancroft's handle their lines. One of them who'd let only Bergdorf Goodman handle his line evidently cut a deal with her—he agreed to let Bancroft's have it exclusively, on the condition that Miss Bancroft herself appear in his gowns. He then designed an entire collection for her to wear, which she was naturally photographed in at various society functions. The media and the public went wild when they saw her wearing his stuff, and women began to arrive in droves in Bancroft's designer departments. The European designer's profits soared, Bancroft's profits soared, and several other designers jumped on the bandwagon and pulled their lines from other stores to give them to Bancroft's."

Farrell sent him an impatient look over the top of the report he'd been reading. "Is there a point to all this?"

"I was coming to it right now: Miss Bancroft is a merchant, like her forebears, but her special talent is actually in expansion and forward planning, and that's what she heads now. Somehow, she managed to convince her father and Bancroft's board of directors, who are anything but progressive, to embark on an expansion program and open stores in other cities. To finance the opening of those stores, they needed to raise hundreds of millions of dollars, which they did in the usual way—they borrowed what they could from their bank, then they took the company public and sold shares on the New York Stock Exchange."

"What *difference* does all this make?" Farrell demanded shortly.

"It wouldn't make any difference were it not for two things, Mr. Farrell: they've expanded so quickly that they're in hock up to their ears, and they've been using most of their profits to open more stores. As a result, they don't have a lot of cash lying around to weather any major economic reversals. Frankly, I don't know how they intend to pay for the Houston land, or if they can. Secondly, there's been a rash of hostile takeovers lately with one department store chain swallowing up another. If somebody wanted to take over Bancroft's, they couldn't afford to put up a fight and win it. They're ripe for a takeover attempt. And," Peter stated, deepening his voice to emphasize the importance of what he was about to say, "I think somebody else has noticed that."

Instead of looking concerned, Peter watched an odd expression cross Farrell's face, an expression that might have been amusement or satisfaction. "Is that right?"

Peter nodded, slightly disconcerted by his strange reaction to what should have been alarming news. "I think somebody is already secretly starting to buy up all the shares in Bancroft's they can get their hands on, and they've been buying them up in blocks small enough not to alert Bancroft's or Wall Street or the SEC yet." Gesturing toward the three computer screens on the credenza behind the desk, Peter said, "May I?"

Farrell nodded and Peter got up and walked over to the credenza. The first two computers processed information from all of Intercorp's reporting divisions, and their screens were lit up with data that Farrell had evidently been looking at earlier. The third computer screen was blank, and Peter used it to key in the codes and requests that he used in his own office. An instant later, the Dow Jones average scrolled across the screen. Interrupting that display, Peter keyed in another set of requests and the screen lit up with the heading:

TRADING HISTORY:
BANCROFT & COMPANY TRADING CODE B&C•
NYSE•

"Look at this." Peter pointed to the columns of data on the screen. "Until six months ago, Bancroft's stock was pretty much where it had been for two years—selling at ten dollars a share. Until then, the average number of shares traded in a week was one hundred thousand. Now look," he said, moving his finger down the column on the left. "In the last six months it's been inching upward until it's now nearly twelve dollars a share, and the volume of shares traded has been hitting new highs about once a month."

He pressed another key, and the screen went dark, then he turned toward Farrell, frowning. "It's just a hunch, but I think someone—some entity—may be trying to acquire control of the company."

Matt stood up, putting an abrupt and permanent end to the discussion. "Either that, or investors simply think B&C is a good long-term investment. We'll proceed with the purchase of the Houston property."

Peter, realizing he was dismissed, had no choice but to pick up the signed contract on the desk and do as he was instructed. "Mr. Farrell," he said hesitantly, "I've been wondering why you're sending me to Houston to handle these negotiations. It's out of my line—"

"It shouldn't be a difficult deal to close," Matt said with a tentative, reassuring smile. "And it will broaden your experience. As I recall, that was part of the reason you gave for wanting to join Intercorp."

"Yes, sir, it was," Peter replied, but the burst of pride he felt at Farrell's obvious confidence in him to handle things took an awful blow when Farrell added, as Peter headed for the door, "Don't bungle it, Peter."

"I won't," Peter assured him, but he was shaken by the unspoken warning he'd heard in Farrell's voice.

Tom Anderson, who'd been quietly standing near the windows through-out Vanderwild's dissertation, spoke up as soon as he left. "Matt," he said with a chuckle as he returned to the chair he'd vacated in front of Matt's desk, "You scare the hell out of that kid."

"That kid," Matt pointed out dryly, "has an I.Q. of one sixty-five, and he's already made Intercorp several million dollars. He's proving to be an excellent investment."

"And is that land in Houston an excellent investment too?"

"I think it is."

"Good," Tom replied, sitting down and stretching his long legs out in front of him. "Because I'd hate to think you were spending a fortune just to retaliate against some society dame who insulted you in front of a reporter."

"Why would you leap to a conclusion like that?" Matt asked, but there was a gleam of sardonic amusement in his eye.

"I dunno. Sunday, I just happened to read in the paper that a chick named Bancroft gave you the cold shoulder at the opera. And tonight, here you are, signing a contract to buy something she wants for herself. Tell me something—how much is that land going to cost Intercorp?"

"Twenty million, probably."

"And how much is it going to cost Ms. Bancroft to buy it from us?"

"A hell of a lot more."

"Matt," he drawled with deceptive casualness, "d'you remember the night eight years ago, when my divorce from Marilyn was final?"

Matt was surprised by the question, but he remembered the time well enough. A few months after Tom started working for him, Tom's wife sud-denly announced that she'd been having an affair and wanted a divorce. Too proud to plead and too crushed to fight, Tom had moved his things out of their house, but he'd believed until the day the divorce went through that she'd change her mind. On that day Tom hadn't come into work or tele-phoned, and at six o'clock that night, Matt understood why—Tom called from the police station, where he'd been taken that afternoon after being arrested for being drunk and disorderly.

"I don't remember much about that night," Matt admitted, "except that we got drunk together."

"I'd already gotten drunk," Tom corrected wryly, "then you bailed me out of jail, and we *both* got drunk together." Watching Matt closely, he con-tinued. "I have a hazy recollection that you commiserated with my misfor-tune that night, by ranting about some dame named Meredith who'd jilted you, or something. Except you didn't call her a dame, you called her a spoiled little bitch. At some point before I passed out, you and I drunkenly agreed that women whose names start with the letter M are no good for anyone."

"Your memory is obviously better than mine," Matt said evasively, but Tom had noticed the imperceptible tightening in Matt's jaw at the mention of her name, and he leapt to the instant and correct conclusion.

"So," he continued with a grin, "now that we've established that the Meredith that night is actually Meredith *Bancroft*, would you care to tell me what happened between you two to make you still hate each other?"

"No," Matt said. "I wouldn't." He stood up and walked over to the coffee table, where he'd laid out the engineering drawings for the Southville facility. "Let's finish our discussion about Southville."

🌿21

*T*raffic was backed up for blocks near Bancroft's corner. Crowds of shoppers huddled tightly in their coats rushed across the intersection, ignoring the DON'T WALK signal, their heads bent against the bitter wind that blasted across Lake Michigan and whirled through the downtown streets. Car horns blared and drivers cursed the pedestrians, who were causing them to miss their green light. In her black BMW, Meredith watched as droves of shoppers paused at Bancroft's windows and then went into the store. The weather had turned cold, and that always brought out the early shoppers who preferred to beat the Christmas rush. Today, however, her mind wasn't on the numbers of shoppers entering the store.

In twenty minutes she had to make a formal presentation to the board of directors on the Houston store, and although they'd already given a tentative nod to the project, she couldn't proceed any further and finalize arrangements without their formal approval this morning.

Four other women were gathered around Meredith's secretary's desk when Meredith got off the elevator on the fourteenth floor. Stopping at Phyllis's desk, she peered over their shoulders, half expecting to see another issue of *Playgirl* magazine like the one they'd huddled over last month. "What's up?" she asked. "Another male centerfold?"

"No, not that," Phyllis said as the other secretaries hastily disbanded and she followed Meredith into her office. Rolling her eyes in amusement, she explained, "Pam ordered another printout of her astrological forecast for next month. This one says true love is coming her way, along with fortune and fame."

Lifting her brows in shared amusement, Meredith said, "I thought that's what the last one said."

"It did. I told her for fifteen dollars, *I'd* do her next one." The two women regarded each other in laughing harmony, and then they switched to business. "You have a board of directors meeting in five minutes," Phyllis reminded her.

Meredith nodded and picked up the folder with her notes in it. "Is the architect's model in the boardroom?"

"Yes. And I got the projector set up for the slides."

"You're a complete jewel," Meredith said, and she meant it. With the folder in hand, she started for the door, then she turned and added, "Call Sam Green and ask him to be available to meet with me as soon as I finish with the board of directors. Tell him I'd like to go over the preliminary purchase contract he's drawn up for the Houston land. I want to get it to Thorp Development by the end of the week. With a little luck," Meredith added, "I'll have the board's approval on the Houston project by this afternoon."

Phyllis picked up the telephone on Meredith's desk to call the chief counsel and gave a thumbs-up sign. "Knock 'em dead," she said.

The boardroom was very much as it had been fifty years earlier; only now, in the age of glass and brass and chrome, there was a nostalgic grandeur about the immense room with its Oriental carpeting, the intricate molding on dark-paneled walls, and the English landscapes hanging in their baroque frames. Stretching down the center of the huge room was a massive carved mahogany table, thirty feet in length, with twenty ornately carved chairs upholstered in scarlet velvet arranged around it at precise intervals. In the center of the table was an enormous and elaborate antique sterling silver bowl filled with red and white roses. Beside it was a matching tea and coffee service with delicate Sèvres porcelain coffee cups rimmed in gold and hand-painted with tiny roses and vines. Silver pitchers, frosted from the ice water within them, had also been placed at intervals down the table.

The room, with its oversize, heavily carved furniture, had the atmosphere of a throne room, which Meredith often suspected was exactly what her grandfather had wanted when he commissioned the furnishings to be made a half century before. There were times when she couldn't decide whether the room was impressive or ugly, but either way, every time she entered it, she felt as if she were stepping into history. This morning, however, her thoughts were more on making history by opening another store than on feeling a part of past history. "Good morning, gentlemen," she said with a bright, businesslike smile at the twelve conservatively dressed men fanned around the table who had the power to accept or reject her proposal for the Houston project.

With the exception of Parker, whose smile was warm, and old Cyrus Fortell, whose smile was lecherous, there was a marked reticence in the chorus of polite "good mornings" that answered her greeting. Part of their reserve, Meredith knew, sprang from their awareness of the power and responsibility they held; part of it was due to the simple fact that she had repeatedly forced and cajoled them into investing Bancroft's profits into expansion rather than using it to pay large dividends to shareholders—including themselves. Most of all, however, they were restrained and guarded with her because she was an enigma and because they didn't know exactly how to deal with her. Although she was an executive vice president, she was not a member of the board, therefore they outranked her. On the other hand, she was a Bancroft—a direct descendant of the founder of the company—and entitled to be treated with a measure of respect. And yet her own father, who was both a Bancroft and a member of the board, treated her with curt tolerance and nothing more. It was no secret that he'd never wanted her to work for Bancroft & Company; it was also no secret that she'd excelled in every way, and that her contribution to the company had been great. As a result of all that, the board members were caught in a situation guaranteed to make successful, confident men become temperamental and brusque—uncertainty. And because Meredith was indirectly the cause of that unpleasant feeling for them, they reacted to her with frequent and unprovoked negativity.

Meredith understood all that, and she refused to let their unencouraging expressions ruffle her confidence as she took her place at the foot of the table where the projector had been set up, and wait for her father's permission to begin.

"Since Meredith is here," he said, his tone implying she was late and had kept them waiting, "I believe we can now get down to business."

Meredith waited through the interminable reading of the minutes of the last board meeting, but her attention was on the architectural scale model of the Houston store that Phyllis had wheeled in earlier. Looking at the magnificent Spanish-style mall the architect had designed with space for other shops in its enclosed courtyard, she felt her resolve harden and her confidence soar. Houston was the perfect place for this newest and largest member of Bancroft's growing family, and the proximity of the land to Houston's Galleria would ensure its success from the moment Bancroft's opened its doors. When the minutes had been accepted as read, Nolan Wilder, who was the board's chairman, formally stated that Meredith wished to present the final figures and plans for the Houston store for their approval.

Twelve perfectly groomed, masculine heads turned to her as she stood up and walked over to the slide projector. "Gentlemen," she began, "I gather you've all had ample opportunity to look over the architect's model?"

Ten of them nodded, her father glanced at the model, but Parker quietly regarded her with the half-proud, half-puzzled smile he usually wore whenever he watched her perform her job—as if he couldn't quite fathom how or why she insisted on doing it, but was pleased with how well she did it. His position as Bancroft's banker gave him his seat on the board, but Meredith knew she couldn't always count on his support. He was his own man; she'd understood that from the beginning, and she respected him for it.

"We've already discussed most of these cost figures in past meetings," Meredith said, reaching behind her and dimming the lights, "so I'll try to go over these slides as quickly as possible." She pressed the button on the projector's remote control, and the first slide showing the anticipated costs for the proposed store dropped into place. "As we agreed earlier this year, the Houston store will be approximately three hundred thousand square feet. Our projected building costs are thirty-two million dollars, which includes our new store, fixtures, parking lot, lighting—everything. The land we intend to purchase from Thorp Development will be an additional twenty to twenty-three million depending upon our final negotiations with them. We'll need another twenty million for inventory—"

"That's seventy-five million maximum," one of the directors interrupted, "but you're asking us to approve an expenditure of seventy-seven million for the store."

"The other two million is to cover pre-opening expenses," Meredith explained. "If you'll look at line four on the screen, you'll see that it covers grand-opening expenses, advertising, et cetera."

She pressed the button and the next slide fell into place, showing much higher figures for the project. "This next slide," she explained, "shows our projected costs for building the entire mall when we build our store rather than waiting until later to expand. You already know that I feel strongly that we ought to build the entire mall at the same time we build our store. The added costs are fifty-two million, but we'll recover that from leasing out space in the mall to other retail tenants."

"Recover it, yes," her father stated irritably, "but not immediately, as you implied, Meredith."

"Did I imply that?" Meredith asked politely, knowing she'd done no such thing. She smiled at him and let a pulse beat of silence reprimand him for his injustice and impatience. It was, she'd learned, the most effective way to deal with him when he was unreasonable. Even so, his voice sounded strained, as it often had since his heart attack, and she had to subdue a sharp jab of worry.

"We're waiting," he warned.

In a tone of calm reason, Meredith continued. "Some of you feel we ought to wait before constructing the entire mall. I think there are three strong reasons to build it all at once."

"For the record, what are those reasons?" another board member asked as he filled his glass with ice water.

"In the first place, we'll have to pay for all the land whether we're using it for the mall or not. If we go ahead and build the mall on it at the same time we build our store, we'll save several million dollars in construction costs, because as you all know, it is cheaper by the square foot to build it all at once rather than to add on later. Second, construction costs are bound to rise as Houston's economy continues to improve. Third, if we have other, carefully selected tenants in our mall, they will help bring traffic into our store. Are there any other questions?" she asked, and when there were none, Meredith proceeded to the remaining slides. "As you can see from these graphs, our area research team has thoroughly evaluated the location I've chosen for the Houston store, and they've given it the highest possible rating. The demographics of the primary trade area are perfect, there are no geographic barriers—"

Her explanation was interrupted by Cyrus Fortell, an eighty-year-old reprobate who'd been on Bancroft's board for fifty years, and whose ideas were as antiquated as the brocaded vest and ivory-handled cane he always carried. "That's all a bunch of jibberish to me, missy," he exclaimed in his reedy, irate voice. " 'Demographics' and 'primary trade areas' and 'area research teams' and 'geographic barriers.' What's it *mean*, that's what I want to know!"

Meredith felt a mixture of exasperation and affection for Cyrus, whom she'd known since she was a child. The other board members thought he was getting senile, and they planned to retire him. "It means, Cyrus, that a team of people who specialize in studying the best places to open retail stores have gone to Houston and studied the site I've chosen. They think the demographics—"

"Demowhatsas?" he scoffed. "We didn't even *have* that word when I was opening up drugstores across the nation! What does it mean?"

"In the way I'm using it now, it means the characteristics of the human population in the surrounding area of our store—how old they are and how much money they make—"

"I didn't pay any attention to all that in the old days," he persisted irritably, glaring at the impatient faces around the table. "Well, I didn't. When I wanted to open up a drugstore, I just sent people out to build one and filled it up with inventory, and we were in business."

"It's a little different today, Cyrus," Ben Houghton said. "Now, just listen, so you can vote on what Meredith is talking about."

"I can't vote on something I don't understand, now, can I?" he said, turning up the control in his pocket that was connected to his hearing aid. He looked at Meredith. "Proceed, my dear. I understand now that you sent a bunch of experts to Houston who discovered that there are people living in the area who are old enough to get to your store on foot or by motor car, and who have enough money in their pockets to share some of it with Bancroft's. Is that about it?"

Meredith chuckled and so did several of the others. "That's about it," she admitted.

"Then why didn't you just say so? It baffles me why you young people have to complicate every little thing by inventing high-sounding words to confuse us. Now, what are 'geographical barriers'?"

"Well," Meredith said, "a geographical barrier is anything that a potential customer might not want to have to drive through in order to get to our store. For example, if customers had to drive through an industrial area or an unsafe neighborhood to get to our store, those would be geographical barriers."

"Does this Houston site have any of those?"

"No, it doesn't."

"Then I vote in favor of it," he announced, and Meredith swallowed a giggle.

"Meredith"—her father's curt voice cut Cyrus off from further comment—"do you have anything else to add before the board votes on the Houston project?"

Meredith glanced at the inscrutable faces of the men seated at the table, and shook her head. "Inasmuch as we've discussed the details of the Houston project in great depth in prior board meetings, I have nothing to add to all that. I would, however, like to state once again that only by expanding can Bancroft's hope to compete successfully with other full-line department stores." Still slightly uncertain as to whether the board would actually vote in favor of the Houston project or not, Meredith made a final effort to gain their support by adding, "I'm sure I don't have to remind the members of the board that every one of our five new stores is showing profits that equal or surpass our projections. I believe much of that success is due to the care with which we've picked the locations we open in."

"The care with which *you* pick the locations," her father corrected her, and he looked so cold and stern that it took a moment before Meredith realized he had just paid her a compliment. It was not the first time he'd paid her a grudging compliment, but coming now, with the board present, Meredith took it as a highly encouraging sign that he was not only going to support the Houston project, but that he meant to ask the board to approve her as interim president during his leave of absence. "Thank you," she said with quiet simplicity, and sat down.

As if he hardly knew what she was thanking him for, he turned to Parker. "I gather your bank is still willing to commit the funds for a loan to finance the Houston project if the board so approves it?"

"We intend to, Philip, but only under the terms we discussed at the last meeting."

Meredith had known about those terms for weeks, but even so, she had to bite her lip to hide her moment of panic at his mention of them. Parker's bank—more accurately his own board of directors—had reviewed the enormous sums of money they'd loaned to Bancroft's in the last few years, and they'd grown nervous about the astronomical figures. In order to make the loans for the Phoenix and now the Houston store, his board had insisted on some new terms. Specifically, they were requiring she and her father to personally guarantee the loans as well as to put up additional collateral, including their personal stock in Bancroft's, to secure the loans. Meredith was gambling with her own money, and she found it slightly terrifying. Beyond her stock in Bancroft's and her salary, the only money she had was her inheritance from her grandfather, and it was that which she was going to put up as additional collateral for the Houston store.

As her father spoke, however, it was obvious he was still angry at what he regarded as outrageous demands from his banker. "You know how I feel about your special terms, Parker. Given the fact that Reynolds Mercantile has been Bancroft's only bank for more than eighty years, this sudden demand for personal guarantees and additional collateral is not only uncalled for, it's insulting."

"I understand your feelings," Parker said calmly. "I even agree with you, and you know that. This morning I met again with my board and tried to persuade them to either relinquish their insistence on these tighter terms or at least to lessen their demands, but without success. However," he continued, looking at the men assembled around the table in order to include them in his remarks, "their insistence on added collateral and personal guarantees is no reflection on their opinion of Bancroft & Company's worthiness as a borrower."

"Sounds to me like it is," old Cyrus announced.

"Sounds to me like your bank thinks Bancroft's is a potential deadbeat!"

"They think nothing of the sort. The fact is that in the last year the economic climate for department store chains has been less than healthy. Two of them have filed Chapter 11 to escape being shut down by their creditors while they try to reorganize. That's one factor that influenced our decision, but of equal importance is the fact that banks have been failing in numbers unequaled since the Great Depression. As a result of that, most banks are becoming increasingly cautious about lending too much to any one borrower. Then, too, we have to satisfy the bank examiners who are now scrutinizing all our loans more closely than ever before. Lending requirements are stricter now."

"Sounds to me like we ought to go to another bank," Cyrus suggested with a bright, eager look at the faces around the table. "That's what I'd do! Tell Parker here to go to Hades and we'll find our money elsewhere!"

"We could try to find other financing," Meredith told Cyrus, struggling to separate her personal feelings for Parker from this discussion. "However, Parker's bank is giving us a very advantageous interest rate that we'd have difficulty getting from any other bank. He's naturally—"

"There's nothing natural about it," Cyrus interrupted, passing an appreciative glance over her that verged on lecherous before he turned accusingly on Parker. "If I were going to marry this gorgeous young woman, the natural thing would be to give her any little thing she wants instead of tying up her assets!"

"Cyrus," Meredith warned, wondering why some old men, like Cyrus, abandoned dignity in favor of acting and speaking like pubescent teenagers, "this is business."

"Women shouldn't be involved in business—unless they're ugly and can't get a man to look after them. In my day, a beautiful girl like yourself would be at home, doing natural things like having babies and—"

"This isn't your day, Cyrus!" Parker snapped. "Go ahead, Meredith— what were you about to say?"

"I was about to say," Meredith replied, feeling her cheeks warm with embarrassment as the other men at the table exchanged smirking glances, "that your bank's special conditions are of little serious concern, since Bancroft & Company is going to make all loan payments on a timely basis."

"That's quite true," her father averred, his attitude becoming resigned and impatient. "Unless anyone has anything to add to this discussion, I believe we can close the Houston topic and vote on it at the end of this meeting."

Picking up her file, Meredith formally thanked the board for their consideration of the Houston project and left the boardroom.

"Well?" Phyllis asked, following Meredith into her office. "How did it go? Is there going to be a Houston branch of Bancroft's or not?"

"They're voting on it right now," Meredith said, leafing through the morning mail Phyllis had laid on her desk.

"I have my fingers crossed."

Touched by Phyllis's dedication to her and to Bancroft's, Meredith smiled reassuringly. "They'll approve the Houston store," she predicted. Her father was reluctantly in favor of that, so she had little doubt on that score. What she couldn't ascertain from his remarks during the past weeks was whether or not he was in favor of building the complete mall at the outset. "All that's really in doubt is whether they'll approve the building of the entire mall or only our store. Will you call Sam Green and ask him to bring the Thorp contracts?"

When she hung up the phone a few minutes later, Sam Green was standing in her doorway. Sam was only five feet five with hair the color and texture of steel wool, but there was an aura of competence and authority about him that was immediately recognizable—particularly to anyone who found themselves on the opposite side of any legal issue he was handling. Behind his wire-rimmed glasses, his green eyes were sharp with intelligence. At the moment, however, they were peering expectantly at Meredith. "Phyllis said you're ready to start finalizing a contract for the Houston land," he said, walking into her office. "Does this mean we have the board's approval?"

"I'm assuming we'll have it in a few minutes. How much do you think our opening offer to Thorp should be?"

"They're asking thirty million," he replied, thinking aloud as he sat in one of the chairs in front of her desk. "How about an opening offer of eighteen million, and we settle at, say, twenty? They've got a mortgage on that land and they need cash badly. They might sell it for twenty."

"Do you really think so?"

"Probably not," he said with a chuckle.

"If we have to, we'll go to twenty-five. It's worth a maximum of thirty, but they haven't been able to sell it for that—" The phone rang on her desk and Meredith answered it instead of finishing her sentence. Her father's voice was curt and final: "We will proceed with the Houston project, Meredith, but we will postpone building the entire mall until we have some profits out of our store there."

"I think you're making a mistake," she told him, hiding her disappointment behind a brisk, businesslike tone.

"It was the board's decision."

"You could have swayed them," Meredith said baldly.

"Very well, then, that was *my* decision."

"And it's a mistake."

"When you are running this company, you can make the decisions—"

Meredith's heart gave a funny little lurch at his words. "And am I going to be doing that?"

"Until then *I* will make them," he said, avoiding her question. "For now, I'm going home. I'm not feeling well. In fact, I'd have postponed the meeting this morning if you hadn't been so adamant about needing to get going on the land deal."

Uncertain whether he was really ill or simply using that as a ploy to avoid a discussion with her, Meredith sighed. "Take care of yourself. I'll see you at dinner Thursday night." When she hung up the phone, she allowed herself a silent moment of regret that the entire mall couldn't be built, and then she did what she'd learned to do years before, after her disastrous marriage: She faced reality and found something in it to look forward to and work toward. Smiling at Sam Green, she injected a note of pleasure and triumph into her voice. "We have approval to proceed on the Houston project."

"The entire mall, or just the store?"

"Just the store."

"I think it's a mistake."

He'd obviously heard her say as much to her father, but Meredith didn't comment on his remark. She'd made it a policy to keep her comments and thoughts about her father's policies to herself whenever possible. Instead, she said, "How soon can you get a contract ready and take it to Thorp?"

"I can have the contracts ready by tomorrow night. But if you want me to negotiate the deal personally, I won't be able to go down to Houston until the week after next. We're still preparing that lawsuit against Wilson Toys."

"I'd rather you handle it," she said, knowing that he'd be able to negotiate a better deal than anyone else, but wishing he could do it sooner. "I suppose the week after next will be all right. By then we may have a written commitment from Reynolds Mercantile, and we won't need to make the contract contingent on financing."

"That land has been for sale for years," he said with a smile. "It will still be available in two weeks. Besides, the longer we wait, the more likely Thorp will be to take our low-ball-park offer." When she still looked concerned, he added, "I'll try to get my people moving quicker on the Wilson lawsuit. As soon as we wrap it up, I'll head to Houston."

It was after six when Meredith looked up from the contracts she'd been reading and saw Phyllis heading toward her with her coat on and Meredith's evening newspaper in her hand. "I'm sorry about the Houston deal," Phyllis said, "sorry that they wouldn't approve the entire mall, I mean."

Meredith leaned back in her chair and smiled wearily. "Thank you."

"For being sorry?"

"No," Meredith replied, reaching for the newspaper, "for caring. Basically, though, I'd say it's been a pretty good day."

Phyllis nodded toward the newspaper which she'd already opened to the second page. "I hope that this doesn't make you change your mind."

Puzzled, Meredith unfolded it and saw Matthew Farrell looking back at her beside some starlet who'd evidently flown to Chicago in his private jet to accompany him to the party of a friend last night. Snatches of newspaper copy imprinted itself on Meredith's mind as she glanced at the glowing article about Chicago's newest entrepreneur and most eligible bachelor, but when she looked up at Phyllis, her face was perfectly composed. "Is this supposed to bother me?"

"Check the business section before you decide," Phyllis advised.

It occurred to Meredith to tell Phyllis that she was out of line, and, just as quickly, she dismissed the notion. Phyllis had been her first secretary, and Meredith had been her first boss. In the past six years they'd worked hundreds of nights together as well as dozens of weekends; they'd eaten cold sandwiches at Meredith's desk while they worked to meet project deadlines. They were a dedicated team, they liked and respected each other.

The first page of the business section contained another picture of Matt and a glowing article about his leadership of Intercorp, his reasons for relocating to Chicago, the fabulous manufacturing facility he intended to build at Southville, and yet another mention of the lavish penthouse apartment he'd bought and furnished in the Berkeley Towers. Beside his picture and slightly below it was a picture of Meredith, accompanied by an article that quoted her remarks about Bancroft's successful expansion into the national retailing market.

"They gave him top billing," Phyllis noted, perching her hip on the edge of Meredith's desk, watching her read the article. "He's been here for less than two weeks and the newspapers are full of stories about him."

"Newspapers are also full of stories about muggers and rapists," Meredith reminded her, disgusted by the lavish praise the article heaped on his leadership, and furious with herself because for some reason, seeing his picture was making her hands tremble. No doubt her reaction was the result of knowing he was in Chicago now instead of thousands of miles away.

"Is he really as handsome as he looks in his pictures?"

"Handsome?" Meredith said with careful indifference as she got up and headed to the closet for her coat. "Not to me."

"He's a jerk, right?" Phyllis said with an irrepressible grin.

Meredith smiled back at her and walked over to lock her desk. "How'd you guess?"

"I read Sally Mansfield's column," Phyllis replied. "And when she wrote that you gave him the 'cut direct' in front of everyone, I figured he must be a world-class jerk. I mean, I've seen you deal with men you couldn't stand and you managed to smile at them and be polite."

"Actually Sally Mansfield misunderstood the whole episode. I hardly know the man." Deliberately changing the subject, Meredith said, "If your car's still in the shop, I can give you a ride home."

"No thanks. I'm going to my sister's for dinner, and she lives in the other direction."

"I'd give you a ride to her place, but it's late and this is Wednesday—"

"And your fiancé always has dinner at your apartment on Wednesday, right?"

"Right."

"It's a lucky thing you like routine, Meredith, because it would drive me crazy knowing the man in my life always did particular things on particular days, day after day . . . year after year . . . decade after—"

Meredith burst out laughing. "Stop it. You're depressing me. Besides, I like routine and order and dependability."

"Not me. I like spontaneity."

"Which is why *your* dates rarely show up on the right night, let alone on time," Meredith teased.

"True."

🌿 22

*M*eredith would have liked to forget about Matthew Farrell entirely, but Parker arrived at her apartment with the newspaper in his hand. "Did you see the article about Farrell?" he asked after kissing her.

"Yes. Would you like a drink?"

"Please."

"What would you like?" she asked, walking over to the nineteenth-century armoire she'd had converted to a liquor cabinet and opening its doors.

"The usual."

Her hand stilled in the act of reaching for a glass, while Lisa's remark ran through her mind, followed by Phyllis's comment today. *You need someone who'll make you do something really adventurous, like voting for a Democrat. . . . It would drive me crazy knowing the man in my life always did a particular thing on a particular day. . . .* "Are you sure you wouldn't like something different?" Meredith said hesitantly, looking at him over her shoulder. "How about a gin and tonic?"

"Don't be silly. I always drink bourbon and water, honey, and you always have white wine. It's practically a custom."

"Parker," Meredith said hesitantly, "Phyllis said something today, and Lisa had made a remark a week ago, that make me wonder if we're . . ." She trailed off, feeling silly, but she nevertheless took out the gin and tonic for herself.

"Made you wonder if we're what?" he asked, sensing her dismay and coming up behind her.

"Well, in a rut."

His arms slid around her. "I like ruts," he said, kissing her temple. "I like routines and predictability, and so do you."

"I know I do, but don't you think that—in years to come—too much of that might make us bored, and boring, people. I mean, don't you think excitement can be nice too?"

"Not particularly," he said, then he turned her in his arms and said with gentle firmness, "Meredith, if you're angry with me for asking you and your father to put up personal collateral for the Houston loan, then say so. If you're disappointed in me because of it, say so, but don't go blaming it on other reasons."

"I'm not," Meredith promised sincerely. "In fact, I got my stock certificates out of the safe to give to you. They're over there in that big folder on my desk." Ignoring the folder for the moment, he studied her face, and Meredith added reluctantly, "I'll admit it's frightening to hand over everything I have, but I believe you when you say you couldn't convince your board to forgo the extra collateral."

"You're sure?" he asked, looking handsome and worried.

"I'm positive," she averred with a bright smile, and turned to finish fixing his drink. "Why don't you look over the certificates and make certain they're in order while I set the table and see what Mrs. Ellis left us for dinner." Mrs. Ellis no longer worked for her father, but she came to Meredith's apartment on Wednesdays to clean and do the marketing, and she always left a meal ready for them to eat.

Parker walked over to her desk while Meredith spread pale pink linen place mats on the dining room table.

"Are they in here?" he asked, holding up a manila envelope.

She glanced over her shoulder at the envelope. "No. That's my passport, birth certificate, and some other papers. The stock certificates are in a larger envelope."

He held one up, looking at the return address on the outside, and frowning with confusion. "In this one?"

"No," she said with another glance over her shoulder. "That's my divorce papers."

"This envelope has never been opened. Haven't you ever read them?"

She shrugged as she took out linen napkins from the side table. "Not since I signed them. I remember what they say, though. They say that in return for a ten-thousand-dollar payoff from my father, Matthew Farrell grants me a divorce and relinquishes all right to any claims on me or anything I ever have."

"I'm certain they aren't worded exactly like that," Parker said with a grim chuckle, turning the envelope over in his hand. "Do you mind if I have a look?"

"No, but why would you want to?"

He grinned. "Professional curiosity—I am an attorney, you know. I'm not entirely the boring, fastidious banker your friend Lisa likes to think I am. She needles me about that all the time, you know."

It was not the first time Parker had made a remark that indicated Lisa's joking jibes got under his skin, and Meredith made a mental note to tell Lisa, very firmly this time, that it had to stop. Parker had much to be proud of. Taking all that into consideration, she decided it was unwise and unnecessary to add to his pique by reminding him that he had specialized in tax law, not domestic law. "Look all you like," she replied, and leaning forward, she pressed a kiss on his temple. "I wish you didn't have to go to Switzerland. I'm going to miss you every day."

"It's only for two weeks. You could go with me."

He was scheduled to address the World Banking Conference there, and she would have loved to watch him do it, but it wasn't possible. "You know I'd love to. But this season is—"

"Your busiest time of the year," he finished without resentment. "I know."

In the refrigerator Meredith found a beautifully arranged platter of cold, marinated chicken and a salad of hearts of palm. As usual, there was little for her to do except open a bottle of wine and put the platter in the center of the dining room table—which was about the extent of her culinary abilities anyway. Cooking was something she'd tried to do a few times and failed, and since she didn't enjoy it anyway, she was content to spend her time working and leave domestic chores to Mrs. Ellis. If food couldn't go directly to the table via the microwave or oven, Meredith had no desire whatsoever to bother with it.

Rain was spattering against the windows, and she lit the candles in the antique candelabra, then she carried out the chicken and salad and chilled white wine and put them on the table. Standing back, she surveyed the effect of the table setting. Fresh pink roses reposed in an ornate bowl in the center of the table, and the antique silver flatware looked lovely against the pink linen place mats. Thinking she ought to contribute something more to the meal than merely setting the table and putting the platters and wine there, she reached out and poked gently at two of the fresh pink roses in the centerpiece.

"Dinner is ready," she said, walking over to Parker. For a moment he seemed not to hear her, then he pulled his gaze from the documents he was reading and looked at her, frowning. "Is something wrong?"

"I'm not certain," he said, but he sounded as if something was very wrong. "Who handled your divorce?"

Unconcerned, she perched on the arm of his wing chair and glanced distastefully at the papers that were headed Decree of Divorce: Meredith Alexandra Bancroft vs. Matthew Allan Farrell. "My father took care of everything. Why do you ask?"

"Because I find these documents very irregular from a legal standpoint."

"In what way?" Meredith asked, noticing that her father's lawyer had misspelled Matt's middle name as Allan instead of Allen.

"In *every* way," Parker said, flipping back and forth through the pages, truly agitated.

The tension in his voice communicated itself to Meredith, and because she hated thinking of Matt and the divorce, she immediately tried to reassure Parker and herself that whatever Parker was concerned about was meaningless, even though she hadn't the vaguest idea *what* he was concerned about. "I'm certain everything was done legally and correctly. My father handled everything, and you know what a stickler for detail he is, Parker."

"Well, he might be, but this lawyer—Stanislaus Spyzhalski, whoever *that* is—wasn't concerned with details. Look here," he said, flipping back to the cover letter that had been addressed to her father. "This letter says he's enclosed the entire file, and that the court has sealed the records, as your father asked."

"What's wrong with that?"

"What's *wrong* is that this 'entire file' does not contain a notice that Farrell was ever served with the petition for divorce, or that he ever appeared in court, or that he ever waived his right to appear—and that's only a small part of what bothers me."

Meredith felt the first twinges of genuine alarm, but she firmly ignored them. "What difference does all this make now? We're divorced, that's all that matters."

Instead of replying, Parker flipped back to the first page of the divorce petition and began reading it slowly, his scowl deepening with every paragraph. When Meredith couldn't stand the suspense anymore, she stood up. "What," she demanded in a calm, no-nonsense tone, "is bothering you now?"

"This entire document is bothering me," he replied with unintended curtness. "Divorce decrees are drawn up by lawyers and signed by the judge, but this decree reads like none *I've* ever seen written by any reasonably competent attorney. Look at the wording of this!" he said, jabbing his index finger at the last paragraph on the last page as he read.

"In return for $10,000 and other good and valuable consideration paid to Matthew A. Farrell, Matthew Farrell relinquishes all claim to any property or possessions owned now or in the future by Meredith Bancroft Farrell. Furthermore, this court herewith grants a decree of divorce to Meredith Bancroft Farrell."

Even now the memory of the way she'd felt eleven years ago when she learned that Matt had accepted money from her father made Meredith wince. He'd been such a liar, such a rotten hypocrite when they were married and he'd protested that he'd never touch a cent of her money.

"I cannot believe the wording of this!" Parker's low, angry voice pulled her from her brief reflections. "It reads like a damned real estate contract: 'In return for $10,000 and other good and valuable consideration,' " he said again. "Who in the hell *is* this guy?" he demanded of Meredith. "Look at his address! Why would your father hire an attorney whose practice was on the South Side, practically in the slums?"

"Secrecy," Meredith said, glad at least to have an answer for something. "He told me at the time that he'd deliberately hired 'a nobody lawyer' on the South Side—someone who wouldn't guess who I am or who Father is either. He was very upset about everything, as I told you before. What are you doing?" she asked as he reached for the phone on her desk.

"I'm going to call your father," he said, and then with a brief grim smile to silence her protest, he added, "I'm not going to alarm him. I'm not sure there's anything to be alarmed *about*." True to his word, when her father answered his phone, Parker indulged in small talk with him for a few moments, and then he casually remarked that he'd been looking over Meredith's divorce decree. As if teasing her father about his choosing a lawyer on the fringe of the slums, he asked him who had recommended Mr. Stanislaus Spyzhalski, Esquire. He laughed at whatever Philip replied, but when he hung up the phone, Parker's smile vanished.

"What did he say?"

"He said he got his name from the Yellow Pages."

"So what?" Meredith said, trying desperately not to react to the generalized alarm shaking through her. She felt as if she were being thrust into dark, dangerous territory and threatened by something vague and unidentifiable. "Now who are you calling?" she asked when Parker took out the slender black phone book he carried inside his coat pocket and picked up the phone.

"Howard Turnbill."

Torn between concern and anger at his uninformative replies, she said, *"Why* are you calling Howard Turnbill?"

"We were at Princeton together," he replied unhelpfully.

"Parker, if you are trying to make me really angry, you're going to succeed," she warned him as he began pressing the keypad on her phone. "I want to know *why* you're calling your old Princeton classmate now."

Inexplicably, he grinned at her. "I love that particular tone of voice of yours. Reminds me of my kindergarten teacher. I had a crush on her." Before she could strangle him, which she looked ready to do, he added hastily, "I'm calling Howard because he's president of the Illinois Bar Association, and—" He broke off as Howard answered the phone. "Howard, this is Parker Reynolds," he began, then he paused while the other man said something to him. "You're right, I'd forgotten I owe you a rematch on that squash game. Call me at the office tomorrow, and we'll set up a date." He paused again and laughed at whatever Howard said, then he said, "Do you happen to have a roster of the Illinois Bar members handy? I'm not at home right now, and I'm curious to know whether a certain individual is a member. Could you check your roster and tell me if he is?" Howard obviously said he could do that, because Parker then said, "Good. The man's name is Stanislaus Spyzhalski. That's S-p-y-z-h-a-l-s-k-i. I'll hold on."

Covering the mouthpiece of the phone, Parker gave her a reassuring smile. "I'm probably worrying needlessly. Merely because the man's incompetent doesn't mean he isn't a legitimate attorney." A moment later, however, when Howard returned to the phone, Parker's smile faded. "He's not on the roster? You're certain?" For a moment Parker was lost in thought, then he said, "Could you get a hold of a current roster for the American Bar Association and see if he's listed there?" He paused, listening, then he said with forced joviality, "No, it's not an emergency. Tomorrow will be fine. Give me a call at my office and we'll set up the squash game then too. Thanks, Howard. Give my love to Helen."

Lost in his own thoughts, Parker slowly replaced the phone on its cradle.

"I don't think I understand what you're worrying about," Meredith said.

"I think I'd like another drink," he announced, getting up and walking over to the liquor cabinet.

"Parker," Meredith said firmly, "since this involves me, I think I have a right to know what you're thinking."

"At this moment I'm thinking of several known cases of men who set themselves up as attorneys—usually in poorer neighborhoods—and who took money from clients who believed they were going to handle legal work for them. One of the cases involved a man who was actually an attorney, but who pocketed the filing fees charged by the courts and who then 'granted' his clients an uncontested divorce by simply signing the document himself."

"How could he do that?"

"Lawyers draw up the petitions for divorce. Judges merely sign them. He signed the judge's name to them."

"But how could he—they—get away with that?"

"They got away with it by handling only uncontested matters, including divorces."

Meredith swallowed half her drink without realizing what she was doing, then she brightened. "But surely in those instances, when both parties acted in good faith, then the courts would honor the divorce decrees even though they weren't filed?"

"Like hell they did."

"I don't like the tone of this conversation," Meredith said, feeling a little woozy from the potent drink. "What *did* the courts do about those people who thought they were divorced?"

"If they'd remarried, the courts allowed them to be innocent of bigamy."

"Good."

"But the second marriage was invalidated and the first one had to be dissolved through the proper channels."

"Dear God!" Meredith said, and sank into a chair. But she knew in her heart, she absolutely *knew* her divorce was legal and valid. She knew it because the alternative was unthinkable.

Belatedly realizing how upset she was, Parker reached out and gently ran his hand over her silky hair.

"Even if Spyzhalski doesn't belong to the bar, even if he's never been to law school, your divorce could still be legitimate—so long as he presented that absurd divorce petition to a judge and somehow got it signed." She glanced up at him and her eyes were the same lovely blue-green as the sweater and slacks she wore—only darker now, and troubled. "I'll have someone go over to the courthouse tomorrow and try to find out if the divorce was filed and recorded. As long as it was, there's nothing more to worry about."

23

*B*ad night?" Phyllis asked her the next morning as Meredith walked past her desk with an absentminded nod.

"It wasn't the greatest. What's on my calendar this morning?"

"You have a meeting here with the advertising division at ten o'clock to discuss the grand opening for the New Orleans store. Jerry Keaton in personnel asked to see you about some raises you need to approve, and I told him you could see him at eleven. Is that okay?"

"Fine."

"And at eleven-thirty Ellen Perkvale from legal needs to discuss a lawsuit that's just been filed against us. It pertains to a lady who claims she broke a tooth in the Clarendon Room."

Meredith rolled her eyes in disgust. "She's suing us because she broke her tooth while eating in our dining room?"

"Not exactly. She's suing us because she broke it on a nutshell that was in her trout amandine."

"Oh," Meredith said, unlocking her desk and accepting the likelihood of having to reach a settlement. "That changes matters."

"True. Is eleven-thirty okay for that meeting?"

"Fine," Meredith replied as the phone on her desk began to ring. "I'll get it," Phyllis said, and the day launched itself with the usual frenetic rush of store business that Meredith sometimes found exhausting yet always exhilarating. Occasionally, she had a moment to herself, and when that happened, she found herself staring at the phone, willing Parker to call and to say there was absolutely nothing amiss with her divorce.

It was nearly five o'clock when Phyllis finally said that Parker was on the phone. Racked with sudden tension, Meredith snatched the receiver from its cradle. "What did you find out?" she asked him.

"Nothing conclusive yet," he replied, but there was a new, strained quality to his voice. "Spyzhalski isn't a member of the ABA. I'm waiting to hear from someone at the Cook County courthouse. He'll call me with the information I've asked for as soon as he has it. I'll know exactly where we stand within the next few hours. Are you going to be home tonight?"

"No," she sighed, "I'll be at my father's. He's giving a small birthday party for Senator Davies. Call me there."

"I will."

"The moment you get your answers?"

"I promise."

"The party will break up early because Senator Davies has to leave for Washington on a midnight flight, so if I've already left, call me at home."

"I'll find you, don't worry."

24

Trying not to worry became increasingly impossible as the evening wore on. Half convinced she was agonizing over nothing, and yet unable to quell her mounting sense of alarm, Meredith managed to smile and nod and be reasonably gracious to her father's guests, but it took a supreme effort. Dinner had been over for an hour, and *still* Parker hadn't phoned. Trying to distract herself, she lingered in the dining room, supervising the clearing of the table, then she wandered into the library, where the guests had gathered for a brandy before leaving for their homes.

Someone had turned on the television and several of the men were standing near it, watching the news. "Lovely party, Meredith," Senator Davies's wife said, but the rest of her words seemed to vanish into the nether as Meredith heard the television commentator say, "Another Chicagoan was in the news today—Matthew Farrell was Barbara Walters's guest on a taped broadcast earlier this evening. Among other things, he commented on the recent rash of corporate takeovers. Here's a clip from that interview . . ."

The guests, who'd all read Sally Mansfield's column, naturally assumed Meredith would be interested in seeing what Farrell had to say. After glancing at her with curious smiles, the roomful of people turned in unison to the television set as Matt's face and voice filled the room.

"How do you feel about the growing number of hostile corporate takeovers?" Barbara Walters asked him, and Meredith noted with disgust that even the journalist was leaning forward in her chair, as if fascinated by him.

"I think it's a trend that's bound to continue, until such time as guidelines are set up to control it."

"Is anyone immune from a forced merger with you—friends, and so forth? I mean," she added with joking alarm, "is it possible that our own ABC could find itself your next prey?"

"The object of a takeover attempt is called the *target*," Matt said evasively, smiling, "not the *prey*. However," he said with a lazy, disarming smile, "if it will set your mind at rest, I can assure you that Intercorp does not have an acquisitive eye on ABC." The men in the room chuckled at his quip, but Meredith kept her face perfectly blank.

"Can we talk a little more about your private life now? During the past few years you've reportedly had torrid love affairs with several movie stars, a princess, and most recently with Maria Calvaris, the shipping heiress. Were these widely publicized love affairs real, or were they invented by the gossip columnists?"

"Yes."

Meredith heard again the appreciative laughter that filled the library at Matt's sangfroid, and her eyes sparked with resentment over the ease with which he could win people over.

"You've never married, and I was wondering if you have any plans to marry in the future?"

"It's not out of the question."

His brief smile emphasized the impertinence of the question, and Meredith gritted her teeth, remembering how that smile had once made her heart hammer. Abruptly, the television cameras switched back to the local newscasters, but Meredith's moment of relief was squelched by the senator, who turned to her with friendly curiosity. "I imagine all of us here read Sally Mansfield's column, Meredith. Would you care to satisfy our curiosity and tell us why you don't like Farrell?"

Meredith managed to imitate Matt's lazy smile. "No."

They all laughed, but she saw the heightened curiosity in their faces, and she hastily busied herself plumping up the sofa pillows as the senator said to her father, "Stanton Avery has put Farrell's name up for membership at the country club."

Mentally cursing Matt Farrell for coming to Chicago, Meredith shot her father a warning look, but his temper had already overruled his judgment. "I'm quite certain that those of us in this room have enough influence among us to keep him out—even if everyone else who belongs to Glenmoor wants him in, which they won't."

Judge Northrup heard that and broke off his conversation with another guest. "Is that what you want us to do, Philip? Blackball him?"

"You're damned right it is."

"If you're convinced he's an undesirable, that's good enough for me," said the judge, looking around at the others. Slowly but emphatically, all her father's guests nodded their unanimous agreement, and Meredith knew that Matt's chances of belonging to Glenmoor were now zero.

"He's bought a huge tract of land out in Southville," the judge told her father. "Wants it rezoned so he can build a big high-tech industrial complex on it."

"Is that right?" her father said, and Meredith realized from his next words that he planned to squelch that too, if he could. "Who do we know on the Southville zoning commission?"

"Several people. There's Paulson and—"

"For heaven's sake!" she interrupted with a forced laugh, sending her father a pleading look. "There's no need to roll out the heavy guns just because I don't like Matt Farrell."

"I'm certain you and your father must have excellent reasons to feel as you do," Senator Davies said.

"You're damned ri—"

"Not at all!" Meredith said, cutting off her father and trying to stop a vendetta from getting under way. With a bright artificial smile, she told everyone, "The truth is that Matt Farrell made a pass at me years ago, when I was eighteen, and father has never forgiven him for it."

"Now I know where I've met him!" Mrs. Foster exclaimed, looking at her husband. Turning to Meredith, she said, "It was years ago at Glenmoor!

I remember thinking what an extraordinarily attractive young man he was . . . and, Meredith—*you* were the one who introduced us to him!"

Whether by accident or design, the senator spared Meredith the need to reply by saying, "Well, I hate to break up my own birthday party, but I have to be on a plane to Washington at midnight. . . ."

A half hour later the last of the guests departed, and Meredith was bidding them good-bye beside her father when she saw a car turn into the drive. "Who the hell is that?" her father said, scowling at the headlights swooping toward them.

She peered at the car and identified it as a light blue Mercedes when it passed beneath one of the lamps along the drive. "It's Parker!"

"At eleven o'clock at night?"

Meredith began to tremble with foreboding, and that was before the porch lights illuminated his tense, grim face. "I was hoping the party would have broken up by now. I need to talk to both of you."

"Parker," Meredith began, "don't forget my father's been ill—"

"I won't distress him unduly," Parker promised, almost propelling them down the hall with a hand against both their backs, "but he needs to be apprised of the facts so that they can be dealt with properly."

"Stop talking about me like I'm not here," Philip said when they entered the library. "Facts about what? What the hell is going on?"

Pausing to close the library doors, Parker said, "I think you both ought to sit down."

"Dammit, Parker, nothing upsets me *more* than being kept in suspense—"

"Very well. Philip, last night I happened to have a look at Meredith's divorce decree, and there were several irregularities about it. Do you recall, about eight years ago, reading of a Chicago attorney who was accepting fees from clients, then pocketing the fees without ever filing their cases?"

"Yes. So what?"

"And about five years ago there was another batch of stories about an alleged attorney on the South Side named Joseph Grandola who was convicted of fifty-some counts of fraud for misrepresenting himself as an attorney and charging fees to handle cases that never actually went near a courthouse." He waited for a comment, but short of a sudden rigidity in Philip's stance, there was no response, and so he went on. "Grandola had a year of law school before they kicked him out. A few years later he opened an office in a neighborhood where most of his 'clients' were undereducated. For over a decade he got away with his scam by taking only cases that wouldn't require a trial and that were unlikely to ever involve an opposing attorney—such as uncontested divorces, wills that needed to be drawn up, and so forth—"

Meredith sank down onto the sofa, her stomach beginning to churn, her mind already numbly accepting what Parker was going to tell her father, while her heart screamed a denial that it couldn't be true. Parker's voice droned on as if from a great distance. "He'd had some law school training, and he knew just enough legal jargon to draw up a fair representation of a legal pleading. When a client came to him wanting a divorce, he first made certain the other spouse was either in full agreement—or nowhere to be found. If that was so, he charged his client whatever he could get them to pay him, then he drew up a petition for divorce. Knowing he'd never be able to pass himself off as an attorney long enough to get a judge to sign the petition, he signed them himself."

"Are you trying to tell me," Philip said, his voice strained almost to the point of unrecognizability, "that this lawyer I hired eleven years ago was *not* a lawyer?"

"I'm afraid so."

"I don't believe it!" he said in a low shout, as if he could frighten the possibility away with his own fury.

"There's no point in giving yourself another heart attack over it, because it won't change anything," Parker pointed out quietly and reasonably, and Meredith felt a mild sense of relief as she saw her father make an effort to calm himself.

"Go on," he said after a moment.

"Today, after I verified that Spyzhalski isn't a member of the bar association, I sent an investigator over to the courthouse—a very *discreet* investigator we use for bank matters," he reassured Philip, who had clutched the back of a chair. "He spent the day and part of the night verifying and reverifying that Meredith's divorce is nowhere in the court records."

"I'll kill that bastard!"

"If you mean Spyzhalski, you'll have to find him first. He's vanished. If you mean Farrell," Parker continued in a resigned voice, "I strongly suggest you reconsider your attitude."

"Like hell I will! Meredith can solve the whole thing very simply by flying to Reno or somewhere and getting a quiet, quick divorce."

"I've already thought of that, and it won't help." He held up his hand to silence Philip's angry outburst. "Listen to me, Philip, because I've had time tonight to think this thing through. Even if Meredith did as you suggest, it wouldn't unsnarl the legal tangle of their property rights. That would still have to be done through the Illinois courts."

"Meredith would never need to tell him that there is a snarl!"

"Besides being morally and ethically wrong, it's also completely impractical." With a frustrated sigh, Parker explained. "The ABA has already had two complaints against Spyzhalski, and they've turned the matter over to the authorities. Let's assume Meredith did as you just suggested, and Spyzhalski is arrested and he confesses. The minute he does, the authorities will notify Farrell that his divorce isn't legal—assuming he doesn't read about it in the newspaper first. Do you have any idea of the lawsuit he could slap against you for all this? In good faith, he allowed you and Meredith to assume the responsibility for handling the divorce, and you were negligent; furthermore, you've exposed him to bigamy all these years, and—"

"You seem to have the problems figured out," Philip snapped. "What do you suggest we do?"

"Whatever we *have* to do in order to pacify him and make him agree to a quick, uncomplicated divorce," Parker replied with calm implacability, then he turned to Meredith. "I'm afraid that job is going to fall to *you*."

During the entire discussion, Meredith had been sitting, reeling from it all, but that remark served to stir her out of her blank stupor. "Just exactly why does he have to be pacified by me or by anyone else?"

"Because there are enormous financial implications here. Like it or not, Farrell is your legal husband of eleven years standing. You are a wealthy young woman, Meredith, and Farrell, as your legal husband, could conceivably demand a share of what you have—"

"Stop calling him that!"

"It's true," Parker said, but gently this time, "Farrell could refuse to cooperate in getting a divorce. He could also sue you for negligence—"

"Dear God!" she cried, standing up and beginning to pace. "I can't believe this! No, wait—we're overreacting," she said after a moment. Forcing herself to start thinking logically, as if she were dealing with a problem at work, she paused and then said, "If what I've read is true, Matt is far wealthier than we are—"

"Far wealthier," Parker confirmed, smiling approvingly at her for the calm logic she was exercising. "In which case, he would have a hell of a lot more to lose in a fight over property than you do."

"So there's nothing to worry about," she concluded, "because he'll want to get this thing over with just as badly as I do, and he'll be relieved that I don't want anything from him. In fact, we have the upper hand—"

"That's not quite true," Parker denied. "As I just explained, your father and you assumed the responsibility for obtaining the divorce, and since you failed to do it, Farrell's attorneys could probably convince the courts that the fault is yours. In which case, the judge might even grant him punitive damages. You, on the other hand, would have a hard time getting any money out of Farrell, because you were supposed to handle the divorce from here, and I suspect his attorneys could convince the court that you deliberately failed to do that out of some premeditated belief that you might later be able to squeeze him for money."

"He can rot in hell before he gets one more cent out of us," Philip snapped. "I already paid the bastard ten thousand dollars to get out of our lives and forgo any money of Meredith's or mine."

"How did you pay it to him?"

"I—" Philip's face fell. "I did what Spyzhalski told me to do which wasn't extraordinary—I wrote a check made jointly payable to Farrell and him."

"Spyzhalski," Parker pointed out sarcastically, "is a swindler. Do you honestly think he'd have scruples against forging Farrell's endorsement and cashing it himself?"

"I should have killed Farrell the day Meredith brought him back here!"

"Stop it!" Meredith cried. "Don't give yourself another coronary over this. We'll simply have an attorney contact *his* attorney—"

"I hardly think so," Parker interrupted. "If you want the man to cooperate and keep this mess *quiet*—which, I think, is a primary goal for all of us—then you'd better start by smoothing things over with him."

"What things?" Meredith demanded hotly.

"I would suggest you begin," Parker stated, "with a personal apology for that remark of yours that appeared in Sally Mansfield's column—"

The recollection of the benefit ball hit her then, and Meredith sank onto the chair in front of the fire, staring into the flames. "I can't believe this," she whispered, but her father's voice was a near shout as he glared at Parker.

"I'm starting to wonder about you, Parker. What sort of man are you to suggest she apologize to that bastard! *I'll* deal with him."

"I'm a practical, *civilized* man, that's what I am," he replied, walking over and laying a consoling hand on Meredith's shoulder. "And you're a volatile man, which is why you're the last person in the world who ought to try to deal with him. Furthermore, I have faith in Meredith. Look, Meredith has told me the whole story about what happened between Farrell and her. He married her because she was pregnant. What he did when she lost the baby was cruel, but it was also practical and possibly kinder than dragging out a marriage that was doomed from the start—"

"Kind!" Philip spat out. "He was a twenty-six-year-old fortune hunter who seduced an eighteen-year-old heiress, got her pregnant, and then 'kindly' condescended to marry her—"

"Stop it!" Meredith said again with more force. "Parker is right. And you know perfectly well he didn't 'seduce' me. I told you what happened and why." With an effort, she got herself under control. "This is all beside the point. I'll deal with Matt once I decide how best to do it."

"That's my girl," Parker said. He glanced at Philip, ignoring his thunderous expression. "All Meredith has to do is meet with him in a civilized way, explain the problem, and suggest that they obtain a divorce with no financial claims against one another." With a wry smile he studied her pale, drawn face. "You've handled tougher adversaries and tougher assignments than that, haven't you, honey?"

Meredith saw the encouragement and pride in his face, and she looked at him in helpless consternation. "No."

"Of course you have!" he argued. "You can put most of this behind you by tomorrow night if you can get him to agree to see you tomorrow—"

"See me!" she burst out. "Why can't I just talk to him on the phone?"

"Is that how you'd handle it if it were a messy business situation of vital importance to you?"

"No, of course not," she sighed.

For several minutes after Parker left, Meredith and her father remained in the library, both of them staring into space in a kind of angry stupor. "I suppose you blame me for this," her father stated finally.

Rousing herself from her self-pity, Meredith turned her head and looked at him. He looked defeated and pale. "Of course not," she said quietly. "You only tried to protect me by hiring a lawyer who didn't know us."

"I'll call Farrell myself in the morning!"

"No, you can't," she said quietly. "Parker was right about that. You become irrationally angry and defensive at the mention of Matt's name. If you tried to talk to him, you'd lose your temper in ten seconds and end up giving yourself another heart attack in the process. Why don't you go to bed now and get some sleep," she added, standing up. "I'll see you at work tomorrow. This will all seem less—well—threatening in the morning. Besides," she added, somehow managing to give him a reassuring smile as they walked toward the front door, "I'm not an eighteen-year-old girl anymore, and I'm not afraid of confronting Matthew Farrell. Actually," she lied, "I'm rather looking forward to outwitting him!" He looked as if he was desperately trying to think of an alternative, and he was growing paler because he couldn't.

With a cheery wave she left and hurried down the front steps. Her car was parked in the driveway, and she opened the front door, slid into its freezing interior, and closed her door. Then she put her forehead on the steering wheel and closed her eyes. "Oh, my *God!*" she whispered, terrified at the prospect of confronting the dark-haired demon from her past.

🌿25

"Good morning," Phyllis said brightly, following Meredith into her office.

"I might call this morning a lot of things," Meredith replied as she walked over to the closet to hang up her coat, "but *good* isn't one of them." Trying to delay calling Matt, she said, "Do I have any phone messages?"

Phyllis nodded. "Mr. Sanborn in personnel phoned because you haven't returned your updated insurance application form. He says he needs it right away." She handed it to Meredith and stood waiting.

Sighing, Meredith sat down at her desk, picked up her pen, and filled out her name and address, then she stared in revolted confusion at the next question: "Marital Status" it said. "Circle one: Single Married Widowed." A hysterical laugh welled up within her as she looked at the middle choice. She was *married.* For eleven years she had been *married* to Matt Farrell.

"Are you feeling all right?" Phyllis asked anxiously when Meredith put her forehead in her hand and gazed at the form, paralyzed.

Lifting her eyes to Phyllis, she said, "What can they do to you for lying on an insurance form?"

"I guess they could refuse to pay off your legal heir if you die."

"Fair enough," Meredith replied with bitter humor, and with an angry flourish, she circled Single. Oblivious to Phyllis's worried frown, she handed her the completed form and said, "Will you close my door when you leave, and hold my calls for a few minutes?"

When Phyllis left, Meredith removed the phone book from the credenza behind her, looked up Haskell Electronics' phone number, and jotted it down. Then she put away the phone book and sat there, staring at the telephone as if it had fangs, knowing the moment she'd dreaded all night had arrived. Closing her eyes for a moment, she tried to put herself in the right frame of mind by rehearsing her plan again: If Matt was angry about what she'd said at the opera—which he would surely be—she would apologize with simple dignity. An apology, with no excuses, followed by a polite, impersonal request to meet with him about an urgent matter. That was her plan. In slow motion she lifted her shaking hand and reached for the telephone. . . .

For the third time in an hour, Matt's intercom buzzed on his desk, interrupting a loud and heated debate among his executives. Angry at the continued interruptions, he glanced apologetically at the men and reached for the intercom button as he explained, "Miss Stern's sister is ill, and she's on the Coast. Go on with your conversation," he added as he pressed the button and snapped at the secretary who was filling in for Miss Stern, "I told you to hold my calls!"

"Yes, sir, I—I know"—Joanna Simons's voice came over the speaker phone—"but Miss Bancroft said it's extremely important, and she insisted I interrupt you."

"Take a message," Matt snapped. He started to release the button, then he stopped. "Who did you say was calling?"

"Meredith Bancroft," the secretary emphasized meaningfully, her tone telling him that she, too, had read of his confrontation with Meredith in Sally Mansfield's column. So, obviously, had the men seated in a semicircle around his desk, for the announcement of Meredith's name caused a pulse beat of stunned silence followed instantly by an explosion of nervous, heightened conversation meant to cover the previous silence.

"I'm in the middle of a meeting," Matt said curtly. "Tell her to call me back in fifteen minutes." He put the phone down, knowing that courtesy dictated that he should have volunteered to call *Meredith* back. He didn't really give a damn; they had nothing left to say to each other. Forcing himself to concentrate on business, he looked at Tom Anderson, and continued the conversation that Meredith's call had interrupted. "There won't be any zoning problem in Southville. We have a contact on the zoning commission who's assured us that the county and the city of Southville are both eager to have us build the factory there. We'll have approval from them on Wednesday, when they meet to vote. . . ."

Ten minutes later he ushered the men out of his office, closed the door, and sat down behind his desk again. When Meredith hadn't called after thirty minutes, he leaned back in his leather chair and glowered at the silent telephone, his hostility growing with every passing moment. How like Meredith, he thought, to call him for the first time in more than a decade, then insist that his secretary interrupt him in the middle of a meeting, and when he didn't take the call, to then make him sit and wait. She had always behaved as if she were royalty. She had been born with an inflated sense of her own worth and brought up to believe that she was better than everyone else. . . .

Drumming her fingernails on her desk, Meredith leaned back in her chair, angrily watching the clock, deliberately waiting forty-five minutes before calling him again. How like that arrogant, swaggering braggart to make *her* call *him* back! she thought wrathfully. Obviously he hadn't acquired any manners along with his wealth, or he'd know that since she had courteously taken the first step in contacting him, it was his duty to take the next step. Of course, good manners would never mean anything to Matthew Farrell. Beneath his newly acquired veneer of urbanity, he was still nothing but a crude, ambitious—Meredith abruptly checked her bitter thoughts; bitterness would only make what lay ahead of her more difficult. Besides, she reminded herself yet again, it was unfair to blame Matt for everything that had happened years before. She had willingly participated in their lovemaking the night they met, and she had disregarded her responsibility to protect herself against pregnancy. When she got pregnant, Matt had decently volunteered to marry her. Later, she had convinced herself that he loved her, but he had never said so. He had never actually deceived her, and it was stupid and childish to blame him for not having lived up to her naive expectations. It was as foolish and pointless as the way she'd spoken to him at the opera. Feeling far more calm and reasonable now, Meredith put aside her hurt pride and promised herself to maintain her philosophical composure. The hands on the clock lurched into position at 10:45, and she reached for the telephone.

Matt jumped at the buzz of his intercom. "Miss Bancroft is on the line," Joanna said.

He picked up the phone. "Meredith?" he said, his voice clipped, impatient, "this is an unexpected surprise."

Distractedly, Meredith noted that he had not said an "unexpected pleasure," as was customary, and that his voice was deeper and more resonant than she remembered.

"Meredith!" His irritation vibrated across the distance separating them and snapped her out of her nervous preoccupation. "If you've called me to breathe in my ear, I'm flattered but a little confused. What do you expect me to do now?"

"I see you're still as conceited and ill-mannered as—"

"Ah—you've called me to criticize my manners," Matt concluded.

Meredith sternly reminded herself that her goal was to soothe him, not antagonize him. Carefully reining in her temper, she said with sincerity, "Actually, I'm calling because I'd like to—to bury the hatchet."

"In what part of my body?"

It was close enough to the truth to wrench a helpless laugh from her, and when Matt heard it, he suddenly remembered how enchanted he'd once been by her infectious laugh and sense of humor. His jaw tightened and his tone hardened. "What do you want, Meredith?"

"I want, that is, I need to talk to you—in person."

"Last week you turned your back on me in front of five hundred people," he reminded her icily. "Why this sudden change of heart?"

"Something has happened, and we have to discuss it in a mature, calm fashion," she said, desperately trying to avoid being specific until she could deal with him face-to-face. "It's about, well, us—"

"There is no us," he said implacably, "and it's obvious from what happened at the opera that calm maturity is beyond your capability."

An angry retort sprang to Meredith's lips, but she stifled it. She didn't want a battle, she wanted a treaty. She was a businesswoman and she had learned to deal successfully with stubborn men—Matt was bent on being difficult; therefore, she needed to maneuver him into a more reasonable frame of mind. Arguing with him would not accomplish that. "I had no idea Sally Mansfield was nearby when I behaved that way to you," she explained tactfully. "I apologize for what I said, and particularly for saying it in front of her."

"I'm impressed," he said in a mocking tone. "You've obviously studied diplomacy."

Meredith grimaced at the phone, but she kept her voice soft. "Matt, I'm trying to call a truce, can't you cooperate with me just a little?"

The sound of her saying his name jolted him, and he hesitated a full five seconds, then he said abruptly, "I'm leaving for New York in an hour. I won't be back until late Monday night."

Meredith smiled with triumph. "Thursday is Thanksgiving Day. Could we do it before then, say on Tuesday, or are you impossibly busy that day?"

Matt glanced down at his desk calendar which was covered with meetings and appointments scheduled for Thanksgiving week. He was impossibly busy. "Tuesday will be fine. Why don't you come to my office at eleven forty-five?"

"Perfect," Meredith instantly agreed, more relieved than disappointed by her five-day reprieve.

"By the way," he said, "does your father know we're meeting?"

His acid tone told her that his dislike for her father had not diminished. "He knows."

"Then I'm surprised he hasn't had you locked and chained to prevent it. He must be getting soft."

"He's not soft, but he's older now and he's been very ill." Trying to lessen Matt's inevitable animosity when he discovered her father inadvertently hired a sham lawyer and that they were still legally married, she added, "He could die at any time."

"When he does," Matt countered sarcastically, "I hope to God someone has the presence of mind to drive a wooden stake through his heart."

Meredith muffled a horrified giggle at his quip and politely said goodbye. But when she hung up, the laughter faded from her face and she leaned back in her chair. Matt had implied her father was a vampire, and there was a time when she felt as if he had indeed been draining her life from her. At the very least, he had stolen much of the joy from her youth.

🌿 26

By Tuesday, as she stood before the mirror in the private bathroom that adjoined her office, Meredith had managed to convince herself that she could definitely have a polite, impersonal meeting with Matt, as well as persuade him to agree to an uncomplicated, quick divorce.

She touched up her lipstick, brushed her shoulder-length hair into an artful windblown style, then she stepped back to study the effect of the softly draped black wool jersey dress with its high collar, sarong skirt, and long, full sleeves. A wide, shiny gold choker at her neck gleamed brightly against the stark black dress, and at her wrist was a matching bracelet. Pride and good sense demanded that she look her best; Matt dated movie stars and sexy, glamorous models, and she knew she could deal with him better if she felt confident rather than dowdy. Satisfied, she shoved her cosmetics into her purse, picked up her coat and gloves, and decided to take a taxi to his office so that she wouldn't have to fight traffic or look for a parking space in the rain.

In the taxi she gazed out the window, watching the pedestrians dashing across Michigan Avenue, holding umbrellas and newspapers over their heads. Rain pounded like tiny hammers on the roof of the cab, and she snuggled deeper into the luxurious folds of the fur coat her father had given her on her twenty-fifth birthday. For five days and nights she'd planned her strategy, rehearsed what she would say and how she would say it. Calm, tactful, businesslike—that was how she would act. She would not descend to criticizing him for his past actions. For one thing, he had no conscience; for another, she was adamantly unwilling to give him the satisfaction of knowing how terribly his betrayal had hurt her. No recriminations, she reminded herself—calm, businesslike, and tactful. By behaving that way, she'd set the tone and, hopefully, an example for him to follow. And she wouldn't just burst out with the information about their problem—she'd *ease* into it.

Her hands were beginning to shake, and she shoved them into the deep pockets of her coat, her fingers curling into fists of nervous tension. Rivers of rain poured down the cab's windshield, blurring the traffic signal ahead, turning it into colorful flashes of green, yellow, and red, flashes that reminded her of the fireworks exploding on that Fourth of July evening that had altered the entire course of her life.

The cab driver's voice snapped her out of her reverie. "Here we are, miss."

Meredith fumbled in her purse, paid him, and dashed through the downpour into the soaring glass and steel building that housed Matt's newest business acquisition.

When she stepped off the elevator on the sixtieth floor, she found herself in a spacious silver-carpeted private reception area. She walked over to the receptionist, a chic brunette who was seated at a round desk, watching Meredith approach with ill-concealed fascination. "Mr. Farrell is expecting you, Miss Bancroft," she said, obviously recognizing Meredith from her pictures. "He's in a meeting at the moment, but it should be over in a few minutes. Please have a seat."

Annoyed because Matt intended to make her wait like a peasant trying to get an audience with a king, Meredith pointedly looked at the clock on the wall. She was ten minutes early.

Her anger left as abruptly as it had come, and she sat in a leather and chrome chair. As she picked up a magazine and opened it, a man hurried out of the corner office, leaving the door ajar. Over the top of the magazine Meredith discovered she had a clear view of the man who was her husband, and she studied him with reluctant fascination.

Matt was seated behind his desk, his dark brows knitted in a thoughtful frown as he leaned back in his chair, listening to the men who were talking to him. Despite his relaxed pose, his jaw was stamped with authority, his chin set with confidence, and even in his shirt-sleeves he seemed to exude an aura of dynamic power that Meredith found slightly surprising and strangely disturbing. The other night, at the opera, she'd been too unstrung to look at him well, let alone study him. But now, as she had the time and opportunity, she noted that his features were much the same as she'd remembered them from eleven years ago . . . and yet subtly different. At thirty-seven, he had lost the brashness of youth, and in its place his face had acquired a hard-bitten strength that made him look even more attractive— and more uncompromising. His hair was darker than she had recalled, his eyes lighter, but there was the same blatant sensuality in that chiseled mouth. One of the men said something funny, and the glamour of Matt's sudden white smile made her heart contract. Firmly ignoring that unexplainable reaction, she concentrated on the discussion that was under way in his office. Apparently Matt was planning to merge two divisions of Intercorp into one, and the purpose of the meeting taking place was to discuss the smoothest way to handle it.

With mounting professional interest, Meredith noted that Matt's method of conducting a meeting with his executives was very different from her father's. Her father called a meeting to give orders, and he was outraged if anyone dared to contradict him. Matt, on the other hand, obviously preferred a lively give-and-take, a free expression of differing opinions and conflicting suggestions. He listened, quietly weighing the merit of each idea, each objection as it was expressed. Instead of bullying his staff into humiliated submission, as her father did, Matt was utilizing the talent of each man, benefiting from each man's particular expertise. To Meredith, Matt's way seemed far more sensible and far more productive.

She sat, openly eavesdropping now, while a tiny seed of admiration took root and began to grow. She lifted her arm to lay the magazine aside, and as if the movement caught his attention, Matt suddenly turned his head and looked directly at her.

Meredith froze, the magazine still in her hand as those penetrating gray eyes locked onto hers. Abruptly he pulled his gaze away and looked at the men seated around his desk. "It's later than I thought," he said. "We'll resume this discussion after lunch."

Within moments the men were filing out, and Meredith's throat went dry as Matt came stalking toward her. *Calm, tactful, businesslike,* she reminded herself in a nervous chant as she forced her gaze upward, past the smoothly tailored gray trousers that hugged his long, muscled legs and hips, and looked into his shuttered eyes. *No recriminations . . . Ease into the problem, don't blurt it out.*

Matt watched her stand up, and when he spoke his voice was as completely impersonal as his feelings toward her. "It's been a long time," he said, deliberately choosing to forget their brief, unpleasant meeting at the opera. She'd apologized for that on the phone; she'd proved her desire for a truce by coming here, and he was willing to meet her halfway. After all, he'd gotten over her years ago, and it was foolish to nurse a grudge over something—and someone—who no longer mattered one damn bit to him.

Encouraged by his apparent lack of animosity, Meredith extended her black-gloved hand and struggled to keep her own nervousness from showing in her voice. "Hello, Matt," she managed to say with a composure she didn't at all feel.

His handclasp was brief, businesslike. "Come into my office for a moment; I have to make a phone call before we leave."

"Leave?" she said as she walked beside him into a spacious silver-carpeted office with a panoramic view of the Chicago skyline. "What do you mean, leave?"

Matt picked up the telephone on his desk. "Some new artwork has arrived for my office, and they're going to be hanging the paintings in a few minutes. Besides, I thought we could talk better over lunch."

"Lunch?" Meredith repeated, thinking madly for a way to avoid it.

"Don't tell me you've already eaten, because I won't believe you," he said, punching out a number on the telephone. "You used to think it was uncivilized to eat lunch before two in the afternoon."

Meredith remembered saying something like that to him during the days she spent at the farm. What a smug little idiot she had been at eighteen, she thought. These days, she normally ate lunch at her desk—when and if she had time to eat at all. Actually, lunch in a restaurant wasn't a bad idea, she realized, because he wouldn't be able to curse or shout or make a scene when she told him her news. Rather than stand there while he waited for the person he was calling to come to the phone, Meredith wandered over to inspect his collection of modern art. At the far end of the room, she noted and identified the only piece she liked—a large Calder mobile. On the wall beside it was a huge painting with blobs of yellow, blue, and maroon on it, and she stood back, trying to see what *anyone* found to like in such stuff. To her, the painting looked like fish eyes swimming in grape jelly. Beside it was another painting which appeared to depict a New York alley . . . she tipped her head to one side, studying it intently. Not an alley—a monastery, perhaps—or possibly upside-down mountains with a village and a stream running in a slash diagonally across the entire canvas, and trash cans . . .

Standing behind his desk, Matt watched her while he waited for his call to go through. With the detached interest of a connoisseur, he studied the woman standing in his office. Wrapped in a mink coat, with a gold choker glittering at her throat, she looked elegant, expensive, and pampered—an impression that was at striking variance with the madonnalike purity of her profile as she gazed up at the painting, her hair sparkling like minted gold beneath the spotlights overhead. At nearly thirty, Meredith still projected that same convincing aura of artless sophistication and unconscious sex appeal. No doubt that had been a major part of her allure for him, he thought sardonically—her heart-stopping beauty combined with a superficial but convincing air of regal aloofness and a touch of nonexistent sweetness and goodness. Even now, a decade older and wiser, he would still find her exquisitely appealing if he didn't already know how heartless and selfish she really was.

When he hung up the phone, he walked over to where she was studying the painting and waited in silence for her comments.

"I—I think it's wonderful," Meredith lied.

"Really?" Matt replied. "What do you like about it?"

"Oh, everything. The colors . . . the excitement it conveys . . . the imagery."

"Imagery," he repeated, his voice incredulous. "What specifically do you see when you look at it?"

"Well, I see what could be mountains—or gothic spires upside down—or . . ." Her voice trailed off in sublime discomfort. "What do *you* see when you look at it?" she asked with forced enthusiasm.

"I see a quarter-of-a-million-dollar investment," he replied dryly, "which is now worth a half million."

She was appalled, and it showed before she could hide it. "For *that?*"

"For that," he replied, and she almost thought she saw a glint of answering humor in his eyes.

"I didn't mean that exactly the way it sounded," she said contritely, reminding herself of her plan: *Calm, tactful* . . . "I know very little about modern art, actually."

He dismissed the subject with an indifferent shrug. "Shall we go?"

When he went to get his coat from the closet, Meredith noticed the framed photograph on his desk of a very pretty young woman sitting on a fallen log with her knee drawn up near her chest, her hair tossing in the wind, her smile dazzling. Either she was a professional model, Meredith decided, or judging from that smile, she was in love with the photographer.

"Who took the picture?" she asked when Matt turned toward her.

"I did, why?"

"No reason." The young woman wasn't one of the famous starlets or socialites Matt had been photographed with. There was a fresh, unspoiled beauty to the girl in the picture. "I don't recognize her."

"She doesn't move in your circles," he said sardonically, shrugging into his suit jacket and coat. "She's just a girl who works as a research chemist in Indiana."

"And she loves you," Meredith concluded, turning in surprise at the veiled sarcasm in his voice.

Matt glanced at his sister's picture. "She loves me."

Meredith sensed instinctively that this girl was important to him, and if that was true—if he was possibly thinking of marrying her—then he would be as eager as she to get a swift, simple divorce. Which would make her task this afternoon much easier.

As they walked through his secretary's office, Matt stopped to talk to the gray-haired woman. "Tom Anderson is at the Southville zoning commission hearing," he told her. "If he gets back while I'm at lunch, give him the number at the restaurant and have him call me there."

❧27

A silver limousine was waiting at the curb for them. Standing beside it was a burly chauffeur with a broken nose and the physique of a buffalo, who held the back door open for her. Normally, Meredith found riding in a limousine restful and luxurious, but as they charged away from the curb, she grasped the armrest in uneasy surprise. She managed to keep her alarm from showing as the chauffeur hurtled the limo around corners, but when he ran a red light and bluffed out a CTA bus, her gaze darted nervously to Matt.

He responded to her unspoken comment with a mild shrug. "Joe hasn't given up his dream of driving at Indy."

"This *isn't* Indy," Meredith pointed out, clutching the armrest tighter as they swerved around another corner.

"And he isn't a chauffeur."

Determined to imitate his nonchalance, Meredith pried her fingers loose from the padded armrest. "Really? What is he, then?"

"A bodyguard."

Her stomach lurched at this proof that Matt had done things to make people hate him enough to do him physical harm. Danger had never attracted her; she liked peace and predictability and she found the idea of a bodyguard a little barbaric.

Neither of them spoke again until after the car lurched to a stop at the canopied entrance of Landry's, one of Chicago's most elegant, exclusive restaurants.

The maître d', who was also a part owner of the restaurant, was stationed at his usual post near the front door, clad in a tuxedo. Meredith had known John ever since her boarding school days, when her father used to bring her there for lunch and John sent soft drinks to her table, fixed up like exotic bar drinks, with his compliments.

"Good afternoon, Mr. Farrell," he intoned formally, but when he turned to Meredith, he added with a twinkling smile: "It's always a pleasure to see you, Miss Bancroft." Meredith shot a swift look at Matt's unreadable face, wondering how he felt at the discovery that she was better known at the restaurant he'd chosen than he was. She forgot about that as they were escorted toward their table, and she realized there were several people whom she knew dining there. Judging from their shocked stares, they recognized Matt and were undoubtedly wondering why she was lunching with a man she'd publicly shunned. Sherry Withers, one of the biggest gossips in Meredith's circle of acquaintances, lifted her hand in a wave, her gaze leveled on Matt, her brows raised in amused speculation.

A waiter led them past banks of fresh flowers and around a fanciful white trellis to a table that was far enough away from the ebony grand piano in the center of the room to enjoy the music, but not so close that it hindered conversation. Unless you were a regular patron of Landry's, it was nearly impossible to reserve a table with less than two weeks notice; reserving a good table, which this one certainly was, was virtually impossible, and Meredith wondered idly how Matt had accomplished it.

"Would you like a drink?" he asked her when they were seated.

Her mind shifted abruptly from aimless conjecture over how he got reservations to the very dire confrontation that lay immediately before her. "No, thank you, just ice water—" Meredith began, then she decided a drink might help steady her nerves. "Yes," she corrected herself. "I would."

"What would you like?"

"I'd like to be in Brazil," she mumbled on a ragged sigh.

"I beg your pardon?"

"Something strong," Meredith said, trying to decide what to drink. "A Manhattan." She shook her head, negating that drink. It was one thing to be calmed, another to be lulled into saying or doing something she shouldn't. She was a nervous wreck, and she wanted something to soothe her tension. Something she could sip slowly until it did its job. Something she didn't like. "A martini," she decided with an emphatic nod.

"All of that?" he asked, straight-faced. "A glass of water, a Manhattan, and a martini?"

"No . . . just the martini," she said with a shaky smile, but her eyes were filled with frustrated dismay and an unconscious appeal for his patience.

Matt was temporarily intrigued by the combination of startling contrasts she presented at that moment. Wearing a sophisticated black dress that covered her from throat to wrist, she looked both elegant and glamorous. That alone wouldn't have disarmed him, but combined with the faint blush that was staining her smooth cheeks, the helpless appeal in those huge, intoxicating eyes of hers, and her girlish confusion, she was nearly irresistible. Softened by the fact that she had asked for this meeting to make amends, he abruptly decided to follow the same course of action that he had tried to follow the night he spoke to her at the opera—and that was to let bygones be bygones. "Will I throw you into another bout of confusion if I ask what kind of martini you'd like?"

"Gin," Meredith said. "Vodka," she amended. "No, gin—a gin martini."

Her flush deepened and she was too nervous to notice the glint of amusement in his eyes as he solemnly asked, "Dry or wet?"

"Dry."

"Beefeater's, Tanqueray, or Bombay?"

"Beefeater's."

"Olives or onion?"

"Olives."

"One or two?"

"Two."

"Valium or aspirin?" he inquired in that same bland voice, but a grin was tugging at the corner of his mouth, and she realized he'd been teasing her all along. Gratitude and relief built inside her, and she looked at him, returning his smile. "I'm sorry. I'm, well, a little nervous."

When the waiter had departed with their drink order, Matt considered her admission about being nervous. He looked about him at the beautiful restaurant where a meal cost as much as he used to make in an entire day working at the mill. Without actually intending to, he made an admission of his own: "I used to daydream about taking you to lunch in a place like this."

Distracted by how best to open the subject on her mind, Meredith's glance skimmed over the magnificent pink floral sprays in massive silver containers and the tuxedo-clad waiters hovering solicitously at linen-covered tables agleam with china and crystal. "A place like what?"

Matt laughed shortly. "You haven't changed, Meredith; the most extravagant luxury is still ordinary to you."

Determined to maintain the fragile goodwill that had begun while she debated over what to drink, Meredith said reasonably, "You wouldn't know whether I've changed or not—we spent only six days together."

"And six nights," he emphasized meaningfully, deliberately trying to make her blush again, wanting to shake her composure, to see again the uncertain girl who'd been unable to decide what to drink.

Pointedly ignoring his sexual reference, she said, "It's hard to believe we were ever married."

"That's not surprising since you never used my name."

"I'm sure," she countered, striving for a tone of serene indifference, "that there are *dozens* of women who are more entitled to do that than I ever was."

"You sound jealous."

"If I sound jealous," Meredith retorted, holding on to her temper with an effort, and leaning closer across the table, "then there's something terribly wrong with your hearing!"

A reluctant smile drifted across his features. "I had forgotten that prim boarding-school way you have of expressing yourself when you're angry."

"*Why,*" she hissed, "are you deliberately trying to goad me into an argument?"

"Actually," he said dryly, "that last was a compliment."

"Oh," Meredith said. Surprised and a little flustered, she shifted her gaze to the waiter who was placing their drinks on the table. They gave him their lunch order, and she decided to wait until Matt had finished part of his drink, until the alcohol in it had soothed him a bit, before she broke the news to him about their nonexistent divorce. She left the next topic up to him to choose.

Matt picked up his glass, annoyed with himself for having needled her, and said with genuine courtesy and interest, "According to the society columns, you're active in a half-dozen charities, the symphony, the opera, and the ballet. What else do you do with your time?"

"I work fifty hours a week at Bancroft's," Meredith replied, vaguely disappointed that he'd never read about her achievements anywhere.

Matt knew all about her supposed accomplishments at Bancroft's, but he was curious about how good an executive she really was, and he knew he could judge that simply by listening to her talk. He began questioning her about her work.

Meredith answered—haltingly at first and then more freely, because she dreaded telling him the reason for this meeting and because her work was her favorite topic. His questions were so astute, and he seemed so genuinely interested in her answers, that before long she was telling him of her achievements and her goals, her successes and her failures. He had a way of listening that encouraged confidences—he concentrated exclusively on what was being said to him, as if each word were interesting and important and meaningful. Before she realized it, Meredith had even confided the problem she faced with accusations of nepotism at the store and how difficult it was to deal with that as well as the chauvinism her father fostered among his staff with his own attitude.

By the time the waiter cleared away their luncheon plates, Meredith had answered all his questions and finished nearly half the bottle of Bordeaux that he'd ordered. It occurred to her that the reason she'd been so vocal was because she'd been stalling about telling him her upsetting news. But even now, when that could no longer be put off, she felt vastly more relaxed than at the beginning of the meal.

In companionable silence they regarded each other across the table. "Your father is lucky to have you on his staff," Matt said, and he meant it sincerely. He had no doubt that she was one hell of an executive—possibly even a gifted executive. While she'd spoken, her management style had become clear to him; so had her dedication and intelligence, her enthusiasm and, most of all, her courage and wit.

"I'm the lucky one," Meredith said, smiling at him. "Bancroft's means everything to me. It's the most important thing in my life."

Matt leaned back in his chair, absorbing this newly discovered side of her. He frowned at the wine in the glass he was holding, wondering why in the hell she talked about those damned department stores as if they were people whom she loved. Why was her career the most important thing in her life? Why wasn't Parker Reynolds—or some other suitably prominent socialite—more important to her? But even while he asked himself the questions, Matt thought he knew the answer: Her father had succeeded after all; he had dominated her so ruthlessly and so effectively, that in the end he had turned her off men almost completely. Whatever her reason for marrying Reynolds was, she apparently wasn't in love with him. Based on what she said, and the way she looked when she spoke of Bancroft's, she was wholly committed to and in love with a department store.

Pity drifted through him as he looked at her. Pity and tenderness—he had experienced those emotions the night he met her, along with a raging desire to possess her that had obliterated his common sense. He had walked into that country club, taken one look at her jaunty smile and glowing eyes, and lost his mind. His heart softened as he remembered the way she had gaily introduced him as if he were a steel magnate from Indiana. She had been so full of laughter and life, so innocently eager in his arms. God, he had wanted her! He had wanted to take her away from her father, to cherish and pamper and protect her.

If she had stayed married to him, he would have been incredibly proud of her now. In an impersonal sort of way, he was proud as hell of what she'd become.

Pamper and protect her? Matt realized the direction of his thoughts and clenched his teeth in self-disgust. Meredith didn't need anyone to protect her; she was as deadly as a black widow spider. The only human being who mattered to her was her father, and to appease him, she'd murdered her unborn child. She was spoiled, spineless, and heartless—an empty, beautiful mannequin who was meant to be draped in beautiful clothes and propped at the end of a dining room table. That was all she was good for, it was her only use in life. It was her appearance that had made him forget that for the past few minutes—that gorgeous face of hers with those captivating aquamarine eyes fringed with curly lashes; the proud way she held herself; that soft, generous mouth; the musical sound of her voice; the hesitant, infectious smile. Christ, he'd always been a fool where she was concerned, he thought, but his hostility was suddenly doused by the realization that this spurt of anger was foolish and pointless. Regardless of what she had done, she had been very young and very frightened, and it had happened long ago. It was over. Idly twirling the stem of the wineglass in his fingers, he looked at her and paid her a casual, impartial compliment: "From the sound of things, you've become a formidable executive. If we'd stayed married, I'd probably have tried to lure you over to my organization."

He had unwittingly tossed her the opening she needed, and Meredith seized it. Trying to inject a note of humor into the dire moment, she said with a nervous, choked laugh, "Then start trying to lure me over."

His eyes narrowed. "What is that supposed to mean?"

Unable to maintain her wavering smile, Meredith leaned forward, crossed her arms on the table, and drew a long, steadying breath. "I—I have something to tell you, Matt. Try not to get upset."

With a disinterested shrug, he lifted his wineglass toward his mouth. "We have no feelings for each other, Meredith. Therefore, nothing you could tell me could upset me—"

"We're still married," she announced.

His brows jerked together. "Nothing except that!"

"Our divorce wasn't legal," she plunged on, inwardly shrinking from his ominous gaze. "The—the lawyer who handled the divorce wasn't a real lawyer, he was a fraud, and he's being investigated right now. No judge ever signed our divorce decree—no judge even saw it!"

With alarming deliberation he put his glass down and leaned forward, his low voice hissing with anger. "Either you're lying or else you don't have enough sense to dress yourself! Eleven years ago, you invited me to sleep with you without giving a thought to protecting yourself from pregnancy. When you *got* pregnant you came running to me and dumped the problem in my lap. Now you're telling me you didn't have the brains to hire a real lawyer to get you a divorce, and we're still married. How in the hell can you run an entire division of a department store and still be that stupid?"

Each contemptuous word he spoke cracked against her pride like a whip, but his reaction was no worse than what she'd expected, and she accepted the tongue-lashing as her due. Fury and shock temporarily robbed him of further speech, and she said in a low, soothing voice, "Matt, I can understand how you feel. . . ."

Matt wanted to believe she was lying about the whole mess, that this was some sort of crazy attempt to get money from him, but his every instinct told him she was telling him the truth.

"If our positions were reversed," she continued, trying to speak in a calm, rational voice, "I would feel just as you do—"

"When did you find this out?" he interrupted tightly.

"The night before I called you to arrange this meeting."

"Assuming you're telling me the truth—that we're still married—just exactly what do you want from me?"

"A divorce. A nice, quiet, uncomplicated, *immediate* divorce."

"No alimony?" he jeered, watching the angry flush steal up her cheeks. "No property settlement, nothing like that?"

"No!"

"Good, because you sure as hell aren't going to get any!"

Angry at his deliberate and rude reminder that his wealth was now far greater than hers, Meredith looked at him with well-bred disdain. "Money was all you ever thought about, all that mattered to you. I never wanted to marry you, and I don't want your money! I'd rather starve than have anyone know we were ever married!"

The maître d' chose that untimely moment to appear at their table to inquire if their meal had been satisfactory or if they wanted anything else.

"Yes," Matt said bluntly. "I'll have a double shot of scotch on the rocks, and my *wife*," he emphasized, taking petty, malicious satisfaction out of doing exactly what she'd just said she never wanted to do, "will have another martini."

Meredith, who never, ever had engaged in a public scene, glowered at her old friend and said, "I'll give you a thousand dollars to poison his drink!"

Bowing slightly, John smiled and said with grave courtesy, "Certainly, Mrs. Farrell," then he turned to a furious Matt, and added drolly, "Arsenic or do you prefer something more exotic, Mr. Farrell?"

"Don't you dare ever to call me by that name again!" Meredith warned John. "It is *not* my name."

The humor and affection vanished from John's face, and he bowed again. "My sincerest apologies for having taken undue liberties, Miss Bancroft. Your drink will be delivered with my compliments."

Meredith felt like a complete witch for taking her anger out on him. Morosely, she glanced at John's stiff, retreating back and then at Matt. She waited a moment longer for their tempers to cool, then she drew a long, calming breath. "Matt, it's counterproductive for us to sling insults at one another. can't we please try to treat each other at least with courtesy? If we could, it would make it much easier for us to deal with all this."

She was right, he knew, and after a moment's hesitation he said shortly, "I suppose we can try. How do you think things ought to be handled?"

"Quietly!" she said, smiling at him in relief. "And *quickly*. The need for secrecy and haste is far greater than you probably realize."

Matt nodded, his thoughts finally becoming more organized. "Your fiancé," he assumed. "According to the papers, you want to marry him in February."

"Well, yes, there is that," she agreed. "Parker already knows what's happened. He's the one who discovered that the man my father hired isn't a lawyer, and that our divorce doesn't exist. But there's something else—something vitally important to me that I could lose if this comes out."

"What's that?"

"I need a discreet—preferably secret—divorce so that there won't be any gossip or publicity about us. You see, my father is going to take a leave of absence because of his health, and I desperately want the chance to fill in for him as interim president. I need that chance to prove to the board of directors that when he retires permanently, I'm capable of handling the presidency of the corporation. The board is hesitant to appoint me interim president—as I told you, they're very conservative and they already have doubts about me because I'm relatively young for the position, and because I'm a woman. I already have those two strikes against me, and the press hasn't helped by portraying me as a frivolous social butterfly, which is what they like to do. If the press gets hold of our situation, they'll turn it into a carnival. I've announced my engagement to a very upright, important banker and you're supposed to be marrying a half-dozen starlets, but here we are— still married to each other. Potential bigamy doesn't get people appointed to the presidency of Bancroft's. I promise you, if this comes out, it will put an end to my chances."

"I don't doubt you believe that," Matt said, "but I don't think it would be as damaging to your chances as you think it would."

"Don't you?" she said bitterly. "Think how you reacted when I told you the lawyer was a fraud. You instantly leapt to the conclusion that I am an inept imbecile incapable of managing my own life, let alone anything else, like a department store chain. That is exactly how the board will react, because they're not one bit fonder of me than you are."

"Couldn't your father simply make it clear he wants them to appoint you?"

"Yes, but according to the bylaws of the corporation, the board of directors has to unanimously agree on the election of a president. Even if my father did control them, I'm not certain he'd intercede in my behalf."

Matt was spared the need to reply to that because a waiter was bringing their drinks and another was approaching the table, carrying a cordless telephone. "You have a call, Mr. Farrell," he said. "The caller said you instructed that he call you here."

Knowing the call had to be from Tom Anderson, Matt excused himself to Meredith, then he picked up the receiver and said without preamble, "What's the story on the Southville Zoning Commission?"

"It's not good, Matt," Tom said. "They've turned us down."

"Why in God's name would they turn down a rezoning request that can only benefit their community?" Matt said, more stunned than angry at that moment.

"According to my contact on the commission, someone with a lot of influence told them to turn us down."

"Any idea who it is?"

"Yeah. A guy named Paulson heads the commission. He told several members of it, including my contact, that *Senator Davies* said he'd consider it a personal favor if our rezoning request was denied."

"That's odd," Matt said, frowning, trying to recall if he'd donated money to Davies's campaign or to his opponent, but before he could remember, Anderson added in a voice reeking with sarcasm, "Did you happen to see a mention of a birthday party given for the good senator in the society column?"

"No, why?"

"It was given by one Mr. Philip A. Bancroft. Is there any connection between him and the Meredith we were talking about last week?"

Fury, white hot and deadly, exploded in Matt's chest. His gaze lifted to Meredith, noting her sudden pallor which could only be attributed to his mention of the Southville Zoning Commission. To Anderson he said softly, icily, "There's a connection. Are you at the office?" Anderson said he was, and Matt told him, "Stay there. I'll be back at three o'clock and we'll discuss the next steps."

Slowly, deliberately, Matt placed the phone back on its cradle, then he looked at Meredith, who'd suddenly developed a consuming need to smooth nonexistent creases in the tablecloth with her fingernail. Guilt and knowledge were written across her face, and he hated her at that moment, despised her with a virulence that was almost uncontainable. She had asked for this meeting not to "bury the hatchet," as she'd claimed, but because she wanted something—several things: She wanted to marry her precious banker, she wanted the presidency of Bancroft's, and she wanted a quick, quiet divorce. He was glad she wanted those things so badly, because she wasn't going to get them. What she and her father *were* going to get was a war, a war they were going to lose to him . . . along with everything they had. He signaled the waiter for the check. Meredith realized what he was doing, and the alarm that had quaked through her when he mentioned the Southville Zoning Commission escalated to panic. They hadn't agreed to anything yet, and suddenly he was putting a premature end to the discussion. The waiter presented the check in a folded leather case, and Matt yanked a hundred-dollar bill from his wallet, tossed it on top of the check without ever looking at it, and stood up. "Let's go," he snapped, already coming around the table and pulling out her chair.

"But we haven't agreed on anything," Meredith said desperately as he took her elbow in a tight grip and began urging her toward the door.

"We'll finish our discussion in the car."

Rain was pounding the red canopy in heavy sheets when they emerged, and the uniformed doorman who was stationed at the curb opened his umbrella, holding it over their heads as they climbed into the limousine.

Matt instructed his chauffeur to drive to Bancroft's department store, and then he gave her his full attention. "Now," he said softly, "what is it you want to do?"

His tone suggested he was going to cooperate, and she felt a mixture of relief and shame—shame because she knew why the zoning commission had turned him down, just as she knew why he was going to be denied membership at the Glenmoor Country Club. Mentally vowing to somehow *force* her father to undo the damage he'd done to Matt in those two places, she said quietly, "I want us to get a very quick, secret divorce—preferably out of state or out of the country—and I want the fact of our having been married to remain secret."

He nodded, as if giving the matter favorable consideration, but his next words jarred her. "And if I refuse, how can you retaliate? I suppose," he speculated in a coldly amused voice, "you could continue to cut me dead at boring society functions and your father could have me blackballed at every other country club in Chicago."

He already knew about her father blackballing him at Glenmoor! "I'm sorry about what he did at Glenmoor. Truly I am."

He laughed at her earnestness. "I don't give a damn about your precious country club. Someone nominated me after I'd told him not to bother."

Despite his words, Meredith didn't believe he didn't care. He wouldn't be human if he hadn't been deeply embarrassed at being denied membership. Guilt and shame for her father's petty viciousness made her glance slide away from his. She'd enjoyed his company at lunch, and he'd seemed to enjoy hers too. It had felt so good to talk to him as if the ugly past didn't exist. She didn't want to be his enemy; what had happened years ago wasn't entirely his fault. They both had new lives now—lives they'd made for themselves. She was proud of her accomplishments; he had every right to be proud of his. His forearm was resting on the back of the seat, and Meredith gazed at the elegant, wafer-thin gold watch that gleamed at his wrist, and then at his hand. He had wonderful, capable, masculine hands, she thought. Long ago, those hands had been callused, now they were manicured—

She had a sudden, absurd impulse to take his hand in her own and say, *I'm sorry. I'm sorry for the things we've done to hurt each other; I'm sorry we were so wrong for each other.*

"Are you trying to see if I still have grease under my fingernails?"

"No!" Meredith gasped, her gaze shooting to his enigmatic gray eyes. With quiet dignity she admitted, "I was wishing that things could have ended differently . . . ended so that we could at least be friends now."

"Friends?" he repeated with biting irony. "The last time I was friendly with you, it cost me my name, my bachelorhood, and a hell of a lot else."

It has cost you more than you know, Meredith thought miserably. *It has cost you a factory you want to build in Southville, but somehow I will make that right. I'll force my father to rectify the damage he's done and make him agree never to interfere with you again.* "Matt, listen to me," she said, suddenly desperate to make things right between them. "I'm willing to forget the past and—"

"That's gracious of you," he jeered.

Meredith stiffened, sorely tempted to point out that *she* was the injured party, the abandoned spouse, but then she squelched the impulse and continued doggedly. "I said I was willing to forget the past, and I am. If you'll agree to a quiet, congenial divorce, I'll do everything I can to smooth things over for you here in Chicago."

"Just how do you think you can smooth things over for me in Chicago, princess?" he asked, his voice reeking with sarcastic amusement.

"Don't call me princess! I'm not being condescending, I'm trying to be fair."

Matt leaned back and regarded her, his eyes shuttered. "I apologize for being rude, Meredith. What is it that you intend to do for me?"

Relieved by his apparent chance in attitude, she said quickly, "For a start, I can make certain you aren't treated like a social outcast. I know my father blocked your membership at our club, but I will try to make him change that—"

"Let's forget about me," he suggested smoothly, revolted by her wheedling and hypocrisy. He'd liked her better when she'd stood her ground at the opera and haughtily insulted him. But she needed something from him now, and Matt was glad it was desperately important to her. Because she wasn't going to get it. "You want a nice, quiet divorce because you want to marry your banker and because you want to be president of Bancroft's, right?" When she nodded, Matt continued. "And the presidency of Bancroft's is very, very important to you?"

"I want it more than I've ever wanted anything in my life," Meredith averred eagerly. "You—you will cooperate, won't you?" she said, searching his unreadable face as the car pulled to a stop in front of Bancroft's.

"No." He said it with such polite finality that for a moment Meredith's mind went blank.

"No?" she repeated in angry disbelief. "But the divorce is—"

"Forget it!" he snapped.

"Forget it? Everything I want hinges on it!"

"That's too damned bad."

"Then I'll get one *without* your consent!" she flung back.

"Try it and I'll make a stink you'll never live down. For starters, I'll sue your spineless banker for alienation of affection."

"Alienation of—" Too stunned to be cautious, Meredith burst out with a bitter laugh. "Have you lost your mind? If you do that, you'll look like an ass, like a heartbroken, jilted husband."

"And *you'll* look like an adulteress," he countered.

Fury erupted through Meredith's entire body. "Damn you!" she raged, her color rising. "If you *dare* to publicly embarrass Parker, I'll kill you with my own two hands! You're not fit to touch his shoes!" she exploded. "He's ten times the man you are! He doesn't need to try to bed every woman he meets. He has principles, he's a gentleman, but you wouldn't understand that because underneath that tailor-made suit you're wearing, you're still nothing but a dirty steelworker from a dirty little town with a dirty, drunken father!"

"And you," he said savagely, "are still a vicious, conceited bitch!"

Meredith swung, palm open, then swallowed a gasp of pain as Matt caught her wrist an inch from his face, holding it in a crushing grip, while he warned in a silky voice: "If the Southville Zoning Commission doesn't reverse their decision, there will be no further *discussion* of a divorce. If I decide to give you a divorce, I'll decide the terms and you and your father will go along with them." Increasing the pressure on her wrist, he jerked her forward until their faces were only inches apart. "Do you understand me, Meredith? You and your father have no power over me. Cross me one more time, and you'll wish to God your mother had aborted *you!*"

Meredith jerked her arm free of his grasp. "You are a monster!" she hissed. Rain spattered on her cheek and she snatched up her gloves and purse and threw a quelling look at the chauffeur/bodyguard, who had opened the door for her, and was watching their altercation with the enthusiastic intensity of a spectator at a tennis match.

As she climbed out of the car, Ernest rushed forward, belatedly recognizing Meredith, ready to defend her from whatever peril she might be in. "Did you see the man in that car?" she demanded of the Bancroft doorman. When he said that he had indeed, she said, "Good. If he ever comes near this store, you are to call the police!"

28

Joe O'Hara pulled the car over to the curb in front of Intercorp's building, and before it came to a complete stop, Matt flung open the door and climbed out.

"Tell Tom Anderson to come up here," he ordered Miss Stern as he stalked past her on the way into his office after having lunch with Meredith. "And then try to find me some aspirin."

Two minutes later, she appeared at his desk with a glass of cold water and two aspirin. "Mr. Anderson is on his way up," she said, studying his face as he tossed down the tablets. "You have a very busy schedule. I hope you aren't getting the flu. Mr. Hursh is out sick with it, and so are two of the vice presidents and half the word processing department. It starts with a headache."

Since she'd never shown any overt interest in his personal well-being, Matt naturally assumed her only concern was that he be able to stick to his working schedule. "I am not getting the flu," he said shortly. "I never get sick." He ran a hand around the back of his neck, absently massaging the aching muscles. The headache that had been only a minor, nagging discomfort this morning was beginning to pound.

"If it is the flu, it can last for weeks and even turn into pneumonia. That's what happened to Mrs. Morris in advertising and Mr. Lathrup in personnel, and they're both in the hospital. Perhaps you ought to plan on resting instead of going to Indiana next week. Otherwise your schedule—"

"I do not have the flu," Matt enunciated tightly. "I have a common, garden-variety headache."

She stiffened at his tone, turned on her heel, and marched out, bumping into Tom Anderson on the way.

"What's Miss Stern's problem?" Tom asked, glancing over his shoulder.

"She's afraid she'll have to reschedule my appointments," Matt said impatiently. "Let's talk about the zoning commission."

"Okay, what do you want me to do?"

"For the time being, ask for a postponement of any ruling."

"And then what?"

In answer, Matt picked up the phone and called Vanderwild. "What's Bancroft selling for?" he asked Peter, and when the other man answered, he said, "Start buying it. Use the same technique we used when we decided to acquire Haskell. Keep it quiet." He hung up and looked at Tom. "I want you to check out every member on Bancroft's board of directors. One of them may be for sale. Find out who he is and what his price is."

Not once in the years they'd been together, in the corporate battles they'd fought and won, had Matt ever resorted to anything as indefensible as bribery. "Matt, you're talking about plain bribery—"

"I'm talking about beating Bancroft at his own game. He's using influence to buy votes on the zoning commission. We'll use money to buy votes on his board. The only difference between what he's doing and what I'm doing is the medium of exchange. When I'm through with that vindictive old bastard, he'll be taking his orders from me in his own boardroom!"

"All right," Tom said after a hesitant pause. "But this will have to be handled very discreetly."

"There's more," Matt instructed, walking into the conference room that adjoined his office. He pressed a button on the wall and the mirrored panel that concealed the bar slid silently away. Matt jerked a bottle of scotch out of the cabinet, poured some into a glass, and took a long swallow. "I want to know everything there is to know about Bancroft's operation. Work with Vanderwild on it. In two days I want to know everything about their finances, their executives. Most of all, I want to know exactly where they're the most vulnerable."

"I gather you intend to take them over."

Matt tossed down another long swallow of his drink. "I'll decide that later. What I want right now is enough stock to control them."

"What about Southville? We've got a fortune invested in that land."

A mirthless smile twisted Matt's lips. "I phoned Pearson and Levinson from the car," he said, referring to the Chicago law firm he kept on retainer, "and told them what I want to do. We'll get our rezoning and we'll also make a handsome profit from Bancroft's."

"How?"

"There's the little matter of that Houston property they want so badly."

"And?"

"And we now own it."

Anderson nodded, took two steps toward the door, stopped, and turned back. Hesitantly, he said, "Since I'm going to be in the front lines alongside you in this battle with Bancroft, I'd like to at least know how it got started in the first place."

Had any of his other executives asked that question, Matt would have verbally flayed him. Trust was a luxury that men in Matt's financial stratum couldn't afford. He had learned, as others who'd made it to the top had also learned, that it was risky, even dangerous to confide too much to anyone. More often than not, they used the information to garner favors elsewhere; sometimes they used it simply to prove they were truly a confidant of a famous and successful man. Of all the people he knew, there were only four whom Matt trusted implicitly: his father, his sister, Tom Anderson, and Joe O'Hara. Tom had been with him since the old days, when he was getting by on daring and guts, building an empire on a foundation of audacity and hunches—and very little real capital. He trusted Anderson and O'Hara because they'd *proven* their loyalty. And, to a certain extent, he trusted them because, like him, they didn't come from privileged backgrounds and fancy prep schools. "Ten years ago," Matt replied after a reluctant pause, "I did something Bancroft didn't like."

"Jesus, it must have been pretty damned bad for him to keep up a vendetta all this time. What did you do?"

"I dared to reach above myself and to intrude on his own elite little world."

"How?"

Matt took another swallow of his drink to wash away the bitterness of the words, the memory. "I married his daughter."

"You married his—*Meredith Bancroft?* That daughter?"

"The very same," Matt averred grimly.

When Anderson gaped at him in stunned silence, Matt added, "There's something else you might as well know. She told me today that the divorce she thought she got eleven years ago wasn't legal. The lawyer was a fraud who never filed the petition with the court. I told Levinson to check that out, but I have a hunch it's the truth."

After another moment of stunned silence, Anderson's agile mind began to function. "And now she wants a fortune as a settlement, right?"

"She wants a divorce," Matt corrected, "and she and her father would like to ruin me, but beyond that, she claims she doesn't want anything."

Tom reacted with angry loyalty and a bitter, sarcastic laugh. "When we're through with them, they're going to wish to God they hadn't started this war," he promised, heading for the door.

When he was gone, Matt walked over to the windows and stood looking out on a day as bleak and dreary as his soul. Anderson was probably right about the outcome of all this, but Matt's sense of triumph was already dissolving. He felt . . . empty. As he stared out at the rain, Meredith's parting words revolved around and around in his mind: *you're not fit to touch Parker's shoes! He's ten times the man you are! Underneath that tailor-made suit you're wearing, you're still nothing but a dirty steelworker, from a dirty little town, with a dirty, drunken father!* He tried to blot those two sentences out of his mind, but they stayed, taunting him with his own stupidity, forcibly reminding him again of what a fool he was where she was concerned. For years after he thought they were divorced, he had not been able to drive her completely out of his heart. He had worked himself half to death to build an empire, driven by some stupid, half-formed plan to come back someday and impress Meredith with all he'd achieved and become.

His mouth twisted with bitter self-mockery. Today he'd had his chance to impress her: He was a financial success; the suit he was wearing cost more than the truck he had owned when they met; he'd taken her to a beautiful, expensive restaurant in a chauffeur-driven limousine—and after all that, he was still "nothing but a dirty steelworker" to her. Normally, he was proud of his origins, but Meredith's words had made him feel like some slimy monster dredged up from the bottom of a stagnant swamp, a monster who'd exchanged his scales for skin.

It was nearly seven P.M. when he finally left the building. Joe opened the door of the car, and Matt slid inside. He was inordinately tired, and he leaned his aching neck against the back of the seat, trying to ignore the faint scent of Meredith's soft perfume that lingered in the car. His thoughts drifted to their lunch, and he thought of the way she had smiled into his eyes while she talked to him about the store. With typical Bancroft arrogance she had smiled at him and asked him for a favor—a quiet, friendly divorce—at the same time she was publicly humiliating him and privately collaborating with her father to ruin him. Matt was perfectly willing to let her have her divorce, but not quite yet.

The car swerved suddenly, and horns blared beside and behind it. Matt's eyes snapped open, and he caught Joe watching him in the rearview mirror. "Did it ever occur to you," he said curtly, "to glance at the road now and then? It might make the trip less adventurous, but more restful."

"Naw. I get traffic-hypnosis if I stare at the road too much. So," he said, launching into the topic that was obviously on his mind after witnessing the altercation between Matt and Meredith in the car, "that was your wife today, huh, Matt?" He glanced at the road, then returned his gaze to the rearview mirror. "I mean, you were arguing about a divorce, so I figured she must be your wife, right?"

"Right," Matt snapped.

"She sure is a spitfire," Joe chuckled, ignoring Matt's narrowed gaze. "She doesn't like you very much, does she?"

"No."

"What's she got against steelworkers?"

Her parting words shot through Matt's brain. *You're nothing but a dirty steelworker.* "Dirt," Matt said uninformatively. "She doesn't like dirt."

When it was obvious his employer was not going to offer any further information, Joe reluctantly changed the subject. "Are you gonna need me when you're in Indiana at the farm next week? If not, your father and I thought we'd have a two-day orgy of checkers."

"No. Stay with him." Although his father had been sober for over a decade, Patrick was very emotional about the sale of the farm despite the fact that it had ultimately been his decision to sell it. Because of that, Matt felt a little uneasy about leaving him entirely alone while he was going to be out there, packing up their personal belongings.

"What about tonight? Are you going out?"

Matt had a date with Alicia. "I'll use the Rolls," he said. "Take the night off."

"If you need me——"

"Dammit! I said I'll use the Rolls."

"Matt?"

"What!"

"Your wife sure is a knockout," Joe said with another chuckle. "Too bad she makes you so grouchy."

Matt reached out and rudely closed the communicating window.

With Parker's arm around her shoulders offering silent comfort, Meredith stared at the fire crackling in her fireplace, her mind riveted in helpless anger on her ill-fated meeting with Matt. He'd been so *nice* in the beginning, teasing her because she'd been unable to make up her mind about what to drink . . . listening to her talk about her work.

The call he'd gotten about the Southville Zoning Commission had changed everything; Meredith realized that, now that she'd had time to think. But there were some things she didn't understand, things that made her feel uneasy because they made no sense: Even before Matt had gotten the phone call she'd felt as if he harbored some sort of underlying anger—no, *contempt*—for her. And despite what he had done eleven years earlier, he had not once been on the defensive today. Far from it. Instead, he'd acted as if he thought *she* should be! He had wanted a divorce, she had been the injured party, yet today Matt had called *her* a vicious, conceited bitch.

With an irritated mental shrug, Meredith shoved those useless thoughts aside. She was looking for reasons to justify his actions, she realized with disgust, trying to find excuses for him. From the night she'd met him, she'd been so dazzled by his hard-bitten strength and rugged looks, that she'd set out to make a knight in shining armor of him. To a lesser degree she was doing the same thing now—and all because, today, he'd had almost the same mesmerizing effect on her senses that he had years ago.

A glowing red log tumbled off the grate in a shower of orange sparks, and Parker glanced at his watch. "It's seven o'clock," he said. "I suppose I'd better leave." Sighing, Meredith stood up and accompanied him to the door, grateful for his considerate departure. Her father had been having tests run at the hospital all afternoon, and had insisted on coming over that night to hear a full accounting of Meredith's meeting with Matt. What she had to tell him was undoubtedly going to make him angry, and though Meredith was used to his ire, it embarrassed her to have him unleash it in front of Parker. "Somehow," she said, "I have to make him agree to reverse his stand about the Southville zoning commission. Until he does that, I haven't a prayer of making Matt agree to a quiet divorce."

"You'll succeed," Parker predicted, his arms sliding around her as he drew her close for a reassuring kiss. "For one thing, your father has very little choice. He'll realize that."

She was closing the door when she heard Parker greeting her father down the hall, and Meredith drew a long breath and braced herself for the confrontation that lay ahead of her.

"Well?" Philip said to her as he strode into her apartment. "What happened with Farrell?"

Meredith ignored that for the moment. "What did your doctor say about the test results? What did he say about your heart?"

"He said it's still in my chest," Philip sarcastically replied, taking off his coat and tossing it over a chair. He hated all doctors in general and his own doctor in particular, because Dr. Shaeffer could not be bullied or intimidated or bribed to give Philip what he wanted—a strong heart and a clean bill of health. "Never mind all that. I want to know exactly what Farrell said," he announced, walking over and pouring himself a glass of sherry.

"Don't you *dare* drink that!" she warned, then her mouth dropped open when he took a slender cigar out of his inside jacket pocket. "Are you trying to kill yourself? Put that cigar down!"

"Meredith," he snapped icily, "You are causing my heart more stress by not answering my question than this drop of brandy and puff of cigar could possibly do. I am the parent, not the child, kindly remember that."

After a day of frustration, that unfair attack sent sparks of anger to her eyes. He looked better than he had all week, which meant the test results must have been encouraging, particularly since he was deciding to risk the sherry and cigar. "Fine!" she replied, glad he was feeling strong, because she suddenly felt incapable of trying to gloss over the meeting. He wanted a blow-by-blow accounting, and Meredith gave it to him. Strangely, when she was finished, he looked almost relieved.

"That's it? That's everything Farrell said? He didn't say anything that seemed"—he glanced at his cigar as if trying to think of exactly the right word—"anything that seemed *odd?*" he emphasized.

"I've told you everything that was said," Meredith replied. "Now I'd like some answers." Looking him straight in the eye, she said with quiet force,

"Why did you block Matt's membership at Glenmoor? Why did you get his rezoning request denied? Why, after all these years, are you still carrying on this crazy vendetta? *Why?*"

Despite his angry tone, her father looked uneasy. "I kept him out of the club to protect you from having to see him there. I got his rezoning request denied because I want him to get the hell out of Chicago so we don't have to see him everywhere we go. That's beside the point, what's done is done."

"It's going to have to be *un*done," Meredith informed him flatly.

Philip ignored that. "I don't want you talking to him again. I went along with it today only because I let Parker convince me there was no other way. He should have volunteered to go with you. Frankly, I'm beginning to think Parker is weak, and I don't like weak men."

Meredith choked on a laugh. "In the first place, Parker is not at all weak, and he was intelligent enough to know his presence would only have complicated a difficult situation. In the second place, if you ever met any-one as strong as you, you'd hate him."

He had started to pick up his coat from the back of the chair where he'd tossed it, and he glowered at her over his shoulder. "Why would you say a thing like that?"

"Because," Meredith said, "the only man I've ever known who can equal you for sheer, fearless strength of will is Matthew Farrell! It's true, you know," she said gently, "in some ways he's very much like you—shrewd, invulnerable, and willing to go to any lengths to get what he wants. In the beginning you hated him because he was a nobody, and because he dared to sleep with me. But you hated him even more because you couldn't intimidate him—not that first night at the country club when you had him evicted, and not later, after we were married and I brought him home." She smiled, a sad smile devoid of anger, as she finished calmly, "You despise him because he's the only man you've ever met who is as indomitable as you are."

As if indifferent to her answer, he said coolly, "You don't like me, do you, Meredith?"

Meredith considered that with a mixture of fondness and wariness. He had given her life and then tried to direct every breath she took, every day of that life. No one could ever accuse him of not caring for her, or of neglect-ing her, for he had hovered over her like a hawk since she was a child. He had spoiled so much for her, and yet he had acted out of love—a possessive, strangling love. "I love you," she answered with an affectionate smile to take the sting out of her words, "but I don't like many of the things you do. You hurt people without regret, just as Matt does."

"I do what I think needs to be done," he replied, pulling on his coat.

"What needs to be done at the moment," Meredith reminded him, standing up so that she could walk him to the door, "is for you to immediately reverse the damage you've done to him at Glenmoor and the Southville zoning commission. Once you have, I'll contact him again and smooth things over."

"And you think he'll settle for that and agree to the divorce you want?" he replied with sarcastic disbelief.

"Yes, I do. You see, I have one advantage here: Matthew Farrell doesn't want to be married to me any more than I do to him. Right now he wants revenge, but he isn't insane enough to complicate the rest of his own life for the sake of retaliating against you and me. I hope. Now," she finished, "will you give me your word to get on the phone tomorrow and get the zoning commission moving on his request?"

He looked at her, his will on a collision course with her needs. "I'll look into the matter."

"That's not good enough—"

"It's as far as I'm willing to go."

He was bluffing, Meredith decided after studying his set face, and she placed a relieved kiss on his cheek. When he left, she wandered back to the sofa and sat down. She'd been staring blankly into the dying embers of the fire for a quarter of an hour before she remembered that Parker had told her tonight that Bancroft's board was meeting tomorrow to try to decide on an interim president. He would not be voting on this particular issue because of his involvement with Meredith. Tonight, however, she was too exhausted to feel much suspense or excitement over a meeting that might be inconclusive.

The television's remote controller was on the coffee table, and as she reached for it, she suddenly thought of Barbara Walters's interview with Matt. They'd talked about his success and the famous women he'd been with, and Meredith wondered how she could have *ever* believed she and Matt could be happy together. She and Parker understood each other; they came from the same social background, the same class—a class of people who endowed hospitals with new wings and donated their time to charity of civic causes. They did *not* discuss their wealth on public television—or talk about their tawdry little affairs there either!

No matter how much money Matthew Farrell made, she thought bitterly, or how many beautiful, famous women he slept with, he would still be what he had always been—ruthless, arrogant, and vicious. He was greedy, unscrupulous and . . . She frowned at the television screen in blank confusion—he was all of that and yet, today, she'd had the feeling he harbored an equally low opinion of *her!* When she thought of the way she'd attacked his family and called him a dirty steelworker, she didn't have a very high opinion of herself. That had been a cheap shot, and the truth was that she had a kind of tacit admiration for people with enough strength of body and spirit to do hard physical labor; it took a lot of courage to return, day after day, to a job that offered no mental challenge—only a paycheck. She'd attacked Matt's background because it was his only vulnerable spot.

The phone jarred her out of her thoughts, and Meredith answered it. Lisa's worried voice came out in a rush. "Mer, what happened with Farrell today? You said you'd call me after you'd met with him."

"I know, and I had you paged after I got back to the office, but you didn't answer."

"I left the building for a few minutes. So, what happened?"

Meredith had told the whole story twice already, and she was too weary to tell it again. "It wasn't a successful meeting. Could I tell you the details tomorrow instead?"

"I understand. How about dinner?"

"Okay. But it's my turn to cook."

"Oh, no!" Lisa teased. "I still have indigestion from the last time you did that. Why don't I pick up some Chinese food on my way over?"

"All right, but I'll pay for it."

"Fair enough. Should I bring anything else?"

"If you want to hear about my meeting with Matt," Meredith replied with bleak humor, "You'd better bring a full box of Kleenex."

"That bad?"

"Yep."

"In that case, maybe I ought to bring a gun instead," she joked, "and after we eat we could go out hunting for him."

"Don't tempt me!" Meredith replied, but she smiled a little at Lisa's quip.

🌿29

At 1:30 the following afternoon, Meredith left the advertising department and headed toward her own office. All day long, wherever she went, people were turning to stare at her, and she had no doubt about why they were doing it. She slapped the button for the elevator, thinking of Sally Mansfield's infuriating blurb in this morning's *Tribune*:

Friends of Meredith Bancroft who were stunned to see her snub Chicago's most eligible bachelor, Matthew Farrell, at the opera benefit two weeks ago, have another shock in store for them: The couple was lunching together at one of Landry's cozy back tables! Our newest bachelor is certainly a busy man—that same night he escorted gorgeous Alicia Avery to the opening of *Taming of the Shrew* at the Little Theater.

In her office, Meredith opened her desk drawer with an angry jerk, marveling anew at the petty vindictiveness of the columnist who was a close friend of Parker's ex-wife. That mention of her lunch with Matt was nothing but a ploy to make Parker look like a fool in imminent danger of being jilted.

"Meredith," Phyllis said, her voice tense. "Mr. Bancroft's secretary just called. She said he wants to see you in his office immediately."

Unscheduled, abrupt summonses from Meredith's father were extremely rare; he preferred to oversee the activities of his executives with regularly scheduled weekly meetings and to handle anything else by telephone. In the moment of silence that Meredith and her secretary looked at each other, they both assumed the reason might be related to the naming of an interim president.

That conclusion was borne out when Meredith reached the reception area outside her father's office and saw that all the other executive vice presidents had also been summoned, including Allen Stanley, who'd been on vacation for the past week.

"Miss Bancroft," her father's secretary said, motioning her forward, "Mr. Bancroft would like you to go right in." Meredith's heart soared as she walked toward his door—since she was the first to be advised of the board's choice, it was only logical that she *was* that choice. Like her father, and his father, and all the other Bancrofts before them, Meredith Bancroft was going to be granted her birthright. More correctly, she was going to be allowed to prove her worthiness for the next six months.

Foolishly close to sentimental tears, Meredith knocked on the door and walked into his office. No one but a Bancroft had ever occupied this office or sat behind that desk; how could she have imagined that such a grand tradition would be ignored by her father?

Her father was standing at the windows, his hands clasped behind him. "Good morning," she said brightly to his back.

"Good morning, Meredith," he said, turning around, his voice and expression unusually friendly. He sat down behind his desk, watching her as she came forward. Although there was a sofa and coffee table at the far end of his office, he never sat there or offered anyone else a seat there. Instead, it was his habit to sit in the high-backed swivel chair behind his desk and to speak to people formally, across the expansive barrier of a large, antique baronial desk. Meredith wasn't certain whether he did that unconsciously, or whether it was with the deliberate intention of intimidating people. Either way, it was subtly unnerving to everyone, including Meredith at times, to have to traipse across the wide expanse of carpet to reach his desk, while he sat there, watching and waiting.

Now, Meredith noted, he waited with an unusual degree of patience, although he did not stand up. While good breeding and custom caused him to stand up whenever a woman arrived anyplace else, if that woman worked for Bancroft's at the management level or above, he remained seated, even when every other man arose. It was, Meredith knew, his way of silently criticizing their presence in the executive ranks. And yet, when she was with him away from the store, he observed all the formalities. In the years she'd worked at the store, Meredith had learned to accept his two distinct and very different personas, even though there were still times when it disconcerted her to kiss him good night and have him walk past her the next morning at work with barely a curt nod.

"I like that dress you're wearing," he said, looking at her beige cashmere dress.

"Thank you," Meredith replied with surprised sincerity.

"I hate seeing you in those business suits you wear most of the time. Women should wear dresses." Without giving her a chance to reply, he inclined his head toward one of the chairs in front of his desk, and Meredith sat down, desperately trying to hide her nervousness.

"I've sent for the entire executive staff because I have an announcement to make, but I wanted to speak with you first. The board of directors has decided upon an interim president." He paused, and Meredith leaned forward in her chair, tense with expectation. "They've chosen Allen Stanley."

"What?" she said in a gasp, reeling from a combination of shock, anger, and disbelief.

"I said, they've chosen Allen Stanley. I'm not going to lie to you—they did it on my recommendation."

"Allen Stanley," Meredith interrupted, coming to her feet and speaking in a stunned, furious voice, "has been on the verge of a nervous breakdown ever since his wife died! Furthermore, he doesn't have the expertise or experience to run a retail operation—"

"He's been Bancroft's controller for twenty years," her father snapped, but Meredith wasn't intimidated and she wasn't finished. Outraged, not only because she'd been cheated of the opportunity she should have been given, but at the sheer stupidity of the choice of successor, she braced her hands on his desk. "Allen Stanley is a glorified accountant! You couldn't have made a *worse* choice, and you know it! Any one of the others, *any* of them, would have been a better choice. . . ." It hit her then, a realization that nearly sent her to her knees. "That's why you recommended Stanley, isn't it? Because he can't possibly run Bancroft's as well or better than you have. You're deliberately jeopardizing this company because your *ego*—"

"I won't tolerate that sort of talk from you!"

"Don't you dare try to exert parental authority on me now!" Meredith warned furiously. "You've told me a thousand times that at this store our relationship doesn't exist. I am not a child, and I am not speaking as your daughter. I am a vice president and major shareholder of this company."

"If any of the other vice presidents dared to speak to me as you are now, I'd fire them on the spot—"

"Then fire me!" she flung back. "No, I won't give you that much satisfaction! I resign. Effective immediately. You'll have a letter on your desk in fifteen minutes."

Before she could take the first step to leave, he sank into his chair. "Sit down!" he ordered her. "Since you're determined to have it out at this inopportune moment, let's lay *all* our cards on the table."

"That will be a welcome change!" Meredith retorted, sitting down.

"Now," he said with biting sarcasm, "the truth is that you are not angry about my choosing Allen Stanley, you're angry because I didn't choose *you*."

"I'm angry about *both* those things."

"Either way, I had sound reasons for not choosing you, Meredith. For one thing, you are not old enough or experienced enough to take over the reins of this company."

"*Really?*" Meredith shot back. "How did you arrive at that conclusion? You were less than a year older than I am now when Grandfather put you in charge."

"That was different."

"It certainly was," she agreed, her voice shaking with anger. "Your record at this store when you were put in charge was a great deal less impressive than mine is! In fact, the only thing you really accomplished was to come to work on time!" She saw him put his hand to his chest, as if he were having a pain, and that only made her more furious. "Don't you dare fake a heart attack, because it won't stop me from saying what I should have said years ago." His hand fell from his jacket and he glared at her white-faced as she pronounced, "You are a *bigot*. And the real reason you won't give me a chance is because I am a female."

"You're not far from wrong," he gritted out with a suppressed rage that nearly matched hers. "There are five *men* out there in that reception room who have invested decades of their lives in this store. Not a few years, but *decades!*"

"Really?" she retorted sarcastically. "How many of them have invested four million dollars of their own money in it? Furthermore, you're not only bluffing, you're lying. Two of those men came to work here the same year I did, and for higher salaries, I might add."

His hands closed into fists on his desk. "This discussion is pointless."

"Yes, it is," she agreed bitterly, standing up. "My resignation still stands."

"Just where do you think you'll go from here?" he said in a voice that implied she'd never find a comparable job.

"To any major retailer in the country!" Meredith countered, too furious to consider the anguish such an act of disloyalty would cause her. Bancroft's was her history, her life. "Marshall Field's would hire me in five minutes, so would the May Company or Neimans—"

"Now *you're* bluffing!" he snapped.

"Just watch me!" she warned, but she was already sickened by the thought of working for Bancroft's competitors and exhausted by the holocaust of emotions inside her. Almost wearily, she said, "Just once, could you possibly be completely honest with me—"

When he waited in stony silence for her question, she said, "You never intended to turn the store over to me, did you? Not now, and not in the future, no matter how long or how hard I worked here?"

"No."

In her heart she'd always known that, but even so, she reeled from the shock of having him say it. "Because I'm a woman," she stated.

"That's one reason. Those men out there won't work for a woman."

"That's garbage," Meredith replied numbly, "And it's illegal. It's also untrue, but you already know that. Dozens of men report to me, directly or indirectly, in the departments under my control. It's your own egotistical bigotry that makes you believe I shouldn't run this organization."

"Maybe it's partly that," he shot back. "And maybe it's also because I refuse to aid and abet you in your blind determination to build your entire life around this company! In fact, I will do anything in my power to prevent you from building your life around any career with *any* store! Those are my motives for keeping you from inheriting this office, Meredith. And whether you like my motives or not, at least I *know* what they are. You, on the other hand, don't even know why you're determined to turn yourself into Bancroft's next president."

"What!" she uttered in blank, angry confusion. "Suppose you tell me why you think I am."

"Very well, I will. Eleven years ago you married a bastard who was after your money and who'd gotten you pregnant; you lost his baby and you discovered you could never have more children. And suddenly," he finished with bitter triumph, "You developed an abiding love for Bancroft and Company and a driving ambition to mother it!"

Meredith stared at him while all the flaws in his argument raged through her brain and a lump of emotion swelled painfully in her throat. Fighting to keep her voice steady, she said, "I have loved this place since I was a little girl; I loved it before I met Matthew Farrell and I loved it after he was out of my life. In fact, I can tell you exactly when I decided to work here and be president someday. I was six years old, and you brought me here to wait for you while you met with the board. And you told me," she continued raggedly, "that I could sit there, in your chair, while I waited for you. And I did. I sat there, touching your fountain pens and I buzzed your secretary on the intercom, and she came in and let me dictate a letter. It was a letter to *you*," she said—and from the way his face paled, she knew he suddenly remembered that letter. "The letter said"— she paused to draw another shattered breath, adamantly refusing to let him see her cry—'Dear Father, I am going to study and work very hard, so that someday you will be so proud of me that you'll let me work here like you and Grandfather. And if I do, will you let me sit in your chair again?'

"You read the letter that day, and you said 'of course,'" Meredith finished, looking at him with proud disdain. "I kept my word; you never meant to keep yours. Other little girls played house, but not me," she added on a choked laugh. "I played department store!"

Lifting her chin, she added, "I used to think you loved me. I knew you wished I'd been a boy, but I never realized you didn't give a damn about me because I was merely a girl. All my life you've made me despise my mother for leaving us, but now I wonder if she left or you *drove* her away, exactly as you've just driven me away. My resignation will be on your desk tomorrow." She saw the look of knowing satisfaction on his face at her postponement, and she lifted her chin higher. "I have meetings scheduled, and I won't be able to get to it before then."

"If you aren't here when I make the announcement to the others," he warned her as she turned toward the side door of his office that led through the conference room and then out into the hall, "they'll all suspect you ran out of here crying because you weren't the choice."

Meredith paused long enough to give him a look of magnificent contempt. "Don't fool yourself, Father. Even though you treat me like an unwanted millstone, there isn't one of them who truly believes you are as heartless and indifferent to me as you actually are. They'll think you told your own daughter days ago who the choice was going to be."

"They'll know differently when you resign," he warned, and for a split second there was something like alarm in his voice.

"They'll be too busy helping poor Allen Stanley run this place to think about it."

"*I'll* be running Allen Stanley."

She paused with her hand on the doorknob and looked at him over her shoulder, so numb inside that she actually managed to laugh. "I know that. Did you think I was arrogant enough to believe I could handle Bancroft's on my own, without guidance from you while you're on leave? Or were you afraid I'd try?" Without waiting for his reply, Meredith opened the door into the conference room and left him standing there.

Her disappointment at not having the chance to prove herself as Bancroft's temporary president was completely eclipsed by the pain of having just realized that she actually meant very little to him. For years she'd been telling herself he loved her, but he just didn't know how to show it. Now, as she waited for the elevator, Meredith felt as if someone had turned her world upside down and inside out. The doors opened and she stepped inside, then she stared at the double panel of lit numbers, not knowing which one to press because she didn't know where she was going. Or who she really was. All her life she'd been Philip Bancroft's daughter. That was her past. Her future had always been here, at the store. Now her past was a lie and her future was . . . a void. Masculine voices were coming down the hall and she reached out and pressed the button for the mezzanine, praying the doors would close before anyone saw her.

The mezzanine was actually a balcony that looked out across the first floor of the store, and not until Meredith walked over to the polished brass railing and looked down did she realize that she had automatically come here, to her favorite place. Her hands gripping the cool, smooth brass railing, she stood there looking down at the noisy bustle in the aisles below, feeling isolated and entirely alone in a crowded department store teeming with Christmas shoppers while "White Christmas" played over the speaker system. Off to her right, at the lingerie counters, women were pawing through slips and nightgowns, while Mrs. Hollings, the manager of the lingerie department and Meredith's former supervisor, presided over the main counter with the same stern, unflappable calm she'd exhibited for all twenty-five of her years at Bancroft's. She gave Meredith a brief smile, but Meredith turned away, pretending not to have seen the silent greeting. She turned away because she could not manage even a pretense of a smile in return.

Behind her, shoppers were searching through the racks of silk peignoirs. On the balcony across the store from where she stood, the men's lounge wear department was doing a brisk business in bathrobes. She heard the voices, and the music, and the constant hum of computerized cash registers churning out sales tickets, but she felt nothing. Overhead, the store's paging system began to chime—two short bells, a pause, then one more; it was her paging code, but she didn't react. Not until someone actually spoke directly to her did she manage to move. "Do you work here?" an impatient shopper demanded.

Did she work here? With an effort Meredith dragged her mind into focus. "I mean," the woman continued as she thrust a peignoir at Meredith, "since you aren't wearing a coat, I assume you do."

"Yes," Meredith replied. For today, she worked here.

"Then where will I find the sale peignoirs in your ad? This one is $425.00 and the ad in Sunday's *Tribune* said you had them for $89.95."

"Those are on the fifth floor," Meredith explained.

Her paging code sounded again, and still she stood there—not certain whether she was saying good-bye to the store, her dreams, or merely tormenting herself.

The third time the page sounded, Meredith reluctantly walked over to the counter near the bathrobes and dialed the number for the store's main operator. "This is Meredith Bancroft," she said. "You paged me?"

"Yes, Miss Bancroft. Your secretary says it's urgent that you call your office."

When she hung up, Meredith glanced at her watch. She had two more meetings scheduled for that afternoon—assuming she could make it through them as if everything were normal. And even if she could, what was the point of putting herself to the trouble of doing it? Reluctantly Meredith called Phyllis's extension. "It's me," she said. "You had me paged?"

"Yes, I'm sorry to bother you, Meredith," Phyllis began, and from her sad, uneasy tone Meredith assumed that the meeting her father had called to announce his temporary successor was over, and the news was already out.

"It's Mr. Reynolds," Phyllis continued. "He's called twice in the last half hour. He says he has to talk to you. He sounds awfully upset."

Meredith realized Parker had apparently heard the news too. "If he calls again, please tell him I'll get back to him later." She couldn't bear his sympathy right now without breaking down. And if he tried to tell her this was somehow for the best . . . she couldn't bear that either.

"All right," Phyllis said. "You have a meeting with the director of advertising in a half hour. Do you want me to cancel it?"

Again Meredith hesitated, her gaze roving almost lovingly over the frenetic activity all around her. She couldn't bear to just walk out—not with the Houston deal still up in the air and several other projects still needing her attention. If she worked hard for the next two weeks, she could complete much of her work and get the rest of it ready to be turned over to her successor. To leave things in a mess—to leave without taking care of some of her projects—was not in the best interest of her store. Her store. Hurting Bancroft's was like hurting herself. No matter where she went or what she did, this place would always be a part of her and she of it. "No, don't cancel anything. I'll be up there in a little while."

"Meredith?" Phyllis said hesitantly. "If it's any consolation, as far as most of us are concerned, you should have been given the president's job."

Meredith's laugh was short and choked. "Thanks," she said, and hung up the phone. Phyllis's words of support were sweet, but just now they didn't do much to lift her heavy spirits.

30

*P*arker glanced at the ringing telephone in Meredith's living room, and then at her. She was standing at the window, looking pale and withdrawn. "That's probably your father again."

"Let the answering machine take it," Meredith replied with a shrug. She'd left the office at five o'clock, and by then she'd already refused to take two calls from her father and several more from reporters who were eager to ask how she felt about being passed over for the presidency today.

Her father's voice crackled with fury as soon as her recorded message was finished: "Meredith, I know you're there, dammit. Answer this phone! I want to talk to you."

Sliding his arm around her waist from behind, Parker drew her against him. "I know you don't want to talk to him," he said with sympathetic logic, "but he's already called four times in the past hour. Why not talk to him and get it over with?"

Parker had insisted on seeing Meredith to lend her moral support, but all she wanted was to be alone. "I don't want to talk to anyone right now, especially him. Please try to understand. I'd really like to be . . . by myself."

"I know," he said with a sigh, but he remained where he was, offering silent sympathy while Meredith stared listlessly out the window into the darkness. "Come over to the sofa," he whispered, his lips brushing her temple. "I'll fix you a drink." She shook her head, declining the drink, but she walked over to the sofa and sat in the circle of his arms. "Are you certain you'll be all right if I leave?" he asked an hour later. "I have some things I have to do if I'm going to leave tomorrow, but I hate to go when you're in a mood like this. Tomorrow's Thanksgiving and you're not going to want to spend it with your father as you'd planned. Look," he said abruptly, coming to a decision, "I'll cancel my flight to Geneva. Someone else can give the address to the banking conference. Hell, they won't notice—"

"No!" Meredith burst out, forcing herself to display an energy she didn't feel as she stood up. In all the pathos of the moment, she'd forgotten Parker was supposed to leave tomorrow for three weeks of meetings with his European counterparts and to give the keynote address at the World Banking Conference. "I'm not going to throw myself out of a window," she promised with a wry smile, sliding her hand around his neck and giving him a gentle kiss good-bye. "I'll have Thanksgiving dinner with Lisa's family instead. By the time you come back, I'll have made new career plans, and I'll have my life back in order. I'll finalize the arrangements for our wedding."

"What do you intend to do about Farrell?"

Closing her eyes, Meredith wondered briefly how anyone was supposed to deal with so many complications, setbacks, and disappointments. In the face of today's crushing revelations, she'd actually *forgotten* that she was still married to that loathsome, impossible—"My father will have to agree to stop blocking Matt's rezoning request. He *owes* me that much," she added bitterly. "When he does, I'll have a lawyer contact Matt and offer him that as a peace offering."

"Do you think you can handle the wedding arrangements when you're feeling like this?" he asked gently.

"I can and I will," she promised, forcing enthusiasm into her voice. "We'll be married in February—on schedule!"

"There's one more thing—" he added, cupping her cheek in his palm. "Promise me you won't commit yourself to a new job until I get back."

"Why not?"

Drawing a long breath, he said very carefully, "I've always understood why you've insisted on working at Bancroft's, but since you can't anymore, I'd like you to at least give some thought to making a career out of being my wife. You'd have plenty to do. In addition to running our home and entertaining, there's civic and charitable work—"

Overwhelmed by a despair beyond anything she'd known in years, Meredith started to protest, and then gave up. "Have a safe trip," she whispered as she pressed a kiss on his cheek.

They were partway to the door when someone began determinedly pressing the buzzer from the lobby in a jaunty, familiar rhythm. "That's Lisa," Meredith said, filled with guilt at having forgotten their dinner date and frustration because she wasn't going to be permitted the solitude she desperately needed. She pressed the button that unlocked the security door on the bottom floor, and a minute later Lisa marched into the apartment wearing a determinedly cheerful smile and carrying containers of Chinese food. "I heard what happened today," she announced, giving Meredith a brief, hard hug. "I figured you'd forget our dinner plans, and I figured you wouldn't be hungry," she added, putting the cartons on the polished surface of the dining room table and shrugging out of her coat, "but I couldn't stand the thought of you spending the evening alone, so here I am—want me or not." Pausing to glance over her shoulder, she added, "Sorry, Parker, I didn't know you'd be here. I guess the food will stretch."

"Parker's just going," Meredith told her, hoping the two of them would forgo their usual verbal sparring. "He's leaving tomorrow to attend the World Banking Conference."

"How fun!" Lisa said dramatically, turning a dazzling smile on Parker. "You can compare techniques for foreclosing on widows with bankers from all over the world."

Meredith saw his face freeze, saw his eyes narrow with fury, and she was dimly aware of feeling surprised again that Lisa's jibes dug that deep, but at the moment her own problems outweighed all else. "Please, you two!" she warned, looking at the two people she loved and who struck sparks off each other. "Don't bicker. Not tonight. Lisa, I can't eat a mouthful of food—"

"You have to eat to keep your strength up."

"And," Meredith continued determinedly, "I'd rather be alone—honest."

"Not a chance. Your father was pulling up across the street just as I came up." As if to confirm that, the buzzer began to sound.

"He can stay down there all night for all I care," Meredith said, opening her apartment door for Parker.

Parker swung around. "For God's sake, I can't leave yet if he's down there. He'll expect me to let him up here."

"Don't do it," she told him, fighting to control her emotions.

"What the hell am I supposed to tell him when he asks me to hold the security door open for him?"

"Allow me to offer a suggestion, Parker," Lisa replied sweetly, tucking her hand through his arm and marching him toward the open door. "Why don't you just treat him like any poor sucker with a dozen kids to support who needs a loan from your bank—and tell him *no!*"

"Lisa," he said between his teeth, yanking her hand off his arm, "I could really learn to hate you." To Meredith, he added, "Be reasonable, the man is not only your father, we're also involved in business."

Plunking her hands on her hips, Lisa gave him a bright, daring smile. "Parker, where is your spine, your character, your courage?"

"Mind your own goddamned business. If you had any class, you'd realize this is a private matter and you'd go wait in the kitchen."

The rebuke had a surprising effect on Lisa; normally able to take as much as she gave, Parker's statement caused a humiliated flush to stain her cheeks. "Bastard," she said under her breath, and turning on her heel, she headed toward the kitchen. As she passed Meredith, she said, "I came here to console you, not upset you, Mer. I'll wait in the kitchen." In the kitchen, Lisa angrily brushed away the tears stinging her eyes as she snapped on the radio. "Go ahead and rant, Parker," she called, and gave the volume knob a hard twist, "I won't hear a word." From the radio came the sound of a screeching soprano weeping vociferously while performing an aria from *Madame Butterfly.*

In the living room, another long, demanding blast from the lobby buzzer joined the shrieking din of the soprano's plaintive wailing, and Parker drew in a harsh breath, torn between the urge to break the radio and strangle Lisa Pontini. He looked at his fiancée, who was standing a few feet away, too immersed in misery to notice the deafening racket, and his heart softened. "Meredith," he said gently when the buzzer went silent, "is that really what you want me to do—refuse to let him up here?"

She glanced at him, swallowed, and nodded.

"Then that's what I'll do."

"Thank you," she whispered.

Her father's furious voice as he stalked into the room brought them both lurching around in surprise. "Goddammit! It's a hell of a note when I have to sneak past the security door with another tenant! What is this, a party?" he demanded, raising his voice to be heard above the opera blasting from the radio. "I left two messages with your secretary this afternoon, Meredith, and four more on your answering machine!"

Anger at his intrusion banished her exhaustion. "We have nothing to say to each other."

He flung his hat onto the sofa and jerked a cigar out of his pocket. Meredith watched him light it and stoically refused to comment. "On the contrary," he snapped, clamping the cigar between his teeth and glowering at her, "Stanley turned the presidency down. He said he didn't think he could handle it."

Too hurt by their earlier meeting to feel anything at this news, Meredith said matter-of-factly, "So you decided to offer it to me?"

"No, I did *not!* I offered it to my—the board's—second choice, Gordon Mitchell."

That piece of painful information hardly touched her. She shrugged. "Then why are you here?"

"Mitchell turned it down."

Parker reacted with the same surprise Meredith felt. "Mitchell's ambitious as hell. I'd have thought he'd be dying for a shot at it."

"So would I. However, he feels he can make a greater contribution to the store by remaining in merchandising. The well-being of Bancroft's is obviously more important to *him* than personal glory," he added with a pointed look at Meredith that silently accused her of self-aggrandizement. Brusquely, he finished, "You're the third choice. That's why I'm here."

"And I suppose you expect me to leap at the chance?" she retorted, still so hurt by what he'd said to her earlier that she couldn't feel elated over what he'd just told her.

"I expect you," he said, his face turning an angry, alarming red, "to behave like the executive you seem to think you are, which means putting our personal differences aside for the time being so that you can take advantage of the opportunity you're being offered!"

"There are other opportunities elsewhere."

"Don't be a fool! You'll never have a better chance to show us what you can do."

"Is that what you're giving me—a chance to prove myself?"

"Yes!" he bit out.

"And if I do prove myself, then what?"

"Who knows?"

"Under those circumstances, I'm not interested. Get someone else."

"Goddammit! There *is* no one as qualified as you are to do it, and you know it!"

The words burst from him in an explosion of resentment, frustration, and desperation. To Meredith his reluctant admission was infinitely sweeter than any ordinary praise. The excitement she'd refused to feel before began to build inside her, but she struggled to sound nonchalant. "In that case, I accept."

"Fine, we'll discuss business at dinner tomorrow. We have five days to go over pending projects before I leave on my cruise." He started to reach for his hat, intending to go.

"Not so fast," she said, her mind snapping into sudden focus. "First, but not most important, there's the matter of an increase in salary."

"One hundred fifty thousand dollars a year, effective one month after you move into my office."

"One hundred seventy-five thousand dollars a year, effective *immediately*," she argued.

"With the understanding," he angrily agreed, "that your salary returns to what it is now if—when—I come back from my leave of absence."

"Agreed."

"And," he added, "you're to make no—repeat, *no*—major changes in policy without consulting with me first."

"Agreed," she said again.

"Then it's settled."

"Not quite—there's one more thing I want from you. I intend to devote myself completely to my work, but I have two personal matters that I also have to take care of."

"What are they?"

"A divorce and a marriage. I can't have the latter without the former." When he remained rigid and silent, she walked forward. "I believe Matt will agree to a divorce if I can offer him an olive branch—the approval of his zoning request—and the further guarantee that there'll be no more interference in his private life from our end. In fact, I'm almost certain he will."

Her father studied her with a grim smile. "Do you really think so?"

"Yes, but you evidently don't. Why?"

"Why?" he said, sounding amused. "I'll tell you why. You said he reminded you of me, and *I* wouldn't settle for such a puny offering. Not now. Not anymore. I'd make him regret the day he ever tried to thwart me, and when I'd accomplished that, I'd drive a bargain on *my* terms—a bargain he'd choke on!"

The words sent a chill of apprehension up her spine. "Nevertheless," she persisted, "before I agree to take over, I want your word that he'll have his zoning request approved as soon as he petitions again for it."

He hesitated, then he nodded. "I'll attend to it."

"And you'll also give your word not to interfere in anything else he does if he'll agree to a swift, quiet divorce?"

"You have my word. Parker," he said, bending down to retrieve his hat from the sofa, "have a good trip."

When he left, Meredith looked at Parker. He grinned at her as she said softly, "My father couldn't say he was sorry or that he was wrong, but conceding to everything I asked for was his way of making amends. Don't you agree?"

"It probably was," Parker said without complete conviction.

Meredith didn't notice; she threw her arms around him in sudden, exuberant glee. "I'll manage everything—the presidency, the divorce, and our wedding plans," she promised gaily. "You'll see!"

"I know you will," he said, smiling and linking his hands behind her back, drawing her close.

Seated at the kitchen table with her feet propped up on the seat of a chair, Lisa had decided Puccini's opera wasn't just boring, it was intolerable, when she looked up and saw Meredith standing in the doorway. "Are Parker and your father gone?" she asked, switching off the radio. "God, what a night," she added when Meredith nodded.

"It happens to be a wonderful, marvelous, fantastic night!" Meredith declared with a dazzling smile.

"Has anyone ever told you that you have alarming mood swings?" Lisa demanded, eyeing her in amazement. She'd heard Philip's raised voice in the living room a few minutes ago.

"Kindly address me with a little more respect."

"How do you wish to be addressed?" Lisa asked, studying Meredith's face.

"How about Madam President?"

"You're joking!" Lisa cried with delight.

"Only about the way you should address me. Let's open a bottle of champagne. I feel like celebrating!"

"Champagne it is," Lisa agreed after giving her a hug. "And afterward you can tell me what happened with you and Farrell yesterday."

"It was awful!" Meredith cheerfully declared, taking a champagne bottle from the refrigerator and stripping off the foil.

31

*I*n the week that followed, Meredith threw herself into her role as interim president; she made decisions with caution and skill, she met with the executive committee, listening to their opinions, suggesting new ideas, and within a few days they began to respond to her with confidence and enthusiasm. At the same time, she managed to keep up with much of the work she'd handled as operations vice president—something that was made far easier by Phyllis's competence, her unflagging loyalty, and her willingness to work long hours beside Meredith.

After several days of successfully fulfilling her dual role, Meredith had learned to pace herself, and her earlier exhaustion gave way to euphoria. She even managed to devote some time to her wedding plans; she ordered invitations from Bancroft's stationery department, and when the bridal salon called to say they had some new designs, she went down to see them. One of the designs, a glorious sheath of pearl-encrusted ice-blue silk with a deep, wide V carved out of the back was exactly what she'd been looking for and hadn't been able to find. "It's perfect!" she exclaimed, laughing and hugging the sketch while the staff in the bridal salon, caught up in her unaffected, contagious delight, beamed at her.

With the sketch in one hand and a sample of the wedding invitation in the other, she sat at the ornate desk that had belonged to her father and grandfather. Sales at all of Bancroft's stores were at a record high, she was dealing well with every matter that crossed her desk, no matter how complicated, and she was marrying the finest, the best of men—the man she had loved since she was a child.

Leaning back in the swivel chair, she grinned at the portrait of Bancroft's founder that hung in a wide, heavily carved frame on the opposite wall. Suddenly bursting with sentimentality and happiness, she looked at the bearded man with the twinkling blue eyes, and fondly whispered, "What do you think of me, Great-grandfather? Am I doing all right?"

As the week spun out, she continued to feel challenged and happy and absorbed. Success smiled upon every task she took on . . . except one: Before her father left on his cruise, he'd kept his promise about Matt's rezoning request, but she could not get through to Matt to tell him that.

No matter when she called his office, his secretary curtly informed her that he was either out of the office or out of town. On Thursday afternoon, when he still hadn't returned her phone calls, Meredith tried again. This time his secretary relayed a message from Matt: "Mr. Farrell," she announced in a clipped frosty voice, "instructed me to tell you that you are to deal with his attorneys, Pearson and Levinson, not with him. He will not take your phone calls now or in the future, Miss Bancroft. He also told me to say that if you persist in calling him here, he will take legal action for harassment." And then the woman hung up!

Meredith held the phone away from her ear, glaring at it. She considered going to Matt's office and *insisting* on seeing him, but there was every possibility that in his present mood he'd simply have her forcibly escorted out of the building by his security people. Realizing that it was imperative for her to remain unemotional and objective, she calmly reviewed her alternatives—exactly as she would have were this a business problem. She knew it would be futile to call Matt's attorneys. They represented the opposition, and they'd try to intimidate her for the sheer fun of it. Furthermore, she'd known from the beginning that she was ultimately going to need an attorney to draw up the legal papers once Matt had agreed to proceed with an amicable divorce. Obviously, she needed one sooner than she'd anticipated—one who would go through the irritating formality of relaying her peace offering to Pearson & Levinson so *they* could relay it to their client.

But she couldn't choose just any competent attorney, not when Matt was being represented by a firm as powerful and prestigious as Pearson & Levinson. Whoever she chose had to have as much political clout and as much skill as Matt's renowned lawyers possessed; otherwise his lawyers would intimidate hers into submission with the sort of legal muscle-flexing and out-of-court game-playing that lawyers seemed to especially enjoy. Secondly, and equally important, whoever she chose had to be someone who would guard her privacy as well as he guarded her legal interests; someone who wouldn't discuss her case with his friends over drinks at the Lawyers' Club . . . someone she could trust implicitly.

Parker had suggested a friend of his, but Meredith wanted someone *she* knew and liked. She didn't want to mix business problems with personal ones, so Sam Green was out of the question. Idly, she picked up her pen and wrote down the names of attorneys she knew socially, then she slowly crossed out each one. All of them were very successful, and all of them belonged to her country club; they played golf with one another; they also probably *gossiped* together.

There was only one man who met her criteria, although she hated to tell him about all this. "Stuart," she sighed with a mixture of reluctance and affection. Stuart Whitmore had been the only boy to like her when she was a homely thirteen-year-old, the only boy to voluntarily ask her to dance at Miss Eppingham's party. At thirty-three, he was as physically unimpressive as ever, with narrow shoulders and thinning brown hair. He was also a brilliant lawyer from a long line of brilliant lawyers, a fascinating conversationalist, and—most of all—her friend. Two years ago he'd made his last—and most determined—effort to get her to go to bed with him; he did it in a typical Stuart fashion: As if he were delivering a well-prepared legal argument to a jury, he itemized all the reasons that she *ought* to go to bed with him, ending with "including, but not limited to, the future possibility of matrimony."

Surprised and touched that he'd considered marrying her, Meredith had gently turned him down while trying to make him understand that his friendship mattered very much to her. He'd listened intently to her rejection, and dryly replied, "Would you then consider letting me represent you in some legal action? That way I can tell myself that ethics, not lack of reciprocity of feelings, prohibit our getting involved." Meredith was still trying to decipher that sentence when she belatedly heard the wry humor in it, and her answering smile had been filled with gratitude and affection. "I will! I'll steal a bottle of aspirin from a drugstore tomorrow morning, and you can bail me out of jail."

Stuart had grinned at her, and stood up, but his good-bye was warm and endearing. Handing her his business card, he said, "Plead the fifth until I get there."

The following morning, Meredith had coerced Mark Braden into calling a friend of his—a lieutenant at the local precinct, who then called Stuart and told him that Meredith had been busted for shoplifting in a drugstore. Suspecting a prank, Stuart had hung up, called back, and discovered there *was* a Lieutenant Reicher, and that Meredith *was* supposedly in custody.

Perched on a step outside the police station, Meredith watched Stuart's Mercedes sedan screech to a stop in the towaway zone in front. Not until she saw him leap out of the car, leaving it with the motor running, did she realize how much he really cared for her.

"Stuart!" she called when he ran up the steps right past her. He paused and spun around, and instantly realized he was the victim of a joke. "I'm so sorry," she whispered. "I only meant to show you how far I was willing to go to preserve a friendship that means very much to me."

The anger drained from his expression, he drew a long, steadying breath, then he grinned. "I left two opposing parties of a bitter divorce alone in our conference room, waiting for the other attorney. By now they've either killed each other or, worse, reconciled, and in so doing cheated me out of my very exorbitant fee."

Still smiling at the memory, Meredith picked up the phone and pressed the intercom button. "Phyllis, would you please get Stuart Whitmore at Whitmore and Northridge on the phone for me?"

The moment she put down the phone, nervous tension began to build in her, and her hand trembled as she reached for a stack of computer printouts on her desk. She hadn't seen Stuart more than twice in the last year. What if he didn't return her call . . . what if he didn't want to get involved with her personal problems . . . what if he was out of town? The sharp, short buzz of the intercom made her jump.

"Mr. Whitmore is on line one, Meredith."

Meredith drew a steadying breath and picked up the phone. "Stuart, thank you very much for calling me back so quickly."

"I was on my way to a deposition when I heard my secretary take your call," he replied, his tone businesslike but polite.

"I have a small legal problem," she explained. "Actually, it isn't a small problem. It's rather large. No, enormous."

"I'm listening," he said when she hesitated.

"Do you want me to tell you what it is now? On the phone, when you're in a hurry to leave?"

"Not necessarily. You could give me a hint though—to whet my legal appetite."

She heard it then—the dry veiled humor in his voice—and she breathed a sigh of relief. "To put it briefly, I need advice about—about my divorce."

"In that case," he gravely and immediately replied, "my advice is to marry Parker first. We can get a better settlement that way."

"This isn't a joke like the last time, Stuart," she warned, but there was something about him that inspired so much confidence that she smiled a little. "I'm in the most amazing legal mess you've ever encountered. I need to get out of it right away."

"I normally like to drag things out—it builds up the fees," he drolly replied. "However, for an old friend, I suppose I could sacrifice avarice for compassion just once. Are you free for dinner tonight?"

"You're an angel!"

"Really? Yesterday the opposing counsel told the judge I was a manipulative son of a bitch."

"You are not!" Meredith protested loyally.

He laughed softly. "Yes, my beauty, I am."

32

*F*ar from being judgmental, or appalled by her behavior as an eighteen-year-old, Stuart listened to her entire tale without a sign of emotion—not even surprise when she told him the identity of the father of her baby. In fact, so disconcerting was his bland expression and unwavering silence, that when Meredith finished her recitation, she said hesitantly, "Stuart, have I made everything clear?"

"Perfectly clear," he said, and as if to prove that, he added, "You've just finished telling me that your father is now willing to use his influence to get Farrell's zoning request approved with the same disregard for the illegality of influence peddling that he displayed when he had Senator Davies block it? Right?"

"I—I think so," she replied, uneasy about his smoothly worded condemnation of her father's actions.

"Pearson and Levinson represent Farrell?"

"Yes."

"That's it, then," he declared, signaling the waiter for the check. "I'll call Bill Pearson in the morning and tell him that his client is unjustly putting my favorite client to a lot of needless mental anguish."

"Then what?"

"Then I will ask him to have his client sign some nice papers, which I will draw up and send over to him."

Meredith smiled with a mixture of hope and uncertainty. "Is that all there is to it?"

"Could be."

Late the next afternoon, Stuart finally called.

"Did you speak to Pearson?" Meredith asked, her stomach churning with anticipation and apprehension.

"I just hung up a minute ago."

"Well?" she prodded eagerly when he didn't go on. "Did you tell him about my father's offer? What did he say?"

"He *said*," Stuart replied sardonically, "that the entire matter between you and Farrell is a highly *personal* one, which his client wishes to first deal with from that aspect and later—when his client is ready—*his client* will dictate the terms under which a divorce will be obtained."

"My God," she breathed. "What does that mean? I don't understand!"

"In that case, I shall endeavor to strip away the polite legalese and translate for you," Stuart offered. "Pearson was telling me to go fuck myself."

The profanity, which was completely out of character for Stuart, told Meredith that he was far more annoyed than he was letting on, and that alarmed her almost as much as the incomprehensible attitude of Matt's lawyer. "I still don't understand!" she said, lurching forward in her chair. "Matt was very cooperative that day at lunch—until he got the phone call about the Southville rezoning thing. Now I'm offering to see that his rezoning request is approved, and he won't even *listen.*"

"Meredith," Stuart said firmly. "Did you hold anything back when you described your relationship with Farrell to me?"

"No, nothing. Why do you ask?"

"Because," he replied, "from everything I've read and heard about him, Farrell is a logical, intelligent man—coldly, almost inhumanly logical according to some people. Logical, busy men don't go out of their way to get revenge for petty grievances. It's a waste of their time, and in Farrell's case, his time is worth a great deal of money. But every man has a limit to what he's willing to take. It's as if Farrell's been pushed past that limit, and he *wants* a fight, he's spoiling for it! And that makes me very, very uneasy."

It made Meredith more than uneasy. "Why would he want a fight?"

"I have to assume he wants the satisfaction of revenge."

"Revenge for what?" Meredith implored in an alarmed cry. "Why would you say such a thing?"

"It was something Pearson said—he warned me that any attempt on your part to push this divorce through court without prior and complete approval from his client would result in what he called even more unpleasantness for you."

"More unpleasantness?" she repeated, flabbergasted. "Why would he want that now? When I had lunch with him last week, he tried to be nice. He honestly did. He joked with me even though he really despises me—"

"Why?" he interrupted intently. "Why would he despise you? What makes you think he does?"

"I don't know. It's just something I sense." Dismissing that unanswerable question, she continued. "He's understandably furious over the Southville thing, and he was undoubtedly offended by the things I said to him in the car after lunch. Could that be what got under his skin and 'pushed him past the limit'?"

"Could be," Stuart replied, but he sounded unconvinced.

"What are we going to do now?"

"I'll think about it over the weekend. I'm leaving for Palm Beach in an hour to spend the weekend with Teddy and Liz Jenkins on their yacht. We'll work out our strategy when I get back. Try not to worry too much."

"I'll try," Meredith promised, and when she hung up she made a herculean effort to thrust Matthew Farrell out of her mind by immersing herself in work. She'd succeeded reasonably well two hours later when Sam Green asked to see her right away. As he'd promised, Sam had rushed his staff to complete the project that was preventing him from going to Houston and negotiating with Thorp for the Houston property. Three days ago, Sam had called them, hoping to arrange a meeting this week, only to have Ivan Thorp tell him there was no point in coming down until next week.

Smiling, Meredith watched him heading toward her desk. "Are you ready for your Houston trip?"

"Thorp just called me and canceled our meeting," he said, and sank into the chair across from her, looking angry and harassed. "It seems that they accepted a twenty-million-dollar contract on that land. The purchaser wanted the deal kept confidential until now, which is why Thorp stalled about meeting with me. The property is now owned by the real estate division of a large conglomerate."

Sick with disappointment and adamantly unwilling to accept defeat, Meredith said, "Contact the new owners, and find out if they'll sell it."

"I already have, and they're perfectly willing to sell," Sam said, his voice edged with sarcasm.

Surprised by his tone, Meredith prodded, "Then let's stop wasting time and start negotiating with them."

"I've already tried. They want thirty million and that figure *isn't* negotiable."

"Thirty million! That's ridiculous!" Meredith exclaimed, half rising from her chair. "It's insane! The property is worth twenty-seven million, tops, in today's economy and they paid only twenty for it!"

"I pointed that out to the director of their real estate division, but his attitude is take it or leave it."

Meredith got up and restlessly walked over to the windows, trying to decide what to do next. The Houston property, with its location near The Galleria, was the most desirable site for a Bancroft's branch that she'd ever seen anywhere. She wanted that store built there, and she wasn't going to relent.

"Are they planning to develop it themselves?" she asked, returning to her desk and leaning on the edge, her arms crossed over her chest, lost in thought.

"No."

"You said a conglomerate owns it. Which one?"

Sam Green, like nearly everyone else at Bancroft's, was obviously aware that Meredith's name had been linked with Matthew Farrell's in the gossip column, and he hesitated several seconds before he answered. "Intercorp."

Disbelief and fury made her lurch upright and glare at him. "Are you joking!" she exploded.

His scowl turned ironic. "Do I look like a man who's joking?"

Aware that Sam's reluctance to mention Intercorp made it unnecessary to pretend this was purely a business battle, Meredith said furiously, "I'll kill Matthew Farrell for this!"

"I consider that threat to be privileged lawyer-client communication so I won't have to testify against you if you do."

Emotions ran riot through her entire body; she stared at Sam in rage and disbelief while Stuart's prediction that Matt was out for vengeance banished any doubt that Intercorp's purchase of the land had been a coincidence. Obviously this was some of the unpleasantness Pearson had warned Stuart about today.

"What do you want to do next?"

Her stormy blue eyes snapped to his. "Next, after I kill him? Then I want to feed him to the fish! That vicious, scheming—" She broke off, schooling her features into a semblance of calm, and walked behind her desk. "I'll have to think this over, Sam. Let's discuss it on Monday."

When Sam left, Meredith began to pace. She paced the length of her office, back and forth across the windows, trying to conquer her fury so that she could be objective and effective. It was one thing for Matt to make her personal life a nightmare; she could deal with that through Stuart somehow. But now he was attacking Bancroft & Company, and that panicked and infuriated her more than anything he might have tried to do to her personally. He had to be stopped—and now. God knew what else he planned to do—or worse, what schemes he'd already put into motion.

Angrily, she shoved her fingers through the hair at her nape, and continued to pace until slowly she calmed down and began to think. "Why is he *doing* this?" she said aloud to the empty room. The answer was clear—it had to be his way of retaliating for having his Southville zoning request turned down. Matt had been pleasant at lunch last week—until he got that phone call about Southville. Her father's interference with Matt's zoning request was obviously the cause of this battle.

But it was all so unnecessary now! Somehow she had to make him listen to her, had to make him understand that he'd won his battle, and her father was conceding it. All Matt had to do to get his rezoning request approved was to resubmit it to the commission! Since Stuart wasn't available to advise her not to do it, Meredith took the only course open to her: She marched over to the desk and dialed Matt's office.

When his secretary answered his phone, Meredith deliberately deepened her voice, trying to disguise it. "This is—Phyllis Tilsher," she lied, using her secretary's name. "Is Mr. Farrell in?"

"Mr. Farrell has gone home. He won't be in until Monday afternoon."

Meredith glanced at her watch, surprised to see it was already five o'clock. "I didn't realize it was so late. I don't have his home phone number with me at the moment. May I have it please?"

"I am not permitted to give out Mr. Farrell's home number to anyone," she said. "Those are Mr. Farrell's instructions."

Meredith hung up. She couldn't bear to wait until Monday before trying again, and calling him at the office was a waste of time anyway. Even if she gave a false name, his secretary would undoubtedly insist on knowing what she wanted before putting her through. She could go to his office on Monday, but in the mood he was in, he'd probably refuse to see her and then have his security people toss her out of the building. If she couldn't make him listen to her at his office, and she didn't dare wait until Monday to try, she had to get to him at . . . "Home!" she said aloud. Reaching him at home was a *much* better plan; he wouldn't have a secretary at his home who'd already been told to refuse to let her talk to him. On a wild chance that he might have a listed phone number, she picked up the phone and called information.

The operator was sorry to inform her that his number was unpublished.

Disappointed but not defeated, Meredith hung up. Now that she'd decided to talk to him at his home, she wasn't going to give up. With a viable plan in mind, and the opportunity to see it through, Meredith possessed a calm, iron resolve that was in complete contrast to her delicate appearance and soft voice. Trying to think of someone who might know his private number and be willing to give it to her, she closed her eyes and concentrated. Matt had escorted Alicia Avery to the opera, and Stanton Avery had sponsored Matt as a prospective member at the Glenmoor Country Club. Smiling with satisfaction, she looked up Stanton Avery's number in her private phone directory and dialed it.

According to the Avery butler, Mr. Avery *and* his daughter were staying at their St. Croix residence and were not expected to return for another week. Meredith considered trying to pry their phone number in St. Croix out of the servant, but on quick reflection she realized Stanton wouldn't be likely to give her Matt's number. He'd be more likely to guard Matt's privacy from the woman who'd insulted him at the opera, and whose father had blackballed Matt's membership at Glenmoor. Meredith hung up, and then called Glenmoor, intending to ask the club's manager to get Matt's phone number from his application for membership.

But Timmy Martin had already left for the day. And the office was closed.

Biting her lip, she accepted the fact that she now had no choice but to go to Matt's apartment. The prospect of confronting an infuriated Matthew Farrell, especially on his own ground, was chilling. A shiver ran down her spine when she recalled the savage look on his face when she'd called his father a dirty drunk. Tipping her head back, she closed her eyes, while within her regret mingled with fear and anger. *If only* her father hadn't interfered with Matt's zoning request . . . or humiliated him by blackballing him at Glenmoor. *If only* she hadn't lost her temper in the car . . . *then* their lunch would have concluded as pleasantly as it had begun, and none of this would be happening.

Regrets, however, weren't going to solve her monumental problem, and she opened her eyes, bracing herself for what she had to do. She didn't know Matt's phone number, but she knew exactly where he lived. So did everyone else who read the *Chicago Tribune*. Last month's Sunday supplement had contained a four-page color layout of the fabulous penthouse apartment that Chicago's newest and richest entrepreneur had bought and furnished in the Berkeley Towers on Lake Shore Drive.

33

Lake Shore Drive traffic was moving at a crawl, and Meredith found herself hoping nervously that the weather, which was turning foul, wasn't a portent of events to come. Rain mixed with sleet had started falling when she pulled out of the parking garage, and the wind was howling like a banshee as it buffeted her car. Ahead of her was a vast sea of glowing red taillights; to the east, Lake Michigan was undoubtedly churning like a boiling pot.

In the warmth of her car, Meredith tried to concentrate on exactly what she would say to Matt when she first saw him—something that would soothe his fury and convince him to let her stay. Something diplomatic. Very diplomatic. Her sense of humor, which hadn't had much reason to assert itself lately, chose that unlikely moment to present her with a sudden vision of herself, knocking on his apartment door, and when he opened it, waving a white handkerchief in his face in a request for a truce.

The image was so preposterous that she smiled, but her next thought made her groan in dismay: Before she could reach his door, she'd undoubtedly have to get past the inevitable security desk and security guard which all of the luxury buildings provided to protect their tenants. If her name wasn't on their list of expected guests, they'd never let her get to the elevators.

Her hands tightened reflexively on the steering wheel; panic and frustration started to overwhelm her, and she made herself draw a long, calming breath. Traffic had started to move, and she accelerated. Somehow, some way, she would just have to bluff her way past the guards. If Berkeley Towers' security system was anything like that of other luxury residences, it wasn't going to be easy. A doorman would probably admit her to the lobby, where a security guard would ask her name. He would look at a list that contained the names of everyone who was expected by the various tenants, and when he didn't find her name on it, he would offer to let her use the phone to call Matt. And that was the problem. . . . She didn't *know* Matt's phone number and, even if she did, she was certain now that he'd refuse to see her. Somehow, she was going to have to bluff her way past the guards and up to the penthouse without alerting Matt in advance that she was there.

Twenty minutes later, when Meredith braked her car to a stop at the curb in front of Matt's building, she still wasn't certain how she was going to manage it, but she had the beginnings of a plan.

A doorman met her with an umbrella to shield her from the rain, and she handed him her car keys, then reached into her briefcase and took out a large manila envelope that contained some mail for her father.

From the moment she stepped into the luxurious lobby and walked over to the reception desk, everything went exactly as she'd feared and anticipated it would. The uniformed security guard asked her name, then he checked the list on his desk and, failing to find her name, he gestured to the ivory and gold phone on his desk. "Your name doesn't seem to be on tonight's list, Miss Bancroft. If you would like to use this phone, you can call Mr. Farrell. I'll need clearance from him to let you up. I'm sorry for the inconvenience."

He was only twenty-three or twenty-four, she noted with relief; therefore more likely to fall for her performance than an older, hardened security guard. Meredith gave him a smile that could have melted brick. "There's no need to apologize." She glanced at the name tag on the breast of his uniform. "I understand perfectly, Craig. I have the number in my address book."

Aware of his admiring stare, Meredith dug through her Hermès hand-bag, searching, ostensibly, for her little address book. With another apolo-getic smile, she rifled through her handbag again, then she patted her coat pockets, and finally she looked in the manila envelope. "Oh, no!" she burst out, looking devastated. "My address book. I don't have it with me! Craig, Mr. Farrell is waiting for these papers." She fluttered the large manila enve-lope. "You *have* to let me go up."

"I know," Craig murmured, his gaze roving over her beautiful, stricken face, then he checked himself. "But I can't. It's against the rules."

"I really have to go up there," she pleaded, and then, because she was desperate, she did something she'd never normally do. Meredith Bancroft, who prized her privacy and hated name-droppers, looked the young man straight in the eye and said with a sudden smile, "Haven't I seen you some-where? I know I have. Yes, of course—in the store!"

"What—what store?"

"Bancroft and Company! I'm Meredith Bancroft," she announced, cringing inwardly at the breathy enthusiastic sound of her voice. Pompous. Disgustingly pompous, she thought.

Craig snapped his fingers. "I *knew* it! I knew I recognized you. I've seen you on the news and in the papers. I'm a big fan of yours, Miss Bancroft."

Her lips twitched at the exuberant, naive admiration that caused him to act as if she were a movie star. "Well, now that you know for certain that I'm not some criminal, couldn't you make an exception for me just this once?"

"No." When she opened her mouth to argue, he explained. "It wouldn't do you any good anyway. You can't get off the elevators at the penthouse because the elevator doors won't open there unless you have a key or unless someone up there buzzes you through."

"I see." Meredith was disheartened and frustrated, but his next offer nearly made her faint with alarm.

"Tell you what I'll do," he said, picking up the phone and pressing a series of buttons. "Mr. Farrell instructed us not to call him about unlisted guests, but I'll call up there myself and tell him you're here."

"No!" she burst out, knowing what she was likely to hear from Matt. "I—I mean, rules are rules and you probably shouldn't break them."

"For you I'll break a rule," he said with a grin, then he spoke into the phone. "This is the security guard in the lobby, Mr. Farrell. Miss Meredith

Bancroft is here to see you. Yes, sir, Miss Meredith Bancroft. . . . No, sir, not Banker. Bancroft. You know—the department store Bancroft."

Unable to bear seeing his face when Matt told him to throw her out, she closed her purse, intending to beat an ignominious retreat.

"Yes, sir," Craig said. "Yes, sir, I will. Miss Bancroft," he said as she started to turn away, "Mr. Farrell said to tell you—"

She swallowed. "I can imagine what he said to tell me."

Craig drew the elevator keys out of his pocket and nodded. "He said to tell you to come up."

Matt's chauffeur/bodyguard answered Meredith's knock, wearing rumpled black trousers and a white shirt with the sleeves rolled up on his thick forearms. "This way, ma'am," he said in a gravelly, Bronx-accented voice that was right out of a 1930s gangster movie. Quaking with tension and determination, she followed him across the foyer, past pairs of graceful white pillars, down two steps, and halfway across an immense living room with white marble floors, to a trio of light green sofas that formed a broad U around a huge glass cocktail table.

Meredith's gaze bounced nervously from the checkerboard and checkers that rested on the table's surface to the white-haired man who was seated on one of the sofas, then back to the chauffeur, who she assumed had been playing checkers with the other man when she arrived. That assumption was reinforced when the chauffeur walked around the cocktail table, sat down on one of the sofas, spread his arms across the back of it, and eyed her with an expression of fascinated amusement. In uneasy confusion Meredith glanced at the chauffeur and then at the white-haired man who was watching her in wintry silence. "I—I've come to see Mr. Farrell," she explained.

"Then open your eyes, girl!" he snapped, standing up. "I'm right in front of you."

Meredith stared at him in blank confusion. He was slim and fit, with thick wavy white hair, a neatly trimmed mustache, and piercing pale blue eyes. "There must be some mistake. I've come to see Mr. Farrell—"

"You sure have a problem with names, girl," Matt's father interrupted with biting contempt. "My name is Farrell, and yours isn't Bancroft, it's still Farrell, from what I hear."

Meredith suddenly realized who he was, and her heart skipped a beat at the hostility emanating from him. "I—I didn't recognize you, Mr. Farrell," she stammered. "I've come to see Matt."

"Why?" he demanded. "What the hell do you want?"

"I—I want to see Matt," Meredith persisted, almost unable to believe this towering, robust, angry man could possibly be the same brooding, dissipated person she'd met at the farmhouse.

"Matt isn't here."

Meredith had already been through a great deal this afternoon, and she had no intention of being thwarted or bullied by anyone else. "In that case," she replied, "I'll stay until he returns."

"You'll have a long wait," Patrick said sarcastically. "He's in Indiana at the farm."

She knew that was a lie. "His secretary said he was at home."

"That's his home!" he said, advancing on her. "You remember it, don't you, girl? You should. You walked around, looking down your nose at it."

Meredith was suddenly very frightened of the rage that was gathering force behind his rigid features. She backed away as he started toward her. "I've changed my mind. I—I'll talk to Matt another time." Intending to leave, she turned on her heel, then gasped in terror as Patrick Farrell gripped her arm and spun her around, his thunderous face only inches from hers. "You stay away from Matt, do you hear me! You almost killed him before, and you're not going to walk back into his life now and tear him to pieces again!"

Meredith tried to jerk her arm free, and when she couldn't, fury overcame her fear. "I don't want your *son*," she informed him contemptuously, "I want a *divorce*, but he won't cooperate."

"I don't know why he wanted to marry you in the first place, and I sure as hell don't know why he'd want to stay married to you now!" Patrick Farrell spat out, flinging her arm away. "You murdered his baby rather than have a lowly Farrell in that hallowed womb of yours!"

Pain and rage ripped through Meredith, slashing at her like a thousand knives. "How dare you say a thing like that to me! I *miscarried!*"

"You had an *abortion!*" he shouted. "You had an *abortion* when you were six months pregnant, then you sent Matt a telegram. A goddamned telegram, after it all was done!"

Meredith's teeth clenched against the hurt she'd kept bottled inside her for so many years, but it couldn't be contained any longer. It exploded from her, aimed at the father of the man who had caused all her suffering: "I sent him a telegram all right—a telegram telling him that I'd miscarried, and your precious son never even bothered to call me!" To her infuriated horror, she felt tears leap to her eyes.

"I'm warning you, girl," he began in a terrible voice, "don't play games with me. I know Matt flew back to see you, and I know what that telegram said, because I *saw* him and I saw that telegram!"

Meredith didn't immediately register what he said about the telegram telegrams. "He—he came back to see me?" Something strange and sweet burst into bloom in her heart, and just as abruptly, it died. "That's a lie," she said flatly. "I don't know why he came back, but it wasn't to see me, because he didn't do it."

"No, he didn't see you," he jeered furiously. "And you know *why* he didn't! You were in the Bancroft wing of the hospital, and you had him barred from it." As if he'd finally expended most of his rage, his shoulders slumped, and he looked at her with helpless, angry despair. "I swear to God, I don't know how you could do a thing like that! When you murdered your baby, he was wild with grief, but when you wouldn't let him see you, it nearly killed him. He came back to the farm and stayed there. He said he wasn't going back to South America. For weeks I watched him drowning himself in a bottle. I saw what he was doing—what *I'd* been doing to myself for years. So I sobered him up. Then I sent him back to South America to get over you."

Meredith scarcely heard the last part of that; alarm bells were exploding in her brain and clanging in her ears. The Bancroft wing was named after *her father* because he had donated the money that built it. Her private nurse was employed by *her father;* her doctor was *her father's* crony. Everyone she'd seen or talked to in the hospital had been accountable to her father, and her father despised Matt. Therefore he might have . . . he could have . . . A piercing happiness shot through her, shattering the icy shell that had surrounded her heart for eleven long years. Afraid to believe Matt's father, and afraid *not* to believe him, she lifted her tear-glazed eyes to his stony face. "Mr. Farrell," she whispered shakily. "Did Matt really come home to see me?"

"You know damned well he did!" Patrick said, but as he stared at that stricken face of hers, what he saw was confusion, not cunning, and he had an agonizing premonition he'd been dead wrong; that she *didn't* know anything about any of this.

"And you saw that—that telegram I supposedly sent him—about my having an abortion? Exactly what did it say?"

"It—" Patrick hesitated, searching her eyes, torn between doubt and guilt. "It said you'd had an abortion and you were getting a divorce."

The color drained from Meredith's face, the room began to spin, and she reached out for the back of the sofa, her fingers biting into it as she tried to steady herself. Fury at her father pounded in her brain, shock shook through her, and regret almost sent her to her knees, regret for those anguished, lonely months after her miscarriage and all the years of suppressed pain at Matt's desertion that followed them. But most of all what she felt was sorrow; deep, fresh, wrenching sorrow for her lost baby and for the victims of her father's manipulations. It tore at her, ravaging her heart and sending hot tears pouring from her eyes and down her cheeks. "I didn't have an abortion, and I didn't send that telegram—" Her voice broke as she stared at Patrick through a blur of tears. "I swear I didn't!"

"Then who sent it?"

"My father," she cried. "It must have been my father!" Her head fell forward, and her shoulders began to shake with silent sobs. "It had to have been my father."

Patrick stared at the weeping girl his son had once loved to distraction. Torment was etched in every line of her body, torment and anger and sorrow. He hesitated, shattered by what he was seeing, and then with a violent oath he reached out and pulled his daughter-in-law into his arms. "I may be a fool to believe you," he muttered fiercely. "But I do."

Instead of haughtily rejecting his touch, as he half expected her to do, his daughter-in-law put her arms around his neck and clung to him while deep, wrenching sobs racked her slender body. "I'm sorry," she wept brokenly, "I'm so sorry—"

"There, there," Patrick whispered over and over again, holding her tightly, helplessly patting her back. Through the moisture gathering in his eyes, he saw Joe O'Hara get up and walk into the kitchen, and he held her tighter. "Go ahead and cry," he whispered to her, fighting back his rampaging fury at her father. "Cry it all out." Holding the weeping girl in his arms, Patrick stared blindly over her head, trying to think. By the time she quieted, he knew what he wanted to do. He wasn't so sure how to get it done. "Feel better now?" he asked, tipping his chin down to look at her. When she nodded a little sheepishly and accepted his handkerchief, he said, "Good. Dry your eyes and I'll get you something to drink. Then we'll talk about what you're going to do next."

"I know exactly what I'm going to do next," Meredith said fiercely, dabbing at her eyes and nose. "I'm going to murder my father."

"Not if I get to him first," Patrick said gruffly. He drew her toward the sofa, pushed her down, and vanished into the kitchen, returning a few minutes later with a steaming cup of hot chocolate.

Meredith found his gesture completely endearing, and she smiled as he handed it to her and sat down beside her.

"Now," he said when she'd finished the chocolate, "let's talk about what you're going to tell Matt."

"I'm going to tell him the truth."

Trying unsuccessfully to hide his delight, Patrick nodded emphatically. "That's just what you should do. You're still his wife, after all, and he has a right to know what happened. And because he's your husband, he has an obligation to listen and believe you. Both of you have other obligations too—to forgive and forget, to comfort and solace. To honor your wedding vows—"

She realized then what he was getting at, and she paused in the act of putting her cup on the table. Patrick Farrell was the son of Irish immigrants. Obviously he had deep convictions about people being bound to each other for life, and now that he knew the truth about what had happened to his grandchild, he was prodding hard. "Mr. Farrell, I—"

"Call me Dad." When Meredith hesitated, the warmth faded from his eyes. "Never mind, I shouldn't have expected someone like you to want to—"

"It isn't that!" Meredith said, her face burning with shame as she recalled the contempt she'd felt for him before. "It's just that you mustn't get your hopes up about Matt and me." She needed to make him understand that it was much too late to salvage their marriage, but after the pain she'd just put him through, she couldn't bear to hurt him more by telling him bluntly that she did not love his son. What she *did* want was a chance to explain to Matt about the miscarriage; she wanted to ask for his understanding and forgiveness. And she wanted to give him hers. She wanted that desperately. "Mr. Farrell—Dad—" she corrected herself awkwardly when he frowned, "I know what you're trying to accomplish, and it won't work. It can't. Matt and I knew each other for only a few days before we separated, and that isn't enough time to—to . . ."

"To know if you love someone?" Patrick finished when Meredith trailed off into helpless silence. His bushy white brows lifted in mockery. "I knew the moment I laid eyes on my wife that she was the only woman for me."

"Well, I'm not that impulsive," Meredith said, and then felt like sinking through the floor because Patrick Farrell's eyes suddenly gleamed with knowing amusement. "You must have been pretty impulsive eleven years ago," he reminded her meaningfully. "Matt was with you in Chicago for only one night, and you were pregnant. He told me himself you hadn't been intimate with anyone before him. So it looks to me like you must have made up your mind pretty fast that he was the one for you."

"Please don't go into that," Meredith whispered shakily, holding her hand up to fend off his words. "You don't understand how I feel—how I've felt about Matt all this time. Lately, some things have happened between Matt and me. It's all so complicated—"

Patrick shot her a disgusted glance. "There's nothing complicated about it. It's very simple. You loved my son. He loved you. You made a baby together. You're married. You'll need some time together to find the feelings you used to have for each other. And you will. It's as simple as that."

Meredith almost laughed at his gross misstatement of the entire situation, and his brows shot up when he saw that she found his remarks humorous. "You'd better make up your mind about what you're going to do pretty fast," Patrick said, shamelessly trying to force her hand by implying Matt was considering remarrying, "because there's a girl who loves him plenty, and he just might decide to marry her."

She assumed he was referring to the girl whose picture was on Matt's desk, and her heart gave a funny little lurch as she stood up to leave. "The one in Indiana?" He hesitated then nodded, and she tossed a halfhearted smile in his direction as she picked up her purse. "Matt's been refusing to take my calls. I need to talk to him now, more than ever," she said in a voice that implored him for help.

"The farm is the perfect place to do it," Patrick announced, grinning as he abruptly arose. "You'll have plenty of time on the way there to think of the best way to tell him everything, and he'll have to listen. It'll take you only a couple hours to get there."

"What?" she blinked. "No, really. Absolutely not. Seeing Matt alone at the farm isn't a good idea at all."

"You think you need a chaperon?" he demanded incredulously.

"No," Meredith said half seriously. "I think we need a referee. I was hoping that you'd volunteer and that the three of us could meet here, when he gets back."

Putting his hands on her shoulders, he said urgently, "Meredith, go to the farm. You can say all the things you need to say to him right there. You'll never have a better chance," he cajoled her when she hesitated. "The farm's been sold. That's why Matt is there now; he's packing up our personal things. The phone's been disconnected, so you won't be interrupted. He can't get in his car and drive off because he had car trouble on the way there, and his car had to be towed into the shop. Joe's not supposed to pick him up until Monday morning." He saw her begin to waver and he joyously increased the pressure he was applying. "There's been eleven long years of hatred and hurt between the two of you, and you could put an end to it this very night! Tonight! Isn't that what you really want? I know how you must have felt when you thought Matt didn't care about you or the baby, but think how *he's* felt all these years! By nine o'clock tonight, all that misery could be behind both of you. You could be friends like you used to be." She looked ready to capitulate, yet she still hesitated, and Patrick guessed the reason. Slyly he added, "After you're done talking, you can go to the Edmunton Motel and stay there."

The more Meredith considered his arguments, the more she realized he was right. Without a phone at the farm, Matt couldn't call the police to have her arrested for trespassing; without a car he couldn't drive off and leave her. He would *have* to listen. She thought of how Matt must have felt—and must still feel—about that telegram he'd gotten, and suddenly she wanted desperately to do what Patrick had suggested, to put an end to all the ugliness between them right away and to part friends. "I'll have to stop at my apartment and pack an overnight case," she said.

He smiled down at her with such heartwarming tenderness and approval that a lump of emotion grew in her throat. "You make me proud, Meredith," he whispered, and she realized he knew that confronting an angry Matt was not going to be nearly so easy as he'd made it seem. "I guess I'd better go," she said, and then she rose up on her toes and pressed an impulsive kiss to his rough cheek. His arms went around her, enfolding her in a tight bear hug, and the affectionate gesture almost undid her. She could not remember the last time her own father had hugged her.

"Joe will drive you," he said, his voice thick with emotion. "It's started snowing, and the roads could get bad."

Meredith stepped back and shook her head. "I'd rather take my own car. I'm used to driving in the snow."

"I'd still feel better if Joe drove you," he persisted.

"I'll be fine," she countered emphatically. Meredith turned to leave, then she remembered she was supposed to have dinner with Lisa that night and attend a showing at an art gallery of Lisa's boyfriend's latest work. "May I use your phone?" she asked Patrick.

Lisa was more than disappointed. She was a little angry when Meredith canceled, and she demanded an explanation. When Meredith told her where she was going and why, Lisa was furious—at Philip Bancroft. "God, Mer, all these years, and you and Matt each thought the other . . . and all because your bastard father—" She broke off in the midst of her disjointed tirade and said somberly, "Good luck tonight."

After Meredith left, Patrick was silent for a long moment, then he looked over his shoulder at Joe, who'd been eavesdropping in the kitchen doorway. "Well," he said with a beaming grin, "what do you think of my daughter-in-law?"

Joe shoved away from the kitchen doorframe and sauntered into the living room. "I think it would've been better if I'd taken her out to the farm, Patrick. That way, she wouldn't be able to leave, because *she* wouldn't have a car either."

Patrick chuckled. "She figured that out for herself. That's why she wouldn't let you drive her there."

"Matt's not gonna be happy to see her," Joe warned. "He's mad as hell at her. No, he's worse than mad. I've never seen him like he is now. I mentioned her name to him yesterday, and he gave me a look that chilled my blood. From some phone calls I heard in the car, he's thinking of movin' in on that department store of hers and taking it over. I've never seen anybody get under his skin like she can."

"I know that," Patrick softly agreed, his smile widening. "I also know she's the only one who ever has."

Joe studied Patrick's pleased expression, his brow furrowed. "You're hoping that after she tells Matt about what her father did and after Matt cools down, he might not let her leave the farm, aren't you?"

"I'm counting on it."

"Five dollars says you're wrong."

Patrick's face fell. "You're betting against it?"

"Well, normally I wouldn't. Normally I'd bet ten bucks, not five, that Matt would look at that beautiful face of hers, and see the way her eyes look when she cries, and then he'd take her straight to bed to try to make it up to her."

"Why don't you think he'll do that?"

" 'Cause he's sick, that's why."

Patrick relaxed and grinned smugly. "He's not *that* sick."

"He's sick as a dog!" Joe persisted stubbornly. "He's had that flu all week, and he still went off to New York. When I picked him up at the airport yesterday, he coughed in the car and it made me shudder."

"Care to raise the bet to ten dollars?"

"You're on."

They sat back down to continue their checker game, but Joe hesitated. "Patrick, I'm calling the bet off. It's not fair for me to take your ten bucks. You haven't seen Matt hardly at all this week. I guarantee you, he's going to be too sick and too mad to want to keep her there."

"He may be that mad, but he won't be that sick."

"What makes you so sure?"

"I happen to know," Patrick said, feigning absorption in his next move on the checkerboard, "that Matt got a prescription from the doctor before he left for Indiana, and he took it with him. He called me from the car on the way to the farm and said he was feeling better."

"You're bluffing—your eye's twitching!"

"Care to raise the bet?"

34

When Meredith left her apartment with her overnight bag, it had merely been snowing, but by the time she drove across the Indiana line, the storm was becoming a blizzard. Sand trucks and snowplows were working the highway, their yellow lights swirling like beacons. A moving van passed her, throwing slush onto her windshield; two miles ahead, she passed the same moving van—jackknifed in a ditch, the driver standing outside it, talking to another trucker, who had already pulled off to help him.

According to the radio, the temperature was twenty-two degrees and dropping, with a total snowfall of twelve inches expected, but Meredith was only semi-aware of the treacherous weather. All her thoughts were concentrated on the past, and on her need to get to the farm and make Matt understand what had actually happened. When Patrick had insisted she go to the farm, she'd still been half numb with the shock of her discoveries. Now that the shock had worn off, she felt a sense of urgency to make amends, to explain, that far surpassed Patrick's.

Even now, thinking of the way Matt must have felt when he got that telegram made her sick to her stomach. And still he had flown home to see her in the hospital—only to be refused admittance like some beggar without rights of any kind. He had never abandoned her or their baby. The knowledge filled her with sweetness and a consuming desperation to make him understand that she had not done away with their baby or barred him from her life.

Her headlights gleamed ominously on the highway ahead, and Meredith eased off the accelerator, her breath catching as the car slid onto the patch of ice, racing forward without traction, then grabbing on the snow-covered ground again. As soon as the BMW was under control, her thoughts returned to Matt. Now she understood the reason for the underlying enmity she'd sensed in him. She understood it all, including his furious parting remark in the car last week: "Cross me one more time, just once more, and you'll wish to God your mother had aborted *you!*"

Given the incredible injustices done to him, Meredith could understand why he was retaliating in ways that had seemed so extraordinarily vicious.

Considering everything he believed she'd done years before, it was amazing that he'd tried to be friendly at the opera and at lunch. In his place, Meredith wouldn't have been able to be civil, let alone friendly.

The thought struck her that Matt might have sent himself that telegram so that he could acquit himself to his father for abandoning Meredith, and, just as quickly, she discarded it. Matthew Farrell did as he damned well pleased and offered excuses to no one. He had gotten her pregnant, married her, and then confronted her father's wrath without concern or apology. He had built a business empire with nothing but sheer daring and strength of will. He wouldn't have cowered before his own father and sent himself a telegram. The telegram she'd received, telling her to get a divorce, had obviously been sent in bitter response to the obscene one he'd received. And even so, he'd flown home to try to see her before sending it. . . .

Tears stung her eyes, and she accelerated without realizing it. She had to get to him, to talk to him, to make him understand. She needed his forgiveness and he needed hers, and she didn't think it was the least bit odd or in any way threatening to her future with Parker that she felt such piercing regret and aching tenderness for Matt now. Visions of how the future would be paraded across her mind: Next time, when Matt extended his hand, as he had at the opera, and smiled at her and said, "Hello, Meredith," she would smile at him and put her hand in his. Their friendship wouldn't have to be limited to chance social encounters either; they could be business friends too. Matt was a brilliant tactician and negotiator; in the future, she decided warmly, perhaps she might call him for advice occasionally. They'd meet for lunch and smile at each other; she'd tell him her problem, and he'd offer advice. Old friends were like that. The warmth within her built to a rosy glow.

The country roads were treacherous, but Meredith scarcely noticed. Her delightful imaginings of future friendly meetings with Matt had been obliterated by the reality that she had absolutely no proof to offer him that what she was going to tell him was the truth. He already knew how badly she wanted a quiet divorce. If she walked into the house and went straight to the point about the miscarriage, he'd undoubtedly think she'd invented the entire tale to play on his sympathy and get him to agree to the divorce. Worse, he'd bought the Houston land she wanted for twenty million dollars, and he was holding Bancroft & Company in a ten-million-dollar financial vise by demanding thirty million for it. No doubt he'd assume her tale about the miscarriage was nothing but a desperate, transparent ploy to trick him into loosening the screws on that vise. Therefore, her only choice was to first smooth things over with him by telling him that his rezoning request would now go through. Once he understood that her father had agreed never to interfere with Matt again, then Matt would surely be as reasonable about the divorce as he'd tried to be at lunch—before he got that phone call. Then and only then—when he would know she had nothing more to gain—she could explain what really happened to their baby. He'd surely believe her at that point, because there'd be no reason to doubt her.

The wooden bridge across the creek on his property was covered in snow several inches deep. Meredith accelerated to prevent herself from bogging down, and held her breath. The BMW plowed across it, tires skidding, rear end slipping sideways, then it plunged ahead toward the front yard of the farmhouse. In the reflected light from the snow-covered fields and the moon overhead, the barren trees in the yard were eerie, distorted versions of what they had been that long-ago summer. Like forbidding skeletons, they cast twisted shadows on the white frame house, warning her away, and Meredith felt a shiver of foreboding as she cut the headlights and turned off the engine. A light shone dimly through a curtain in an upper window; Matt was here, and he was still awake. And he was going to be infuriated when he saw her.

Leaning her head back against the seat, she closed her eyes, trying to gather the courage she needed to get through whatever was going to happen in the next few minutes. And at that moment, alone in the car, facing an impossibly difficult and desperately important task, Meredith asked for help for the first time in eleven years. "Please," she whispered to God, "make him believe me."

Opening her eyes, she sat up, pulled her keys out of the ignition, and picked up her purse. Eleven years ago her prayers that Matt would come to her at the hospital had been answered, only she hadn't known it, and she'd stopped praying after that. No doubt God was now thoroughly hacked off at her for that. It was amazing, she thought with a bubble of hysterical laughter as she got out of the car, that she'd managed to make everyone angry with her, when she'd tried so hard to be a nice person.

The light on the porch suddenly snapped on, and her laughter vanished; her heart leapt into her throat, and she looked up to see the front door opening. In her preoccupied alarm, she lost her footing in the deep snow, grabbed the car fender for balance and dropped her keys into the snow beside her right tire. She bent down to reach for them, but she realized she had another set in her purse, and didn't see the point of digging around in the snow. Not at a time like this, when she was facing the most important confrontation of her life.

The porch light spilled into the yard, and Matt stood in the doorway, staring in disbelief at the disconcerting scene before him: A woman had just gotten out of her car, a woman who looked impossibly like Meredith, and then she had ducked down and disappeared. She reappeared again, walking around the front of her car through the swirling snow. Groping for the door frame, he clutched it, trying to keep the weakness and dizziness at bay. He stared at her, half convinced that his fever was causing him to hallucinate, but when the woman reached up and pushed her heavy mane of snow-dusted hair off her forehead, the gesture was so achingly familiar to him that his heart contracted almost painfully.

She walked up the porch steps and lifted her face to his. "Hello, Matt."

Matt decided he was definitely hallucinating. Or else he was dreaming. Possibly, he was dying upstairs in his bed. He didn't know which of the three it was, but he did know that the chills that had racked his body in the house were coming with alarming frequency now. The apparition before him smiled—a sweetly tentative smile. "May I come in?" she asked. She looked and sounded like an angelic version of Meredith.

A furious blast of arctic wind threw snow into his face and snapped him out of his daze. This was no damned apparition, this *was* Meredith, and the realization belatedly sent adrenaline pumping furiously through his veins. Too ill to march her back to her car or freeze to death arguing with her about leaving, he straightened, stepped back from the doorway, and rudely turned his back, leaving her to follow him inside. Grateful that the shock of finding her on his doorstep was giving him a burst of strength, he walked into the darkened living room. "You must have the instincts of a bloodhound and the tenacity of a bulldog to come all the way out here after me," he informed her as he reached out in the dark and switched on the overhead light. His voice sounded hoarse and strange to his own ears.

Meredith had braced herself for a far worse, far more explosive reception than this one. "I had some help finding you," she said, searching his haggard face, shaken by a stab of poignant tenderness for him. Suppressing the urge to reach up and take his face in her hands and say "I'm sorry," she contented herself for the time being with shrugging out of her coat and handing it to him.

"It's the butler's night off," Matt mocked, ignoring her coat. "Hang it up yourself." Instead of retorting as he expected, she turned and draped the coat over a chair. His eyes narrowed with anger and confusion as he compared her quiet humility with his last encounter with her. "Well?" he snapped. "Let's hear it. What do you want?"

To his surprise, she laughed—a funny, breathless laugh. "I think I want a drink. Yes, I definitely want a drink."

"We're out of Dom Pérignon," he informed her. "You have your choice of scotch or vodka. Take it or leave it."

"Vodka is fine," she said quietly.

Matt's knees felt like water as he walked into the kitchen, poured some vodka into a glass, and returned to the living room. She took the glass he thrust at her and glanced around at the room. "It—it seems odd to see you here again after all these years—" she began haltingly.

"Why? This is where I come from—and where you think I still belong. I'm nothing but a dirty steelworker, remember?"

To Matt's dumbfounded disbelief, her color heightened with embarrassment and she started apologizing. "I'm very sorry I said that. I wanted to hurt you and I said that because I knew it would. I didn't mean it, and there's nothing wrong with being a steelworker—they're hardworking, decent men who—"

"What the hell are you trying to pull?" Matt exploded, then almost keeled over from the stabbing pain in his head. The room reeled, and he put his hand against the wall, trying to steady himself.

"What's wrong?" Meredith cried. "Are you ill?"

Matt had a sudden premonition that he was either going to collapse like a damned baby or throw up in front of her. "Get out of here, Meredith." His head swam and his stomach churned as he turned on his heel and started toward the stairs. "I'm going to bed."

"You *are* ill," she burst out, running toward him when he grabbed the banister and swayed on the second step. She reached for his arm to help him, and he jerked it away, but not before she felt the fiery heat of his skin.

"My God, you're burning up!"

"Go *away!*"

"Shut up, and lean on me," she commanded, and he didn't have the strength to stop her from picking up his arm and draping it over her shoulders.

When Meredith got him up to his bedroom, he staggered forward and collapsed on the bed, his eyes closed. Still as . . . death. Terrified, she picked up his limp arm, felt for a pulse, and in her panic she couldn't find any. "Matt!" she cried, grabbing his shoulders and shaking him. "Matt, don't you *dare* die!" she warned hysterically. "I've come all this way to tell you things you have to know, to ask for your forgiveness and—"

The raw fear in her voice, the frantic way she was shaking him, finally penetrated Matt's befuddled senses, and in his dazed state he was incapable of nourishing any further animosity for her at all. All that seemed to matter was that she was there and that he felt terribly sick. "Stop—" he whispered, "shaking me! Dammit."

Meredith let go of him and almost cried with relief, then she got a grip on herself and tried to gather her wits. The last time she'd seen someone collapse like this, it had been her father and he *had* nearly died, but Matt was young and strong. He had a fever, he did not have a bad heart. Not certain what to do to help him, she looked around the room and saw the two prescription bottles on the table beside the bed. Both labels said he was to take one every three hours. "Matt," she said urgently, thinking it might be time for him to take more medicine, "when did you take these pills?"

Matt heard her and tried to force his eyes open, but before he could, she was clutching his hand, leaning close to his ear, and imploring him. "Matt, can you hear me?"

"I am not deaf," he rasped hoarsely, "and I am not dying. I have the flu and bronchitis. I just took more pills."

He felt the bed sink as she sat down beside him, and he actually imagined her fingertips gently smoothing the hair off his forehead. He was obviously very close to delirium, and the whole scene that he saw behind his eyes was taking on the quality of a comic dream: Meredith hovering frantically over him, touching his forehead, smoothing his hair back. Quite hilariously, impossibly funny.

"Are you certain that's all it is—the flu and bronchitis?" she asked from the other side of his closed eyelids.

His mouth quirked in a fevered smile. "How much worse do you want it?"

"I think I should call a doctor."

"I need a woman's touch."

She answered with a shaky, worried laugh. "Will I do?"

"Very funny," he whispered.

Meredith felt her heart lurch because he'd almost sounded as if she would *more* than suffice. "I'll leave you alone to rest."

"Thank you," he murmured, turning his face away from the overhead light, already drifting into sleep.

Meredith pulled the blankets over him, noticing for the first time that he'd been barefoot. He'd fallen asleep in the clothes he'd been wearing when he let her in, and she supposed they'd keep him warmer than pajamas. Walking over to the door, she put her hand on the light switch, then she turned back, watching his chest rise and fall in the steady rhythm of sleep. His breathing was ragged, his face was pale beneath his tan, but even sick and fast asleep he looked like a very large and formidable adversary. "Why is it," she wryly asked the sleeping man, "that every time I come near you, *nothing* happens the way it should?"

Her smile faded, and she turned out the light. She really hated chaos and uncertainty in her personal life; hated the helpless, endangered feeling it gave her. At work, chaos was fine—challenging, stimulating, exciting. Because at work, when she took risks or played hunches, they almost always paid off. If they didn't, the result was failure, not disaster. In her entire adult life she'd taken only two major personal risks, and they'd both proven to be catastrophic mistakes: She'd slept with Matthew Farrell and she'd married him. Even now, after eleven years, she was still trying to disentangle herself from the second one. Lisa was forever criticizing Parker's predictable, reliable nature, but Lisa couldn't understand that predictability and reliability were two things Meredith treasured, craved in her personal life. The ramifications of spontaneous personal risk, in her case, were more than she was willing to endure. In business she had a knack for gambling on the right things; in her personal life she just didn't!

Stopping to pick up her coat from the chair, Meredith went out to the car and got her overnight bag, then she brought it back inside. She started toward the stairs, then she paused to look around the room with a mixture of nostalgia and vague sadness. It was the same; the old sofa facing a pair of wing chairs in front of the fireplace, the books on the shelves, the lamps. The same, only smaller, and forlorn in a way with the packing boxes open on the floor, some of them already filled with books and knickknacks wrapped in newspaper.

35

*I*t was still snowing in the morning when Meredith crept into Matt's room to check on him. He was a little feverish, but his forehead felt much cooler.

In the gray light of day, after a night's sleep and a hot shower, her unexpected reception at the farmhouse last night seemed more comic than unsettling.

Putting on a pair of pleated navy slacks and a bright yellow and navy V-neck sweater, she walked over to the mirror to brush her hair—and she started grinning. She couldn't help it. The more she thought about last night, the funnier it seemed in retrospect. After all her nervousness and determination, after her harrowing drive through a blizzard, they'd said only a half-dozen sentences to each other before Matt had practically collapsed at her feet, and they'd both gone to bed for the night! Obviously, she decided with a suppressed giggle, there was some perverse supernatural influence at work whenever she went near Matt.

Actually, the fact that he was too ill to forcibly eject her was something of a boon. Although she couldn't very well unload all her news on him when he was so sick, by this afternoon he should be feeling well enough to discuss the whole thing rationally, and yet too weak to refuse to listen. If he still tried to make her leave, she'd buy time by telling him a half truth—that she'd lost her keys in the snow and couldn't go.

Content with her plan, she brushed her hair and fluffed it with her fingers until it fell in casual waves and curls over her shoulders. Satisfied, she put on lipstick and mascara, then backed up and checked her appearance in the mirror. Her hair was getting too long, she thought, but apart from that, she looked fine.

Intent on rounding up some sick-room things like a thermometer and aspirin, she headed down the hall and into the bathroom. The cabinet behind the bathroom mirror yielded up a thermometer and several bottles, most of them with labels yellowed with age. Meredith surveyed them, her brow furrowed with uncertainty. Illness, other than an occasional bout of menstrual cramps or a rare headache, was practically unknown to her; she'd had two colds in her entire life, and the last time she'd had the flu she was twelve years old!

What did one do for someone with the flu and bronchitis, she wondered. The flu was rampant among employees at the store, and Meredith tried to remember what Phyllis had told her about her own symptoms. She'd had a splitting headache, Meredith recalled, and nausea and aching muscles. Bronchitis was something else again—that caused congestion and coughing.

Reaching up, Meredith took out a bottle of aspirin and the thermometer, which were the only things she was actually familiar with, then she selected a bottle with an oily orange label: merthiolate. The label said it was for cuts, so she put it back and picked up a tube of stuff that said it was for muscular aches. She opened it, squeezed a little onto her finger, and the smell of it made her eyes water.

In stupefaction she scanned the shelves. The problem, she realized, was that the contents of the medicine cabinet were so old and outdated that the brand names meant nothing to her.

A large brown bottle said SMITH'S CASTOR OIL, and her shoulders started to rock with laughter. It would serve him right, she decided, it really would. She had no idea what castor oil was supposed to cure, but she knew it was purported to taste utterly vile. So she added that to the things in the crook of her arm, intending to put it on his tray as a joke. It dawned on her that she was in remarkably high spirits for someone who was marooned on a farm with a sick man who hated her, but she attributed that to the fact that she was going to be able to put an end to that hatred. That, and the fact that she very much wanted to help him feel better. She owed him that much after everything she'd inadvertently put him through in the past. Added to all that, there was a youthful nostalgia associated with being there that made her feel eighteen again.

She spotted a short blue jar and recognized its label; it was supposed to relieve the symptoms of congestion, and it didn't smell a whole lot better than the stuff in the tube, but it might help make him more comfortable. She added it to what she had and looked it all over. The aspirin would help his headache, she knew, but it might also upset his stomach. She needed an alternative. "Ice," she said aloud. An ice bag would definitely help his headache.

She went down to the kitchen with her store of medicines, opened the freezer, and was relieved to see that there was plenty of ice. Unfortunately, after searching through all the cupboards and drawers, she couldn't find anything suitable for use as an ice bag. And then she remembered the red rubber bag she'd seen in the cabinet beneath the bathroom sink that morning when she was looking for a towel after her shower. Upstairs, she bent down and pulled the rubber bag out of the cabinet, but it had no cap on it. Crouching down, she felt around for a cap, then she crawled partway into the cabinet to look for it. She saw it at the back, behind a can of cleanser, and she pulled it out, only to discover the cap was attached to a three-foot length of slender red rubber tubing with a curious metal clamp on it.

Straightening, Meredith surveyed the peculiar cap-and-tubing arrangement, then she tried to pull the threaded cap loose from the tube, but the manufacturer had, for some unknown reason, made the whole thing as one piece. With no alternative but this one, Meredith checked the clamp, then she tied a tight knot in the tubing to be on the safe side, and brought the contraption downstairs to fill it with ice and water.

With that task completed, the only remaining problem she confronted was breakfast, and she had precious little to choose from. It had to be something bland and easy to digest, which eliminated almost everything in the cabinets except the loaf of fresh bread on the counter. In the refrigerator she found a package of fresh lunch meat, another of bacon, a pound of butter, and a carton of eggs; the freezer contained two steaks. Cholesterol count was evidently not one of Matt's priorities. She took out the butter and put two slices of bread into the toaster, then she looked through the cupboards again to see what he might be able to eat for lunch. Other than some cans of soup, everything else was spicy or rich: stew, spaghetti, tuna fish—and a can of sweetened condensed milk. Milk!

Elated, she found a can opener, and poured some into a glass. It looked awfully thick, and when she read the directions they said it could be used directly from the can or diluted with water. Not certain which way Matt preferred it, she tasted it and shuddered. Diluting wasn't going to help this stuff, and she couldn't imagine why he liked it, but he evidently did. When the toast was ready, she went into the living room, took the top off a TV snack table, and used that as a tray so that she could carry medicines, ice bag, and breakfast upstairs in one trip.

Matt's throbbing head tugged him from a drugged sleep to an aching semi-awareness that it must be morning. Turning his face on the pillow, he forced his eyes open, and was momentarily confused by the sight of an old-fashioned white plastic alarm clock with black hands indicating 8:30, instead of the digital clock radio in his bedroom. Memory came drifting back then; he was in Indiana, and he'd been sick. Judging from the amazing effort it took to roll over and lean up on his forearm so that he could reach for the bottles of pills beside the clock, he was *still* sick. Trying to clear his head, he shook it, then winced at the trip-hammers that began to thunder in his temples. His fever had broken, though, because his shirt was drenched with sweat. As he picked up the glass of water on the table and swallowed the pills, he considered trying to get up so that he could take a shower and get dressed, but he felt so exhausted, he decided to sleep another hour and then give it a try. The label on one of the bottles warned, CAUTION. CAUSES DROWSINESS, and he dimly wondered if that was the reason he couldn't shake off this stupor. He lay back down on the pillows and closed his eyes, but some fuzzy memory was hovering at the edges of his mind. Meredith. He'd had that demented dream that she'd come in a snowstorm and helped him up to bed. He wondered how his subconscious had conjured up an image as bizarre as *that* one. Meredith might help him off a bridge or over the edge of a mountain or into bankruptcy if she thought she could, but anything less destructive was ludicrous.

He'd just started to drift back to sleep when he heard footsteps moving stealthily up the creaky steps. Jolted into startled awareness, he lurched into a sitting position, reeling dizzily from the sudden movement, but as he started to shove back the covers, the intruder knocked on the door. "Matt?" a soft voice called, a unique voice, musical, cultured.

Meredith's voice.

His hand froze as he stared blankly at the wall across from him, and for one crazy moment he was completely disoriented.

"Matt, I'm coming in—" The doorknob turned, and reality hit him—it had not been a bizarre dream. Meredith was there.

Using her shoulder to shove open the door, Meredith backed slowly into the room, deliberately giving him time to get under the covers in case he was up but not yet dressed. Lulled into a false sense of security because he'd been reasonably pleasant the previous night, she almost dropped the tray when his infuriated voice erupted behind her like steam hissing from a volcano. "What are *you* doing here!"

"I brought you a tray," she explained, turning toward him and heading around the bed, surprised by his furious expression. But that expression was *nothing* compared to the menace that tightened his face an instant later when his gaze riveted on the red rubber bag.

"What in the living hell," he exploded, "do you think you're going to do with *that?*"

Determined not to let him ruffle or intimidate her, Meredith lifted her chin and calmly replied, "It's for your head."

"Is that supposed to be your idea of a *dirty joke?*" he demanded, looking murderous.

Completely disconcerted, Meredith put the tray down on the bed beside his hip and said soothingly, "I put ice in it for you—"

"You *would,*" he bit out, and then he said in an awful voice, "I'll give you exactly five seconds to get the hell out of this room and one minute more to get out of this house, before I throw you out." He leaned forward, and Meredith realized he intended to shove back the bedcovers and overturn the tray.

"No," she cried, but there was as much pleading as protest in her voice. "There's no use threatening me, because I can't leave. I lost my car keys out in front when I got out of the car. And even if I hadn't, I still couldn't leave until I tell you everything I came here to say."

"I'm not interested," Matt said savagely, reaching out to jerk the covers off, furious because he had to wait for a wave of dizziness to pass.

"You weren't behaving like this last night," she argued desperately, and whisked the tray off the blankets before he dumped it onto the floor. "I didn't think you'd get this upset just because I made an ice bag for your head!"

He stopped, his hand arrested on the edge of the blankets, an indescrib-able expression of blank, comic shock on his chiseled features. "You did what?" he uttered in a choked whisper.

"I just told you. I made up an ice bag for your head—"

Meredith broke off in alarm as he suddenly covered his face with his hands and fell backward against the pillows, his shoulders shaking. His body shook from head to foot, and muffled sounds came from behind his hands. He shook so violently, his head left the pillows and the bedsprings squeaked. He shook so hard that Meredith thought he was having a seizure or choking to death.

"What's wrong?" she burst out. Her question seemed to make the bed shake harder and his strangled sounds increase. "I'm calling an ambulance!" she cried, putting the tray down and running for the door. "There's a phone in my car—" She was out of the room and starting down the steps when Matt's laughter exploded behind her: great, gusty shouts of laughter; huge, prolonged bursts of uncontrollable mirth . . .

Meredith stopped dead, turned, and listened, realizing that the seizure she'd witnessed had in actuality been a fit of wild hilarity. Arrested on the steps, her hand on the railing, she reflected upon his outburst of laughter and speculated uneasily over its possible cause. That long rubber tube had bothered her from the beginning, but the assembled contraption had borne not the *slightest* resemblance to the disposable hygiene products one usually saw in drugstores. Furthermore, she thought a little fiercely in her own defense as she started slowly back up the stairs, that red rubber bag had been hanging on the back of the bathroom door the last time she'd been there! Surely, if it *was* a hygiene product, it shouldn't have been left in full view.

Outside his door, she paused, feeling excruciatingly self-conscious. It occurred to her then that whatever discomfort she felt, it was probably worth it. After all, mirth had diverted him from his furious attempt to eject her. Even when he was flat on his back, Matthew Farrell was the most for-midable foe she'd ever confronted. And when he was angry, he was actually terrifying. But no matter what he said or did, no matter how angry or unrea-sonable he might become, it was time for her to try to make peace with him.

Her mind made up, Meredith shoved her hands into her pockets, affected an expression which she hoped looked like well-bred confusion, and walked back into the bedroom.

The moment he saw her, Matt had to bite back a fresh onslaught of laughter. Despite her furious blush, she was sauntering toward him with her hands in her pockets, trying to look as if she didn't have the *slightest* idea why he'd laughed. All she needed to do to complete the comic picture of blank innocence she was trying to effect was to gaze up at the ceiling and start whistling.

In the midst of that thought it suddenly hit him why she was there, and the smile that had been lurking at the corner of his mouth abruptly vanished. Obviously, Meredith had discovered he'd bought the land she wanted in Houston and that it was now going to cost her ten million dollars more. She'd come racing out there to wheedle and cajole and do whatever else it took to make him change his mind—even if that meant fixing him a bed tray and hovering solicitously at his bedside. Disgusted by her clumsy, transparent attempt to manipulate him, he waited for her to speak, and when she didn't he curtly demanded, "How did you find me?"

Meredith was instantly aware of an alarming change in his mood. "I went to your apartment last night," she admitted. "About the tray—"

"Forget that," he snapped impatiently. "I asked you how you found me."

"Your father was at your apartment, and we talked. He told me you were here."

"You must have put on one hell of an act to convince him to help you," he said with unconcealed contempt. "My father wouldn't give you the time of day."

So desperate was Meredith to make him listen and believe, she sat down on the bed beside him without thought as she began, "Your father and I talked, and I explained some things to him. And he believed me. After we—understood each other—he told me where you were so that I could come here and explain to you too."

"Then start explaining," he said tersely, leaning back against the pillows. "But keep it short," he added, so astonished that she'd been able to wheedle her way around his father that he was suddenly curious to witness a little of whatever performance she'd given last night.

Meredith looked at his cold, forbidding face, and drew a steadying breath, forcing herself to meet his eyes. Moments ago those eyes had been warm with laughter; now they were like shards of ice. "Are you going to talk," he snapped, "or sit there studying my face?"

She flinched at his tone, but didn't drop her eyes. "I'm going to talk," she said. "The explanation is a little complicated—"

"But hopefully convincing," he jeered.

Instead of retorting with that haughty fury she'd used on him in the past, she nodded and smiled wryly. "Hopefully."

"Then get on with it! But just stick to the salient points—what you want me to believe, what you're offering, and what you want from me in return. In fact, you can skip the last part, I *know* what you want, I'm just interested to see how you plan to get it."

His words flicked against her lacerated conscience like whips, but she kept her eyes on his and began to speak with quiet sincerity. "What I want you to believe is the truth, which I'm about to tell you. What I'm offering are some peace-offerings which I'd intended to make to you last night when I went to your apartment. And what I want from you in return," she continued, ignoring his order to skip that part, "is a truce. An understanding between us. I want that very much."

Sardonic amusement twisted his mouth when she said the last part. "And that's *all* you want—a truce and an understanding?" The biting irony in his voice gave her the uneasy feeling that he was referring to the Houston land. "I'm listening," he prodded rudely when she hesitated. "Now that I understand your purely altruistic motives, let's hear what you're willing to offer."

He made it sound not only as if he doubted her motives, but as if he doubted she could offer anything that wasn't paltry and insignificant, so Meredith played her trump card, presenting him with the most important concession she had to give—and one that she knew was *vitally* important to him. "I'm offering you the approval of your rezoning request by the Southville zoning commission," she said, and saw his momentary surprise at her frank admission that she knew about the situation. "I know my father had it blocked, and I'd also like you to understand that I *never* agreed with that. I quarreled with him about it long before you and I had lunch."

"How fair-minded you've suddenly become."

Her lips turned up into a funny little smile. "I thought you'd react like that. In your position, so would I. However, you can believe this, because I can prove it: The Southville zoning commission will approve your request just as soon as you resubmit it. My father has given me his word that he'll not only stop blocking it, he'll reverse his position and use his influence to get it approved. In turn, I give you my word to make certain he keeps his."

He gave a short, unpleasant laugh. "What makes you think I'd take your word, or his, for anything? Now I'll make *you* a deal," he added in a silky, threatening voice. "If my rezoning request is approved by five o'clock Tuesday night, *without* being resubmitted, I'll call off the lawsuits my attorneys are preparing to file on Wednesday—a lawsuit against your father and Senator Davies for illegally attempting to influence public officials, and another lawsuit against the Southville zoning commission for deliberately failing to act in the best interest of their community."

Meredith's stomach lurched sickly at the discovery he'd planned to do that—and at the incredible speed with which he mobilized the forces for revenge. What had *Business Week* said of him—*A man who's a throwback to the days when an eye for an eye was regarded as justice, not cruel and inhuman revenge.* Suppressing a shudder of fear, Meredith reminded herself that despite all that had been written of him, despite the fact that Matt had every reason to despise her, he had still tried to treat her cordially at the opera, and had been willing to try again that day at lunch. Not until he'd been pushed past all bounds of endurance was he turning his power against her father and her. The knowledge restored her courage and it did something more—it sent a shaft of piercing tenderness through her for this angry, dynamic man who had shown so much restraint.

"What else?" Matt snapped impatiently and was stunned by the soft expression in her eyes when she raised them to his and said, "There will be no further acts of vengeance on my father's part—petty or large."

"Does this *mean*," he asked with mocking delight, "that I can be a member of that exclusive little country club of yours?"

Flushing, she nodded.

"I'm not interested. I never was. What else are you offering?" When she hesitated, and twisted her fingers in her lap, he lost patience. "Don't tell me that was it? That's your entire offer? And now I'm supposed to forgive and forget and give you what you really want?"

"What do you mean, really want?"

"Houston!" he clarified icily. "Among your unselfish motives for this visit, you left out the thirty-million-dollar motive that sent you scurrying to my apartment last night. Or am I misjudging the purity of your actions, Meredith?"

She surprised him again by shaking her head and quietly admitting, "I found out yesterday that you'd bought the Houston land, and you're right— it was the catalyst that sent me to your apartment."

"And then brought you running out here," he added sarcastically. "And now that you're here, you're prepared to say or do whatever it takes to make me change my mind and sell you the property for what I paid for it. Just how far are you willing to go?"

"What do you mean?"

"I mean, is that it? Surely those few paltry concessions aren't the best you can do?"

She opened her mouth to reply, but Matt had enough of this disgusting charade. "Let me save you the trouble of answering that," he said nastily. "Nothing you can do or say, now or in the future, will make one damned bit of difference to me. You can hover solicitously by my bedside, you can offer to climb into bed with me, and the Houston property is still going to cost you thirty million if you want it. Is that clear?"

Her reaction stunned him utterly. He'd been hammering at her with every sentence he spoke, threatening her with public lawsuits and devastating scandal that would ensue, insulting her with every nuance of his voice; in short, he'd subjected her to the sort of intimidation that made hardened business adversaries either sweat or rage, but he hadn't been able to break her control. In fact, she was looking at him with an expression that, if Matt didn't know it was impossible, looked almost like tenderness and contrition.

"That's very clear," she replied softly, and she slowly stood up.

"You're leaving, I take it?"

She shook her head and smiled a little. "I'm going to take the cover off your breakfast plate and hover solicitously at your bedside."

"For Christ's sake!" Matt exploded, his own rigid control over the situation slipping a notch. "didn't you understand what I just said? Nothing you do is going to make me change my mind about the Houston property!"

Her expression sobered, but her eyes remained soft, looking into his. "I believe you."

"And?" he demanded, his anger giving way to complete bafflement which he blamed upon the drug that was making it hard to concentrate.

"And I accept your decision as—as a sort of, well, penance for past misdeeds. You couldn't have found a better one either, Matt," she admitted without rancor. "I wanted that property for Bancroft and Company, and it's going to hurt terribly when it goes to someone else. We can't afford to pay thirty million." He stared at her in shocked disbelief as she continued with a somber smile. "You've taken away from me something I wanted desperately. Now that you have, will you call it even between us and agree to a truce?"

His first instinct was to tell her to go to hell, but that was a purely emotional reaction, and when it came to bargaining, Matt had learned long before never to let his emotions overrule his judgment or interfere with his logic. And logic reminded him that some sort of civilized relationship with her was exactly what he'd hoped to achieve in their last two encounters. Now she was offering it to him—and at the same time she was conceding victory to him with a grace that was astounding. And nearly irresistible. Standing there, waiting for his decision, with her hair tumbling in artless waves and curls over her shoulders, and her hands shoved into her pants pockets, Meredith Bancroft looked more like a contrite high school girl who'd been summoned to the principal's office than like a corporate executive. And at the same time, she still managed to look like the proud young socialite she was—quietly regal, serenely unattainable, enticingly beautiful.

Looking at her now, Matt finally and completely understood his long-ago obsession with her. Meredith Bancroft was the quintessential woman—

changeable and unpredictable, haughty and sweet, witty and solemn, serene and volatile, incredibly proper . . . unconsciously provocative.

What was the point in carrying on this ridiculous war with her, he asked himself. If he called it off, they could go their own ways without any more regrets. The past should have been buried years earlier; it was long past time to do it now. He'd had his revenge—ten million dollars' worth, because he didn't believe for a minute that she wouldn't find a way to raise the extra money. He was already wavering when he suddenly remembered her carrying that tray into him, and he had to stifle the urge to chuckle. The moment his expression altered, she seemed to sense that he was on the verge of capitulating; her shoulders relaxed a little and her eyes lit with relief. The fact that she could read him that well was just irksome enough to make him decide to prolong her suspense. Crossing his arms over his chest, Matt said, "I don't make deals when I'm flat on my back."

She wasn't fooled. "Do you think some breakfast might sweeten your disposition?" she asked with a teasing smile.

"I doubt it," he replied, but her smile was so contagious that he started to grin in spite of himself.

"So do I," she joked, then she offered him her hand. "Truce?"

Matt reacted automatically to the gesture, starting to extend his hand, but she suddenly pulled her hand just out of reach, and with a winsome smile she said, "Before you agree, there's one thing I ought to warn you about."

"And that is?"

Her voice was half serious. "I was thinking of suing you over the Houston property. I wouldn't want my earlier remark to mislead you into thinking I'm voluntarily accepting the loss of it as penance. When I said that, I only meant that if the courts won't force you to sell it for current market value, I'll accept that without hard feelings toward you. I hope you'll understand that whatever happens on that matter, it's only business, not personal."

Matt's eyes gleamed with suppressed laughter. "I admire your honesty and tenacity," he told her truthfully. "However, I suggest that you reconsider taking me to court. It will cost you a fortune to sue me for fraud or whatever grounds you're considering, and you'll still lose."

Meredith knew he was probably right, and losing the Houston property didn't matter so very much at that moment; she was overjoyed because she had *already* won something just as important as a lawsuit: Somehow, some way, she'd actually diverted this proud, dynamic man from fury to laughter; she'd made him accept a truce. Determined to cement that truce and lighten the atmosphere even more if possible, she teasingly confided, "Actually, I was thinking more of suing you for restraint of trade, or something like that. What do you think of my chances then?"

He pretended to give that consideration, then he shook his head. "That won't hold up in court either. However, if you're absolutely determined to sue, I'd sue me for collusion and conspiracy."

"Could I win that one?" she asked with a widening smile.

"No, but it would be a more entertaining trial."

"I'll give that some thought," she promised with sham gravity.

"You do that."

He grinned at her. Meredith smiled back at him. And in that prolonged moment of warmth and understanding, the eleven-year barrier of anger and sorrow between them began to crumble, and then it collapsed. Slowly, uncertainly, Meredith lifted her hand and held it out to him in a gesture of truce and friendship. Overwhelmed with the poignancy of the moment, she watched Matt's hand reach out for hers, felt his long fingers sliding across hers, his palm grazing her palm, and then his fingers, strong and warm, curled tightly, engulfing her hand. "Thank you," she whispered, lifting her eyes to his.

"You're welcome," he quietly replied, holding her hand for a moment longer, and then letting go. Letting go of the past.

Like two strangers who've accidentally shared something more profound than they intended or expected, they both sought at once to withdraw to safer ground. Matt leaned back into the pillows and Meredith quickly turned her attention to her neglected tray of food and medicine. From the corner of his eye Matt watched her as she picked up the offending red rubber item with the tips of thumb and forefinger only, and in an excess of fastidious modesty, she put it on the floor out of sight. When she turned back to him and put the tray on the table beside the bed, she'd recovered her smiling composure. "I didn't know how you'd feel this morning, and I didn't think you'd be very hungry, but I brought you some breakfast."

"It all looks very tasty," Matt lied, surveying the items on the tray. "Castor oil is a great favorite of mine—as an appetizer, of course. And I gather that smelly goo in the blue jar is the main course?"

Meredith burst out laughing and picked up a plate with a bowl upended on it. "The castor oil was a *joke*," she promised.

Now that the emotional battle between them was over, Matt felt himself beginning to lose the battle to stay awake. Waves of drowsiness were sweeping over him, pulling him down, making his eyelids feel as heavy as boulders. He no longer felt ill; he felt exhausted. Obviously, those damned pills were partly the cause of it. "I appreciate the gesture, but I'm not hungry," he told her.

"I didn't think you would be," she said, studying his features with the same gentleness that had softened her luminous turquoise eyes all morning. "But you have to eat anyway."

"Why?" he demanded a little testily, and then it belatedly dawned on him that Meredith had actually made up a tray for him—Meredith, who hadn't known how to turn on a stove eleven years ago, and hadn't wanted to try. Touched by her thoughtfulness, he forced himself back into a sitting position, resolved to eat whatever she had prepared.

She sat down beside him on the bed. "You have to eat in order to keep your strength up," she explained, then she reached out and picked up the glass of white liquid from the tray, holding it out to him.

He took it, turning it in his hand, eyeing it warily. "What is this?"

"I found a can of it in the cupboard. It's warm milk."

He grimaced, but obediently raised it to his lips and swallowed.

"With butter in it," Meredith added when he choked.

Matt thrust the glass into her hand, leaned his head back against the pillows, and closed his eyes. "Why?" he whispered hoarsely.

"I don't know—because it's what my governess used to give me when I got sick."

His lids opened, and humor flickered briefly in his gray gaze. "To think I used to envy rich kids—"

Meredith sent him a laughing look and started slowly to lift the cover off the plate of toast.

"What's under there?" he demanded warily.

She swept off the cover then, revealing two slices of cold toast, and Matt sighed with a mixture of relief and weariness; he didn't think he could possibly stay awake long enough to chew it. "I'll eat it later, I promise," he said, making a superhuman effort to keep his eyelids from slamming shut. "Right now I just want to sleep."

He looked so tired and drained that Meredith reluctantly agreed. "All right, but at least take these aspirin. If you take them with milk, they're less likely to bother your stomach." She handed them to him along with the glass of buttered milk. Matt grimaced at the warm white liquid, but he obediently took the aspirin and chased the tablets down with it.

Satisfied, Meredith stood up. "Can I get you anything else?"

He shuddered convulsively. "A priest," he gasped.

She laughed. And the musical sound lingered in the room after she left, drifting through his sleep-drugged mind like a soft melody.

36

By noon the pills had worn off, and Matt felt vastly better, although he was surprised to discover how weak he was after doing nothing more strenuous than take a shower and put on a pair of jeans. Behind him the bed beckoned invitingly, and he ignored it. Downstairs, Meredith was evidently making lunch, and he could hear her moving about in the kitchen. He took the tiny electric travel shaver he'd bought in Germany out of its case, plugged it into the current converter, looked in the mirror, and forgot the shaver was running quietly in his hand. Meredith was downstairs . . .

Impossible. Inconceivable. But true nonetheless. Fully awake now, her motives for being here and her calm acceptance of his verdict about Houston seemed improbable at best. Matt knew it, but as he began to shave, his mind skated away from reexamining her behavior too closely. No doubt the reason was that it was far more pleasant *not* to do that right now. Outside, it was snowing again, and cold as the Arctic, judging from the icicles clinging to the tree limbs. But inside there was warmth, and unexpected companionship, and the simple truth was he wasn't fit to resume his packing tasks and he wasn't sick enough to be contented lying in bed staring at the walls. Meredith's company, although not restful by any wild stretch of the imagination, was going to be a pleasant diversion.

In the kitchen, Meredith heard him moving above her head, and she smiled as she put the canned soup she'd prepared into a bowl and the sandwich she'd made for him onto a plate. From the moment Matt's hand had closed around hers, a strange peace had swept over her, a peace that had now burst into bloom like roses in springtime. She had never really known Matt Farrell, she realized, and she wondered if anyone truly did. According to everything she had read and heard about him, his business foes feared and hated him; his executives admired and were awed by him. Bankers courted him, CEOs asked his advice, and the Securities & Exchange Commission that presided over the stock exchange watched him like a hawk.

With few exceptions, she realized as she considered the stories she'd read, even people who admired him subtly gave the impression that

Matthew Farrell was a dangerous predator to be handled gently and never angered.

And yet, Meredith thought with another soft smile, he had lain upstairs in that bed, still believing that she had coldly aborted his child and divorced him as if he were some insignificant beggar . . . and he had *still* taken her hand in his. He had been willing to forgive her. The memory of that moment, the sweetness of it, was incredibly poignant.

Obviously, Meredith decided, all those people who talked of him with fear and awe didn't know Matt well at all! If they did, they'd realize that he was capable of enormous understanding and great compassion. She picked up the tray and headed upstairs. Tonight, or in the morning, she would tell him about what had happened to their baby, but not right now. On the one hand, she was desperately eager to have it done with, to eradicate completely and forever the hurt, the anger, the confusion that they had both felt. Then the slate would be wiped clean; they could find real peace with each other, perhaps even real friendship, and they could put a graceful, congenial end to this ill-fated, tumultuous marriage of theirs. But as much as Meredith wanted to have it all out in the open, she was dreading the actual confrontation as she'd never dreaded anything before. This morning Matt had been willing to let bygones be bygones, but she did not like to think about his probable reaction when he discovered the extent of her father's treachery and duplicity.

For now she was content to let him exist in blissful ignorance of what was coming, and to give herself a short respite from what had been a wildly stressful and draining twenty-four hours . . . and what was bound to be a painful and wrenching discussion for her as well as for him. It occurred to her that she was inordinately satisfied at the prospect of spending a quiet evening in his company, if he was well enough, but she didn't think that was in the least significant or alarming. After all, they were old friends in a way. And they deserved this chance to renew their friendship.

Pausing outside his door, she knocked and called, "Are you decent?"

With amused dread, Matt sensed instinctively that she was bringing him another tray. "Yes. Come in."

Meredith opened the door and saw him standing in front of the mirror with his shirt off, shaving. Stunned by the odd intimacy of seeing him like that again, she jerked her gaze from the sight of his bronze back and rippling muscles. In the mirror his brows rose when he noted her reaction. "It's nothing you haven't seen before," he remarked dryly.

Chastising herself for acting like an inexperienced, unsophisticated virgin, she tried to say something suitably flippant and blurted out the first banal thing that came to mind. "True, but I'm an engaged woman now."

His hand stilled. "You've got yourself a problem," he said lightly after a pulsebeat of silence. "A husband *and* a fiancé."

"I was homely and unpopular with boys when I was young," she joked, putting down the tray. "Now I'm trying to collect men to make up for lost time." Turning toward him she added on a more sober note, "From something your father said, I gather I'm not the only one who has a problem with a spouse as well as a fiancé. Evidently you're thinking of marrying the girl whose picture is on your desk."

With an outward appearance of nonchalance, Matt tipped his head back and ran the shaver up his neck to his jaw. "Is that what my father said?"

"Yep. Is it true?"

"Does it matter?"

She hesitated, oddly unhappy with the direction the conversation was taking, but she answered honestly. "No."

Matt unplugged the razor, feeling physically weak and loath to deal with the future right now. "Could I ask a favor?"

"Yes, of course."

"I've had an exhausting two weeks, and I was actually looking forward to coming out here to find some peace and quiet—"

Meredith felt as if he'd slapped her. "I'm sorry I've interrupted your peace."

Warm amusement sent a wry smile to his lips. "You've *always* cut up my peace, Meredith. Every time we come within sight of each other, all cosmic hell breaks loose. I didn't mean that I'm sorry you're here, I only meant that I'd like to spend a pleasant, restful afternoon with you, and not have to deal with anything heavy right now."

"I feel the same way, actually."

In complete accord, they stood silently contemplating each other, and then Meredith turned away and picked up the heavy navy-blue bathrobe with a Neiman-Marcus label that was lying over the back of the chair. "Why don't you put this on, and then you can sit here and eat your lunch."

He shrugged obligingly into the robe, knotted it at the waist, and sat down, but Meredith saw the uneasy way he was looking at the covered plates. "What's under that bowl?" he asked warily.

"A string of garlic," she lied with sham solemnity, "to hang around your neck." He was still laughing when she swept off the cover. "Even I can manage to cook a can of soup and slap sandwich meat between two slices of bread," she informed him, smiling back at him.

"Thank you," he said sincerely. "This is very nice of you."

After he finished eating, they went downstairs and sat in front of the fire he insisted on building. For a while they talked pleasantly about nothing more controversial than the weather, his sister, and finally the book he'd been reading. Obviously, Matt had amazing recuperative powers, she thought, but even so, she could see that he was getting tired. "Wouldn't you like to go back up to bed?" she asked.

"No, I like it better down here," he answered, but he was already stretching out on the sofa, leaning his head against a throw pillow. When Matt awoke an hour later, he had the same thought he'd had that morning when he first opened his eyes—that he'd only dreamed Meredith was there. But when he turned his head slightly and looked over at the chair she'd been sitting in earlier, he saw that it was no dream. She was there—jotting notes on a yellow writing tablet propped on her lap, her legs curled beneath her. Firelight gilded her hair, brushed her smooth cheeks with a faint rosy glow, and cast shadows off her long curly lashes. He watched her as she worked, smiling inwardly because she looked more like a schoolgirl doing her homework than the interim president of a national retail chain. In fact, the longer he watched her, the more impossible the truth seemed. That misconception was immediately disproved when he quietly asked, "What are you working on?"

Instead of "algebra" or "geometry," the woman in the chair smiled and said, "I'm writing a market trend summary to present at the next board of directors meeting—one that I hope will convince them to let me expand our private label merchandise. Department stores," she explained when he looked genuinely interested, "particularly stores like Bancroft's, make a large profit from selling merchandise with their own labels on it, but we're not taking full advantage of it the way Neiman's and Bloomingdale's and some of the others have."

As he had been last week at lunch, Matt was instantly intrigued by this business persona of hers, partially because it was in such contrast to the other images he'd had of her in the past. "Why haven't they taken advantage of it?" he asked. Several hours later, when their discussion had ranged from Bancroft's merchandising to its financial operations, to its problems with product liability and expansion plans, Matt was no longer merely intrigued, he was impressed as hell with her . . . and, in a crazy way, extremely proud of her.

Sitting across from him, Meredith was vaguely aware of having somehow earned his approval, but she was so wrapped up in their discussion, so awed by his instantaneous grasp of complicated concepts, she'd lost all track of time. The page she'd been writing on was now filled with notes she'd made about his suggestions, suggestions that she was eager to think about further. His last suggestion, however, was out of the question. "We'd never be able to pull that off," she explained when he urged her to look into buying their own clothing production facilities in Taiwan or Korea.

"Why not? Owning your own facilities would eliminate all your problems with quality control and loss of consumer confidence."

"You're right, but I couldn't possibly afford it. Not now and not in the near future."

His brow furrowed at her apparent lack of understanding. "I'm not suggesting you use your own money! Borrow it from the bank—that's what bankers are for," he added, forgetting for the moment that her fiancé was a banker. "Bankers lend you your own money when they're certain that what you're borrowing it for is a sure thing, then they charge you interest for borrowing it back from them—and when the loans are paid off, they tell you how lucky you are to have them taking risks on you. You surely know how that works by now."

Meredith burst out laughing. "You remind me of my friend Lisa—she's not very impressed with my fiancé's profession. She thinks Parker ought to just give me the money whenever I need it without insisting on the usual collateral."

Matt's smile faded a little at the reminder of her fiancé's existence, and then it turned to shock when she added lightly, "Believe me, I'm becoming an expert on commercial borrowing. Bancroft's is borrowed out, and so am I, to be honest."

"What do you mean, so are you?"

"We've been expanding very rapidly. If we go into a mall that's being developed by someone else, the costs go down but so do the profits, so we usually develop the mall ourselves, then lease part of it out to other retailers. It costs a fortune to do that, and we've been borrowing the money for it."

"I understand, but what does that have to do with you personally?"

"It takes collateral to get loans," she reminded him. "Bancroft and Company has already put up all the collateral it has, as well as the actual stores, of course. The corporation ran out of collateral when we built the store in Phoenix. I wanted to go into New Orleans and Houston, so I'm putting the stocks and property in my trust fund up for collateral. I'll be thirty in a week, and the trust my grandfather set up for me comes under my control then."

She saw him scowl and hastily added, "There's no reason to be concerned. The New Orleans store has been easily able to make the payments on its loan, just as I knew it would. So long as the store can make its payments, I have nothing to worry about."

Matt was utterly dumbstruck. "You're not telling me that in addition to putting up your own things as collateral, you've also personally guaranteed that loan for the New Orleans store?"

"I had to," she explained calmly.

Matt tried, with incomplete success, not to sound like an irate professor lecturing a backward student from his lofty podium of superior knowledge. "Never do that again," he warned her. "Never, ever put your own money up for a business deal. I told you, that's what banks are for. They make the profit on the interest, let them take the risk. If business were to fall off, and the New Orleans store couldn't make its payments, you'd have to, and if you couldn't, the bank would clean you out."

"There was no other way—"

"If your bank told you that, it's a crock," he interrupted. "Bancroft and Company is an established, profitable corporation. The only time a bank has the right to ask you to personally guarantee a business loan or put up your own holdings as collateral is when you're an unknown quantity without a decent credit history." She opened her mouth to object, and Matt forestalled her by raising his hand. "I know they'll *try* to get you to sign personally," he admitted, "they'd love to have fifty cosigners on an ordinary home mortgage if they could get it, because it eliminates their risk. But never, ever agree to sign your name for a Bancroft loan again. Do you think for a damn second that General Motors executives are asked by a lender to sign corporate loans for GM?"

"No, of course not. But our case is a little different."

"That's what banks always try to tell you. Who the hell is Bancroft's banker, anyway?"

"My fiancé . . . Reynolds Mercantile Trust," she clarified, watching shock and then annoyance chase across his face in the firelight.

"That's one great deal your fiancé cut for you," he said sarcastically.

Meredith wondered if that remark came from male competitiveness. "You're not being reasonable," she quietly informed him. "There's something *you're* forgetting. There are bank examiners who scrutinize a bank's loans, and now, with banks failing everywhere, the examiners are frowning on banks getting too heavily invested in any one borrower. Bancroft and Company is in debt to the tune of hundreds of millions to Reynolds Mercantile. Parker couldn't continue to loan us money, particularly now that he and I are engaged, without bringing down censure on himself—unless we put up enough collateral."

"There must have been some other form of collateral you could have used as security. What about your stock in the store?"

She chuckled and shook her head. "I've already used that, and so has my father. There's only one major family stockholder in B and C who hasn't already put her stock up."

"Who's that?"

Meredith was already wishing for a way to divert the conversation to another track, and he'd just handed her the opportunity. "My mother."

"Your mother?"

"I did have one of those, you know," she reminded him dryly. "She was given a large block of stock as part of the divorce settlement."

"Why doesn't your mother put her stock up for the bank? It's not unreasonable, since she's going to reap the profits. The value of her stock is going up every day that B and C continues to expand and prosper."

Laying aside the notepad, Meredith looked at him. "She hasn't done it because she hasn't been asked to do it."

"Would you feel comfortable telling me why not?" Matt asked, hoping she wouldn't think he was prying instead of trying to help.

"She wasn't asked because she lives in Italy somewhere, and neither my father nor I have had anything to do with her since I was a year old." When he heard that without any outward sign of emotion, Meredith suddenly decided to tell him something she normally chose to forget. Watching him for reaction, she said with a smile, "My mother was—is—Caroline Edwards."

His dark brows drew together into a baffled frown, and she prodded, "Think about an old Cary Grant movie, where he was on the Riviera, and the princess of a mythical kingdom was running away—"

She knew from his smile exactly when he identified the movie—and its female star. Leaning against the back of the sofa, he regarded her with smiling surprise. "She is your mother?"

Meredith nodded.

In thoughtful silence, Matt compared the elegant perfection of Meredith's features to the memory he had of the star of the movie. Meredith's mother had been beautiful, but Meredith was more so. She had a glow that lit her from within and illuminated her expressive eyes; a natural elegance that she hadn't acquired in some acting school. She had a dainty nose that sculptors would envy, delicate cheekbones, and a romantic mouth that invited a man to kiss it at the same time everything else about her warned a man to keep his distance.

Even if that man was her husband . . .

Matt pushed that thought out of his mind the moment he had it. They were married to each other only by a technicality; in reality, they were strangers. *Intimate* strangers, the demon in his mind reminded him, and Matt suddenly had to force himself not to look below the bright yellow V at the throat of her sweater. He didn't need to look. Once he had explored and kissed every inch of the breasts that were now filling out that sweater so provocatively. He still remembered exactly the way they filled his hands, the softness of her skin, the tautness of her nipples, the scent . . . Annoyed with the persistent sexual direction his thoughts were suddenly taking, he tried to tell himself it was merely the natural, appreciative reaction of any male who was confronted by a female who had the alluring ability to look both innocent and seductive in a simple sweater and slacks. Realizing that he'd been looking at her without speaking, he returned to the discussion at hand. "I always wondered where you got that beautiful face of yours—God knows your looks couldn't have come from your father."

Shocked by his unprecedented compliment and inordinately pleased that he evidently thought her face beautiful even now, when she was crowding thirty, Meredith acknowledged the compliment with a smile and a slight shrug, because she honestly didn't know what to say.

"How is it I never knew who your mother is until now?"

"There wasn't much time to talk before."

Because we were too busy making love, his mind replied, forcibly reminding him of those hot, endless nights he'd held her in his arms, joining his body to hers, trying to satisfy the need he'd felt to please her and be close to her.

Meredith was finding it surprisingly pleasant to confide in him, and so she told him something else: "Have you ever heard of Seaboard Consolidated Industries?"

Matt mentally sifted through the disjointed names and facts he'd accumulated over the years. "There's a Seaboard Consolidated somewhere in the southeast—Florida, I think. It's a holding company that originally owned a couple of large chemical companies and later diversified into mining, aerospace, computer component manufacturing, and chains of drugstores."

"Supermarkets," Meredith corrected him with that jaunty sideways smile of hers that used to make him yearn to drag her into his arms and kiss it off her lips. "Seaboard was founded by my grandfather."

"And now it's yours?" Matt said, abruptly recalling that a woman supposedly headed Seaboard.

"No, it's owned by my stepgrandmother and her two sons. My grandfather married his secretary seven years before he died. Later he adopted her two sons, and when he died he left Seaboard to them."

Matt was impressed. "She must be quite a businesswoman—she's built Seaboard into a large and very profitable conglomerate."

Meredith's dislike of her stepgrandmother prompted her to deny the woman any such undue praise, and in doing so she revealed more than she intended. "Charlotte has expanded it, but the corporation was always very diversified. In fact, Seaboard owned everything the family had acquired for generations, and Bancroft and Company—the department store, I mean—was less than one quarter of its total assets. So you see, it's not as if she built Seaboard up from nothing."

Meredith saw Matt's surprised expression and realized he'd already noted that the division of her grandfather's estate seemed very off balance. At any other time, she wouldn't have confided as much as she already had, but there was something special about today. There was the pleasure of sitting across from Matt in quiet friendship after all these years; the warmth of knowing that she was mending a relationship that never should have ended with enmity in the first place; the flattering realization that he seemed to be very interested in whatever she said. All of that, combined with the coziness of a fire crackling in the grate while snow piled up on the windows, created an atmosphere that positively encouraged confidences. Since he'd courteously refrained from prying any further into the matter they'd been discussing, Meredith voluntarily provided the answers. "Charlotte and my father detested each other, and when my grandfather married her, it caused a breach between the two men that never truly healed. Later on—perhaps in retaliation because my father was shunning him, my grandfather legally adopted Charlotte's sons. We didn't even know he'd done it until his will was read. He divided his estate into four equal parts, and left one to my father and the rest to Charlotte and her sons, with Charlotte in control of their share, of course."

"Do I detect a note of cynicism in your voice every time you mention the woman?"

"Probably."

"Because she got her hands on three quarters of your grandfather's estate," Matt speculated, "instead of half of it, which would be more normal?"

Meredith glanced at her watch, realized she needed to do something about dinner, and hurried through the rest of her explanation. "That isn't why I can't stand her. Charlotte is the hardest, coldest woman I've ever known, and I think she deliberately widened the breach between my father and grandfather. Not that it took much effort on her part," Meredith concluded with a wry smile. "My father and grandfather were hardheaded and hot-tempered—entirely too much alike to have a nice, peaceful relationship. Once, when they were quarreling about the way my father was running the store, I heard my grandfather shout at my father that the only *smart* thing my father had ever done in his life was to marry my mother—and then he'd loused that up just like he was lousing up the store." With an apologetic glance at the clock, she stood up then and said, "It's gotten late, and you must be hungry. I'll fix something for dinner."

Matt realized he was famished, and he stood up too. "Was your father really lousing up the store?" he asked as they walked into the kitchen.

Meredith laughed and shook her head. "No, I'm certain he wasn't. My grandfather had a weakness for beautiful women. He was crazy about my mother and furious at the time because of the divorce. He's the one who gave her the block of Bancroft's stock, actually. He said it served my father right because he'd know that every time the store made one dollar of profit, she was getting a piece of it in dividends."

"He sounds like a great guy," Matt said sarcastically.

Meredith's mind had already shifted to dinner, and she opened the cupboard, trying to decide what he might be able to eat. Matt went straight to the refrigerator and took out the steaks. "How about these?"

"Steaks? Do you feel like eating something that heavy?"

"I think so. I haven't eaten a full meal in days." Despite his interest in dinner, Matt was strangely reluctant to end their conversation, perhaps because idle conversation like this between the two of them was such a novel experience. Almost as novel, but not quite as unbelievable, as having her there now, playing the part of a devoted, attentive wife looking after her recuperating husband. As he unwrapped the meat, he watched her standing at his shoulder, tying a towel around her narrow waist for a makeshift apron. Hoping to get her to talk to him again, he made a joking reference to one of the last things she'd said. "Does your father tell you that *you're* lousing up the store?"

Taking down the loaf of bread, she gave him a bright sideways smile, but the smile didn't quite reach those expressive eyes of hers. "Only when he's in an unusually good mood."

Meredith saw sympathy flicker in his eyes, and she immediately endeavored to show him that it wasn't necessary. "It's embarrassing when he rants at me in meetings with store executives, but they're all accustomed to it by now. Besides, all of them have come under fire from him too, though not as often or in the same way I get it. You see, they realize my father is the sort of man who—who hates to be confronted with proof that someone else is perfectly capable of accomplishing something without his advice or interference. He hires competent, knowledgeable people with good ideas, then he bullies them into submitting to his own ideas. If the idea works, he takes the credit; if it fails, they're his scapegoat. Those who defy him and stick to their guns get promotions and raises if their ideas succeed, but they don't get thanks or recognition. And they're in for the same battle the very next time they want to do something innovative."

"And you," Matt asked, leaning a shoulder against the wall beside her, "how do you handle things now that you're running the show?"

Meredith paused in the act of taking silverware from the drawer and looked at him, her thoughts drifting to the meeting he'd held in his office the day she'd gone there. Unfortunately, she was distracted by the sight of his bare chest, which was now at eye level and which was clearly exposed to view by the gaping front of his robe. Looking at all that bronze skin and muscle with its sprinkling of dark curly hairs had an unexpected and disquieting effect on her. With a funny catch in her breath, she lifted her gaze to his and the feeling subsided, but not the intimacy of the moment. "I handle things the way you do," she said softly, not bothering to hide the admiration she'd felt.

He quirked a dark brow at her. "How do you know how I handle things?"

"I watched you the day I came to your office. I've always known there was a better way to deal with executives than what I've seen my father do, but I wasn't certain if I'd be mistaken for being weak and feminine if I tried for a more open dialogue when I became president."

"And?" he prodded, grinning slightly.

"And you were doing exactly that with your staff that day—yet no one would *ever* accuse you of being weak or feminine. And so," she finished with a breathless, self-conscious laugh as she turned back to the silverware drawer, "I decided to be just like you when I grow up!"

Silence hung in the room like a living, breathing thing—Meredith uneasily self-conscious, and Matt far more pleased by her praise than he wanted to admit. "That's very flattering," he said formally. "Thank you."

"You're welcome. Now, why don't you sit down and I'll fix dinner."

After dinner they went back to the living room, and Meredith wandered over to the bookcase, surveying the old books and games there. She'd had a beautiful, unforgettable day, and that fact was making her feel guilty about Parker and vaguely uneasy about . . . about something she couldn't quite name. Yes, she could, she thought with brutal honesty, she could name it easily, though she couldn't understand why it was affecting her. There was too much overpowering masculinity in this house for her peace of mind, too much male charm, too many memories starting to stir. She hadn't anticipated any of that when she came here. She hadn't expected a close-up view of Matt's bare chest to set off a chain of memories of other times when she'd seen it— times when she was lying on her back with Matt above her, inside her.

She ran her finger slowly along dusty spines of novels without actually seeing their titles, and she wondered idly how many other women shared those same intimate memories of Matt's body joined with theirs. Dozens, she decided, no hundreds, probably. And in a funny, purely impartial way, she no longer condemned Matt for all his well-publicized sexual exploits any more than she could find it in her heart to continue looking down her nose at the women who offered him their bodies. Now, as a grown woman herself, she fully recognized what she had only partially understood as a girl, and that was that Matt Farrell positively exuded bold sex appeal and potent masculinity. In itself, that was a lethal attraction, but when one added in the enormous wealth he'd accumulated and the power he now wielded, she could see why the combination would be absolutely irresistible to most women.

She herself wasn't endangered by it. Not a bit! The last thing she wanted in her life was an unpredictable sexual athlete who had women panting for him. She vastly preferred dependable, morally upright men. Like Parker. But she enjoyed Matt's company, she admitted that much to herself. Possibly, she was enjoying it too much.

On the sofa, Matt watched her, hoping she wouldn't find a book and lose herself in it for the rest of the evening. When she remained in front of the shelf with the old games on it for a rather long time, he thought maybe she was looking at the Monopoly game . . . and remembering the last time they'd played it. "Would you like to play?" he asked.

Her head jerked around, her expression inexplicably wary. "Play what?"

"I thought you were looking at one of the games—the one on top."

Meredith saw it then, the Monopoly game, and all her preoccupation and worries vanished in the anticipation of spending the next few hours doing something as completely frivolous and silly as playing Monopoly with him. She smiled at him over her shoulder, reaching for it. "Do you want to?"

Matt suddenly wanted to as much as she apparently did. "I suppose we could," he said, already pulling the quilt off the sofa so they could sit there with the game board between them.

Two hours later, Matt owned Boardwalk, Park Place, the set of green properties, the set of red properties, the set of yellow properties, all four railroads, and both utilities; and the board was literally covered with his houses and hotels, which Meredith had to pay rent for every time her token landed on one of his properties. "You owe me two thousand dollars for that last move," he pointed out, utterly contented with his evening—and utterly enchanted with the woman who could turn a Monopoly game into one of the most enjoyable nights he'd had in years. "Hand it over."

Meredith gave him a limpid look that made him chuckle even before she said, "I have only five hundred left. Would you consider a loan?"

"Not a chance. I've won. Hand it over."

"Slumlords have no heart," she said, and she plopped the money into his open palm. She tried to scowl and ended up smiling at him. "I should have known from the last time we played this game—when you bought up everything in sight and took everyone's money—that you were going to turn out to be a famous, rich tycoon."

Instead of smiling, he looked at her for a moment and then asked quietly, "Would it have mattered if you had known?"

Meredith's heart skipped a beat at the sheer unexpectedness of such a momentous question. Trying desperately to pass the matter off lightly and restore their former mood, she gave him a comic look of a woman who has been grievously maligned and began to clear the game board. "I'll thank you not to imply that I might have been mercenary in my youth, Mr. Farrell. You've humiliated me enough for one night by winning away all my money."

"You're right, I have." Matt matched her light tone, but he was amazed that he'd asked the question out loud and furious with himself for suddenly starting to wonder what he might have done to make her want to stay married to him. Getting up, he made certain the fire wouldn't flare up while they slept. By the time he finished, he'd gotten himself under firm control. "Speaking of money," he said as she put the game back on the shelf, "if you ever personally guarantee a loan for your company again, at least insist that your fiancé's bank agree to release you from that guarantee after two or three years. That's long enough for them to have proof that the loan is solid."

Relieved by the change of topic, Meredith turned around. "Do banks do that?"

"Ask your fiancé." Matt heard the sarcasm in his voice, and he hated the absurd stab of jealousy that was causing it. And while he was still berating himself for what he'd already said, he said even more. "And if he won't agree, get yourself another banker."

Meredith knew she was suddenly on shaky ground, but she couldn't understand how she got there. "Reynolds Mercantile," she explained patiently, "has been Bancroft's bank for nearly a century. I'm certain, if you knew all the details of our finances, you'd agree that Parker has been more than accommodating."

Irrationally annoyed by her persistent defense of Parker, he purposely said something he'd wanted to say all night. "Is he responsible for that ring you're wearing on your left hand?"

She nodded, watching him warily.

"He has lousy taste. It's ugly as hell."

He said it with such magnificent disdain, and what he said was so true about the ring, Meredith felt uncontrollable laughter welling up inside her. He stood still, brows raised in challenge, *daring* her to deny it, and she bit down on her lip, trying not to giggle. "It's an heirloom."

"It's ugly."

"Well, an heirloom is a—"

"It is any object," Matt said bluntly, "with deep sentimental value that is too ugly to sell and too valuable to throw out."

Instead of being irate, as he half expected her to be, Meredith burst out laughing, slumping against the wall. "You're right," she laughed.

Watching her, Matt struggled to remember that she meant nothing to him anymore, then he tore his gaze from that flushed, intoxicating face of hers and glanced at the clock on the mantel. "It's after eleven o'clock," he said. "We may as well call it a night."

Startled by his curt tone, Meredith quickly turned off the lamp beside the sofa. "I'm sorry. I shouldn't have kept you up so late. I didn't realize what time it is."

Like Cinderella's magic coach that turned into a pumpkin at the end of the night, the mood of pleasant conviviality had completely disintegrated when they walked up the stairs together to go to bed. Meredith sensed it, but she didn't know why it was happening. Matt sensed it, and he knew exactly why it was happening. With cool courtesy he escorted her to Julie's room and said good night.

37

*A*t midnight Matt was still awake, his eyes shut, his mind obsessed with the fact that Meredith was sleeping down the hall. At 12:30 he rolled over onto his back and, in sheer frustration, he opened the prescription bottle and took one of the pills that the label warned would cause drowsiness. At 1:15 he yanked the cap off the bottle and took another one.

They put him to sleep, but in that drug-induced state, he dreamed of her . . . endless, heated dreams, where Meredith turned into his arms, naked and eager, running her hands over him, making him groan with pleasure. He made love to her over and over again until he finally scared her because he couldn't stop. . . . *"Matt, stop this, you're scaring me!"*

He drove into her deeper and deeper, while she begged him to stop. . . . *"Matt, please stop!"*

While she told him he was dreaming . . . *"Stop it, you're dreaming!"*

And threatened to call the doctor . . . *"If you don't wake up, I'm going to call a doctor!"*

He didn't want a doctor, he wanted her. He tried to roll on top of her again, but she held him down, and put her hand on his forehead . . . And offered him coffee . . .

"Please wake up! I've brought you coffee."

Coffee?

And whispered gently in his ear . . . *"Dammit, you are dreaming! You're smiling in your sleep! Now, wake up!"*

It was the curse that got through to him. Meredith never swore, therefore something was wrong with his dream. Something was wrong. . . .

He forced his eyes open and gazed at her beautiful face, struggling to reorient himself. She was bending over him, her hands grasping his shoulders, and she looked worried. "What's wrong?" he asked.

Meredith relaxed her hold and sank down beside him on the bed with a sigh of relief. "You were thrashing around and talking in your sleep so much that I heard you out in the hall. When I couldn't wake you up, I started to panic, but your head felt cool. Here, I brought you some coffee," she added, nodding at the mug on the nightstand.

Matt obediently forced himself to a sitting position. Leaning back against the headboard, he raked his hand through his hair, trying to shake off the lingering vestiges of sleep. "It's those pills," he explained. "Two of them must pack the wallop of a nuclear warhead."

She picked up the bottle and read the label. "This says you're only supposed to take one."

Without replying, Matt reached for the mug and drank most of the coffee, then he leaned his head back and closed his eyes for several minutes, letting the heat and caffeine work their magic, blissfully unaware and unconcerned with the things that had plagued him the night before.

Meredith, who remembered his waking-up ritual and his lack of conversation for the first few minutes after he awakened, stood up and idly straightened the things on the nightstand, then she absently picked up his robe and laid it across the foot of the bed. When she turned back, his eyes were more alert, his face relaxed and almost boyish. And very handsome. "Feel better?" she asked, smiling.

"Much better. You make very good coffee."

"Every woman is supposed to have *one* major culinary accomplishment to her credit—something she can show off whenever the occasion calls for it."

He caught the gleam of amusement in her eye and grinned lazily. "Who said that?"

"A magazine I read in the dentist's office," she replied, chuckling. "My major culinary achievement is coffee. Now, do you feel like breakfast?"

"That depends on whether or not you plan to serve it from bottles and jars like yesterday," he joked.

"I'd be more careful if I were you about insulting the cook. There's some powdered cleanser under the kitchen sink that would look just like sugar if I were to put it on your cereal."

His shoulders shook with laughter, and he drained the last of his coffee.

"Seriously," she said, smiling back at him from the foot of his bed, a golden goddess in blue jeans; an angel with devilment in her eyes. "What would you like for breakfast?"

You, he thought, and desire began to roar through his entire body. He wanted *her* for breakfast. He wanted to reach out and drag her into his bed, to shove his hands into the rumpled silk of her hair and join his famished body with hers. He wanted to feel her hands on him, he wanted to bury himself inside her and make her moan for him. "Whatever you fix will be fine," he said tightly, shifting the blankets to hide his arousal. "I'll have it downstairs after I shower."

When she left the room, Matt closed his eyes and clenched his teeth, caught between fury and disbelief. Despite everything that had happened in the past, she could still do this to him! If all he felt for her was lust, he could have forgiven himself, but he couldn't forgive himself for this sudden hopeless yearning to be a part of her again . . . to be loved by her.

Eleven years ago he had fallen in love with her almost the moment he laid eyes on her, and for years afterward, his life had been haunted by a laughing, haughty, prim eighteen-year-old.

In the last decade he had gone to bed with dozens of women, all of them more experienced sexually than Meredith had been. With them, the sexual act was an act of mutual gratification. With Meredith, it had been an act of profound beauty. Exquisite. Tormenting. Magic . . . At least, that's how he'd felt at the time—very probably, he decided now, because he'd been so insane about her he didn't know the difference between imagination and reality. She had captivated him at eighteen, but at twenty-nine she was far more dangerous to his peace of mind because she had changed, and the changes intrigued and beckoned to him. Her youthful sophistication had acquired the added gloss of elegance, yet that same soft vulnerability still glowed in her eyes, and her smile still changed from provocative to sunny, according to her moods. At eighteen she possessed an unaffected candor that had charmed and surprised him; at twenty-nine she was a successful businesswoman, and yet she seemed as natural and unaffected as she had before. Equally surprising, she seemed completely indifferent to, or unaware of, her own beauty. Not once yesterday had she stopped to primp at the mirror in the dining room, nor had she glanced at it in passing. Unlike other beautiful women he'd known, she didn't pose or posture or run her fingers through that gorgeous hair of hers to draw attention to it. Her beauty had matured and her figure had acquired a lush ripeness that enabled her to look as alluring in jeans and a sweater as she did in the mink coat and black dress she'd worn to lunch the other day.

Matt's blood stirred hotly, and his hands itched to explore and caress those new curves she'd acquired. Suddenly his treacherous mind presented him with a tantalizing solution: Perhaps if he had her just one more time, he could quench this thirst for her and get her completely out of his system. . . . Swearing under his breath, Matt got out of bed and pulled on his robe. He was insane to even consider being intimate with her again.

Again? He stopped cold. For the first time since she'd arrived, he was able to think without being weakened by the aftereffects of illness or those damned pills. Why in the hell had she come to the farm in the first place?

She'd answered that question herself: *I want a truce . . .*

Fine, he'd agreed to her truce. So why was she still there? Meredith hadn't come to play house with him, that was for damned sure—so why was she hanging around, bringing him coffee in bed, and doing her very effective utmost to charm and disarm him?

The answer hit him like a bucket of icewater, leaving him dumbstruck by his own stupidity: *I wanted that Houston property for Bancroft's,* she'd said, *but we can't afford to pay thirty million.*

Christ, she was like a narcotic! She completely drugged his mind. Meredith wanted that Houston land for the original price, and she was obviously willing to do anything to get it, including pandering to him. Her abject apology, her alleged desire for a truce, her wifely vigilance this week-end—it was all a sham designed to lull him into capitulating! Thoroughly revolted by her duplicity and his gullibility, Matt walked over to the window and shoved the curtain aside, looking out at the snow that had piled up in the drive, while in his mind he saw her standing meekly beside his bed: *I'll accept that as a sort of penance . . .*

Penance? he thought furiously. Meekness? Meredith didn't have a meek bone in her body; she and her father ran roughshod over anyone who got in their way, and they did it as if it were their divine right! The only thing that had changed in Meredith was that she'd learned tenacity. No doubt, she'd climb into that bed with him if she thought it would get her that land, he thought with revulsion, not lust.

Turning on his heel, Matt picked up his briefcase from the floor, opened it, and yanked out the cellular phone he always kept in it. When Sue O'Donnell answered his call at the neighboring farm, Matt impatiently replied to her inquiries about his family, then he said, "I'm snowed in over here. Would you ask Dale to plow the drive right away?"

"You bet I will," she agreed at once. "He's due home this afternoon, and I'll have him come right over."

Angry with the delay, but unable to come up with an alternative, Matt hung up and headed into the bathroom for a shower. Before his lust drove him to do something that would cost him what little pride and self-respect he had left, he was going to get Meredith out of there! All he had to do now to accomplish that was find her keys. He had a dim recollection of seeing her get out of her car the night she arrived, and then bend down near the car's front tire on the driver's side. He'd find her keys near there. The prospect of groping around in the snow was far less distasteful than having her under his roof for another day. Or another night. If he couldn't find them, he'd hot-wire her car to start without the damned keys. Reaching into the tub, he turned on the water, wondering if she had an electronic alarm on the car that would disable the vehicle if he tried that. If she did, he'd think of something else, but one way or another, he was getting her out of there. As soon as the drive was plowed, he was going to give her five minutes to pack up and get out.

38

Still buttoning his shirt, Matt strode purposefully down the stairs. Meredith whirled around as he stalked past the kitchen doorway, pulling on a leather flight jacket, heading for the front door. "Where are you going?"

"I'm going outside to find your keys. Do you remember where you dropped them?"

Her lips parted in surprise when she saw the granite determination that hardened his jaw. "I—I dropped them as I walked around the front of the car, but there's no reason for you to go out there now——"

"Yes," he said flatly, "there is. This charade has gone on long enough. don't look so surprised," he snapped. "You're as bored with this pretense at marital bliss as I am." She drew in a sharp breath as though he had slapped her, and Matt added coldly, "I admire your tenacity, Meredith. You want the Houston property for twenty million, and you need a quick, congenial divorce with no publicity. You've spent two days catering to me so that I'll be more agreeable to both. You tried and you failed. Now, go back to the city and behave like the competent executive you are. Take me to court over the Houston property and file for divorce, but knock off this nauseating farce! The role of humble, loving wife doesn't suit you, and you must be as sick of it as I am."

He turned on his heel and strode out the front door. Meredith stared at the place where he had stood, her heart twisting with panic, disappointment, and humiliation. He'd suddenly decided these last two days were a *boring* charade! Blinking away frustrated tears, she bit down on her lip and turned back to the frying pan. She'd obviously passed up her best opportunities to tell him she hadn't had an abortion, and she didn't have the slightest, the vaguest idea why his mood had suddenly turned so hostile. She hated that volatile unpredictability that was Matt; he'd always been that way. You never knew what he thought or what he was going to do next! Before she left this house, she was going to tell him the truth about what had happened eleven years ago, but now she wasn't certain he was going to care, even if he believed her. She picked up an egg and hit it so hard against the side of the frying pan that the yolk slid down the outside.

For ten minutes Matt pawed through the snow near the BMW's front tire in a futile effort to find Meredith's damned keys; he dug and sifted until his gloves were soaked and his hands were frozen, and then he gave up and checked out her alarm system, looking through the window. There was no sign of a keypad, which probably meant hers could be disabled only with her car key. Even if he jimmied her door lock and got in to hot-wire the damned car, an alarm system like hers was designed to disable the vehicle so it couldn't be driven.

"Breakfast is ready," Meredith said uneasily, walking into the living room when she heard the front door slam. "Did you find the keys?"

"No," Matt said, striving to keep his temper under control. "There's a locksmith in town, but he isn't open on Sunday."

Meredith served the scrambled eggs she'd made, then she sat down across from him. Desperately trying to restore some semblance of the relationship they'd shared yesterday, she asked in a quiet, reasonable voice, "Do you mind telling me why you've suddenly decided this whole weekend has been a boring plot on my part?"

"Let's just say my faculties have returned along with my health," he said shortly. For ten minutes, while they ate, Meredith tried to engage him in conversation, only to have him rebuff her attempts with curt, brief replies. The moment he was finished eating, he got up and said he was going to start packing up the things in the living room.

With a sinking heart, Meredith watched him go, then she automatically began to tidy up the kitchen. When the last dish had been washed and put away, she went into the living room. "There's a lot to pack," she said, determined to find a way to make him more receptive. "What can I do to help?"

Matt heard the soft plea in her voice and his body responded with a fresh surge of lust as he straightened and looked at her. *You could go upstairs with me and offer me that delectable body of yours.* "Suit yourself."

Why, Meredith wondered fiercely, did he have to be so damned unapproachable now, and why did he suddenly find her boring and irritating? His father had said Matt had been wild with grief over her alleged abortion and that, when Meredith had refused to see him, it nearly killed him. She'd thought at the time Patrick must be grossly exaggerating Matt's feelings for her; now she was certain of it, and the certainty made her feel strangely, inexplicably, despondent. It didn't surprise her though. Matt had always been capable of shouldering great responsibility, but it was impossible to know what he was really thinking and feeling. Hoping against hope his mood would improve if she left him alone, she went upstairs and spent the morning packing away linens and bedding and the contents of the closets, most of which he'd told her at breakfast were to be donated to a charity. Only the family mementos were being kept, and she carefully sorted through his parents' closet, making certain that nothing of sentimental value went into the boxes destined for charity. When she took a break, she sat down on the bed and opened a photograph album that had evidently belonged to Matt's mother. It was filled with pictures that were so old, most of them were fading. Many of them were of relatives in the old country: sweet-faced girls with long hair and bonnets, and handsome, unsmiling men with Irish surnames like Lanigan, O'Malley, and Collier. Beneath each picture was the date it was taken and the name of whoever was in the photograph. The last picture in the album was the most current—it was a wedding photograph of Matt's mother and father. *April 24, 1949* was written beneath the picture in her neat script. Judging from the variety of names in that album, Elizabeth Farrell had lots of cousins and aunts and uncles in the old country, Meredith thought with a soft smile, wondering wistfully what it would be like to come from a big family.

At noon she went downstairs. They had sandwiches for lunch, and although Matt wasn't friendly, at least he answered her questions and comments with aloof courtesy, and she took that as an encouraging sign that his mood was improving. When she'd finished cleaning up after lunch, she gave a final satisfied glance at the gleaming kitchen, then she walked into the living room, where Matt was methodically packing books and knickknacks into boxes. She paused in the doorway, watching the way his chamois shirt stretched taut across his broad, muscled shoulders and tapered back whenever he lifted his arm. He'd taken off the jeans that had gotten damp while he was searching outside for her keys, and in their place he was wearing a pair of gray slacks that molded themselves to his hips and the long length of his muscled legs. For one hopeless moment she actually considered walking up behind him, wrapping her arms around his waist, and laying her cheek against the solid wall of his back. She wondered what he'd do. Push her away, probably, Meredith decided dismally.

Mentally, she braced herself for a rebuff and stepped forward, but after a half day of enduring his unpredictable temper, her nerves were scraped raw and her own temper was strained to the breaking point. She watched him taping the last box of books shut, and said, "Can I do anything to help you?"

"Hardly, since I'm already finished," he said without bothering to turn.

Meredith stiffened, her frayed temper sending bright spots of warning color to her high cheekbones. With a last effort to sound polite, she said, "I'm going up to Julie's room to pack some things she left behind. Would you like me to fix you a cup of coffee before I do?"

"No," he snapped.

"Is there anything else I can get for you?"

"Oh, for God's sake!" he exploded, swinging around. "Stop acting like a patient, saintly wife, and get out of here!"

Fury blazed in her eyes, and she clenched her hands into fists, fighting back tears and the simultaneous urge to slap him. "Fine," she retorted, trying valiantly to hold on to her shattered dignity. "You can make your own damned dinner and eat it alone." Turning on her heel, she stalked up the stairs.

"What the hell is that supposed to mean?" he demanded.

She turned on the landing, looking down at him like an angry, haughty goddess, her hair tumbling over her shoulders. "It means I think you're rotten company!"

That was such an understatement that Matt would have laughed if he weren't already so furious with himself for wanting her—even now as she stood up there, glowering at him. He watched her turn her back on him and disappear down the hall, then he wandered over to the window. Bracing his hand high on the sill, he stared out across the drive. The *plowed* drive. Dale O'Donnell had evidently come while they'd been having lunch. For several minutes Matt stood at the windows, his jaw clenched, fighting against the impulse to go upstairs and discover for himself if Meredith actually wanted the Houston property badly enough to climb into bed with him. There were worse ways to spend a wintry day and night—and no better revenge than to let her do it, then send her on her way, empty-handed. And still he hesitated, held back by some vague scruple . . . or sense of self-preservation. Shoving away from the window, he got his jacket from the closet and went back outside, absolutely determined to find her car keys this time. He found them only inches away from where he'd stopped looking before.

"The drive is clear," he announced, walking into Julie's room where Meredith was putting old scrapbooks into a box. "Pack your things."

Meredith lurched around, stung by his icy tone, her hopes for a reprieve, for a return to the mood of yesterday, dying. Gathering her courage, she slowly finished wrapping the last scrapbook. Now that it was time to tell him about her miscarriage, she fully expected him to react with the equivalent of "Frankly, my dear, I don't give a damn." Just thinking of that possibility made her seethe with anger. After a half day of enduring his sarcasm and frigid silence, her nerves and her temper were strained to the breaking point. Carefully, she put the wrapped book into the box, then she straightened and looked at him. "Before I leave, there's something I have to tell you."

"I'm not interested," he bit out, striding forward. "Get going."

"Not until I tell you what I actually came here to say!" she said, then cried out in shocked alarm when he grabbed her arm.

"Meredith," he snapped, "cut the crap and get moving!"

"I can't!" she burst out, jerking her arm free. "I—I don't have my keys." He saw it then; the small suitcase lying beside the bed. Matt wasn't clear on much about the night she arrived, but he sure as hell would have noticed if she'd been carrying a suitcase when she got out of that car. The shock of seeing it would have registered on him. Her car was supposedly locked, but she'd managed to get a suitcase out of it! Turning on his heel, he yanked her purse off the dresser, turned it upside down, and unceremoniously dumped the contents out. A set of car keys landed on top of her wallet and makeup case. "So," he said in a silky voice, "You don't have any keys?"

In her panic and desperation, Meredith unthinkingly put her hand on his chest. "Matt, please listen to me—" She watched his gaze rivet on her hand, then it slowly lifted to her face, and when his eyes met hers, there was a distinct change in him, though she was unaware that it was the intimacy of her gesture that caused it. The rigidity left his jaw, his body relaxed; his eyes were no longer hard and indifferent, but lazy and speculative; even his voice was different—smooth, soft, like satin over cold steel. "Go ahead and talk, sweetheart, I'm hanging on to every word."

Meredith's mind rang out an alarm as she looked into those heavy-lidded gray eyes, but she was too desperate to speak to heed the warning or even to notice that his hands were slowly gliding up and down her arms. Drawing a quick, steadying breath, she launched into the speech she'd rehearsed all morning: "Friday evening, I went to your apartment to try to reason with you—"

"I already know that," he interrupted.

"What you don't know is that your father and I had a raging argument."

"I'm sure you didn't rage, sweetheart," he said with thinly veiled sarcasm. "A well-bred woman like you would never stoop so low."

"Well, I did," Meredith said, shaken by his attitude but determined to forge ahead. "You see, your father told me to stay away from you—he accused me of destroying our baby and nearly destroying your life. I—I didn't know what he was talking about at first."

"I'm sure the fault was his for not making himself clear—"

"Stop talking to me in that condescending way," Meredith warned with a mixture of panic and desperation. "I'm trying to make you understand!"

"I'm sorry. What is it I'm supposed to understand?"

"Matt, I didn't have an abortion—I had a miscarriage. A miscarriage," she repeated, searching his impassive features for some sign of reaction.

"A miscarriage. I see." His eyes dropped to her lips and his hand slid up her arm, curving around her nape. "So beautiful . . ." he whispered huskily. "You always were so damned beautiful . . ."

Stunned into blank immobility by his words and the husky timbre of his voice, she stared at him, not certain what he was thinking, unable to believe he'd accepted her explanation so easily and calmly. "So beautiful," he repeated, his hand tightening on her nape, "and such a *liar!*" Before she could summon a coherent thought, his mouth swooped down, seizing hers in a kiss of ruthless sensuality, grinding her lips apart. His fingers shoved into her hair and twisted, forcing her head back and holding her captive as his tongue drove insolently into her mouth.

The kiss was intended to punish and degrade her, and Meredith knew it, but instead of fighting him as he obviously expected her to do, she wrapped her arms around his neck, pressed her body to his, and kissed him back with all the shattering tenderness and aching contrition in her heart, trying to convince him in this way that she spoke the truth. Her response made him stiffen in shock; he tensed, as if he intended to shove her away, and then with a low groan he gathered her into his arms and kissed her with a slow, melting hunger that demolished her defenses completely and drove her mad with helpless yearning. The kiss deepened dramatically, his mouth moving urgently, persuasively, on hers, and against her, Meredith felt the rigid pressure of his aroused body.

When he finally lifted his head, she was too dazed to immediately grasp the meaning of his caustic question, "Are you using birth control? Before we get into bed so you can show me how badly you really want that Houston property, I want to be certain there won't be another child from this encounter—or another abortion."

Meredith lurched back, staring at him in stunned anger.

"Abortion!" she choked. "Didn't you hear what I just told you? I had a *miscarriage.*"

"Damn you, don't lie to me!"

"You have to listen—"

"I don't want to talk anymore," he said roughly, and his mouth captured hers in a bruising kiss.

Frantic to stop him, to make him listen before it was too late, Meredith struggled and finally managed to tear her mouth from his. "No!" she cried, wedging her hands against his chest, burying her face against his shirt. His hand clamped against the back of her head as if he intended to force her head up again, and Meredith fought with a strength born of terror and panic, shoving his hands away and tearing out of his grasp. "I didn't have an abortion—I *didn't!*" she cried, backing up a step, her chest rising and falling in sharp, shallow breaths, her words spilling out with all the pent-up pain and fury she felt. Gone was the carefully rehearsed speech she'd planned, and in its place came a torrent of anguished words. "I had a miscarriage, and I nearly died. A miscarriage! No one will perform an abortion when you're nearly six months pregnant—"

Minutes ago his eyes had been smoldering with desire, now they raked over her with savage contempt. "Evidently they will if you've given an entire wing to the hospital where it's performed."

"It's not a question of legality, it's too dangerous!"

"Apparently it was, since you were in there for almost two weeks."

Meredith realized he'd already considered all this long ago, arrived at his own logical, if erroneous, conclusions, and that nothing she said was going to make any difference. The realization was shattering, and she turned her head aside, brushing at the tears of futility starting to spill from her eyes, but she could not stop talking to him. "Oh, please," she implored brokenly, "listen to me. I hemorrhaged, and I lost our baby. I asked my father to send you a telegram to tell you what happened and to ask you to come home. I never imagined he'd lie to you, or stop you from getting into the hospital, but your father said that's what he did . . ." The dam of tears broke loose, flooding her eyes and shattering her voice as she wept. "I thought I was in love with you! I waited for you to come to the hospital. I waited and waited," she cried, "but you never did."

She bent her head, her shoulders jerking with sobs she couldn't suppress any longer. Matt knew she was crying, but he was rendered incapable of reaction by a memory that had started screaming through his brain when she mentioned her father—a vision of Philip Bancroft standing in his study, white-faced with rage: *You think you're tough, Farrell, but you don't even know what tough is yet. I'll stop at nothing to get Meredith free of you!* After that tirade, after Bancroft's rage was spent, he'd asked Matt if they could try to get along for Meredith's sake. Bancroft had seemed sincere. He'd seemed to accept the marriage, albeit reluctantly. But had he really, Matt wondered now. *I'll stop at nothing to get Meredith free of you . . .*

Meredith raised her eyes to his then, wounded blue-green eyes. In a state of paralyzed uncertainty, Matt looked into those eyes, and what he saw nearly sent him to his knees: They were filled with tears and pleading. And truth. Naked, soul-destroying, unbearable truth. "Matt," she whispered achingly, "we—we had a baby girl."

"Oh, my *God!*" he groaned, and he yanked her into his arms. "*Oh, God!*"

Meredith clung to him, her wet cheek pressed against his shirt, unable to stop the outpouring of grief and sorrow, now that she was in his arms. "I—I named her Elizabeth for your mother."

Matt scarcely heard her; his entire being was tormented with the image of Meredith, lying alone in a hospital room, waiting in vain for him. "Please, no," he pleaded with fate, clasping her tighter to him, rubbing his jaw against her hair. "Please no."

"I couldn't go to her funeral," she whispered hoarsely, "because I was so sick. My father said he went . . . you d-don't think he lied about that too, do you?"

The agony Matt felt when she mentioned a funeral and being sick almost doubled him over. "Oh, Christ!" he groaned, holding her tighter, running his hands over her back and shoulders, helplessly trying to heal the hurt he had unwittingly caused her years before. She lifted her tear-drenched face to his and begged him for reassurance: "I told him to be sure Elizabeth had dozens of flowers at her funeral. I told him they had to be pink roses. You . . . you don't think he lied to me when he said he sent them?"

"He sent them!" Matt promised her fiercely. "I'm sure he did."

"I couldn't—couldn't bear it if she didn't have any flowers . . ."

"Oh, please, darling," Matt whispered brokenly. "Please don't. No more."

Through the haze of her own sorrow and relief, Meredith heard the anguish clogging his voice, saw the ravaged sorrow on his face, and tenderness poured through her, its sweetness filling her heart until she ached with it. "Don't cry," she whispered, her own tears falling unchecked as she reached up and laid her fingers on his hard cheek. "It's all over now. Your father told me the truth. That's why I came here, you see . . . I had to tell you what really happened. I had to ask you to forgive me—"

Leaning his head back, Matt closed his eyes and swallowed, trying to clear the painful lump of emotion that was clogging his throat. "Forgive you?" he repeated in a ragged whisper. "For what?"

"For hating you all these years."

He forced his eyes to open and he looked down at her beautiful face. "You couldn't possibly have hated me as much as I hate myself at this moment."

Meredith's heart lurched at the naked remorse in his eyes; he'd always seemed so completely invulnerable that she'd thought him incapable of deep feeling. Or perhaps her judgment had been clouded by her youth and inexperience. But whatever the case, she thought nothing of trying to comfort him now. "It's over. don't think about it," she said softly, leaning her face against the hard wall of his chest, but it was a hopeless suggestion because in the silence before he spoke again, that was all either of them could think about. "Were you in much pain when it happened?" he said finally.

Meredith started to ask him again not to think of it, but she realized in some part of her mind that he was asking her to share with him now the things that would have been his right to share with her long ago. At the same time, he was offering her the belated chance to turn to him for the comfort that she'd needed from him. And Meredith slowly realized that she wanted that, even now. Standing in the circle of his arms, she felt the slow, soothing strokes of his hand against her nape and shoulders, and suddenly she wasn't twenty-nine anymore; she was eighteen, and he was twenty-six, and she was in love with him. He was strength and security and hope. "I was sleeping when it started," she began. "Something woke me up—I felt strange, and I turned on the lamp. When I looked down, the blankets were soaked with my blood. I screamed." She stopped, and then made herself continue. "Mrs. Ellis had just come back from Florida that day. She heard me and woke up my father and someone called an ambulance. The pains started coming, and I begged my father to try to call you, and the paramedics arrived. I remember them carrying me out of the house on a stretcher, and they were running. And I remember the sound of the siren screaming and screaming and screaming in the night. I tried to cover my ears to block out the sound, but they were giving me an injection and the paramedic held my arms down." Meredith drew a shuddering breath, not sure she could go on without starting to cry, but Matt's hand was drifting down her spine, holding her pressed against the solid strength of his body, and she found the courage to finish. "The next thing I remember was the sound of a machine beeping, and when I opened my eyes, I was lying in a hospital bed with all sorts of plastic tubes attached to me and a machine monitoring my heartbeats. It was daylight, and a nurse was there, but when I tried to ask her about our baby, she patted my hand and told me not to worry. I asked her if I could see you, and she said you weren't there yet. When I opened my eyes again, it was night and there were doctors and nurses all around the bed. I asked them about the baby too, and they said my doctor was on his way and everything was going to be just fine. I *knew* they were lying to me. So I asked—no," she amended with a sad smile as she tipped her head back and looked at him, "I *ordered* them to let you come in because I knew they wouldn't dare lie to you."

He tried to smile back at her but it didn't reach his tormented gray eyes, and she laid her cheek against his chest. "They told me you weren't there, but that my father was, and then my doctor arrived, and my father came in, and everyone else left the room. . . ."

Meredith stopped, cringing from the memory of what came next. As if Matt sensed what she was feeling, he laid his hand against her cheek, pressing her face to the rhythmic beating of his heart. "Tell me," he whispered, his deep voice ragged with tenderness and sorrow. "I'm here, and it can't hurt as much this time."

Meredith took his word for it, her hands sliding up his chest to his shoulders, instinctively clutching them for support, but fresh tears were flooding her eyes and clogging her voice. "Dr. Arledge told me that we'd had a baby girl, and that everything humanly possible had been done to save her, but they couldn't because—because she was too little." Tears raced down her cheeks. "Too *little!*" she repeated on a heartbroken sob. "I thought baby girls were supposed to be little. Little is such a—a *pretty* word . . . so *feminine . . .*"

She felt Matt's fingers digging into her back, and somehow the suppressed force of his reaction gave her strength. Drawing a long breath, she finished, "Because she was so little, she couldn't breathe properly. Dr. Arledge asked me what I wanted to do, and when I realized he was asking me if I wanted her to have a name and a—a funeral, I started begging him to let me see you. My father was furious at him for upsetting me, and he told me he'd sent you a telegram, but that you weren't there. Dr. Arledge said I couldn't wait for days to make these decisions. And so I—I decided," Meredith concluded brokenly. "I named her Elizabeth because I thought you would like that, and I told my father I wanted her to have dozens and dozens of pink roses. And I said I wanted all the cards to be from us and to say 'We loved you.'"

Matt's voice was raw. "Thank you," he whispered, and she suddenly realized the wetness on her cheek was not only from her tears, but also his.

"And then I waited," she told him with a ragged sigh. "I waited for you to come, because I thought that somehow, if you were there, everything would start to be better." Within moments after she finished, Meredith felt a sense of relief, of calm sweeping over her.

When Matt finally spoke, he, too, had gotten control of his emotions. "Your father's telegram reached me three days after he sent it. It said that you'd had an abortion, and that you wanted nothing more from me except a divorce, which you were already instituting. I flew home anyway, and one of your maids told me where you were, but when I got to the hospital, they informed me you'd specifically said you didn't want me allowed up to see you. I went back the next day with some half-formed plan of getting past the security guards at the desk of the Bancroft Wing, but I never got that far. A cop was waiting at the doors to serve me with a signed court injunction that made it a criminal act for me to go near you."

"And all that time," she whispered, "I was in there, waiting for you."

"I promise you," he said tightly, "that if I'd thought there was a chance you wanted to see me, no court order, no force on this earth, would have stopped me from getting to you!"

She tried to reassure him with a simple truth: "You couldn't have helped me."

His body seemed to stiffen. "I couldn't?"

She shook her head. "Everything medically possible was already being done for me, just as it had been for Elizabeth. There wasn't anything you could have done to help." Meredith was so relieved to have the truth out in the open at last that she abandoned her pride and took it one step further. "You see, despite what I had put on the cards with the roses, I knew in my heart how you *really* felt about the baby—and about me."

"Tell me," he said gruffly, "how did I really feel?"

Surprised by the sudden terseness in his tone, Meredith tipped her head back. With a soft smile to prove she meant no criticism, she said, "The answer to that is as obvious now as it was then: You were stuck with both of us. You slept one time with a silly eighteen-year-old virgin who did her best to seduce you, and who didn't have sense enough to use birth control, and look what happened."

"What happened, Meredith?" he demanded.

"What happened? You know what happened. I came looking for you to give you the glad news, and you did the noble thing—you married a girl you didn't want."

"Didn't *want?*" he exploded, his harsh voice in complete opposition to the poignancy of his words. "I've wanted you every day of my godforsaken life."

Meredith stared at him, mesmerized, doubtful, joyous, shattered.

"And you were wrong about something else too," he said, his expression gentling as he framed her tear-streaked face between his palms, his fingers brushing the wetness away. "If I'd been able to see you in the hospital, I *could* have helped."

Her voice dropped to a shaken whisper. "How?"

"Like this," he said, and still cradling her face, he bent his head and brushed his lips over hers. The exquisite tenderness of his kiss, the caressing way his fingers slid over her face, destroyed Meredith's defenses completely, and fresh tears welled up just when she thought she had cried them all. "And like this—" His mouth slid to the corners of her eyes, and she felt the touch of his tongue on her tears. "I'd have taken you home from the hospital with me, and held you in my arms—like this—" he promised achingly, drawing her against his full length, his breath against her ear sending shivers down her spine. "When you were well enough, we'd have made love, and later, when you wanted me to, I'd have given you another baby—" He didn't say "like this," but when he shifted her backward onto the bed and followed her down, Meredith knew that was what he meant. She knew it as surely as she knew it was wrong to let him take off her sweater and unfasten her jeans, as surely as she knew it was impossible for her to have another baby. But, oh, the sweetness of pretending, just this once, that all of this was reality and the past was only a dream that could be altered.

Her heart wanted desperately to try, but some tiny voice of reason warned that it was a mistake. "This is wrong—" she whispered when he leaned over her, his chest and arms bare and bronze.

"This is *right*," he said fiercely, and his lips covered hers, parting them with familiar, insistent skill.

Meredith closed her eyes and let the dream begin.

Only in this dream she wasn't merely an observer; she was a participant—hesitant at first; as shy and awkward as she'd always been when confronted with his bold sexuality and unerring expertise. His mouth tormented and enticed hers, his tongue sliding on her lips, flicking at the crease, while his hands shifted endlessly down her sides, her legs, sliding with tantalizing languor upward toward her breasts. Meredith moaned inwardly with a combination of awakening delight and recurring inhibition, and slid her hands uncertainly into the crisp, curly hairs on his muscular chest, touching. His mouth became more demanding, his hands so near her aching breasts, but not touching, thumbs playing over her ribs. Just when she thought she would die from the need, he drove his tongue into her mouth, and his hands took hard possession of her breasts, kneading, teasing, instinctively rubbing hardened nipples, and the cry that Meredith had been suppressing erupted at the same moment her restraint broke. Her body arched toward his, and she ran her hands feverishly down the bunched muscles of his arms, welcoming the invasion of his tongue, giving him hers, rolling with him onto her side. He tore his mouth from hers, and she moaned in protest at the loss, then shivered in delight as he kissed her ear, sliding his lips down her neck, then over her breasts, until they closed hard on her nipples. Lost in the dark, silent wanting, she felt his hand slide to the triangle between her legs, seeking and finding every hot, damp place, touching and caressing, until she writhed against him.

Matt knew the exact moment that she relinquished her body entirely to him; he felt the tension leave her, her legs relaxing, then opening for him, and the poignant sweetness of her well-remembered surrender sent desire raging uncontrollably through him. It made his heart thunder and his body throb until even his limbs began to tremble as he shifted on top of her. Gone was his hazy hope of prolonging this unbelievable, momentous joining; all that mattered was being a part of her again. The veins in his arms stood out as he held himself above her, his eyes clenched shut, easing himself into her an inch at a time, fighting the overpowering need to bury himself full-length in her incredible warmth, to devour her with his hands and mouth.

His control began to slip when she arched her hips, and again when she slid her hands over his shoulders and whispered his name, but when he opened his eyes and looked down at her Matt was lost: This wasn't a figment of his fevered imagination—the girl he had loved was the woman in his arms; the beautiful face that had haunted his dreams was inches from his, flushed with desire, her shining hair spilling over his pillow. She'd been waiting for him in that hospital; she had never tried to rid herself of his baby or him. She had come to him here, endured his hatred and braved his anger—and then she had asked for *his* forgiveness. The realization was overpoweringly poignant, and even then Matt might have been able to continue moving slowly and steadily inside her—if Meredith hadn't chosen that moment to run her fingers through the hair at his nape, and lift her hips, and whisper, "Please, Matt." The exquisite sweetness of his name on her lips and the arousing shift of her body reaching for his tore a silent groan from him, and he drove into her, plunging again and again, until they were both wild with wanting, reaching together for it . . . finding it in the same moment, exploding together and then shattering. Limbs entwined, hearts thundering, he wrapped her in his arms, and still he kept thrusting, wanting to spill eleven years of yearning into her, and Meredith held him to her, her body beginning to convulse again, until her rhythmic spasms had finally drained him of everything except a feeling of overwhelming joy and peace.

He collapsed against her, his skin fiery, his breathing labored, and then he moved onto his side to keep himself from crushing her, taking her with him, his arm around her back, his fingers buried in the bunched satin of her hair. Silent, floating, still intimately joined to her, he let his hand drift up and down her spine, reveling in the sensation of being held inside her wet warmth and the brush of her lips against his collarbone.

He closed his eyes, savoring it, filled with reverence for all the things she was and for all the things she made him want to be. Eleven years ago he'd been cheated of heaven; he'd found it again this weekend, and there was nothing that he wouldn't do to avoid losing it again. Then he'd had nothing to offer her except himself; now he could give her the world—and himself.

He felt her breathing even out and realized she was falling asleep. He smiled to himself, a little embarrassed by his lack of restraint that had worn them both out so completely and so quickly. . . . He'd let her sleep for an hour, he decided, and himself too. Then he would wake her up and make love to her more properly and thoroughly. After that they would talk. They were going to have to make plans. Even though he expected that she might be hesitant to break off her engagement on the strength of one afternoon in bed with him, Matt knew he could persuade her of the simple truth: They were meant to be together. They had always been meant to be together. . . .

Nudged from his sleep by a sound somewhere in the house, Matt opened his eyes and stared in mild confusion at the empty pillow beside him. The room was dark, and he rolled onto his side, squinting at his watch. It was almost six o'clock, and he leaned up on his elbow, surprised that he'd slept for almost three hours. For a moment or two, he was perfectly still, listening, trying to decide where Meredith was, but the first sound he heard was the last one he expected: It came from outdoors—a car engine firing, motor revving.

For a moment of ignorant bliss he decided she must have been worried about her battery running down in the cold, and he tossed off the quilts and rolled out of bed. Combing his hand through his hair, he walked over to the window and pushed the curtain aside, intending to open the window and call to her to let him take care of that. What he saw was a pair of red taillights glowing brightly as the BMW sped down the long drive toward the main road.

He was so stunned that his first reaction was to worry that she was driving too damned fast—and then reality hit him. She had left! For a split second his mind couldn't seem to absorb the shock. She had crawled out of bed and crept off in the night! Swearing savagely under his breath, he turned on the lamp and yanked on his pants, then he stood, hands on his hips, glaring at the empty bed in a state of near paralysis. He could not believe she'd run away as if they'd done something she was ashamed of and couldn't bear to face in daylight.

He saw it then—the note propped on the nightstand, written on the same pad of yellow paper she'd used to make her notes for the board of directors meeting. He snatched it up, hope flaring in his chest that she'd merely gone to find a grocery store or something.

"Matt," she'd written, "what happened this afternoon should never have happened. It was wrong for both of us—understandable, I suppose—but terribly wrong. We both have our own lives and plans for the future, and we have people in our lives who love and trust us. We betrayed them by doing what we did. I'm ashamed of that. And even so, I will always remember this weekend as something beautiful and special. Thank you for it."

Matt stood staring in furious disbelief at the words, feeling absurdly—stupidly—as if he'd been raped! No, not raped, used, like some paid stud who she could take to her bed when she wanted a "special" time, and then dismiss afterward like an insignificant peon whom she was ashamed to have been with.

She hadn't changed one damned bit in all these years! She was still spoiled and self-centered and so convinced of her own superiority that it wouldn't *occur* to her that maybe, just maybe, someone from a less privileged class than her own might be worth consideration. No, she hadn't changed at all, she was still a coward, still—

Matt checked himself in mid-thought, amazed that his anger could actually obliterate his memory of everything that he'd discovered. For the last few minutes he'd been judging her based on all the erroneous things he'd believed of her for eleven years. That was habit; it was not reality. Reality was what he'd learned of her in this room; truths so painful, and so beauti-ful—that they'd made him ache. Meredith was no coward, she had never run away from him, from motherhood, or even her tyrannical father who she'd had to deal with at the store all these years. She had been eighteen, and she had thought she loved Matt—a slight smile touched his eyes at the memory of her astounding admission—but it vanished when he thought of her lying in the hospital waiting for him. She had sent flowers for their baby, and named her Elizabeth for his mother. . . . And when he never came back, she had picked up the pieces of her life, gone back to college, and faced what-ever else the future handed her. Even now it made him cringe to remember the things he'd said and done to her in the last few weeks. Jesus, how she must have hated him!

He had threatened her and bullied her . . . and yet, when she discovered the facts from Matt's father, she had braved a snowstorm to come and tell him the truth, and she had done it knowing that when she arrived, she was going to find brutal hostility.

Leaning a shoulder against the bedpost, he gazed at the bed. His wife, Matt decided with mounting pride, didn't run away from things that would make most people take to their heels.

But tonight she had run from him.

What, he wondered, would make Meredith flee like a frightened rabbit, when, for the first time all weekend, there could have been total harmony between them?

In his mind he quickly reviewed the past two days, looking for answers. He saw her reaching for his hand, asking for a truce, and he remembered the way she'd watched their hands joining—as if the moment was profoundly meaningful to her. Her fingers had trembled when he touched them. He saw her smiling up at him with those glowing blue-green eyes of hers—*I've decided to be just like you when I grow up.* But most of all he remembered the way she had cried in his arms when she was telling him about their baby . . . the way she had put her own arms around him too, holding him to her as naturally as she had in this bed . . . the way she had moaned beneath him, her nails biting into his back, her body welcoming his with the same exquisite, shattering ardor she had shown him when she was eighteen.

Matt slowly straightened, struck by the most obvious answer. Meredith had very likely run away tonight because what had happened between them was as shattering to her as it was to him. If it was, then all her plans for her future with Parker and the rest of her life were jeopardized by what had happened in this house and especially in this bed.

She was no coward, but she was cautious. He'd noticed that when they'd talked about the department store. She took calculated risks, but only when the rewards were great and the likelihood for failure was comparatively small. She'd admitted that herself downstairs.

Given that, she sure as hell wasn't going to want to risk her heart or her future on Matthew Farrell again if she could possibly avoid it. The ramifications of making love with him, of getting involved with him again, were too overwhelming for her to face. The last time she'd done it, her life had become a living hell. He realized that to Meredith, the likelihood for failure with him was enormous, and the rewards were . . .

Matt laughed softly—the rewards were beyond her wildest imaginings. Now all he had to do was convince her of it. To do that, he was going to need time, and she wasn't going to want to give it to him. In fact, considering the way she'd fled tonight, he half expected her to fly to Reno or somewhere else immediately in order to sever all ties with him at the first possible moment. The longer he thought, the more convinced he became that she'd do exactly that.

In fact, there were only two things he was *more* sure of, and that was that Meredith still felt something for him, and that she was going to be his wife in every way. To accomplish that, Matt was now prepared to move heavenand earth; in fact, he was even prepared to permanently forgo the gratification of finding her lousy father and making her an orphan. In the midst of those thoughts, he suddenly realized something that made him stiffen in alarm: The roads that Meredith was driving on were bound to be treacherous in places, and she was not likely to be concentrating very well right now.

Turning, he headed swiftly down the hall to his room.

Walking over to his briefcase, he took out the phone and made three calls. The first call was to Edmunton's new chief of police. Matt instructed him to have a patrolman watch for a black BMW on the overpass and to discreetly escort the car back to Chicago to make certain the driver got home safely. The police chief was perfectly willing to comply with the extraordinary request; Matthew Farrell had contributed a very large sum to his election campaign.

His next phone call was to the home of David Levinson, senior partner in Pearson & Levinson. Matt instructed Levinson to appear, with Pearson in tow, in Matt's office at eight sharp the next morning. Levinson was perfectly willing to comply. Matthew Farrell paid them an annual retainer of $250,000 to do their legal utmost—whenever and wherever he wanted it done.

The last call was to Joe O'Hara. Matt instructed him to get out to the farm and pick him up immediately. Joe O'Hara balked. Matt Farrell paid him a lot of money to be at his beck and call, but Joe also regarded himself as Matt's protector, and his friend. He didn't figure it was in Matt's best interests to have a means of escape from the farm if Meredith wanted him to stay. Instead of agreeing to leave at once, Joe said, "Is everything all patched up between you and your wife?"

Matt scowled at this unprecedented failure to follow instructions at once. "Not exactly," he said impatiently.

"Is your wife still there?"

"She's already left."

The sadness in O'Hara's voice banished Matt's annoyance with his prying and made him again realize the depth of his driver's loyalty. "So you let her go, huh, Matt?"

Matt's smile was in his voice. "I'm going after her. Now, get your tail out here, O'Hara."

"I'm on my way!"

When he hung up the phone, Matt stared out the window, planning his strategy for tomorrow.

39

Good morning," Phyllis said, her forehead creasing in a worried frown as Meredith walked past her Monday morning without her usual greeting, two hours late for work. "Is anything wrong?" she asked, getting up from her new desk outside the president's office and following Meredith inside. Miss Pauley, who'd been Philip Bancroft's secretary for twenty years, had decided to take a long-overdue vacation while her employer was on leave.

Meredith sat down at her desk, leaned her elbows on it, and massaged her temples. Everything was wrong. "Nothing, really. I have a slight headache. Do I have any phone messages?"

"A pile of them," Phyllis said. "I'll get them, and I'll bring you some coffee too. You look like you could use some."

Meredith watched Phyllis leave, and she leaned back in her chair, feeling like she'd aged a hundred years since she'd left this office on Friday. Besides having lived through the most cataclysmic weekend of her life, she'd also managed to demolish her pride by going to bed with Matt, betraying her fiancé, and then compounding her wrongs by running away and leaving Matt a note. Guilt and shame had haunted her throughout the drive home, and to finish it all off nicely, she'd actually thought she was being followed by some demented Indiana patrolman who slowed down whenever she did, stopped for gasoline when she did, and then stayed behind her until she lost sight of him a few blocks from her apartment. By the time she got home she was a mass of guilt and shame and fear—and that was *before* she played back the messages on her answering machine and listened to the ones from Parker.

He'd called Friday night to say that he missed her and needed to hear the sound of her voice. His Saturday morning message had been mildly confused at her lack of reply. Saturday night he'd been worried by her silence, and he'd asked if her father had gotten ill on his cruise. Sunday morning he said he was alarmed and that he was going to call Lisa. Unfortunately, Lisa had evidently explained that Meredith had gone to see Matt on Friday to tell him the truth and get things straightened out. Parker's Sunday night message was furious and hurt: "Call me, dammit!" he'd said. "I want to believe you have a legitimate reason for spending the weekend with Farrell, if that's what you've done, but I'm running out of excuses." Meredith sustained that part better than his next words, which were filled with confusion and tenderness. "Darling, where are you, really? I know you aren't with Farrell. I'm sorry I said that, my imagination is running wild. Did he agree to a divorce? Has he murdered you? I'm terribly worried about you."

Meredith closed her eyes, trying to banish the sensation of impending doom so that she could attempt to get on with her day. The note she'd left Matt had been cowardly and childish, and she couldn't understand why she'd been unable to stay there until he woke up and then say good-bye to him like a mature adult. Every time she went near Matt Farrell, she said and did things that she'd never do under ordinary circumstances—foolish, wrong, dangerous things! In less than forty-eight hours with him, she'd thrown away her scruples and forgotten about things that mattered to her, like decency and principles. Instead, she'd gone to bed with a man she didn't love, and she had betrayed Parker. Her conscience was on a rampage.

She thought of the way she'd responded to him in bed, and bright color ran up her pale cheeks. At eighteen she'd been awed by the fact that Matt seemed to know all the right places to touch her, all the right things to whisper to her, in order to drive her into a frenzy of defenseless desire. To discover, when she was twenty-nine, that he could still do it—only much more so—filled her with despondent shame. Yesterday she'd practically begged him for a climax—she, who was helplessly modest in bed with her own fiancé.

Meredith drew herself up short. These sorts of recriminations, these thoughts, weren't fair to either Matt or her. The things she'd told him yesterday had shaken him deeply. They'd gone to bed together as a way to . . . to console each other. He had *not* merely used that as an excuse to get her into bed. At least, she thought a little wildly, it hadn't *seemed* like it at the time.

She was doing it again, she realized in frustrated alarm—losing focus, concentrating on all the wrong things. It was counterproductive to sit, on the verge of tears, filled with remorse and obsessed with anything as silly as his sexual expertise. She needed to take action, to do something to banish this strange, nameless panic that had been growing inside her from the moment she'd left Matt's bed. At four o'clock that morning she'd arrived at certain conclusions, and she'd made a decision. Now she needed to *stop* going over the problems and follow through with that decision.

"I had to wait for a fresh pot of coffee to brew," Phyllis said, heading toward Meredith's desk with a steaming mug in one hand and a fistful of pink message slips in the other. "Here are your messages. don't forget, you rescheduled the executive committee meeting for today at eleven."

Meredith managed not to look as harassed and miserable as she felt. "Okay, thanks. Will you get Stuart Whitmore on the phone for me? And will you see if you can reach Parker at his hotel in Geneva? If he isn't in his suite, leave a message."

"Who do you want first?" Phyllis asked with her usual cheerful efficiency.

"Stuart Whitmore," Meredith said. First she would tell Stuart of her decision. Next she would talk to Parker, and try to explain. Explain? she thought miserably.

Trying to think of something less daunting, she picked up the phone messages and leafed disinterestedly through them. The fifth one brought her halfway to her feet, her heart beginning to hammer. The message said that Mr. Matthew Farrell had called at 9:10 A.M.

The harsh buzz of her intercom jerked Meredith's attention to the phone, and she saw that both her lines were lit up, their hold buttons flashing.

"I have Mr. Whitmore on line one," Phyllis said when Meredith answered the intercom, "and Matthew Farrell is on line two. He says it's urgent."

Meredith's pulse rate doubled. "Phyllis," she said shakily, "I don't want to speak to Matt Farrell. Would you tell him that I want us to communicate with each other through our attorneys from now on? And also tell him I'm going out of town for a week or two. Be polite to him," she added nervously, "but very firm."

"I understand."

Meredith put down the phone, her hand shaking, watching the flashing light on line two become constant. Phyllis was giving Matt the message. She started to reach for the phone; she should at least talk to him and find out what he wanted, she thought, then she jerked her hand back. No, she shouldn't! It didn't matter. As soon as Stuart told her where to go to get a quick, legal divorce, whatever Matt wanted would be irrelevant. She'd arrived at the obvious solution of a Reno divorce—or something like it—in the small hours of the morning, and it made perfect sense. Now that there was no more enmity between them, she knew Matt wouldn't consider carrying out the threats he'd made in the car that day after lunch. All that was in the past.

The light on Matt's call went out, and she couldn't stand the suspense. She buzzed Phyllis and asked her to come in. "What did he say?" Meredith asked her.

Phyllis bit back a puzzled smile at Meredith's complete loss of serenity. "He said he understood perfectly."

"Was that all?"

"Then he asked if your trip was a sudden, unscheduled one, and I told him it was. Is that okay?"

"I don't know," Meredith said helplessly. "Did he say anything when you told him my trip was sudden?"

"Not exactly."

"What do you mean by *that?*"

"What he did was laugh, but not loud. I guess you'd call it a chuckle— sort of low and deep. Then he thanked me and said good-bye."

For some reason, Matt's entire reaction made Meredith feel acutely uneasy. "Was there anything else?" she asked when Phyllis continued to hover in the doorway.

"I was just wondering," the secretary replied a little sheepishly. "I mean, do you think he has *really* dated Michelle Pfeiffer and Meg Ryan, or do you think the movie magazines just make that stuff up?"

"I'm sure he has," Meredith said, struggling to keep her voice and face completely blank.

Nodding, Phyllis glanced at the phone. "Did you forget Stuart Whitmore is still on your line?"

Horrified, Meredith snatched up the phone and asked Phyllis to close her door. "Stuart, I'm sorry for making you wait," she began, nervously raking her hair off her forehead. "I'm not having a very good morning."

Stuart's reply was amused. "I'm having a *fascinating* morning, thanks to you."

"What do you mean?"

"I mean that Farrell's attorneys suddenly want a parlay. David Levinson called me at nine-thirty this morning so filled with goodwill that you'd almost think the arrogant bastard had had a profound religious experience over the weekend."

"What exactly did he say?" Meredith asked, her trepidation mounting.

"Well, first Levinson treated me to a lecture on the sanctity of marriage, particularly among Catholics, which he delivered in his most pious voice. Meredith," Stuart pointed out on a suffocated laugh, "Levinson is an orthodox Jew on his fourth marriage and sixth mistress! Jesus, I couldn't believe his nerve!"

"What did you say?"

"I told him I couldn't believe his nerve," Stuart said, then he stopped trying to make her see the humor of it all because he sensed she couldn't.

"All right, never mind all that. According to Levinson, his client is suddenly willing to let the divorce go through, which strikes me as odd, and odd always makes me nervous."

"It isn't that odd," Meredith said quietly, ignoring the painful and irrational thought that Matt was dumping her with embarrassing abruptness after she'd gone to bed with him. He was only doing the decent thing by calling an end to hostilities immediately. "I saw Matt this weekend, and we talked."

"About what?" When she hesitated, he said, "Don't keep secrets from your lawyer. Levinson's sudden eagerness for a meeting is setting off all kinds of alarm bells in my head. I smell an ambush."

Because Meredith knew it wasn't fair or wise to keep the events of the weekend from Stuart, she told him what had happened—from her discovery that Matt had purchased the Houston land to her stormy confrontation with Matt's father. "Matt was too sick to listen to me when I first got to the farm," she continued, "but yesterday I told him the truth about what my father had done, and he believed me." She didn't tell Stuart she'd gone to bed with Matt; that was something no one had a right to know except, perhaps, Parker.

When she was done, Stuart was silent for such a long time that she was afraid he was guessing the truth, but when he spoke, all he said was "Farrell's got more control than I have. I'd be gunning for your father."

Meredith, who still had to deal with her father over his treachery when he returned from his cruise, let that remark pass. "In any case," she said, "that's obviously why Matt has decided to be cooperative."

"He's being more than cooperative," Stuart said dryly. "According to Levinson, Farrell is deeply concerned about your well-being. He wants to make a financial settlement for you. He also volunteered to sell you the Houston land for very agreeable terms—though at the time I didn't know what land Levinson was talking about."

"I don't want, nor am I entitled to, a financial settlement from him," Meredith said emphatically. "If Matt's willing to sell us the Houston land, that's wonderful, but there's no need for a meeting with Matt's attorneys. I've decided to fly to Reno or somewhere and get a divorce right away. That's why I was calling you—I wanted to ask where I could go to that would be fast and legal."

"No dice," Stuart said flatly. "If you attempt to do that, Farrell's offer is withdrawn."

"What makes you say that?" Meredith cried, feeling as if an invisible trap were closing around her.

"Because Levinson made that very clear. It seems his client wants to do this thing properly and completely or not at all. If you refuse to meet with him tomorrow, or try to get a quickie divorce, Farrell's offer to sell you the Houston land will be permanently withdrawn. Levinson implied that either of those actions would be construed by his client as a personal rejection of his goodwill. It boggles the mind," Stuart concluded with heavy irony, "to discover that Farrell's reputation for cold ruthlessness is only a cover to hide his sensitive heart, doesn't it?"

Meredith sank back into her chair, her attention momentarily diverted by several members of the executive committee who were walking past her office and into the adjoining conference room. "I don't know what to think," she admitted. "I've been judging Matt so harshly for so long, I don't know who he really is."

"Well," Stuart cheerfully informed her, "we're going to find out tomorrow at four o'clock. Farrell wants the meeting at his office, with his attorneys, myself, and you in attendance. I can cancel an appointment. Shall I meet you there, or would you rather I pick you up?"

"No! I don't want to go. You can represent me."

"Nope. You have to be there. Levinson said his client is not flexible on the date, place, or attendees. Inflexibility," Stuart remarked with a return of irony, "is an odd trait for a man of such extraordinary benevolence and generosity as we're being led to believe that Farrell is by his attorneys."

Harassed, Meredith glanced at her watch. The meeting was scheduled to begin now. She was loath to relinquish the Houston land if Matt was willing to sell it back to her, and almost as reluctant to endure the emotional strain of having to deal with him face-to-face.

"Even if you got your Reno divorce," Stuart reminded her when she didn't say anything, "You'd still have to deal with the property issue when you came back. There's an eleven-year snarl of property rights here that can be easily unraveled if Farrell is willing—or that he can drag out in court for years if he isn't."

"God, what a mess," she said weakly. "All right, I'll meet you in the lobby at Intercorp at four o'clock. I'd rather not go up there alone."

"I understand," Stuart said kindly. "See you tomorrow. don't think about all this until then."

Meredith tried, very hard, to follow his advice as she sat down at the head of the conference table. "Good morning," she said with a bright, artificial smile. "Mark, do you want to begin? Any problems to report from the security division?"

"One nice big fat one," he said. "Five minutes ago the New Orleans store had a bomb threat. They're clearing the store, and the bomb squad is on its way."

Everyone at the table jerked to attention.

"Why wasn't I notified?" Meredith demanded.

"Both your phone lines were busy, so the store manager followed procedure and called me."

"I have a private direct line too."

"I know and so does Michaelson. Unfortunately, he panicked and couldn't find the phone number."

At 5:30 that night, after a day of raw tension and helpless waiting, Meredith finally received the phone call she'd been praying for: The New Orleans Bomb and Arson Squad had found no trace of explosives and were going to remove the barriers around the store. That was the good news. The bad news was that the store had lost an entire day's sales in the most important season of the year.

Limp with relief and exhaustion, Meredith notified Mark Braden of the news, then she packed a briefcase full of work and went home. Parker hadn't returned her call yet, but she knew he'd call her as soon as he received her message.

In her apartment she dumped her coat, gloves, and briefcase onto the chair, and walked over to the answering machine to check her messages, thinking Parker might have called, but the red light was not on. Mrs. Ellis had been there, though, and left a note beside the phone saying she'd done the marketing today instead of Wednesday because she had a doctor's appointment Wednesday morning.

The continued silence from Parker was making Meredith increasingly uneasy, and as she walked into the bedroom, she began to imagine him in a Swiss hospital, or, worse, soothing his wounded feelings with some other woman, dancing in some Geneva nightclub. . . . Stop it, just stop it! she warned herself. The mere proximity of Matthew Farrell was causing her to start expecting disaster to befall her at every turn. It was foolish, she knew, but given her past experiences with Matt, not entirely incomprehensible.

She'd taken her shower and was tucking a silk shirt into her slacks when the hard knocking on her door made her turn in surprise. Whoever it was had a pass key to get through the downstairs security door, which meant it had to be Mrs. Ellis, since Parker was in Switzerland. "Did you forget something, Mrs.—" she began as she opened her door, then she froze in surprise at the sight of Parker's grim face.

"I was wondering if *you* forgot something," he said curtly, "like the fact that you have a fiancé?"

Overwhelmed with remorse that he'd actually flown home, Meredith flung herself into his arms, noting the way he hesitated before putting them around her. "I didn't forget," she said, kissing his rigid cheek. "I'm so sorry!" she said, pulling him into the apartment. She expected him to take off his coat, but all he did was study her with a cool, hesitant look. "What is it you're sorry about, Meredith?" he finally asked.

"For worrying you so much that you thought you needed to leave the conference and fly home! Didn't you get my message at your hotel this morning? I left word for you at ten-thirty our time."

At her answer, the rigidity left his face, but there was a haggard, drawn look about him that she'd never seen before. "No, I didn't. I'd like a drink," he said, shrugging out of his coat. "Anything you have is fine, just make it a stiff one."

Meredith nodded, but she hesitated, worriedly studying the deep lines etched into his handsome face by strain and fatigue. "I can't believe you flew home because you couldn't reach me."

"That is one of two reasons I flew home."

She tipped her head to the side. "What was the other reason?"

"Morton Simonson is going to file Chapter 11 tomorrow. I got the word in Geneva last night."

Meredith wasn't certain why he should feel the need to come home because an industrial paint manufacturer was going to file bankruptcy, and she said so as she turned to fix his drink.

"Our bank has loaned them in excess of one hundred million," Parker said. "If they go belly-up, we'll lose most of that. Since I also seemed to be on the verge of losing my fiancée," he added, "I decided to fly home and see what I could do to salvage one or both."

Despite his attempt at flippancy, Meredith now understood the gravity of the Morton Simonson issue, and she felt even worse for adding to Parker's worry. "You were never on the verge of losing me," she said with an ache in her voice.

"Why the hell didn't you return my phone calls? Where were you? What's going on with Farrell? Lisa told me what you found out from Farrell's father. She said you drove to Indiana to see Farrell on Friday night so you could tell him the truth and get him to agree to a divorce."

"I did tell him the truth," Meredith said gently, handing him his drink, "and he's agreeable to a divorce. Stuart Whitmore and I are going to meet with Matt and his lawyers tomorrow."

He nodded, watching her in speculative silence. His next question was one she dreaded—and expected. "Were you with him all weekend?"

"Yes. He—he was too ill to listen to anything Friday night." Belatedly recalling that Parker didn't know Matt had bought the Houston property in retaliation for having his rezoning request denied, Meredith told him about it. Next she explained why she'd felt she needed to get Matt to agree to a truce *before* she told him about her miscarriage. Finished, she stared at her hands, consumed with guilt for what she hadn't told Parker, not certain if confessing it was a selfish way of unburdening herself or whether it was the morally and ethically correct thing to do. If the latter were the case, and she still felt that it was, this didn't seem like the right time to tell him—not when he'd already had one major blow with Morton Simonson.

She was still trying to decide, when Parker said, "Farrell must have been furious on Sunday when he realized your father had duped him about your miscarriage."

"No," Meredith said, thinking about the wrenching sorrow and regret on Matt's face. "He's probably angry with my father now, but he wasn't then. I started to cry when I told him about Elizabeth's funeral, and I think Matt was trying very hard *not* to cry. It wasn't a time for anger somehow."

The guilt she felt for what happened after that was in her eyes, and Parker saw it.

"No, I suppose it wasn't." He'd been sitting hunched slightly forward, his forearms braced on his legs, holding his glass between his knees, watching her. Now he jerked his gaze from her face and began idly rolling the glass in his palms, his jawline tightening. And in the endless moments of lengthening silence, Meredith knew—she knew he'd guessed that she had gone to bed with Matt.

"Parker," she said shakily, ready to confess, "if you're wondering whether Matt and I—"

"Don't tell me you went to bed with him, Meredith!" he bit out. "Lie to me if you have to, and then make me believe it, but don't tell me you slept with him. I couldn't stand it."

He'd already judged her and handed her her penance—and to Meredith, who wanted only to tell the truth and make him understand and someday forgive her, it seemed like a lifelong sentence to purgatory. He waited a minute, evidently to give them both time to put the subject to rest, and then he put the glass down. Putting his arm around her shoulders, he drew her close and tipped her chin up, trying to smile into her shadowed eyes. "From what you told me about your phone call with Stuart this morning, it sounds like Farrell's going to be reasonably decent about all this."

"He is," Meredith said, but guilt and misery made her smile wobble.

Parker kissed her forehead. "It's almost over, then. Tomorrow night we'll toast your successful divorce negotiations and maybe even the acquisition of that Houston property you want so badly." He sobered then, and what he said made Meredith belatedly realize how deeply concerned he was about matters at the bank. "I may have to look around and find you another lender to finance that store and the land. Morton Simonson is the third large borrower to file Chapter 11 on us in the last six months. If we aren't taking the money in, we can't lend it out unless we borrow it from the fed, and we're already heavily borrowed there."

"I didn't know you'd had two other big loans go bad."

"The economy is scaring the hell out of me. Never mind," he added, standing up and pulling her to her feet, smiling reassuringly. "The bank isn't going to collapse. We're in better shape than most of our competitors. Could you do me a favor though?" he asked half seriously.

"Anything," she stated without hesitation.

He grinned and put his arms around her for a good-night kiss. "Could you make certain that Bancroft and Company continues to make all its loan payments to Reynolds Mercantile Trust on time?"

"Absolutely!" Meredith replied, smiling tenderly at him. He kissed her then, a long, tired, gentle kiss that Meredith returned with more fervor than ever before. When he left, she refused to compare that kiss to Matt's demanding, hot, ardent ones. Passion was what Matt's kisses offered. Parker's offered love.

40

Matt stood in the center of the mammoth conference room that adjoined his office, his hands on his hips, looking at everything through narrowed, critical eyes. In thirty minutes Meredith would be there, and he was desperately, boyishly, determined to impress her with all the trappings of his success. A secretary and the receptionist, whose names he'd heretofore never bothered to learn, had been summoned to the conference room so that he could seek their opinion of the overall effect. He'd called Vanderwild's office too, and left him an urgent message to come up immediately. Vanderwild was closer to Meredith's age than Matt was, and he had good taste—it wouldn't hurt to get his opinion on things. "What do you think, Joanna?" he asked the secretary now, his hand on the dimmer switch that controlled the tiny spotlights high above in the ceiling. "Is this too little light or too much?"

"I—I think it's just right, Mr. Farrell," Joanna replied hastily, trying very hard not to show how shocked she was to discover that their formidable employer was actually subject to a human frailty like doubt, and that, moreover, he had finally put himself to the trouble of learning their names. The fact that he also had a devastating smile was not exactly a surprise. They'd seen him smile in meetings with his executives, in magazines, and newspapers, but until today, no woman at Haskell Electronics had ever had that smile focused upon herself, and both Joanna and Valerie were trying hard not to look as flustered or flattered as they felt.

Valerie stood back, studying the effect of the centerpiece on the conference table. "I think the fresh flowers on the conference table are a lovely touch," she assured him. "Shall I arrange to have the florist bring a similar spray every Tuesday?"

"Why would I want to do that?" Matt asked, so absorbed in the matter of lighting that he momentarily forgot that he'd led both women to think his sudden interest in the appearance of his office and conference room was purely aesthetic and not related to today's guests in any way. "That looks nice," he said, watching Joanna arrange a $2,000 crystal water pitcher and matching glasses on one end of the rosewood conference table. When she straightened and backed away from the table, Matt passed a slow, critical glance over the vast room with its silver carpeting and burgundy suede sofas and chairs. Although his office and this conference room took up an entire side of the glass high rise and offered a breathtaking view of the Chicago skyline, he'd decided to close the opaque draperies. With the draperies closed and the room dim, the spotlights highlighted the satin sheen of the thirty-foot rosewood table and sent prisms of light flashing off the deeply faceted crystal on the table. Like the conference table, the interior walls were of rosewood, and a circular bar had been recessed into one of them. The doors to the bar were open now with light glancing off thousands of crystal facets on the gold-rimmed tumblers and decanters that stood upon the shelves.

Despite that, Matt continued to deliberate about the room. With the draperies closed, the room looked more lush, cozier. Or else like an expensive restaurant, he wasn't certain anymore. "Open or closed?" he asked the two women, then he pressed a button that sent eighty feet of draperies gliding open across the glass wall so that the skyline was revealed, and they could help him decide.

"Open," Joanna said.

"Open," Valerie echoed.

Matt looked out at the hazy, overcast day. The meeting with Meredith would go on for at least an hour, by which time it would be dark, and the view would be spectacular. "Closed," he said, pressing the button and watching the draperies whoosh across the glass walls. "I'll open them when it's dark out," he said, thinking aloud.

Brushing back the sides of his suit coat, he considered the coming meeting, knowing that his obsession with minor details was foolish. Even if Meredith was duly impressed with $40,000 worth of crystal and all the other trappings of his little kingdom—even if she was cordial and relaxed and gracious when she walked in—she sure as hell wasn't going to like her surroundings, or her host, once the meeting began.

He sighed, half eager and half reluctant for the battle to begin, then he absently remembered the two women who were waiting to see if he needed anything else. "Thank you both very much. You've been very helpful," he said, his mind going back to the appearance of the suite. He flashed a smile at both women, a warm smile that made them feel appreciated and noticed and admired at last, then he spoiled that utterly by demanding of the secretary, "If you were a woman, would you find this room attractive?"

"I find it attractive," Joanna said stiffly, "even as a lowly robot, Mr. Farrell."

It took a moment for her icy retort to register on Matt, but when he glanced over his shoulder, both women were walking through the double doors past Eleanor Stern. "What's she miffed about?" he demanded of his own secretary, whose sole interest, like his own, was on getting work done at the office, not socializing or flirting.

Miss Stern straightened her severely cut gray suit and removed the pencil she'd tucked behind her ear. "I assume," she said with unhidden disdain for the other secretary, "that she hoped you'd be aware that she is a woman. She's been hoping you'd notice that since the day you arrived here."

"She's wasting her time," Matt advised. "Among other things, she's an employee. Only an idiot fools around with his employees."

"Perhaps you ought to get married," Miss Stern sensibly replied, but she was flipping pages in her dictation notebook, looking for some figures she wanted to discuss with him. "In my day, that would have put a stop to female aspirations."

A slow smile broke across Matt's face and he perched his hip on the conference table, suddenly eager to tell someone his newly discovered truth. "I am married," he quietly said, watching for her stunned reaction.

Miss Stern flipped a page, and without looking up, said, "My heartiest congratulations to you both."

"I'm serious," Matt said, his brows pulling together.

"Shall I relay that information to Miss Avery?" she asked with a dead-pan look. "She's called twice today."

"Miss Stern," Matt said firmly, and for the first time in their sterile working relationship he truly regretted that he'd never befriended her. "I married Meredith Bancroft eleven years ago. She's coming here this after-noon."

She looked at him over the top of her steel-rimmed glasses. "You have dinner reservations at Renaldo's tonight. Will Miss Bancroft be joining you and Miss Avery? If so, shall I change the reservations to a party of three?"

"I canceled my date with—" Matt began, then his mouth dropped open, and a lazy grin spread across his face. "Do I detect a note of *censure* in your voice?"

"Certainly not, Mr. Farrell. You made it very clear at the beginning that censuring your actions was not part of my job. As I recall, you specifically said that you didn't want my personal opinions, and you didn't want cake on your birthday; you merely wanted my skills and my time. Now, do you want me to be present at this meeting to take notes?"

Matt swallowed back a startled laugh at the discovery that his long-ago remark had evidently been rankling her for all these years. "I think it might be a good idea for you to take notes. Pay particular attention to anything at all that Miss Bancroft or her attorney agree to; I intend to hold them to every concession."

"Very well," she said, and turned to leave.

Behind her, Matt's voice checked her in midstep. "Miss Stern?" She turned back, her posture primly erect, her pencil poised for his instructions. Teasingly, Matt asked, "Do you have a first name?"

"Certainly," she replied, her eyes narrowing.

"May I use it?"

"Of course. Although, I don't think Eleanor suits you quite as well as Matthew."

Matt gaped at her deadpan expression and swallowed a sharp bark of laughter, uncertain whether she was serious or making a joke. "Do you sup-pose," he said gravely, "You and I could be . . . a little less formal around here?"

"I assume you're suggesting a more relaxed relationship, the sort one might find more typical between a secretary and her employer?"

"Yes, actually I was."

She lifted a thoughtful gray brow, but this time Matt saw it—the gleam of an answering smile in her pale eyes. "Will I have to bring you cake on your birthday?"

"Probably," he said with a sheepish grin.

"I'll make a note of it," she replied, and when she actually did, Matt burst out laughing. "Will there be anything else?" she asked, and for the first time in all these years Eleanor Stern smiled at him. The smile had an electrifying effect on her face.

"There is one more thing," Matt added. "It's very important, and I'd like your complete attention."

She sobered immediately. "You have it."

"In your opinion, is this conference room extremely impressive, or merely ostentatious?"

"I feel quite confident," she replied straightfaced, after looking the room over, "that Miss Bancroft will be dumbstruck with admiration."

Matt gaped as she turned on her heel without asking if he wanted anything and practically fled from the room, but he could have sworn her shoulders were shaking.

Peter Vanderwild was pacing nervously in Miss Stern's office, waiting for the old bat to emerge from Farrell's office and give him permission to enter. She came walking out with unusual haste, and Peter braced himself to be made to feel a truant schoolboy facing the principal. "Mr. Farrell wants to see me," he told her, trying to hide his agitation over Matt's urgent summons. "He said it was *very* important, but he didn't say what it was about and I—I didn't know which files to bring."

"I do not think," she said in an odd, choked voice, "You will need your files, Mr. Vanderwild. You may go in."

Peter gave her a queer, curious glance, then he hurried in to see Mr. Farrell. Two minutes later Peter backed out of Matt's office, inadvertently banging into the corner of Miss Stern's desk in his state of preoccupied worry.

She looked up at him. "Were you able to answer Mr. Farrell's question without your files?"

Desperately in need of reassurance, Peter braved what he knew would be her scorn. "Yes, but I—I'm not certain I gave the right answer. Miss Stern," he implored, "in your opinion, is the conference room impressive or ostentatious?"

"Impressive," she said.

Peter's shoulders sagged with relief. "That's what I said."

"That was the right answer."

Peter stared at her in amazement; she was looking at him, her eyes positively glinting with sympathetic amusement. Shocked at the realization that there was actually some warmth beneath her glacial surface, he wondered if his own rigidity had somehow caused her to regard him with such disfavor in the past. He decided to buy her a box of candy at Christmas.

Stuart was waiting, briefcase in hand, when Meredith walked into the lobby of Intercorp's building. "You look wonderful," he said, taking Meredith's hand in his. Perfect. Calm and collected."

After an hour's deliberation that morning, Meredith had finally decided to wear a jonquil-yellow wool dress with a contrasting navy coat trimmed in jonquil, for the sole reason that she'd read somewhere that men interpreted yellow as being assertive but not hostile. In hopes of carrying that assertive impression one step further, she'd twisted her hair into a chignon instead of wearing it loose.

"Farrell will take one look at you and give us anything we ask for," Stuart gallantly predicted as they walked toward the elevators. "How could he resist?"

It was the fact that Matt's last look at her had been when she was naked in bed with him that was making Meredith so excruciatingly uneasy about confronting him now. "I don't have a good feeling about this," she said shakily, stepping into the elevator in front of Stuart.

She stared blindly at the shiny brass doors, trying to concentrate on the memory of the laughter and quiet conversation she'd shared with Matt at the farm. It was wrong to think of him as her adversary now, she reminded herself. She'd cried in his arms over the loss of their baby, and he'd held her, trying to comfort her. That's what she needed to remember, so she wouldn't be so foolishly nervous. Matt was not her adversary.

The receptionist on the sixtieth floor stood up as soon as Stuart gave her their names. "Right this way, please. Mr. Farrell is expecting you both. The others are already here."

The poise Meredith was clinging to took a minor blow when she walked into Matt's office and didn't completely recognize it. The wall at the left end had been slid back so that his office opened into a conference room the size of an indoor tennis court. Two men were seated at the conference table, talking desultorily with Matt. He glanced up, saw her, and instantly arose, starting toward her with long, purposeful strides, his expression warm and relaxed. He was wearing a beautiful dark blue suit that fit him to perfection, a gleaming white shirt, and a handsome maroon and blue silk tie. For some reason, his formal business attire made her feel even more uneasy about this meeting. "Let me help you with your coat," he said ignoring Stuart, who shrugged out of his own coat.

Too nervous and self-conscious to meet his gaze, Meredith obeyed automatically, turning slightly, trying to stop the compulsive shiver that ran through her as he lifted her coat and his fingers brushed her shoulders. Afraid he'd noticed her reaction, she bent her head and concentrated on stripping off her navy kid gloves and transferring them to the hand with her navy handbag. Stuart had walked over to the conference table to shake hands with the opposing counsel, so Meredith headed toward him, but when he would have introduced her to the other two attorneys, Matt suddenly arrived at her elbow and began to act incongruously, as if this were an intimate social gathering being hosted by him in her honor. "Meredith," he said with a smile in his eyes as he looked at her, "I'd like you to meet Bill Pearson and Dave Levinson."

Aware of the subtly possessive, protective way Matt was standing beside her, Meredith tore her startled gaze from his and looked at the two men, extending her hand to each of them. They were both over six feet tall, impeccably dressed in tailor-made three-piece suits with an aura of confident elegance and decisiveness about them. In comparison to their height and distinguished looks, Stuart, who was standing opposite them, appeared small in stature and insignificant in appearance, with his thinning brown hair and studious horn-rimmed eyeglasses. In fact, Meredith thought nervously as Stuart introduced himself to Matt, Stuart looked outnumbered, outflanked, and outclassed.

As if he sensed her thoughts, Matt said, "Bill and Dave are here to safeguard your interests as much as my own." That remark caused Stuart to pause in the act of sitting down, and to give Meredith a look of unabashed derision that warned her not to believe that for an instant. Meredith saw the look and felt vastly reassured. Stuart might be younger and shorter than the other two, but he was neither fooled nor outflanked.

Matt saw the look too, but he ignored it. Turning to Meredith, who was about to sit down, he put his hand under her elbow to stop her, beginning to execute his plan. "We'd just decided to have a drink when you arrived," he lied when she was standing again, looking at him in confusion. He glanced pointedly at his attorneys. "What will you have, gentlemen?"

"Scotch and water," Levinson promptly replied, understanding that he'd just been told to have one whether he wanted it or not, and obediently shoving aside the folder he'd been about to open.

"The same," Pearson echoed, taking his cue and relaxing back in his chair as if they had all the time in the world.

Turning to Stuart, Matt said, "What would you like to drink?"

"Perrier," he said succinctly. "With a lime, if you have it."

"We have it."

Matt looked to Meredith, but she shook her head and said, "I don't care for anything."

"In that case, will you help me carry the drinks?" he countered, determined to get the chance to speak privately with her. "These three men have faced one another across conference tables before, I'm told. I'm certain they'll be able to find something to talk about while we get their drinks." Having thus instructed Levinson and Pearson to keep Stuart occupied, he put his hand under Meredith's elbow. Behind him, Levinson was already launching into an animated dialogue about a controversial trial in the newspapers, with Pearson contributing additional remarks—all of it done in sufficiently loud voices to give Matt the cover of privacy they understood he wanted with Meredith.

The bar was a deep half circle made entirely of narrow, vertical strips of beveled mirror, and because it was recessed into a wall, Matt was out of sight of the men at the conference table the moment he stepped around the counter. Meredith, however, was stubbornly hovering on the opposite side of the counter, gazing fixedly at the beveled mirrors as if hypnotized by the reflection of colored light dancing off crystal glasses. Removing the top of the ice bucket, Matt put ice into five glasses, then he pulled the stopper out of a crystal decanter and splashed scotch into three glasses, and vodka into another. Glancing at the refrigerator that was beneath the counter on his side, he casually said, "Would you mind getting me the Perrier?"

She nodded, and he watched her move with visible reluctance around the bar to do as he asked. Scrupulously avoiding his gaze, she took out a bottle of Perrier and a lime, and put both on the counter, then she started to turn. "Meredith," Matt said quietly, putting a detaining hand on her arm, "why can't you look at me?"

She jumped at his touch and he let go of her arm, but she lifted her eyes to his, and when she did, much of the tension drained from her elegant face. She even managed a rueful little smile as she admitted, "I don't know why exactly, but I'm finding this whole ordeal excruciatingly awkward."

"It serves you right," he teased, trying to divert her with humor. "Didn't anyone ever tell you it's not nice to leave a man in bed with nothing but a note to say good-bye? It makes him wonder if you still respect him."

She swallowed a startled giggle at his pointed quip, and he grinned back at her. "Leaving you that way was foolish," she admitted, and it didn't occur to either of them to wonder why, no matter how long their separation, or how tense the circumstances surrounding each meeting, they fell easily into conversation with each other. "I can't explain why I did it. I don't understand it myself."

"I think I do," Matt said. "Here, drink this." He handed her the vodka and soda he'd made for her. When she started to decline and give it back to him, he shook his head. "It will help make this meeting a little easier to endure." He waited until she'd taken a sip and then he said what he'd gotten her over there to say. "I'd like to ask a favor of you now."

Meredith heard the sudden solemnity in his voice, and she looked at him closely. "What sort of favor?"

"Do you remember at the farm—you asked me for a truce?"

She nodded, remembering with poignant clarity the way she'd stood beside his bed, watching his hand close over hers.

"I'm asking you for the same thing now— a kind of a truce, a cease-fire, from the time my attorneys begin talking until you leave this room."

Alarm tingled through her, vague and unfocused, and she slowly put her glass down, warily searching his unreadable features. "I don't understand."

"I'm asking you to listen to the terms of my offer and to remember that, no matter how—" Matt paused, trying to think of a suitably descriptive word for how his terms were likely to strike her. *Infuriating? Outrageous? Obscene?* "No matter how *unusual* my terms may seem, I'm doing what I honestly believe is best for both of us. My attorneys are going to explain my legal alternatives if you refuse my offer, and you're bound to feel backed into a corner at first, but I'm asking you not to get up and walk out of here, or to tell the three of us to go to hell, no matter how angry you become. Last, I'm asking you to give me five minutes in here alone with you, after the meeting, during which time I will try to convince you to go along with what I'm suggesting. If I can't do that, you're free to tell me to go to hell and walk out of here. Will you agree to that?"

Meredith's alarm escalated to new heights, and yet he was only asking her to stay there, and stay calm, for an hour or so.

"I agreed to your terms at the farm," he reminded her. "Is it so much to ask that you agree to mine now?"

Unable to withstand the quiet force of his argument, Meredith slowly shook her head. "I suppose not. All right, I agree. Truce," she said, then watched in surprise as Matt held his hand out to her just as she had held hers out to him at the farm, except that he turned his hand palm-up. Her heart gave an inexplicable little bump as she laid her hand in his and his fingers closed tightly around it.

"Thank you," he said.

It hit her that she had said exactly that to him. Amazed that this moment at the farm had obviously seemed poignant to him, too, she tried to smile back at him as she echoed his former words: "You're welcome."

Fully aware of the ploy that Farrell had used to draw Meredith away, Stuart permitted the two attorneys to carry on their barrage of diversionary conversation while he mentally ticked off the amount of time necessary to fix five drinks. When that time had elapsed, he swiveled around his chair, rudely turned his back on Levinson and Pearson and, without bothering to hide what he was doing, he craned his neck to see the occupants of the bar. He half expected to see Farrell trying to badger Meredith; what he saw was a couple in profile, captured in a pose so thoroughly startling that Stuart felt momentarily disoriented. Far from trying to badger her, Farrell was holding his hand out to her, looking at her with a somber smile that struck Stuart as decidedly . . . tender. And Meredith, who was almost *always* completely composed, was putting her hand in his and looking up at him with an expression that Stuart had never seen on her face before: a vulnerable expression of naked caring.

Abruptly, he pulled his gaze from the couple and turned to the attorneys, but he still hadn't come up with a suitable explanation for Meredith's expression a minute later, when she and Farrell brought the drinks to the conference table.

When Farrell had seated Meredith, Pearson said, "Matt, shall we begin?" The seating arrangement had struck Stuart as odd from the minute he'd walked into the room: Pearson was deliberately positioned at the head of the conference table, where Farrell would normally have been. Meredith had been seated on Pearson's left, with Stuart next to her. Levinson was on Pearson's right, directly across from her, and now Farrell walked around the table, sitting down next to Levinson. Ever aware of subtleties, Stuart wondered if Farrell had deliberately put Pearson in the hot seat to make Meredith think that Pearson rather than himself was responsible for whatever she was about to hear. Either that, Stuart decided, watching Farrell angle his chair back and prop his ankle atop his knee, or else Farrell wanted to be able to observe Meredith throughout the proceedings without having to make it obvious, which it would have been if he'd been at the head of the table.

A moment later Pearson began to speak, and what he said was so unexpected, so incongruous that Stuart's brows drew together in wary surprise. "There is much to be considered here," he said, addressing his remarks to

Stuart—remarks that Stuart instantly realized were deliberately designed to have an emotional effect on Meredith. "We have here a couple who took vows eleven years ago, *solemn* vows. They both knew at the time that marriage is an estate not to be entered into lightly or—"

Caught somewhere between annoyance and amusement, Stuart said, "You can dispense with reciting the entire wedding ceremony, Bill. They already went through it eleven years ago. *That's* why we're here now." He turned to Matt, who was idly rolling a gold pen between his fingers and said, "My client isn't interested in your attorneys' assessment of the situation. What do you want and what are you offering? Let's get down to business."

Instead of reacting to Stuart's deliberate provocation, Matt glanced at Pearson and, with a slight inclination of his head, he instructed him to do exactly that.

"Very well," Pearson said, dropping the role of kindly mediator. "Here's where we stand. Our client has sufficient grounds for a very ugly and damaging lawsuit against your client's father. As a result of Philip Bancroft's *unconscionable* interference in our client's marriage, our client was deprived of his right to attend the funeral of his child, he was deprived of his right to comfort his wife and be comforted by her after the death of that child, and he was misled into believing she wanted to divorce him. In short, he was deprived of eleven years of marriage. Mr. Bancroft has also interfered with Mr. Farrell's business by illegally trying to influence the Southville zoning commission. These are matters that can, of course, be dealt with in a court of law. . . ."

Stuart glanced at Farrell, who was watching Meredith, who, in turn, was staring fixedly at Pearson, the color draining from her face. Angry that she was unexpectedly being subjected to this, Stuart looked at Pearson and said disdainfully, "If every married man with interfering in-laws could sue them for it, there'd be a fifty-year back-up on the dockets. They'll laugh him out of court."

Pearson regarded him with brows raised in challenge. "I doubt that. Bancroft's interference was malicious and extreme; I think a jury would relish ruling against Bancroft for what were, in my opinion, indefensible actions of astonishing viciousness. And that's before we start talking about Bancroft's illegal attempt to influence the Southville zoning commission. However," he said, holding up a hand to silence Stuart, "whether we won our case or not, the mere filing of those cases would create a storm of unpleasant publicity—publicity that would be damaging to Mr. Bancroft and very possibly Bancroft and Company as well. It's common knowledge that Mr. Bancroft is seriously ill, and, of course, the effect of such publicity and a trial might further jeopardize his health."

A knot of fear and panic was growing in Meredith's stomach, but at that moment her strongest feeling was one of betrayal. She had driven to the farm to tell Matt the truth about the baby and her father's telegram; now he was threatening to use it against her. Her spirits lifted, however, when Pearson said, "I've mentioned all that, Miss Bancroft, not to alarm or distress you, but merely to remind you of the facts and to acquaint you with our point of view. However, Mr. Farrell is willing to overlook all of those things I've been mentioning, and to waive his rights to all legal proceedings against your father for all time . . . for a few simple concessions from you. Stuart," he said as he handed a two-page document to Stuart and an identical copy of it to Meredith, "the verbal offer I am about to make is detailed in this document, and to relieve any doubts you may have about Mr. Farrell's sincerity, he has offered to sign it for you at the conclusion of this meeting. However, there is one stipulation, and that is that this offer must be accepted or rejected before your client leaves here today. If it is rejected, it is withdrawn forthwith and we will file legal proceedings against Philip Bancroft by the end of the week. Would you care to take a few minutes to look it over before I summarize it?"

Refusing to even glance at the document, Stuart tossed it on the table, leaned back in his chair, and regarded his adversary with a smile of acid disdain. "I'd much rather hear it from *you*, Bill. I never fully appreciated your flair for drama before this. The only reason I haven't told you to go to hell and meet us in court before now is that I can't bring myself to leave before I see the last act." Despite his apparent lack of concern over their threats, Stuart was not only worried, he was furious at Pearson's deliberate attempt to frighten and intimidate Meredith.

At a curt nod from Matt, Levinson suddenly stepped in, his voice conciliatory. "Perhaps it would be better if *I* summarize the offer contained in that document."

"I don't know about that," Stuart drawled insolently. "Are you the understudy or the star?"

"The star," the older man replied imperturbably. "I prepared the document." Directing his attention to Meredith, Levinson smiled and said, "As my associate has just explained, Miss Bancroft, if you agree to what your husband asks, he is willing to forgo taking legal action against your father, but he is also offering much more than that in this document: He is also offering to give you a generous settlement—a lump sum alimony payment if you prefer to think of it that way—in the amount of five million dollars."

That did it. The alarm Meredith had been feeling combined with shock; she looked at Stuart and said, "Agree to what? What is happening here?"

"It's just a game," Stuart reassured her. "First they threaten you with what they'll take away from you if you refuse to play. Now they're telling you what they'll give you if you do."

"A game?" she cried softly. "What *game?*"

"That's the part they're saving for the very end."

Her eyes clinging to his, Meredith nodded, gathered her wits, and looked at Levinson, studiously avoiding looking at Matt. "Go on, Mr. Levinson," she said, lifting her chin in a show of dignity and courage.

"In addition to the five-million-dollar settlement," Levinson said, "Your husband will sell to Bancroft and Company a certain piece of property in Houston for the sum of twenty million dollars."

Meredith felt the room reel, and she turned her head then, looking at Matt, her face filled with confusion, gratitude, and misgivings. He held her gaze without flinching while Levinson added, "Last, if you agree to what your husband is proposing, he will sign a waiver on the usual two-year separation required by this state in order to obtain a divorce on the grounds of irreconcilable differences. That will reduce the waiting period to six months."

Stuart dismissed that concession with a shrug. "We don't need a waiver from Farrell in order for the court to agree to reduce the waiting period. The law clearly states that if the couple has not cohabited for a period of two years, and irreconcilable differences exist, then the waiting period can be shortened to six months. These two people haven't cohabited in eleven years!"

Levinson leaned back in his chair, and Meredith had a sickening premonition of what he might be angling toward when he quietly said, "They spent last weekend together."

"So what?" Stuart said. He was no longer angry, he was stunned by Farrell's $5 million offer and completely preoccupied with discovering what concession Farrell wanted in return for it. "They did *not* cohabit in the marital sense of the word. They merely slept in the same house. No judge alive would think their marriage might be preserved, and insist on a two-year waiting period, merely because they managed to stay under the same roof for two days. What they did was certainly not cohabiting."

Deafening silence ensued.

Levinson lifted his brows and looked steadily at Stuart. Stuart, who was growing angry again, glared at Farrell. "You shared a roof, not a bed." But Farrell said nothing. Instead, he shifted his gaze and looked quietly and pointedly at Meredith.

Stuart knew then. He knew, even before he turned his head and saw the look of betrayal shimmering in Meredith's eyes and the angry, embarrassed flush on her pale cheeks as she yanked her gaze from her husband's and stared at her hands. Despite the disjointed thoughts whirling through his mind, he lifted his shoulders and said with convincing unconcern, "So they slept together. Big damned deal. I still repeat—why would your client consider refusing to sign a waiver on the two years? Why prolong the inevitable divorce?"

"Because," Levinson said calmly, "Mr. Farrell is not convinced a divorce *is* inevitable."

Stuart's laugh was genuine. "That's ridiculous."

"Mr. Farrell doesn't think so. In fact, he's willing to offer all the concessions we've discussed here—a five-million-dollar alimony settlement, the property in Houston, the dismissal of all legal action against Philip Bancroft, and a waiver on the two-year waiting period—all of that in return for only one concession for himself."

"What concession?"

"He wants one week for every year of marriage he was denied. Eleven weeks. Eleven weeks with his wife, so that they can get to know each other better . . ."

Meredith half rose out of her chair, her eyes shooting sparks at Matt. "You want *whaat!*"

"Define how he intends to get to know her," Stuart snapped, convinced that the phrase carried blatant sexual overtones.

"I think we can leave it to them to work that out," Levinson began, but Meredith's furious voice interrupted him.

"Oh, no, you can't!" She stood up, her eyes alive with fury as she said to Matt, "You've subjected me to everything in this meeting from terrorism to humiliation. Don't stop now. Let's be specific, so they can write it all down with the rest of your offer. Tell them exactly how you intend to get to know me. This is nothing but blackmail, so stipulate your terms, you—you bastard!"

Matt looked at the attorneys. "Leave the two of us alone now."

Meredith, however, was past the point of caring who heard anything anymore. "Sit down!" she warned the attorneys. Nothing mattered. She was trapped; she'd understood the terms; she just hadn't anticipated the Grotesque payment Matt was going to exact. Either she slept with him for the next eleven weeks, or he was going to drag her father through the courts, and very likely kill him with the stress. She saw something else then—the gray-haired secretary who'd slipped in and seated herself on a sofa and was busily taking down what everyone said. Like an animal who is cornered, Meredith struck out, mentally circling as she leaned her palms on the table, glaring at Matt, her eyes filled with contempt and hatred. "Everyone stays while you list your obscene terms. Either you kill my father with your lawsuits or you get your pound of flesh from me—that's it, isn't it? Now, start telling these lawyers of yours how you intend to take it! Tell them how often and which way, damn you! But you draw up receipts, you bastard, because I'll make you sign them."

Her gaze shot to the secretary. "Are you having a stimulating time over there? Are you getting this all down? This monster you work for is going to dictate how he wants his kicks, how often—"

Suddenly everyone was in motion. Matt jumped out of his chair and headed around the table, Levinson grabbed for his sleeve and missed, Stuart shoved his chair back and tried to thrust Meredith behind him, but Meredith flung him off. "Stay away from me!" she warned Stuart before whirling on Matt, her hands clenched into fists at her sides. "Bastard!" she hissed. "Stuart dictating your terms. How *often* do you want it—how—" Matt reached for her at the same moment Meredith swung, her palm crashing against his face with a force that snapped his head sideways.

"Stop it!" he ordered, grabbing her upper arms, but his gaze was on Stuart, who was heading forward, reaching for him.

"Bastard!" she sobbed, glaring at Matt. "You bastard, I trusted you!"

Matt yanked her against his chest, shrugging Stuart off. "Listen to me!" he said tautly, turning Meredith aside. "I am not asking you to sleep with me! Do you understand me? I'm asking for a chance, dammit! Just a chance for eleven weeks!"

Everyone was standing; everyone froze, even Meredith stopped struggling, but her whole body was trembling and she covered her face with her hands. Glancing at their spectators, Matt ordered sharply, "Get the hell out of here."

Levinson and Pearson gathered up their papers to leave, but Stuart stayed where he was, watching Meredith, who was neither returning nor resisting Matt's embrace. "I'm not going anywhere until you take your hands off her and she tells me she wants me to leave."

Matt knew he meant it, and since Meredith had stopped resisting, he dropped his arms, reaching into his pocket for a handkerchief to give her.

"Meredith?" Stuart said uncertainly to the back of her head. "Do you want me to wait outside or stay here? Tell me what you want me to do."

Humiliated past all endurance at the realization she'd jumped to erroneous conclusions and made such a scene, and furious because she'd been prodded into doing both, Meredith ungraciously snatched Matt's handkerchief.

"What she wants to do right now," Matt told Stuart with a grim effort at humor, "is throw another punch at me—"

"I can speak for myself!" Meredith gritted out, dabbing at her eyes and nose and stepping back a pace. "Stay here, Stuart." She raised liquid, angry, mistrustful eyes to Matt, and said, "You wanted this all legal and formal. Tell my attorney what you mean by wanting a chance, because I obviously don't understand."

"I'd rather do it in private."

"Well," she said with a haughty glance that was spoiled by the tears still sparkling on her lashes, "that's just too bad! You're the one who insisted on doing this today, and in front of your lawyers! You couldn't possibly have spared me this and discussed it with me in private some other time—"

"I called you yesterday to try to do exactly that," he told her. "You instructed your secretary to tell me to deal with you only through your attorney."

"Well, you could have tried again!"

"When? After you flew to Mexico or Reno or wherever you intended to go on your sudden trip this week to divorce me?"

"And I was *right* to try," she said ferociously, and Matt bit back a smile of pride. She was splendid—already recovering her composure, her chin up, her shoulders square. She wasn't able to look the lawyers in the face yet, though, so he glanced over her shoulder at them. His own lawyers were heading out with their coats and briefcases, but Meredith's lawyer stubbornly remained where he stood, arms crossed over his chest, watching Matt with a mixture of antagonism, suspicion, and blunt curiosity. "Meredith," Matt said. "Would you at least ask your attorney to wait in my office. He can see everything from there, but he doesn't need to hear any more than he has."

"I have nothing else to hide," she said wrathfully. "Now, let's get this over with. What exactly do you want from me?"

"Fine," Matt said, deciding he didn't give a damn what Whitmore heard. Sitting down on the edge of the conference table, he crossed his arms over his chest. "I want a chance for us to get to know each other for the next eleven weeks."

"And just how do you intend for us to do that?" she demanded.

"The usual ways—we'll have dinner together, go to plays—"

"How often?" she interrupted, looking angrier than ever.

"I hadn't thought about it."

"I'm sure you were too busy refining your blackmail and thinking up ways to ruin my life!"

"Four times a week!" Matt snapped out the answer to her question about how often. "And I am not trying to ruin your life!"

"What *days* of the week?" she fired back.

His anger died, and he fought back another smile. "Friday, Saturday, Sunday, and—Wednesday," he said after a moment's thought.

"Has it occurred to you that I have a career and a fiancé?"

"I don't want to interfere with your career. Your fiancé will have to back off for eleven weeks."

"This isn't fair to him—" Meredith cried.

"Tough!"

The harsh word, his cold tone and implacable features, were so eloquent of his entire ruthless personality, Meredith finally realized nothing she said or did would dissuade him from accomplishing his goal. She was his latest target for a hostile takeover. "Every rotten thing they say about you—it's all true, isn't it?"

"Most of it," he bit out, looking like she'd slapped him again.

"It doesn't matter who you hurt or what you have to do to get what you want, does it?"

His face tightened. "Not in this case."

Her shoulders sagged, her bravado fleeing. "Why are you doing this to me? What have I done to you—deliberately, I mean—to make you try to tear my life to pieces like this?"

Matt couldn't think of an answer he could give her now that she'd accept without either laughing in his face or getting furious. "Let's just say that I think there's something between us—an attraction—and I want to see how deep it goes."

"God, I cannot believe this!" she cried, wrapping her arms around her stomach. "There is *nothing* between us! Nothing but a horrible past."

"And last weekend," he pointed out bluntly.

Meredith hid her chagrin in anger. "That was—that was *sex!*"

"Was it?"

"You ought to know!" she shot back, remembering something she'd overlooked of late. "If half of what I've read about you is true, you hold the world's record for cheap affairs and meaningless flings. God, how could you sleep with that rock star with the pink hair?"

"Marianna Tighbell?"

"Yes! don't bother denying it! It was all over the front page of the *National Tattler.*"

Matt swallowed a shout of laughter, watching her pace slowly back and forth, loving the way she moved, the way she clipped her words when she was angry, the way she clutched him when she was close to a climax—as if she weren't certain she could count on one. Maybe she wasn't always able to count on one with her other lovers. . . . She was gorgeous and innately passionate; he knew better than to hope she hadn't been to bed with dozens of men. He settled for hoping they'd all been selfish, inept, or dull. Preferably, all three. And impotent.

"Well?" she said, rounding on him. "How could you sleep with that—that woman?"

"I've been to a party in her home. I have never slept with her."

"Am I supposed to believe that?"

"Apparently not."

"It doesn't matter," Meredith said, giving herself a mental shake. "Matt, please," she implored him, trying for one last time to make him abandon his insane plan. "I'm in love with someone else."

"You weren't on Sunday when you and I were in bed—"

"Stop talking about that! I'm in love with Parker Reynolds, I swear to you I am. I've been in love with him since I was a girl. I was in love with him before I met you!"

Matt was about to brush that off as highly unlikely for the same reason he thought it was unlikely now, when she added, "Only he had just gotten engaged to someone else, and I'd given up."

That information cut him deeply enough to make him stand and brusquely say, "You heard my offer, Meredith, take it or leave it."

Meredith stared at him, aware that he'd suddenly turned aloof and hard. He meant it—the discussion was over. Stuart realized it too, and he was already putting on his coat and walking toward Matt's office, pausing in the doorway to wait for her. Deliberately turning her back on Matt, she walked over to get her purse, taking vengeful pleasure in making him think she was scorning his bargain, but her mind was whirling in panic. She picked up her purse from the conference table, feeling his eyes boring holes through her back, then she walked purposefully to the sofa to get her coat.

Behind her, Matt spoke in an icy, ominous voice. "Is this your answer, Meredith?"

Meredith refused to reply. She swallowed, trying for one last moment to think of some way to reach him, to touch his heart. But he had no heart. Passion was all he was capable of; passion and ego and revenge were what he was made of. She picked up her coat from the sofa and draped it over her arm, leaving Matt in the conference room without so much as glancing over her shoulder at him. "Let's go," she told Stuart, wanting Matthew Farrell to think, at least for a minute or two, that she'd thrown his ultimatum in his face . . . hoping against hope that he would call out to her that he'd only been bluffing, that he wouldn't do this to her father or her.

But the silence behind her was unbroken.

Matt's secretary had evidently gone home for the day, and when Stuart had closed the connecting door behind the two offices, Meredith stopped and spoke for the first time. In a suffocated voice, she said, "Can he do what he's threatening to do to my father?"

Angry about several different things, including Meredith's being put under this unreasonable pressure to make a decision, Stuart sighed. "We can't prevent him from filing the lawsuits, or bringing your father to trial; I don't think he stands much chance of gaining anything except revenge, if he does it. Win or lose, though, the day he files those lawsuits, your father's name will be all over the headlines. How is your father's health?"

"Not good enough to risk being put to the strain of that kind of publicity." Her eyes dropped to the documents he was holding, then lifted beseechingly to his. "Are there any loopholes in there we could use?"

"Not one. No traps either, if that's any reassurance. They're fairly simple and forthright, they say exactly what Levinson and Pearson said aloud." He put them on the secretary's desk for Meredith to read, but she shook her head, avoiding the sight of the words, and, picking up a pen from the desk, she scribbled her name on the bottom.

"Give them to him and make him sign them," she said, tossing the pen aside as if it were dirty. "And make that—that maniac write down the days of the week that he named and initial the changes. And make it read so that if he misses a day, he can't make it up with another!"

Stuart almost smiled at that, but he shook his head when she handed the papers back to him. "Unless you want the five million dollars or the Houston land more than you seemed to in there, I don't think you need to go through with this. He's bluffing about your father."

Her face lit up with eagerness and hope. "Why do you think so?"

"It's a hunch. A strong hunch."

"A hunch, based on what?"

Stuart thought of the solemn tenderness on Farrell's face when he was holding Meredith's hand. He thought of the way he'd looked when she slapped him and the lack of roughness in the way he'd restrained her afterward. And, although Stuart had originally thought that Farrell had some sort of eleven-week orgy in mind, the man had seemed genuinely taken aback by that accusation. Rather than tell her such nebulous things, Stuart said something more concrete: "If he's ruthless enough to do this to your father, then why is he being so generous in his offers to you? Why not simply threaten you with suing your father to make you give in?"

"I suppose he thinks he'll have more fun if I'm less resistant. I also think he likes my knowing—and my father knowing—that he can throw that kind of money around and not even miss it. Stuart, my father humiliated him terribly when he was twenty-six, and he's still trying! I can imagine the kind of malice Matt must feel for him, even if you can't."

"I am still willing to bet you that man won't lift a legal hand against your father whether you agree to this or not."

"I want to believe you," she said, calmer now. "Give me a sound reason to, and we'll walk out of here and throw those papers in the wastebasket."

"This is going to sound . . . odd . . . given what I've seen of Farrell today and the reputation he has, but I don't think he'd do anything to hurt you."

She laughed—a short, bitter laugh. "How do you explain intimidation and humiliation, not to mention blackmail? What do you call what he put me through in there?"

Stuart shrugged helplessly. "Not blackmail—he's paying you the money, not the reverse. I would call it pulling out all the stops, using every single means you have to get what you want because you want it so badly. I also think it got out of hand in there, thanks to Pearson's strong-arm tactics and flair for drama. I was watching Farrell most of the time, and every time Pearson got tough with you, Farrell looked angry. I think he picked the wrong attorneys for a gentle finesse attempt like this was supposed to be. Levinson and Pearson play the game only one way—they go for the throat and they play to win."

Meredith's heart sank at Stuart's flimsy rationale. "I can't bet my father's life on anything as flimsy as all that. And I'll tell you something," she added sadly. "Matt picked lawyers who think exactly like he does. You could be right when you say Matt doesn't want to hurt me personally, but you're wrong about what he's after. I figured it out just as we left." She drew a shaky breath. "Matt isn't after me. He doesn't even know me. What he wants is revenge against my father, and he's figured out two ways to get it: Either he takes my father to trial, or he gets his revenge an even sweeter, better way—by using me. I'm the sweetest revenge of all. Forcing my father to see us together after all these years, making him think there's a chance we'll stay together—to Matt that's an eye for an eye. So," she said, putting her hand on his sleeve, "will you do me a favor when you take this in to him?"

Stuart nodded, covering her hand. "What do you want me to do?"

"Try to make Matt agree that this bargain and our marriage will remain a secret. He probably won't agree—that will deprive him of some of his pleasure, some of his revenge, but try."

"I will."

When she left, Stuart flipped to the second page, wrote in the terms he hoped to get Farrell to agree to, then he straightened. Rather than politely knock on Farrell's office door, Stuart opened it. When he saw that Farrell wasn't there, he headed quietly toward the conference room, hoping to catch him off guard, to see something—some expression—that would give a clue about the man's real feelings.

The draperies had been drawn back in the conference room, and Farrell was standing at the windows, his drink in one hand, staring out at the night skyline, his jaw rigid. He looked, Stuart thought with some satisfaction, like a man who had just suffered an enormous defeat and was trying to come to grips with it. In fact, standing in the vast conference room, surrounded by all the trappings of his wealth and power, there was an incongruous quality of isolation in the way he bent his head and stared at the glass in his hand. He lifted his glass then and tossed down the drink as if trying to wash away a bitter taste, and Stuart spoke. "Should I have knocked?" Farrell's head jerked around, and even in that unguarded instant of surprise, Stuart wasn't certain whether he saw profound relief—or merely tremendous satisfaction, so quickly did Farrell's guard go up. He'd been fairly easy to read when Meredith was present—now Stuart watched him become aloof and completely inscrutable as he flicked a glance at the papers in Stuart's hand to confirm what they were, then started toward the bar.

"I was about to have another drink," Farrell said, showing no apparent eagerness to get his hands on the signed documents. "Would you care for one, or would you rather get down to business?"

He sounded as if it didn't matter to him which option Stuart chose, but Stuart seized the opportunity to try to discover some clue to the man's feelings about Meredith. "The business part won't take long," he said, following him over to the bar. "I'll take you up on the offer of a drink."

"Another Perrier?" Farrell asked, stepping into the mirrored half circle.

"Bourbon," Stuart said succinctly. "Straight up."

That earned a dubious look from Farrell. "Really?"

"Would I lie to a clever, ruthless mogul like yourself?" Stuart said dryly.

Farrell flicked a sarcastic glance at him and reached for the decanter of bourbon. "You'd lie to the devil himself for the sake of a client."

Surprised and annoyed by the partial truth of that assessment, Stuart put his briefcase down and laid the documents on the bar. "You're right in this instance," he admitted. "Meredith and I are friends. In fact," Stuart continued, striving for a more relaxed atmosphere of confidence, "I used to have a huge crush on her."

"I know."

Surprised again, and half convinced Farrell was lying, Stuart said, "Considering that I don't think Meredith knew it, I have to say you're remarkably well informed. What else do you know?"

"About you?" Farrell asked casually.

When Stuart nodded, Farrell began fixing his own drink. Dropping ice cubes into his glass, he launched into a brusque, dispassionate recitation of Stuart's personal history that left him completely astonished and a little chilled. "You're the oldest son in a family of five," Farrell said. "Your grandfather and his two brothers founded the law firm where you're now a senior partner, carrying on with the family tradition of practicing law. At the age of twenty-three you graduated first in your class from Harvard Law School—also a family tradition—where you distinguished yourself by being president of your class and making *Law Review*. When you graduated, you wanted to work in the district attorney's office, specializing in prosecuting cases of landlord abuse, but you yielded to family pressure and joined the family firm instead, where you handle cases for wealthy corporate clients, mostly from your own social circle.

"You hate corporate law, but you have a genius for it; you're a tough negotiator, a brilliant strategist, and a good diplomat unless your personal feelings are involved, as they were today. You're thorough and you're meticulous, but you're lousy with juries because you try to sway them with dry facts instead of emotional logic. For that reason, you usually do the pretrial preparation, then you hand jury cases over to an associate and supervise them. . . ."

Farrell paused in that recitation to hand Stuart his drink. "Shall I go on?"

"By all means, if there's more," Stuart replied a little stiffly.

Picking up his own glass, Farrell took a swallow and when Stuart had done likewise, he said, "You're thirty-three, heterosexual, with a penchant for fast cars, which you don't indulge, and a love of sailing, which you do. When you were twenty-two, you thought you were in love with a girl from Melrose Park whom you met at the beach, but she was from a blue-collar Italian family, and the cultural gap was too wide for both of you to bridge. You both agreed to call it off. Seven years later you fell in love with Meredith, but she couldn't reciprocate, so you became friends. Two years ago your family put on a push to marry you off to Georgina Gibbons, whose daddy is also a socialite lawyer, and the two of you got engaged, but you called that one off. You're worth about eighteen million right now, mostly in blue chip stocks, and you'll inherit another fifteen when your grandfather dies—less if he continues his junkets to Monte Carlo, where he nearly always loses."

Pausing in that recitation that had Stuart trapped somewhere between amazement and anger, Farrell gestured to the sofas near the windows, and Stuart picked up the documents and his drink and followed him there. When he was seated across from him, Farrell said blandly, "Did I leave anything important out?"

"Yes," Stuart replied with a sardonic smile as he lifted his drink in a mocking toast, "what's my favorite color?"

Farrell looked him straight in the eye. "Red."

Stuart choked. "You're right about everything but my thoroughness. Obviously you were better prepared for this confrontation than I was. I'm still waiting for the background check I ordered on you, and it won't be half so complete. I'm amazed and reluctantly impressed."

Farrell shrugged. "You shouldn't be. Intercorp owns a credit reporting bureau as well as a large investigative agency that does a lot of work for multinational corporations."

It struck Stuart as odd that Farrell had said, "Intercorp owns," not "I own," as if he felt no real desire to be personally associated with the corporate empire he had created. In Stuart's experience, most entrepreneurs with newly amassed wealth were braggarts who were transparently proud of their accomplishments and embarrassingly eager to remind everyone of what they owned. Stuart had expected something like that of Farrell, particularly because the news media normally portrayed him as a flamboyant, international playboy-tycoon who led the completely sybaritic, richly satisfying life of a modern-day sultan.

Stuart had the feeling that the truth was far from that; that at best, Farrell was a guarded, solitary man who was difficult to get to know. At worst, he was a cold, calculating, unemotional man with a wide streak of ruthlessness and an iron control that was almost chilling. This was undoubtedly how his business adversaries thought of him. "How did you know what my favorite color is?" he asked finally, ready to try again to get a better reading on Farrell. "You didn't get that off a credit report."

"That was a guess," Farrell said dryly. "Your briefcase is maroon and so is your tie. Also, most men like red. Women like blue." For the first time, Farrell actually let his attention stray to the document Stuart had put on the table. "Speaking of women," he said casually, "I gather Meredith signed that."

"She added some conditions," Stuart replied, watching him closely, noting the imperceptible tensing of his adversary's jaw. "She wants the days you mentioned stipulated in the document and she wants it clarified that if you miss one, you can't make it up."

Farrell's expression softened, and even in the subdued lighting Stuart saw amusement glinting in those gray eyes. Amusement and . . . pride? He had no time to confirm that, however, because Farrell abruptly got up, walked over to the conference table, and returned with a gold fountain pen he'd left there. When he flipped to the signature page where Stuart had written in the added terms and uncapped the pen, Stuart added, "You'll see that she also wants it agreed that you will not publicly reveal either this marriage of yours or the eleven-week trial dating period to anyone."

Farrell's eyes narrowed, but just as Stuart opened his mouth to argue for Meredith's terms, Farrell looked down and quickly initialed all three stipulations, then he signed the document and tossed it across the table to Stuart. "Was secrecy your advice," he asked, "or Meredith's idea?"

"Hers," Stuart replied, and then because he was itching to see Farrell's reaction, he added smoothly, "If she'd have taken *my* advice, she would have thrown that agreement in the trash."

Farrell leaned back, studying Stuart with unnerving intensity and something that might have been a glimmer of respect. "If she'd done that," he countered, "she'd have risked her father's health and his good name."

"She wouldn't have risked anything," Stuart contradicted flatly. "You were bluffing." The other man lifted his brows and said nothing, so Stuart pressed harder. "What you're doing is unethical and extreme. Either you're a world-class bastard, or you're insane, or you're in love with her. Which is it?"

"Definitely the first," Farrell replied. "Possibly the second. Possibly all three. You decide."

"I already have."

"Which is it?"

"The first and the third," Stuart replied, suddenly enjoying himself, noting Farrell's slight, reluctant smile at Stuart's unflattering conclusion. "What do you know about Meredith?" Stuart asked after another swallow of his drink, determined to reaffirm his conclusion that Farrell was in love with her.

"Only what I've read in the magazines and newspapers in the last eleven years. I'd rather find out the rest by myself."

For a man who checked out an attorney right down to the size of his shoe, Stuart thought it was meaningful that Farrell, who was supposedly interested only in revenge, hadn't done an equally impersonal background check on Meredith. "Then you don't know the little things about her," Stuart said as he continued watching him over the rim of his glass, "like the fact that in the summer after her freshman year of college there was a rumor going around that she'd had some sort of tragic love affair, and that's why she wouldn't go out with anyone. You, of course, were probably inadvertently the cause of that." He paused, watching the flare of intense interest and emotion that Farrell belatedly tried to conceal by lifting his glass and taking a swallow of his drink. "And of course," he continued, "You wouldn't know that in her junior year a rejected fraternity boy started the rumor that she was either a lesbian or frigid. The only thing that stopped the lesbian thing from sticking to her was her friendship with Lisa Pontini, who was dating the president of the kid's fraternity. Lisa was so far from being a lesbian, and so loyal to Meredith, that she made the kid a laughingstock with the help of her current boyfriend. The part about being frigid stuck though. They nicknamed her the 'ice queen' at school. When she finished grad school, and came back here, the nickname got whispered, but she was so damned beautiful that it added to her allure because it made her a challenge. Besides, showing up with Meredith Bancroft on your arm, looking at that face of hers across a restaurant table, was such an ego boost that you didn't much care that she wouldn't sleep with you."

Stuart waited, hoping Farrell would finally take the bait and start asking questions, which would have been a tip-off about his true feelings, but Farrell either had no feelings for her—or else he was too smart to risk giving any hints that might cause her attorney to tell her that her husband was definitely in love with her and that she could tear up that document without risk of having him carry out his threats. Irrationally convinced the latter was still the case, Stuart said idly, "Can I ask you something?"

"You can *ask*," Farrell emphasized.

"What made you decide to double-team her today with two attorneys, particularly two attorneys whose methods are notoriously heavy-handed?"

For a second Stuart thought he wasn't going to answer, but then Farrell admitted with an ironic smile, "That was a tactical error on my part. In my haste to get the agreement drawn up in time for this meeting, I failed to make Levinson and Pearson understand that I wanted her convinced to sign, not bludgeoned to death." Putting his half-empty glass down on the table, he stood up, making it obvious that their little tête-à-tête was over.

Left with no choice, Stuart did likewise, but as he bent to pick up the papers, he added, "That was more than a mistake, it was the kiss of death. Besides bullying and coercing her, you betrayed and humiliated her by letting Levinson tell us all that she'd slept with you last weekend. She's going to hate you for that for a lot longer than eleven weeks. If you knew her better than you do, you'd realize that."

"Meredith is incapable of lasting hatred," Farrell informed him in an implacable voice that was tinged with pride, and Stuart had to hide his shock because every word Farrell was saying now was inadvertently confirming his own suspicion. "If she weren't incapable of it, she'd hate her father for spoiling her childhood and for belittling her success at work. She'd be hating him now for what she's just discovered he did to us eleven years ago. Instead, she's trying to protect him from me. Rather than hating, Meredith looks for ways to excuse the inexcusable in people she loves—including me, by telling herself I was justified in leaving her because I'd been *forced* to marry her in the first place." Oblivious to Stuart's stunned fascination, Farrell eyed him across the cocktail table and added, "Meredith can't stand to see people hurt. She sends flowers to dead babies with notes to tell them they were loved; she cries in an old man's arms because he's believed for eleven years that she aborted his grandchild, and then she drives four hours in a storm because she has to tell me the truth right away. She's softhearted, and she's overly cautious. She's also smart, astute, and intuitive, and those things have enabled her to excel at the department store without being devoured by back-biting executives or turning into one herself." Leaning down, he picked up his fountain pen and shot a cool, challenging look at Stuart. "What else could I possibly need to know about her?"

Stuart returned the look with one of his own—satisfied triumph. "I'll be damned," he said softly, laughing. "I was right—you *are* in love with her. And because you are, you wouldn't do a damned thing to hurt her by prosecuting her father."

Brushing the sides of his jacket back, Farrell shoved his hands into his pockets, spoiling some of Stuart's triumph by showing no concern over his conclusion. He spoiled the rest of it by saying blandly, "You *think* that, but you aren't sure enough to risk having Meredith put me to the test. You aren't even sure enough to broach the subject with her again, and if you were sure, you'd still hesitate to do it."

"Really?" Stuart retorted, smiling to himself. As he walked over to the bar to get his briefcase, he was already debating what to tell Meredith and how to do it. "What makes you think so?"

"Because," Farrell replied calmly behind him, "from the moment you realized Meredith slept with me last weekend, you haven't been completely certain about anything—particularly how she feels about me." He walked forward, angling toward his office and politely escorting Stuart out.

Stuart suddenly remembered the indescribable look on Meredith's face earlier, when she'd stood with her hand in Farrell's. Hiding his growing uncertainty behind a convincing shrug, he said, "I'm her lawyer—it's my job to tell her what I think, even when it's a hunch."

"You're also her friend and you were in love with her once. You're personally involved, and because you are, you're going to hesitate and contemplate, and in the end you'll decide to let this run its course. After all, if nothing comes of this, she's lost nothing by doing what I've required of her, and she gains five million dollars."

They'd reached his desk and Farrell walked behind it, but he remained politely standing. Thoroughly annoyed by the probable accuracy of Farrell's psychological summation, Stuart looked around for something to say to shake *him* up, and his gaze fell on the framed picture of a woman on Farrell's desk. "Are you planning to keep that picture there while you're trying to court your wife?"

"Absolutely."

Something in the way he said that made Stuart revise his original impression that the woman was a girlfriend or mistress. "Who is she?" he asked bluntly.

"My sister."

Farrell was watching him with that same infuriating calm, so Stuart shrugged, and with a deliberate effort to be offensive, he said, "Nice smile. Nice body too."

"I'll ignore the last part of that," Farrell said, "and politely suggest that the four of us have dinner when she's in town next time. Tell Meredith I'll pick her up tomorrow night at seven-thirty. You can phone my secretary in the morning and give her the address."

Summarily dismissed and duly cut down to size, Stuart nodded and opened the door, then he walked out and closed it. Outside Farrell's office he began to wonder if he was doing Meredith a favor by not warning her to run, not walk, from the agreement she'd signed, whether she was in love with her husband or not. The man was like a machine; unyielding, detached, uncompromising, and completely unemotional. Not even a slur against his sister could rile the bastard.

On the opposite side of the connecting door, Matthew Farrell sank heavily into his chair, leaned his head back, and closed his eyes. "Christ!" he whispered, heaving a long, shaking breath of relief. "Thank you."

It was the closest he'd come to a prayer in more than eleven years. It was the first easy breath he'd drawn in over two hours.

41

*H*ow did it go with Farrell?" Parker asked the minute he walked into Meredith's apartment to take her out for what he'd predicted would be a dinner to celebrate her almost-divorced status. His smile faded as she raked her hair off her forehead and mutely shook her head. "Meredith, what happened?" he said, putting his hands on her arms.

"I think you'd better sit down," she warned him.

"I'll stand," he said, already looking upset.

Ten minutes later, when she'd finished telling him the whole thing, he no longer looked upset, he looked furious—with her. "And you agreed to that?"

"What choice did I have?" Meredith cried. "I didn't have anything to bargain with. He was holding all the cards, and he handed out the ultimatum. It's not so very bad," she said, trying to smile and make him feel better. "I've had a couple hours to think it over, and it's more of a gross inconvenience—an annoyance—than anything else. I mean, when you're objective."

"I'm damned objective, and I disagree," Parker said harshly.

Unfortunately, Meredith was so overwrought, so guilt-stricken, she failed to consider that Parker might feel better if she felt worse about having to go out with Matt. "Look," she said with another encouraging smile, "even if I could have flown somewhere and gotten a divorce, I'd still be all snarled up in the property issues after the divorce because they have to be settled separately. As it stands now, everything will be completely settled and finished in six months—the divorce, the property, the works."

"Right," Parker snapped furiously. "And three of those six months are supposed to be spent with Farrell!"

"I told you, he specifically said that we wouldn't have to be intimate. And—and that still leaves almost half of every week for us to be together."

"That's certainly fair-minded of the son of a bitch!"

"You're losing your perspective!" Meredith warned, stunned at the belated realization that everything she was saying was angering him more. "He's doing this to retaliate against my father, not because he wants me!"

"Don't bullshit me, Meredith! Farrell's not gay or blind, and he intends to have a piece of you whenever and however he can get it. As you pointed out to me three times in your recitation of the meeting, that bastard's lawyers repeatedly said that Farrell regards himself as your husband! And do you know what I find the most infuriating about all this?"

"No," she said, feeling frustrated tears in her throat, "suppose you tell me, if you can do it without being vulgar and overbearing—"

"*I'm* vulgar and overbearing, am I? Farrell flips you a proposition like this, and *I'm* the one who's being vulgar and overbearing? I'll tell you what I find the most painful, the most disgusting, about all this—it's that you aren't particularly upset about it! He offers you five million dollars for rolling in the hay with him four times a week, and I'm vulgar? That's what—a hundred thousand dollars or so per time?"

"If you want to get all technical and precise," Meredith flung back as her exhaustion and frustration built to a mindless fury, "he is technically my husband!"

"What the hell am I technically—a wart?"

"No, you're my fiancé."

"How much do you intend to charge me?"

"Get out, Parker." She said it quietly. She meant it utterly.

"Fine." He snatched up his coat from the back of the chair, and Meredith tugged her engagement ring off her finger, fighting back tears.

"Here," she said hoarsely, thrusting it at him, "take this with you."

Parker looked at the ring in her hand and much of his anger faded. "Keep it for now," he said. "We're both too angry to think clearly. No, that's wrong, and that's what bothers me. I'm furious and you're trying to pass this whole thing off like a goddamned lark!"

"Dammit, I was trying to soothe things over so you wouldn't be so angry."

He hesitated uncertainly, then reached out and closed her fingers over the ring. "Is that what you were doing, Meredith, or is that what you think you were doing? I feel like the world has caved in, and you—who have to face the next three months—are taking it better than I am. I think maybe I should stay away until you've had time to decide just how important I really am to you."

"And I think," Meredith countered tautly, "You ought to spend some of that time wondering why you couldn't have offered me some sympathy and understanding instead of seeing this whole thing like some sexual challenge to your private property!"

He left then, closing the door behind him, and Meredith sank down on the sofa. The world, which had seemed so bright and promising just a few days before, had collapsed around her feet—exactly as it always did when she went near Matthew Farrell.

42

I'm sorry, sir, you aren't allowed to park here," the doorman said as Matt got out of his car in front of Meredith's apartment building.

His mind on his impending first date with his wife, Matt put a $100 bill into the man's gloved hand and continued toward the entrance without breaking stride.

"I'll keep an eye on it for you, sir," the doorman called behind him.

The oversize tip was also payment for future favors as needed, but Matt didn't pause to tell him that, nor would it have been necessary; doormen all over the world were masters of diplomacy and economics who understood that enormous tips such as that were advance payment for small future services, not merely present ones. At the moment Matt wasn't certain what future services he might require, but ingratiating himself with Meredith's doorman seemed like a wise precaution in any case.

The guard at the desk checked his guest list, saw Matt's name, and nodded politely. "Miss Bancroft—Apartment 505," he said. "I'll buzz her to let her know you're on the way up. Elevators are right there."

Meredith was so tense that her hands shook as she combed her fingers through the sides of her hair, shoving it into a casual, windblown style that fell about her shoulders. Stepping back from the mirror, she glanced at the bright green silk shirt and matching wool crepe skirt she was wearing, adjusted the slender hammered-gold belt at her waist, then she clipped a pair of large gold squares at her ears and slid a gold bracelet onto her wrist. Her face was abnormally pale, so she applied more blusher to her cheekbones; she was just about to add more lipstick when the buzzer shrilled twice, and the tube slid from her trembling fingers, leaving a coral streak across the polished wood of her dressing table. Ignoring the fact that Matt was obviously on his way up, she picked up the tube, intending to use it, then she changed her mind, capped it, and tossed it into her purse. Looking nice for Matthew Farrell, who hadn't even had the courtesy to let her know where they were going so that she could have a clue as to what to wear, was completely unnecessary. In fact, if he had seduction in mind, the worse she looked the better!

She walked to the door, stoically ignoring her trembling knees, jerked it open, and, raising her eyes no higher than his chest, she said very truthfully, "I was hoping you'd be late."

The ungracious greeting was no less than Matt expected, but she looked so damned beautiful in emerald green with her shining hair swinging loose and artless about her shoulders, he had to suppress the urge to laugh and drag her into his arms. "How late were you hoping I'd be?"

"About three months, actually."

He did laugh then, a rich, throaty chuckle that made Meredith's head snap up a few inches, but she couldn't quite look him in the face yet. "Are you enjoying yourself already?" she asked, staring fixedly at a pair of very broad shoulders encased in a soft fawn cashmere sport coat and an open-necked cream shirt that seemed to glow against his tanned throat.

"You look lovely," he said quietly, ignoring her jibe.

Still without looking at him, she turned on her heel and walked over to the closet to get a coat. "Since you didn't have the courtesy to let me know where we're going," she said to the inside of the closet, "I had no idea what I should wear."

Matt said nothing, he knew she was going to put up a fight when she found out, and so he'd simply not told her. "You're dressed perfectly," he said instead.

"Thank you, that's extremely informative," Meredith answered. She pulled out her coat from the closet, turned around, and collided with his chest. "Would you mind moving?"

"I'll help you with your coat."

"Don't help me!" she said, stepping sideways and tugging her coat. "Don't help me with anything! don't ever help me again!"

His hand locked on her upper arm, pulling her gently but forcibly around. "Is this the way it's going to be all night?" he asked quietly.

"No," she said bitterly, "this is the *good* part."

"I know how angry you are—"

Meredith lost her fear of looking at him. "No, you don't know!" she said, her voice shaking with ire. "You think you know, but you can't even begin to imagine!" Abandoning her vow to stay aloof and silent and to *bore* him to death, she said, "You asked me to trust you in your office, then you took everything I told you about what happened eleven years ago, and used it against me! Did you honestly think you could tear my life to pieces on Tuesday, and walk in here on Wednesday, and everything would be all sweet and rosy, you—you heartless hypocrite!"

Matt gazed into her stormy eyes and honestly considered saying, "I'm in love with you." But she wouldn't believe that after what happened yester-day—and if by some chance he could make her believe it, she'd use it against him and walk out on their agreement. And that he could not let her do. Yesterday she'd told him that all there was between them was a horrible past. He desperately needed the time he'd bargained for—time to breach her defenses and prove to her that a future relationship with him would not cause a repeat of the pain of the past. So instead of trying to explain or argue, he embarked on phase one of the psychological campaign he'd men-tally mapped out—which was to get her to break the habit of blaming him completely for that past. Taking her coat, he held it out for her. "I know I seem like a ruthless hypocrite to you now, and I don't blame you for think-ing it. But at least do me the justice of remembering that I was *not* the villain eleven years ago." She slid her arms into the sleeves and wordlessly started to step away, but he put his hands on her shoulders and turned her around, waiting until she lifted her resentful eyes to his. "Hate me for what I'm doing now," he told her with quiet force, "I can accept that, but don't hate me for the past. I was as much a victim of your father's scheming as you were!"

"You were heartless even then!" Meredith said as she shrugged off his hands and picked up her purse. "You hardly bothered to write when you were in South America."

"I wrote you dozens of letters," he said, and opened the door for her. Wryly he added, "I even mailed half of them. And you're in no position to criticize on that score," he added as they started down the carpeted hallway. "You only wrote six to me in all those months!"

Meredith watched his hand rise and press the down button for the ele-vator, telling herself that to exonerate himself, he was lying about the letters, but something was niggling at the back of her mind, something he'd told her during his phone call from Venezuela that she'd interpreted at the time as a criticism of her letter writing style. *You aren't much of a correspondent, are you . . . ?*

Until the doctor had restricted her activity, she'd been in the habit of taking her letters to Matt out to the mailbox at the end of the driveway her-self but anyone could have removed those letters afterward—her father, a servant. The only five letters she'd gotten from Matt were ones that had come when she was hovering at the mailbox and got the mail herself from the postman's hand. Perhaps the only letters Matt received were the ones she'd given to the postman personally.

The awful suspicion grew inside her, and she glanced unwillingly at Matt, fighting down an impulse to question him further about the letters.

The elevator doors slid open and he ushered her through the lobby and outside to the street, where a maroon Rolls-Royce was waiting at the curb, gleaming like a polished jewel in the light of a streetlamp.

Meredith slid into the luxurious barley leather interior, and gazed fixedly out the windshield as Matt put the car into gear and they glided into traffic. The Rolls was beautiful, but she'd have died rather than say anything that sounded admiring about his car, and besides, her mind was still on the letters.

Evidently, so was Matt's, because as they stopped at a light, he said, "How many letters did you actually get from me?"

She tried not to answer, honestly tried to ignore him, but while she could hold her own in an open confrontation, she was incapable of silent sulking. "Five," she said flatly, staring at her gloved hands.

"How many did you write?" he persisted.

She hesitated, then she shrugged. "I wrote you at least twice a week at first. Later, when you didn't answer, I cut back to once a week."

"I wrote dozens of letters to you," he said again, more emphatically. "I presume your father was intercepting our mail, and evidently failed to catch the five that got through?"

"It doesn't matter now."

"Doesn't it?" he said with biting irony. "God, when I think of the way I used to wait for mail from you, and the way I felt when it never came!"

The intensity of his voice stunned her almost as much as the words he'd uttered. She glanced at him in shock because he'd never given the slightest indication back then that she meant anything to him as a person. In bed, yes, but not out of it. The muted light of the dashboard played over the harsh, rugged contours of his face and jaw, highlighting the sculpted mouth and arrogant chin. Suddenly she was hurtled back in time, and she was sitting beside him in the Porsche, watching the wind ruffle his thick, dark hair, attracted and repelled by those sternly handsome features and his blatant sensuality. He was more handsome than ever, and the relentless ambition she'd sensed in him in the past had been channeled and realized; it was power now—irrefutable, harsh, and terribly potent. And it was being used on her. After several minutes she finally said, "Is it too much to expect to be told where you're taking me?"

She saw him smile because she'd at last broken the silence. "Right here," he said, and he flipped on the turn indicator and swung the Rolls into the underground parking garage beneath his apartment building.

"I should have known you'd try this," she burst out, fully prepared to get out of the car the instant he stopped and walk home if necessary.

"My father wants to see you," Matt said calmly, pulling into a parking space directly in front of the elevator, between a limousine with California license plates and a midnight-blue Jaguar convertible that was so new it had only temporary license plates. Reluctantly willing to go upstairs if his father was there, Meredith got out of the car.

Matt's burly chauffeur opened the door, and behind him, Patrick Farrell was already walking up the foyer steps, his face wreathed in a smile.

"Here she is," Matt told his father with grim humor, "delivered to you just as I promised she'd be—safe, sound, and mad as hell at me."

Patrick held his arms out to Meredith, beaming at her, and she walked into his embrace, turning her face away from Matt.

Looping his arm over her shoulders, he turned her to the chauffeur. "Meredith," he said, "this is Joe O'Hara. I don't think you two have ever been formally introduced."

Meredith managed a weak, embarrassed smile as she recollected the two highly emotional scenes that the chauffeur had witnessed. "How do you do, Mr. O'Hara."

"It's a pleasure t'meet you, Mrs. Farrell."

"My name is Bancroft," Meredith said firmly.

"Right," he said, shooting a challenging grin at Matt. "Pat," he said, starting for the door, "I'll pick you up out front later on."

The last time she'd been there, Meredith had been too distracted to notice the extravagant luxury of the apartment. Now she was too tense to look at anyone, so she glanced around her and was reluctantly impressed. Since Matt's penthouse occupied the entire top floor, all the exterior walls were made entirely of glass, offering a spectacular view of the city lights. Three shallow steps led down from the marble foyer to the various living areas, but instead of being divided by walls, they were left wide open, indicated only by pairs of marble columns. Directly ahead of her was a living room large enough to accommodate several sofas and numerous chairs and tables. To the right of the living room was a dining room, which was elevated like the foyer, and just above and behind that was a cozy sitting room with its own intricately carved English bar to serve it. It was an apartment that had been designed and furnished to entertain in; it was showy and impressive and opulent with its various levels and marble floors; it was also the exact opposite of Meredith's own apartment. And even so, she liked it immensely.

"So," Patrick Farrell said, beaming, "how do you like Matt's place?"

"It's very nice," she admitted. It hit her then that Patrick's being there could be the answer to her prayer. Not for a moment did she believe he knew the full extent of Matt's heavy-handed tactics, and she vowed to speak to him, privately if possible, and beg him to intervene.

"Matt likes marble, but I'm not so comfortable around it," he teased, grinning. "It makes me feel like I've died and been interred."

"I can imagine how you must feel in his black marble bathtubs, then," Meredith said with a slight smile.

"En*tombed*," Patrick promptly agreed, walking beside her past the dining room and up the three steps to the sitting room.

When she sat down, Patrick remained standing and Matt walked over to the bar. "What would you both like to drink?"

"Ginger ale for me," Patrick said.

"I'll have ginger ale too," Meredith said.

"You'll have sherry," Matt countered arbitrarily.

"He's right," Patrick said. "It doesn't bother me a bit to watch everyone else drink. So," he said, "You know all about Matt's marble bathtubs?"

Meredith devoutly wished she'd never blurted that out. "I—I saw some pictures of the apartment in the Sunday newspaper."

"I knew it!" Patrick declared, winking at her. "All these years, whenever Matt's picture was in a magazine or somewhere, I'd say to myself, I hope Meredith Bancroft sees this. You were keeping track of him, weren't you?"

"No!" Meredith exclaimed defensively. "I most certainly was not!"

Oddly, it was Matt who rescued her from the embarrassing discussion. Glancing up from the bar, he said to her, "While we're on the subject of notoriety, I'd like you to tell me how you expect to keep our seeing each other a secret, which is what your attorney said you want."

"A secret?" Patrick said to her. "Why do you want to do that?"

Meredith thought of at least a dozen angry and highly descriptive reasons, but she couldn't very well tell them to his father, and Matt interceded anyway. "Because Meredith is still engaged to someone else," he told his father, then he shifted his gaze to her. "You've been all over the news here for years. People will recognize you wherever we go."

Patrick spoke up. "I think I'll go see when dinner can be ready," he said, and walked off toward the dining room, leaving Meredith with the impression that he was either starving or eager to make himself scarce.

Meredith waited until he was out of earshot, then she said with angry satisfaction, "I won't be recognized, but you will. *You're* America's corporate sex symbol; you're the one whose motto is 'If it moves, take it to bed.' You're the one who sleeps with rock stars and then seduces their housemaids—are you *laughing* at me?" she gasped, her gaze riveting on his shaking shoulders.

Uncapping the ginger ale, he slid her a sideways grin. "Where are you getting all this junk about housemaids?"

"Several of the secretaries at Bancroft's are among your *many* admirers," Meredith retorted with scathing disdain. "They read about you in the *Tattler.*"

"The *Tattler?*" Matt said, trying to hide his laughter behind a thoughtful frown. "Is that the tabloid that said I was taken aboard a UFO and told by clairvoyant aliens what business decisions to make?"

"No, that was *The World Star!*" Meredith retorted, growing more frustrated by his amused dismissal of the whole topic. "I saw it in the grocery store."

His amusement vanished and his voice took on an edge. "I seem to recall reading somewhere that *you* were having an affair with a playwright."

"That was in the *Chicago Tribune,* and they didn't say I was having an affair with Joshua Hamilton, they said we were seeing a lot of each other!"

He picked up the glasses and carried them over to her. "Were you having an affair with him?" he persisted.

Hating the feeling of being dwarfed by him, Meredith stood up and took the glass from his hand. "Hardly. Joshua Hamilton happens to be in love with my stepbrother, Joel."

She had the satisfaction of finally seeing Matthew Farrell at a complete loss. "He's in love with your *what?*"

"Joel is my step-grandmother's son, but he's close to my age, so we agreed years ago to call each other stepbrother and sister. Her other son's name is Jason."

Matt's lips twitched. "I gather," he said dryly, "that Joel is gay?"

Meredith's satisfied smile vanished and her eyes narrowed at his tone. "Yes, but don't you dare say anything ugly about Joel! He's the kindest, dearest man I've ever known! Jason is straight and he's an utter pig!"

His expression softened at her militant defense of the one brother, and he lifted his hand, unable to restrain the urge to touch her. "Who would have guessed," he said, smiling into her stormy eyes as he brushed his knuckles over her arm, "that the prim and proper debutante I met long ago would actually have so many skeletons in her closet?"

Oblivious to Patrick Farrell, who was arrested on the bottom step, listening to their altercation with fascinated interest, Meredith jerked her arm away. "At least I haven't *slept* with all of mine," she retorted hotly, "and not one of them," she added, "has pink hair!"

"Who," Patrick asked in a choked, laughing voice as he finally made his presence known, "has pink hair?"

Matt glanced up distractedly and saw the cook carrying in a tray and placing it on the dining room table. "It's too early for dinner," he said, frowning.

"That's my fault," Patrick said. "I thought my plane left at midnight tonight, but just after you went to get Meredith, I realized it leaves at eleven o'clock. I asked Mrs. Wilson to set dinner forward an hour."

Meredith, who was eager to get the evening over with, was delighted with an early dinner, and immediately decided to ask Patrick to drop her off at home when he left. Buoyed up by that, she managed to make it through the entire meal with relative equanimity, and Patrick made that easier by keeping up a stream of impersonal conversation in which she participated only when and if Matt didn't. In fact, though Matt was seated at the head of the table and she was on his immediate right, Meredith managed to avoid not only speaking to him, but looking at him—until dessert was cleared away. The end of the meal seemed to chart an entirely new course for the evening.

Before that, she'd believed that Patrick had no idea of the unethical extremes his son had gone to, but as he arose from the table, she discovered his apparent lack of knowledge, and even his neutrality, was an illusion. "Meredith," he said in a censorious tone, "You haven't spoken a word to Matt since we sat down at this table. Silence isn't going to get you anywhere. What you two need is a nice big fight to get everything out in the open and clear the air." He glanced at Matt with a meaningful smile. "You can start just as soon as I kiss Meredith good-bye. Joe will be waiting out in front."

Meredith stood up quickly. "We're not going to have a fight. In fact, I have to leave. Could you drop me off at home on your way to the airport?"

Patrick's tone was as implacable as it was paternal and kind. "Don't be foolish, Meredith. You'll stay here with Matt and he'll take you home later."

"I'm not being foolish! Mr. Farrell—"

"Dad."

"I'm sorry—Dad," she corrected herself, and then because she realized this was going to be her only chance to enlist his support, she said, "I don't think you realize why I'm here right now. I'm here because your son has blackmailed and coerced me into seeing him for an eleven-week period."

She expected him to be surprised, to demand an explanation from Matt. She did not expect him to look at her unflinchingly, and then side with his son against her. "He did what was necessary to stop you from doing something you might both regret for the rest of your lives."

Meredith stepped back as if he had slapped her, and she struck back verbally with quiet force. "I never should have told either one of you the truth about what happened years ago. Tonight, all night, I've thought you didn't realize why I'm here now—" Her voice dropped and she shook her head at her own naivete. "I was planning to explain it to you, and to ask you to intercede."

Patrick lifted his hand in a gesture of helpless appeal to be understood, then he looked worriedly to Matt, who stood there, unmoved by the little tableau. "I have to go," he said, and lamely added, "Do you want me to give a message to Julie for you?"

"You can give her my sympathy," she quietly replied, turning around and looking for her purse and coat, "for being raised in a family of heartless men." She missed the tensing of Matt's jaw, but she felt Patrick's hand on her shoulder, and though she stopped, she refused to turn back. His hand dropped away and then he left.

The moment the door closed behind him, silence fell over the apartment . . . heavy, waiting, stifling. Meredith took one step, intending to get her things, but Matt caught her arm and drew her back. "I'm getting my coat and purse and I'm leaving," she said.

"We're going to talk, Meredith," he said in the cool, authoritative tone she particularly hated.

"You'll have to physically restrain me to make me stay here," she warned him, "and if you try, I'll swear out a warrant for your arrest in the morning, so help me God!"

Torn between frustration and amusement, Matt reminded her, "You said you wanted our meetings to be private."

"I said *secret!*"

Matt realized he was getting nowhere, that her animosity was building by the moment, and so he did the last thing he wanted to do; he issued a threat. "We had a bargain! Or do you no longer care what happens to your father?" The look she gave him was so filled with contempt that for the first time, he wondered if he'd been wrong about her ability to hate. "We're going to talk tonight," he said, gentling his tone, "either here or at your place. You decide where."

"My place," she said bitterly.

They made the fifteen-minute trip in complete silence. By the time she opened her apartment door, the atmosphere was vibrating with tension.

Meredith went directly to a lamp, turned it on, then she walked over to the fireplace because it was as far as she could possibly get from him. "You said you wanted to talk," she reminded him ungraciously. Crossing her arms over her chest, she leaned her shoulders against the mantel, waiting for him to start trying to bully and coerce her, which she was positive he meant to do. For that reason, she was slightly disconcerted when he made no effort to do either, and instead shoved his hands into his pockets and stood in the center of the living room, slowly looking around at the cozy room as if he were fascinated by every piece of furniture and each knickknack.

Baffled, she watched as he took one hand out of his pocket and picked up a photograph of Parker in an ornate antique frame from the end table near his hip. He put the picture back, and then let his gaze drift from the antique secretary she used as a desk to the dining room table with its silver candlesticks, to the chintz-covered Queen Anne chairs before the fire. "What are you doing?" Meredith demanded warily.

He looked around at her then, and the quiet amusement in his eyes was almost as startling as what he said. "I'm satisfying years of curiosity."

"About what?"

"About you," he said, and if Meredith hadn't known better, she'd have believed there was tenderness in his expression. "About how you live."

Wishing she'd stayed out in the open instead of backing herself into a wall, she watched him walk forward, finally stopping in front of her, both hands in his pockets again. "You like chintz," he said with a boyish half smile. "Somehow I never imagined you with chintz. It suits you though— the antiques and bright flowers; it's warm and inviting. I like it very much."

"Good, then I can die happy," Meredith said, increasingly wary of the warmth in his eyes and his smile. "Now, what did you want to talk about?"

"For one thing, I'd like to know why you're even angrier tonight than you were yesterday."

"I'll tell you why," she said, her voice shaking with suppressed resentment. "Yesterday I yielded to your blackmail and agreed to see you for eleven weeks, but I will not—*will not*—participate in this farce you apparently want to enact!"

"What farce?"

"The farce of pretending you want a reconciliation, which is what you did in front of the lawyers on Tuesday and your father tonight! What you want is revenge, and you found a subtler, cheaper way of getting it than suing my father!"

"In the first place," he pointed out, "I could have staged a public massacre in a courtroom for the five million dollars I'm giving you if this doesn't work out. Meredith," he said forcefully, "this is not about revenge! I told you at that meeting exactly why I was asking for this time with you. There's something between us—there has *always* been something between us—and not even eleven years could kill it! I want it to have a chance."

Meredith's mouth fell open, and she gaped at him, torn between ire at his outrageous lie and mirth that he actually expected her to believe it. "Am I supposed to think"—she had to stop to swallow back an angry, hysterical laugh—"that you've been carrying some sort of torch for me for all these years?"

"Would you believe it if I said it's true?"

"I'd have to be an idiot to believe it! I told you tonight that I and everybody who subscribes to a magazine or reads a newspaper knows about hundreds of your affairs!"

"That statement is an outrageous exaggeration, and you damned well know it!" In skeptical silence she raised her brows. "Dammit!" Matt swore, angrily shoving a hand through the side of his hair. "I didn't expect this. Not this." He walked away from her, then he turned on his heel, his voice ringing with harsh irony. "Will it help convince you if I admit that you haunted me for years after our divorce? Well, you did! Would you like to know why I worked myself into the ground and took insane gambles, trying to double and triple every cent I made? Would you like to know what I did the day my net worth actually reached one million dollars?"

Dazed, incredulous, and unwillingly enthralled, Meredith stared at him, and without meaning to she nodded slightly.

"I did it," he snapped, "out of some obsessive, demented determination to prove to you I could do it! The night an investment paid off and put me over the one-million-dollar mark, I opened a bottle of champagne, and I toasted you with it. It wasn't a friendly toast, but it was eloquent in its way. I said, To you, my mercenary wife—may you long regret the day you turned your back on me.

"Shall I tell you," he continued bitterly, "how I felt when I finally realized that every woman I took to bed was blond, like you, with blue eyes, like yours, and that I was unconsciously making love to you?"

"That's disgusting," Meredith whispered, her eyes wide with shock.

"That's exactly how I felt!" He walked back to stand in front of her, and he softened his voice, but not much. "And since we're having confession time here, it's your turn."

"What do you mean?" Meredith said, unable to believe everything he'd said, and yet half convinced that somehow he was telling her what he believed was true. . . .

"Let's start with your incredulous reaction when I said I think there's been something between us all this time."

"There is nothing between us!"

"You don't find it odd that neither of us remarried during all these years?"

"No."

"And, at the farm, when you asked for a truce, you weren't feeling anything for me then?"

"No!" Meredith said, but she was lying and she knew it.

"Or in my office," he demanded, firing questions at her like an inquisitor, "when I asked you for a truce?"

"I didn't feel anything, either of those times, except . . . except a casual sort of friendship," she said a little desperately.

"And you're in love with Reynolds?"

"Yes!"

"Then what the hell were you doing in bed with me last weekend?"

Meredith drew a shaky breath. "Well, it was something that just happened. It didn't mean anything. We were trying to comfort each other, that's all. It was . . . pleasant enough, but no more than that."

"Don't lie to me! We couldn't get enough of each other in that bed, and you damned well know it!" When she remained stubbornly, resistantly silent, he pushed her harder. "And you have absolutely no desire to make love with me again, is that it?"

"That's it!"

"How would you like to give me five minutes to prove you're wrong?"

"I wouldn't," Meredith flung back.

"Do you honestly think," he said more quietly, "I'm naive enough not to know you wanted me as badly as I wanted you, that day in bed?"

"I'm sure you're experienced enough to gauge how a woman feels to within a fraction of a sigh!" she shot back, too angry to realize what she was admitting as she added, "But at the risk of wounding your damnable confidence, I'll tell you *exactly* how I felt that day! I felt like I've always felt in bed with you—naive, clumsy, and gauche!"

He looked ready to explode. "You *what?*"

"You heard me," she said, but her satisfaction at his stunned reaction was short-lived, because instead of being enraged at his overestimation of her feelings, he put his hand against the mantel for support and started to laugh. He laughed until Meredith got so angry that she tried to move away, and then he sobered abruptly.

"I'm sorry," he said contritely, a strange, tender light in his eyes. Lifting his hand, Matt laid it against her smooth cheek, amazed and shamelessly delighted that for all her innate sensuality, she obviously hadn't slept around very much. If she had, instead of feeling gauche in bed with him, she'd surely know she turned his body into an inferno with a simple touch. "God, you are lovely," he whispered. "Inside and out." He bent his head, intending to kiss her, but she turned her face away, so he kissed her ear.

"If you'll kiss me back," he whispered huskily, brushing his lips along the curve of her jaw, "I'll make it six million. If you'll go to bed with me tonight," he continued, losing himself in the scent of her perfume and the softness of her skin, "I'll give you the world. But if you'll move in with me," he continued, dragging his mouth across her cheek to the corner of her lips, "I'll do much better than that."

Unable to turn her face farther because his arm was in the way, and unable to turn her body because his body was in the way, Meredith tried to infuse disdain in her voice and simultaneously ignore the arousing touch of his tongue against her ear. "Six million dollars and the whole world!" she said in a slightly shaky voice. "What else could you possibly give me if I move in with you?"

"Paradise." Lifting his head, Matt took her chin between his thumb and forefinger and forced her to meet his gaze. In an aching, solemn voice he said, "I'll give you paradise on a gold platter. Anything you want—everything you want. I come with it, of course. It's a package deal." Meredith swallowed audibly, mesmerized by the melting look in his silver eyes and the rich timbre of his deep voice. "We'll be a family," he continued, describing the paradise he was offering while he bent his head to her again. "We'll have children . . . I'd like six," he teased, his lips against her temple. "But I'll settle for one. You don't have to decide now." She drew in a ragged breath and Matt decided he'd pushed matters as far as he dared for one night. Straightening abruptly, he chucked her under her chin. "Think about it," he suggested with a grin.

Meredith watched in a stupor of shock and disbelief as he turned and headed to the door without another word. It closed behind him, and she stared at it, riveted to the spot, her mind trying to absorb everything he'd said. Reaching blindly for the back of a chair, she walked around it and sank into it, not sure whether to laugh or cry. He had to be lying. He had to be *crazy*. That alone would explain his resolute pursuit of a foolish goal he'd evidently set for himself eleven years earlier—of proving he was good enough to be married to her, to a Bancroft. She'd read articles about his occasional business clashes with competitive companies or takeover targets, and they'd implied that he was almost inhumanly single-minded.

Evidently, Meredith realized with a hysterical, panicky giggle, she really *was* Matthew Farrell's newest "takeover target." She could not—would not—let herself believe he'd actually been hung up on her for years after their parting. My God, he'd never even said I love you to her when they were married—not even at the height of passion or the afterglow.

She did, however, believe some things he'd told her tonight: He probably *had* spent those early years working himself into the ground to prove to her, and undoubtedly her father, that he could make a fortune. That sounded just like Matt, she thought with a wry smile—and so did the champagne toast he said he drank to her the night he was worth a million dollars. Vengeful to the very end, she decided with amusement. No wonder he'd become such a force to be reckoned with in the business world! It occurred to her that her thoughts were a little mild, given the circumstances, and she reluctantly faced the reason for that: One other thing that Matt had said was true—there *had* always been something between them. From the very first night she'd met him, there'd been an immediate and inexplicable rapport that had sprung up between them, a bond that swiftly drew them closer together during those long-ago days at the farm. She'd felt it then, but it came as a shock to discover that Matt had been aware of it too. That same inexplicable rapport had already been struggling to resurface the day of their ill-fated lunch when he had teased her about not knowing what she wanted to drink. It had burst into bloom again at the farm, when she put her hand in his and asked for a truce, then grown stronger, more vibrant, when they sat together in the living room that night, talking about business. In a way, it was almost as if they'd been born friends. It was impossible for her to truly hate Matt for anything.

With a baffled sigh Meredith got up, turned out the lamp, and started toward her bedroom. She was standing beside her bed, unbuttoning her blouse, when the rest of his words, the ones she was adamantly trying not to remember, whispered forcefully through her mind, and her hands stilled on the buttons. *Go to bed with me tonight and I'll give you the world. Move in with me, and I'll give you paradise on a gold platter. Anything you want—everything you want. I come with it, of course. It's a package deal.*

Mesmerized by the memory, Meredith stood still, then she gave her head a hard shake and finished unbuttoning her blouse. The man was absolutely lethal. No wonder women fell at his feet. Just the memory of his voice whispering those things in her ear was making her hands tremble! Really, she decided as she tried to suppress a halfhearted smile, if he could bottle all that awesome sex appeal, he wouldn't need to work to make money. Her smile faded as she wondered how many other women he'd offered his paradise to, and then she realized the answer had to be none. In all the rabid press coverage of his personal life, she'd never seen a single piece of information that implied he lived other than alone. She felt unaccountably better now that she'd remembered that. And she was too exhausted from the emotional turmoil of the past two days to wonder if that wasn't a little odd.

When she got into bed, her thoughts turned to Parker and her spirits plummeted. She'd hoped all day that he would call. Despite the way they'd parted, she knew in her heart that neither of them wanted to end their engagement. It dawned on her that perhaps he was waiting for her to call. Tomorrow, she decided, she'd call him tomorrow and try again to make him understand.

43

"Mornin', Matt," Joe said as Matt slid into the back seat of the limo at 8:15 the next morning, then he glanced uneasily at the folded newspaper in Matt's hand and added, "Is—is everything okay? With you and your wife, I mean?"

"Not exactly," Matt replied dryly. Ignoring the *Chicago Tribune*, which he normally read in the car every morning, Matt stretched his legs out in front of him and gazed out the side window. A faint smile played about his mouth as the limo pulled into traffic, and his thoughts drifted to Meredith. Several minutes had passed before Matt noticed that his car was not making its usual daring assault on traffic this morning. Puzzled, he looked up and saw Joe watching him in the rearview mirror. "Something on your mind?" Matt asked.

"No, why?"

"You passed up a chance to cut off that delivery truck." Wordlessly, Joe withdrew his gaze from the mirror, stepped on the accelerator, and Matt let his thoughts return pleasurably to Meredith. He let them linger on her until he arrived at Haskell's building, then he forced himself to start thinking of the business day that lay ahead as he got out of the car in the underground garage.

"Good morning, Eleanor," he said with a grin as he walked through his secretary's office and opened his door. "You're looking very well this morning."

"Good morning," she managed to say in an odd, shocked voice. In accordance with their usual morning ritual, she followed him into his office and stood beside his desk with a notepad in one hand, his mail and phone messages in the other, ready to write down his instructions for dealing with each item. Matt saw her gaze ricochet to the newspaper when he tossed it onto his desk, but his attention was diverted by the thick stack of phone messages she was holding. "Who are those calls from?"

"The news media," she replied with disgust as she began flipping through them. "The *Tribune* has called four times and the *Sun-Times* has called three. UPI is on hold on my desk right now, and the Associated Press is downstairs in the main lobby, along with the reporters from the local television and radio stations. All four of the major networks have called, so has CNN. *People* magazine wants to talk to you, but the *National Tattler* wanted to talk to me—they said they 'want to know the dirt from a secretary's point of view.' I hung up on them. You've also had two crank calls from anonymous individuals who inferred you must be homosexual, and one from Miss Avery, who said to tell you that you are a deceitful bastard. Tom Anderson called to ask if he can do anything to help, and the guard in the lobby phoned for reinforcements to stop the press from barging up here." She paused and glanced at him. "I've already handled that."

Frowning, Matt mentally sorted through the business activities of Intercorp's various companies, trying to think which would have caused a public furor. "What's happened that I don't know about?"

She nodded grimly to the folded newspaper lying on Matt's desk. "Have you opened that paper yet?"

"No," Matt said, reaching for the *Tribune* and irritably snapping it open, "but if something happened last night to cause an uproar in the press, Anderson should have called me at ho—" He glanced at the front page of the paper and froze, momentarily unable to absorb the shock: Pictures of Meredith, himself, and Parker Reynolds were staring back at him beneath a headline that screamed:

FAKE LAWYER CONFESSES TO DUPING FAMOUS CLIENTS

He snatched up the paper, scanning the accompanying story, his jaw clenching.

Last night, police in Belleville, Illinois, arrested Stanislaus Spyzhalski, 45, on charges of fraud and practicing law without a license. According to the Belleville police department, Spyzhalski has confessed to duping hundreds of clients over the past fifteen years by falsifying judges' signatures on documents that he never filed, including a divorce decree which he claims to have been hired to obtain a decade ago for department store heiress Meredith Bancroft from her alleged husband, industrialist Matthew Farrell. Meredith Bancroft, whose impending marriage to financier Parker Reynolds was announced this month . . .

With a savage curse Matt looked up from the story, rapidly calculating the possible consequences of all this, then he looked at his secretary, and began issuing rapid-fire instructions: "Get Pearson and Levinson on the phone, then find my pilot. Call Joe O'Hara in the car and tell him to stand by for instructions, and get my wife on the phone."

She nodded and left, and Matt finished scanning the article.

Officials say they were originally alerted to Spyzhalski by a Belleville man who tried to obtain a copy of his marriage annulment from the St. Clair County courthouse. Belleville police have already recovered some of Spyzhalski's files, but the suspect has refused to turn over the rest prior to his hearing tomorrow, where he plans to represent himself. Neither Farrell, Bancroft, nor Reynolds were available for comment tonight. . . . Details of the alleged Bancroft-Farrell divorce remain undivulged, but a spokesman for the Belleville police department said that they are confident that Spyzhalski, who they describe as flamboyant and unrepentant, will provide them . . .

Matt's heart froze at the thought of the details of the divorce being divulged. Meredith had divorced him on grounds of desertion and mental cruelty, which, respectively, would make his proud young wife look pitiful and helpless when the press got through with her. Neither image was anything but devastating for the temporary president of a national corporation who hoped to be permanently appointed to that post when her father retired.

The story was continued on page three, and Matt yanked the page over and ground his teeth at what he saw. Beneath a bold caption that read *Menage à Trois?* there was a picture of Meredith smiling at Parker as they danced at some Chicago charity affair, and a similar picture of Matt—dancing with a redhead at a charity ball in New York. Beneath those was a story that began with a report about Meredith having snubbed Matt at the opera a few weeks before, and then went into the details of their individual dating habits. Matt punched the intercom button just as Eleanor hurried into his office. "What the hell's happening with those calls?" he demanded.

"Pearson and Levinson aren't expected in until nine," she recited. "Your pilot is doing a check flight right now with the new engine, and I left word for him to call the instant he lands, which should be in about twenty minutes. Joe O'Hara is on his way back here with the car. I told him to wait in the parking garage, to avoid the reporters in the lobby—"

"What about my wife?" Matt interrupted, unaware that he'd automatically called her that for the second time in five minutes.

Even Eleanor looked tense. "Her secretary says she's not in yet, and that even if she was, Miss Bancroft's instructions were to tell you that all future communications between the two of you are to be handled through your lawyers."

"That's changed," Matt said shortly. Reaching up, he ran a hand around his nape, absently rubbing the tense muscles, wanting to get to Meredith before she tried to deal with the press on her own. "How did her secretary sound when you talked to her—did she sound like everything was normal over there."

"She sounded like she was under siege."

"That means she's getting the same calls you've gotten this morning." Moving out from behind his desk, Matt grabbed his coat, and headed for the door. "Have the attorneys and the pilot call me at her number," he ordered. "And call our public relations department. Tell whoever's in charge to keep the press on ice here and not to antagonize them. In fact, treat them very nicely and promise them a statement this afternoon at—one o'clock. I'll call from Meredith's office and notify P.R. where to tell them to assemble this afternoon. In the meantime, give them a damned brunch or something while they're waiting."

"You're serious about the food?" she said, knowing his normal method of dealing with the press when they intruded on his private life was either to avoid them or to tell them, in slightly different words, to go to hell.

"I'm serious," Matt gritted out. He paused at the door for one last instruction. "Get through to Parker Reynolds. He'll be surrounded by press too. Tell him to call me at Meredith's office, and in the meantime tell him he is to tell the press *exactly* what we're telling them here."

At 8:35 Meredith stepped off the elevator and headed toward her office, glad of the chance to work and escape the thoughts of Matt that had kept her awake most of the night and then made her oversleep. Here, at least, she'd be forced to put her personal problems aside and concentrate on business.

"Good morning, Kathy," she said to the receptionist, then she glanced around at the nearly deserted area. The executives, who worked late hours, rarely came in before nine o'clock, but the clerical staff was normally in evidence long before now, ready to go to work promptly at 8:30. "Where is everyone? What's going on?" she asked.

Kathy gaped at her and swallowed nervously. "Phyllis went downstairs to talk to security. She's having your phone calls held at the switchboard. Nearly everyone else is in the coffee room, I think."

Frowning, Meredith listened to the persistent ringing of unanswered telephones up and down the corridor. "Is it someone's birthday?" she asked. It was a ritual for everyone on the two administrative floors to wander up to the coffee room sometime during the day to have coffee and cake on the occasion of an employee's birthday, but never before had that created such an unusual and unacceptable dearth of needed personnel. Her own birthday was two days away on Saturday, Meredith realized, and for a split second she wondered if there was some sort of early surprise party being given for her.

"I don't think it's a party," Kathy said uneasily.

"Oh," Meredith said, dumbfounded by this unprecedented negligence on the part of a normally conscientious clerical staff. Stopping in her office to drop off her coat and briefcase, she headed directly for the coffee room. The minute she walked over to the coffeepots, two dozen pairs of eyes riveted on her. "It sounds like a fire drill out there, ladies and gentlemen," Meredith said with a matter-of-fact smile, dimly surprised by the taut silence and gaping stares of the assembly, who all seemed to be clutching newspapers. "How about answering some of those phones?" she added—needlessly, because they were already stampeding out of there, mumbling "good morning" and "excuse me."

She'd just sat down at her desk and was taking the first sip of her coffee, when Lisa raced into her office, clutching a huge armload of newspapers. "Mer, I'm so sorry!" she burst out. "I bought every damned copy from the newspaper stand out front so they wouldn't have any more to sell. It's the only way I could think of to help you!"

"Help me?" Meredith asked with a startled smile.

Lisa's mouth fell open, and she clutched the newspapers tighter, as if to hide them. "You haven't seen the morning paper, have you?"

Alarm traced a finger up Meredith's spine. "No, I overslept and didn't have time. Why? What's wrong?"

With visible reluctance, Lisa slowly laid the stack on Meredith's desk. Meredith tore her eyes from Lisa's pale face, looked at the paper, then half rose from her chair. "Oh, my God!" she breathed, her stricken gaze flying over the print. She put down her coffee cup and stood up, forcing herself to read more slowly. Then she turned to page three and read the more sensational and personal article on that page. Finished, she looked at Lisa with glazed panic in her eyes. "Oh, my God," she whispered again.

They both jumped as Phyllis slammed Meredith's door and rushed toward them. "I've been in security," she said, her short hair disheveled, as if she'd been raking her fingers through it. "We were swarming with reporters at the main doors, waiting for us to open. They started getting in at the employee entrance, so Mark Braden let them all in and told them to go to the auditorium. The phone has been ringing off the hook. Most of the calls are from reporters, but you also had calls from two of the board members who want to talk to you immediately. Mr. Reynolds has called three times and Mr. Farrell called once. Mark Braden wants instructions. So do I!"

Meredith tried to concentrate, but her insides were trembling with sick dread. Sooner or later a reporter would dig up the reasons for her marriage to Matt. Someone would talk—a servant, an orderly at the hospital—and the world was going to know that she had been a silly, pregnant teenage bride of an unwilling husband. Her pride and her privacy were about to be torn to shreds. Other people made mistakes and broke rules, she thought bitterly, and got by with it. But not her—she had to pay again and again and again.

It suddenly hit her then, what else everyone was going to think when that sham lawyer revealed the details of her divorce, and she felt the room tilt sickeningly. Because her father hadn't settled for something nice and decent like irreconcilable differences, she was not merely going to be portrayed as some promiscuous teenager without enough sense to use birth control, she was also going to be the pathetic object of desertion and mental cruelty!

And Parker—dear God, Parker was a respectable banker and the papers were going to drag him into this mess.

She suddenly thought of Matt and what this was going to do to him, and she felt violently ill. When people learned he'd subjected his sad little pregnant wife to mental cruelty and then deserted her, his reputation and character would be destroyed beyond recall. . . .

"Meredith, please—tell me what to do." Phyllis's imploring voice seemed to come from very far away. "The phone on my desk is ringing right now."

Lisa held up her hand. "Give her time to think—she just saw the newspaper when you walked in."

Meredith sank down in her chair, shaking her head to clear it, knowing she had to do something—anything. For lack of any other ideas, she said slowly, "We'll follow the same procedure we follow whenever something newsworthy happens at the store—notify the switchboard to screen all calls and have those from reporters transferred to public relations." She swallowed painfully. "Tell Mark Braden to keep herding the reporters who come here to the auditorium."

"Yes, but what do you want public relations to *tell* the reporters?"

Raising her gaze to Phyllis's, Meredith drew a ragged breath and admitted, "I don't know yet. Just tell them to wait——" She broke off at the knocking on her door, and all three of them turned as the receptionist poked her head inside and said anxiously, "I'm sorry to disturb you, Miss Bancroft, but Mr. Farrell is here, and he's—he's very, very insistent about seeing you. I don't think he's going to take no for an answer. Shall I use your phone and call security?"

"No!" Meredith said, bracing herself to face Matt's justifiable fury. "Phyllis, go bring him in here, will you?"

Having carefully observed what office the receptionist had headed for, Matt waited impatiently at the reception desk, ignoring the fascinated interest his presence was generating among the secretaries and clerks and the executives getting off the elevators. He saw the receptionist emerge from Meredith's office with another woman, and he took a step forward, fully prepared to go over or around both women if Meredith was foolish enough to refuse to see him. "Mr. Farrell," an attractive brunette in her late twenties said, managing to sound professional despite her wavering smile, "I'm Phyllis Tilsher, Miss Bancroft's secretary. I'm sorry you were made to wait. Will you come with me please?"

Forcing himself not to outpace her, Matt let her usher him to Meredith's office, where she swung open the door and stepped aside. At any other time, the incredible sight that Matt beheld would have made his chest swell with pride: Seated behind a baronial desk at the far end of a richly paneled office that shouted of hushed wealth and quiet dignity, with her golden hair caught up in a shining chignon, Meredith Bancroft looked like a regal young monarch who should have been sitting on a throne instead of a high-backed leather chair—a very pale and worried monarch at the moment. Tearing his eyes from her, he glanced at the secretary and unconsciously began taking charge. "I'm expecting two calls here," he told her quickly, "let me know the instant they come through. Tell anyone else who calls that we're in a budget meeting and can't be disturbed, and don't let anyone else past that door!"

Phyllis nodded and hastily left, closing the door behind her, and Matt headed for Meredith, who was slowly standing up and walking around to his side of the desk. Jerking his head toward the redhead standing near the windows who was studying him with unconcealed fascination, Matt said, "Who is she?"

"Lisa Pontini," Meredith said absently, "an old friend. Let her stay. Why," she added in a state of numb confusion, "are we having a *budget* meeting in here?"

Matt remembered Lisa Pontini's name from years before. Suppressing the urge to pull Meredith into his arms and try to comfort her—both of which he knew she'd reject—he smiled reassuringly and tried to inject a teasing note into his voice. "It'll throw the employees off the track temporarily if they think it's business at its most boring usual up here. Can you think of anything more boring than budgets?" She tried to smile at his humorous logic and couldn't, so Matt said with quiet force, "With a little luck we're going to pull through this with only a few scrapes and no scars. Now, will you trust me and do what I ask?"

Meredith stared at him while it sank in that instead of blaming her and her father for this calamity, he was actually going to step in and help. She straightened slowly, feeling a sudden return of her strength and wits. With a nod she said, "Yes. What do you want me to do?"

Instead of replying, Matt smiled at how quickly and valiantly she was rallying. "Very nice," he said softly. "Chief executive officers never cower."

"They bluff," she concluded, trying to smile.

"Right." He grinned. He started to say more, but the intercom buzzed. Meredith picked up the receiver, listened, and held the phone out to him. "My secretary says David Levinson is on the first line and someone named Steve Salinger is calling you on the other line."

Instead of reaching for it, he said, "Is this a speaker phone?" Realizing he wanted her to be able to listen, Meredith leaned over and pressed the button that enabled everyone in the room to hear what the caller was saying. As soon as she had, Matt jabbed his finger at the flashing light on the second line. "Steve," he said, "is the Lear ready to fly?"

"Sure thing, Matt. I just had her up for a check flight and she's running strong and sweet."

"Good. Hold on." Matt put that call on hold, picked up the other line, and said to Levinson without preamble, "Have you seen the newspapers?"

"I've seen them, and so has Bill Pearson. It's a mess, Matt, and it's going to get worse. Is there anything you want us to do?"

"Yes. Get down to Belleville and introduce yourselves to your new 'client,' then bail the bastard out of jail."

"Do *what?*"

"You heard me. Bail him out of jail and convince him to turn over his files to you as his attorney. When he has, you can do whatever is necessary to keep our divorce decree from getting into the hands of the press— assuming the son of a bitch still has a copy of it. If he doesn't, then do what you have to in order to convince him to forget all the details."

"What were the details? What grounds did he put on the petition?"

"I wasn't in a rational frame of mind when I received a copy of the damned thing, but as I recall, it was desertion and mental cruelty. Meredith is here, I'll ask her." Looking at Meredith, he gentled his voice. "Do you remember any other details—anything else that could be embarrassing to either of us?"

"There was the check for ten thousand dollars my father gave you to pay you off."

"What check? I don't know anything about that, and there's no mention of it in any of my papers."

"My copy of the decree refers to it and says you acknowledge receiving it."

Levinson heard all that, and his voice reeked with irony. "That's just damned great! The press will have a field day conjecturing about what was so wrong with your wife that you, who didn't have a cent at the time, couldn't stomach her, even with her money."

"Don't be an ass!" Matt interrupted furiously before Levinson said anything else to upset Meredith. "They'll paint me as a gold digger who deserted his wife. All of this conjecture is irrelevant if you get down to Belleville and get Spyzhalski under control before he starts spilling the works tomorrow."

"That may not be so easy. According to the news, he's determined to represent himself. He's obviously a crank who's looking forward to putting on a big show for the benefit of the court and the press."

"Change his mind!" Matt snapped. "Get a postponement on his hearing, and get him out of town where the press can't find him. I'll take care of the bastard after that."

"If he has files, they'll have to be turned over eventually as evidence. And his other victims are going to have to be notified."

"You can deal with that later with the prosecuting attorney," Matt said curtly. "My plane is waiting for you at Midway. Call me when you've taken care of everything."

"Right," Levinson said.

Without bothering to say good-bye, Matt ended that call, and returned to his pilot. "Get ready to take off for Belleville, Illinois, within the hour. You'll have two passengers. There'll be three passengers on the way back, and you'll be making a stop somewhere to unload one of them. They'll tell you where."

"Okay."

When he hung up, Meredith gazed at him, a little dazed by his methods and speed. "How," she asked on a choked laugh, "do you intend to take care of Spyzhalski?"

"Leave that to me. Now, get Parker Reynolds on the phone. We're not out of this yet."

Meredith obediently called Parker. The moment he answered, it was obvious he regarded the situation as grave. "Meredith, I've been trying to reach you all morning, but they're holding your calls."

"I'm so sorry about all this," she said, too worried to consider the inadvisability of having this conversation on the speaker phone. "Sorrier than I can say."

"It's not your fault," he said with a harsh sigh. "Right now we have to decide what to do. I'm getting bombarded with warnings and advice. That arrogant son of a bitch you married actually had his secretary call me this morning to give me instructions about how I should handle things. His *secretary!* Then my board of directors decided I should make a public statement disclaiming all knowledge of any of this—"

"Don't!" Matt interrupted furiously.

"Who the hell said don't?" Parker demanded.

"I said it, and I'm the son of a bitch she married," Matt snapped, his eyes narrowing on Lisa Pontini, who was suddenly sliding down the wall, convulsed with laughter, her hand clamped over her mouth. "If you make a statement like that, it will look to everyone like you're throwing Meredith to the wolves."

"I have no intention of doing anything of the sort!" Parker countered angrily. "Meredith and I are engaged."

Tenderness and gratitude poured through Meredith at his words. She'd thought that he wanted out of their engagement and now, when things were worse than ever, he was standing by her. Unaware of what she was doing, she smiled softly at the phone.

Matt saw the smile and his jaw tightened, but he kept his mind on the problem at hand. "At one o'clock today," he informed Parker, and Meredith as well, "You, Meredith, and I are going to give a joint press conference. If and when the details of our divorce decree are made public, Meredith will look like she was the victim of desertion and mental cruelty."

"I realize that," Parker bit out.

"Good," Matt replied sarcastically. "Then you ought to be able to follow the rest of this: During our press conference we're going to make a show of solidarity. We're going to proceed on the assumption that the details of the divorce will come out, and we're going to neutralize them in advance."

"How?"

"By standing up in front of everyone and behaving like a nice close-knit little family who are wholeheartedly in empathy with one another and particularly with Meredith. I want every journalist who's present to be able to get enough of an earful and an eyeful this afternoon to last them for weeks so they'll get out of our lives and stay out. I want them to leave that press conference room drowning in sympathy and convinced there's no ill will among us." Pausing, Matt looked at Meredith and said, "Where can we assemble all the reporters? Intercorp's shareholders room isn't very large—"

"Our auditorium is," Meredith said quickly. "It's already decorated for our annual Christmas pageant, so it's clean and ready."

"Did you hear that?" Matt demanded of Parker.

"Yes!"

"Then get over here as soon as you can so we can prepare a statement," Matt ordered, and immediately hung up. He glanced over at Meredith, and the way she was looking at him went a long way to banish the jealousy that had been eating him since she'd smiled at Parker's voice; her eyes were filled with admiration, gratitude, and a little awe. And a lot of apprehension.

He was about to say something reassuring, when Lisa Pontini suddenly shoved away from the wall, her lips trembling with amusement. "I used to wonder how you managed to make Meredith throw caution aside and go to bed with you, get pregnant, get married, and nearly go to South America with you—all within a few days. Now I understand what happened. You're not a tycoon, you're a *typhoon*. By any chance," she asked, "have you ever voted democrat?"

"Yes," Matt admitted dryly. "Why?"

"I just wondered," she lied, noting Meredith's quelling frown. Sobering, Lisa held out her hand to him, and quietly said, "I'm very happy to meet Meredith's husband at last."

Matt grinned at her and returned her handclasp. He decided he liked Lisa Pontini immensely.

44

*A*t Matt's suggestion, Meredith had invited all the store's senior executives and upper level managers to attend the news conference, in an effort to eliminate speculation among store employees by providing them with fact, albeit secondhand fact, from their managers. In order to soften up the press,

Bancroft's deli department had been ruthlessly raided on Meredith's orders, and all 150 reporters who were now taking their seats in the auditorium had been partaking of liberal amounts of imported food and expensive wine.

As she waited in the wings offstage with the two men who'd rushed to her aid, Meredith felt not only gratitude, but an odd sense of well-being. Forgotten was the bargain Matt had inflicted on her and the argument she'd had with Parker the other night; all that mattered right then was that both men had wanted to help when she needed them. Trying to hold off an inevitable attack of nervousness, she looked at Matt. He was standing just a few feet away from Parker, glancing over the public statement they'd all collaborated on, but which he had mostly written. Parker was doing exactly the same thing, and Meredith knew *why* they were: Both men were deliberately avoiding the need to speak to, or even look at, each other. In her office they'd treated each other with cool civility while they debated the exact wording of the statement that was about to be read by Bancroft's head of public relations, but their mutual dislike had been glaringly obvious. Both of them had agreed that when they walked out on that stage, there would be a show of friendly unity, but Meredith wasn't certain they'd be able to put up a convincing pretense when they so obviously couldn't stand each other.

Now, as she studied the pair of them, their instinctive animosity seemed almost funny, because she was suddenly struck with how very similar they were in some ways. Both of them were unusually tall and undeniably handsome—Parker in an impeccably tailored blue three-piece suit with his Phi Beta Kappa key pinned discreetly to his vest pocket, and Matt in a beautiful charcoal suit with a faint gray pinstripe that made his shoulders look even broader. Parker, with his sun-streaked blond hair and blue eyes, had always reminded her of Robert Redford, and never more than today. Glancing at Matt to make a comparison, she studied the tough angles of his jaw and cheek, the sternly molded lips and the thick dark brown hair that had been beautifully cut and shaped. On second thought, Meredith decided abruptly, the two men were not alike at all. Parker was the image of cultured, civilized urbanity, while Matt was . . . not. Even now there was a reckless, brash forcefulness about Matt that not even eleven years of acquired social polish could hide. In all actuality, his face was too rugged, too harsh, to be conventionally handsome—except for his eyelashes, Meredith thought with an inner smile. He had absurdly thick, lush eyelashes.

Suddenly the noise level in the auditorium dropped, lights brightened, a microphone squealed, and Meredith's pulse began to hammer, banishing all thoughts of anything but the next few minutes. "Ladies and gentlemen," Bancroft's P.R. director said, "before Miss Bancroft, Mr. Reynolds, and Mr.

Farrell come out here to answer any additional questions you may have, they have asked me to read the following statement, which contains the facts, as they know them, of the incident that has caused you to assemble here today. The statement is as follows: 'Three weeks ago, the irregularities in the divorce decree supposedly obtained by one Stanislaus Spyzhalski were first noted by Mr. Reynolds. Immediately thereafter, Miss Bancroft and Mr. Farrell met to discuss the matter . . . ' "

As the statement neared its end, Parker and Matt put down their copies of it and started toward Meredith, positioning themselves on either side of her. "Ready?" Parker asked her. She nodded, nervously smoothing the collar of her pink wool suit. "You look lovely," he reassured her, but Matt frowned worriedly at her tense features.

"Relax," he warned her. "We are all victims, not perpetrators, so don't go out there looking stiff and secretive or they'll keep digging, looking for something we're hiding. Be natural and smile at them. Meredith," he said urgently, watching her struggling to draw an even breath. "I can't pull this off alone! I need your help!"

That remark seemed so incredible coming from a man who'd barged past every obstacle she tried to put in his way lately that it wrung a laugh from her when only a moment before she'd been consumed with angry dread at having to discuss her private life in public. "That's my girl," he said with an approving grin.

"Like hell she is!" Parker snapped as the P.R. director finished reading and spoke their names, which was their cue to walk onstage.

Blinding flashes exploded the instant they walked onstage, minicam lights tracked them like bright white eyeballs as the trio stepped up to the bank of microphones at the podium. As had been decided, Matt opened up the interview to questions, but Meredith was startled by the humorous tack he used to do it: "So nice of you to attend our little impromptu gala, ladies and gentlemen," he said. "If we'd have known yesterday that you were going to be here today, we'd have brought in some circus elephants to do justice to the occasion." He paused for the laughter to subside, and then he said, "We'll be up here for only five minutes, so let's keep the questions short and to the point. I have all the time in the world to spend with you," he joked, pausing again for the laughter to subside, "but Meredith has department stores to run and Parker has meetings this afternoon."

His deliberate, congenial use of Parker's and Meredith's first names caused a momentary startled silence, but the anticipated pandemonium erupted almost instantly with questions being shouted from everywhere—

the loudest from a CBS reporter in the front row: "Mr. Farrell, why was your marriage to Miss Bancroft kept secret?"

"If you're asking why you didn't know about it at the time," Matt replied smoothly, "the answer is that neither Meredith nor I were of any particular public interest eleven years ago."

"Mr. Reynolds," a *Chicago Sun-Times* reporter called out, "will your marriage to Miss Bancroft be postponed?"

Parker's smile was brief and cool. "As you heard in the statement that was read, Meredith and F—and Matt," he corrected himself trying to smile pleasantly at Matt, "will have to go through the process of a legal divorce. Naturally, our marriage will have to be postponed until that's final. To do otherwise would make Meredith guilty of bigamy."

The word *bigamy* was a mistake, and the instant he said it, Meredith could sense Parker's anger with himself. She could also feel the reporters' collective mood switch from the relaxed one Matt had tried to create to one of businesslike intensity. Even the questions changed in tone: "Mr. Farrell, have you and Miss Bancroft filed for a divorce yet?" a reporter demanded. "If so, on what grounds and where?"

"No," Matt said, smoothly stepping in. "We haven't yet."

"Why not?" a woman from WBBM demanded.

Matt gave her a look of comic chagrin. "My confidence in attorneys is a little low right now. Would you care to recommend one?"

Meredith knew how hard he was trying to keep the mood light, and when the next question was fired at her, she swore to help him by doing her share. "Miss Bancroft," a man from *USA Today* was shouting, "how do you feel about all this?" She saw Matt lean slightly forward and open his mouth to try to fend the question off, but she stepped in herself. "The truth is," she said with an unconsciously endearing smile, "I haven't felt this painfully *conspicuous* since I had to walk onstage in the sixth-grade nutrition play, dressed up like a prune."

Her unexpected reply startled shouts of laughter from the crowd, but Matt's unguarded reaction caused flashes to explode all over the room as he turned his head and gazed down at her with a startled, beaming grin.

The question Meredith had dreaded came next: "Mr. Farrell, on what grounds did you two file for divorce eleven years ago?"

"We aren't certain," Matt joked with the woman reporter, giving her a disarming smile. "We've discovered that the documents we each received from Spyzhalski don't match."

"For Miss Bancroft," a *Tribune* reporter said, and when Meredith looked at her she said, "Could you tell us why your marriage broke up?"

Meredith knew this was one question Matt couldn't answer for her and desperation provided inspiration. In what she hoped was an amused voice, she said ruefully, "At the time, I seemed to think that life with Mr. Farrell might be . . . boring." While they were still laughing, she added more seriously, "I was a city girl, and very young, and Matt left for the wilds of South America just a few weeks after we were married. Our lives were on very different courses."

"Is there any chance of a reconciliation?" an NBC newsman asked.

"Of course not," Meredith replied automatically.

"That's ridiculous after all these years," Parker added.

"Mr. Farrell?" the same newsman prodded. "Would you care to answer that question?"

"No," he said implacably.

"Is that your answer, or are you declining to answer?"

"Take it whichever way you'd like," Matt replied with a slight smile that didn't reach his eyes, then he nodded to another reporter to ask his question. They came fast and furious, but the worst ones had already been asked, and Meredith let the noise swirl around her, feeling strangely calm. A few minutes later Matt looked around at the audience and said, "Our time is about up. We all hope that you've had your questions answered. Parker," he said with an admirable imitation of conviviality, "do you have anything to add?"

Parker matched his smile. "I think everything has already been said that needed to be, Matt. Now let's clear out of here and let Meredith get back to running this place."

"Before you go," one woman called out imperatively, ignoring the attempt to close the conference, "I'd like to say that you—all three of you are handling this with extraordinary grace. Particularly you, Mr. Reynolds, since you're rather caught in the middle of something you had no control over—then or now. One might expect you to be feeling a certain amount of antagonism for Mr. Farrell for partially causing the delay of your marriage to Miss Bancroft."

"There's no reason for antagonism," Parker said with a killer smile. "Matt Farrell and I are civilized men and we're handling this in the friendliest of ways. We—all three of us—are caught in unusual circumstances that can and will be easily remedied. In fact, this whole problem is little different from a business contract that wasn't properly executed originally and now has to have the T's crossed."

❧

Lisa was waiting in the wings to catch Meredith's hand and give her a hug. "Come upstairs with us," Meredith whispered, hoping Lisa's presence might force Matt and Parker to behave more civilly to each other. As they rode upstairs in the same elevator that was crowded with shoppers, a woman in the back nudged the woman beside her. "That's Meredith Bancroft with her husband and her fiancé," she said in a carrying whisper. "One of each—isn't that something? And *that's* Matthew Farrell, the husband. He dates movie stars!"

Meredith's color rose at the first sentence, but no one said anything until they were safely within the privacy of Meredith's office. Lisa broke the silence by giving Meredith another hug and a laughing look. "You were wonderful, Mer! Brilliant!"

"I wouldn't go that far," Meredith said weakly.

"No, you were! I couldn't believe it when you said you'd had to dress up like a prune in the sixth grade. That's not at all like your usual proper self." Turning to Matt, she added, "You have an excellent effect on her."

"Don't you have something you're being paid to do?" Parker snapped.

Lisa, who worked incredibly long hours, often after the store was closed, shrugged. "I put in more hours here than I'm paid for as it is."

"I do have things I have to do," Meredith said wryly. Parker stepped forward and kissed her cheek. Smiling into her eyes, he said, "I'll see you Saturday night."

Matt gave Meredith two seconds to decline, and when she hesitated, he looked at Parker and stated flatly, "I'm afraid you won't."

"Now, look, Farrell! Saturdays may be yours for the next eleven weeks, but this one is mine. It happens to be Meredith's thirtieth birthday, and our plans were made weeks ago. We're going to Antonio's."

Turning to Lisa, Matt said shortly, "Do you have plans for Saturday?"

"Nothing I can't change, actually," Lisa said, startled.

"Fine, we'll make it a foursome," he decreed. "But not at Antonio's. It's too public and too bright in there. We'll be recognized in seconds. I'll pick the place." Irrationally annoyed because Meredith hadn't told Parker no, he nodded curtly and left.

Parker followed on his heels, but Lisa lingered, a dazed expression on her face as she sank down on the arm of a chair. "My God, Mer," she said, laughing, "no wonder you agreed to his bargain. That is the most amazing man I've ever met—"

"There's nothing funny about any of this," Meredith replied, refusing to comment on Matt's personal qualities. "My father isn't supposed to read or watch anything on his cruise that isn't completely frivolous. If he decides to break the doctor's rules and watch the news, I'll be lucky if we don't have to send a medical evacuation plane for him."

"If I were you," Lisa said in disgust, "I'd be sending fighter jets out to get him, after what he did eleven years ago!"

"Don't make me think about that now, it only drives me insane with frustration. When he comes home, he and I will have it out. I've thought about all this for days, though, and in fairness to my father, I think he probably believed he was protecting me from a fortune hunter who would break my heart in the end."

"So he broke it instead!"

Meredith hesitated then quietly admitted, "Something like that." Then she forced her personal life out of her mind for now, because that was the only way she could cope. "I'll see you Saturday," she told Lisa.

45

At 4:30 the following afternoon Matt glanced up from the conference table where he was meeting with three of his executives and reached for the telephone. "If it's not an emergency," he told Eleanor before she could give a reason for interrupting him, "I don't want to hear about it until I'm done here."

"Miss Bancroft is on the line," she said with a smug smile in her voice. "Does that constitute an emergency?"

"Yes, it does," he said wryly, but as he answered Meredith's call, he wasn't feeling especially pleasant. He'd phoned her late the previous afternoon to tell her Spyzhalski was under control and in a place reporters couldn't get to him. Her secretary had said Meredith was going to be in meetings for several hours, so rather than let her stay in suspense, Matt dictated a carefully worded message to the secretary and asked her to take it to Meredith. When she didn't bother to call him back last night, he'd wondered if she was too busy celebrating the news in bed with Reynolds to bother. All week the possibility that she was still sleeping with her fiancé had been haunting him. Last night it had kept him awake until dawn. Flicking a curt glance of apology at the men seated around the conference table, Matt picked up the phone.

"Matt," she said, sounding harassed, "I know this is your night, but I have a meeting at five o'clock, and I'm swamped with work."

"At the risk of sounding inflexible," he said in a cool, implacable voice, "a deal's a deal."

"I know," she replied with an exasperated sigh, "but besides having to be here late, I also have to bring some work home with me, and come in again tomorrow morning. I'm really not up to a big night out or a big confrontation with you either," she added with a trace of wry humor.

In a tone that conveyed his unwillingness to cooperate, he said, "What are you suggesting?"

"I was hoping you'd be willing to meet me here, and we could have an early dinner, somewhere casual and close by."

Matt's annoyance evaporated, but on the off chance she was trying to taper him off by setting a precedent for quick public dates, he added in a polite but firm voice, "That's fine. I have a briefcase full of my own work. I'll bring it along and after dinner we can spend a quiet, productive evening at—your place or mine?"

She hesitated. "Will you promise we'll work? I mean, I don't want to have to . . . to have to . . ."

His lips twitched with a smile as her voice trailed off. Obviously she did have pressing work, and equally obviously she was worried that he would try to maneuver her into bed. "We'll work," he promised.

Her relief came out in a laughing sigh. "Okay. Why don't you meet me here about six o'clock? There's a good restaurant just across the street. We can go to my apartment afterward."

"Good enough," he said, completely willing to adapt his schedule to hers as long as she didn't try to avoid him. "Are the reporters leaving you alone?"

"I've had a few calls, but we gave them such a show yesterday, I think it's all going to die a natural death now. I talked to Parker last night and again this morning, and he's being left alone too."

Matt didn't give a damn if reporters devoured Parker alive, and he wasn't thrilled by the discovery that she'd talked to him twice since the press conference when she'd not bothered to call Matt until then. Conversely, he was vastly relieved that she apparently hadn't been with him last night, so he said that was good news, and that he'd come up to her office around six o'clock.

After shouldering his way through the crowds of Christmas shoppers on the main floor at six o'clock, the relative silence on Meredith's floor when Matt stepped off the elevator was a welcome relief. Off to his right, two secretaries were working late, but the receptionist and all the others had already left. At the opposite end of the carpeted corridor, Meredith's office door was open and he could see a group of men and one woman seated in there. Her secretary's desk was cleared, her computer covered for the night, so rather than sitting down in the reception area, Matt took off his coat and perched his hip on the secretary's desk, pleased with this unexpected opportunity to see how Meredith worked and what sorts of things occupied her days. Everything about her intrigued him. It always had.

Unaware of Matt's presence outside her office, Meredith looked at the invoice Gordon Mitchell, the general merchandise manager in charge of women's dresses and accessories, had just handed her. "You bought three hundred dollars' worth of gold metal buttons?" she said with a puzzled smile. "Why are you showing me this? It's certainly within your budget."

"Because," he replied blandly, "those gold buttons are the reason for that sales increase in women's dresses and ready to wear that you've been watching happen all week. I thought you'd like to know."

"You bought them and had them sewn on locally, is that it?"

"That's it," he said, stretching out his legs and looking pleased. "If a dress or a suit has gold metal buttons on it, they walk out of here. It's a craze."

Meredith gazed at him levelly, avoiding looking at Theresa Bishop, the vice president of creative merchandising, whose job it was to predict fashion trends far in advance. "I can't completely share your satisfaction," she told him quietly. "Theresa advised us long ago, after she returned from a trip to New York, that one of the continuing fashion trends was going to be clothing decorated with gold metal buttons. You ignored her. The fact that you belatedly bought the buttons and had them sewn on now can't possibly compensate for the sales we lost before and while you were doing it. What else do you have to report?"

"Very little," he snapped.

Ignoring his attitude, Meredith reached out and pressed a button on the computer screen that showed sales in the past four hours in all the departments under his supervision there and in the branch stores across the country. "Your accessory sales are fifty-four percent higher than over this same day last year. You're doing something right there."

"Thank you, Madam President," he said snidely.

"I seem to recall that you hired a new manager for accessories, and he brought in a new buyer. Is that right?"

"Perfectly correct, as always!"

"What's happening with Donna Karan's DKNY line you bought so much of?" she continued, impervious to his tone.

"It's doing fantastic, exactly as I thought it would."

"Good. What do you intend to do with all those moderate skirts and blouses you bought?"

"I'm going to keystone them and get them out of here."

"All right," she said reluctantly, "but mark them all Special Purchase and keep our labels out of them. I mean that. I was on the third floor today and I saw some blouses with Bancroft labels in them and a price tag of eighty-five dollars. They weren't worth forty-five dollars."

"They are when they have a Bancroft label in them!" he shot back. "That label is worth something to customers. I shouldn't have to remind you of that."

"It *won't* be if we start sticking it on junk. Get those blouses off that floor and onto clearance racks tomorrow. I mean that, and cut the labels out of them. You know which ones I mean. What about the bucket goods you were so high on?"

"I bought them. I've seen the merchandise—mostly costume jewelry, some of it very nice."

Ignoring his sulky, clipped reply, Meredith said levely, "Just keep the bucket goods on the right counters. I don't want to see that stuff mixed in with expensive costume jewelry."

"I said," he bit out, "it's nice stuff."

Meredith leaned back in her chair, studying him in lengthening silence, while the other vice presidents looked on. "Gordon, why are you and I suddenly at odds over the kind of merchandise that Bancroft's will and will not sell? You used to be adamant about maintaining only high-quality merchandise. All of a sudden you're making buying decisions that are better suited to a low-end department store chain than to us."

When he didn't deign to reply, Meredith abruptly leaned forward in her chair, dropped the subject, dismissed him as if he weren't still there, and turned her attention to Paul Norman, the general merchandising manager in charge of home products, and the only one she hadn't yet addressed. "As usual, your departments are all looking good, Paul," she said, smiling at him. "Appliances and furniture sales are up twenty-six percent over this week last year."

"Twenty-seven," he corrected her with a grin. "The computers adjusted from twenty-six to twenty-seven just before I walked in."

"Nice work," she said sincerely, then she chuckled, recalling the sales flyers they'd been able to put in the newspapers, offering stereo components for extraordinarily low prices. "Electronic items are running out of our stores like they had legs. Are you trying to put Highland Superstores out of business?"

"I would *love* to."

"So would I," she admitted, then she sobered and looked at the entire group assembled around the desk. "We're looking good nationwide—everywhere but the New Orleans store. We lost sales the day of the bomb scare, and they stayed down for the next four days for the same reason." She glanced at the vice president of advertising. "Is there any possibility that we'll get some additional advertising time on any of the New Orleans radio stations, Pete?"

"Not in a time slot worth having. We've gone ahead with the increased print advertising. That will help recover some of our losses from the bomb scare."

Satisfied they'd covered everything, Meredith glanced around at the group and smiled warmly. "That about does it. We're acquiring the property for the Houston store, and we're hoping to break ground on the project in June. Have a nice weekend, everyone."

As the group started to stand, Matt went over to a sofa in the reception area and picked up a magazine as if he'd been reading it, but he was so damned proud of the way she'd handled herself that he couldn't stop grinning. The only thing that hadn't pleased and impressed him was her interaction with the one executive who'd hassled her; it seemed to Matt that stronger measures had been called for, then and there, to cut him down to size. The executives filed out of her office and passed him by without a glance, their conversations a jumbled garble of retailing terms and wishes for a good weekend. Putting the magazine down, Matt started back to Meredith's doorway, then drew up short because two men had remained in her office. And Meredith wasn't smiling at whatever they were telling her.

With equal parts of guilt and curiosity, Matt resumed his former position at the secretarial desk, only now he stood in open view with his coat folded over his arm.

Unaware of how late it was, Meredith studied the memo Sam Green had just handed her, which showed a continuing and dramatic increase in the number of shares of Bancroft's stock being bought up on the stock exchange. "What do you make of it?" she asked the attorney, frowning.

"I hate to tell you this," he said, "but I did some checking today, and there are whispers on Wall Street that someone wants to take us over."

Meredith made a physical effort to look calm and collected, but inwardly she was reeling from the thought of a takeover attempt. "Not now.

It wouldn't make any sense. Why would another department store chain, or any other entity, decide to take us over at a time like this, when we're in debt up to our ears for all our expansion costs?"

"For one thing, because we couldn't afford to fight off an attempt right now—we don't have the money to put up a long, serious battle."

Meredith already knew that, but she still shook her head and said, "It wouldn't make sense to go after us now. All they'd get by acquiring us is a lot of debts they'd have to pay off." But she and Sam both knew that as a long-range investment, Bancroft & Company could be a very attractive acquisition. "How long before you'll know the names of whoever is buying our stock?"

"Another few weeks before we get notification from all the stockbrokers who handle the individual transactions, but we're only notified if the new shareholder actually takes custody of the stock certificates. If the certificates stay in the brokers' custody, we're never notified of the shareholder's identity."

"Can you put together an updated list of new shareholders whose names we do know?"

"Sure thing," he said, and turned, leaving Meredith alone in the office with Mark Braden. Since what she needed to discuss with the director of security was very confidential, Meredith got up to close her office door and glanced at her watch to see how much time she had until Matt arrived. Her gaze ricocheted from her watch, which showed 6:20, to the tall figure in her doorway, and her heart gave an inexplicable lurch at the sight of him. "How long have you been waiting?" she asked Matt, starting forward.

"Not long." Unwilling to rush her when she obviously had something more to do, he added, "I'll wait out here until you finish."

Meredith paused to consider if there was any reason to close Matt out of the discussion she needed to have with Mark about Gordon Mitchell. Deciding there wasn't, she smiled at him and said, "You can come in, but will you close the door?" Matt did as she asked, and Meredith quickly introduced Mark Braden to him, then she turned to Mark. "You heard Gordon's explanations and you witnessed his attitude for yourself. It's a complete departure from everything he used to say and do. What do you think?"

Mark shot a speculative glance at Matt, but when Meredith nodded for him to go on, he said bluntly, "I think he's on the take."

"You keep saying that, but can you show me one piece of evidence to prove he's getting kickbacks from anyone?"

"No," he said, looking frustrated. "He hasn't acquired any expensive new toys like boats and planes, and he hasn't bought any new real estate that

I can trace. He has a mistress, but she's been around for years. He and his wife and kids still live pretty much like they always have. In short, there's no evidence he's living any higher than before, and there's no motive either—he doesn't have expensive habits like drugs or gambling."

"Maybe he's innocent," Meredith said, but she didn't believe it.

"He's not innocent, he's cautious and he's smart," Mark argued. "He's been in retailing long enough to know how closely we watch merchandisers and buyers for any sign they're taking kickbacks. He's covering his tracks. I'll keep digging around," Mark promised, and with a curt nod he walked past Matt.

"I'm sorry," Meredith told Matt as she loaded her briefcase with work she needed to do tonight. "I didn't realize how long that other meeting went."

"I enjoyed listening to it," he said, and she shot a stunned look at him as she snapped the locks closed on her briefcase.

"How much of it did you hear?"

"About twenty minutes of it."

"Any questions?" she teased, but the warmth of his smile, the lazy boldness in his heavy-lidded gray gaze, made her feel overheated, so she hastily looked away and kept her gaze averted.

"Three questions," Matt said, watching the way she was avoiding looking at him. "Four, actually," he amended.

"What questions are those?" she asked, coming toward him and feigning absorption in flicking an imaginary speck off her coat.

"What are bucket goods, what is keystone, and why are you avoiding my eyes?"

She made a valiant attempt to give him a long, direct, calm look, but his wicked grin was almost her undoing. "I didn't realize I was avoiding your eyes," she lied, then she explained. "Keystone means to sell something for only twice what we paid for it. Bucket goods are things like jewelry and accessories that we occasionally buy in large quantities, sight unseen, for a dollar each—usually they're overstock from our regular suppliers. What was your fourth question?" she asked while they waited for the elevators.

How long is it going to be before you trust me? he thought. *How long before you'll go to bed with me? How long before you stop dancing out of my reach?* He asked the last question because it was the least inflammatory one, and because he was curious to see her reaction: "How long are you going to keep dancing this avoidance waltz with me?"

She started at his bluntness, then she shot him an amused, cocky look that made him long to kiss her. "Just as long as you keep trying to call the tune."

"I think you're starting to enjoy it," Matt remarked with a disgruntled sidelong glance.

Meredith stared at the lighted down arrow on the elevator buttons, but she smiled and said with more candor than she'd intended, "I always enjoyed your company, Matt. I don't like your motives this time around."

"I told you the other night what my motives are," Matt said firmly, the footsteps behind them silenced by the thick blue carpet.

"I don't like the motives behind your motives," she clarified.

"I don't *have* motives behind my motives!" Matt said in a low, forceful voice.

Behind them a laughing male voice said, "Maybe not, but what you do have are people behind you people, and your conversation is getting awfully deep for us to follow without a map."

Their heads jerked around in unison, and Mark Braden raised his brows, his smile veiling the warning that he'd deliberately given them that other employees were listening. "Have a nice weekend, everyone," Meredith said with a bright artificial smile at the three secretaries.

On the first floor they wended their way, leading with their briefcases, through the throngs of shoppers as they headed for the restaurant across the street. At one of the counters, however, Meredith stopped. "I want to introduce you to Mrs. Millicent," she told Matt. "She retired a year ago and comes back to help us out at Christmas. She'll be thrilled to meet you— she's kept a record of all the famous people she's seen here for over twenty-five years, and she especially dotes on movie stars."

"I don't qualify in either category," Matt pointed out.

"You are famous, and besides, you've dated all sorts of glamorous movie stars, so she'll think she's died and gone to heaven."

Vaguely displeased at Meredith's deliberate and ostensibly unconcerned reminder of what she perceived to be the women he'd slept with, Matt automatically followed her as she sidled through a six-deep throng of women shoppers blocking the counter and part of the aisle.

His briefcase banged into a wide derriere and hooked on a purse strap, but Meredith was obviously an old hand at this, because she sidled right through. He was looking down, untangling his briefcase handle from the purse strap when the owner of the purse, mistaking him for an inept purse-snatcher, let out an outraged cry of alarm and yanked on her purse. "Your strap caught on my briefcase—" Matt explained, glancing up at her.

Her mouth dropped open in shock as she recognized his face. "Aren't you—aren't you Matt Farrell?"

"No," Matt lied, and rudely shouldered past her, trying to get to Meredith through the sea of coats and purses. Meredith looked over her shoulder, obviously impatient at his delay, and held out her gloved hand to pull him forward through the throng, then she turned back to the elderly salesclerk she was talking to. The loudspeakers were playing "Jingle Bells," and the page system was chiming, and over it all was the loud hum of women calling for salesclerks to help them. In growing discomfort Matt waited beside her at a crowded counter which he now realized was surrounded by women who were pawing through the nylon stockings and pantyhose that dripped from revolving chrome racks. They hung from overhead wires, too, waving in front of his nose, blowing enticingly in the air currents from the heating vents and revolving doors just beyond.

With relief he heard Meredith say his name, and he leaned forward to meet the fascinated sixty-two-year-old who was scrutinizing his every feature. "How do you do," Matt said, leaning forward to shake her outstretched hand. As he did so, a stocking draped itself across his head from the overhead wire, and he had to pause to untangle himself from it. He held out his hand again, and it draped itself languorously over his cashmere-clad shoulder.

"Why, Meredith!" Mrs. Millicent burst out excitedly, watching him bat the nylon off his shoulder. "He reminds me of Cary Grant!" Meredith cast a skeptical glance at him just in time to see another stocking drape itself over his ear. He yanked this one down and put it on the counter, and she tore her laughing gaze from him, then she quickly concluded her conversation with Mrs. Millicent.

With Matt in the lead, they retraced their way through the crowd. Unfortunately, when they were almost to the aisle, the shopper who'd mistaken him for a purse-snatcher pointed him out to everyone within hearing. "That's him!" she called, oblivious to Meredith, who was right on his heels, blocked from view by his shoulders. "That's Matthew Farrell—Meredith Bancroft's husband, the one who used to date Meg Ryan and Michelle Pfeiffer!"

A lady on Matt's right thrust her shopping bag at him. "Could I have your autograph?" she pleaded, searching in her purse for a pen in the apparent hope he would sign the bag. Matt reached for Meredith's arm, shouldering past the woman. Behind him, she announced in offended anger to everyone else, "Who wants his autograph anyway? I just remembered that he also dated a porn queen!"

Matt could feel the tension radiating from Meredith even after they dashed through the revolving doors and were outside in the frigid night air. "Despite what you're thinking," he said defensively, knowing how much she hated notoriety, "people don't ask me for autographs. It's only happening now because our faces are plastered all over the local news."

She flashed him a dubious look and said nothing.

The situation in the restaurant across the street was worse than her store. The place was packed with Christmas shoppers having early dinners, and they were waiting in double lines in the vestibule. "Do you think we should wait?" Meredith asked him. And before the words were out of her mouth, the buzzing started around them. Opposite them, a woman leaned across the three-foot space that separated her line from the one Matt and Meredith were in. "Excuse me," she said, speaking to Meredith with her eyes on Matt. "Aren't you Meredith Bancroft?" Without waiting for Meredith to answer, she said to Matt, "And that makes *you* Matthew Farrell!"

"Not really," Matt said shortly, and it didn't take the pressure he was exerting on Meredith's arm to make her agree to get out of there.

"Let's go to my apartment and order a pizza," she said when they reached her car in its reserved spot in the parking garage.

Furious with fate for doing this to him, Matt waited while she unlocked the car and got into it, but he stopped her from closing the door. "Meredith," he said firmly, "I have *never* dated a porn queen."

"That's a load off my mind," she said with a sidelong smile, and Matt was surprised and relieved that she'd evidently regained much of her humor and equilibrium. "And I will admit," she added, turning on the ignition and waiting for the old BMW to catch, "Meg Ryan and Michelle Pfeiffer *are* both blondes."

"I know Michelle Pfeiffer very casually," he said, helpless not to defend himself, "and I've never met Meg Ryan."

"Really?" Meredith dryly replied, her hand on the door handle to close it. "Mrs. Millicent was all excited because she was supposedly on your yacht for a cruise."

"She was. I wasn't!"

46

They had pizza and wine at her place—picnic-style, on the floor in front of the fire. They'd finished eating and were having the last of the wine before they tackled the work they'd brought in. Matt leaned forward and reached for his wineglass, surreptitiously watching her gazing into the fire, her arms wrapped around her updrawn knees. She was, he thought, an utterly captivating bundle of contradictions. A few weeks ago he'd watched her walk down the grand staircase at the opera, looking like a regal socialite. At her office today, in a business suit, surrounded by her staff, she was every inch an executive. Tonight, sitting before the fire in jeans that hugged her shapely bottom and a bulky cable-knit sweater that came almost to her knees, she was . . . the girl he had known long ago. Maybe that change from executive to artless girl was why he couldn't gauge her mood or guess her thoughts. Earlier, he'd thought she was upset over the mention of the women allegedly in his life, but all during their meal she'd been delightful company.

Now, as he watched her staring into the fire, he wondered about the faint smile at her lips that had appeared at odd times throughout their meal.

"What's so funny?" he asked idly, and his question unexpectedly made her eyes widen and shoulders start to shake with laughter. "Well?" he prodded, frowning, when she shook her head, folded her arms on her knees, and hid her laughing face in them. "Meredith?" he said a little curtly, and she laughed harder.

"It's you," she managed, giggling. "You, with those stockings clinging to you—" Matt started to grin even before she added merrily, "If you could have seen the look on your face!" She got herself under control, and with her head still in her arms, she turned her laughing face toward him and stole a peek. What she saw made her roll her eyes and dissolve with laughter again. "Cary Grant!" she chortled, her shoulders shaking. "Mrs. Millicent must be getting senile! You no more resemble Cary Grant than a p-panther resembles a p-pussy cat!"

"Which one am I?" he chuckled, but he already knew she likened him to the panther. Lying back, he folded his arms beneath his head and smiled up at the ceiling, utterly contented with his lot in life—for the first time in his life.

"I suppose we'd better get to work," she said finally. "It's eight forty-five already."

Matt rolled reluctantly to his feet, helped her clear away the few remnants of their meal, then walked over to the sofa, unlatched his briefcase, and took out a thirty-page contract he needed to read.

Across from him, Meredith sat down in a chintz-covered chair and took out her own work. Despite her earlier merriment, she'd been vibrantly and uneasily aware of his nearness throughout their meal. Having Matt there, behaving as tamely as the kitten she'd laughed about, was anything but amusing or soothing to her nerves. For unlike Mrs. Millicent, she didn't underestimate the threat he posed—he was that panther, patiently stalking his prey. Unhurried, graceful, predatory, and dangerous. She understood the threat he posed—and even so, she was more hopelessly attracted to him with each hour he was near.

She glanced covertly at him. He was sitting across from her on the sofa, his shirt-sleeves folded back on his forearms, his ankle propped on the opposite knee. As she watched, he put on a pair of gold wire-rimmed glasses that looked incredibly sexy on him, opened a file folder on his lap, and started to read the documents inside it.

He felt her watching him, and he glanced up and saw her staring at the glasses in surprise. "Eyestrain," he explained mildly, then he bent his head and returned his attention to the documents.

Meredith admired his ability to reach a state of instant, intense concentration, but she couldn't come near matching it. She stared into the fire, thinking about what Sam Green had told her. From there her thoughts drifted to the bomb scare in the New Orleans store, the problem with Gordon Mitchell, and the phone call from Parker yesterday, telling her that he'd have to find her another lender to make her the loan for the Houston land. All of it revolved around and around in her mind as fifteen minutes became twenty and then thirty.

Across from her, Matt said quietly, "Want to talk about it?"

Her head jerked around and she saw him watching her, the contract he'd been reading lying discarded in his lap. "No," she said automatically. "It's probably nothing. Nothing you'd be interested in at least."

"Why don't you try me?" he offered in that same calmly reassuring voice.

He looked so competent, so decisive and invincible, sitting there, that Meredith decided to take advantage of what he was offering. She leaned her head against the back of her chair and briefly closed her eyes, but her voice was a ragged sigh. "I have the strangest—the uneasiest—feeling," she admitted, lifting her head and looking at him with unguarded candor, "that something is happening, or going to happen, and it's terrible. Whatever it is, it's terrible."

"Can you isolate the source of your uneasiness?"

"I thought you'd laugh at what I just said," she admitted.

"It's not a laughing matter if you're actually sensing something you're unconsciously aware of. That's instinct, and you should pay close attention to it. On the other hand, your feeling could be coming from stress, or even from my reentry into your life. The last time I was in your life, all hell broke loose for you. You could be superstitiously fearing the same thing will happen again."

She flinched at his accurate summary of her feelings, but she shook her head at the idea that this was the source of her uneasiness. "I don't think it's coming from stress or you. I can't seem to put my finger on what's bothering me."

"Start with remembering as closely as you can—to the hour, if possible—when you first felt it. I don't mean when you stopped to notice it and think it out, but before that. Think back to a sudden feeling of restlessness, or mild confusion, or—"

She gave him a weary, laughing look. "I feel that way most of the time lately."

Matt returned her grin. "That's my fault, I hope." She caught his meaning, drew a shaky breath, obviously to warn him that he'd promised not to get personal tonight, so he returned to the subject at hand. "I meant more a feeling that something is odd—even if it seemed very good, very fortunate at the time."

His last words led her effortlessly to the way she felt when her father told her the presidency was hers, but only because Gordon Mitchell had turned it down. She told Matt about that and he considered it, and said, "Okay, good. That was your instinct warning you that Mitchell wasn't acting predictably or sensibly. Your instincts were right. Look what's happened since then: He's become an executive you can't trust—one who you suspect is taking bribes. Furthermore, he's violating established standards for your store's merchandise and openly opposing you in meetings."

"You put a lot of faith in your instincts, don't you?" she asked with surprise.

He thought of how much he was already gambling on his instinctive belief that the feelings she'd had for him before were still there—faint embers that he was trying to fan into a blaze again. He was letting himself dream of their heat, letting the need for it grow within him with every additional moment he spent with her. If he failed, his defeat would be even more devastating because he was counting so desperately on success. And knowing all that, he was still taking the full risk. "You have no idea," he said with feeling, "how *much* faith I place in them."

Meredith considered all that, and finally said, "The source of my feeling of impending disaster is probably easier to locate than I made it seem. For one thing, we had a bomb scare at our New Orleans store on Monday that cost us a great deal in lost revenue. That's our newest store, and it's barely breaking even. I'm personally guaranteed on its loans. If it starts running at a loss, the income from our other stores will make up the difference, of course."

"Then why are you worried about it?"

"Because," she said with a sigh, "we've expanded so quickly that our debt level is very high. We didn't have much choice—Bancroft's either had to go forward and get into the mainstream of competition or face becoming obsolete. The problem is, we don't have much money on hand to cover us now if something should happen to cause several of our stores to suddenly start losing money."

"Couldn't you borrow it if that happens?"

"Not too easily. We're borrowed up to the teeth right now for all our expansion costs. I'm worried about more than just that though." When he continued to regard her in waiting silence, she admitted, "There's a record number of shares of our stock being traded on the stock market every day. I'd noticed it in the newspapers for the past couple of months, but I assumed investors were reading about us and realizing we're a good long-term investment for their money, and we are. But," she said, drawing a steadying breath before she could make herself say the words, "Sam Green, our attorney, thinks all those shares may be going because someone is getting ready to try to take us over. Sam has contacts on Wall Street, and evidently there are whispers about a takeover attempt on us. Parker caught wind of a similar rumor in October, but we ignored it. It may be true after all. It'll be weeks before we know the names of those who've bought our stock lately. Even when we do, it may not tell us anything significant. If a company wants to keep their intention of taking us over a secret, they won't be buying our stock in their own names. They'll have other people buy it for them as well. They may even be illegally parking the stock in accounts with fake names." She caught herself and gave him a wry look. "You already know all about how it's done, don't you?"

He quirked an amused brow at her. "No comment."

"One company you started to take over a few months ago paid you fifty million just to go away and leave them alone. We couldn't do that, and we don't have the kind of money right now that it would take to try to fight a takeover. God," she finished miserably, "if Bancroft's were to become nothing but a division of some big corporate conglomerate, I couldn't bear it."

"There are steps you can take to protect yourself in advance."

"I know, and the board of directors has been discussing them for two years, but they haven't *done* anything really effective yet." Restlessly, she got up and poked at the fire.

Behind her, Matt said, "Is that the extent of your worries or is there more?"

"More?" she said on a choked laugh, straightening. "There's more, but what it all boils down to, I guess, is that things that never happened before are happening now, and it's giving me a generalized feeling of doom. There's the fear of being a takeover target, and bomb scares, and now Parker can't lend us the money for Houston, so we'll have to deal with a new lender."

"Why can't he?"

"Because Reynolds Mercantile is looking for money right now, not lending big sums of it to overborrowed customers like us. I wouldn't be surprised if poor Parker isn't worried about Bancroft's being able to keep making payments on the loans we already have with him."

"He's a big boy," Man said flatly, shoving papers back into his briefcase, "he can take the heat. If he lent you more money than he should have, it's his own fault, and he'll figure out a way to cut his losses." Every time she mentioned Reynolds, jealousy ate at him like acid, and this was no exception; his mood took a sudden turn for the worse. "You need to get a good night's sleep," he told her, and Meredith simultaneously realized that there was an edge to his voice and that he was getting ready to leave. Surprised by his rather abrupt departure, she walked him to the door, berating herself for dumping all her concerns on him.

He turned in the doorway. "What time are we assembling here for your birthday tomorrow?"

"Seven-thirty?" she suggested.

"Fine."

He stepped into the hall and Meredith moved to the open doorway. "About tomorrow night," she said, "since it's my birthday, I'd like to ask a favor of you."

"What's that?" he asked, putting down his briefcase and shrugging into his coat.

"That you and Parker talk to each other—no stony silences," she warned, "like the way you two acted before the press conference. Agreed?"

That was one mention too many of her precious Parker. Matt nodded, started to say something, hesitated, and then took a step forward and said it. "Speaking of Reynolds," he asked with deceptive calm, "are you still sleeping with him?"

Her mouth dropped open, and she demanded, "What is that supposed to mean?"

"It means that I assume you were sleeping with him, since you were engaged to him, and I'm asking you if you still are."

"Who the hell do you think you are!"

"Your husband."

For some reason the solemn finality of the statement made her heart slam into her ribs. Her hand tightened on the doorknob in a reflexive grab for support. He saw her reaction and added with a slight smile, "It has a nice sound, once you get used to it."

"No, it doesn't," she replied mutinously. But it did—a little.

His smile vanished. "Then let me introduce you to a word that has an even worse sound. If you are still sleeping with Reynolds, that word is *adultery*."

Meredith gave the door a shove that would have sent it crashing into its frame if he hadn't stopped it with his foot and simultaneously hauled her into the hall with his hands on her shoulders. His mouth claimed hers in a kiss that was both rough and tender, his arms drawing her tightly against him. And then he gentled the kiss, brushing his parted lips on hers in a light, exquisite touch that was even harder to resist than the other one. He trailed his lips to her ear and nipped the lobe, his whisper sending shivers down her spine. "I know you want to kiss me back, I can feel it. Why not indulge the impulse," he invited her huskily. "I'm more than willing and completely available . . ."

To her horror, his teasing statements doused her anger and gave her simultaneous impulses to giggle and to do exactly what he suggested.

"If I die in an accident on the way home tonight," he cajoled softly, his mouth sliding over her cheek toward her lips again, "think how guilty you'll feel if you don't."

Pushed another step toward laughter, Meredith opened her mouth to say something duly flippant or, better yet, sarcastic, and the instant she did, his mouth captured hers. His hand clamped the back of her head, holding her mouth to his while his other arm angled down across her back, holding her hips tightly to his. And Meredith was lost. Locked to him from toe to head, possessed by his hands and mouth and tongue, she went down to ignominious defeat. Against his chest, her fists flattened, her hands sliding up his shirt inside his coat, her fingers splaying wide of their own accord, spreading against the muscled warmth of his chest. His tongue stroked intimately against hers, his mouth inexorably forcing hers to open wider, and suddenly Meredith was welcoming the invasion of his tongue, helplessly kissing him back with all the desperation and confusion rioting inside her. As soon as she did, his arm tightened, his mouth starting to move with fierce, devouring hunger over hers, and Meredith felt his own desire beginning to pour through her veins.

In sheer panic she tore free of his mouth and then his grasp. She stepped back into the doorway, her chest heaving, fists clenched at her sides.

"How could you even *consider* sleeping with Reynolds when you kiss me like that?" he demanded in a low, accusing voice.

Meredith managed a look of angry scorn. "How could you break your promise to behave impersonally tonight?"

"We aren't in your apartment," he pointed out, and his ability to twist everything and everyone to suit himself was the last straw. She stepped back, checked the impulse to slam the door in his face and, at the last second, she shut it with a hard snap. Once inside the protection of her own apartment, however, she slumped against the door and her head bent in anguished defeat. The mere fact that he had blackmailed and coerced her into this arrangement would have been enough to make any woman with a spine be able to withstand him for three short months. But not her, she thought furiously, shoving away from the door. Not her. She hadn't even lasted three weeks! She was spineless where he was concerned, putty in his hands. Filled with self-disgust, Meredith wandered toward the sofa, stopping at the end table to pick up Parker's picture. He looked back at her, smiling, handsome, dependable, filled with integrity. Furthermore, he loved her! He'd told her so dozens of times. Matt hadn't—not once! But was that going to stop her from surrendering her pride, her self-respect, to Matthew Farrell? Probably not, she thought bitterly. Not at this rate.

Stuart had said Matt didn't want to hurt her. Based on the way he'd swooped to her rescue yesterday, Meredith was inclined to accept that even now, when she was battered by emotions she didn't want and couldn't control. No, Matt didn't want to hurt her. For a variety of obscure and convoluted reasons, what Matt *did* want was to have her back with him, and *that* was where she'd get hurt. Matt's reputation for womanizing was legendary; he was also completely unpredictable and unreliable. The combination was absolutely guaranteed to break her heart.

She sank down on the sofa and put her face in her hands. He didn't want to hurt her. . . . For a few minutes Meredith contemplated trying to appeal to his protective instinct—the same one that had made him move heaven and earth to help her yesterday. She could tell him honestly, "Matt, I know you don't really want to hurt me, so please go away. I have a nice life planned for myself. don't spoil it for me. I don't mean anything to you—not really. I'm just another conquest to you, a passing fixation you have . . ."

She considered it, but she knew it would be a waste of time. She'd already said as much to him, but to no avail. Matt meant to fight this battle to the very end and emerge victorious—and he was doing it for reasons that were probably clearer to her than to him.

Lifting her head, she stared into the fire, remembering his words: *I'll give you paradise on a gold platter. We'll be a family, we'll have children . . . I'd like six, but I'll settle for one.*

If she told him she couldn't have children, that might make him give up his whole scheme. And the moment she realized it might, Meredith felt as if her heart would shatter, and that reaction made her furious with herself and him. "Damn you!" she told him aloud. "Damn you for making me feel vulnerable like this again."

He didn't want to be a family; he just wanted the novelty, the accomplishment of having her live with him for a while. Sexually she would bore him within days, Meredith knew. Matt was an entirely sensual being; he'd slept with movie stars and exotic models. Meredith was sexually repressed and embarrassingly inept, and she knew it. She'd felt that way eleven years ago with Matt. After their divorce it had taken two years to regain just a little of her self-esteem and the ability to feel some desire. Lisa had insisted that the only complete cure was to sleep with someone else, and Meredith had tried. She'd gone to bed with a university track star who'd been chasing her for months, and it had been disastrous. His panting and pawing had revolted her, while her reticence and ineptitude had frustrated and angered him. Even now she could remember his taunts and they made her shudder: *C'mon, baby, don't just lie there, do something for me. . . . What the hell's the matter with you anyway. . . . How can anybody who looks as hot as you be so cold?* When he tried to consummate the act, something inside her had snapped and she'd fought him off, grabbed her clothes, and fled. Sex, she'd decided, was not for her.

Parker had been her only other lover, and he was different—tender, sweet, undemanding. And even he was disappointed with her in bed; he'd never criticized her openly, but she sensed how he felt.

Meredith flopped back and let her head rest against the arm of the sofa, staring dry-eyed at the ceiling, refusing to cry the tears that ached in her throat. Parker could never have made her feel as miserable as she did now. Never. Only Matt could do this to her. And even so, she wanted him.

The realization hit her unbidden, terrifying, unacceptable. Undeniable.

In just a few days Matt had led her this far along the path of utter and humiliating capitulation. Tears of shame and futility sparkled in her eyes. He didn't even have to say I love you to make her want to throw all her plans for her life away.

Across the room, the antique grandfather clock began to chime the hour of ten. To Meredith it was tolling the end of her peace and serenity.

Matt maneuvered the Rolls out from behind two trucks that were blocking his lane, then he reached for the car phone. The clock on the dash showed ten o'clock, but he didn't hesitate to make his call. Peter Vanderwild answered Matt's call on the second ring, sounding startled and honored by this unprecedented late-night call. "My trip to Philadelphia was a complete success, sir," he told Matt on the erroneous assumption that was why his boss was calling.

"Never mind that now," Matt said impatiently. "What I want to know is if there's any way at all that there could be a leak about us buying up

Bancroft's stock—a leak that would start takeover rumors on Wall Street?"

"No way. I've taken all the usual precautions to cover our identity until it's time to file the SEC papers. Their stock is climbing steadily, so it's naturally costing us more to get it lately."

"I think there's another player in the game," Matt said tersely. "Find out who the hell it is!"

"Someone else actually wants to take them over?" Vanderwild repeated. "I thought that too before, but why? They're a lousy investment right now unless you have a personal reason like yours."

"Peter," Matt warned, "keep your face out of my personal business or you'll be looking through the want ads."

"I didn't mean—that is, I read the newspapers—I apologize—"

"Fine," Matt interrupted. "Get busy checking out the rumors, find out if there really is another player, and if there is one, find out who the hell it is."

The luxury liner lifted gracefully over the heavy Atlantic swells, then glided down in what seemed to Philip Bancroft to be the most annoying, boringly repetitious movement he'd ever been forced to endure. Seated at the captain's table between a senator's wife and a Texas oilman, he listened with feigned interest to the woman who was speaking to him. "We should make port late in the afternoon, the day after tomorrow," she was saying. "Have you enjoyed the cruise so far?"

"Immensely," he lied, stealing a glance at his watch beneath the edge of his tuxedo jacket. It was ten o'clock in Chicago. He could be watching the news right now, or playing cards at the country club, instead of being held prisoner on this floating hotel.

"Will you be staying with friends while we're in Italy?" she asked.

"I don't have friends there," Philip replied. Despite the exasperating tedium, he felt better, stronger, every day. His doctor had been right—he had needed to absent himself completely from the concerns of the world and his business for a while.

"No friends in Italy?" she repeated, trying valiantly to carry the one-sided conversation.

"No. Just an ex-wife," Philip retorted absently.

"Oh. Will you be visiting her?"

"Hardly," Philip replied, and then his hand stilled in shock that he had even referred to the woman he'd thrown out of his home and his life all those years ago. Obviously, all this enforced relaxation was numbing his brain.

47

*F*rom the moment Matt had suggested her birthday celebration become a foursome, Meredith had felt grave doubts about the evening, but when Parker and Lisa arrived within moments of each other, they both looked so determinedly cheerful and festive, she was lulled into thinking it might not be a disaster after all. "Happy birthday, Mer," Lisa said, wrapping her in a tight hug and handing her a gaily wrapped box. "Happy birthday," Parker said, and gave her a small, rather heavy oblong box. "Farrell's not here yet?" he added, glancing around.

"Not yet, but there's wine and hors d'oeuvres in the kitchen. I was just fixing a tray."

"I'll finish and bring it out," Lisa volunteered. "I'm famished." She vanished into the kitchen in a cloud of fringed plum silk.

Scowling at her back, Parker demanded of Meredith, "Why does she dress like that? Why can't she dress like normal people?"

"Because she's special," Meredith said with a firm smile. "You know," she added, giving him a puzzled look, "most men think Lisa is stunning."

"I like the way *you* dress," he said, casting an appreciative glance over her bright red velvet bolero jacket trimmed in gold braid and an attached ascot tie that gave the outfit an air of deceptive innocence. The jacket was open now, revealing a strapless red dress that was nipped in at her narrow waist and gently shirred at the hem. Pointedly ignoring her comment about Lisa, he smiled and said, "Why don't you open my present before Farrell gets here?"

Inside the silver wrapping paper was a blue velvet box, and nestled in satin within it was a stunning sapphire and diamond bracelet. Meredith carefully removed it. "It's beautiful," she whispered while her chest contracted painfully and her stomach clenched into knots. Tears burned her eyes, causing the glittering jewels to blur and waver, and at that moment she knew— she knew that neither the bracelet nor Parker could be hers to keep. Not when she'd already betrayed Parker in her mind and her heart because of her helpless obsession with Matt. Lifting her head, she forced herself to meet

Parker's expectant gaze and held the bracelet out to him. "I'm sorry," she said in a suffocated voice. "It's magnificent, but I—I can't accept this, Parker."

"Why not?" he began, but he already knew the answer to that, had sensed this moment was coming. "So that's the way it is," he said harshly. "Farrell's won."

"Not completely," she said quietly, "but whatever happens between Matt and me, I still couldn't marry you. Not now. You deserve more than a wife who can't seem to control her feelings for another man."

After a moment of tense silence, he said, "Does Farrell know you're breaking our engagement?"

"No!" she explained a little wildly. "And I'd just as soon he *doesn't* know. It will only make him more persistent."

Again he hesitated, and then he reached out, took the bracelet from her hand, and firmly fastened it on her wrist. "I'm not giving up," he said with a grim smile. "I regard this as a minor setback. I really hate that bastard."

The buzzer sounded, Parker looked up, and his gaze riveted on Lisa, who was standing in the kitchen doorway, holding a tray. "How the hell long have you been there, eavesdropping?" he demanded while Meredith went to let Matt into the apartment.

"Not long," she said in what struck him as an unusually gentle voice. "Would you like a glass of wine?"

"No," he said bitterly, "I'd like the whole bottle."

Instead of gloating over his predicament, she filled a glass and brought it to him, her eyes soft and strangely luminous.

Matt stepped through the doorway, and to Meredith it seemed as if the entire living room was overwhelmed by the sheer force of his presence. "Happy birthday," he said, smiling down at her. "You look fantastic," he added, running his eyes over her from the top of her shining golden hair to the tips of her red shoes.

Meredith said thank you and tried not to notice how breathtakingly handsome he looked in a gray suit and vest, gleaming white shirt, and conservative striped tie. Lisa made the first move to lighten the atmosphere. "Hi, Matt," she said, beaming at him. "You look more like a banker tonight than Parker."

"I don't have a Phi Beta Kappa key," Matt joked reluctantly reaching out to shake Parker's hand which was extended to him with equal reluctance.

"Lisa hates bankers," Parker said, letting go of Matt's hand and walking over to the wine bottle. He filled his glass and tossed it down.

"Well, Farrell," Parker said with unprecedented bad manners, "it's Meredith's birthday. Lisa and I remembered it. Where's *your* gift?"

"I didn't bring it here."

"You mean you forgot, don't you?"

"I mean I didn't bring it here."

"Why don't we get going, everyone," Lisa burst out, sharing Meredith's desire to get both men to a public place—preferably a noisy one, where they couldn't spar. "Meredith can open my gift later."

Matt's limousine was waiting at the curb. Lisa got in first, and Meredith followed, deliberately sitting down next to her and effectively eliminating the possibility that the two men would engage in a skirmish over who sat next to whom. The only person who didn't look tense was Joe O'Hara, who added to the tension by saying with a grin, "Evenin', Mrs. Farrell."

Two bottles of Dom Pérignon were reclining in sterling ice buckets beside the car's liquor cabinet. "How about some champagne? I'd love—" Lisa began, but just then the limo rocketed forward into traffic, plastering her to the back of the seat and making her gasp.

"Jesus Christ!" Parker burst out, fighting for balance as he was pressed forward in his rear-facing seat by the same force. "Your idiot driver just cut across four lanes of traffic and ran a red light!"

"He's perfectly competent," Matt replied, raising his voice to be heard over the blaring horns of irate motorists, and no one noticed that an old Chevrolet was racing along in their wake, changing lanes whenever they did, with a kind of defiant desperation. While the limo hurtled toward the expressway, scattering cars in its wake, Matt lifted a bottle of champagne from its icy nest and opened it. "Happy thirtieth birthday," he said, handing Meredith the first glass of champagne. "I'm sorry I missed the last eleven of them—"

"Meredith gets sick on champagne," Parker interrupted. Turning to Meredith with an intimate smile, he added, "Remember the time you got sick on champagne at the Remingtons' anniversary party?"

"Not sick, exactly. Dizzy," Meredith corrected him, puzzled by his tone and his choice of topic.

"You were definitely dizzy," he teased. "And a little giddy. You made me stand out on the balcony with you in the freezing cold. Remember—I gave you my coat to wear. And then Stan and Milly Mayfield joined us and we made a tent out of our coats and stayed outside." He glanced at Matt and said in a coldly superior voice, "Do you know the Mayfields?"

"No," Matt replied, handing Lisa a glass of champagne.

"No, of course you wouldn't," he said dismissively. "Milly and Stan Mayfield are old friends of Meredith's and mine." He said it with the intention of making Matt feel like an outsider, and Meredith hastily brought up a new subject. Lisa quickly joined in, drawing Matt into the discussion. Parker had four more glasses of champagne and contributed two more amusing stories about people he and Meredith knew and whom Matt did not.

The restaurant Matt had chosen was one Meredith had never seen or heard of before, but she loved it the moment they walked into the foyer. Patterned after an English pub, with stained-glass windows and dark wood paneling, the Manchester House had a large lounge that stretched across the entire back of it. The dining rooms, which were on both sides of the foyer, were small and cozy, separated from the lounge section with ivy-covered trellises. The lounge, where they were escorted to wait until their table was ready, was filled with Christmas revelers, including a party of about twenty. Judging from the raucous bursts of laughter from that table and some of the occupants seated on the stools at the bar, nearly everyone had been indulging liberally in Christmas cheer.

"This sure as hell isn't the sort of place I'd have picked to celebrate Meredith's birthday," Parker said with a scornful look at Matt as they all sat down.

Keeping his impatience under control for Meredith's sake, Matt said flatly, "It's not what I'd have picked either, but if we wanted to eat in peace, it had to be somewhere relatively dark and out of the way."

"Parker, it's going to be fun," Meredith promised, and she really did like it—the English atmosphere and the upbeat music being played by a live band.

"The band is good," Lisa agreed, leaning forward in her chair and watching the musicians. A moment later her eyes widened as Matt's chauffeur sauntered into the lounge and sat down on a stool at the far end of the bar. "Matt," she said with laughing incredulity, "I think your chauffeur just decided to come in out of the cold and have a beer."

Without looking in that direction, Matt replied, "Joe drinks Coke not beer, when he's on duty."

A waiter appeared to take their drinks order, and Meredith decided there was no need to inform Lisa that Joe was also a bodyguard, especially not when she preferred to forget that herself.

"Will that be all, folks?" the waiter asked, and when they told him it was, he walked over to the end of the bar. He was starting to hand the order over to the bartender, when a short man wearing an unusually bulky overcoat walked up beside him and said, "How'd you like to make a quick hundred bucks, buddy?"

The waiter swung around. "How?"

"Just let me stand over there behind that trellis for a while."

"Why?"

"You've got yourself some important guests at one of those tables, and I've got myself a camera under this coat." He held out his hand, and in it was a press pass showing that he was employed by a well-known tabloid, and a neatly folded $100 bill.

"Stay out of sight," the waiter said, palming the money.

At the maître d's desk in the front foyer, the owner of the restaurant picked up the phone and dialed the home phone number of Noel Jaffe, who rated restaurants in his newspaper column. "Noel," he said, turning his shoulder a little to avoid being overheard by the new crowd of customers coming in the doors, "this is Alex over at the Manchester House. You remember I told you someday I'd repay you for the nice write-up you gave my place in your column? Well, guess who's sitting in my restaurant right now."

"No kidding." Jaffe laughed when Alex told him who they were. "Maybe they are the happy little family they seemed like at that press conference."

"Not tonight, they aren't," Alex said, his whisper rising a little. "The fiancé has a face on him like a storm cloud, and he's had plenty to drink."

There was a brief, thoughtful pause, and then Jaffe chuckled and said, "I'll be right there with a photographer. Find us a table where we can see without being seen."

"No problem. Just remember—when you write about this, spell the name of my place right and put in the address."

Alex hung up the phone, so delighted with the prospect of free publicity about Chicago's rich and famous eating in his restaurant, he called several radio and television stations too.

By the time the waiter brought the second round of drinks—and the third for Parker—Meredith was well aware that Parker was drinking too much, too fast. That in itself wouldn't have been quite so alarming if he wasn't also determined to infuse the conversation with a steady stream of little vignettes about things he and Meredith had done, most of them beginning with "Remember when . . ."

Meredith didn't always remember, and she was, moreover, becoming increasingly aware that Matt was getting angry.

Matt wasn't getting angry, he was already coldly furious. For three quarters of an hour he'd been forced to listen to Reynolds relating cute tales about himself and Meredith, designed to point out to Matt that he was, hopelessly and irrevocably, Meredith's and Reynolds's social inferior, no matter how much money he had. Included among them was a story about the time Meredith broke her tennis racquet in a doubles tournament she played with him at the country club when she was a teenager . . . another about some damned dance given by some ritzy private school where she'd dropped her necklace . . . and yet another about a polo game he'd recently taken her to.

When he started talking about a charity auction they'd worked on together, Meredith stood up quickly. "I'm going to the ladies' room," she said, deliberately interrupting Parker. Lisa stood up too. "I'll go with you."

As soon as they reached the ladies' room, Meredith walked over to the sink, bracing her hands on the tiled counter in a posture of complete misery. "I can't stand much more of this," she told Lisa. "I never imagined tonight would be as bad as this."

"Should I pretend I'm sick and make them take us home?" Lisa said, grinning as she leaned forward to reapply her lipstick. "Remember when you did that for me that time we double-dated when we were at Bensonhurst?"

"Parker wouldn't care if we both passed out at his feet tonight," Meredith said irritably. "He's too busy doing everything he can to provoke Matt into an argument."

The tube of lipstick in Lisa's hand stilled, and she shot Meredith an irate sideways glance. "Matt is goading him!"

"He isn't saying a word!"

"*That* is how he's goading him. Matt is leaning back in his chair, watching Parker like he's a performing clown! Parker isn't used to losing, and he's lost you. And Matt is sitting there, silently gloating because he knows he's going to win."

"I cannot believe you!" Meredith burst out in a low, angry voice. "For years you've criticized Parker when he was right. Now he's wrong and he's drunk, and you're taking his side! Furthermore, Matt hasn't won anything. And he is *not* gloating. He may be trying to look bored and amused by Parker's antics, but he isn't! Believe me, he's angry—really angry because Parker is making him look like a—a social outcast."

"That's the way you see it," Lisa said with such fierce indignation that Meredith stepped back in astonishment. It turned to guilt as Lisa added, "I don't know how you could have considered marrying a man for whom you haven't the least bit of sympathy!"

The waiter had just told Matt that his table was ready, and over his shoulder Matt saw Lisa and Meredith emerge from the ladies' room and wend their way through the crowded lounge.

Parker had stopped talking about the things he and Meredith had done and was now thoroughly antagonizing Matt by questioning him about his background and sneering at Matt's answers. "Tell me, Farrell," he said in a loud, slurred voice that made several people at neighboring tables turn around, "where did you go to college? I've forgotten."

"Indiana State," Matt bit out, watching Lisa and Meredith.

"I went to Princeton."

"So what!"

"I was just curious. What about sports? Did you play any?"

"No," he clipped, sliding back his chair and standing up so that the four of them could go to their table in the dining room as soon as the women arrived.

"What did you do with your free time?" Parker persisted, sliding back his chair and standing up, too, a little unsteadily.

"I worked."

"Where?"

"In the steel mills and as a mechanic."

"I played some polo, boxed a little bit. And," he added with a disdainful look down Matt's entire length, "I gave Meredith her first kiss."

"I took her virginity," Matt snapped back, baited past endurance, but his eyes were on Meredith and Lisa, who were less than ten feet away.

"You son of a bitch!" Parker hissed, and, drawing back his arm, he aimed a punch at Matt.

Matt barely saw it coming in time to avoid it. Reacting instinctively, he threw up his left arm and swung hard with his right. Pandemonium erupted; women screamed, men jumped out of their chairs, Parker crashed to the floor, and white lights exploded in the background. Lisa called him a bastard, Matt looked toward her, and a small fist connected with his eye at the same instant Meredith bent down to help Parker off the floor. Matt instinctively drew back his fist to return the blow, realized it was Lisa who'd hit him, and checked the motion, but his elbow connected with something hard behind him and Meredith cried out. Joe was hurtling forward, plowing through the fleeing diners, and Matt caught Lisa's wrists to stop the hellcat from punching him again while photographers appeared out of nowhere, crowding in for more shots. With his free hand Matt yanked Meredith away from Parker's prone body and thrust her at Joe. "Get her out of here!" he yelled, trying to block her from view of the cameras with his own body. "Take her home!"

Suddenly Meredith felt herself being half lifted off her feet and shoved through the shouting crowd toward the kitchen's swinging doors. "There's a back way out," Joe panted, dragging her in his wake past startled cooks hovering over steaming pots and gaping waiters with loaded dinner trays. He threw his shoulder at the back door, sending it flying open and crashing against the back of the brick building, and they plunged into the frigid night air and into the rear parking lot, ignoring the parking lot attendant. Jerking the door of the limo open, Joe shoved her into the back of it and down onto the floor. "Stay down," he shouted, already slamming her door and running for the driver's door.

In a blur of unreality, Meredith stared at the fuzzy threads of the dark blue carpet a half inch from her wide eyes, unable to *believe* this was happening! Refusing to cower on the floor, she shoved herself upward, trying to crawl into the seat just as the car engine roared to life. The Cadillac blasted out of the parking lot, tires screaming, careening around the corner on two wheels, dumping Meredith back onto the floor in an ignominious heap. Streetlights flew by the windows in a white blur as the car raced crazily down one street and up another, and it belatedly occurred to her that they weren't circling and going back to the restaurant for Lisa.

Gingerly, she crawled up into the seat that faced the rear of the car, so that she could order Matt's maniac chauffeur to slow down and go back. "Excuse me—Joe," she called, but he was either too busy breaking the speed limit and traffic laws to hear her, or the blaring horns from irate motorists they were cutting off had drowned out her voice. With an angry sigh Meredith got up onto her knees, leaned her chest against the seat back, and poked her head through the connecting window. "Joe," she said, her voice breaking with fear as they swerved onto the right shoulder and passed a semi truck with only inches between them. "Please! You're scaring me!"

"Don't you worry none, Miz Farrell," he said, glancing at her in the rearview mirror, "ain't nobody goin' to stop us. Even if they could catch us, they won't bother us, because I'm packin'."

"Packing?" Meredith repeated numbly, glancing at the empty seat beside him, half expecting to see an open suitcase. "Packing what?"

"A rod."

"Pardon me?"

"I'm packin' a rod," he reiterated.

"You're going fishing? *Now?*"

He let out a sharp bark of laughter, shook his big head, and by way of explanation he pulled open his black suit coat. "I'm packin' a rod," he repeated, and Meredith stared in wide-eyed horror at the butt of the handgun that protruded from a lethal-looking shoulder holster.

"Oh, my God," she breathed and, turning limply, she slid back down on the seat and devoted herself to agonizing over Lisa's fate. In her current frame of mind she didn't particularly care if Matt and Parker both spent the night in jail for disturbing the peace, but she was worried about Lisa. Meredith had seen Parker swing at Matt first; she had no doubt who'd started the fistfight, but she also saw Parker miss his target, and she wasn't the least bit inclined to forgive Matt, who was sober, for turning a missed, drunken punch into a barroom brawl! Lisa, Meredith recalled, had been fiddling with the catch on her purse at about the time Parker had swung at Matt, and she'd looked up only when someone screamed—just in time to see Matt floor Parker. Which was why she'd launched herself into the fray out of some misbegotten—and incomprehensible—desire to defend Parker, whom she'd always seemed to dislike. The entire scenario passed before Meredith's eyes, and if she weren't so disgusted with the lot of them, she'd have laughed at the memory of Lisa drawing back her fist to poke Matt right in the eye. Having a lot of brothers certainly paid off at such times, Meredith decided grimly. She had no idea if Lisa had actually connected with her target, because, at the time, she herself had been bending down to help Parker up, and when she looked up, Matt's elbow had smacked her in the eye. It dawned on her then that the area around her right eye felt funny and she touched her fingertips to it. It felt tender.

A few minutes later she jumped when the phone rang, its ordinary sound glaringly out of place in a fleeing Cadillac limousine being driven by a man who was probably an ex-mobster.

"It's for you," Joe called cheerfully. "It's Matt. They got out of the restaurant okay. Everyone's fine. He wants to talk to you."

The news that Matt was calling her now, after everything he'd put her through, had an effect on Meredith like spontaneous combustion. She jerked the phone out of its built-in cradle in the side panel and put it to her ear. "Joe says you're fine," Matt began, his deep voice subdued. "I have your coat and—" Meredith didn't hear the rest of what he said. Very slowly, very deliberately, and with infinite satisfaction, she hung up on him.

Ten minutes later, when the curb in front of her apartment building was already racing by the side windows, Matt's chauffeur finally slammed on the brakes and, with all the delicacy of a pilot landing a 727 on the far end of a short runway, he brought the car to a teeth-jarring stop. Having failed to kill her on the highway or cause her to die of fright, he then got out of the car while it was still rocking, opened the back door with a flourish, and, with a satisfied grin, announced, "Here we are, Miz Farrell, safe and sound."

Meredith doubled up her fist.

Thirty years of civilized behavior and good breeding could not be overcome, however, so she forced her fingers to relax, climbed out of the car on legs that shook like jelly, and courteously, if dishonestly, wished him a good night. She walked into the building, escorted by Joe, who insisted he had to do it, and everyone in the lobby turned to stare at her askance—the doorman, the desk guard, and several tenants who were returning from an early evening. "G-good evening, Miss Bancroft," the desk guard babbled, gaping at her open-mouthed.

Meredith assumed her appearance must be a sight. She put up her chin and brazened it out. "Good evening, Terry," she replied with a gracious smile while yanking her arm from Joe's protective grasp.

A few moments later, however, when she unlocked her apartment door and saw herself reflected in the foyer mirror, she stopped dead, her eyes widening, her breath catching on a burst of horrified laughter. Her hair was standing straight out on one side, and the other side looked like it had been arranged with an electric mixer; her bolero jacket, which had looked pert earlier, was hanging drunkenly off the back of one shoulder, and the ascot tie was slung over the other shoulder. "Very nice," she sarcastically informed her reflection, and closed the apartment door.

"I should really go home," Parker said, gingerly rubbing his sore jaw. "It's eleven o'clock."

"Your place will be crawling with news people," Lisa told him firmly. "You may as well stay here tonight."

"What about Meredith?" he said a few minutes later when she returned from the kitchen and handed him another cup of tea.

Lisa felt a funny ache in her heart at his frustrating concentration on a woman who was not in love with him and who was, moreover, the last woman in the world he should be in love with. "Parker," she said softly, "it's over."

He lifted his head and looked at her in the muted light from the lamp, realizing she was referring to his future with Meredith. "I know," he said somberly.

"It's not the end of the world," Lisa continued, sitting beside him. Parker noticed, not for the first time, the way lamplight struck ruby lights off her hair. "The relationship was comfortable for you and Meredith, but do you know what happens to comfortable after a few years?"

"No, what?"

"It degenerates to dull."

Without answering, he drank the tea and put the mug down, then he looked around her living room because he felt an odd reluctance to look at her. The room was an eclectic combination of starkly modern and charmingly traditional, with unusual art pieces thrown in. It was like her—daring, dazzling, unsettling. An Aztec mask stood upon a modernistic mirrored pedestal beside a chair upholstered in pale peach leather with a basket of ivy next to it. The mirror above the fireplace was modern American; the Chelsea porcelain figurines on the mantel were English. Restless and uneasy with the questions drifting persistently through his mind, Parker stood up and went over to the fireplace to inspect the porcelain figurines. "This is beautiful," he said sincerely. "Seventeenth century, isn't it?"

"Yes," Lisa said quietly.

He came back and stopped in front of her, gazing down at her but carefully keeping his eyes from the cleavage above the bright plum V of her dress, then he asked the question that baffled him the most. "What made you take a swing at Farrell, Lisa?"

Lisa started and stood up abruptly, picking up the cup. "I don't know," she lied, angry because his nearness in the apartment, the implied and longed-for intimacy of his being there, was making her voice tremble.

"You can't stand me, yet you went leaping to my defense like an avenging angel," Parker persisted. "Why?"

Swallowing, Lisa debated about what to tell him; whether to shrug the question off with a joke about his need for a defender, or whether to risk everything and tell him the truth before some other woman grabbed him again. He was puzzled and he wanted an explanation, but she knew instinctively he didn't want or anticipate an avowal of love. "What makes you think I can't stand you?"

"You're joking," he said sarcastically. "You've never failed to make it eloquently clear how you feel about me and my profession."

"Oh, that," she said. "That was—that was teasing." Her gaze skated away from those piercing blue eyes of his, and she headed for the kitchen, dismayed when he picked up the tea tray and followed.

"Why?" he persisted, referring to her assault on Farrell.

"Why have I teased you, you mean?"

"No, but you could start with that."

Lisa shrugged, making an adventure in fastidiousness out of putting away the tea things and wiping the sink, but her mind was working frantically. Parker was a banker; everything had to add up to him, and her actions and explanations weren't doing that. She could either try to bluff, which she was dismally aware wasn't going to work—not with him—or she could take the biggest gamble of her life and tell him the truth. She decided to gamble. She had lost her heart to him long ago; she had nothing left to lose now but her pride. "Can you remember when you were a kid, say nine or ten years old?" she began, hesitantly continuing to wipe nonexistent crumbs from the countertop.

"I'm capable of that, yes," he said dryly.

"Did you ever like a girl back then, and try to get her attention?"

"Yes."

Swallowing audibly, she plunged ahead because it was too late to turn back. "I don't know how preppy boys did it, but in my neighborhood a boy usually threw a stick at you. Or teased you terribly. They did that," she finished achingly, "because they didn't know any other way to make you *notice* them."

Gripping the countertop with both hands, Lisa waited for him to speak behind her, and when he said absolutely nothing, her stomach clenched. Drawing a long, shattered breath, she stared fixedly ahead and said, "Do you have any idea how I feel about Meredith? Everything I am and have— all the good things—are because of her. She is the kindest, the finest person I've ever known. I love her more than my own sisters. Parker," she finished brokenly, "can you imagine how . . . how horrible it feels to be in love with a man—and have him propose to the friend you also love?"

Parker spoke then, his voice blunt and incredulous. "I've obviously passed out somewhere, stinking drunks, and I'm hallucinating," he pronounced. "In the morning when they bring me around, some psychoanalyst is going to want to know all about this dream. Just so I can be completely accurate when I describe it, are you trying to tell me you've been in *love* with *me?*"

Lisa's shoulders shook with teary laughter. "It was very stupid of you not to notice."

His hands settled on her shoulders. "Lisa, for God's sake . . . I don't know what to say. I'm sorr—"

"Don't say anything!" she cried. "And especially not that you're *sorry!*"

"Then what am I supposed to do?"

She tipped her head back, tears streaming from her eyes, and addressed the ceiling in a tone of frustrated misery. "How could I possibly fall in love with such an unimaginative man?" The pressure on her shoulders increased, and she reluctantly let him turn her around. "Parker," she said, "on a night like this, when two people are badly in need of comfort, and they happen to be a man and a woman, doesn't the answer seem obvious to you?"

Her heart stopped beating when he remained still, then it hammered madly when his fingers touched her chin, tipping it up. "The odds are that it's a very *bad* idea," he said, looking down at her wet lashes, surprised and touched by what she'd said and what she was offering.

"Life is one big gamble," she told him, and Parker belatedly realized that she was laughing and crying at the same time. And then he forgot to think at all, because Lisa's arms were twining around his neck and he was suddenly the recipient of the sweetest, hottest kiss . . . a kiss that brought his arms reflexively around her, pulling her tighter and closer. Lisa matched his ardor, subtly pushing it one step further, almost daring him to hold back. And then he wasn't holding back anymore. . . .

❧48

Wrapped in a bathrobe, Meredith sat in her living room, the television's remote control in her hand. Sunday morning cartoons were on most of the local channels, and she passed them by with an impatient press of the button, looking for the channel that replayed the previous night's late news so that she could torture herself with what she was already certain would be news coverage of the debacle. On the sofa beside her, where she'd flung it down a minute ago, was the Sunday morning newspaper with its sensational front-page story and pictures of the brawl. The *Tribune* had taken a tongue-in-cheek approach by quoting Parker's remark from their press conference and putting it above the pictures of the fight:

> "Matt Farrell and I are civilized men and we're handling this in the friend-liest of ways. This whole problem is little different than a business contract that wasn't properly executed, and now has to have the T's crossed."

Beneath that, the caption read:

FARRELL AND REYNOLDS—
"CROSSING THE T'S"

Below it were pictures of Parker swinging his fist at Matt, another of Matt's fist connecting with Parker's jaw, and a third of Parker lying on the floor with Meredith bending down to help him.

Meredith sipped her coffee as she watched the newscaster finish the national news and switch to his co-anchor for local coverage. "Janet," he said, grinning at the woman beside him, "I hear there's something new tonight on the Bancroft-Farrell-Reynolds menage à trois."

"There certainly is, Ted," she replied, turning full face to the camera, her voice filled with amused glee. "Most of you will recall that at their recent press conference, Parker Reynolds, Matthew Farrell, and Meredith Bancroft all seemed like a congenial little family. Well, tonight the three of them dined at the Manchester House, and it seems there was a little family fight. I mean, folks, a real, full-fledged fistfight! It was Parker Reynolds in one corner and Matthew Farrell in the other; husband against fiancé; Princeton University versus Indiana State; old money squaring off against new . . ." She paused to laugh at her own wit, and then said wryly, "Wondering who won? Well, place your bets, folks, because we have pictures that tell all."

A picture of Parker swinging at Matt and missing flashed on the screen, followed by one of Matt leveling Parker.

"If you put your money on Matt Farrell, you won," she concluded, laughing. "Second place in the match goes to Miss Lisa Pontini, a friend of Miss Bancroft's, who, we're told, landed a right hook on Matt Farrell right after that picture was taken. Miss Bancroft didn't wait around to congratulate the winner or console the loser. We're told she made a hasty getaway in Matt Farrell's limousine. The three combatants left together in a taxi and—"

"Dammit!" Meredith exclaimed, punching the remote control's off button, then she stood up and headed into her bedroom. As she passed her dresser, she automatically turned on the radio. "And now for the nine o'clock local news," the announcer said. "Last night, at the Manchester House on the North Side, open hostilities broke out between none other than industrialist Matthew Farrell and financier Parker Reynolds. Farrell, who is married to Meredith Bancroft, and Reynolds, who is engaged to her, were reportedly both having dinner with her when—"

Meredith slapped the off button on the top of the radio. "Unbelievable!" she gritted out. From the instant Matt crossed her path at the opera, nothing in her life was the same. Her entire world was being turned upside down! Sinking down on the bed, she picked up the phone and called Lisa's number again. She'd tried until late last night to reach her, but either Lisa wasn't answering her phone or she wasn't home. Neither was Parker, for that matter, because Meredith had tried to call him too.

Parker answered on the fifth ring, and for a split second Meredith went blank. "Parker?" she uttered.

"Mmmm," he said.

"Are—are you all right?"

"I'm fine," he mumbled, sounding groggily as if he'd been up all night and had just fallen into a deep sleep. "Hung over."

"Oh. I'm sorry. Well, is Lisa around?"

"Mmmm," he said again, and a second later Lisa's husky whisper murmured sleepily into the phone, "Whosethis?"

"It's Meredith," she answered just as it hit her that they were both sleeping in such proximity that Parker could hand Lisa the phone. Lisa had two phones in her apartment—one in the kitchen, and one beside the bed. They weren't sleeping in the kitchen. Shock sent her to her feet. "Are—are you in bed?" Meredith blurted out before she could stop herself.

"Mmm-hmm."

With Parker? Meredith thought, but she didn't ask. She already knew the answer, and she clutched the headboard to steady herself in a room that seemed to tilt crazily. "Sorry I woke you both up," she managed to get out, and hung up. The world had spun off its axis . . . or she was spinning off hers. Everything was completely out of control. Her best friend was in bed with her fiancé. Equally shocking, she didn't feel betrayed or crushed. She felt dazed. Turning, she glanced around at the bedroom as if to assure herself that it, at least, hadn't changed completely in the last few hours. The cream lace and satin bedspread was where it belonged with its ruffles cascading to a half inch above the Oriental carpet, like they always did. All ten of the matching throw pillows were artfully propped in *exactly* the order she always placed them. She was so shaken by everything else that she felt absurdly better knowing her bedspread hadn't picked itself up and left the room, taking all her throw pillows with it. But then she looked up and caught the reflection of her face in the mirror. Even that had changed.

An hour later Meredith picked up her keys, slid a pair of large, dark sunglasses onto her nose, and left her apartment. She would go to the office and spend the day working. That at least was something she could understand and control. Matt hadn't bothered to call, and that would have surprised her if she hadn't passed the point where anything could do that. The elevator doors opened on the lower level parking garage beneath her apartment building, and she headed toward her reserved parking space. She rounded the corner, car keys in hand, and stopped dead.

Her car was gone.

Her car was gone, and someone had already parked a new Jaguar sports car in her space.

Her car had been stolen! Her parking space had been usurped!

That did it! She had finally reached her breaking point. She gaped at the shiny, dark blue Jaguar, and she had a sudden insane impulse to shriek with laughter, a mad urge to put her thumb to her nose and wiggle her fingers at fate. There was nothing else, absolutely nothing more that fate could do to her! She was ready to fight back—spoiling for it.

Turning on her heel, Meredith went back to the elevator, slapped the button for the lobby level, and walked up to the security clerk at the lobby desk. "Robert," she said, "there is a blue Jaguar in my parking space—L12. Please have it towed out of there. Immediately."

"But it's probably just a new tenant who doesn't—"

Meredith picked up the phone on the desk and held the receiver toward him. "Now," she said in a dangerously strained voice, "call that garage on Lyle Street and tell them to get that car out of my space in fifteen minutes!"

"Okay, Miss Bancroft. Okay. No problem."

Partially satisfied, Meredith marched toward the lobby doors, intending to take a taxi to her office and call the police from there about her stolen car. Determined to flag down the taxi that was just pulling up at the curb, she rushed forward, then halted abruptly when she saw the throng of reporters milling around outside her building. "Miss Bancroft—about last night," one of them called, and two photographers took pictures of her through the glass windows. Unaware that the man climbing out of the cab wearing pilot's sunglasses was Matt, Meredith turned on her heel and stalked to the elevator. So what if she was now a prisoner in her own apartment building? No problem. She would go upstairs and phone for a taxi to pick her up at the delivery entrance, then she'd sneak out there, crouch down behind the trash cans, and leap into the cab when it pulled up. No problem at all! She could do that. Of course she could.

She had just picked up the telephone in her apartment when someone knocked on her door. Completely overwhelmed by the trials and tribulations of her recent life, Meredith opened the door without bothering to ask who was there, then she gazed distractedly at the sight of Matt filling her doorway, his sunglasses reflecting her own image back at her. "Good morning," he said with a hesitant smile.

"Oh, is that what it is?" she replied, letting him in.

"What does that mean?" Matt asked, trying to see her eyes behind the big round amber sunglasses perched on her small nose so that he could gauge her mood.

"That means," she primly replied, "that if this is a *good* morning, I'm locking myself in a closet so I don't have to see what tomorrow is like."

"You're upset," he concluded.

"*Me?*" she said sarcastically, pointing to her chest. "Me, upset? Just because I'm a prisoner in my own apartment building, and I can't go near a newspaper, radio, or television without finding us the main topic? Why on earth should *that* upset me?"

Matt bit back a wayward smile at her harassed tone. She saw it. "Don't you *dare* laugh," she warned indignantly. "This is all your fault. Every time you come near me, things start happening to me!"

"What's happening to you?" he asked in a laughter-tinged voice, longing to drag her into his arms.

She threw up her hands. "Everything is going crazy! At work, things are happening that have *never* happened before—I have bomb scares to deal with and our stock is fluctuating. So far this morning my car has been stolen, someone else is using my parking space, *and* I've discovered my best friend and my former fiancé spent the night together!"

He chuckled at her logic about her problems at the office. "And you think *all* of that is *my* fault?"

"Well, how do you explain it?"

"Cosmic coincidence?"

"Cosmic catastrophe, you mean!" she corrected him. Putting her hands on her slim hips, she informed him, "One month ago I was leading a nice life. A quiet life. A *dignified* life! I went to charity balls and danced. Now I go to barrooms and get into brawls, and then I go careening through the streets in a limousine driven by a demented chauffeur who assures me that he—he *packs* a *rod!* We are talking about a handgun here—a murder weapon to shoot someone with!"

She looked so beautiful and so flustered and so irate that Matt's shoulders began to shake with laughter. "Is that all?"

"No. There's one more little thing I didn't mention about last night."

"What's that?"

"This—" she announced triumphantly, and pulled off her sunglasses. "I have a black eye! A shiner. A—a—"

Torn between laughter and regret, Matt lifted his finger and touched the tiny blue smudge at the outer corner of her lower lid. "That," he said with a sympathetic grin, "doesn't have the dignity of a shiner or a black eye; it's just a little mouse."

"Oh, good," she said. "I've learned a new term!"

Ignoring her jibe, Matt studied the well-concealed little bruise with thoughtful admiration. "It barely shows. What are you using to hide it?"

"Makeup," she answered, disconcerted by his question. "Why?"

Almost choking with laughter, Matt took off his sunglasses. "Do you think I could borrow some?"

Meredith gaped incredulously at the identical mark at the corner of his eye, and suddenly her emotions veered crazily to mirth. She saw the wry grin tugging at his lips, and she started to giggle. She clamped her hand over her mouth to stifle the sound, her eyes widened, and the giggles erupted into great gales of gusty mirth. She laughed so hard that her eyes teared, and Matt started laughing too. When he reached out and drew her quaking body against his own, she collapsed against him and laughed harder.

Wrapping his arms around her, Matt buried his laughing face in her hair, filled with the joy of her. Despite his surface nonchalance a few minutes earlier, the things she'd accused him of were mostly true. He'd been guilt-stricken when he saw the morning papers; he *was* turning her life upside down, and if she'd have raged at him, he'd have deserved it. The fact that she was seeing the humor while she recognized the dire consequences filled him with profound gratitude.

When most of her hilarity had passed, Meredith leaned back in his arms. "Did," she asked, swallowing another irrepressible giggle, "Parker give you your— mouse?"

"I'd be less mortified if he had," Matt teased. "The truth is, your friend Lisa nailed me with a right hook. How did you get yours?"

"You did it."

His smile faded. "I did not."

"Yes, you did." She nodded emphatically, her intoxicating face still flushed with merriment. "Y-you hit me with your elbow when I bent down to rescue Parker. Although, if it happened today, I'd probably jump on him with both feet!"

Matt's smile widened with delight. "Really? Why?"

"I told you," she said, drawing a shaky, laughing breath. "I called Lisa this morning to see if she was all right, and they were in bed together."

"I'm shocked!" he said. "I gave her credit for better taste!"

Meredith bit her lip to stop herself from laughing at his quip. "It's really terrible, you know—your best friend in bed with your fiancé."

"It's an outrage!" Matt declared with sham indignation.

"Yes, it is," she agreed, grinning helplessly at the laughter gleaming in his eyes.

"You have to get even."

"I can't," she said on a suffocated giggle.

"Why not?"

"Because," she said, dissolving into fresh gales of laughter. "Lisa doesn't *have* a fiancé!" She collapsed in his arms again, overcome with the absurdity of her own joke, burying her laughing face in his chest, her hands sliding around his nape as they used to—clinging to him as instinctively as they had during those long-ago nights of passion. Her body knew she still belonged to him, Matt realized. He tightened his arms around her, his voice turning low-pitched and suggestive. "You can still get even."

"How?" she chuckled.

"You can go to bed with me instead."

She stiffened and backed away a hasty step, still smiling, but more out of self-consciousness than mirth. "I—I have to call the police about my car," she said, launching into diversionary conversation and hastily starting toward her desk. She peered out the window as she passed. "Oh, good, there's the tow truck now," she babbled brightly, picking up the phone to call the police. "I told the security clerk to have that car removed from my spot."

An odd expression flashed across his face at that announcement, but Meredith was too preoccupied by the fact that he was following her to her desk to wonder about it. When he reached out and firmly pressed down on the button to disconnect her call to the police, she eyed him with wary alarm. He wasn't finished trying to get her into bed, she knew, and her resistance was almost gone. He was so appealing, and it had felt so good to laugh with him . . . Instead of reaching for her, as she half expected him to do, he said mildly, "What's the phone number for the security desk?"

She told him, then watched in startled confusion as he called it.

"This is Matt Farrell," he told the security guard. "Please go down to the garage and tell the tow truck to leave my wife's car where it is." When the security guard argued that Miss Bancroft's car was an '84 BMW, while the car in her parking space was a blue Jag, Matt said, "I know that. The Jaguar is her birthday present."

"My *what?*" Meredith gasped.

He hung up the phone and turned to her, a smile lurking at his mouth, but Meredith wasn't smiling—she was dumbstruck by the overwhelming generosity of the gift, panicked at the web he was weaving around her, and thoroughly alarmed by the treacherous leap her heart gave at the sound of his deep voice quietly saying "my wife." She started with the least important issues first, because she wasn't quite ready to address the others yet. "Where is my own car?"

"In the night clerk's space, one level below yours."

"But—but how did you start my car to move it? You said at the farm that even if you could start it without the keys, the alarm would disable it."

"That wasn't a problem for Joe O'Hara."

"I *knew* when I saw that gun that he was probably a—a felon."

"No, he's not," Matt said dryly. "He's an expert with wiring."

"I can't possibly accept the other car—"

"Yes, darling," he said, "You *can.*"

Meredith felt it happening again, that awesome magnetic pull of his body and voice, the melting inside her when he called her darling. She backed away a step, and her voice shook. "I—I'm going to the office."

"I don't think so," Matt said softly.

"What do you mean?"

"I mean we have something more important to do."

"What is it?"

"I'll show you," he promised huskily, "in bed."

"Matt, don't do this to me—" she pleaded, holding her hand up as if to fend him off and backing away two steps.

He stalked her, step for step. "We want each other. We have *always* wanted each other."

"I really do have to go to the office. I have tons of work."

She backed away again in the same avoidance waltz Matt had teased her about, but her eyes were warm and frightened because she knew. . . . She knew it was too late to dance out of his reach now.

"Give in gracefully, darling. This dance is over. The next one is ours."

"Please don't call me that," she cried, and Matt realized that for some reason she was truly frightened.

"Why are you afraid?" he asked, stalking her slowly around the back of the sofa, trying to head her toward the bedroom.

Why was she afraid, Meredith thought a little wildly. How could she explain that she didn't want to love a man who didn't love her . . . that she never wanted to be as vulnerable to being hurt as she'd been eleven years ago . . . that she didn't think he'd be satisfied with her for very long, and she didn't think she could bear it if she lost him again because he wasn't.

"Matt, listen to me. Stand still and listen to me, please!"

Matt stopped short, stunned by the terrified desperation in her voice.

"You said you want children," she blurted out, "and I can't have any. There's something physically wrong with me—it would be too risky."

He didn't miss a beat. "We'll adopt."

"What if I said I don't want any children?" she flung back.

"Then we won't adopt."

"I have no intention of giving up my career—"

"I don't expect you to."

"God, you are making this so hard!" she cried. "Can't you leave me just a little pride? I'm trying to tell you that I couldn't bear being married to you—not living as husband and wife, which is what you say you want."

His face paled as the sincerity in her voice hit him. "Do you mind if I ask you why the hell not?"

"Yes, I *do* mind."

"Let's hear it anyway," he said tautly.

She folded her arms protectively over her chest, absently rubbing them with her hands as if to ward off the sudden chill of his expression. "It's too late for us," she began. "We've changed. You've changed. I can't pretend I don't—don't feel something for you. You know I do. I always did," she admitted miserably, her gaze searching his shuttered gray eyes, looking for understanding and finding only cold impassivity while he waited to hear the rest of what she had to say. "Maybe if we'd stayed together, it would have worked, but it couldn't now. You like sexy movie stars and—and seductive European princesses, and I can't be those things for you!"

"I'm not asking you to be anything but what you are, Meredith."

"It won't be enough!" she argued miserably. "And I couldn't bear living with you and knowing that I'm not enough—knowing that someday you'll start wanting things I can't give you."

"If you're talking about children, I thought we just settled that."

"I don't think we settled it, I think you made a reckless concession because you're willing to say anything right now to make me agree with what you want. But I'm not talking about you wanting children, I'm talking about you wanting other women! I could never be enough for you. I *know* I couldn't."

His eyes widened. "I beg your pardon?"

"I tried to explain to you once before about—about how I feel when we make love. Matt," she said almost choking on her words, "people—men, I mean—they think I'm . . . I'm frigid. Even in college they thought that. I don't think I am exactly, but I'm not—I'm not like most women."

"Go on," he insisted gently when she stopped, but there was an odd light in his eyes.

"In college, two years after you left, I tried to sleep with a boy and I hated it. So did he. Other women on campus were sleeping around and enjoying it, but I didn't. I couldn't."

"If they'd all been through what you had," Matt said, so filled with tenderness and relief that he could hardly keep his voice steady, "they wouldn't have been very damned eager to do it again either."

"I thought that, too, but that wasn't it. Parker isn't a clumsy, oversexed college boy, and I know he thinks I'm not—not very responsive. Parker didn't mind so very much, but you—you would."

"You're out of your mind, sweetheart."

"You're not *used* to me yet! You haven't noticed that I feel awkward and inept. No, I *am* awkward and inept!"

Matt bit back a grin and gravely said, "Inept too? As bad as that?"

"Worse."

"And are those all the reasons you have for being afraid to pick up where we left off eleven years ago?"

You don't love me, dammit, she thought. "Those are all the important ones," she said dishonestly.

Weak with relief, Matt quietly said, "I think we can overcome those hurdles right here. I meant what I said about children. I also meant what I said about your career. That takes care of two out of your three concerns. The situation about other women," he continued, "is only slightly more complex. If I'd have known that this day was going to come for us, I'd have lived my life very differently while I waited for it. Unfortunately, I can't change the past. I can, however, tell you that my past isn't nearly as lurid or indiscriminate as what you've been led to believe. And I can promise you," he added with a tender smile at her upturned face, "that you are enough for me—in every way."

Helplessly affected by the husky timbre of his voice, the sensuality in his beautiful eyes, and the incredibly touching things he was saying, Meredith watched him slowly strip off his sport jacket and toss it over the back of the sofa, but the import of his action didn't register because she was absorbed in what he was saying. "As far as your being frigid is concerned, that is absurd. The memory of what it was like to be in bed with you haunted me for years. And if you think," he continued gravely, "that you're the only one who's harbored some insecurities about those times we spent in bed, then I've got news for you, darling. There were times I felt inadequate. No matter how often I told myself to slow down, to make love to you for hours and make us both wait for a climax, I couldn't seem to do it because being in bed with you made me crazy with wanting."

Tears of relief and joy burned the backs of Meredith's eyes; he'd meant to give her an expensive sports car for a birthday present, but the gift he was giving her with his words meant a thousand times more. Mesmerized, she heard him say, "When I got your father's telegram, I tortured myself for years, thinking you might have stayed married to me if I could have made our lovemaking better, longer, hotter . . ." A smile suddenly drifted across his handsome face, and his tone changed to one of amused gravity. "That takes care of the issue of frigidity, I think."

Matt saw the warm flush on her smooth cheeks—evidence that his words had affected her. "That leaves us with only one minor objection of yours about being married to me."

"What's that?"

"Your feeling that you're inept and—?"

"Clumsy," she provided, distracted by the way he was lazily stripping off his tie. "And . . . and inferior."

"I can see how distressing that might be for you," he agreed with sham gravity. "I suppose we'd better take care of that next." He began unbuttoning the top button of his shirt.

"What are you doing!" she demanded, her eyes widening.

"I'm getting undressed so you can have your way with me."

"Don't unbutton that second button—I mean it, Matt."

"You're right. You should be doing this. Nothing gives a person a greater sense of power and *superiority* than forcing another person to stand perfectly still while they're being undressed."

"You should know. You've probably done it dozens of times."

"Hundreds. Come here, darling."

"Hundreds?!"

"I was joking."

"It wasn't funny."

"I can't help it. When I'm nervous, I make jokes."

She stared at him. "Are you nervous?"

"Terrified," he said half seriously. "This is the greatest gamble of my life. I mean, if everything doesn't go perfectly in this little experiment, I might as well face the fact that we weren't meant for each other, after all."

Meredith's last vestige of resistance crumbled as she looked at him. She loved him; she had always loved him. And she wanted him so badly—almost as badly as she wanted him to love her. "That's not true."

His voice hoarse with tenderness at her words, Matt opened his arms to her. "Come to bed with me, darling. I promise you that you'll never have any doubts about yourself, or me, after this."

Meredith hesitated and then walked straight into his arms.

In the bedroom Matt did exactly four things to make certain his promise was kept: He made her drink some champagne to relax; he told her that any kiss or caress of his that she'd enjoyed, he would find just as exciting. And then he turned his body into a hands-on teaching instrument for a woman whose very voice excited him. Last, he made no effort to hide or control his reactions to anything she did to him. In so doing, Matt managed to turn the next two hours of his life into an agony of almost unendurable passionate torment, a torment which his wife, after overcoming her shyness, was now doing her gloriously effective damnedest to heighten.

"But I'm not completely *certain* you like this," she whispered, touching her lips to his swollen body.

"Please don't do that," Matt gasped.

"You don't like it?"

"You can see that I do."

"Then why do you want me to stop?"

"Keep doing it, and you'll know why in about one minute."

"Do you like this?" Her tongue flicked against his nipples, and he held his breath to stifle his gasp.

"Yes," he finally managed in a strangled voice. He reached up and grabbed the headboard, gritting his teeth as she mounted him and began to move, determined to let her do it all, have it all. "This is what I get for falling in love with a CEO instead of some nice dumb starlet—" he joked, so dazed with passion, he didn't know what he was saying. "I should have known a CEO would want to be on top—"

It took a moment to realize she had gone perfectly still.

"If you stop now, without letting me have a climax, there's every chance I'll die right here, darling."

"What?" she whispered.

"Please, don't stop, or I'll take over no matter what I promised," he gasped, already lifting his hips to get higher and deeper into her tight, wet warmth.

"You're in *love* with me?"

He closed his eyes and swallowed, his voice thick with lust and amusement. "What the hell do you think this is all about?" He opened his eyes, and even in the darkened room he could see the tears shimmering in her eyes.

"Don't look at me like that," he pleaded, letting go of the headboard and pulling her down against his chest. "Please, don't cry. I'm sorry I said it," he whispered, kissing her in helpless desperation because he thought she didn't want to hear how he felt, and he'd spoiled their lovemaking. "I didn't mean to say it so soon."

"Soon?" she repeated fiercely, her shoulders shaking with teary laughter. "*Soon?*" she wept brokenly. "I've been waiting almost half my life for you to say you love me." With her wet cheek pressed to his chest and her body still intimately joined to his, she whispered, "I love you, Matt."

The moment she said it, Matt climaxed involuntarily inside her, shuddering, clutching her fiercely, his fingers digging into her back, his face buried against her neck, helpless yet omnipotent because she'd finally said the words.

Her body tightened, holding him. "I've always loved you," she whispered. "I'll always love you."

The climax that should have been nearly over exploded with new force, his body jerking spasmodically, and he groaned long and low, twisting higher into her, brought to the most volcanic moment of his life, not by stimulation or technique, but words. Her words.

Meredith rolled over in Matt's arms and snuggled closer to him, sated and happy.

In New Orleans, a well-dressed man walked into one of the dressing rooms at Bancroft & Company's crowded store. In his right hand he carried a suit he'd taken off the rack. In his left hand he carried a Saks Fifth Avenue bag with a small plastic explosive in it. Five minutes later he left the dressing room, carrying only the suit, which he returned to the rack.

In Dallas, a woman walked into a stall in the ladies' room at Bancroft & Company, carrying a Louis Vuitton purse and a bag from Bloomingdale's. When she left, she was carrying only her purse.

In Chicago, a man took the escalator to the toy department of Bancroft's downtown store, his arms laden with packages from Marshall Field's. He left one small package stuck beneath the ledge of Santa Claus's house, where children were lined up to have their pictures taken on Santa's knee.

In Meredith's apartment, several miles away and several hours later, Matt glanced at his watch, then he rolled to his feet and helped Meredith clear away the debris from the meal they had eaten after making love again in front of the fire. They'd taken her car out for a test drive, stopped at a little Italian restaurant, and brought their meal back because they both wanted to be alone together.

Meredith was putting the last of the dishes into the dishwasher when he came up silently behind her. She felt his presence like a tangible force even before his hands settled on her waist, and he drew her back against him. "Happy?" he asked huskily, brushing a kiss on her temple.

"Very happy," she whispered, smiling.

"It's ten o'clock."

"I know." Her smile wavered as she braced herself for what she suspected was coming next—and she was right.

"My bed is bigger than yours. So is my apartment. I can have a moving van here in the morning."

Drawing a long, steadying breath, she turned in his arms and laid her hand against his face as if to soften the blow of her refusal. "I can't move in with you—not yet."

Beneath her fingers she felt his jaw tense. "Can't or don't want to?"

"Can't."

He nodded as if accepting her answer, but he dropped his arms. "Let's hear why you think you can't."

Shoving her hands into the deep pockets of her robe, Meredith stepped back and launched her argument. "To begin with, I stood beside Parker last week and let him make a public statement that we were getting married as soon as the divorce was final. If I move in with you now, I'll make Parker look like an ass, and myself like a fool who can't make up her mind—or else a woman who's so shallow and silly that she goes with whatever man wins a fistfight."

She waited for him to argue or agree. Instead, he leaned a hip against the table behind him, his face impassive, and remained silent. Meredith realized that his own disregard for public opinion was probably making him view her concerns as trivial, so she brought up another, larger problem. "Matt, I haven't wanted to think about the ramifications of that fight last night, but I can tell you right now, there's a ninety-percent chance I'll be called before the board of directors to give an explanation. don't you understand the compromising predicament I'm in? Bancroft and Company is an old and dignified operation; the board of directors is rigid, and they didn't want me in the president's office in the first place. A few days ago I stood up in a news conference held at Bancroft and Company and said we hardly know each other and there was no chance of a reconciliation. If I move in with you right away, my credibility as an officer of Bancroft's will suffer just as much as my honesty as a person. And that isn't all. Last night I was part of, and the cause of, a public brawl—a fiasco that could have gotten us all arrested if the police had been called. I'll be lucky if the board doesn't threaten to invoke the morals clause in my contract and ask me to step down."

"They wouldn't dare invoke the morals clause over a thing like that!" Matt said, looking more contemptuous of the notion than alarmed by it.

"They could and they might."

"I'd get myself a new board of directors," he said.

"I wish I could," Meredith said with a wry smile. "I take it your board pretty much does what you want done?" When he nodded curtly, she sighed. "Unfortunately, neither my father nor I control our board. The point is, I'm a woman, and I'm young, and they weren't any too crazy about my becoming interim president in the first place. can't you see why I'm worried about what they're going to think of all this?"

"You're a competent executive, that's all in the hell they need to be concerned with. If they call a meeting and demand an explanation, or threaten to invoke the morals clause if you don't step down, then take the offensive, not the defensive. You weren't pushing drugs or running a house of prostitution; you were present during a fight."

"Is that what you'd tell them—that you weren't running drugs or anything?" she asked, fascinated with his business methods.

"No," he said brusquely. "*I'd* tell them to fuck off."

Meredith swallowed a giggle at the ludicrous prospect of standing up in front of twelve conservative businessmen and doing such a thing. "You aren't seriously suggesting I say that?" she said when he didn't seem to share her humor.

"That's exactly what I'm suggesting. You can alter the words slightly if you think you should, but the point is that you can't live your life to suit other people. The harder you try, the more restrictions they'll put on you just for the fun of seeing you jump through their hoops."

Meredith knew he was right, but not in this instance or in her specific circumstances. For one thing, she wasn't willing to incur the board's wrath; for another, she was using her predicament as an excuse to stall before making the commitment Matt wanted. She loved him, but in many ways he was still a complete stranger to her. She wasn't ready to promise herself completely to him. Not yet. Not until she was absolutely certain the paradise he promised her—the part about the life they would have together—really existed. And from the expression on Matt's face, she had an awful feeling he suspected she was stalling. His next words confirmed that he knew exactly what she was doing and that he didn't like it.

"Sooner or later, Meredith, you're going to have to take a risk and trust me completely. Until you do, you're cheating me and you're cheating yourself. You can't outwit fate by trying to stand on the sidelines and place little side bets about the outcome of life. Either you wade in and risk everything to play the game, or you don't play at all. And if you don't play, you can't win."

It was, she thought, a beautiful philosophy on the one hand and a terrifying one on the other—a philosophy, moreover, that was far better suited to him than her.

"How about a compromise," she suggested with a winsome smile that Matt reluctantly found irresistible. "Why don't I wade in—but stay in the shallow end for a while until I get accustomed to it?"

After a tense moment he nodded. "How long?"

"A little while."

"And while you're debating about how deep you dare to go, what am I supposed to do? Am I supposed to wait and pace and wonder if your father will be able to convince you not to live with me or to go through with the divorce?"

"I have plenty of courage to withstand my father regardless of whether he comes around and sees things our way or not," she said so forcefully that he smiled a little. "What I'm worried about is whether or not you'll try to meet him halfway if he does—for my sake?"

She rather expected him to agree, for her sake, but she'd misjudged the depth of Matt's hatred, because he shook his head. "He and I have an old score to settle first, and it's going to be settled my way."

"He's ill, Matt," she warned, an awful feeling of foreboding shaking through her. "He can't take a lot of stress anymore."

"I'll try to remember that," Matt replied unanswerably. His expression softened a little, and he changed the subject. "Now, who is sleeping where tonight?"

"Do you suppose any of the reporters who saw you come up here this morning are still out there, watching?"

"Probably one or two of the tenacious ones."

She bit her lip, hating to have him leave, but knowing he shouldn't stay. "Then you can't really stay all night, can you?"

"Evidently not," he said in a tone that made her feel like a coward.

Matt saw her eyes darken with consternation, and he relented. "All right, I'll go home and sleep alone. It's nothing less than I deserve for participating in that adolescent fight last night. While I'm on that subject," he added more gently, "I'd like you to know that while I was guilty of saying something that undoubtedly caused your drunken fiancé to take a swing at me, I didn't realize what was happening until after it was over. One second I was looking at you, and the next I saw a fist coming at me from the corner of my eye. For all I knew, it was some drunk at the bar who'd decided to pick a fight, and I reacted instinctively."

Meredith suppressed a shudder, a delayed reaction to the lethal swiftness, the easy brutality, with which Matt had leveled Parker . . . the savage look on his face in that split second when he realized he was being attacked. Then she firmly shoved the thought aside. Matt was not now, and was never going to be, like the fastidious, urbane men she'd known. He had grown up tough, and he was tough. But not with her, she thought with a tender smile, and she reached out and smoothed his dark hair back from his temple.

"If you think," he said wryly, "that you can smile at me like that and make me agree to almost anything, you're right." And then he abruptly reverted to his usual, more indomitable self by adding, "However, while I'm willing to practice extreme discretion in our relationship—read that as sneaking—I'm determined that you're going to spend as much time with me as possible, and that includes some nights together. I'll arrange for a pass so that you can get into the parking garage in my building. If I have to, I'll stand out in front and talk to the damned reporters to divert them every time you drive in."

He looked so irked at the prospect of having to pander to public opinion that she said in a voice of exaggerated gratitude, "You'd do *that*? Just for me?"

Instead of laughing, he took the question seriously and pulled her tightly to him. "You have no idea," he said fiercely, "how *much* I'd do—just for you!" His mouth opened over hers in a rough, consuming kiss that stole her breath and robbed her of all ability to think. When he was finished, she was clinging to him. "Now that you're almost as unhappy with tonight's sleeping arrangement as I am," he said with grim humor, "I'll get out of here before the reporters out in front decide to go home and say we spent the night together anyway."

Meredith walked him to the door, exasperated because he was right—after that kiss she wanted to spend the night in his arms so badly that she ached. She stood while he shrugged into his jacket and put on his tie. When he was finished, he looked at her for a moment and quirked a knowing brow at her. "Something on your mind?" he teased.

There was—she wanted to be kissed. The memory of the stormy, uninhibited hours she'd just spent in bed with him washed over her then, and with a deliberately provocative smile Meredith Bancroft reached out and caught her husband's tie. Slowly and forcefully she pulled on it, smiling daringly into his smoky gray eyes, and then, when he was close enough, she leaned up on her toes, wrapped her arms around him, and gave him a kiss that left him breathless.

When he left, Meredith shut the door and leaned against it, smiling dreamily, her eyes closed. Her lips were tender from his last stormy kiss; her hair was tousled because he'd shoved his hands into it while he kissed her, and her cheeks were glowing. She felt like a woman who had been made love to very thoroughly and who had enjoyed it tremendously. And it was all true.

Her smile deepened as she thought of the sexy, tender things he had said to her, and she could almost hear his deep voice saying them. . . .

I love you, he had whispered . . .

I'll never let anyone hurt you . . .

You have no idea how much I'd do for you!

Forty miles northeast of Belleville, Illinois, another squad car screeched to a halt behind those already parked beside a wooded stretch of lonely county road, their red and blue lights revolving with frantic eeriness in the night. Overhead, the blinding searchlight of a police helicopter moved restlessly over the pines, lighting the way for the teams of searchers and dog handlers who were combing in the dark for clues. In a shallow ditch beside the road, the coroner crouched beside the body of a middle-aged man. Raising his voice to be heard over the whistling roar of the helicopter blades, he called out to the local sheriff, "You're wasting your time with that search party, Emmett. Even in the daylight you won't find any clues in those woods. This guy was dumped out of a moving vehicle and he rolled down here."

"You're wrong!" Emmett shouted triumphantly. Beaming his flashlight at something in the ditch, he bent down and picked it up.

"The hell I am! I'm telling you somebody beat the hell out of this guy and then dumped him out of a moving vehicle."

"Not about that," the sheriff replied, walking forward. "I did find somethin'. I found a wallet."

The coroner tipped his head toward the body. "His?"

"Let's have a look," the sheriff replied, and after beaming his flashlight at the picture on the driver's license, he bent down and pulled the blanket off the victim's face, studying it for comparison. "His!" he pronounced emphatically. Holding the license up to his light, he said, "He's got one of them foreign names you can't hardly pronounce. Stanislaus . . . Spyzhalski."

"Stanis—" the coroner uttered. "Isn't he that fake lawyer they busted down in Belleville?"

"By God, you're right!"

49

With his briefcase in one hand and his coat over his arm, Matt stopped at the desk of the secretary who'd helped him prepare the conference room the day Meredith came. "Good morning, Mr. Farrell," she said.

Displeased by the sulky hostility in her tone and face, Matt made a mental note to transfer her to another floor and instead of pleasantly asking her if she'd had a nice weekend, which he'd been about to do, he said coolly, "Eleanor Stern called me at home this morning to say she isn't feeling well. Fill in for her, will you?" It was an order, not a request, and they both knew it.

"Yes, of course," Joanna Simons replied, and she gave him a smile that was so genuine, so gleeful, Matt almost wondered if he'd misjudged her.

Joanna waited until Haskell's new—and unwanted—president had disappeared into his office, then she rushed over to the receptionist's desk. She'd been hoping to take it easy while her new boss was out of town. This opportunity to work for Farrell, however, offered her an unexpected and exciting opportunity. "Val," she whispered to the receptionist, "did you keep the name and phone number of that reporter from the *Tattler* who called you to get some info on Farrell?"

"Yes, why?"

"Because," she said triumphantly, "Farrell just told me I'm supposed to fill in for hatchet-face today. That means I'll have the keys to her desk." She glanced up to make certain the other secretaries whose desks fanned around the reception area in a broad circle were all busy and preoccupied. Most of them didn't share her animosity for Matthew Farrell, they hadn't been here as long, and their loyalties had been more easily transferred from the old team to the new owner. "Tell me again what that reporter wanted to know."

"He asked how we felt about Farrell and I told him some of us couldn't stand him," Valerie said. "He asked if I ever put calls through to him from Meredith Bancroft or if she came here. He was especially interested in whether or not they're really as friendly as they acted in their news conference. I told him I didn't take Farrell's calls and that Meredith Bancroft had been here only once, for a meeting with Farrell and his attorneys. He wanted to know if anyone else had been in on the meeting, and I told him I knew hatchet-face had been in there, because I had to take her calls out here. He asked if I thought she sat in on it to take notes. I told him she takes notes on almost every meeting he has, and he asked if I could get my hands on those notes from the Bancroft meeting. He said they'd pay for any info on that meeting that we could get for him. He didn't say how much he'd pay though."

"It doesn't matter. I'd do this for free!" Joanna said bitterly. "He'll have to unlock the old bat's desk for me to use today. Maybe he'll unlock the file cabinets too. Those meeting notes should be in one of those two places."

"Let me know if I can help," Valerie said.

When Joanna walked into Eleanor Stern's office, she found that Farrell had already unlocked his secretary's desk and left it open for her to use, but that the file cabinets were still locked. A brief sketchy search of the desk revealed nothing but supplies and a drawer full of nonconfidential files on Haskell's operation. There was nothing about Bancroft. "Damn," she said under her breath, swinging around in her chair and glancing through the door that connected this office with Farrell's. He was standing, looking at the computer on the credenza behind his desk. No doubt he was checking on Haskell's production reports from its factories over the weekend—or some massive stock portfolio he owned, she thought with growing hatred for the man who couldn't be bothered remembering her name . . . who had fired their bosses and changed their benefit packages and salary structures.

Leaning farther back in her chair, Joanna could see the front of his desk. His desk keys were protruding from the lock in the center drawer. The keys to the files would either be on that ring or in one of his desk drawers.

"Good morning," Phyllis said, following Meredith into her office. "How was your weekend?" she asked, then she bit her lip and looked mortified by her question. She had obviously heard about the fistfight Saturday, Meredith realized, and at that moment she didn't care. She was so happy, she felt buoyant. Pausing in the act of unlatching her briefcase, Meredith sent her a wry, laughing look. "How do *you* think it was?"

"Would *exciting* be the right word?" Phyllis ventured, smiling back.

Meredith thought of Matt's lovemaking, the things he'd said and done to her, and her whole body felt deliciously warm. "I'd say that's a pretty apt word," she said, hoping she didn't sound as dreamy as she felt. With an effort she pulled her thoughts from the weekend and made herself think about the work she had to do before she could see Matt again tonight. "Any phone calls this morning?"

"Just one—Nolan Wilder. He wants you to call him back as soon as you get in."

Meredith froze. Nolan Wilder was the chairman of Bancroft's board of directors, and she had little doubt he was calling to demand an explanation of Saturday night's debacle. Which, in the clear light of morning, struck her as being an act of monumental gall, given that Wilder's own divorce had been so ugly and bitter that it had taken two years to get through the courts. "Get him on the phone for me, will you?" she asked.

A minute later, Phyllis buzzed her. "Wilder's on the line."

Pausing a few seconds to compose herself, Meredith picked up the phone and said in a bright, firm voice, "Good morning, Nolan. What's up?"

"That's what I was going to ask you," he said in the cool, ironic tone he used during board meetings and which Meredith particularly loathed. "I've had calls from board members all weekend demanding explanations for that business Saturday night. I shouldn't have to remind you, Meredith, that Bancroft's image, the dignity of its name, is the foundation of its success."

"I hardly think I need to be told that," Meredith said, forcing herself to sound more amused than angry. "It's—" She broke off as Phyllis rushed in, her face stricken.

"You have an emergency call from MacIntire in New Orleans on line two."

"Hold on, Nolan," Meredith said, "I have an urgent call." Alarm was screaming through every fiber of her body as Meredith answered the phone. MacIntire's voice was taut. "We've had another bomb threat here, Meredith. It was phoned to the police department a few minutes ago. The caller said the bomb is set to go off in six hours. I've ordered the store cleared and the bomb squad is on the way. We're following the usual procedure for evacuation, just as we did last time. I think the call's from the same crank who made the last one."

"It probably is," she said, fighting to keep her voice level and her thoughts clear. "The minute you can get back inside, start putting together a list of anyone at all who might have a reason to want to put us through this. Have your security manager draw up a list of everyone who was detained for shoplifting, and have your credit manager give us a list of everyone denied credit in the last six months. Mark Braden, who heads our security division, will fly down there tomorrow to work with your people. Now, get out of there—just in case it wasn't a crank."

"Right," he said reluctantly.

"Call me from wherever you decide to go and give me your phone number so we can keep in touch."

"Got it," he said. "Meredith," he added, "I'm really sorry about this. I don't know why this store is suddenly a target. I assure you we bend over backward for customers, in keeping with company policy, and—"

"Adam," she interrupted emphatically, "get out of that store!"

"Okay."

Meredith hung up and punched the button for the line where she'd left Wilder on hold. "Nolan," she said, "I don't have time to talk about a board meeting now. The New Orleans store just had another bomb threat."

"This is going to play hell with Christmas profits," he predicted furiously. "Keep me posted, Meredith, you know where to reach me."

Meredith mumbled a distracted promise, and then launched into action. Looking at her secretary, who was hovering anxiously in the doorway, she said, "Have the paging operator give out the emergency code. Hold all my calls unless they're critical, and if they are, put them through to me in the conference room."

When her secretary left, Meredith stood up and began to pace, telling herself this was nothing but a false alarm. On the store's intercom system the emergency code was already beginning to ring—three short bells followed by three long ones—notifying all department heads to assemble immediately in the designated emergency location, which was the conference room adjoining Meredith's office. The last time that emergency code had to be used was two years before, when a shopper had died of a heart attack in the store. Then, like today, the purpose for assembling everyone was primarily to keep them informed and, therefore, prevent a hysterical outbreak of gossip among the employees, and to plan what information would be given to the press. Like most large corporations, Bancroft & Company had an established set of procedures for dealing with emergencies such as personal injuries, fires . . . and even bomb scares.

The possibility that a bomb might actually explode in New Orleans and injure people was more than Meredith could bear to contemplate. The thought of a bomb going off after the store was cleared was less horrifying but sickening nonetheless. Like all the Bancroft branch stores, the New Orleans store was beautiful, distinctive, and new. In her mind, Meredith saw its splendid white-pillared façade gleaming in the sunshine, then she saw it exploding and collapsing, and she shuddered. There wasn't a real bomb in it, she told herself, it was another false alarm. A false alarm that would cost the store dearly in lost Christmas profits.

The store's executives were hurrying past her doorway, assembling in the conference room, but Mark Braden, according to established procedure, came straight into her office. "What's happening, Meredith?"

Meredith told him, and he swore under his breath, looking at her in angry consternation. When she finished telling him about the instructions she'd given MacIntire, he nodded. "I'll catch a flight out there in a few hours. We've got a good security man in that store. Between us and the police, maybe we can turn up something that will point to a suspect."

The atmosphere in the crowded conference room was heavy with tension and curiosity. Rather than sitting down at the conference table, Meredith walked to the center of the room, where she could be seen and heard more easily by the men and women who'd assembled there. "We've had another bomb scare in New Orleans," she began. "The bomb squad is on its way there. Since this is the second one we've had, we're going to be hit with a lot of calls from the press. No one . . . no one," she emphasized, "is to make any statements. Refer all inquiries from the media to public relations." She glanced at the P.R. director and said, "Ben, you and I can work out a statement after this meeting, and—" She broke off as the phone rang on the conference table. "Excuse me," she said, and picked it up.

The manager of the Dallas store sounded frantic. "We've had a bomb threat, Meredith! The caller told the police that the bomb is set to go off in six hours. The bomb squad is on the way, and we're clearing the store." Meredith automatically gave him the same instructions she'd given the manager of the New Orleans store, then she hung up the phone. For a moment she was unable to think, then she slowly looked at the assembly. "We've had another bomb threat—at the Dallas store. They're clearing it now. The call went to the police, just like the one in New Orleans, and the caller said the bomb is set to go off in six hours."

A flurry of furious exclamations and outraged curses erupted around the room, then died in the shock of the telephone shrilling yet again. The sound made Meredith's heart stop, but she reached out and picked it up. "Miss Bancroft," the policeman's voice said urgently, "this is Captain Mathison over at the First District. We've just received an anonymous phone call from a man who said a bomb has been placed in your store and is set to go off in six hours."

"Hold on," Meredith said, her dazed eyes leveling on Mark Braden as she stretched the receiver out to him. "Mark," she said, automatically following procedure for the Chicago store and handing the matter over to him. "It's Mathison."

She waited in a paralysis of fury and pain while Mark snapped questions at the captain, whom he knew well. After Braden hung up, he turned to the silent group in the conference room. "Ladies and gentlemen," he said, his voice tight with anger, "we've had a bomb threat against this store. We'll use the same procedure you're familiar with for fire. You all know what to do and say to your people. Let's get at it and get everyone out of here. If you're feeling panicky, Gordon," he snapped, looking straight at Meredith's problem vice president who'd started to mumble frantically, "keep it to yourself until your staff has cleared out!" He threw a quick glance at the other faces in the room. They looked tense but composed, and he nodded curtly, already turning to leave and instruct his own staff to supervise the evacuation procedures. "In case you don't normally use them," he called behind him, "don't forget to take your pagers with you when you leave."

Within ten minutes Meredith was the only one present on the executive floor. Standing at her window, she listened to the sirens wailing and watched as more fire trucks and squad cars jammed into Michigan Avenue to reinforce those that were already there. From her vantage point fourteen stories above street level, she watched the police cordoning off the store and shoppers pouring out of it in droves, while the knot in her chest grew and twisted until she could hardly drag air through her lungs. Although she'd ordered the heads of the other two stores to evacuate, she herself had no intention of leaving this one until she absolutely had to. This store lived and breathed for her; it was her heritage and her future; she refused to desert it or be driven out until the bomb squad needed it completely cleared. Not for a moment did she believe there was a bomb in any of her stores, but even if the threats were just that, the damage they were going to do to the company's profits would be great. Like many other department stores, Bancroft's depended on the Christmas season for over forty percent of its annual gross sales.

"It's going to be all right," she told herself aloud. She turned away from the window, her attention caught by the twin computer screens on her credenza. They were flashing now because the computers were updating sales figures from the Phoenix and Palm Beach stores. Reaching out, Meredith pressed the combination of keys that showed the Phoenix store's sales figures for this same day last year, and then those from the Palm Beach store, so that she could see the comparison. Both stores were doing much better this year than last, and she tried to take consolation from that. It dawned on her then that Matt might be near a radio and hear what was happening. Rather than worry him, she picked up the phone and called him. It felt strangely reassuring to know he'd be concerned.

Matt wasn't concerned when she told him what was happening, he was frantic. "Get out of that store, Meredith," he ordered. "I mean it, darling, hang up the phone and get the hell out of there!"

"Nope," she said softly, smiling at his autocratic command and alarmed tone. He loved her, and she loved hearing his voice whether he was calling her darling or issuing orders. "It's a hoax, Matt, just like the one a few weeks ago."

"If you don't leave that building," he warned, "I'm coming over there and hauling you out of there myself."

"I can't," she said firmly. "I'm like the captain on a ship. I don't leave until I know *everyone* else is safely out of here." She paused while he expressed his opinion of that with a long and eloquent curse. "Don't give me orders you wouldn't follow yourself," she said with a smile in her voice. "In less than a half hour we should be cleared out. I'll leave then."

Matt expelled his breath in a harsh sigh, but he stopped trying to persuade her to leave because he knew it was useless—and because he knew he couldn't get to her before thirty minutes and drag her out of there. "All right," he said, standing up and glowering worriedly at his office, "but call me when you're out, because I'm going to be going crazy until I know you are."

"I will," she promised. Teasingly, she added, "My father left his cellular phone in his desk. Do you want the number so you can reach me—in case the suspense gets too great?"

"You're damned right I want the number."

Meredith opened the desk, took out the phone, and gave him the number.

When she hung up, Matt began to pace, too agitated to sit and wait without knowing what was happening to her. Raking his hand through his hair, he walked over to the window, trying unsuccessfully to see the roof of her building through the maze of skyscrapers. She was so cautious by nature that he could hardly believe she was insisting on staying in that damned store. He hadn't expected that. It hit him then that if he had a radio, he might be able to keep abreast of what was happening twelve blocks away as well as at Meredith's other stores. He didn't have one in his office, but he thought Tom Anderson did.

Turning away from the windows, he headed toward his secretary's office. "I'll be with Tom Anderson," he said, "extension 4114. If Meredith Bancroft calls me, I want that call put through to me there. Is that clear? It's an emergency," he warned her, wishing to God that Eleanor Stern were there.

"Perfectly clear, sir," she said, but Matt didn't notice the hostility in her tone. He was too worried about Meredith to notice a secretary; he was too worried to remember to take his keys out of his desk.

Joanna waited until the elevator doors closed behind him, then she turned and looked at his desk. His gold key ring was still in the center drawer. The third key she tried unlocked the file cabinets; the file on Meredith Bancroft was neatly labeled with her name and filed in its appropriate place, under B. Her palms perspiring with nervous excitement, Joanna removed the file and opened it. In it were some shorthand notes not yet transcribed, and which she didn't dare take the time to try to decipher—and a two-page typewritten agreement signed by Meredith Bancroft. The terms of that agreement made Joanna's eyes widen and her mouth slowly curve into a smile of malicious glee. The same man who *Cosmopolitan* magazine named as one of the country's ten most eligible bachelors—the man who dated movie stars and famous models and who women drooled over—that same man was having to pay his own wife five million dollars just to see him four nights a week for eleven weeks. He was also having to sell her some land in Houston she evidently wanted. . . .

🌿

"I need a radio," Matt said without preamble as he stalked into Anderson's office. He saw it on the windowsill and turned it on. "The bomb squad is swarming all over Bancroft's. They've evacuated all three stores," he said disjointedly. He'd had dinner with Tom last Tuesday after his tumultuous meeting with Meredith, and Matt had told Tom all that led up to it. Now he glanced distractedly at his friend and added, "Meredith won't leave the damned store!"

Tom lurched forward in his chair. "My God! Why not?"

Meredith's call to tell Matt that she was out of the building was put through to him in Tom's office. Matt was still talking to her when the newscaster on the radio announced that a bomb had just been found in the New Orleans branch of Bancroft & Company and that the bomb squad was attempting to disarm it. It was Matt who had to tell her the news. Within the next hour another bomb was discovered in the Dallas store, and a third one was found in the toy department of the Chicago store.

50

With his hand on the iron gate, Philip stood looking at the picturesque little villa Caroline Edwards Bancroft had lived in for nearly thirty years. Perched high on a rocky hill, it overlooked the sparkling harbor far below, where his ship had put into port early that morning. Flowers bloomed riotously in neatly tended beds and pots, basking in the late afternoon sunlight. An aura of beauty and tranquillity pervaded the place, and he found it nearly impossible to imagine his frivolous film-star ex-wife living happily in such relative seclusion as this.

The house had been given to her by Dominic Arturo, the Italian she'd had an affair with before they were married, he knew, and now he assumed she must have gone through every cent of her divorce settlement, or she wouldn't be living there. The large block of stock she owned in Bancroft & Company paid dividends, but she was legally prohibited from selling or transferring it to anyone other than himself. Beyond that, all she could do with her stock was exercise her right to vote her shares, and she always voted in accordance with whatever the board of directors recommended. That much Philip knew, because he'd made it a point over the years to watch how she voted. Now, as he stood looking at the house, he assumed she must have been trying to live on the dividends alone, because nothing short of poverty could have induced his party-loving wife to live like this.

He took his hand away from the black iron gate. He hadn't intended to go there, until that foolish woman at the captain's table had asked if he planned to visit his ex-wife. Once she'd put the idea into his head, he'd found it hard to ignore. He was older now, and he didn't know how long he had to live. Suddenly it had seemed like a good idea to make peace with the woman he'd once loved. She'd been an adulteress and he'd retaliated by keeping her away from her own daughter and forcing her to agree never to come near Meredith or him again. At the time it had seemed like justice. Now that he was facing death without warning, it seemed a little . . . harsh. Perhaps.

However, having seen the way Caroline had been living made him decide against entering the courtyard and knocking on the front door. Curiously, his reason for that was one of pity: He knew how vain she was, and he knew that her ego would take a terrible blow if he saw her living like this. On those occasions when he'd thought of Caroline during the last three decades, he'd always imagined her living in high style, looking as beautiful as ever, and participating in the same social whirl she'd adored before they were married. The woman who lived here must surely have turned into a hag and a hermit, with nothing to do but wile away the years watching ships put into port or shopping in the tiny nearby village.

His shoulders drooping with a strange kind of despair for long-forgotten dreams and shattered lives, Philip turned toward the little path that wound around the side of the hill toward the port below. "You've come a long way, just to turn back, Philip," an unforgettable voice said.

His head jerked around, and he saw her then, standing perfectly still beneath a tree on the hillside to his far left, a basket of flowers over her arm.

She started toward him, her gait long and graceful, her blond hair hidden beneath a peasant scarf that somehow looked good on her. She wasn't wearing any makeup, he realized as she came closer, and she looked much older, and—in some ways—lovelier. The restlessness in her face was gone now; in its place was a calm serenity she'd never possessed in her youth. Oddly, she reminded him more of Meredith now than when she was Meredith's age. And she still had fantastic legs.

He stared at her, feeling his unreliable heart beating a little faster than normal, and he couldn't think of what to say, which made him feel gauche, which in turn made him angry with himself. "You look older," he announced bluntly.

She replied with a soft laugh and no rancor at all, "How nice of you to say so."

"I just happened to be in the neighborhood——" He nodded toward his ship in the harbor, realized how inane his words sounded, and scowled at her because she appeared to be laughing at his discomfiture.

"What takes you away from the store?" she said, putting her hand on the gate but not opening it.

"I've taken a leave of absence. Bad heart."

"I know you've been ill. I still read the Chicago newspapers."

"May I come in?" Philip said without meaning to, and then he remembered that there were always men around her. "Or are you expecting company?" he added with unhidden sarcasm.

"It's good to know that while everything and everyone else in the world seems to change," she remarked dryly, "you and you alone remain the same—as jealous and suspicious as ever." She opened the gate, and he followed her up the path, already regretting that he'd come.

The floors of the villa were stone, covered with bright patches of carpet and huge urns of flowers from her garden. She nodded to a chair in the small room that doubled as living room and parlor. "Would you like a drink?" He nodded, but instead of sitting down, he walked over to the big window, looking out at the harbor. He stayed there until he was forced to turn and accept the glass of wine she held out to him. "Are you doing—all right?" he asked lamely.

"Very well, thank you."

"I'm amazed Arturo couldn't have given you something better than this. This place is little more than a cottage." She said nothing, and that goaded Philip into mentioning her last lover, the one who had caused their divorce. "Spearson never amounted to anything, did you know that, Caroline? He's still trying to eke out a living by training horses and giving riding lessons."

Unbelievably, she smiled at that and, turning, she poured herself a glass of wine. In silence she took a sip, her big blue eyes studying him over the rim. Caught off guard and feeling stupid and churlish, Philip returned her gaze unflinchingly.

"Surely you aren't finished?" she said quietly after a long moment. "You must have dozens more of my imagined indiscretions and infidelities to throw in my face. Evidently, they still bother you after thirty years."

Taking a long breath, Philip tipped his head back and sighed. "I'm sorry," he said truthfully. "I don't know why I started in on you like that. What you do is none of my business."

She smiled, that same serene, unruffled smile he found so unsettling. "You started in on me," she said, "because you're still completely unaware of the truth."

"What truth?" he asked sarcastically.

"Dennis Spearson didn't break up our marriage, Philip, and neither did Dominic. You did." Anger sparked in his eyes and she shook her head, her voice gentle. "You couldn't help it. You're like a frightened little boy who's scared to death that someone is going to take something or someone away from you, and who can't bear the fear and uncertainty of it happening. And so, rather than sitting around and impotently waiting for it to happen, you take matters into your own hands and *force* it to happen—so that you can get the pain over with. You begin by putting restrictions on the people you love—restrictions that they can't bear, and when they finally break one, you feel betrayed and furious. Then you avenge yourself on them—on the same people who you forced to hurt you, and because you're not a boy, but a man with money and power, your revenge against imaginary trespassers is terrible. Your father did virtually the same thing to you."

"Where did you acquire that piece of psychological garbage—from some shrink you had an affair with?" he demanded scathingly.

"I acquired it from a lot of books I read to try to figure you out," she replied, her gaze level.

"And that's what you want me to believe happened to our marriage? That you were innocent and I was irrationally jealous and possessive?" he asked, draining his glass.

"I'll be happy to tell you the whole truth if you think you're well enough to handle it."

Philip frowned at her, taken aback by her unshakable calm and the gentle beauty of her smile. She had been glamorous in her twenties; in her fifties she had faint lines at her eyes and some lines on her forehead; her face had acquired character and it made her strangely more appealing. And quite disarming.

"Give the truth a try," he suggested dryly.

"Okay," she said, walking closer to him. "Let's see if you're old enough and sensible enough now to believe it when you hear it. I have a feeling you will believe it."

Philip had pretty much decided to the contrary already. "Why is that?"

"Because," she answered, leaning her left shoulder against the window, "You're going to realize that I have absolutely nothing to gain or to lose by admitting it all to you, do I?"

She waited, forcing him to admit that much. "No, I suppose not."

"Then, here is the truth," she said calmly. "When we met, I was utterly dazzled by you. You weren't a Hollywood phony; you weren't like any of the men I'd known before. You had breeding and class and style. I fell in love with you on our second date, Philip." She watched shock and then disbelief flicker across his face at that, but she continued with quiet determination. "I was so much in love and so filled with insecurity and inferiority that I could hardly breathe when we were together, for fear I'd make a mistake. Instead of telling you the truth about my background and the men I'd slept with, I told you the same fiction about my origins that the studio publicity office had invented for me. I told you I grew up in an orphanage, and that I'd had one tiny little affair when I was a foolish teenager."

When he didn't say anything, she drew an unsteady breath and said, "The truth is that my mother was a whore who had no idea who my father was, and that I ran away when I was sixteen. I took a bus to Los Angeles and got a job in a cheap diner, where this jerk who worked as a messenger for a film company discovered me. I auditioned for him on the couch in his boss's office that night. Two weeks later I met his boss and got auditioned again—the same way. I couldn't act, but I was photogenic, so the boss got me an appointment at a modeling agency, and I started making money doing magazine ads. I went to acting school, and eventually I got some bit parts in movies after I auditioned for them in someone's bed, of course. Later I got some better parts, and then I met you."

Caroline waited for him to react, but all he did was shrug and say coldly, "I know all that, Caroline. I had you investigated a year before I actually filed for divorce. You aren't telling me anything I didn't find out or assume on my own."

"No, but I'm about to. By the time I met you, I'd gotten some pride and confidence, and I no longer slept with men because I was desperate or too weak to say no."

"You did it because you liked it!" he spat out. "And not with one but with hundreds of them!"

"Not nearly hundreds," she corrected him with a sad smile, "but many of them. It was just—just something you did. It was part of the business, like shaking hands is to men in your business."

She heard his snort of contempt and ignored it. "And then I met you, and I fell in love, and for the first time in my life I felt shame—shame for all the things I'd been and done. And so I tried to change my past by reinventing it to suit your standards. Which, of course, was a hopeless endeavor."

"Hopeless," he agreed shortly.

Her eyes were soft as they looked into his, her voice ringing with quiet sincerity. "You're right. But what I could—and *did*—change was the present. Philip, no man touched me but you from the day we met."

"I don't believe you," he snapped.

But Caroline only smiled wider and shook her head. "You have to believe me—because you already agreed that I have absolutely nothing to gain by lying to you. What possible reason could I have to humble myself like this? It's the sad truth," she continued, "that I actually thought I could atone for my past by cleaning up my present. Meredith is your daughter, Philip. I know you used to think she was either Dominic's or Dennis Spearson's, but all Dennis ever gave me was riding lessons. I wanted to fit in with your crowd, and all the women knew how to ride, so I was sneaking out to Spearson's for lessons."

"That was the lie you told at the time."

"No, my love," she said without thinking, "that was the truth. I won't pretend that I didn't have an affair with Dominic Arturo before I met you. He gave me this house as a way to atone for that stupid, drunken pass that you caught him making at me."

"It wasn't a pass," Philip hissed, "he was in our bed when I came home a day early from a business trip."

"I wasn't in it with him!" she retorted. "And he was out cold."

"No, you weren't in it with him," he agreed sarcastically. "You had snuck off to Spearson's, leaving a house full of guests, all of whom were gossiping about your absence."

To his shock, she laughed at that—a sad, whimsical laugh—and confidingly asked, "Isn't it ironic that I never got caught up in any of the lies about my past? I mean, everyone in the world believed that fairy tale about my being an orphan, and the affairs I did have before we were married never came out." She shook her head, making her heavy, shoulder-length hair shimmer in the waning sunlight. "I got away unscathed when I was guilty, but when I was truly innocent, you convicted me on circumstantial evidence. Is that poetic justice, do you think?"

Philip was utterly at a loss for words, unable to believe her, unable to completely doubt her. It wasn't so much the things she'd told him that made him believe she'd been innocent, it was her *attitude* toward it all—the serene acceptance of her fate, the lack of rancor, the frankness and honesty in those eyes of hers. Her next question made his head jerk toward her in surprise. "Do you know why I married you, Philip?"

"Presumably you wanted the financial security and social prestige I could offer."

She chuckled at that and shook her head. "You underrate yourself. I already told you I was dazzled by your looks and breeding, and I was in love with you, but I'd never have married you if it hadn't been for one more thing."

"What was that?" Philip asked in spite of himself.

"I believed," she confessed somberly, "I honestly believed that I had something to offer you too—something you needed. Do you know what it was?"

"I can't imagine."

"I thought I could teach you how to laugh and enjoy life."

Silence hung over the room for a long moment, then she looked at him from beneath her thick lashes and there was a funny catch in her voice as she asked softly, "Did you ever learn how to laugh, darling?"

"Don't call me that!" Philip almost shouted, but his chest felt tight with emotions he didn't want to feel—hadn't felt in decades—and he slammed his empty glass down on a table. "I should be going."

She nodded. "Regrets are an awful burden. The sooner you leave, the sooner you'll be able to convince yourself you were actually right thirty years ago. But if you stay, who knows what would happen?"

"Nothing would happen," he said, referring to going to bed with her, startled then that the idea would even occur to him.

"Good-bye," she said quietly. "I'd ask you to give my love to Meredith, but you won't, will you?"

"No."

"She doesn't need it," Caroline said with a winsome smile. "From everything I've been reading, she's remarkable and wonderful. And," she added with pride, "whether you like it or not, there's a part of me in her. She," Caroline informed him, "*knows* how to laugh."

Philip stared at her in blank confusion. "What do you mean, from what you've been reading? What are you talking about?"

Caroline tipped her head toward the pile of Chicago newspapers and gave a throaty chuckle. "I was referring to the way she's handling being married to Matthew Farrell and engaged to Parker Reynolds—"

"How the hell do you know about that?" Philip exploded, his face turning cold and pale.

"It's all over the papers," Caroline began, then she faltered, watching him stalk over to the newspapers and yank them up. His entire body seemed to vibrate with fury as he clutched the paper that broke the news of the arrest of Stanislaus Spyzhalski, and he glared at the pictures of Meredith, Matt, and Parker on the front page. He threw that one down and yanked up the next one, which contained excerpts from their joint news conference with a picture of Farrell grinning at her. Another newspaper was opened to an article about a bomb scare in the New Orleans store, and it slid from his fingers. "He warned me what he'd do eleven years ago," he said in a strangled whisper, more to himself than to her. "He warned me, and he's *doing* it!" He looked up at Caroline, his eyes alive with fury. "Where's the nearest telephone?"

🌿51

Matt was pacing in the foyer of his apartment when Meredith finally arrived at seven o'clock that night—thirty minutes late. He pulled open the door, jerked her into his arms, and said furiously, "Dammit, if you're going to be late, and bombs are going off all over the place, call me to let me know you're all right!" He held her away, tempted to shake her, and instantly regretted his outburst. She looked exhausted.

"I'm sorry," she said. "I didn't think you'd imagine anything like that."

"I evidently have an overactive imagination where you're concerned," Matt said wryly, smiling to take the sting out of his greeting. He led her toward the back of the apartment and up the steps to the lounge area because it was the coziest part of the place, and because the view from the corner windows was the best.

"I was at the police station most of the afternoon," she explained as she sat down on the leather sofa, "trying to give them any information I could that might help them find whoever put the bomb in the store. When I went home to change and come over here, Parker called, and we were on the phone for almost an hour."

Meredith trailed off, remembering Parker's phone call. Neither of them had brought up the fact that he'd spent the night at Lisa's. Parker was no liar, and his deliberate failure to offer an explanation was silent confirmation to Meredith that the night had not been platonic. It felt strange to imagine those two being involved—strange and yet almost reassuring somehow, because Meredith loved them both.

Before he hung up, Parker had wished her happiness, but he'd sounded dubious and worried about her ability to be happy with Matt. About Matt he'd said little—except that he regretted starting the fistfight with him. "The only thing I regret more," Parker had said dryly, "is that I missed my punch."

The rest of their conversation had been about business, and it had not been either reassuring or pleasant.

Pulling herself out of her reverie, she said, "I'm sorry if I seem preoccupied. This has been an incredible day, from beginning to end."

"Do you want to talk about it?"

Meredith looked up at him, struck anew by the aura of quiet command, of absolute competence that surrounded him. Casually dressed in dark trousers with his white shirt open at the throat and the cuffs folded back on his forearms, Matthew Farrell positively exuded indomitable power and strength. It was stamped on his jaw and etched into every one of his hard, chiseled features.

And yet, she thought with an unconscious smile, in bed she could make this bold, powerful man groan with need and turn to her in stormy desperation. She loved knowing that. She loved him.

His question pulled her back to less pleasant thoughts: "Would you rather try to forget about the day?"

"I feel guilty about burdening you," Meredith said, though she was longing for his advice and perhaps reassurance.

His lips quirked, and there was a decidedly sensual note in his eyes. "Having you burden me again is a fantasy that kept me awake until dawn." He watched the telltale glow of knowledge and memory in her eyes and he smiled, but he didn't try to distract her further. Sobering, he said, "Let's hear about your day."

With a conscious effort Meredith pulled herself from the sensual spell of his fantasy. "Actually, it's easy to sum up," she said, curling her legs beneath her and twisting toward him. "Last but not least, our stock closed down three points this afternoon."

"It'll come back up once the bomb thing dies down," Matt said.

Nodding, she continued. "This morning, the chairman of the board called. They want an explanation from me about the fight Saturday night. I was talking to him when the first bomb call came through, so we never finished our conversation."

"The bomb scares will distract them for a while."

With a weak attempt at humor, she added, "I guess every cloud really does have a silver lining." Averting her gaze from Matt's quiet scrutiny, she stared out the windows.

"What else is bothering you?"

It was obvious from his insistent tone that Matt knew there was something else and that he fully intended to hear about it. Feeling excruciatingly self-conscious, she looked at him and said, "Could I have more time to arrange financing to buy the Houston land from you? Parker had arranged for another lender to make us the loan since his bank couldn't. Today, when that lender heard about the bomb threats, they called Parker and pulled out of the deal. They said they want to wait and see what happens at Bancroft's for a couple of months."

"It was nice of Reynolds to unload all that on you today," Matt said sarcastically.

"He called to be certain I was all right and to apologize for what happened Saturday. The rest—the part about the money—came up because we'd had a meeting scheduled to negotiate the terms of the loan tomorrow with the new lender. Parker had to tell me the new lender had called off the meeting—" A loud beeping noise from her pager made Meredith stop talking and reach for the purse she'd put down beside the sofa. She removed the pager, looked at the message on it, and with a silent, frustrated moan she let her head fall back against the sofa, her eyes closed. "This is all I needed to make today perfect."

"What's wrong?"

"It's my father," she sighed, reluctantly looking at Matt. The warmth had left his eyes at the mention of her father, and his jaw was rigid. "My father wants me to call him. It's two or three A.M. in Italy. Either he's calling to say hello in the middle of the night, or else he's finally seen a newspaper. May I use your phone?"

Her father was in Rome at the airport, waiting for a flight home, and when his voice exploded over the phone, Matt scowled and Meredith flinched. "What in the living hell are you doing!" he shouted the moment the operator connected him.

"Calm down, please," Meredith began, but there was no calming him.

"Have you lost your mind!" he thundered. "I leave you alone for a couple of weeks and your face is plastered all over the newspapers next to that bastard's face and then we have bomb threats—"

Ignoring the issue of Matt for the time being, Meredith tried to soothe him about that day's bomb scares, which she thought he'd discovered. "Don't give yourself a stroke over them," she pleaded, holding on to her temper and her strained nerves. "All three bombs were found and removed with no harm to anyone—"

"*Three!*" he roared. "Three bombs? What are you talking about?"

"What were *you* talking about?" she asked, but too late.

"I was talking about the fake scare in New Orleans," he said, and she could feel him striving for control. "There were three bombs found? When? Where?"

"Today. In New Orleans, Dallas, and here."

"What's happened to our sales?"

"The inevitable happened," she said, trying to sound both matter-of-fact and encouraging. "We had to close down for the day, but we'll make it up later. I'm already working on some sort of special sale—Advertising wants to call it a bomb sale in lieu of a fire sale," she tried to joke.

"What happened to our stock?"

"It was down three points at closing today."

"And Farrell?" he demanded with renewed fury. "What's happening with him? You stay the hell away from him. No more press conferences—nothing!"

He was talking so loud that Matt could hear him, and Meredith looked at him in helpless consternation, but instead of giving her an encouraging smile, or any form of moral support, Matt waited for her to refuse her father's orders, and when she didn't do it immediately, he turned on his heel and walked over to the windows, standing with his back to her.

"Now, listen to me," Meredith pleaded with her father in a shaky, calming voice, "there is no point in working yourself up and having another attack over any of this."

"Don't speak to me like an idiot invalid!" he warned, but his voice was straining and she was certain she heard him pause to swallow a pill. "I'm waiting for an answer about Farrell."

"I don't think we should discuss this on the phone."

"Stop stalling, dammit!" he raged, and Meredith realized that it was probably better to deal with the issue now instead of trying to delay it, since he seemed to be getting more worked up over her evasiveness.

"All right, fine," she said quietly, "we'll deal with it now, if that's what you want." She paused, thinking madly for the best way to go about it. It seemed wisest to first try to relieve him of the anxiety he'd undoubtedly have over whether or not she'd discovered his duplicity eleven years before, so she started there. "I realize you love me and you did what you believed was best eleven years ago . . ." Taut silence followed that, so she cautiously added, "I'm talking about the telegram you sent Matt telling him I'd had an abortion. I know about it—"

"Where the hell are you right now?" he demanded suspiciously.

"I'm at Matt's apartment."

His voice shook with rage and something that sounded to Meredith like fear. Panic. "I'm coming home. My plane leaves in three hours. Stay away from him! Don't trust him. You don't know that man, I tell you!" Reverting to blazing sarcasm, he added, "See if you can manage to keep us out of bankruptcy until I get there."

He slammed the phone down, and Meredith slowly hung up, then she looked at Matt, whose back was still turned on her, as if accusing her of not taking a stronger stand. "This has been quite a day," she said bitterly. "I suppose you're angry because I didn't come right out and tell him more about us."

Without turning, Matt lifted his hand and wearily rubbed the tense muscles at the base of his neck. "I'm not angry, Meredith," he said in a flat, emotionless voice. "I'm trying to convince myself you won't back down when he gets here, that you won't start doubting me and yourself, or, worse—start weighing what you have to gain by staying with me against what you have to lose if you do."

"What are you talking about?" she said, walking over to him.

He gave her a grim sideways look. "For days I've been trying to second-guess what he'll do when he gets back here and finds out you want to stay with me. I've just figured it out."

"I repeat," she said softly. "What are you talking about?"

"Your father's going to play his trump card. He's going to make you choose: him or me; Bancroft and Company, along with the president's office—or nothing if you choose me. And I'm not sure," he added on a ragged sigh, "which way you'll go."

Meredith was too worn out, too spent, to take on a problem she didn't have yet. "It won't come to that," she said, because she honestly believed she could, with time, persuade her father to accept Matt. "I'm all he has, and he loves me in his own way," she said, her eyes pleading with him not to make things harder on her now than they already were. "And because he does, he'll rant and rave, and he may threaten me with that, but he'll relent. I've thought a lot about what he did to us. Matt, please, just put yourself in his place," she urged. "Suppose you had an eighteen-year-old daughter whom you'd sheltered from every reality and ugly thing in life. And suppose she met a much older man who you honestly believed was a—a gold digger. And that man took her virginity and got her pregnant. How would you feel about him?"

After a moment of silence Matt said tersely, "I'd hate his guts," and just when Meredith thought she'd scored her point, he added, "but I'd find some way to accept him for her sake. And I sure as hell wouldn't crush her by making her think he'd walked out on her. Nor would I try to bribe him into doing exactly that," he added.

Meredith swallowed. "Did he try to do that?"

"Yes. The day I took you home to him."

"What did you say?"

Matt gazed into her wide, troubled blue eyes, smiled reassuringly, and put his arm around her. "I told him," he whispered as his mouth came down on hers for a long, drugging kiss, "that I didn't think he ought to interfere in our lives. But," he murmured thickly, kissing her ear as she melted against him, "not quite in those words."

It was midnight when he walked her down to her car. Exhausted from the trials of the day and deliciously limp from his lovemaking, Meredith sank into the driver's seat of the Jaguar. "Are you certain you're awake enough to drive?" he asked, his hand on the open door.

"Just barely," she said with a languorous smile, turning the key in the ignition. The heater and radio came on as the engine throbbed to life.

"I'm giving a party for the cast of *Phantom of the Opera* on Friday night," he said. "A lot of people you know are coming to it. My sister will be here too, and I thought I'd invite your lawyer. I think the two of them would hit it off."

When he hesitated, as if afraid to voice the question, Meredith said teasingly, "If that was an invitation, my answer is yes."

"I wasn't going to ask you to come as a guest."

Embarrassed and confused, Meredith glanced at the steering wheel. "Oh."

"I'd like you to act as my hostess, Meredith."

She realized then the reason for his hesitation. He was asking her for what constituted a semi-public declaration that they were a couple. She looked into those compelling gray eyes of his and smiled helplessly. "Is it black tie?"

"Yes, why?"

"Because," she said with a jaunty glance, "it's very important for a hostess to be dressed just right."

With a half-laugh, half-groan, Matt pulled her out of the car and into his arms, seizing her lips in a long kiss of gratitude and relief.

He was still kissing her when the newsman on the radio announced that the body of Stanislaus Spyzhalski, who'd been arrested for falsely representing himself as an attorney to clients including Matthew Farrell and Meredith Bancroft, had been found in a ditch on a county road outside of Belleville, Illinois.

Meredith jerked back and she stared at Matt in shock. "Did you hear that?"

"I heard it earlier today."

His complete indifference and his failure to mention it to her struck Meredith as a little odd, but exhaustion had rendered her incapable of rational thought, and Matt's mouth was already opening on hers again.

52

Inquest, the investigative agency owned by Intercorp, was headquartered in Philadelphia and headed by a former CIA man, Richard Olsen. Olsen was waiting in the reception area when Matt got off the elevator at 8:30 the next morning. "It's good to see you, Matt," he said as they shook hands.

"I'll be with you in five minutes," Matt promised. "Before we get started, I need to make a phone call."

Closing his office door behind him, Matt sat down at his desk and called a private number that rang on the desk of the president of a large Chicago bank. It was answered on the first ring by the president of that bank. "It's Matt," he said without preamble. "Reynolds Mercantile is pulling out on the Bancroft loan, just as we thought they would. So did the other lender they'd lined up for B and C."

"The economy's shaky and lenders are nervous," the banker remarked. "Also, Reynolds Merc had two megaloans go bad on them this quarter, so they'll be looking for money for a while."

"I know all that," Matt replied impatiently. "What I don't know is whether the bomb scares are enough to make them decide B and C is becoming risky, and to start selling off some of the loans they're holding on them."

"Shall we give it a try?"

"Do it today," Matt ordered.

"The same approach we talked about before?" the banker reconfirmed. "We buy up the B and C loans on behalf of the Collier Trust and you arrange to take them off our hands within sixty days."

"Right."

"Is it all right to mention the name Collier to Reynolds? He won't connect it with you?"

"It was my mother's maiden name," Matt said, "no one will connect it to me."

"If this bomb-scare business comes to an end without doing serious damage to B and C's overall worth," the banker added, "we might be interested in retaining the loans ourselves—once they're stabilized."

"In that case, we'll discuss terms then," Matt agreed, but his main concern was more immediate. "Once you've offered to take the loans off Reynolds's hands, make certain you tell him the Trust wants to finance the Houston project for Bancroft as well. Get him to call Meredith Bancroft right away and tell her that. I want her to know she's got the funds available to her."

"We'll handle it."

After hanging up the phone, Matt asked Eleanor to bring Richard Olsen into his office. He waited with strained patience as Olsen surrendered his coat, but before the man had settled into a chair across from him, Matt asked the question that was uppermost on his mind: "What do the police know about the bombings?"

"They don't know a great deal," Olsen said, unlocking his briefcase and removing a file which he opened on his lap. "They've drawn some interesting conclusions however, and so have I."

"Let's hear them."

"For starters, the police think the bombs were meant to be discovered before they went off—a theory which is borne out by the fact that warnings were phoned to the police in plenty of time, and the bombs were placed where they'd be easy to find. The bombs themselves were the work of a pro. My gut feeling is that we aren't dealing with a demented crank here who's retaliating for some imagined offense or indignity he suffered at a Bancroft store. If the police are right—and I think they are—then whoever planted those bombs obviously didn't intend to cause harm to the stores themselves or anyone in them. If that's true, the only remaining logical motive is to cause harm to the store's profits by scaring away shoppers. I understand B and C's sales plummeted all over the country yesterday and the value of their stock has already dropped significantly. Now, the question is, who would want to cause that to happen and why?"

"I don't know," Matt said, striving to keep the frustration out of his voice. "I told you on the phone yesterday that there's a rumor that some entity—other than myself—has been planning to try to take them over. Whoever that is has been quietly buying up their shares. When I got into the game and started buying too, I drove the price of Bancroft's shares up. Presumably, there's a predator company out there, other than mine, who decided to either scare me off with the uproar over bombings and the risk to Bancroft's earnings, or they're simply trying to drive down the price of the shares so they could grab them cheaper."

"Do you have any idea who that company could be?"

"None whatsoever. Whoever it is wants B and C so badly that they aren't thinking straight. The corporation's in debt and B and C is a bad buy for the short-term gain."

"Obviously you don't care about that."

"I'm not in it for profit," Matt replied.

With characteristic bluntness Olsen said, "Why are you buying up their shares, then?" When his question was answered with a quelling stare and total silence, Olsen lifted his hands. "I'm looking for motives other than profit, Matt. If I know yours, maybe I can find someone else with a similar motive or motives and that will give me some leads."

"My original motive was revenge against Philip Bancroft," Matt said when his desire for privacy lost out to his greater desire to get this solved.

"Is there anyone else—with a great deal of money—who might also want revenge against him?"

"How the hell should I know?" Matt said, getting up and beginning to pace. "He's an arrogant son of a bitch. I can't be his only enemy."

"Okay. We'll start there—we'll look for enemies he might have made who now see a long-term shot at revenge and profit, and who can afford to go after it by taking over B and C."

"That sounds absolutely ridiculous."

"Not nearly as much when you consider the fact that no legitimate corporation with motives of pure profit would resort to bomb threats as a means of weakening their prey."

"It's still ridiculous," Matt argued. "Sooner or later they're going to have to make their intentions known, and the minute they do, they're going to be suspect in the bomb threats."

"Being suspect doesn't mean anything unless there's proof," Olsen said flatly.

53

By midafternoon, business had not picked up at any of the stores, and Meredith was trying not to hover at the computers in her office. Mark Braden was due back from New Orleans at any moment, and she'd been expecting her father to descend on her since early morning. Phyllis's announcement that Parker was on the phone was a welcome diversion from her present worries. He'd called her once already to cheer her up, and she assumed this was another such friendly call. It dawned on her, not for the first time as she reached for the phone, that her feelings for Parker couldn't have been nearly as deep as she'd thought they were if she could shift from being his fiancée to his friend so easily. And the fact that Parker seemed to be adapting to that switch as easily as she made her wonder why on earth they'd ever considered getting married in the first place. Lisa's repeated jibes that Parker and Meredith's relationship lacked fire were obviously founded in fact. But Meredith now had good reason to wonder if Lisa's objections to their engagement hadn't been selfishly motivated. That possibility hurt a little, and if Meredith weren't so deluged with problems, she'd have called Lisa and tried to talk to her. On the other hand, it seemed to her that Lisa was the one who should initiate that talk, and she should have done so before now. Dismissing that problem for the time being, Meredith picked up her phone.

"Hi, beautiful," Parker said with a smile in his voice. "Could you stand a little good news for a change?"

"I'm not certain I'll know how to handle it, but give me a try," Meredith replied, and she was smiling too.

"I have lenders who'll make the loan to buy the Houston land, *and* who'll finance the whole building project for you when you're ready to go on it. They walked into my office like angels from heaven this morning, looking for loans to take off our hands."

"That's wonderful news," Meredith replied, but her enthusiasm was dampened by worry about how they were going to make payments on all three existing expansion loans six months from now if business were to stay bad.

"You don't sound very elated."

"I'm worried about poor sales in all our stores," she admitted. "I shouldn't be telling Bancroft and Company's banker that, but he's my friend too."

"As of tomorrow morning," Parker said a little hesitantly, "I'll be your friend—period."

Meredith stiffened in her chair. "What does that mean?"

"We need cash, he said with a reluctant sigh, "so we're selling your loans off to the same investors who are going to lend you the money for the Houston project. You'll be making your payments to the Collier Trust from now on."

Meredith wrinkled her nose, lost in thought. "Who?"

"A partnership called the Collier Trust. They use Criterion Bank right around the corner from you, and Criterion vouched for them. In fact, Criterion's people approached me on their behalf. The Collier Trust is a private partnership with plenty of capital to lend, and they've been looking for good loans to buy up. Just to be on the safe side, I checked them out with my own sources. They're solid and completely aboveboard."

Meredith felt vaguely uneasy. A few months before, everything seemed so stable and predictable—like Reynolds Mercantile's relationship with Bancroft & Company, and her personal life. Now all of it was in a state of sudden and complete flux. She thanked Parker for getting her the Houston financing, but when she hung up, something about the Collier Trust continued to bother her. She'd never heard it before, and yet it seemed almost familiar.

A minute later Mark Braden walked into her office, grim and unshaven, and she prepared to deal with the more urgent problem of the bombings. "I came here straight from the airport, just as you wanted me to do," he explained by way of apology for his appearance. He was shrugging out of his coat and tossing it over a chair, when there was a flurry of surprised greetings outside her office as secretaries exclaimed, "Welcome back, Mr. Bancroft!" and "Good afternoon, Mr. Bancroft!" Meredith stood up, bracing herself for the confrontation with her father that she'd been dreading.

"All right, let's hear it!" Philip began, slamming his office door. "The damn plane had mechanical trouble or I'd have been here hours ago." Taking over in his inimitable style, he walked forward, flinging off his coat, and demanded of Mark Braden, "Well? What have you found out about these bomb scares? Who's behind it? Why aren't you in New Orleans—that store seems to be the prime target!"

"I just got back from New Orleans, and all we have now are theories," Mark began patiently, then he paused as Philip marched over to the computer screens on the credenza behind the desk and punched in commands on the keyboard that brought onto the screen the total sales in all the stores for the day. When he compared that figure with last year's, on the other screen, his face turned an alarming shade of gray beneath his newly acquired tan. "Good God!" he whispered. "It's worse than I expected."

"It'll get better soon," Meredith said, trying to sound soothing as he belatedly pressed an absentminded kiss on her cheek. If things hadn't been so dire, she'd have laughed at his appearance. Never less than impeccably attired, her father now wore a suit wrinkled from the long transatlantic flight, he needed a shave, and his hair looked as if he'd been combing it with his fingers. "People are staying away from our stores right now," she added, "but in a couple of days, when the publicity about the bombs is over, they'll come back." She started to move away from his desk so that he could sit in the chair behind it, but he surprised her by distractedly motioning her to stay there. Walking over to one of the guest chairs, he eased himself into it, and she realized that he was more exhausted and strained than he looked.

"Start from the day I left," he told her. "Sit down, Mark. Before I hear your theories, I want to hear some facts from Meredith first. Did you complete the purchase of the land in Houston yet?"

Meredith froze at the mention of that particular project, then she glanced at Mark. "Would you mind waiting outside for a few minutes, Mark, while I discuss this with my—"

"Don't be ridiculous, Meredith," her father said. "Braden can be trusted, and you should know it."

"I do know it," she said, chafing at his tone, but she remained firm. "Mark, would you please give us five minutes?"

She waited until he left, then she came around the desk. "If we're going to talk about the Houston project, we're going to have to talk about Matt. Are you calm enough to listen without going into a rage?"

"You're damned right we're going to talk about Farrell! But first I want to try to salvage my business—"

Instinct told Meredith that this was the right time to tell him about everything, including her involvement with Matt—now, when he was distracted with business concerns and Braden was outside waiting to fill them in on whatever he knew. For one thing, he wouldn't have much time to rant and rave over each event. "You said you want to hear everything that's happened, and I'm going to tell you all of it—I'll keep it short and in chronological order, so it'll only take a few minutes, but you're going to have to understand that Matt is involved in some of it."

"Start talking," he ordered, scowling.

"Fine," she said, and reached out for the diary she'd kept at his instruction before he went on the cruise. As she flipped through pages she said, "We did try to buy the Houston land, but in the midst of the negotiations, someone else bought it." Glancing up, she said levelly, "Intercorp bought it—"

He half rose out of his chair, his eyes blazing with fury and shock. "Sit down and stay calm," she warned him quietly. "Intercorp bought it for twenty million and upped the price to thirty million. Matt did it," she emphasized, "in retaliation against you—because he discovered that you'd had his rezoning in Southville blocked. He also planned to sue you and Senator Davies and the Southville zoning commission." He paled at that and she quickly added, "It's all been settled already. There'll be no lawsuits, and Matt is selling us the property for the original twenty million."

She watched him, hoping to see some sign of softening toward Matt after that, but he was rigid with the effort to control his hatred and anger, and she dragged her gaze back to the business diary, flipping through the pages. Glad that the next matter didn't involve Matt, she said, "Sam Green said there's been an unusual amount of interest in our stock on the market. It drove the price up until this week, when the price began dropping because of the bomb scares. We should know any day now who the new shareholders are and how large a block they own—"

"Did Sam happen to use the word *takeover?*" he demanded, his voice tight.

"Yes," Meredith said reluctantly, and flipped to the next page, "but we all agreed that's probably an imaginary worry, because we'd be a poor takeover target right now. As you already know, we had a bomb threat in the New Orleans store, which proved to be false. It slowed down sales for several days; then they returned to normal." For the next few minutes she continued leafing through the pages until she'd brought him up-to-date on everything, including Parker's call that morning about their new lenders. "That takes care of business," she said, watching him for signs that the strain was more than his heart could take. He looked like a stone statue in that chair, but his color had returned to normal. "Now let's take care of personal matters— Matthew Farrell in particular." Deliberately phrasing the question as a challenge, she said, "Can you handle a discussion of him now?"

"Yes," he snapped.

Gentling her voice, she said, "When I discovered he'd bought the Houston land, I went to his apartment to force a showdown. Instead of finding Matt there, I found his father, who warned me to stay away from Matt, and who accused me of trying to ruin his life and of having an abortion eleven years ago." His jaws clamped, and Meredith calmly continued. "I went to see Matt at the farm that weekend, and together we realized what you had done, including preventing him from seeing me in the hospital. When I had time to think," she said with a sad smile, "I realized you obviously thought you were protecting me from—from a man you believed to be a social-climbing gold digger, which is what you called him back then. You shouldn't have interfered," she added somberly. "I loved him, and I never got completely over the pain of believing he'd deserted me and the baby. In the end you caused me more hurt than he ever could have. But I know you didn't mean to," she added, searching his rigid face.

When he didn't move or speak, Meredith continued. "The week after I came back from seeing Matt at the farm, the bogus lawyer you hired was arrested, and he started naming his clients' names, which caused an uproar in the press about Matt, Parker, and me. Matt had him bailed out of jail and taken care of, then the three of us gave a joint press conference. We tried to pass the matter off as lightly as possible and to put up a show of solidarity. Unfortunately, last week four of us went out to dinner for my birthday, and Parker had too much to drink . . . and, well, there was a fight, and that got us in the newspapers again. About all I can say," she added, trying desperately to joke and find something positive from it, "is that our business had an upward surge for several days after the press conference, which probably came from all the publicity."

Her father didn't smile. When he finally spoke, his voice shook with angry disbelief. "You've broken your engagement to Parker, haven't you?"

"Yes."

"Because of Farrell."

"Yes." Softly, but with absolute conviction, she said, "I love him."

"Then you're an idiot!"

"And he loves me."

That brought her father out of his chair, his lip curled with contempt. "That monster doesn't want *you* or love *you*—what he wants is revenge against *me!*"

His tone hurt as much as his words, but Meredith didn't falter. "Matt understands that I can't live with him for a few weeks—not after I stood in the auditorium downstairs and publicly announced that we scarcely knew each other and there was no possibility of a reconciliation. Now," she concluded with quiet finality, "the fact is that the two of you are going to have to learn to accept each other. I won't pretend that Matt isn't still angry with you for what you did, but he loves me, and because he does, he'll forgive you for the past eventually, and even try to find a way to be friends with you—"

"Did he actually tell you that, Meredith?" he demanded with biting scorn.

"No," she admitted, "but—"

"Then let me tell you what he told *me* eleven years ago," he grated out, leaning his fists on the desk. "That bastard warned me—he threatened me in my own home—that if I came between you and him, he'd buy me and then he'd bury me. He didn't have a thousand dollars to his name eleven years ago, so that was an empty threat, but it isn't now, by God!"

"What were you doing at the time to make him say such a thing?" Meredith demanded, already guessing at the answer.

"I won't hide it from you. I tried to pay him off to go away, and when he refused the money, I took a swing at him!"

"And did he hit you back?" she asked, knowing he wouldn't.

"He wasn't that stupid! We were in my house, and I'd have called the police. Besides, he didn't dare alienate you by attacking me. He knew you were going to inherit millions from your grandfather, and he intended to get his hands on all of that. He *warned* me what would happen if I got in his way, and now he intends to make it happen!"

"It wasn't a warning, it was an empty threat," Meredith said slowly, trying to put herself in Matt's place and think how he would have felt. "What would you expect him to do, stand there and let you humiliate and bully him, and then thank you for it? He had as much pride as you have, and he's just as strong-willed as you. That's why you two can't stand each other."

His mouth dropped open at her naivete, and he stared at her in speechless wonder, his anger draining. "Meredith," he said almost gently, "You're a very smart young woman, and yet you're still a gullible little fool where Farrell is concerned! You've been sitting here updating me on a series of dramatic events that are having dire effects on our business. And yet it hasn't seemed to occur to you they *all*, including these bomb threats, coincided with Farrell's reentry into our lives!"

"Oh, don't be ridiculous!" she said, shocked into laughter.

"We'll see who's ridiculous," he warned fiercely, and leaning across the desk, he picked up the intercom and said, "Send Braden in here. And tell Sam Green and Allen Stanley I want them to join us immediately."

As soon as the corporation's lawyer and its controller arrived a few minutes later, Philip launched into action. "We're not going to play games in this meeting," he told them. "I'm going to lay all my cards on the table, but nothing that is said in here is to leave this room. Is that clear?"

The three men nodded immediately, and Philip turned to Braden. "Let's hear your theory about the bomb scares."

"The police believe, and I agree," Mark explained, "that the bombs weren't meant to do actual damage to the stores. Just the opposite, in fact, because they were carefully placed where they'd be easily discovered before they could explode—and where they'd do minimal damage if they did. In every instance, warnings were called to the police, well in advance of the time they were set to go off. Also, here in Chicago, where it took the longest to locate the bomb, someone actually called in just before it was discovered, to give a *hint* where it was. It's as if whoever is behind all this was taking infinite care that no serious damage was done to the stores. It's bizarre," he said frankly.

"I don't think so," Philip jeered. "It makes *perfect* sense to me!"

"How?" Braden asked, staring at him in bewildered silence.

"It's simple! If you're getting ready to launch a takeover attempt at a department store chain, and you're vicious enough to put bombs in their stores so their stock will drop and you can buy it up cheaper, then you take *great* care that those bombs don't actually do any harm to the stores—because you're planning to own the goddamn stores!"

In the deafening silence he turned to Sam Green. "I want a list of the names on record of every person, every company, every institution, that's bought more than one thousand shares of our stock at a time in the last two months."

"I can get you that tomorrow," Sam Green said. "I'd just about finished drawing it up at Meredith's request."

"I want it first thing in the morning!" Philip ordered, then he turned to Braden. "I want you to run a thorough investigation on Matthew Farrell and get me every scrap of information on him that you can find."

"It would help if I knew what sort of information you're looking for," Mark said.

"For starters, I want to know the names of every single company he owns a major share in, and every single name he does business under. I want to know everything you can find out about his personal financial setup, where he keeps his money, and under what names. I want names. He'll have trusts set up and shelters—get me *names.*"

Meredith already knew what he intended to do with those names—he was going to start looking for those names on the list of new stockholders that Sam was getting together.

"Allen," he said to the controller, "You work with Sam and Mark. I don't want anyone else involved in this hunt for information, because I don't want every damned clerk in this store finding out through the grapevine that we're hunting for information on the same felon my daughter is married to—"

"That's the last time you'll say anything like that about him unless you've already proved it," Meredith said furiously.

"Agreed," he said, so convinced he was right that he didn't hesitate. When the men left, Meredith watched in angry silence as he leaned over and picked up a paperweight, turning it over in his hand as if he were suddenly too self-conscious to look at her. What he said floored her. "We've had our differences, you and I," he began hesitantly. "We've been at cross purposes too often, and much of it has been my fault. While I was marooned on that ship, I thought a lot about what you said to me when I told you I didn't want to see you take over as president. You accused me of not"—he paused to clear his throat—"of not loving you, but you were wrong." He shot an uneasy glance at her, then he glowered at the paperweight and admitted, "I saw your mother for a few hours while I was in Italy."

"My *mother?*" Meredith repeated blankly, as if such a person were more myth to her than reality.

"It wasn't a reconciliation or anything like that," he quickly and defensively stated. "We argued, in fact. She accused me of blaming her for infidelities she never committed. . . ." His voice trailed off for a moment, and from the preoccupied look on his face, it occurred to Meredith that he evidently thought that was possible. Before she could begin to react to that shock, he continued. "Your mother said something else too, something I thought about during the flight back here."

He drew a long, fortifying breath and lifted his eyes to Meredith. "She accused me of being jealous and trying to control the people I love. She said I place unfair restrictions on them because I'm afraid of losing them. Maybe in your case that's been true in the past."

Meredith felt a sudden, painful lump of emotion in her throat, but his next words were blunt and cold. "My feelings for Farrell at this moment have nothing to do with jealousy over you, however. He's trying to destroy everything I've built, everything I have, and all of this is going to be yours someday. I'm not going to let him do that. I'll do anything, *anything* to stop him. I mean that."

She opened her mouth to defend Matt, but he held up his hand and cut her off. "When you realize I'm right, you're going to have to make a choice, Meredith—Farrell or me—and I'm betting that you'll make the right choice despite your attraction to that man."

"There won't be a choice like that, because Matt isn't doing what you think he is!"

"You were always blind where he was concerned. However, I'm not going to let you close your eyes this time and pretend none of this is happening. You will continue to act as president of this corporation while we're investigating him. Bancroft and Company is your birthright, and I was wrong to try to stop you from taking control of it. You've acted wisely and swiftly from what I just heard from Sam and Allen Stanley. Your only mistake was an understandable one—you dismissed the possibility of a takeover attempt because you couldn't see a logical business reason for anyone to want to move in on us. The reason wasn't logical, and it wasn't business, it's vengeance, so you naturally overlooked it. When we have all the facts," he warned, "You'll have to take an official stand. You'll have to decide whether you want to side with our enemy or fight for your birthright as president of this corporation. And you're going to have to inform the board of directors of your choice."

"God, you are so wrong about Matt!"

"I hope I'm not wrong about *you*," he interrupted, "because I'm going to trust you not to alert him that we're on to him so he can cover his tracks." He reached for his coat, suddenly looking weary and old, and said, "I'm exhausted. I'm going home to rest. Tomorrow I'll be coming back in, but I'll use the conference room next door for now. Call me if Braden turns up anything before then."

"I will, but," she said with calm challenge, "I want a commitment from you now."

He turned with his hand on the doorknob. "What commitment?"

"I want you to agree that when Matt turns out to be innocent of all this, you will not only apologize to him for the things you've done, but that you will honestly and sincerely try to befriend him! Furthermore, I want you to promise that you will inform Mark and Sam and anyone else you've slandered him to that you were completely wrong." He tried to brush that unlikely event aside with an angry shrug, but Meredith was determined to strike a bargain. "Yes or no?"

"Yes," he bit out.

After he left, Meredith sank down in her chair. Not for one second did she think there was anything to warn Matt about, and yet she felt vaguely as if she'd been subtly manipulated by the need for silence into siding against him. And at the same time, she was profoundly touched by her father's tacit announcements that he loved her and approved of the job she'd done in his absence. But most of all, what she felt was hope—hope that when the facts all came out and her father apologized to Matt, Matt would be generous enough to accept the apology. The possibility of having the two men she loved become, if not friends, at least not foes, was heady stuff indeed.

Despite her optimism and confidence, one thing her father had said stayed with her, hovering at the edge of her mind. She had dinner with Matt that night in a dimly lit corner of a local restaurant. When he questioned her about her confrontation with her father, she told him about most of it, excluding her father's absurd belief that Matt was behind the bomb scares and a nonexistent takeover attempt. That much she was willing to keep from him in return for her father's promised apology when he was proven wrong. But she purposely waited until later that night, when they'd gone back to her apartment and made love, to ask him about the one comment her father had made that was bothering her. She waited because she didn't want it to sound like an accusation or a confrontation.

Beside her in bed, Matt leaned up on his elbow, idly tracing his finger along the curve of her cheek. "Come home with me," he whispered achingly, "I promised you paradise, and I can't give it to you when we're living in two different places and pretending we're only half married."

Meredith gave him a distracted smile, and it was enough to alert him that something else was on her mind.

Taking her chin between his thumb and forefinger, he turned her face toward his. "What's wrong?" he said quietly.

Carefully keeping her tone nonjudgmental, Meredith lifted her eyes to his. "It's something my father said," she admitted.

His jaw hardened at the mention of her father. "What did he say?"

"He told me that years ago you threatened that you'd buy him and then bury him if he tried to come between us. You didn't really say that, did you?"

"Yes," he replied shortly, then he added more calmly, "When I said that, your father was trying to bribe and then bully me into leaving you. So I made threats of my own if he came between us."

"But you didn't really mean what you said, did you?" she asked, her gaze searching his.

"At the time I meant every word. I always mean what I say," he whispered as his mouth came down on hers for a long, deep kiss. "But," he murmured, his lips feather-light against her cheek, "sometimes I change my mind . . ."

"And by burying him," Meredith persisted, "did you actually mean kill him?"

"I meant that part of the threat figuratively, not literally, although, at the time, I'd have relished doing him serious bodily injury."

Soothed but not completely satisfied, Meredith put her fingers over his lips to stop him from distracting her with another kiss. "Why did you tell him you intended to buy him?"

He lifted his head, frowning at the doubt in her voice. "I'd just finished refusing his bribe and listening to him accuse me of being after your money, not you. I told him I didn't need your money, that I intended to have enough of my own someday to buy and sell him. I think those were almost my exact words. And I suppose by bury him, I meant the same thing—being able to buy and sell him."

Meredith's expression cleared, and she drew his head down to hers, her fingers sliding caressingly over his cheek. "May I have that kiss now?" she whispered, smiling.

🌿54

*T*he smile was still lingering in her heart the next morning when she reached for the newspaper lying outside her apartment door. The headline almost sent her to her knees:

MATTHEW FARRELL QUESTIONED IN MURDER OF STANISLAUS SPYZHALSKI

Her heart hammering, she picked up the paper and read the accompanying story. It began by rehashing the entire fiasco of the sham attorney who'd provided them with falsified divorce documents and ended with the ominous statement that Matt had been questioned by the police late yesterday afternoon.

Meredith stared at that sentence in cold shock. Matt had been questioned yesterday. *Yesterday.* And he'd not only kept it secret from her last night, he hadn't looked or acted as if anything at all was wrong! Dumbstruck by this incontrovertible proof of his ability to hide his emotions, to deceive even her, she walked slowly into her apartment to get ready to go to work, intending to call him from the office.

Lisa was pacing back and forth when she arrived. "Meredith, I have to talk to you," she said as she closed the door to Meredith's office.

Meredith looked at her childhood friend, and her uncertainty about Lisa's loyalty showed in the hesitancy of her smile. "I was wondering when you were going to get around to that."

"What do you mean?"

Meredith looked blankly at her. "I mean about Parker."

That seemed to hurtle Lisa into distracted despair. "Parker? Oh, God, I've wanted to talk to you about that, only I hadn't gotten up the courage yet. Meredith," she implored, raising her hands and letting them fall helplessly, "I know you must think I'm the biggest liar and phony in the world for the way I made fun of him to you, but I swear I didn't do it to try to stop you from marrying him. I was trying to stop myself from wanting him, trying to convince myself he was nothing but a—a stuffy banker. And, dammit, you weren't really in love with him—look how quickly you fell into Matt's arms when he came back." Her defiant façade crumbled. "Oh, please, don't hate me for this. Please don't. Meredith," she said, and her voice broke, "I love you more than my own sisters, and I've hated myself for loving the man you wanted. . . ."

Suddenly they were two eighth-graders again who'd had a quarrel and were confronting each other on the school playground at St. Stephen's, but they were older now, and wiser, and they knew the value of their friendship. Lisa looked at her, tears shimmering in her eyes, her hands clenched into helpless fists at her sides. "Please," she whispered. "Don't hate me."

Meredith drew a shattered breath. "I can't hate you," she said, her smile wobbling. "I love you too, and, besides, I don't *have* any other sisters—" With a choked laugh Lisa flung herself into Meredith's arms, and as they had that long-ago day when they'd worn eighth-grade uniforms, instead of chic designer fashions, they hugged each other and laughed and tried not to cry. "Does it seem a little—incestuous—to you though?" Lisa asked with a sheepish grin when they were standing apart again. "My being with Parker?"

"Yes, as a matter of fact it did—the morning I called you, and you were both obviously in bed. Together."

Lisa started to laugh, then she sobered abruptly. "Actually, I didn't come up here to talk about Parker. I came to ask you about the police questioning Matt yesterday. I saw it in the morning paper and I"—she looked away, her gaze shifting about the room—"and I, well, I guess I came up here looking for reassurance. I mean—do the police think he killed Spyzhalski?"

Fighting down a surge of angry loyalty, Meredith said calmly, "Why should they? More important, why should *you*?"

"I don't," Lisa protested miserably. "It's just that I keep remembering the morning of your press conference, when he was talking to his attorney on the speaker phone. Matt was furious with Spyzhalski, anyone could see that, and desperately determined to protect you from scandal. And then he said something that seemed sort of . . . odd and . . . threatening even then."

"What are you talking about?" Meredith demanded, more impatient than upset now.

"I'm talking about what Matt said when his attorney warned him that Spyzhalski was a crank who wanted to put on a big show in the courtroom. Matt told his attorney to change Spyzhalski's mind and get him out of town. And then Matt said that he'd 'take care of him' after that. You don't think," Lisa finished, her apprehensive gaze searching Meredith's face, "that Matt's way of 'taking care of him' might have been to have him beaten up and dumped in a ditch, dead, do you?"

"That is the most absurd, the most outrageous thing I've ever heard!" Meredith said in a low, explosive voice, but her father's words brought them both whirling around.

"I don't think the police will find a remark like that absurd," he announced from the connecting doorway of the conference room. "Furthermore, it's your duty to inform them of it."

"No," Meredith said, starting to panic at how the police might construe Matt's remark, and then inspiration struck. She was so relieved, she smiled. "I'm Matt's wife, I have no duty to repeat that, not even in a courtroom."

Philip looked at Lisa. "You heard it, and you're not married to the bastard."

Lisa looked at Meredith and saw the pleading in her eyes. Without further hesitation she took her side. "Actually, Mr. Bancroft," she lied with an apologetic smile, "I don't think that's what Matt said after all. No, I'm sure it wasn't. You know how imaginative I am," she added, backing out of the office, "that's why I'm such a brilliant designer here—a very vivid imagination."

When her father transferred his frustrated glower to her, Meredith pointed out something to him that had just occurred to her. "You know," she told him quietly, "in your desperation to blame Matt for everything, you're tripping on your own faulty logic. On the one hand, you're accusing him of having no feelings for me, and of using me merely to get revenge against you. If that's true, how can you possibly believe he'd actually have Spyzhalski murdered to protect me from scandal?" She scored a point with that one, she knew, because her father swore under his breath and walked out, but an instant later Meredith's heart missed a beat as something else Matt said came back to haunt her. The same night Spyzhalski's body was found, she'd been teasing him about his offer to divert the reporters while she drove into his apartment garage. *You'd do that? Just for me?* she'd joked, but his reply hadn't been joking, it had been said with deadly earnestness. *You have no idea,* he'd answered, *how much I'd do—just for you.*

Meredith walked over to her desk and shook her head, shoving the thought aside. "Stop it!" she warned herself aloud. "You're letting everyone else's suspicions get to you!"

At six o'clock, however, it became almost impossible not to do exactly that. "Here are your first two pieces of evidence, Meredith," her father announced, walking in with Mark Braden, and furiously tossing two reports onto her desk.

Filled with sudden foreboding, Meredith slowly shoved the advertising budget she'd been reviewing aside, glanced at the grim faces of both men, and pulled the reports over in front of her. The first report was a lengthy background check that Mark had run on Matt. On it, Mark had put red circles around the names of every company Matt owned, every legitimate business enterprise he was involved in, and there were dozens of them. Eight of the names had large red X's beside them. She looked at the other report, which contained the names of the people, institutions, and companies that had recently acquired more than a 1,000-share block of stock in Bancroft's, and her heart began to thud with dread: Those eight names with the red X's on the investigative report about Matt also appeared on the list of new shareholders. Combined, Matt had already acquired a gigantic block of stock in B & C, all of it purchased in names other than his own or Intercorp's.

"That's only the beginning," her father said. "That shareholder list isn't up-to-date, and the investigative report on Farrell is incomplete. God knows how many additional shares he's bought or in what names. When our stock prices went up, Farrell obviously decided to put a few bombs in our stores to drive them down, so he could buy them cheaper. Now," he said, leaning his flattened palms on her desk, "will you admit that he's behind what's happening to us?"

"No!" Meredith said stonily, but God help her, she wasn't certain whether she was denying that he was right or denying her ability to admit it. "All this proves is that he—he decided to acquire shares of our stock. There could be several reasons for that. Perhaps he realized we're a good long-term investment and it—it amused him to make money on your own company!" She stood up, her knees shaking, and looked at both men. "That's a far cry from having bombs planted in our stores or having people murdered!"

"Why did I ever think you had sense!" Philip said in frustrated fury. "That bastard already owns the property we want in Houston, and God knows how much he owns of us! He's already got enough shares to vote himself a seat on our board right now—"

"It's late," Meredith interrupted, but her voice was taut with strain as she shoved work into her briefcase. "I'm going to go home and try to work there. You and Mark can continue this—this witch hunt without me!"

"Stay away from him, Meredith!" her father warned as she started for the door. "If you don't, you may end up looking like a co-conspirator in all this. By Friday at the latest we'll have enough proof put together to turn him over to the authorities—"

She turned, trying to look scornful. "What authorities?"

"The Securities and Exchange Commission, for starters! If he's acquired five percent of our stock, and I'm damned sure he has by now, then he's in violation of the SEC rules because he hasn't notified them he's done it! And if he's violated that law, then the police won't think he's as pure as the driven snow when it comes to the death of that lawyer, or bomb threats—"

Meredith walked out and closed the door behind her. Somehow she managed to smile and say good night to the other executives she passed on her way to the parking garage, but when she slid into the front seat of the car Matt had given her, her composure broke. Clutching the steering wheel with both hands, she stared at the cement wall of the parking garage, shivering uncontrollably. She told herself she was panicking needlessly, that Matt would have a logical, reasonable explanation for all of this. She was not, absolutely was *not* going to convict him in her head on such circumstantial evidence. She said it over and over again like a chant. Or a prayer. Slowly, the trembling subsided, and she turned the key in the ignition. Matt was innocent, she knew it with every fiber of her being, and she wouldn't dishonor him by doubting him for one more second.

Despite that noble resolve, her fears and misgivings could not be so easily banished, and by the time she'd changed clothes she was so miserable she couldn't concentrate on anything else. She opened her briefcase, listlessly took out the advertising budget, and realized it was pointless to try to work while her mind was in this state. If she could just see Matt, she told herself, see his face and his eyes, and hear his voice, she'd be reassured that he hadn't done the things her father was accusing him of doing.

She was still telling herself that her only reason for needing to see him was for the reassurance of his company and to stop her imagination from running away with itself when she pressed the buzzer beside the double doors of the penthouse. Matt had already put her name on the permanent guest list at the security desk, so he had no idea that she was coming. Joe O'Hara opened the door, his homely face splitting into a wide grin when he saw her. "Hiya, Mrs. Farrell! Matt's gonna be glad to see you! Nothin' could make him gladder," he predicted as he lowered his voice and peered around her, "except if you happened to have suitcases with you?"

"I'm afraid I don't," Meredith said, smiling helplessly at his outrageous gall. In Matt's bachelor household, Joe seemed to be a jack of all trades— not merely chauffeur or bodyguard, but in his off hours he answered the door, the phone, and he even cooked an occasional meal. Now that she was more accustomed to his bulk and that dark, sinister face of his, he reminded her more of a teddy bear—albeit a lethal one.

"Matt's in the library," he said as he closed the door. "He brought a load of work home with him from the office, but he won't mind the interruption, not a bit! Want me to take you to him?"

"No thanks," she said with a smile over her shoulder. "I know the way."

"I was just leaving for a couple hours," he added meaningfully, and Meredith suppressed a silly surge of embarrassment at what he obviously thought was the reason for her visit.

In the doorway to the library she paused, momentarily cheered and reassured by the sight of Matt. Seated on a leather chesterfield, his ankle propped on the opposite knee, he was reading some documents, making notes in the margins. More documents were spread out on the coffee table in front of him. He glanced up, saw her standing there, and the sudden glamour of his lazy white smile made her heart leap. "This must be my lucky day," he said, getting up and walking toward her. "I thought you weren't going to be able to see me tonight—something about your needing to work and get an uninterrupted night's sleep. I suppose it's too much to hope," he added with another grin, "that you brought some suitcases with you?"

Meredith laughed, but it sounded hollow to her own ears. "Joe asked the same thing."

"I definitely ought to fire him for impertinence," Matt teased, pulling her into his arms for a hungry kiss. She tried to respond, but her heart wasn't in it, and he sensed it almost at once. Lifting his head, he studied her for a puzzled moment. "Why do I have the feeling," he asked, "that your mind is on something other than what we're doing?"

"You're obviously more intuitive than I am."

His hands slid down her arms, then he let her go and stepped back, frowning slightly. "What is that supposed to mean?"

"It means that I'm not nearly so good at guessing what's going on in your mind," Meredith replied with more force than she'd intended, and she realized with a jolt that she hadn't come to reassure herself with the sight of him.

She'd come for some answers.

"Why don't we go in the living room, where it's more comfortable, and you can explain the meaning of that remark."

Meredith nodded and followed him, but once they were there, she was too restless to sit down and too self-conscious to face him with her unspoken accusations. Uneasy under his steady scrutiny, she let her gaze drift over the room . . . past the collage of old photographs of his sister and father and mother framed on a splendid carved marble table, past the leatherbound photo album lying beside it. Sensing her tension, he remained standing, and when he spoke his voice was both puzzled and a little curt. "What's on your mind?"

Startled by his tone, her gaze snapped to his face, and she told him exactly what was on her mind. "Why didn't you tell me last night the police questioned you about Spyzhalski's death? How could you spend most of the night with me and never show a sign that you're a—a suspect in it!"

"I didn't tell you because you had enough to deal with without that. Secondly, the police are questioning many of Spyzhalski's 'clients,' and I am *not* a suspect in his death." He saw the relief and uncertainty she was trying to hide, and his jaw hardened. "Or am I?"

"Are you what?"

"A murder suspect—in your eyes."

"No, of course not!" Raking her hair off her forehead in a nervous gesture of confusion and frustration, she looked away from him, unable to stop herself from continuing to prod and hating herself for the mistrust that was making her do it. "I'm sorry, Matt. I've had an awful day." Turning, she studied him with renewed intensity, watching for his reaction as she said, "My father is convinced that someone is about to launch a takeover attempt on us." His expression remained unchanged, unreadable. Guarded? "He thinks that whoever is putting the bombs in our stores might be the same person or group who's planning to take us over."

"It's possible he's right," he said, and from his cool, clipped tone, she knew he was beginning to realize that she suspected him, and that he was going to despise her for it. In profound misery she looked away again, and her gaze fell on the framed photograph of his mother and father smiling at each other on their wedding day. A similar photo had been in one of the albums she'd packed away at the farm. The photographs . . . The names beneath them . . . *The names.* His mother's maiden name was COLLIER. The Collier Trust had bought up Bancroft & Company's loans. If she hadn't been so beset with other problems, she'd have made the connection before.

Her gaze shot to Matt's face, while the dawning pain of betrayal slashed through her like a thousand jagged knives. "Your mother's name was Collier, wasn't it?" she said, her voice ragged with anguish. "You are the Collier Trust, aren't you!"

"Yes," he said, watching her, as if almost uncertain of how or why she was reacting like this.

"Oh, my *God!*" she said, backing away a step. "You're buying up our stock, and you've bought up all our loans. What are you planning to do, foreclose and take us over if we're late with a payment?"

"That's ridiculous," he said, but there was urgency in his voice as he started toward her. "Meredith, I was trying to help you."

"How?" she cried, wrapping her arms around her stomach and jerking back out of his reach. "By buying up our loans or buying up our stock?"

"Both—"

"You're lying!" she said as everything fell into place, and her blinding obsession with him gave way to agonizing reality. "You started buying our stock the day after we had lunch—right after you found that my father blocked your rezoning request. I've seen the dates. You weren't trying to *help* me!"

"No, not then I wasn't," he answered with desperate sincerity. "I bought the original blocks of stock with every intention of accumulating enough to gain either a seat on your board of directors or possibly a controlling interest."

"And you've kept right on buying them ever since," she flung back. "Only now the shares you're buying are costing you a lot less, aren't they, because our stock has dropped after those bomb threats! Tell me something," she demanded shakily, "just this once, tell me the truth—the complete and entire truth! Did you have Spyzhalski killed? Are you behind those bomb threats?"

"No, goddammit!"

Shuddering with fury and anguish, she ignored his protest. "The first bomb scare took place the same week we had lunch and you found out my father had your rezoning request denied! don't you find that just a little bit coincidental?"

"I'm *not* responsible for any of that," he argued urgently. "Listen to me! If you want the entire truth, I'll give it to you." His voice gentled. "Will you listen to me, darling?"

Her treacherous heart slammed against her ribs at the sound of his voice calling her darling and the expression in those gray eyes. She nodded, but she knew she'd never be able to believe he was telling her the complete truth, not when he'd already hidden so much from her, and so skillfully.

"I've already admitted I started buying shares of your stock to retaliate against your father. Later, after we were together at the farm, I began to realize how important that department store is to you, and I also knew that when your father came home and found us together again, he'd pull out every stop to dissuade you from staying with me. I figured that sooner or later he'll make you choose: him or me. Bancroft and Company and the presidency of it, or nothing, if you choose me. I decided to keep buying up your stock so that he couldn't do that. I was prepared to buy however much stock it would take to gain control of the board of directors so that he couldn't threaten you with the loss of the presidency, because I'd control the board."

Meredith stared at him, her trust demolished by his secrecy over this and all the other things. "But you couldn't confide your *noble* motives to me," she said, glaring her disdain.

"I wasn't sure how you'd react."

"And yesterday you let me make a fool of myself telling you about our new lender—the Collier Trust, when you're the Collier Trust."

"I was afraid you'd see it as—charity!"

"I'm not that stupid," she retorted, but her voice was trembling and tears were burning the backs of her eyes. "It wasn't charity, it was a brilliant tactical move! You promised my father you'd own him someday, and now you do! With the help of a few bombs, and my unwitting cooperation."

"I know it looks that way—"

"Because it is that way!" she cried. "From the day I came to the farm to tell you what really happened eleven years ago, you've been ruthlessly using everything I've told you to manipulate things until they happen the way you want them to. You've lied to me—"

"No, I haven't!"

"You've deliberately misled me, and that's the same thing! Your methods are all dishonest, and yet you expect me to believe your motives are noble? Well, I can't!"

"Don't do this to us," he warned, his voice hoarse with angry desperation as he realized he was losing her. "You're letting eleven years of mistrust color everything you've discovered I've done."

In some part of herself Meredith wasn't sure he was wrong. All she was sure of was that a bogus lawyer who got in Matt's way was dead, and her father, who'd gotten in his way, would soon be little more than a puppet dancing on the end of Matt's financial strings. And so was she. "Prove it to me," she cried on the verge of hysteria. "I want proof."

His face tightened. "Someone has to prove to you I'm not an arsonist or a murderer, is that it? You have to have proof that I'm not guilty of all the rest of that, and if I can't give it to you, you're going to believe the worst?"

Battered by the truth of his words, she looked at him, feeling as if her heart were being torn to pieces. When he spoke again, his deep voice was aching with emotion. "All you have to do is trust me for a few weeks until the authorities find out the truth." He held out his hand for hers. "Trust me, darling," he said tenderly.

With uncertainty clawing at her, Meredith looked at his outstretched hand, but she couldn't move. The bomb threats were too convenient . . . the police weren't questioning *all* Spyzhalski's clients, because they hadn't questioned her.

"Either give me your hand," he said, "or end it now, and put us both out of our misery."

Meredith willed herself to put her hand in his and trust him, but she couldn't do it. "I can't," she whispered brokenly. "I want to, but I just can't!" His hand fell to his side, his face wiped clean of all expression. Unable to endure the way he was looking at her, she turned to leave. Her fingers closed around the keys in her pocket, the keys to the car he'd given her. She pulled them out and turned, holding them toward him. "I'm sorry," she said, fighting to keep her voice from shaking, "I'm not allowed to accept gifts of over twenty-five dollars from anyone with whom my company has business dealings."

He stood unmoving, a muscle leaping in his clenched jaw, refusing to reach for the keys, and Meredith felt as if she were dying inside. She dropped them on the table and fled. Downstairs she hailed a cab.

Sales at the Dallas, New Orleans, and Chicago stores picked up surprisingly well the next morning; Meredith felt relief but no particular joy as she watched the figures change on the computer screen in her office. The way she'd felt eleven years ago when she'd lost Matt could not compare to the anguish she felt now—because eleven years ago, she'd been helpless to change the outcome of events. This time, the choice had been entirely hers, and she could not shake the agonizing uncertainty that she might have made a hideous mistake, not even when Sam Green brought her an updated report that indicated Matt had bought even more shares of Bancroft stock than they'd originally realized.

Twice during the day, she made Mark Braden phone the Bomb and Arson squads in Dallas, New Orleans, and Chicago, hoping against hope that one of them might have turned up a lead and failed to notify her. She was looking for something, anything, that would justify her changing her mind and calling Matt, but there were no leads in the bombings.

After that, she moved listlessly through the rest of her day, her head aching from a sleepless night. The afternoon paper was lying outside her door when she got home that night and, without bothering to take off her coat, Meredith scanned it anxiously, looking for some news that the police had a suspect in Spyzhalski's murder, but there was none. She turned on the television set to catch the 6 o'clock news for the same reason—and with the same result.

In a futile effort to stop herself from wallowing in her misery, she decided to put her Christmas tree up. She'd finished decorating it and was arranging the little nativity scene beneath the tree at 10 o'clock, when the late television news came on. Her heart pounding with hope, she sat on the floor beside the tree, her arms wrapped around her knees, her attention riveted on the screen.

But although the Spyzhalski murder was mentioned, as were Bancroft's bomb scares, there was nothing said that might exonerate Matt.

Despondent, Meredith turned off the television, but remained where she was, staring at the twinkling lights on the Christmas tree. Matt's deep voice spoke in her mind, tormentingly familiar, quietly profound: *Sooner or later, you're going to have to take a risk and trust me completely, Meredith. You can't outwit fate by trying to stand on the sidelines and place little side bets about the outcome of life. Either you wade in and risk everything to play the game, or you don't play at all. And if you don't play, you can't win.* When the time had actually come for her to make the choice, she hadn't been able to take the risk.

She thought of other things he'd said to her too, beautiful things spoken with tender solemnity. *If you'll move in with me, I'll give you paradise on a gold platter. Anything you want—everything you want. I come with it, of course. It's a package deal . . .*

The poignancy of his words made her chest ache. She wondered what Matt was doing now and if he was waiting, hoping she would call. The answer to that question was in his parting words last night. Now, for the very first time, the import of his words, the *finality* of them, actually hit her, and she realized he wouldn't be waiting for her to call now or ever. The choice he'd forced her to make last night had been irrevocable in his opinion: *Either give me your hand, or end it now, and put us both out of our misery.*

When she left him standing there last night, she hadn't completely understood that her decision had to be permanent, that he had absolutely no intention of giving her another chance to go back to him if—when—he was proven innocent of the things she believed he'd done. She understood that now. She should have realized it then. And even if she had, she still wouldn't have been able to trust him and give him her hand. The evidence was against him, all of it.

Permanent . . .

The figures in the little nativity scene wavered as scalding tears filled her eyes, and she put her head in her arms. "Oh, please," Meredith wept brokenly, "don't let this happen to me. Please, don't."

55

At five o'clock the following afternoon, Meredith was summoned to the boardroom where an emergency board of directors meeting had been under way for several hours. When she walked into the room, she was surprised to see that the head of the table had evidently been reserved for her. Trying not to feel overly alarmed by the cold, grim faces that watched her as she sat down, she looked around at everyone, including her father. "Good afternoon, gentlemen." In the chorus of "good afternoons" that answered, the only really friendly voice belonged to old Cyrus Fortell. "Afternoon, Meredith," the old man replied, "and may I say you're looking lovelier than ever."

Meredith looked terrible and she knew it, but she flashed him a grateful smile when normally his patently transparent references to her sex during meetings like this had annoyed her. She'd assumed that part of the reason for this emergency meeting had to do with Matt and that they were going to insist on explanations from her, but she'd also assumed they were going to ask for updates on other matters. So she was completely taken aback when the board's chairman, who was seated on her right, nodded to the folder on the table in front of her and said in an icy voice, "We've had those documents prepared for your signature, Meredith. At the conclusion of this meeting, we'll file them with the appropriate authorities. Take a moment to look them over. Since most of us participated in drafting them, there's no need for us to do likewise."

"I haven't seen them," Cyrus protested, opening his folder at the same time she did.

For a second Meredith couldn't believe what she was seeing, and when she did accept it, bile rose up in her throat, strangling and sickening her. The first document was an official complaint to the Securities and Exchange Commission, stating that she had personal knowledge that Matthew Farrell was deliberately manipulating Bancroft's stock, that he was using the insider information that he'd gleaned from her to make his transactions, and demanding that he be halted and investigated. The second complaint was to the Federal Bureau of Investigation and to the chiefs of police in Dallas, New Orleans, and Chicago, stating that she believed, and had reason to believe, that Matthew Farrell was responsible for the bomb scares in Bancroft & Company's stores in those cities. The third complaint was also directed to the police department; it stated that she had overheard Matthew Farrell threaten the life of Stanislaus Spyzhalski during a phone call with his attorney, and that she was waiving her right to silence as Matthew Farrell's wife, and herewith issuing a public statement that she believed he was responsible for Spyzhalski's murder.

Meredith looked at the grotesque words, the carefully phrased and damning half truths, the vicious accusations, and her entire body began to tremble. A voice screamed in her mind that she'd been a fool and a traitor to ever believe there was a shred of truth in the garbage pile of circumstantial evidence against her husband. The daze of helplessness and suspicion that had held her in a kind of stupor for the two days since she left Matt suddenly evaporated, and she saw everything with crystal clarity—her mistakes, the board's motives, her father's handiwork.

"Sign it, Meredith," Nolan Wilder said, shoving his pen at her.

Sign it.

Meredith made her choice, an irrevocable choice—perhaps even a choice that was already too late. Slowly she stood up. "Sign it?" she repeated contemptuously. "I'll do nothing of the sort!"

"We had hoped you'd appreciate this chance to exonerate yourself and to disassociate yourself from Farrell as well as to see the truth brought out and justice done," Wilder said icily.

"Is *that* what you're interested in?" Meredith demanded, leaning her palms on the table and glaring at all of them. "Truth and justice?" Several of the men glanced away as if they weren't entirely comfortable with the documents she'd been told to sign. "Then I'll tell you the truth!" she continued, her voice ringing with conviction. "Matthew Farrell had nothing to do with those bomb scares, and he had nothing to do with the murder of Stanislaus Spyzhalski, and he is not guilty of violating any SEC rules. The truth," she said with scathing disdain, "is that you're all terrified of him. In comparison to his triumphs, your successes in your own businesses are puny, and the thought of having him as a major shareholder of this company, or on this board, makes you feel insignificant! You're vain and you're terrified and, if you honestly believed I'd sign these papers because you've ordered me to do it, you're also fools!"

"I suggest you reconsider your decision very carefully right now, Meredith," another board member warned her, his face stiff with affront over what she'd said. "Either you are going to act in the best interests of Bancroft and

Company, and sign those documents, which is your duty as acting interim president of this corporation—or we can only assume your loyalties lie with an enemy of this corporation."

"You're talking to me about my duty to Bancroft's and, at the same time, telling me to sign those papers?" she repeated, and suddenly she felt like laughing with the sheer joy of having taken her stand—the right stand. "You're dangerously incompetent if it hasn't occurred to you what Matthew Farrell will do to this company in retaliation for slandering and libeling him with that folder full of garbage. He'll *own* Bancroft's and all of *you* when he's finished suing you!" she finished almost proudly.

"We'll take that risk. Sign the papers."

"No!"

Unaware that the expressions of some of the board members were exhibiting definite signs of doubt about the wisdom of provoking Farrell, Nolan Wilder looked at her and said frigidly, "It appears that your misplaced loyalties are preventing you from fulfilling your responsibility as an officer of this corporation to act in its best interest. Either tender your resignation here and now, or prove me wrong and sign the papers."

Meredith looked him right in the eye. "Go to hell!"

"Good for you, girlie!" she heard old Cyrus shout in the taut, shocked silence as his fist hit the table. "I knew you had more than just great legs!" But Meredith scarcely heard him; she was turning her back on all of them, walking out of the boardroom, slamming the door behind her. Slamming it closed on a lifetime of cherished hopes and dreams.

Matt's words came back to her, cheering and forceful, as she walked swiftly toward her office. She'd asked him what he would do if his board pressured him unreasonably, and he'd replied, *I'd tell them to fuck off.* The memory almost made her laugh. She hadn't quite said that to them, in fact she'd never said that to anyone, but what she had said amounted to the same thing, she decided proudly. Matt's party was tonight, and she was in a hurry to go home and change. The phone on her desk was ringing when she got back to her office, and since Phyllis had already left for the day, Meredith answered it automatically.

"Miss Bancroft," a cool, arrogant voice informed her, "this is William Pearson, Mr. Farrell's attorney. I've been trying to reach Stuart Whitmore all day, and since he hasn't yet returned my calls, I'm taking the liberty of calling you directly."

"That's fine," Meredith said, cradling the phone between her shoulder and ear as she opened her briefcase and began putting all her personal things from her desk into it. "Why are you calling?"

"Mr. Farrell has instructed us to tell you that he no longer has any desire to continue with the rest of the eleven-week trial period you agreed to. He has further instructed us to tell you," he continued in his nastiest, threatening tone, "that you are to file for divorce no later than six days from now, or else we will file in his behalf on the seventh day."

Meredith had already been subjected to all the coercion and threats she was willing to endure. Pearson's ominous, autocratic tone was the last straw! She took the phone away from her ear, glowered furiously at the receiver, then she spoke two crisp, emphatic words into Pearson's ear, and slammed the phone onto its cradle.

Not until she sat down to write out a hasty resignation did the full impact of Pearson's call truly hit her, and her feeling of triumph gave way to burgeoning panic at Matt's action. She'd already waited too long. He wanted a divorce. Immediately. No, that couldn't be true, she told herself desperately, writing faster. She signed her name to her resignation, and stood up, then she looked at what she had written. For the second time in moments she felt the terrible force of reality. Her father walked into her office right then, and it hit her yet again that she was severing herself from everything. Even him.

"Don't do this," he said, his voice harsh as she shoved the resignation toward him.

"You made me do it. You convinced them to draw up those documents, then you led me in there like a lamb to the slaughter. You forced me to choose."

"You chose him, not me, and not your heritage."

Meredith leaned her damp palms against the desk, her voice anguished. "There shouldn't have *needed* to be a choice. Daddy," she said, so distracted that she called him by the name she'd stopped using as a little girl, "why did you have to do this to me? Why did you have to tear me apart like this? Why couldn't I have loved you and him?"

"This isn't about that," he said angrily, but his shoulders were sagging and there was desperation in his voice. "He's guilty, but you won't see it. You'd rather believe I'm guilty of jealousy and manipulation and vengeance—"

"Because," Meredith interrupted, knowing she couldn't bear any more, "it's true. You are. You don't love me, not enough to want me to be happy. And anything less than that isn't love, it's nothing but selfish ownership of another human being." Snapping the locks closed on her briefcase, Meredith picked up her purse and coat and headed for the door.

"Meredith, don't!" he warned as she started past him.

She stopped and turned, looking at his haggard face through eyes swimming with tears. "Good-bye," she said aloud. "Daddy," she whispered in her heart.

She was partway across the reception area when Mark Braden called out to her, his face lit with a triumphant grin as he drew her off to the side. "I need you in my office right away. Gordon Mitchell's secretary is down there, crying her little heart out. I've got Mitchell cold! We were right—the bastard's on the take."

"That's confidential company business," she said quietly, "and I no longer work here."

His face fell and his angry dismay was so genuine, and so touching, that Meredith had to fight even harder for composure. But all he said was an embittered, "I see."

She tried to smile. "I'm sure you do." When she turned to go, he put his hand on her arm and drew her back. For the first time in fifteen rigid years of safeguarding Bancroft's interests, Mark Braden broke his own rule; he divulged company information to someone other than the appropriate manager in charge. He did it because he felt she had a right to know. "Mitchell's been taking big kickbacks from several suppliers. One of them blackmailed him into refusing the presidency."

"And his secretary found out and turned him in?"

"Not exactly," Mark said sarcastically. "She's known for weeks. They've been having an affair and he's been reneging on his promise to marry her."

"And that's why she turned him in," Meredith concluded.

"No, she turned him in because he gave her an annual performance review this morning, and rated her adequate. Can you believe it!" Mark snorted. "The stupid ass rated her adequate and then he reneged on his promise to promote her to an assistant buyer. *That's* why she turned him in. She'd already figured he was lying about wanting to marry her, but she was damned determined to become an assistant buyer."

"Thanks for telling me," she said, pressing an affectionate kiss on his cheek. "I would always have wondered."

"Meredith, I'd like you to know how sorry—"

"Don't," she said, shaking her head, afraid her control would shatter if someone was kind right now. Glancing at her watch, she reached out and pressed the elevator button, then she looked at Mark. With a winsome smile she explained, "I have a very important party to attend, and I'm going to be late. Actually, I'm going to be an uninvited, unwelcome guest—" The elevator doors opened and she stepped inside. "Wish me luck," she added as the doors slid closed.

"I do," he said somberly.

$\mathcal{L}$ 56

Looking in the mirror, Matt tied his black tuxedo tie with the same cold efficiency with which he'd done everything else the past two days. Not long ago he'd dreamed of Meredith standing at his side tonight, greeting their guests, but no more. Not now. He wouldn't allow himself to think about her, or to remember her, or to feel anything. He'd torn her out of his mind and heart, permanently this time, and he wanted to keep her out. Instructing Pearson to notify her to proceed with the divorce had been the first, hardest step. After that the rest had been so much easier.

"Matt—" his father said, walking into the master suite, his forehead furrowed into an uneasy frown, "there's someone here to see you. I told the security guard to let her up. She says she's Caroline Bancroft—Meredith's mother—and she needs to talk to you."

"Get rid of her. I have nothing to say to anyone whose name is Bancroft."

"The reason I let her come up," Patrick continued, braving his son's frigid displeasure, "is that she wants to talk to you about the bomb scares in the department stores. She says she knows who's behind them."

Matt froze momentarily, then he shrugged and reached for his black tuxedo jacket. "Tell her to take her information to the police."

"It's too late, I already let her in. She's here."

Swearing under his breath, Matt swung around and realized his father had actually brought the woman to the doorway of his bedroom. For a split second the resemblance she bore to Meredith tore at him as he looked at the slender blond woman who was hiding her uncertainty behind a façade of cool determination. She had Meredith's eyes and her hair, but not the elegant perfection of Meredith's bones and features. What resemblance there was was enough to make him long to throw her out bodily, just to get her out of his sight.

"I realize you're having a party and I'm intruding," she said cautiously, starting forward and passing Patrick, who was already retreating, "but my plane just got in from Rome, and I didn't have any choice except to come straight here. You see, I realized after I was on the plane that once I got here, Philip would probably refuse to see me, let alone believe me, and even if Meredith would do either one, which I doubt, I don't know where she lives."

"How the hell did you know where I live?" he demanded.

"You are Meredith's husband, aren't you?"

"I'm about to be her *ex*-husband," he stated implacably.

"Oh," Caroline said, studying the coldly unapproachable man her daughter had married. "I think I'm sorry to hear that. But to answer your question, I get the Chicago newspapers in Italy, and there was a big layout a while back about this apartment and the building it's in."

"Fine," Matt snapped impatiently. "Now that you've found me and gotten in here, what did you want to tell me?"

She bristled a little at his tone, and then smiled suddenly. "I can tell you've been involved with Philip. He makes a lot of people react negatively to anyone who has his name."

That was close enough to bring a brief, grim smile to Matt's lips. "What did you come here to tell me?" he asked, but with an effort at courtesy.

"Philip was in Italy last week," she began as she unbuttoned her red wool coat and loosened the scarf at her neck. "I know from what he said there that he thinks you're behind the bombs that have been put in Bancroft's stores, and that he also thinks you're the one who plans to take over Bancroft and Company. But he's wrong."

"It's nice to hear that someone thinks that's possible," Matt said sarcastically.

"I don't think it, I know it." Unnerved by his unencouraging attitude and desperate to make him believe her, Caroline began talking faster. "Mr. Farrell, I own a large block of shares in B and C, and six months ago Charlotte Bancroft—she was Philip's father's second wife—called me. She asked me if I'd like a chance to get back at Philip for divorcing me and shutting me out of Meredith's life. Charlotte heads Seaboard Industries in Florida," she added disjointedly.

Matt remembered Meredith's mentions of her stepgrandmother. "She inherited it from her husband," he said, reluctantly drawn into the discussion.

"Yes, and she's built it into an enormous holding company that owns a great many corporations."

"And?" he said when she hesitated.

Caroline looked at him, trying to gauge his emotions, but he didn't seem to have any at all. "And now," she said, "she's getting ready to add Bancroft and Company to her holdings. She asked if I'd vote my block of shares in her favor when she'd acquired enough shares of her own to equal a controlling interest. She hates Philip too, though she doesn't think I know why she does."

"I'm sure he gave her thousands of reasons," Matt said ironically, turning away and shrugging into his tuxedo jacket. The buzzer at the door was ringing incessantly and the sound of conversation drifted into the bedroom as arriving guests stopped in the foyer to relinquish their coats.

"She hates Philip," Caroline persevered, "because it was Philip she wanted, not his father, and she did her damnedest to get him into her bed even after she was engaged to his father. He turned her down repeatedly, and one day he did more than that. He told his father—Cyril—she was a common, mercenary slut who wanted to marry Cyril for his money and who had the hots for him—Philip. It was all true," she said somberly, "but Philip's father was in love with her. He blamed Philip for saying it, and yet he believed him. He called off his wedding and Charlotte, who'd been Cyril's secretary, had to wait years before he finally decided to marry her. Anyway, a few months ago, I told Charlotte I'd think about voting my shares with her when she made her takeover move, but when I had time to consider it, I started changing my mind. Philip is an infuriating fool, but Charlotte is truly evil. She has no heart. A few weeks ago she called and told me someone else was buying up a lot of shares in B and C, and causing the price to go up."

Matt knew he was responsible for that, but he said nothing as she continued. "Charlotte was panicky. She said she was going to do something to make the price drop way down, and then she was going to make her move. The next thing I knew I was hearing about bombs being found in the stores and how it was destroying B and C's Christmas business and causing the stock to drop."

She'd given Matt the missing pieces of the puzzle—the motive for the carefully placed bombs that had been meant to damage business but not the stores themselves, the motive for taking over a corporation that was a bad bet for short-term profit. Charlotte Bancroft had the motives and she had the vast sums of money needed to execute a takeover of a corporation in debt and then to wait until B & C was again profitable.

"You'll have to tell the police," he said, turning toward the phone beside his bed.

She nodded. "I know. Is that who you're calling now?"

"No. I'm calling a man named Olsen who has contacts with the local police. He'll go with you tomorrow and make certain you aren't treated like a crackpot, or, worse, made into their newest suspect."

Caroline stood perfectly still, her face mirroring astonishment as he called a long distance number and ordered the man named Olsen to Chicago on the first plane in the morning—all of it to ease her way through a difficult situation. She revised her initial opinion that he was the most unapproachable man she'd ever encountered and decided he simply didn't want anything more to do with anyone whose name was Bancroft—including Meredith, judging from the cold way he'd said he was about to become her ex-husband. When he hung up he wrote two phone numbers on a pad beside the phone and tore the sheet off. "Here's Olsen's home phone number. Call him anytime tonight and tell him where to meet you. The second phone number is mine, in case you have a problem." He turned back to her, and the hostility he'd shown her earlier was gone. He was still aloof and obviously reluctant to have any other involvement with her, but he unbent enough to say, "Meredith told me you used to be in films. The road cast from *Phantom of the Opera* is here tonight as well as a hundred and fifty other people, some of whom you probably know. If you'd like to stay for the party, my father will introduce you around."

The party was already shifting into full swing as they walked toward the living room. "I'd rather not be introduced," she said quickly, "and I have no desire to renew my acquaintance with any of the old-guard Chicago socialites out there." She hesitated then, watching black-coated waiters passing trays of drinks among gorgeously dressed women and men in tuxedos. Someone was playing a piano and the lilting music blended with the sound of cultured voices and bursts of laughter. "I—I would like to stay for just a little while though," she said with a sudden jaunty smile that made her look thirty-five instead of fifty-five. "I used to live for parties like this. It might be fun to stay and watch and wonder again why I ever thought they were so wonderful."

"Let me know if you figure that out," he said, his own indifference obviously surpassing even her own.

"Why are you giving the party if you don't enjoy them?" she asked with an uncertain smile, wondering anew at this strange, enigmatic man her daughter had married.

"The proceeds of the performance tomorrow night are going to charity," he said with a shrug.

Matt led her to the edge of the crowd, where his sister was deep in conversation with Stuart Whitmore, and he introduced her simply as Caroline Edwards. Whitmore and his sister had already hit it off, he noted, and he wished he hadn't introduced them. Having Whitmore seeing his sister would be an unwanted reminder of Meredith—especially of that ill-fated afternoon in his conference room when she'd put her hand in his and promised to trust him. She hadn't been capable of doing it that day, and she hadn't been capable of it later when it was more important. Because when it came down to it, he was still a crude nobody to her. She would never have suspected Parker, or anyone else of her own class, of being a murderer or an arsonist. She'd been willing to sleep with Matt—but that was *all*. She'd have kept right on stalling about living with him forever. She'd liked going to bed with him, but when it came down to actually committing herself to him, to living with him, to being married to him, *that* she could not make herself do.

He stepped forward to begin playing host when Caroline put her hand on his sleeve and stopped him. "I won't be staying long," she said. "I suppose this is good-bye."

Matt nodded, hesitated, and then made himself bring up Meredith for her mother's sake. "Stuart Whitmore is an old friend of your daughter's, and also her lawyer," he told Caroline. "If you can find a way to lead the conversation around to her, he's bound to talk about her. Assuming you're interested."

"Thank you," she said with a catch in her voice. "I'm very interested."

By the time Meredith walked into the lobby of Matt's building, she wasn't certain if it was clever or crazy to try to confront him in the middle of his party—particularly when he was so angry with her that he was insisting on an immediate divorce. She wasn't completely sure he wouldn't have her thrown out with everyone watching, and she wasn't completely sure that she didn't deserve it.

In desperate hopes of weakening his resistance, she was wearing her most provocative cocktail dress—a backless black chiffon confection with narrow straps and a deep V at the bodice that was encrusted with tiny black beads sewn tightly into intricate leaves and flowers. They covered her breasts, then dipped below her arms to frame the low back of the dress. Obsessed with the need to look her absolute best, she'd spent almost an hour trying different hairstyles. In the end she'd brushed her hair out and let it fall against her shoulders. The sophistication of the dress required a sophisticated hairstyle, but on the other hand, wearing her hair down gave her a naive, youthful look that she hoped might soften Matt when she tried to talk to him. To accomplish that, she'd have worn *braids* if she'd thought they'd help!

The uniformed guard at the security desk checked his list and Meredith breathed a ragged sigh of profound relief when she saw that Matt hadn't removed her name. With her knees trembling and her pulse pounding, she took the elevator to the penthouse, and there she encountered an obstacle in the last place she'd anticipated it: When she pressed the buzzer at Matt's door, Joe O'Hara opened it, took one look at her, and stepped forward, blocking her way. "You shouldn't have come, Miss Bancroft," he said coldly, and the fact that he hadn't called her Mrs. Farrell for the first time in their acquaintance made her heart ache a little. "Matt doesn't want anything to do with you. I heard him say so. He wants a divorce."

"Well, I don't," Meredith said emphatically. "Please, Joe, let me in so I can convince him he doesn't want one either."

The big man hesitated, torn between loyalty to Matt and the pleading sincerity in her aqua eyes while the roar of laughter and conversation from inside the penthouse surrounded both of them. "I don't think you can do it, and I don't think this is the place you should try. There's a crowd in there, and there's reporters."

"Good," she said with more assurance than she felt. "Then they can all leave here and tell the world that Mr. and Mrs. Farrell were together tonight."

"There's a better chance they'll be telling the world that Mr. Farrell threw you out on your ear and fired my ass for letting you in," he muttered grimly, but he stepped back, and Meredith impulsively threw her arms around him. "Thank you, Joe." She pulled away, too nervous to notice his face had reddened with embarrassed pleasure. "How do I look?" she asked, suddenly filled with quaking doubts. She spread the chiffon skirt of her dress as if she were about to curtsy and waited for his opinion.

"You look beautiful," he replied gruffly, "but it ain't going to matter a damn to Matt."

On that alarming and depressing prediction, Meredith stepped into the noisy gaiety of the penthouse. The moment she started down the foyer steps, heads started to turn and conversations dropped off, then started again with renewed force, and she heard her name being repeated. Ignoring all of that, she scanned the crowded living room, the dining room, and then the raised dais that created a glass-enclosed conversation area at the far corner of the penthouse. Her heart began to hammer as she saw Matt standing there, several inches taller than the people around him, and she started forward on legs that quaked.

As she walked up the steps toward him, she could see faces of the group around him. The star of the musical play was standing beside him, talking animatedly to him, while he gazed indifferently at her stunning face. Meredith was just a few feet away when Stanton Avery, who was standing on

Matt's other side, looked up and saw her. He said something to Matt—obviously warning him that she was there—because Matt turned abruptly toward her. He stared at her, his glass arrested halfway to his lips, his eyes like shards of ice as they leveled on her, his expression so forbidding that Meredith hesitated in midstep, then she made herself walk up to him.

Taking some unspoken cue, or perhaps out of courtesy, the people who'd been talking to him disbanded, leaving the two of them alone on the dais. Meredith waited, hoping he'd say something, do something. When he finally did, he acknowledged her with a curt inclination of his head, and said only one word—her name—in a chilling tone. "Meredith."

Follow your instincts, he'd advised her a week ago, and Meredith tried to do that. "Hi," she said inanely, pleading with her eyes for some help, but Matt wasn't interested in helping her now. "You're probably wondering what I'm doing here."

"Not particularly."

That hurt, but at least he was waiting for her to speak, and her instincts told her he wasn't completely indifferent to her. She smiled a little, dying to surrender, not certain how to do it. "I came here to tell you about my day." Her voice shook with nerves and she knew he heard it, but he didn't say a word, encouraging or otherwise. Summoning her courage, Meredith drew a deep breath and forged ahead. "This afternoon I got called into an emergency board meeting. The board was very upset. Furious, actually. They accused me of having a conflict of interest where you're concerned."

"How foolish of them," he said with acid contempt. "Didn't you tell them Bancroft and Company is your only interest?"

"Not exactly," she said, biting back a queasy smile. "They also wanted me to sign some affidavits and formal complaints—accusations that blamed you for Spyzhalski's death, and for illegally using your contact with me to get control of us, and for having bombs placed in our stores."

"Is that all?" he asked sarcastically.

"Not exactly," Meredith said again. "But that's the gist of it." She searched for some sign, some warmth—anything at all in his face to tell her he still cared about all this. And she couldn't see it. What she did see was people turning everywhere to watch them. "I—I told the directors . . ." She trailed off, her voice strangled with tension and fear that he truly didn't want her anymore.

"What did you tell them?" he asked impassively, and Meredith grasped at his question as a tiny bit of encouragement to continue.

"I told them," she said with a proud tilt of her chin, "what you said they should be told!"

His expression didn't change. "You told them to fuck off?"

"No, not exactly," she said a little contritely. "I told them to go to hell."

He didn't say a word, and her heart was sinking when she suddenly saw it—the amused gleam in his beautiful eyes, the faint quirk of a smile dawning at his lips. "And then," she continued as hope burst in her like sunshine, "Your attorney called to tell me that if I didn't file for a divorce within six days, he was going to file in your behalf on the seventh day. And I told him . . ."

She trailed off, and with warm humor in his voice, Matt asked helpfully, "And you told him to go to hell too?"

"No, I told *him* to fuck off!"

"You did?"

"Yes."

He waited for her to say more, his eyes looking deeply into hers. "And?" he prodded quietly.

"And I'm thinking of taking a trip," she said. "I—I'm going to have a lot of time on my hands now."

"You took a leave of absence?"

"No, I resigned."

"I see," he said, but his voice had suddenly softened to a caress, and she wanted to drown herself in the look in his eyes. "What kind of trip did you have in mind, Meredith?"

"If you're still willing to take me there," she said, swallowing almost painfully, "I thought I'd like to see paradise."

He didn't move or speak, and for a horrible moment Meredith thought she'd been wrong, that she'd only imagined he still cared.

And then she realized he was holding out his hand for hers.

Tears of joy and relief sprang to her eyes as she laid her hand in his palm, feeling his fingers engulf hers in their warm strength, closing tightly on her hand, and then abruptly yanking her forward into arms that wrapped around her like steel bands.

Shielding her from view with his shoulders, he turned her face up to his. "I love you!" he whispered fiercely an instant before he seized her mouth in a smoldering kiss. A flash exploded somewhere as a photographer raised his camera, followed by another, and another. Someone started to clap, and the clapping became bursting applause, and the applause was joined with laughter, and still the kiss went on.

Meredith didn't notice. She was kissing him back, melting against him, utterly oblivious to all of it . . . the cheering, the clapping, the laughter, the white flashes from raised cameras. She was already halfway to her destination.

57

With her eyes closed and a smile on her lips, Meredith awakened slowly in Matt's bed, letting memories of the previous night drift lazily through her mind like soft music. Together they had mingled with their guests, enduring the good-natured jibes about their prolonged kiss and obvious reconciliation, and she had loved playing the part of his hostess. After the party, in bed with him, she'd loved playing the part of his wife a thousand times more. Trust and commitment, she sleepily decided, evidently had a very profound effect on lovemaking, because last night's stormy lovemaking had completely eclipsed everything else that had gone before.

Sunlight filtered through the draperies across the room, and she rolled over onto her back, opening her eyes. Matt had kissed her good-bye a while ago, and said he was going out to get some sweet rolls for their breakfast. He'd left a cup of coffee on the table beside the bed for her, and she eased up onto the pillows.

She'd just taken a sip when he walked into the room with a white bakery bag in his hand, a folded newspaper under his arm, and an odd, tense expression on his handsome face. "Good morning," she said, smiling as he bent over to kiss her. "What's that?" she added, noting the tabloid-size paper.

Matt had promised her last night never to keep things from her, but at that moment he'd have preferred a public flogging to showing her that newspaper. "It's the *Tattler*," he said. "I saw it when I was paying for the sweet rolls. Somehow," he added as he reluctantly held it toward her, "they discovered the terms of our eleven-week agreement, and they've interpreted them in their own inimitable fashion." He watched her reach for it, remembering her disgust at the kind of sensational publicity he'd gotten over the years, knowing that this sort of treatment was going to continue to plague her in the future, partly because she was married to him, and partly because of the public fascination with their aborted divorce. Bracing himself for some sort of condemnation, or an explosion of justifiable outrage, he watched her unfold it and look at it.

Meredith's gaze riveted on the lurid headline:

HEIRESS CHARGES HUSBAND $113,000 A NIGHT FOR SEX

"I couldn't figure at first how they came up with that figure," Matt said. "Then it hit me. They multiplied four dates a week times eleven weeks and divided that into the five million I promised you. I'm sorry," he said. "If I could control it, I—"

Suddenly she pulled the newspaper against her face and let out a shriek of laughter that drowned out his apology. She laughed so hard that she slid limply down the pillows while the room filled with her musical hilarity. "One hundred and th-thirteen th-thousand dollars," she choked, her shoulders lifting off the bed, and Matt broke into a grin of profound relief that turned to tenderness, because he knew what she was doing: She was confronting something she hated and finding a way to deal with it so it couldn't harm them.

"Have I ever told you," he whispered huskily, leaning down and bracing his hands on either side of her heaving shoulders, "how proud I am of you?"

She shook her head hard, still laughing, and he pulled the paper away from her face and kissed her flushed cheeks, silencing her giggles with his mouth.

"Are y-you sure," she whispered, overcome with a fresh surge of hilarity even while she put her arms around his shoulders and pulled him down to her, knowing he wanted to make love again, "that you can a-afford to do this again?"

"I think it's within my budget," he tried to tease, but his hand trembled as he reverently smoothed a strand of golden hair off her cheek.

"Yes, but now that I've accepted this as a permanent *job*, do I get periodic wage increases too—over and above the one hundred thirteen thousand?" she joked, her hands cradling his face, her swimming eyes looking into his, "and a benefits package, with medical insurance and guaranteed bonuses?"

"Absolutely," he promised, turning his face into her hand and kissing her palm.

"Oh, no!" she moaned. "You'll send me soaring straight into a higher tax bracket."

Her husband muffled a laugh against her throat, and Meredith turned into his arms. They spent the next hour sending each other soaring straight into the clouds instead.

58

On Sunday night the feature story on the six o'clock news was the arrest of Ellis Ray Sampson who'd been charged with the murder of Stanislaus Spyzhalski. According to St. Clair County officials, Spyzhalski had not been killed by one of his duped clients, as they'd originally believed, but by the outraged husband of a Belleville woman with whom Spyzhalski had been having a fling. Mr. Sampson, who had turned himself in and confessed to having beaten up Spyzhalski, swore that the bogus attorney had been alive when he dumped him in the ditch. Since the coroner's report indicated that Spyzhalski had also had a heart attack that same night, there was a possibility that the legal charges against Sampson might be reduced from murder to manslaughter.

Matt and Meredith watched the newscast together. Matt sarcastically remarked that Sampson should be given a medal for ridding the world of a human parasite. Meredith, who knew how it felt to be victimized by Spyzhalski, said she hoped the charges against Sampson would be reduced.

Matt sent Pearson and Levinson down to Belleville to make sure of it.

On Tuesday of the following week, Charlotte Bancroft president of Seaboard Industries, and her son Jason were officially questioned in Palm Beach, Florida, regarding a series of bomb threats and stock manipulations against Bancroft & Company. Both of them heatedly denied any connection to either as well as any desire to take over Bancroft & Company. On Wednesday, Caroline Edwards Bancroft voluntarily appeared before a Florida grand jury and testified that Charlotte Bancroft had indeed been planning to take over Bancroft & Company, and that Charlotte had further hinted at having planned something that would force B & C's stock to drop.

In the Cayman Islands, where he was vacationing with his lover, Joel Bancroft, former treasurer of Seaboard Industries, read about the suspicions being cast upon his mother and brother. He had resigned six months earlier, when they had both instructed him to open dummy accounts under false names with a particular stockbroker who was willing to collaborate, and to begin buying up blocks of B & C stock, which was to then be "parked" in the bogus accounts.

Lying on the beach, looking out at the water, Joel thought about his mother, whose thirty-year plan to avenge herself against Philip Bancroft had been a demented, driving obsession, and about his brother, who—like his mother—had despised Joel for being gay. After several hours he reached a decision and made a phone call.

The following day Charlotte and Jason Bancroft were arrested and charged with several counts of illegal activities on a tip from an anonymous caller who'd told police the names of the fraudulent stock accounts. Charlotte denied any knowledge of those accounts. Jason, who'd opened the accounts and paid off the maker of the bombs at his mother's instructions, soon began to fear that he was about to become his mother's sacrificial lamb. He beat her to the punch by offering to testify against her in return for immunity from prosecution.

The board of directors of Seaboard, seeing an immediate need to salvage their corporate image, and acting on Charlotte's instructions, named Joel Bancroft president and chief operating officer.

In Chicago, Meredith watched it all happening on the television news, and the ache of longing she felt every time someone mentioned Bancroft & Company almost outweighed the shock she had felt at discovering that Charlotte and Jason were responsible for the things she'd believed Matt had done.

Sitting beside her on the sofa, Matt saw the sadness that darkened her eyes whenever her company's name was mentioned, and he reached out for her hand, threading his fingers through hers. "Have you thought about what you want to do next, now that you have so much free time?"

Meredith knew he was referring to a new career to substitute for the one she'd given up when she sided with him, but she had a feeling her answer would upset and alarm him. Deliberately choosing to misunderstand his question about her free time, she looked down at their joined hands and smiled at the 14-carat emerald-cut diamond he'd slid onto her ring finger along with a platinum wedding band. "I might have considered making a career out of going shopping every day," she teased, "but you've already bought me jewels and a luxury car. Anything else I could buy would be an awful anticlimax, don't you think? I mean, what's left?"

"How about a small jet," he said, kissing her nose, "or a large yacht?"

"Don't you dare—" she warned him, but he only laughed at her horrified look.

"There must be something else you want," he said.

Meredith sobered, and decided to tell him the truth. "There is. I want it badly, Matt."

"Name it, and it's yours."

She hesitated, her thumb idly rubbing the new gold wedding band he wore on his finger, then she lifted her eyes to his. "I want to try to have another baby."

His reaction was instantaneous and fierce. "No. Absolutely not. You weren't going to risk it if you married Parker, and you're not going to risk it for me!"

"Parker didn't want children," she countered. "And you did say," she reminded him softly, *"anything* I want. And I do want that."

Normally the look in her eyes would have melted him, but she'd explained to him in bed one night that the odds were high that she'd miscarry again late in her pregnancy. He already knew she'd almost died the last time, and the thought of risking that was absolutely beyond consideration. "Don't do this to me," he warned, his voice terse and pleading.

"There are obstetricians who specialize in women who have problem pregnancies. I went to the library yesterday, and did a lot of reading about it. There are new drugs and some new techniques they're trying out—"

"No!" he interrupted, his voice taut. "Absolutely not. Ask anything else of me, but not that. I couldn't endure the worry. I mean that."

"We'll talk about it again later," she said with a smile that was both stubborn and serene.

"My answer will be the same," he told her.

He would have said more, but just then the newscaster announced that they had a late-breaking development in the recent Bancroft & Company takeover furor, and Meredith's gaze snapped to the television screen. "Philip A. Bancroft," said the newscaster, "called a news conference late this afternoon to comment on reports that his daughter, Meredith Bancroft, was fired as B and C's acting president as a result of her connection to industrialist Matthew Farrell."

Dread made Meredith's hand tighten on Matt's as her father's grim, unsmiling face appeared on the television screen. Standing stiffly at the podium in Bancroft's auditorium, he read from a prepared statement:

"In response to reports that my daughter's marriage to Matthew Farrell resulted in her termination as B and C's interim president, the board of directors, including myself, categorically deny any such allegations. My daughter is enjoying a brief and long-overdue honeymoon with her husband, at the end of which she is expected to reassume her role here." He paused and looked directly at the camera, and only Meredith realized that he wasn't issuing a statement, he was issuing an *order. To her.*

Shock had already sent her halfway to her feet, but that was nothing compared to what she felt a moment later when he commented on something that had been appearing all week in the Chicago papers. "In response to published rumors that there is a long history of continuing ill feeling between Matthew Farrell and myself, I wish to state that until very recently I had no opportunity to know my"—he paused to self-consciously clear his throat—"my, er, my son-in-law."

It hit Meredith what he was doing. "Matt," she cried, clutching his arm in laughing disbelief, "he's *apologizing* to you!" Matt shot her a dubious look that abruptly changed to reluctant amusement as Philip Bancroft continued. "As everyone now knows, Matt Farrell and my daughter were married for a few short months many years ago, a marriage which we all believed had been ended by an unfortunate and premature divorce. However, now that they've been reunited, I can only say that having a man of Matthew Farrell's caliber as a son-in-law is something that any father would deem an—" he paused to clear his throat again, and then he absolutely glowered at the camera as he reluctantly but forcefully said—"an *honor!*"

Meredith stared at the screen as it switched to the sports scores, and her laughter faded as she looked at her husband. "I made him promise that he'd apologize to you when he found out you were innocent." Laying her fingers against his cheek in an unconscious gesture of appeal, she whispered achingly, "Could you possibly find it in your heart to put the past behind you and try to be friends with him now?"

Privately, Matt thought that nothing Philip Bancroft did, including the televised statement he'd just made, could begin to atone for what he'd done to them, let alone make Matt regard the man as a friend. He considered telling her that, but as he gazed into his wife's shimmering blue eyes, he couldn't quite make himself say that. "I could try," he said. He heard how revolted he sounded by the idea, and he felt obliged to give her additional reassurance, so he dishonestly but forcefully remarked, "That was a very nice speech that he made."

Caroline Edwards Bancroft thought it was too. Sitting opposite Philip in the living room of the house she'd once shared with him, she waited until the program switched to sports news, then she turned off the VCR and removed the tape she'd made. "Philip," she said, "that was a very nice speech."

He handed her a glass of wine, his expression unconvinced. "What makes you think Meredith will think so?"

"I think she will because I know I would."

"Of course you would. You wrote the speech!"

Serenely taking a sip of her wine, Caroline watched him pace.

"Do you think she saw it?" he asked, rounding on her.

"If she didn't see it, you can bring her this videotape. Better yet, you could go to see her now and ask Matt and her both to watch while you're there." Caroline nodded. "I like that idea. It's more personal."

He blanched. "No, really, I couldn't do that. She probably hates me, and Farrell will throw me out. He's no fool. He knows a few words don't make up for the mistakes I've made. He won't accept an apology from me."

"Yes, he will," she said quietly, "because he loves her."

When he hesitated, Caroline handed him the videotape and said firmly, "The longer you wait, the harder it will become for you and them. Go over there now, Philip."

Shoving his hands into his pockets, Philip sighed. "Caroline," he said gruffly, "would you go with me?"

"No," she said, quailing inwardly at the thought of confronting her daughter for the first time. "Besides, my plane leaves in three hours."

His voice softened, and she glimpsed the irresistibly persuasive man she'd fallen in love with three decades before. "You could go with me," he said quietly, "and I could introduce you to our daughter."

Her heart skipped a beat at the way he'd said *our daughter*, then she realized what he was doing and she shook her head, laughing. "You are still the most manipulative man I've ever known."

"I'm also the only man you ever married," he reminded her with a rare smile. "I must have had some good qualities."

"Stop it, Philip," she warned him.

"We could go to see Meredith and Farrell—"

"Start calling him Matt."

"All right," he conceded. "Matt. And after we leave their place, we could come back here. You could stay on for a while, and we could get to know each other again."

"I already know you," she said heatedly. "And if you want to get to know me, you'll have to do it in Italy!"

"Caroline," he said on a harsh breath. "Please." He saw her waver. "At least come with me tonight. This may be your last chance to meet our daughter. You'll like her. She's like you in some ways—she has a lot of courage."

Closing her eyes, Caroline tried to ignore his words and the urging of her own heart, but the combination was irresistibly powerful. "Call her first," she said shakily. "After thirty years I'm not going to just crash in on her unannounced. Don't be surprised when she refuses to see me," she added, taking the phone number Matt had given her out of her purse and giving it to Philip.

"She's probably going to refuse to see both of us," he said. "And I can't blame her."

He walked into the adjoining room to make the call and reappeared so quickly that Caroline knew Meredith must have hung up on him, and her heart sank.

"What did she say?" she managed to get out when Philip seemed unable to speak.

He cleared his throat as if he felt an obstruction in it, and his voice was strangely hoarse. "She said yes."

 59

Meredith walked out of the building where her obstetricians' offices were located, and suppressed the absurd urge to throw out her arms and twirl around on the sidewalk. Turning her face up to the sky, she stood, letting the autumn breeze caress her skin, smiling up at the clouds. "Thank you," she whispered.

It had taken nearly a year and two long consultations with her obstetricians, who specialized in problem pregnancies, to convince Matt that whatever the outcome of her pregnancy might be, if Meredith followed their instructions and treatments impeccably, including staying in bed for part of her pregnancy, the risk to Meredith herself would be only slightly more than to any woman. It had taken another nine months to hear the words she'd finally heard today: "Congratulations, Mrs. Farrell. You're pregnant."

On an impulse she crossed the street and bought a fistful of roses from a florist shop, then she walked down the block to where Joe was waiting with the car, surprising him by arriving from a different direction. She opened the door herself and slid into the backseat.

Joe looped his arm over the back of the seat and twisted toward her. "What'd the doc say?"

Meredith looked up at him, her face glowing with wonder and awe. And she smiled.

A broad answering grin split Joe's face. "Matt's gonna be one happy man!" he predicted. "After he gets over bein' one very scared man!" Turning back, he put the limousine into gear.

Meredith braced herself to be thrown against the back of the seat when he blasted away from the curb in his usual fashion, but Joe passed up three opportunities to charge into traffic and two more perfectly reasonable chances to do it at moderate speed. Not until there was no one behind them for a block did he finally pull out, and then he did it ever so slowly, as carefully and tenderly as if he were pushing a baby carriage. In the backseat Meredith burst out laughing.

Matt was waiting for her, pacing back and forth across the living room windows, raking his hand through his hair, berating himself for ever agreeing to let her try to get pregnant. He knew she thought she was, and he was half hoping she was wrong, because he didn't know how he was going to endure the fear if she was right.

He lurched around as the front door opened, watching her as she walked toward him with one hand behind her back. "What did the doctor say?" he demanded when he couldn't stand the suspense anymore.

She produced a dozen long-stemmed roses from behind her and held them out to him, her smile bursting out like sunshine. "Congratulations, Mr. Farrell. We're pregnant!"

He yanked her into his arms, crushing the roses between them. "God help me!" he whispered raggedly.

"He will, darling," she promised, kissing his taut jaw.

❧ Epilogue

"I old you we'd make it in time," Joe O'Hara said as he brought the limousine to a screeching stop in front of Bancroft & Company. For once Matt appreciated his driving, because Meredith was late for a very important meeting with the board. Their plane had been late getting in from Italy, where they'd stopped to visit Philip and Caroline on their way back from skiing in Switzerland.

"Here," Matt told O'Hara, handing the chauffeur the briefcase he'd brought to the airport with Meredith's meeting notes in it. "You take Meredith's briefcase, and I'll take Meredith."

"You'll what?" Meredith asked, looking over her shoulder as she reached into the backseat for the crutch she had to use until her sprained ankle healed.

"You don't have time to hobble all the way to the elevators," Matt said, and swept her into his arms.

"This is very undignified," Meredith protested, laughing. "You can't carry me through the store like this!"

"Watch me," he said, grinning.

And he did.

Shoppers turned to gape as he strode toward them. At one of the cosmetic counters, a middle-aged woman exclaimed to her friend, "Isn't that Meredith Bancroft and Matthew Farrell?"

"No, it can't be them," a shopper at the counter across the aisle replied. Meredith turned her face into Matt's chest, her shoulders shaking with embarrassed mirth as the woman continued. "I read in the *Tattler* that they're getting a divorce! She's going to marry Kevin Costner and Matt Farrell is in Greece with some movie star."

When they reached the elevators, Meredith lifted her laughing eyes to Matt's. "Shame on you," she joked. "Another movie star?"

"Kevin Costner?" he retorted, brows raised in amused challenge. "I didn't even know you *liked* Kevin Costner!"

In Meredith's office he put her down so that she could limp into the meeting on her own two feet.

"Lisa and Parker said they'd meet us here with the baby and have lunch with us," she added, looking a little anxiously toward the empty reception area outside.

"I'll wait here for them," Matt promised, handing her the briefcase.

A few minutes later Matt turned as Lisa appeared in the doorway, a baby in her arms. "Parker dropped us off in front," she explained. "He'll be up in a few minutes."

"You're looking," Matt teased with a grin, "very pregnant, Mrs. Reynolds," but his eyes were on the six-month-old baby in her arms, and he was already reaching out to take her.

"I'll go watch for Parker," Lisa said.

When she left, Matt looked down at the baby girl that Meredith had risked her life to bring into the world.

Marissa opened her eyes just then and started to cry. With a tender smile Matt touched his finger to her soft cheek. "Shhh, darling," he whispered. "Future presidents of major corporations don't cry—it's bad corporate protocol. Ask your mommy," he suggested.

She quieted, and after a moment she grinned at him and gurgled something that sounded profound. "I knew it!" he said, grinning back at her. "Aunt Lisa's been teaching you Italian right along with Uncle Parker, hasn't she?"

With time on his hands before Meredith finished her meeting, Matt took his daughter to the eleventh floor to show her his favorite department. It was a new department that Meredith had created for all the Bancroft & Company stores, and it contained articles from all over the world, from jewels to clothing to handmade toys. The only thing they had in common was that they met Meredith's requirement: Each article had to be rare, and it had to be perfect before it was allowed to bear the exclusive new logo that was already famous for symbolizing perfection.

With Marissa in his arms, Matt looked up at the logo above Meredith's special department, and he felt the same constriction in his throat that he felt whenever he stood here. The logo was a pair of hands; a man's hand reaching out for a woman's hand, their fingers touching.

Meredith had named the department Paradise.

Tender
Triumph

With love and gratitude to Janet Tait, who had cheered for my triumphs, wept for my sorrows, and enriched my life with her friendship. And for Roger Tait, who had never objected to the time all that takes.

I

Standing in brooding silence at the windows of the elegant penthouse apartment, the tall dark man gazed at the panorama of twinkling lights fanning out across the dusky St. Louis skyline. Bitterness and resignation were evident in Ramon Galverra's abrupt movements as he jerked the knot of his tie loose, then raised his glass of Scotch to his mouth, drinking deeply.

Behind him, a blond man strode quickly into the dimly lit living room. "Well, Ramon?" he asked eagerly. "What did they decide?"

"They decided what bankers always decide," Ramon said harshly, without turning. "They decided to look out for themselves."

"Those bastards!" Roger exploded. In angry frustration, he raked his hand through his blond hair, then turned and headed determinedly for the row of crystal decanters on the bar. "They sure as hell stayed with you when the money was pouring in," he gritted as he splashed bourbon into a glass.

"They have not changed," Ramon said grimly. "If the money was still pouring in, they would still be with me."

Roger snapped on a lamp, then scowled at the magnificent Louis XIV furnishings, as if their presence in his spacious living room offended him. "I was so certain, so absolutely certain, that when you explained about the state of your father's mental health before he died the bankers would stand by you. How can they blame you for his mistakes and incompetence?"

Turning from the windows, Ramon leaned a shoulder against the frame. For a moment he stared at the remaining Scotch in his glass, then he tipped it up to his mouth and drained it. "They blame me for not preventing him from making fatal mistakes, and for not recognizing the fact of his incompetence in time."

"Not recognizing the—" Roger repeated furiously. "How were you supposed to recognize that a man who always acted like he was God Almighty, one day started believing it? And what could you have done if you'd known? The stock was in his name, not yours. Until the day he died, he held the controlling interest in the corporation. Your hands were tied."

"Now they are empty," Ramon replied with a shrug of broad, muscled shoulders on his six-foot-three-inch frame.

"Look," Roger said in desperation. "I haven't brought this up before because I knew your pride would be offended, but I'm a long way from being poor, you know that. How much do you need? If I don't have it all, maybe I can raise the rest."

For the first time, a glint of humor touched Ramon Galverra's finely sculpted mouth and arrogant dark eyes. The transformation was startling, softening the features of a face that lately looked as if it had been cast in bronze by an artist intent on portraying cold, ruthless determination and ancient Spanish nobility. "Fifty million would help. Seventy-five million would be better."

"Fifty million?" Roger said blankly, staring at the man he had known since they were both students at Harvard University. "Fifty million dollars would only help?"

"Right. It would only help." Slamming his glass down on the marble table beside him, Ramon turned and started toward the guest room he had been occupying since his arrival in St. Louis a week before.

"Ramon," Roger said urgently, "you have to see Sid Green while you're here. He could raise that kind of money if he wanted to, and he owes you."

Ramon's head jerked around. His aristocratic Spanish face hardened with contempt. "If Sid wanted to help, he would have contacted me. He knows I am here and he knows I am in trouble."

"Maybe he doesn't know. Until now, you've managed to keep it quiet that the corporation is going under. Maybe he doesn't know."

"He knows. He is on the board of directors of the bank that is refusing to extend our loan."

"But—"

"No! If Sid was willing to help, he would have contacted me. His silence speaks for itself, and I will not beg him. I have called a meeting of my corporation's auditors and attorneys in Puerto Rico for ten days from now. At that meeting I will instruct them to file bankruptcy." Turning on his heel, Ramon strode from the room, his long purposeful strides eloquent of restless anger.

When he returned, his thick black hair was slightly damp from a shower, and he was wearing Levi's. Roger turned and watched in silence as Ramon folded the cuffs of his white shirt up on his forearms. "Ramon," he said with pleading determination, "stay another week in St. Louis. Maybe Sid will contact you if you give him more time. I tell you, I don't think he knows you're here. I don't even know if he's in town."

"He is in town, and I am leaving for Puerto Rico in two days, exactly as I planned."

Roger heaved a long, defeated sigh. "What the hell are you going to do in Puerto Rico?"

"First, I am going to attend to the corporation's bankruptcy, and then I am going to do what my grandfather did, and his father before him," Ramon replied tautly. "I am going to farm."

"You're out of your mind!" Roger burst out. "Farm that little patch of ground with that hut on it where you and I took those two girls from . . . ?"

"That little patch of ground," Ramon interrupted with quiet dignity, "is all I have left. Along with the cottage on it where I was born."

"What about the house near San Juan, or the villa in Spain, or the island in the Mediterranean? Sell one of your houses or the island; that would keep you in luxury for as long as you live."

"They are gone. I put them up as collateral to raise money for the corporation that it cannot repay. The banks who loaned the money will be swarming over everything like vultures before the year is out."

"Dammit!" Roger said helplessly. "If your father weren't already dead, I'd kill him with my own two hands."

"The stockholders would have already beaten you to it." Ramon smiled without humor.

"How can you just stand there and talk as if you don't even care?"

"I have accepted defeat," Ramon said calmly. "I have done everything that can be done. I will not mind working my land beside the people who have worked it for my family for centuries."

Turning to hide his sympathy from the man Roger knew would reject it and despise him for it, he said, "Ramon, is there anything I can do?"

"Yes."

"Name it," Roger said, looking hopefully over his shoulder. "Just tell me and I'll do it."

"Will you loan me your car? I would like to go for a drive alone."

Grimacing at such a paltry request, Roger dug in his pocket, then tossed his keys to his friend. "There's a problem in the fuel line and the filter keeps clogging, but the local Mercedes dealer can't take it in for another week. With your luck the thing will probably quit in the middle of the street tonight."

Ramon shrugged, his face wiped clean of emotion. "If the car stops, I will walk. The exercise will help me get into condition for farming."

"You don't have to farm that place and you know it! In the international business community you're famous."

A muscle clenched in Ramon's jaw as he made an obvious effort to control his bitter anger. "In the international business community, I have been party to a sin no one will forgive or forget—failure. I am about to become its most notorious failure. Would you have me beg my friends for a position on that recommendation? Shall I go to your factory tomorrow and apply for a job on your assembly line?"

"No, of course not ! But you could think of something. I've seen you build a financial empire in a few short years. If you could build it, you could find a way to save a piece of it for yourself. I don't think you give a damn anymore! I—"

"I cannot work miracles," Ramon cut in flatly. "And that is what it would take. The Lear is in a hangar at the airport waiting for a minor part for one of the engines. When the jet mechanics have finished with it, and my pilot returns Sunday night from his weekend off, I will be flying to Puerto Rico." Roger opened his mouth to protest, but Ramon silenced him with an impatient look. "There is dignity in farming. More dignity, I think, than in dealing with bankers. While my father was alive, I knew no peace. Since he died, I have known no peace. Let me find it in my own way."

2

*T*he huge bar at the Canyon Inn near suburban Westport was packed with the usual Friday night crowd. Katie Connelly glanced surreptitiously at her watch, then let her gaze slide over the laughing, drinking, talking groups, searching for a particular face among them. Her view of the main entrance was obscured by the profusion of lush plants suspended from macrame hangers and the tiffany lamps hanging beneath the stained-glass ceiling.

Keeping the bright smile fixed on her face, she returned her attention to the knot of men and women standing around her. "So I told him never to call me again," Karen Wilson was saying to them.

A man stepped on Katie's foot while stretching around her to get his drink from the bar. In the process of reaching into his pocket to extract some money, he jabbed her in the side with his elbow. He offered no apology, nor did Katie really expect one. It was every man, and every woman, for themselves in here. Equal rights.

Turning away from the bar with his drink in his hand, he noticed Katie. "Hello," he said, pausing to flick an interested glance over her slender, curving figure draped in a clingy blue dress. "Nice," he concluded aloud as he considered everything about her, from the shining reddish blond hair tumbling around her shoulders, to the sapphire blue eyes regarding him beneath long curling lashes and delicately arched brows. Her cheeks were elegantly curved, her nose small, and as he continued to survey her, her creamy complexion took on a becoming tint of pale rose. "*Very* nice," he amended, unaware that the reason for her heightening color was irritation, not pleasure.

Although Katie resented him for looking at her as if he had paid for the privilege, she could not really blame him. After all, she was here, wasn't she? Here in what was, despite what the owners and patrons preferred to think, nothing more than a huge singles' bar attached to a tiny dining room to give it dignity.

"Where's your drink?" he asked, lazily reexamining her beautiful face.

"I don't have one," Katie replied, stating the perfectly obvious.

"Why not?"

"I've already had two."

"Well, why don't you get yourself another one and meet me over in that corner? We can get acquainted. I'm an attorney," he added, as if that one piece of information should make her eager to snatch a drink and leap after him.

Katie bit her lip and deliberately looked disappointed. "Oh."

"Oh, what?"

"I don't like attorneys," she said straight-faced.

He was more stunned than annoyed. "Too bad." Shrugging, he turned and wended his way into the crowd. Katie watched him pause near two very attractive young women who returned his considering glance with one of their own, looking him over with blatant interest. She felt a surge of shamed disgust for him, for all of them in this crowded place, but especially for herself for being here. She was inwardly embarrassed by her own rudeness, but places like this automatically made her feel defensive, and her natural warmth and spontaneity atrophied the moment she crossed the threshold.

The attorney had, of course, forgotten Katie in an instant. Why should he bother spending two dollars to buy her a drink, then put forth the effort to be friendly and charm her? Why should he exert himself when it wasn't necessary? If Katie, or any other woman in the room, wanted to get to know him, he was perfectly willing to let her try to interest him. And if she succeeded sufficiently, he would even invite her to come to his place—in her own car, of course—so that she could indulge her equal, and much publicized, need for sexual gratification. After which he would have a friendly drink with her—if he wasn't too tired—walk her to his door, and allow her to drive herself back to wherever she lived.

So efficient, so straightforward. No strings attached. No commitments made or expected. Today's woman, of course, had equal rights of refusal; she didn't have to go to bed with him. She didn't even have to worry that her refusal might hurt his feelings. Because he had no feelings for her. He might be slightly annoyed that he had wasted an hour or two of his time, but then he would simply make another selection from the numerous willing women available to him.

Katie raised her blue eyes, again scanning the crowd for Rob, wishing she had arranged to meet him somewhere else. The popular music was too loud, adding its clamor to the din of raised voices and forced laughter. She gazed at the faces around her, all different, yet all similar in their restless, eager, bored expressions. They were all looking for something. They hadn't found it yet.

"It's Katie, isn't it?" An unfamiliar male voice spoke behind her. Startled, Katie turned and found herself looking into a confidently smiling male face above an Ivy League button-down shirt, well-tailored blazer and coordinated tie. "I met you with Karen at the supermarket, two weeks ago."

He had a boyish grin and hard eyes. Katie was wary and her smile lacked its normal sparkle. "Hello, Ken. It's nice to see you again."

"Listen, Katie," he said, as if he had suddenly devised a brilliant and original scheme. "Why don't we leave here and go somewhere quieter."

His place or hers. Whichever was closest. Katie knew the routine and it sickened her. "What did you have in mind?"

He didn't answer the question, he didn't need to. Instead he asked another. "Where do you live?"

"A few blocks from here—the Village Green Apartments."

"Any roommates?"

"Two lesbians," she lied gravely.

He believed her, and he wasn't shocked. "No kidding? It doesn't bother you?"

Katie gave him a look of wide-eyed innocence. "I *adore* them." For just a fraction of a second he looked revolted, and Katie's smile widened with genuine laughter.

Recovering almost immediately, he shrugged. "Too bad. See you around."

Katie watched his attention shift across the room until he saw someone who interested him and he left, slowly shoving his way through the crowd. She had had enough. More than enough. She touched Karen's arm, distracting her from her animated conversation with two attractive men about skiing in Colorado. "Karen, I'm going to stop in the ladies' room, and then I'm leaving."

"Rob didn't show up?" Karen said distractedly. "Well, look around—there's plenty more where he came from. Take your pick."

"I'm going," Katie said with quiet firmness. Karen merely shrugged and returned to her conversation.

The ladies' room was down a short hall behind the bar, and Katie worked her way through the shifting bodies, breathing a sigh of relief as she squeezed around the last human obstacle in her path and stepped into the relative quiet of the hallway. She wasn't sure whether she was relieved or disappointed that Rob hadn't come. Eight months ago, she had been wildly, passionately dazzled by him, by his clever mind and teasing tenderness. He had everything: blond good looks, confidence, charm and a secure future as the heir to one of St. Louis's largest stockbrokerage firms. He was beautiful and wise and wonderful. And married.

Katie's face saddened as she recalled the last time she had seen Rob. . . . After a marvelous dinner and dancing they had returned to her apartment and were having a drink. For hours she had been thinking of what was going to happen when Rob took her in his arms. That night, for the first time, she was not going to stop him when he tried to make love to her. During the last months he had told her a hundred times, and shown her in a hundred ways, that he loved her. There was no need for her to hesitate any longer. In fact, she had been about to take the initiative when Rob had leaned his head back against the sofa and sighed. "Katie, tomorrow's paper is going to have a story about me in the society section. Not just about me—but also about my wife and son. I'm married."

Pale and heartbroken, Katie had told him never to call her again or try to see her. He did—repeatedly. And just as tenaciously, Katie refused his calls at her office and hung up the phone at home whenever she heard his voice.

That was five months ago, and only rarely since then had Katie allowed herself the bittersweet luxury of thinking of him, even for a moment. Until three days ago, she had believed she was entirely over him, but when she answered her phone on Wednesday, the sound of Rob's deep voice had made her whole body tremble: "Katie, don't hang up on me. Everything's changing. I've got to see you, to talk to you."

He had argued vehemently against Katie's choice of this for a meeting place, but Katie held firm. The Canyon Inn was noisy and public enough to discourage him from trying to use tender persuasion, if that was his intention, and Karen came here every Friday, which meant Katie would have feminine moral support if she needed it.

The ladies' room was crowded and Katie had to wait in line. She emerged several minutes later, absently digging in her shoulder purse for her car keys as she walked down the hall, then stopped at the crowd blocking her reentry into the bar. Beside her at one of the pay telephones on the wall, a man spoke with a trace of a Spanish accent: "Pardon—could you tell me the address of this place?"

On the verge of pushing her way into the tightly packed mass of humanity, Katie turned to look at the tall, lithe male who was regarding her with faint impatience while holding the telephone to his ear. "Were you speaking to me?" Katie asked. His face was deeply tanned, his hair vitally thick and as black as his onyx eyes. In a place filled with men who always reminded Katie of IBM salesmen, this man, who was wearing faded Levi's and a white shirt with the sleeves rolled up on his forearms, definitely did not belong. He was too . . . earthy.

"I asked," the Spanish-accented voice repeated, "if you could tell me the address of this place. I have had car trouble and am trying to order a towing vehicle."

Katie automatically named the two intersections at the corner of which the Canyon Inn was located, while mentally recoiling from the narrowed black eyes and patrician nose in a foreign, arrogant face. Tall, dark foreign-looking men reeking of coarse masculinity might appeal to some women, but not to Katherine Connelly.

"Thank you," he replied, removing his hand from the mouthpiece of the telephone and repeating the names of the streets Katie had given him.

Turning away, Katie confronted a dark green Izod sweater stretched across the masculine chest that was blocking her way back into the bar area. Eyeball to alligator, she said, "Excuse me, may I get by?" The sweater obligingly moved out of the doorway.

"Where are you going?" its wearer inquired in a friendly voice. "It's still early."

Katie raised her deep blue eyes up to his face and saw his smile broaden with frank admiration. "I know, but I have to leave. I turn into a pumpkin at midnight."

"Your *chariot* turns into a pumpkin," he corrected, grinning. "And your dress turns into rags."

"Planned obsolescence and poor workmanship, even in Cinderella's time," Katie sighed in mock disgust.

"Clever girl," he applauded. "Sagittarius, right?"

"Wrong," Katie said, extracting her keys from the bottom of her purse.

"Then what is your sign?"

"Slow Down and Proceed with Caution," she flipped back. "What's yours?"

He thought for a moment. "Merge," he replied with a meaningful glance that faithfully followed every curve of her graceful figure. Reaching out, he lightly ran his knuckles over the silky sleeve of Katie's dress. "I happen to like intelligent women; I don't feel threatened by them."

Firmly repressing the impulse to suggest that he try making a pass at Dr. Joyce Brothers, Katie said politely, "I really do have to leave. I'm meeting someone."

"Lucky guy," he said.

Katie emerged into the dark, sultry summer night feeling lost and depressed. She paused beneath the canopied entrance, watching with a suddenly pounding heart as a familiar white Corvette ran the red light at the corner and turned into the parking lot, screeching to a stop beside her. "I'm sorry I'm late. Get in, Katie. We'll go somewhere and talk."

Katie looked at Rob through the open car window and felt a surge of longing so intense that she ached with it. He was still unbearably handsome, but his smile, normally so confident and assured, was now tinged with an endearing uncertainty that wrung her heart and weakened her resolve. "It's late. And I don't have anything to say to you if you're still married."

"Katie, we can't talk here like this. don't give me a hard time about being late. I've had a lousy flight and it was delayed getting into St. Louis. Now, be a good girl and get in the car. I don't have time to waste arguing with you."

"Why don't you have time?" Katie persisted, "Is your wife expecting you?"

Rob swore under his breath, then accelerated sharply, swinging the sports car into a shadowy parking space beside the building. He got out of the car and leaned against the door, waiting for Katie to come to him. With the breeze teasing her hair and tugging at the folds of her blue dress, Katie reluctantly approached him in the darkened parking lot.

"It's been a long time, Katie," he said when she stopped in front of him. "Aren't you going to kiss me hello?"

"Are you still married?"

His answer was to snatch her into his arms and kiss her with a combination of fierce hunger and pleading need. He knew her well enough, however, to realize that Katie was only passively accepting his kiss, and by avoiding her question he had told her that he was still married. "Don't be like this," he rasped thickly, his breath warm against her ear. "I've thought of nothing but you for months. Let's get out of here and go to your place."

Katie drew an unsteady breath. "No."

"Katie, I love you, I'm crazy about you. don't keep holding out on me."

For the first time, Katie noticed the smell of liquor on his breath and was unwillingly touched that he had apparently felt the need to bolster his courage before seeing her. But she managed to keep her voice firm. "I'm not going to have a sleazy affair with a married man."

"Before you knew I was married, you didn't find anything 'sleazy' about being with me."

Now he was going to try cajolery, and Katie couldn't bear it. "Please, please don't do this to me, Rob. I couldn't live with myself if I wrecked another woman's marriage."

"The marriage was 'wrecked' long before I met you, honey. I tried to tell you that."

"Then get a divorce," Katie said desperately.

Even in the darkness, Katie could see the bitter irony that twisted his smile. "Southfields do not divorce. They learn to live separate lives. Ask my father and my grandfather," he said with angry pain. Despite the doors opening and closing as people drifted in and out of the restaurant, Rob's voice remained at normal pitch, and his hands slid down her back caressing her, then cupping her hips, forcing her against his hardened thighs. "That's for you, Katie. Only for you. You won't be wrecking my marriage; it was over long ago."

Katie couldn't stand any more. The sordidness of the situation made her feel dirty, and she tried to pull away from him. "Let go of me," she hissed. "Either you're a liar, or you're a coward, or both, and—"

Rob's hands tightened around her arms as she struggled. "I hate you for acting like this!" Katie choked. "Let me go!"

"Do as she says," a faintly accented voice spoke from the darkness.

Rob's head snapped up. "Who the hell are you?" he demanded of the white-shirted figure that materialized from the shadows beside the building. Retaining his grip on one of Katie's arms, Rob glowered menacingly at the intruder and snapped at Katie, "Do you know him?"

Katie's voice was hoarse with mortification and anger. "No, but let go of me. I want to leave."

"You're staying," Rob gritted. Jerking his head toward the other man, he said, "And you're going. Now move, unless you want me to help you on your way."

The accented voice became extremely courteous, almost frighteningly so. "You may try if you wish. But let her go."

Pushed past all endurance by Katie's continued implacable stubbornness, and now this unwanted intrusion, Rob vented all his frustrated wrath on the intruder. He dropped Katie's arm and, in one smooth continuous motion, swung his huge fist directly at his opponent's jaw. A second's silence was followed by the terrible crack of bone connecting with bone, and then a resounding thud. Katie opened her tear-brightened eyes to find Rob unconscious at her feet.

"Open the car door," the foreign voice ordered with an insistence that brooked no argument.

Automatically, Katie opened the door of the Corvette. The man unceremoniously shoved and folded Rob inside, leaving his head lolling over the steering wheel as if he were passed out in a drunken stupor. "Which is your car?"

Katie stared at him blankly. "We can't leave him like this. He might need a doctor."

"Which is your car?" he repeated impatiently. "I have no wish to be here in the event someone saw what happened and called the police."

"Oh, but—" Katie protested, looking over her shoulder at Rob's Corvette as she hurried toward her car. She drew up stubbornly at the driver's door. "You leave. I can't."

"I did not kill him, I only stunned him. He will wake up in a few minutes with a sore face and loose teeth, that is all. I will drive," he said, forcibly propelling Katie around the front of her car and into the passenger seat. "You are in no condition."

Flinging himself behind the steering wheel, he banged his knee on the steering column and uttered what Katie thought must have been a curse in Spanish. "Give me your keys," he said, releasing the seat back into its farthest position to accommodate his very long legs. Katie handed them over. Several cars were coming in and leaving, and they had to wait before finally backing out of the space. They swooped down the rows of parked cars, past a battered old produce truck with a flat tire, which was parked at the rear of the restaurant.

"Is that yours?" Katie asked lamely, feeling that some conversation was required of her.

He glanced at the disabled produce truck, then slid her an ironic sideways look. "How did you guess?"

Katie flushed with mortification. She knew, and he knew, that simply because he was Hispanic she had assumed he drove the produce truck. To save his pride she said, "When you were on the telephone you mentioned that you needed a tow truck—that's how I knew."

They swung out of the parking lot into the stream of traffic while Katie gave him the simple directions to her apartment, which was only a few blocks away. "I want to thank you, er—?"

"Ramon," he provided.

Nervously, Katie reached for her purse and searched for her wallet. She lived so close by, that by the time she had extracted a five-dollar bill they were already pulling into the parking lot of her apartment complex. "I live right there—the first door on the right, under the gaslight."

He maneuvered the car into the parking space closest to her door, turned off the ignition, got out, and came around to her side. Katie hastily opened her own door and scrambled out of the car. Uncertainly, she glanced up into his dark, proud, enigmatic face, guessing him to be somewhere around thirty-five. Something about him, his foreignness—or his darkness—made her uneasy.

She held out her hand, offering him the five-dollar bill. "Thank you very much, Ramon. Please take this." He looked briefly at the money and then at her face. "Please," she persisted politely, thrusting the five-dollar bill toward him. "I'm sure you can use it."

"Of course," he said dryly after a pause, taking the money from her and jamming it into the back pocket of his Levi's. "I will walk you to your door," he added.

Katie turned and started up the steps, a little shocked when his hand lightly but firmly cupped her elbow. It was such a quaint, gallant gesture—particularly when she knew she had inadvertently offended his pride.

He inserted her key into the lock and swung the door open. Katie stepped inside, turned to thank him again, and he said, "I would like to use your phone to find out if the towing vehicle was sent as they promised."

He had physically come to her rescue and had even risked being arrested for her—Katie knew that common courtesy required that she allow him to use her phone. Carefully concealing her reluctance to let him in, she stepped aside so that he could enter her luxurious apartment. "The phone's there on the coffee table," she explained.

"Once I have called, I will wait here for a short while to be certain that your friend"—he emphasized the word with contempt—"does not awaken and decide to come here. By then the mechanic should have finished his repairs and I will walk back—it is not far."

Katie, who had not even considered the possibility that Rob might come here, froze in the act of taking off her slim-heeled sandals. Surely Rob would never come near her again, not after being verbally rejected by her and physically discouraged by Ramon. "I'm sure he won't," she said, and she meant it. But even so, she found herself trembling with delayed reaction. "I—I think I'll make some coffee," she said, already starting for the kitchen. And then because she had no choice, she added courteously. "Would you like some?"

Ramon accepted her offer with such ambivalence that most of Katie's doubts about his trustworthiness were allayed. Since meeting him, he had neither said nor done anything that was in any way forward.

Once she was in the kitchen, Katie realized that in the anxiety about seeing Rob tonight she had forgotten to buy coffee, and she was out of it. Which was just as well, because she suddenly felt the need for something stronger. Opening the cabinet above the refrigerator, she took out the bottle of Rob's brandy. "I'm afraid all I have to offer you is brandy or water," she called to Ramon. "The Coke is flat."

"Brandy will be fine," he answered.

Katie splashed brandy into two snifters and returned to the living room just as Ramon was hanging up the telephone. "Did the repair truck get there?" she asked.

"It is there now, and the mechanic is making a temporary repair so that I can drive it." Ramon took the glass from her outstretched hand, and looked around her apartment with a quizzical expression on his face. "Where are your friends?" he asked.

"What friends?" Katie questioned blankly, sitting down in a pretty beige corduroy chair.

"The lesbians."

Katie choked back her horrified laughter. "Were you close enough to hear me say that?"

Gazing down at her, Ramon nodded, but there was no amusement in the quirk of his finely molded lips. "I was behind you, obtaining change for the telephone from the bartender."

"Oh." The misery of tonight's events threatened to drag her down, but Katie pushed it fiercely to the back of her mind. She would think about it tomorrow when she would be better able to cope. She shrugged lightly. "I only made the lesbians up. I wasn't in the mood for—"

"Why do you not like attorneys?" he interrupted.

Katie stifled another urge to laugh. "It's a very long story, which I'd rather not discuss. But I suppose the reason I told him that was because I thought it was vain of him to tell me he was one."

"You are not vain?"

Katie turned surprised eyes up to him. There was a childlike defenselessness to the way she had curled up in her chair with her bare feet tucked beneath her; an innocent vulnerability in the purity of her features and clarity of her wide blue eyes. "I—I don't know."

"You would not have been rude to me, had I approached you there and said that I drive a produce truck?"

Katie smiled the first genuine smile of the night, soft lips curving with a winsome humor that made her eyes glow. "I would probably have been too stunned to speak. In the first place, no one who goes to the Canyon Inn drives a truck, and in the second place, if they did they'd never admit it."

"Why? It is nothing to be ashamed of."

"No, I realize that. But they would say they were in the transportation business, or the trucking business—something like that, so that it would sound as if they owned a railroad, or at least an entire fleet of trucks."

Ramon stared down at her as if the words she spoke were a hindrance, not a help, to his understanding her. His gaze drifted to the red gold hair tumbling over her shoulders, then abruptly he jerked his eyes away. Raising his glass, he tossed down half the brandy in it.

"Brandy is supposed to be sipped," Katie said, then realized that what she had meant as a suggestion sounded more like a reprimand. "I mean," she amended clumsily, "You can gulp it down, but people who are accustomed to drinking brandy usually prefer to sip it slowly."

Ramon lowered his glass and looked at her with an absolutely unfathomable expression on his face. "Thank you," he replied with impeccable courtesy. "I will try to remember that if I am ever fortunate enough to have it again."

Squirming with the certainty that she had now thoroughly offended him, Katie watched him stroll over to the living-room window and part the nubby beige curtain.

Her window afforded an uninspiring view of the parking lot and, beyond that, the busy four-lane suburban street in front of her apartment complex. Leaning a shoulder against the window frame, he apparently heeded her advice, for he sipped his brandy slowly while watching the parking lot.

Idly, Katie noticed the way his white shirt stretched taut across his broad, muscled shoulders and tapered back whenever he lifted his arm, then she looked away. She had only meant to be helpful, instead she had sounded condescending and superior. She wished he would leave. She was mentally and physically exhausted, and there was absolutely no reason for him to be guarding her like this. Rob would not come here tonight.

"How old are you?" he asked abruptly.

Katie's gaze flew to his. "Twenty-three."

"Then you are old enough to have a better sense of priorities."

Katie was more perplexed than annoyed. "What do you mean?"

"I mean, you think it is important that brandy be drunk in the 'proper' way, yet you do not worry if it is 'proper' to invite any man you meet into your apartment. You risk soiling your reputation and—"

"Invite any man I meet!" Katie sputtered indignantly, no longer feeling the slightest obligation to be courteous. "In the first place, I only invited you in here because you asked to use the phone, and I felt I had to be polite after you had helped me. In the second place, I don't know about Mexico, or whatever country you come from, but—"

"I was born in Puerto Rico," he provided.

Katie ignored that. "Well, here in the United States, we do not have such antiquated, absurd ideas about women's reputations. Men have never worried about their reputations, and we no longer worry about ours. We do as we please!"

Katie absolutely could not believe it. Now, when she *wanted* to insult him, he was on the verge of laughter!

His black eyes were warm with amusement, and a smile was hovering at the corner of his mouth. "Do you do as you please?"

"Of course I do!" Katie said with great feeling.

"What is it that you do?"

"Pardon?"

"What is it that you do that pleases you?"

"Whatever I want."

His voice deepened. "What do you want . . . Now?"

His suggestive tone made Katie suddenly and uncomfortably aware of the raw sensuality emanating from his long muscular frame outlined in the revealing Levi's and closely fitted white shirt. A shudder ran through her as his gaze moved over her face, lingering on her soft full lips, before dropping to leisurely study the thrusting curves of her breasts beneath the clinging fabric of her dress. She felt like screaming, laughing, or weeping—or a combination of all three. After everything else that had happened to her tonight, Katie Connelly had managed to latch onto a Puerto Rican Casanova who thought he was now going to make himself the answer to all her sexual needs!

Forcing herself to sound brisk, she finally answered his question. "What do I want now? I want to be happy with my life and myself. I want to be—to be—free," she finished lamely, too distracted by his dark, sensual gaze to think clearly.

"Of what do you wish to be free?"

Katie stood up abruptly. "Of men!"

As she came to her feet, Ramon started toward her with a slow deliberate gait. "You want to be free of so much freedom, but not of men."

Katie continued backing toward the door as he advanced on her. She had been crazy to invite him in here, and he was deliberately misunderstanding her reason for doing so, because it suited his purpose. She gasped as her back bumped into the door.

Ramon stopped six inches away from her. "If you wished to be free of men as you say, you would not have gone to that place tonight; you would not have met that man in the parking lot. You do not know what you want."

"I know that it's late," Katie said in a shaky voice. "And I know I want you to leave now."

His eyes narrowed on her face, but his voice gentled as he asked, "Are you afraid of me?"

"No," Katie lied.

He nodded with satisfaction. "Good, then you will not object to going to the zoo with me tomorrow, will you?"

Katie could tell that he knew she was acutely uneasy with him and that she had no desire to go *anywhere* with him. She considered saying that she had other plans for tomorrow, but she was positive he would only press her to name another time. Every instinct she possessed warned her that he could become extremely persistent if he chose. In her tired, overwrought state, it seemed more expedient to simply make the date and then not be here when he came. That rejection even he would understand and accept as final. "Okay," she feigned. "What time?"

"I will come for you at ten o'clock in the morning."

When the door closed behind him, Katie felt like a spring that was being wound tighter and tighter by some fiend who wanted to see how far she could be twisted before she snapped. She crawled into bed and stared at the ceiling. She had enough problems without having to cope with some amorous Latin who invites her to the zoo!

Rolling over onto her stomach, Katie thought of the sordid scene with Rob and squeezed her eyes closed, trying to escape her tired misery. Tomorrow she would spend the day at her parents' house. In fact, she would spend the entire Memorial Day weekend there. After all, her parents always complained that they didn't see enough of her.

The alarm's buzzing at eight o'clock the next morning woke her from a deep, exhausted sleep. Bewildered over why she had set it to go off on a Saturday, she groped for the button and pushed it in, silencing the insistent noise.

When she opened her eyes again it was nine o'clock and she blinked at the light flooding into her flowered bedroom. Oh, no! Ramon would be here in an hour. . . .

Tumbling out of bed, she hurried into the bathroom and turned on the shower. Her pulse quickened with each passing minute, while everything else seemed to slow down. Her blow dryer took forever to dry her heavy hair; she kept dropping everything she touched, and she longed for a bracing cup of coffee.

Moving quickly, she opened drawers, putting on a pair of navy blue slacks and a matching top trimmed in white piping. She pulled her hair back and tied it with a red, white and blue printed silk scarf, then threw a random assortment of clothing into her overnight bag.

At 9:35, Katie closed the door of her apartment behind her and stepped into the balmy blue of a May morning. The large apartment complex was quiet: the typical lull of a predominately singles' complex in the aftermath of Friday night dates, parties and revelry.

Katie hurried toward her car, shifting her overnight case to her left hand as she searched in her cavernous canvas shoulder bag for her keys. "Damn!" she breathed, putting her case down besides her car and rummaging frantically for her keys. She threw a nervous, apprehensive look at the traffic passing in both directions on the busy street, half-expecting to see a produce truck rattling into the entrance of the complex. "What did I do with them?" she whispered desperately. Her nerves, already strained to the breaking point, exploded in a stifled scream as a hand locked on her arm.

"I have them," a deep voice said smoothly near her ear.

Katie spun around in fright and fury. "How dare you spy on me!" she raged.

"I was *waiting* for you," Ramon emphasized.

"Liar!" she hissed, her fists clenched at her sides. "It's nearly half an hour before you're supposed to be here. Or don't you even know how to tell time?"

"Here are your keys. I put them in my pocket by mistake last night." He raised his hand and held them out to her, along with a single, long-stemmed red rose that lay across his palm.

Snatching her keys from his hand, Katie scrupulously avoided even touching the unwanted crimson flower.

"Take the rose," he told her quietly, his hand still outstretched. "It is for you."

"Damn you!" Katie raged in desperation. "Leave me alone! This isn't Puerto Rico, and I don't want your flower." Ignoring her, he continued to stand patiently. "I said I don't want it!" Katie snapped in frustrated fury and reached down for her overnight case. In the process she inadvertently knocked the rose out of his hand.

The sight of the beautiful bloom falling to the concrete sent a pang of guilt through Katie that shattered her anger and left her feeling deeply embarrassed. She glanced at Ramon; his proud face was composed, reflecting neither anger nor condemnation—only a deep, inexplicable regret.

Unable to meet his eyes Katie dropped her gaze from his, and her guilt sharpened into shame as she saw that buying her a flower wasn't the only thing he had done to try to please her—he had obviously dressed with great care for their date too. Gone were the worn Levi's, replaced by immaculate black slacks and a short-sleeved black knit shirt; his face was freshly shaven, the scent of spicy cologne clinging to his smooth jaw.

He had only meant to please and impress her; he didn't deserve such treatment, especially after the way he had defended her last night. Katie looked at the waxy red rose lying at her feet, and she was so ashamed that tears stung her eyes and made her throat ache. "Ramon, I'm very, very sorry," she said contritely as she bent down and picked up the rose. Clutching the stem, she dragged her eyes upward and gazed pleadingly into his guarded face. "Thank you for the beautiful flower. And if—if you still want me to, I'll go to the zoo with you, because I promised I would." Pausing to pull more air into her constricted lungs, Katie plunged on. "But I want you to understand that I don't want you to get—well—*serious* about me, and start—start. . . ." Katie trailed off in bewilderment as his eyes began to gleam with laughter.

In a dryly humorous voice he said, "I only offered you a flower and a trip to the zoo, not marriage."

Suddenly Katie found herself smiling back at him. "You're right."

"Shall we go, then?" he suggested.

"Yes, but first let me put my overnight case back in the apartment." She reached for it, but Ramon was quicker. "I will carry it," he said.

When they entered her apartment, she took the case from him and started for her bedroom. Ramon's question stopped her. "Was it me you were running away from?"

Katie turned in the doorway. "Not exactly. After last night, I just felt the need to get away from everything and everyone for a while."

"What were you going to do?"

Katie's soft lips curved into a rueful smile that brought a glow to her lovely eyes. "I was going to do what most independent, self-sufficient, adult American women do when they can't cope—run home to mother and dad."

A few minutes later they left the apartment. As they walked across the parking lot, Katie held up the expensive camera she was carrying in her left hand. "It's a camera," she told him.

"Yes, I know," he agreed with mocking gravity. "We have them even in Puerto Rico."

Katie burst out laughing and shook her head in self-deprecation. "I never realized what an 'ugly American' I am."

Stopping beside a jaunty Buick Regal, Ramon opened the passenger door for her. "You are a beautiful American," he contradicted quietly. "Get in."

To Katie's shame, she was vastly relieved that they were going in a car. Careening down the expressway in a rickety produce truck just wasn't her style. "Is your truck broken down again?" she asked as they glided smoothly out of the parking lot, turning into the stream of Saturday morning shopping traffic.

"I thought you would prefer this to a truck. I borrowed it from a friend of mine."

"We could always have taken my car," she volunteered.

The brief look that he sent her made it clear that if Ramon asked someone to go somewhere with him, he expected to provide the transportation. Chastened, Katie turned on the FM radio, then stole a sideways look at him. With his superb physique and deeply tanned face and arms, he reminded her of a Spanish tennis pro.

Katie had wonderful time with Ramon at the zoo, even though it was crowded with Memorial Day visitors. Side by side they wandered down the wide cement paths. Ramon bought her peanuts to toss to the bears and roared with laughter in the Aviary House when a toucan with an enormous beak swooped down and made Katie shriek with alarm and cover her head.

She accompanied him into the Reptile House, trying to keep her phobic aversion to snakes under control by not actually looking at anything. The hair stood up on her nape as she kept her eyes moving around the room without focusing on any of the reptilian occupants.

"Look there," Ramon said in her ear, nodding toward the huge glass enclosure right beside her.

Katie swallowed. "I don't need to look," she whispered through dry lips. "I already know there's a tree in there, which means there's probably a snake hanging from it." Her palms were beginning to perspire, and she could almost feel the reptile's sinuous slitherings on her own skin.

"What is wrong?" Ramon said sharply, noting her draining color. "Do you not like snakes?"

"Not," Katie croaked, "very much."

Shaking his head, he took her by the arm and marched her outside where Katie drew in great gulps of fresh air and sank down on a nearby bench. "I'm sure they put these benches right outside the Reptile House for people like me. Otherwise we'd be dropping like flies out here."

The slight cleft in Ramon's chin deepened as he grinned. "Snakes are very beneficial to mankind. They eat rodents, insects—"

"Please!" Katie shuddered, holding up her hand in protest. "Do not describe their menu to me."

Regarding her with amusement, Ramon persisted, "The fact remains that they are very useful and entirely necessary to balance nature."

Katie rose a little unsteadily to her feet and gave him an arch look. "Really? Well, I've never heard of one thing that a snake can do that something less repulsive-looking can't do better."

Her delicate nose was wrinkled with distaste, and Ramon smiled thoughtfully down into the brilliant blue of her eyes. "Neither have I," he admitted.

They strolled along and Katie could not remember a more quietly enjoyable date. Ramon was always impeccably courteous, taking her arm when they walked down stairs or ramps, showing her a detached gallantry in the way he acquiesced to her slightest desire.

By the time they came to the island where monkeys and peacocks and other interesting, but not rare, small animals were kept, Katie had used most of the second roll of film. Helping herself to a handful of popcorn from the box Ramon held out to her, she leaned over the fence that isolated the little island, and tossed the kernels one at a time to the ducks. Her unintentionally provocative position caused the navy fabric of her slacks to stretch taut over the graceful contours of her hips and derriere, providing an appreciative Ramon with a delightful view, which he was thoroughly enjoying.

Unaware of where his attention was focused, Katie glanced over her shoulder. "Do you want a picture of this?" she asked.

His lips twitched. "Of what?"

"Of the island," Katie said, puzzled by his laughing expression. "This roll of film is nearly finished. I'll give both of them to you, and then when you have them developed you'll have a souvenir of your trip to the St. Louis zoo."

He looked at her in surprise. "These pictures are for me?"

"Of course," Katie replied, helping herself to another handful of popcorn.

"If I had known they were for me," Ramon grinned, "I would have wanted pictures of more than just bears and giraffes to remind me of this day."

Katie lifted her brows in inquiry. "Snakes, you mean? If you do, I'll show you how to use the camera, then you can go back into the Reptile House while I wait here."

"No," he said wryly, as he guided her from the fence. "Not snakes."

On the way home they stopped at a small market so that Katie could buy some coffee. On an impulse, she decided to invite Ramon in for a snack, and added a bottle of red wine and some cheese to her purchases.

Ramon walked her to her door, but when Katie invited him in he seemed to hesitate before finally nodding his assent.

Less than an hour later, Ramon stood up. "I have work to do tonight," he explained.

Smiling, Katie arose and went over to her camera. "There's one shot left on this roll. Stand there and I'll take a picture of you and give you both rolls to take with you."

"No, save it, and I will take a picture of you tomorrow when we go for a picnic."

Katie deliberated about accepting another date with him. For the first time in ages she had felt lighthearted and carefree, and yet. . . . "No, I shouldn't really. But thanks." Ramon was tall, sexy and virile, no doubt about it, but his dark features and blatant masculinity still repelled rather than attracted her. Besides, they really had nothing in common.

"Why do you look at me and then away, as if you wish you did not see me?" Ramon asked abruptly.

Katie's gaze flew to his. "I—I don't."

"Yes," he said implacably. "You do."

Katie considered lying, but changed her mind under the scrutiny of those piercing black eyes. "You remind me of someone who's dead now. He was tall and dark and, well, just very macho-looking like you."

"His death brought you great sorrow?"

"His death brought me great release," Katie said emphatically. "There were times before he died when I wished I had the courage to kill him myself!"

He chuckled. "What a dark, sinister life you have led for one so young and beautiful."

Katie, who was known and liked for her sunny disposition despite the painful memories she kept buried inside, gave him a jaunty smile. "Better a dark sinister life than a boring one, I suppose."

"But you *are* bored," he said. "I saw it as I watched you in the place where we met." With one hand on the doorknob he looked across the room at her. "I will call for you tomorrow at noon. I will provide the food." Grinning at her surprise and indecision, he added, "And you can provide a lecture on how rude I am to insist, not ask, that you go places with me."

It wasn't until that night, when she left a boisterous party at a friend's apartment early because she was bored, that Katie seriously considered Ramon's parting words. Was boredom the reason for this increasing restlessness, this vague, unexplainable discontent that had been growing inside of her these past months, she wondered as she changed into silky pajamas and a matching robe. No, she decided after a thoughtful pause, her life was anything but boring—at times it was almost too eventful.

Curled up on the living-room sofa, Katie traced a long, manicured fingernail absently over the cover of the novel in her lap, her blue eyes cloudy and somber. If she wasn't bored, then what *was* the matter with her lately? It was a question she'd asked herself more and more often, and with mounting frustration because the answer always eluded her. If she could just figure out what was missing from her life, then she could try to do something about it.

There was nothing missing from her life, Katie told herself firmly. Impatient with her discontent, she mentally recounted all the reasons she had to feel happy: at twenty-three, she already had her college degree and she had a wonderful, challenging job that paid very well. Even without her salary, the trust fund her father had established for her years ago provided her with more money than she needed. She had a beautiful apartment and closets full of clothes. She was attractive to men; she had good friends, both male and female, and her social life was as active as she permitted it to be. She had loving, supportive parents, she had . . . everything! Katie told herself firmly.

What more could she possibly want or need to make her happy? "A man," Karen would say, as she often did.

A faint smile touched Katie's lips. "A man" was definitely not the answer to her problem. She knew dozens of men already, so it was not a lack of male companionship that was responsible for this restless, waiting, empty feeling.

Katie, who positively loathed anything that even approached self-pity, caught herself up short. There was absolutely no excuse for her unhappiness—none whatsoever. She was very lucky! Women all over the world were longing for careers; fighting to be independent and self-sufficient; dreaming of financial security and she, Katie Connelly, had all of that, and at only twenty-three years old. "I have everything," Katie said determinedly as she opened the book in her lap. She stared at the blur of words on the page, while somewhere in her heart a voice cried out, *It's not enough. It doesn't* mean *anything. I don't mean anything.*

4

hey went to Forest Park for their picnic, and Ramon spread the blanket Katie brought beneath a giant cluster of oaks, where they feasted on the wafer-thin delicatessen corned beef, imported ham and thick crusty French bread he had brought.

As they talked and ate, Katie was vaguely aware of his appreciative gaze on her animated face and his absorption with the shining tumble of red gold hair that spilled over her shoulders whenever she reached into the wicker picnic basket. But she was having such a lovely time, she really didn't mind.

"I believe fried chicken is customary for picnics in the States," Ramon said when there was a lull in the conversation. "Unfortunately, I cannot cook. If we have another picnic, I will buy the food and let you prepare it."

Katie almost choked on the hearty Chianti wine she was sipping from a paper cup. "What an utterly chauvinistic supposition to make," she berated him, laughing. "Why do you assume that I can cook?"

Stretching out on his side, Ramon leaned on a forearm and regarded her with exaggerated gravity. "Because you are a woman, of course."

"Are—are you serious?" she sputtered.

"Serious about your being a woman? Or about your being able to cook? Or about you?"

Katie heard the sensuous huskiness that deepened his voice as he asked the last question. "Serious about all women being able to cook," she informed him primly.

His grin widened at her evasiveness. "I did not say that all women were good cooks, merely that women should do the cooking. Men should work to buy the food for them to prepare. That is the way it ought to be."

Katie stared at him in speechless disbelief, half-convinced that he was deliberately goading her. "It may surprise you to hear this, but not all women are born with a burning desire to chop onions and grate cheese."

Ramon muffled a chuckle, then abruptly changed the subject. "What sort of job do you have?"

"I work in the personnel department of a big corporation. I interview people for jobs, things like that."

"Do you enjoy it?"

"Very much," she told him, reaching into the basket and extracting an enormous red apple. Drawing her denim-clad legs up against her chest, she wrapped her arms around them and bit into the juicy apple. "This is delicious."

"That is unfortunate."

Katie looked at him in surprise. "It's unfortunate that I like the apple?"

"It is unfortunate that you enjoy your job so much. You may resent having to give it up when you marry."

"Give it up when I—!" Katie giggled merrily, shaking her head. "Ramon, it's lucky for you that you aren't an American. You aren't even safe in this country. There are women here who could cook *you* for the way you think."

"I am an American," he said, ignoring Katie's dire warning.

"I thought you said you were Puerto Rican."

"I said I was born in Puerto Rico. Actually I am Spanish."

"You just said you were American and Puerto Rican."

"Katie," he said, using her name for the first time and sending an unexplainable thrill of pleasure through her. "Puerto Rico is a U.S. commonwealth. Everyone born there is automatically an American citizen. My ancestors, however, are all Spanish, not Puerto Rican. I am an American, born in Puerto Rico, and of Spanish descent. Just as you are"—he leisurely surveyed her fair complexion, blue eyes and reddish blond hair—"as you are an American, born in the United States, and of Irish descent."

Katie was a little stung by the tone of superiority with which he delivered this lecture. "What you are is a Spanish–Puerto Rican–American male chauvinist—of the worst sort!"

"Why do you use that tone of voice to me? Because I believe that when a woman marries her duty is to take care of her husband?"

Katie gave him a lofty look. "No matter what you believe, the fact remains that many women need to have other interests and accomplishments outside the home, just as men do. We like having a career we can take pride in."

"A woman can take pride in caring for her husband and children."

Katie knew she would say anything, *anything* to wipe that insufferably complacent grin from his face. "Luckily for us, American men who are born in the United States don't object to their wives' having careers. They are more understanding and considerate!"

"They are very understanding and considerate," Ramon conceded derisively. "They let you work, permit you to hand over the money you earn, allow you to have their babies, find someone to care for their babies, clean their houses and," he taunted, "still do the cooking."

Katie was momentarily dumbstruck by this speech, then she flopped down on her back and burst out laughing. "You're absolutely right!"

Ramon lay back beside her, linking his hands behind his head, staring up at the powder-blue sky dotted with cotton-ball clouds. "You have a beautiful laugh, Katie."

Katie took another bite of apple and said cheerfully, "You're only saying that because you think you've changed my mind, but you haven't. If a woman wants a career she must be able to have one. Besides, most women want nicer homes and clothes than their husbands could provide on their salaries alone."

"So she gets her fine house and clothes at the expense of her husband's pride, going to work herself and proving to him, and everyone, that what he can provide for her is not good enough."

"American husbands aren't as proud as Spaniards must be."

"American husbands have abdicated their responsibilities. They do not have anything to be proud of."

"Baloney!" Katie replied unarguably. "Would you want the girl you love and marry to live in someplace like Harlem because that was the best you could give her on the money you make driving that truck; when you knew that if she worked, doing something she liked, you could both have much more?"

"I would expect her to be happy with what I could give her."

Katie shivered inwardly at the prospect of some sweet Spanish girl having to live in a slum because Ramon's pride wouldn't allow her to work. His drowsy voice added, "And I would not like it if she were ashamed of what I do for a living, as you are."

Katie heard the quiet reprimand in his words, but persevered anyway. "Don't you ever wish you did something better than drive a produce truck?"

His answer was long in coming, and Katie suspected that he was marking her down as an ambitious pushy American woman. "I do. I grow produce too."

Katie reared up on both elbows. "You work on a produce farm? In Missouri?"

"In Puerto Rico," he corrected.

Katie couldn't decide whether she was relieved or disappointed that he would not be remaining in St. Louis. His eyes were drifting closed, and she let her gaze wander over his thick slightly curling black hair to his face. There was Spanish nobility stamped on his bronzed features, authority and arrogance in the firm jawline and straight nose, determination in the thrust of his chin. Yet, Katie thought with a smile, the slight cleft in his chin and his long, spiky lashes laying against his cheeks, softened the overall effect. His lips were firm but sensuously molded, and with a tingle of excitement Katie wondered how it would feel to have those lips moving warmly on hers. He had told her yesterday that he was thirty-four, but Katie thought he looked younger now, with his face relaxed in sleep.

She let her gaze travel down the long, superbly fit and muscled body stretched out on the blanket beside her. The red knit shirt he was wearing hugged his wide shoulders and chest, its short sleeves exposing the corded strength of his arms. His Levi's accentuated his narrow hips, flat stomach and hard thighs. Even sleeping, he seemed to exude a raw potent virility, but this no longer repelled her. Somehow, having admitted to him that facially he reminded her slightly of David, had banished all similarity between the two men banished from her mind.

His eyes didn't open, but the mobile line of his mouth quirked in a half-smile. "I hope what you are seeing meets with your approval."

Katie's chagrined gaze flew to the rolling parkland stretching out before her. "It does. The park is beautiful today, the trees as—"

"You were not looking at the trees, *señorita*."

Katie chose not to answer that. She was glad he had called her *señorita*; it sounded alien and odd to her, emphasizing the differences between them and neutralizing the effect his blatant masculinity had been having on her. What had she been thinking of, wanting Ramon to kiss her? Getting further involved with him could only lead to disaster. They had absolutely nothing in common; they came from two completely different worlds. Socially, they were miles apart. Tomorrow, for example, she was expected to attend a barbecue at her parents' elegant home on the grounds of Forest Oaks Country Club. Ramon could never fit in with the sort of people who would be there. He would feel ill at ease if she brought him with her. He would be out of place. And the moment her parents discovered that he was a farm laborer who drove a produce truck during the spring, they would very likely make it obvious to Ramon that they didn't think he belonged in their home, or with their daughter.

She would not see Ramon again after today, Katie decided firmly. There could never really be anything between them, and her dawning sexual response to him was a solid enough reason to break off the relationship immediately. It could never lead to anything meaningful or lasting.

"Why have you drawn away from me, Katie?"

His penetrating black eyes were open, searching her face. Katie made absorbing work of smoothing the blanket beneath her, then lying back on it. "Don't know what you mean," she said, closing he eyes and deliberately shutting him out.

His voice was low-pitched and sensual. "Would you like to know what I see when I look at you?"

"Not," she said primly, "if you're going to sound like an amorous Latin lover when you tell me. And from the tone of your voice, I think that's exactly what you were going to do." Katie tried to relax, but in the charged silence that followed her words it was impossible. A few minutes later, she sat up abruptly "I think it's time I got back home," she announced already scrambling to her knees and beginning to repack the picnic hamper. Without a word, Ramon stood up and began folding the blanket.

The strained silence during the drive home was broken only twice by Katie who, in the hope of atoning for her earlier rudeness, made two attempts a conversation only to be rebuffed by Ramon's monosyllabic replies. She was ashamed of her snobbish thoughts, embarrassed for the way she had spoken to him, and angry because he wouldn't let her smooth things over.

By the time he swung the Buick Regal into the parking space in front of her door, Katie wanted nothing more than to end the day, even if it was only three o'clock. Before Ramon could come around the car for her, she shoved open the door and practically leaped out.

"I will open the door for you," he snapped. "It is a gesture of common courtesy."

Katie, who realized for the first time that he was bitingly angry, was suddenly incensed at his obstinacy. "It may surprise you to hear this," she announced as she stormed up the steps and jammed her key into the lock, "but there is nothing wrong with my hands and I am perfectly capable of opening a damned car door. And I don't see why you should be courteous to me when I have been absolutely obnoxious to you!"

The angry humor of this remark was not lost on Ramon, but it was totally eclipsed by her next one. As she flung open the door to her apartment she turned around in the doorway and said furiously, "Thank you, Ramon. I had a very nice time."

Katie, who had no idea why Ramon had burst out laughing, was relieved that he wasn't still angry, and suddenly very wary of the way he had followed her into her apartment, firmly closed the door behind him, and was now looking at her with an unmistakable expression on his face.

His smoothly spoken words were part invitation, part order: "Come here, Katie."

Katie shook her head and took a cautious step backward, but an answering quiver was tingling up her spine.

"Is it not the custom of liberated American women to show their appreciation for having 'a very nice time' with a kiss?" Ramon persisted.

"Not all of them," Katie croaked. "Some of us just say 'thank you.'"

A faint smile touched his mouth, but his heavy-lidded gaze dropped to the inviting fullness of her lips, lingering there. "Come here, Katie." When she still balked, he added softly, "Are you not curious about how Spaniards kiss and Puerto Ricans make love?"

Katie swallowed convulsively. "No," she whispered.

"Come here, Katie, and I will show you."

Hypnotized by that velvet voice and those mesmerizing black eyes, Katie went to him in a trance that was a combination of fright and excitement.

Whatever she expected when she walked into Ramon's arms, it was not to find herself crushed in an embrace of steel and swept soaring off into some thick sweet darkness where the only feeling was of his parted lips moving ceaselessly on hers; the only sensation, the waves of liquid heat that raced through her in the wake of his caressing hands. "Katie," he whispered hoarsely, dragging his mouth from hers and kissing her eyes, her temple, her cheek. "Katie," he repeated in an aching whisper as his mouth again took possession of hers.

It seemed an eternity before he finally lifted his head. Weak and trembling, Katie laid her cheek against his hard chest and felt the violent pounding of his heart. She was utterly devastated by what had just happened. She had been kissed more times than she could remember, and by men whose technique had been practiced and perfected until it was almost an art form. In their arms, she had felt pleasure—not this mindless burst of joy followed by fierce longing.

Ramon's lips brushed the shining hair atop her head. "Now, shall I tell you what I think when I look at you?"

Katie tried to answer lightly, but her voice was nearly as husky as his. "Are you going to sound like an amorous Latin?"

"Yes."

"Okay."

His chuckle was rich and deep. "I see a beauty with red gold hair and the smile of an angel; and I remember a princess who stood in that singles' bar looking very displeased with her subjects; then I hear a witch telling a man who was making advances to her, that her roommates were lesbians." He laid his hand against the side of her face, his fingers tenderly brushing her cheek. "When I look at you, I think you are my angel-princess-witch."

The way he referred to her as "his" brought Katie's drifting spirit plummeting back to reality. Abruptly pulling free of Ramon's arms, she said with false brightness, "Would you like to walk down to the pool? It opened today, and everybody from the apartment complex will be out there." As she spoke she jammed her hands into her back pockets, caught the way Ramon's glance slipped to the straining fabric of her T-shirt across her breasts, and hastily removed her hands.

One black brow arched in mild inquiry, silently asking why she objected to having his eyes on her when he had just had his hands on her. "Of course," he said, "I would enjoy seeing your pool and meeting your friends."

Once again Katie felt uncomfortable with him. He seemed like a dark, foreign stranger who was too intensely interested in her. Added to that, she was leery of him now, and with good reason. She knew when a man intended to maneuver her into bed, and that was where Ramon wanted her. As soon as possible.

Sliding glass doors opened off the back of her living room onto a small patio enclosed by a stockade fence that provided privacy. Two redwood loungers with thick flowered cushions were strategically placed in the center for sunbathing. Behind them, and on both sides, were scattered a profusion of Katie's lush plants, some of which were already blooming.

She stopped beside a redwood planter overflowing with red and white petunias. With one hand on the door in the stockade fence, Katie hesitated, trying to think of how to phrase what she wanted to say.

"You have a beautiful apartment," Ramon commented behind her. "The rent must be very expensive."

Katie swung around, instantly seizing on Ramon's idle comment as a perfect means of drawing attention to the differences between them, and hopefully, cooling his ardent intentions. "Thank you. As a matter of fact, the rent is very high. I live here because it's reassuring to my parents to know that my friends and neighbors are the right sort of people."

"Rich people?"

"Not rich necessarily, but successful, socially acceptable people."

Ramon's face was a mask, wiped clean of all expression. "Perhaps it would be better then, if you did not introduce me to your friends."

One look at that aloof, handsome face, and Katie again felt ashamed of herself. Raking an agitated hand through her hair, she drew a determined breath and confronted the real issue: "Ramon, despite what had just happened between us in my apartment, I want you to understand that I am not going to go to bed with you. Now or ever."

"Because I am Spanish?" he asked dispassionately.

Katie's fair complexion bloomed with chagrin. "No, of course not! Because. . . ." She smiled derisively. "To use a hackneyed phrase, 'I'm just not that kind of girl.' " Feeling much better now that everything was out in the open between them, she turned back toward the door in the fence. "Well, shall we go down and see what's happening at the pool?"

"I do not think that would be wise," he said sardonically. "Being seen with me could cause you embarrassment in front of your 'successful, socially acceptable' friends."

Katie gazed over her shoulder at the tall man who was now looking down his aristocratic nose at her, his hard eyes ironic and disdainful. She sighed. "Ramon, just because I sounded like a conceited ass, doesn't mean that you have to sound like one, too. Please come down to the pool with me?"

Laughter flickered across his features as he gazed at her. Wordlessly, he reached over her shoulder and pushed the door open for her.

The olympic-size swimming pool was a scene of total chaos, as Katie knew it would be. Four separate games of water polo were under way with all in attendance yelling and splashing. Girls in bikinis and men in brief swimming trunks were sprawled on towels and chaise longues, their bodies slick with suntan lotion, toasting in the sun. Beer cans and portable radios were everywhere, and music was blaring over the clubhouse speakers.

Katie walked over to a nearby umbrella table and pulled out an aluminum chair. "What do you think of opening day at an American swimming pool?" she asked Ramon as he sat down beside her.

His enigmatic gaze swept the colorful pandemonium. "Interesting."

"Hi, Katie," Karen called, emerging from the pool like a graceful mermaid, her voluptuous body shining with rivulets of water. As usual, Karen was accompanied by at least two devoted males, who padded dripping beside her over to Katie and Ramon. "You know Don and Brad, don't you?" Karen said, with a perfunctory nod at the two men who were also tenants in the apartment complex. Katie knew them both almost as well as Karen did, so she was a little surprised, but then, as she soon realized, Karen didn't really care who knew whom, so long as she was introduced to Ramon.

With unaccountable reluctance, Katie performed the introductions. She tried not to notice the warm appreciation in Ramon's flashing white smile when he was presented to Karen, and the answering sparkle in Karen's green eyes as she extended her hand to him.

"Why don't you two change clothes and come back out and swim?" Karen invited, without taking her eyes off Ramon. "There's going to be a big party here at sundown. You should stay for that too."

"Ramon doesn't have any swimming trunks with him," Katie quickly declined.

"No problem," the resourceful Karen replied, tearing her eyes from Ramon for the first time since she had climbed out of the pool. "Brad will loan Ramon a pair, won't you, Brad?"

Brad, who had been in hot pursuit of Karen for nearly a year, looked as if he would rather loan Ramon a one-way ticket out of town, but he politely seconded the offer. And how could he help it? Few men ever wanted to deny Karen anything—her looks promised so much in return. She was the same height as Katie, five feet six, but there was a ripe sexuality about her dark hair and curvaceous body that made her seem like passion fruit ready for the plucking—but only by the man of her choice. The independence that shone in her slanting green eyes made it perfectly clear that she did her own choosing. And from the way Karen was watching Ramon walk away with Brad to change into swimming trunks, it was obvious to Katie that Ramon was Karen's choice. "Where," Karen breathed almost reverently, "did you ever find him? He looks like a Greek Adonis . . . or was Adonis blond? Well, anyway, he looks like a black-haired Greek god."

Katie resisted the uncharitable impulse to cool Karen's interest in Ramon by informing her that he was a black-haired Spanish farm laborer. "I met him at the Canyon Inn, Friday night," she said instead.

"Really? I didn't see him there, and he'd be almost impossible to overlook. What does he do, beside look sexy and gorgeous?"

"He . . ." Katie hesitated, then to spare Ramon any possible embarrassment, she said, "He's in transportation. Trucking, actually."

"No kidding?" Karen said unanswerably, giving Katie a searching look. "Is he your private stock or can anyone sample?"

Katie couldn't help smiling at Karen's bluntness. "Would it matter?"

"You know it would. We're friends. If you say you want him, I won't take him away."

The odd thing was, Katie knew she meant it. Karen had personal ethics; she didn't steal her friends' men. Nevertheless, it rankled Katie that Karen automatically assumed she could take Ramon away, unless, out of the spirit of friendship, she chose not to do it. "Help yourself," Katie said with an indifference she didn't entirely feel. "He's all yours if you want him. I'm going to go change into my suit."

Changing into her bikini in her apartment, Katie was annoyed with herself for not telling Karen to leave Ramon alone. And she was equally annoyed for caring one way or another. She was also a little crushed by the frank admiration she had seen in Ramon's expression when he looked at Karen's lush bikini-clad figure.

Katie stood in front of the mirror in her bathing suit, critically surveying her appearance. The bright blue bikini revealed a stunning figure in all its glory, from full high breasts, narrow waist and gently curving hips, to long shapely legs. With disgust, Katie thought she must be the only woman alive who could look coolly proper when she was practically naked!

Men whistled appreciatively at girls like Karen Wilson; they stared in silence at Katie Connelly. The quiet pride in the tilt of her chin and the natural grace with which she moved always made her seem vaguely aloof, and Katie was powerless to change her image, even if she wanted to, which she normally didn't.

With the exception of singles' bars, Katie was rarely approached by men she didn't know. She didn't look approachable. As a rule, men took one look at her flawless skin and clear blue eyes and saw classic beauty rather than sex appeal. They expected her to be remote, untouchable, and they treated her with restrained admiration. By the time they knew her well enough to realize that she was basically warm and friendly with an irrepressible sense of humor, they also knew her well enough not to press her for more than she was willing to give. They talked with her and laughed with her and asked her for dates, but their sexual overtures were usually verbal rather than physical—softly spoken innuendos that Katie smilingly and pointedly ignored.

Katie pulled a brush through her tumbling mass of waving hair, gave it a quick shake to restore it to its casual, windblown style, and took a last dissatisfied look in the mirror.

When she reached the pool area she found Ramon stretched out on a lounger beside three young women who had spread their towels on the cement pool deck and were sitting there, blatantly flirting with him. Seated at the umbrella table on his other side was Karen, along with Brad and Don.

"May I join your harem, Ramon?" Katie quipped, standing over him with a faint smile.

A lazy, devastating grin swept across his tanned face as he looked up at her, then he lithely rolled to his feet, getting up to give her his coveted lounger. Inwardly, Katie sighed. She may as well have come out here in an overcoat. Not once had Ramon's gaze dropped below her neck.

He sat down at the table with Karen and the other two men.

Trying to ignore her mixed emotions, Katie began rubbing suntan oil on her leg.

"I'm very good at that, Katie," Don grinned at her. "Need some help?"

Katie glanced up with a plucky smile. "My legs aren't that long," she declined. Unlike Brad, Don was not completely obsessed with Karen, and Katie had sensed for the last several months that if she gave him the slightest encouragement, he would easily shift his interest from Karen to herself. She was in the process of spreading the oil onto her left arm when she heard Karen say, "Katie told me that you're in the transportation business, Ramon."

"Oh, she did, did she?" Ramon drawled with enough sarcasm to make Katie pause and stare at him. He was leaning back in his chair with a thin cigar clamped between his white teeth, his piercing eyes leveled on Katie. Katie flushed and hastily pulled her gaze from his.

A few moments later, Karen did her utmost to get him to go swimming with her, but was met with a firmly polite refusal.

"Do you *know* how to swim?" Katie asked Ramon when the others had left.

"Puerto Rico is an island, Katie," he replied dryly. "The Atlantic Ocean on one side, and the Caribbean on the other. There is no shortage of water in which to swim."

Katie looked at him with a puzzled frown. From the moment he had kissed her in her apartment, a subtle shift in power had been taking place. Until then she had been confident and in control of their relationship. Now she felt confused and strangely vulnerable, while Ramon seemed decisive and selfassured. Shrugging, she said, "I was only going to offer to teach you to swim if you didn't know how. There's no need for you to launch into a lecture on Puerto Rican geography."

Ignoring her cross tone, he said, "If you wish to swim, we will swim."

Katie's breath froze as he came to his feet and stood looking down at her in Brad's white swimming trunks. He was six feet three inches of splendid masculinity, wide shouldered and narrow hipped, with the firm muscles of an athlete. His chest was covered with a light furring of black hair, and as Katie arose, she kept her eyes carefully fixed on the silver medallion hanging from a chain around his neck.

Disconcerted and embarrassed by the way the sight of his bronzed body was affecting her, Katie did not look up at him until she realized that he had no intention of moving out of her way. When she finally dragged her eyes to his, he said softly, "I think you look very nice too."

An unbidden smile curved Katie's lips. "I didn't think you noticed," she said as they began walking over to the pool.

"I did not think you wanted me to look at you."

"You certainly looked at Karen," Katie heard herself say. She shook her head bemusedly and spoke her next thought aloud as well. "I didn't mean to say that."

"No," he said with amusement. "I am sure you did not."

Preferring to forget the whole exchange, Katie stood poised at the deep end of the pool. She dived, cutting the water in a clean, graceful line. Ramon was right beside her, pacing himself to her strong strokes with an effortless ease that Katie had to admire. They swam twenty laps together before Katie let her feet touch bottom. She stood watching Ramon finish ten more laps before she laughingly called, "Show off!"

Diving neatly, he disappeared from her sight. Katie let out a startled shriek as hands jerked her feet out from under her and hauled her to the bottom. When she surfaced she was gasping for air, her eyes stinging from the chlorine. "That," she said with laughing severity as Ramon raked his wet curly hair back and grinned at her, "was a very childish thing to do. Almost as childish as—this!" Slicing her hand at the water, she sent a geyser of it spraying into Ramon's face, then ducked around trying to avoid reprisal. There followed a laughing, dunking, racing session that lasted for fifteen minutes and left her breathless and exhausted.

Hauling herself over the side of the pool, Katie padded over to the lawn chair and handed Ramon the towel she had brought for him. "You play too rough," she chided him good-naturedly as she bent over and wrung out her long, heavy hair.

His chest heaving from their exertions, Ramon looped the towel around his neck and put his hands on his hips. Quietly, he said, "I would be as gentle with you as you wished me to be."

Katie turned liquid inside at the meaning she read into his words. Almost certain that he had been referring to making love to her, she flopped down on the lounge on her stomach and laid her head on her arms. Her skin flinched as Ramon drizzled suntan oil onto her back, then sat down beside her. She tensed as his hands began slowly stroking up and down her back, rhythmically massaging the oil into her satiny skin. "Shall I unfasten the back?" he asked.

"Don't even consider trying it," Katie warned. By the time his hands had moved up to her shoulders and his thumbs were circling just below her nape, Katie was breathing in shallow little breaths, and every inch of her skin was vibrantly alive where his hands had touched it.

"Am I bothering you, Katie?" he asked in a husky whisper.

"You know you are," Katie murmured lethargically, before she could stop herself. She heard his satisfied chuckle and turned her head away from him. "You're doing it on purpose, and it's making me very nervous."

"In that case, I will let you relax," he said as his weight lifted from her chaise longue. When he was gone, Katie tried not to wonder what he was doing and firmly closed her eyes to the blazing late-afternoon sun.

Occasionally she heard his deep voice followed by a peal of feminine laughter, or one of the men calling something to him. He certainly fit in well here, Katie mused. But then, why shouldn't he, she though dourly. The only requirement for popularity around here with the opposite sex was having an attractive body, preferably combined with an attractive face, and if you were a man, a good job. Katie, with her small lie, had provided Ramon with the latter.

What was the matter with her, Katie wondered drowsily. She had absolutely no reason to complain. Despite her occasional bouts of discontent lately, when her world seemed populated by phony, shallow people, she enjoyed the clever bantering that she exchanged with the confident, self-assured men she knew. She liked having nice clothes, a beautiful apartment, and being the object of so much masculine admiration. She genuinely enjoyed men's company even though she carefully avoided becoming intimate with any of them, because Katie's physical desires were never stronger than her over-whelming need to retain what pride and self-respect David had left her.

Rob would have been the only other man she had ever let make love to her. Luckily she had discovered he was married before she let that happen. The right man would come along someday and she would hold nothing back. The right man, not just any man. Under no circumstances was Katie Connelly going to find herself sitting around the pool or at one of the singles' bars, with three or four men who all had intimate knowledge of her body. It happened to other women all the time, but Katie found the idea degrading and repulsive.

"Hey, Katie, wake up and roll over," Don commanded.

Katie blinked, surprised that she had fallen asleep, and obediently rolled onto her back.

"It's almost six o'clock. Brad and I are going to get some beer and pizzas for the party tonight. Do you want me to bring anything stronger for you and Ramon?" Was there a sneer in the way he said Ramon's name?

Katie wrinkled her nose at her grinning admirer. "Stronger than Mama Romano's pizzas? Heaven forbid!" She looked around for Ramon and saw him walking toward her with Karen on one side and another woman on the other. Carefully extinguishing the ridiculous flare of jealousy she felt, Katie said to Ramon, "There's going to be a party out here tonight—dancing and that kind of thing. Would you like to stay for it?"

"Of course he would, Katie," Karen said promptly on his behalf.

"Then it's fine with me," Katie said with a shrug. She would enjoy the party with her friends, and Ramon could enjoy it with Karen and whomever else he chose.

By nine-thirty that night the food had been devoured, along with several cases of beer and countless bottles of liquor. The pool lights were lit, giving the water an iridescent green glow, and someone had put on a disco tape to play over the loudspeakers. Katie, who loved to dance, had been doing so for nearly an hour with assorted partners when she noticed Ramon standing far away from the activity, a solitary figure leaning against the fence that sur-rounded the pool, staring out into the distance. Silhouetted in the night, with his swimming trunks a stark band of white in the inky darkness, he seemed very aloof, and yet, somehow, lonely.

"Ramon?" Katie said anxiously, coming up behind him and putting her hand on his arm. He turned slowly and looked down at her, and she saw the pleasure her touch brought to his smile. Cautiously, she removed her hand. "Why are you over here, all by yourself?"

"I needed to escape from the noise so that I could think. Do you never feel the need to be by yourself?"

"Yes," she admitted, "but not usually in the middle of a party."

"We do not have to be here in the middle of a party," he pointed out meaningfully.

Katie's heart gave a funny little lurch, which she steadfastly ignored. "Would you like to dance?"

He tipped his head in the direction of the Neil Diamond recording that was now blasting over the loudspeakers. "When I dance I like to hold a woman in my arms," he answered. "Besides, I would have to wait in line for the privilege of dancing with you."

"Ramon, do you know how to dance?" Katie persisted, certain that he probably didn't, and about to offer to teach him.

Flinging his cigar away in a glowing red arc, he said tersely. "Yes, Katie, I know how to dance. I know how to swim. I know how to tie my own shoes. I have a slight accent, which you seem to think means I am backward and ignorant, but which many women find attractive."

Katie stiffened angrily. Lifting her chin, she stared straight into his eyes and said very quietly and very distinctly, "Go to hell." Intending to walk away, she pivoted on her heel, then gasped in surprise as Ramon's hand clamped on her arm, jerking her around to face him.

In a voice vibrating with anger, he said, "Do not ever speak to me that way again, and do not swear. It does not become you."

"I'll talk to you any way I like," Katie blazed. "And if all the other women find you so *damned* attractive, they're welcome to you!"

Ramon gazed down into her stormy blue eyes and proudly beautiful face, and a reluctant smile of admiration broke across his features. "What a little spitfire you are," he chuckled. "And when you are angry—"

"I am not a little anything," Katie interrupted hotly. "I am nearly five feet seven inches tall. And if you were about to say that I'm beautiful when I'm angry, I warn you, I'll laugh my sides off. Men always say that to women because they heard it in some ridiculous old movie, and—"

"Katie," Ramon breathed as his firm, sensual mouth descended to hers, "you are beautiful when you are angry—and if you laugh, I will toss you into the pool."

A jolt rocketed through Katie's nervous system as his warm lips covered hers in a lingering kiss. When he lifted his head, he slipped his arm around Katie's waist, drew her unresisting body close to his side, and led her to the crowd of dancing couples as a slow love song began to play.

Ramon's low voice murmured something in her ear as they danced, but Katie didn't understand the words he said to her. She was too preoccupied with the unbelievably arousing feel of his bare legs and thighs sliding intimately against hers as they moved in time to the music. Desire was pouring through her, melting her resolve. She wanted to lift her head and feel his mouth claim hers the way it had in her apartment; she wanted to be crushed in his strong arms and swept off into that same sweet, wild oblivion he had shown her before.

Closing her eyes in despair, Katie admitted the truth to herself. Even though she'd only known him for forty-eight hours, she wanted Ramon to make love to her tonight. She wanted it so badly that she was shaken and amazed . . . but at least she could understand her physical attraction to him. What she couldn't understand, and what frightened her, was this strange magnetic pull she felt toward him emotionally. Sometimes, when he spoke to her in that deep, compelling voice of his, or looked at her with those dark penetrating eyes, Katie almost felt as if he were quietly reaching out to her and inexorably drawing her closer and closer to him.

Mentally, Katie gave herself a hard shake. Getting involved with Ramon would be disastrous. They were hopelessly incompatible. He was proud, poor and dominating, while she was also proud, wealthy by his standards, and innately independent. Any relationship between them could only end in hurt and anger.

Like the intelligent, sensible young woman she was, Katie decided the best way to avoid the danger of Ramon's attraction was to avoid Ramon himself. She would stay away from him as much as possible for the rest of the evening and firmly refuse to see him again after tonight. It was as simple as that. Except that when his lips brushed first her temple, then her forehead, Katie nearly forgot that she was sensible and intelligent, and almost lifted her mouth up to his, to receive the stirring kiss she knew he would give her.

The instant the song ended, Katie broke away from him. With a bright smile pinned to her face she met his questioning look and said airily, "Why don't you mingle and have fun? I'll see you later."

For the next hour and a half Katie flirted with every man she knew, and several she didn't. She was her most dazzlingly sociable self, and wherever she went the men followed, each one ready to dance, swim, drink, or make love, according to her slightest preference. She laughed and drank and danced. . . . And every moment she was aware that Ramon had apparently taken her suggestion and was thoroughly enjoying himself with at least four other women, particularly Karen, who never left his side.

"Katie, let's get out of here and go somewhere quiet." Don's breath was hot in her ear as they danced to a throbbing disco beat.

"I hate quiet places," Katie announced, twirling away from him and draping herself across Brad who was surprised, but not displeased, to find her suddenly sitting on his lap. "Brad hates quiet places too, don't you?"

"Sure I do," Brad leered. "So let's go back to my place and make noise in private."

Katie wasn't listening. From the corner of her eye she watched Karen dancing with Ramon. Both of her arms were wound around his neck, her body swaying sensuously against his. Whatever Karen was saying to him certainly must have been amusing, because Ramon, who had been grinning down at her, suddenly threw back his head and burst out laughing. Irrationally, Katie was hurt by his easy defection. Redoubling her efforts to be gay, she stood up and pulled a reluctant Brad to his feet. "Get up, lazy, and dance with me."

Brad relinquished his can of beer, strolled into the dancers with his arm around Katie's shoulders, then caught her in a surprisingly crushing embrace. "What the hell has got into you?" he demanded in her ear. "I've never seen you act like this."

Katie didn't answer because she was frantically looking for Ramon and Karen, who, as she soon realized, were nowhere in sight. Her heart plummeted. Ramon had left the party with Karen.

When they hadn't returned after thirty minutes, Katie abandoned all pretense of enjoying herself. Her stomach was twisted into sick knots and, whether she was dancing or talking, her eyes constantly scanned the shifting bodies, desperately searching for Ramon's tall form.

Katie wasn't the only one who had noted Karen's disappearance with Ramon. Katie was dancing with Brad again, ignoring him entirely while she craned her neck looking for the missing couple, when Brad hissed contemptuously, "You aren't by any wild chance hung up on that spic that Karen's taken to her apartment, are you?"

"Don't call him that!" Katie said fiercely, pulling out of his arms. There were tears in her eyes as she turned and plunged into the throngs of dancing couples.

"Where are you going?" an authoritative voice demanded right behind her.

Katie swung around and faced Ramon, her fists clenched impotently at her sides. "Where have you been?"

One dark brow lifted. "Jealous?"

"Do you know," she said, almost choking, "I don't think I even like you!"

"I do not like you very much tonight, either," Ramon replied evenly. Suddenly his gaze narrowed on her face. "There are tears in your eyes. Why?"

"Because," Katie whispered furiously, "that stupid bastard called you a spic."

Ramon burst out laughing and dragged her into his arms. "Oh, Katie," he laughed and sighed against her hair, "he is just angry because the woman he wants went for a walk with me."

Tipping her head back, Katie searched his face. "You only went for a walk?"

The laughter vanished from his expression. "Only for a walk. Nothing more." His arms tightened, holding her close as they moved in time to the music.

Katie laid her cheek against the reassuring strength of his chest and surrendered to delight as his hands caressed her bare shoulders and back, then slid lower, splaying against her spine to force her pliant body into intimate contact with every hard line of his legs and thighs. One hand lifted and curved around her nape, stroking it sensuously, then tightened in an abrupt command. Drawing an unsteady breath, Katie obediently lifted her head to receive his kiss. His hand plunged into her thick silky hair, holding her captive for the driving hunger of his mouth.

By the time he finally drew back, Ramon's breathing was harsh and Katie's pulse was racing out of control, the blood pounding in her ears. She stared up at him and shakily said, "I think I am getting very scared."

"I know, *querida*," he said gently. "Things are happening too quickly for you."

"What does '*querida*' mean?"

"Darling."

Katie closed her eyes and swallowed, swaying weakly against him. "How long will you be here before you go back to Puerto Rico?"

His answer was a long time in coming. "I can stay until Sunday, a week from today, but no longer. We will spend every day together until then."

Katie was too disappointed to even try to hide it. "We can't. I have to attend a big Memorial Day gathering at my parents' house tomorrow. I have Tuesday off work but Wednesday I have to be back at the office." She could see that he was about to argue, and since she also wanted to be with him as much as possible in the time they had left, Katie said, "Would you like to come to my parents' house with me tomorrow?" He looked uncomfortable and some sanity returned to Katie. "That probably isn't a good idea. You won't like them, and they won't like you."

"Because they are rich and I am not?" He smiled faintly. "I may like them in spite of their wealth, who knows?"

Katie smiled at the way he deliberately misstated the problem, and his arms tightened possessively, drawing her closer to him. He had a very engaging smile that softened his virile handsomeness and could make him look almost boyish. "Shall we go back to my place?" Katie said.

Ramon nodded and Katie went to collect her things while he poured Scotch into two paper cups, added ice and water, and then crossed to where she waited.

When they got to her little enclosed patio area, Katie was surprised that instead of going indoors, Ramon put the drinks down on the small table between the two redwood lounge chairs, then stretched out on one of them. Somehow, she expected that he would try to carry on the rest of their conversation in her bed.

With mingled feelings of disappointment and relief, she curled up on the other lounge and twisted toward him. He lit a cigar, its glowing red tip her only focal point in the darkness. "Tell me about your parents, Katie."

Katie took a fortifying swallow of her drink. "By most people's standards, they're very wealthy, but they weren't always. My father owned an ordinary grocery store until ten years ago, when he talked the bank into letting him expand it into a luxury supermarket. It did very well, and after that he opened twenty more of them. Haven't you passed any modernistic supermarkets with the name 'Connelly's' on them?"

"I believe so."

"Well, that's us. Four years ago my dad joined Forest Oaks Country Club. It isn't quite as prestigious as Old Warson or St. Louis Country Club, but the Forest Oaks members like to pretend it is, and my father built the biggest house on the club grounds, right on the golf course."

"I ask you about your parents, and you tell me about their money. What are they like?"

Katie tried to be honest and objective. "They love me very much. My mother plays golf, and my father works hard. I guess the most important thing to them, outside of their children, is having a gorgeous house, a maid, two Mercedes, and belonging to the country club. My dad is handsome for being fifty-eight, and my mother always looks terrific."

"You have brothers and sisters?"

"One of each. I'm the youngest. My sister, Maureen, is thirty, and she's married. My dad made her husband a vice-president of Connelly Corporation, and now he can't wait to take over when dad retires. My brother, Mark, is twenty-five, and he's nice. He isn't nearly as ambitious and greedy as Maureen, who spends her life worrying that Mark may get a bigger piece of the family business when dad retires than she and her husband will. Now that you know the worst, do you want to come tomorrow? A lot of my parents' friends and neighbors will be there too, and they're pretty much like my parents."

Ramon stubbed out his cigar and wearily leaned his head back against the chair. "Do you want me to come?"

"Yes," Katie said emphatically. "But it's selfish of me, because my sister will look down her nose at you if she finds out what you do for a living. My brother, Mark, will probably go so far out of his way to show you that he isn't like Maureen, that he'll embarrass you even more."

In the deep, velvety voice she was coming to adore, Ramon asked, "What will you do, Katie?"

"Well, I'll—I don't really know."

"Then I guess I will have to come with you so that I can find out." Putting his glass down, he rose to his feet.

Katie, realizing that he intended to leave, insisted that he stay for some coffee, for the simple reason that she couldn't bear for him to go yet. She carried it into the living room on a small tray and sat down beside Ramon on the sofa. They drank their coffee in a long, increasingly uncomfortable silence, which Katie was helpless to break or to understand.

"What are you thinking about?" she asked finally, searching his somber profile in the dim light of the single table lamp.

"You." Almost harshly he asked, "Are the things that are important to your parents, important to you also?"

"Some of them, I suppose," Katie admitted.

"How important?"

"In comparison to what?"

"In comparison to this," he said in a savage whisper. His mouth came down hard on hers, his lips moving roughly back and forth, forcing her lips apart for the invasion of his tongue, while he pulled her down on the sofa and twisted his body so that it was half-covering hers.

Katie moaned in protest and instantly his mouth softened, then began a slow, unbearably erotic seduction that soon had Katie writhing beneath him in wild hunger. His tongue tangled with hers, withdrawing, then plunging deep, slowly receding as she tried to hold it, until Katie was pressing her parted lips fiercely to his, lost in the soul-destroying kiss.

When he started to raise his head she curved her hand around it, trying to keep his mouth on hers, then gasped with shocked delight as he jerked the top of her bikini down, freeing her breasts and lowering his mouth to the pink peaks. Slowly he began sucking hard on first one and then the other, until Katie was reduced to a state of mindless, aching desire.

Ramon braced his weight on his hands and lifted slightly off her, his hot eyes restlessly caressing her swollen breasts, their nipples hardened and erect from his tongue and lips and teeth. "Put your hands on me, Katie," he rasped.

Katie lifted her hands, slowly moving her sensitized fingertips over the sinewy muscles of his chest, watching them flinch reflexively and then relax. "You are beautiful," she whispered, her splayed hands drifting from the taut planes of his bronzed hair-roughened chest, along his broad shoulders, then down the corded muscles of his arms.

"Men are not beautiful," he tried to tease, but his voice was thickened from the effect her hands were having on him.

"You are. The way oceans and mountains are beautiful." Unthinkingly, she let her fingertips trace the narrowing vee of dark hair on his chest toward the place where it disappeared beneath the waistband of the low-slung white trunks.

"Don't!" he ordered hoarsely.

Katie stayed her hand and looked up at his face, dark with the passion he was fighting to keep under control. "You're beautiful and you're strong," she whispered into his burning gaze. "But you're gentle too. I think you are the gentlest man I've ever known—and I don't even know why I think so."

His control snapped. "Oh, God!" he groaned. His mouth took hers with an unleashed passion that sent tidal waves of desire crashing over her. His hands sank into the thickness of her hair, holding her head immobile for the endless plunder of his lips. Katie gloried in the feel of his stiff throbbing manhood pressing intimately to her, then moaned with feverish longing when he began slowly circling his hips against her. "Want me," he ordered roughly. "Want me more than you want the things money can buy. Want me as much as I want you."

Katie was almost sobbing with desire when he suddenly pulled away from her, sat up, and leaned his head against the back of the sofa, closing his eyes. She watched his labored breathing even out and, after a few minutes, she straightened her clothing, ran a shaking hand through her wildly disordered hair, and sat up. Feeling discarded and hurt, she squeezed herself to the farthest end of the sofa from him and curled her legs beneath her.

"Katie." His voice was bleak and harsh.

Warily, Katie eyed him. His head was still back against the sofa, his eyes still closed as he spoke: "I did not want to say this to you while you were in my arms and we were both wild with desire for each other. I did not want to ever say this to you, yet I have known from the very first night that before I left I would still be saying it. . . ."

Katie's heart stopped beating. He was going to tell her that he was married, and she—she was going to become hysterical.

"I want you to come back to Puerto Rico with me."

"*What?*" she whispered.

"I want you to marry me."

Katie opened her mouth, but it was several seconds before any words would come out. "I—I can't. I couldn't. I have a job here, and my family, my friends—they're all here. I belong here."

"No," he said angrily, turning his head and pinning her with his gaze. "You do not belong here. I watched you the first time I saw you in the bar, and I watched you tonight. You do not even like these people; you do not belong with them." He saw the growing apprehension widening her eyes and stretched his arm out to her. "Come," he said softly. "Now I want you in my arms."

Too dazed to do anything but obey, Katie slid across the sofa and into his comforting embrace, leaning her head on his shoulder. Gently, he continued, "There is a fineness in you that sets you apart from these people you call your friends."

Katie slowly shook her head. "You don't even know me, not really. You can't be serious about wanting to marry me."

His hand touched her chin, tipping her face up to his, and he smiled into her glazed blue eyes. "I have known what you are from the moment you knocked the flower I brought you on the ground, then nearly burst into tears with shame for what you had done. And I am thirty-four years old; I know exactly what I want." His lips clung to hers in a shattering kiss. "Marry me, Katie," he whispered.

"Couldn't . . . couldn't you stay in the States, in St. Louis, so that we could get to know one another better? Maybe then, after—"

"No," he said with absolute finality. "I cannot." He stood up and Katie stood with him. "Do not answer me now. There is time yet for you to decide." He glanced at the small glass clock beside the lamp. "It is late. I have to get dressed and then I have work that must be done tonight. When shall I call for you tomorrow to take you to your parents'?"

Numbly, Katie told him. "Oh, and I think my mother said it was a barbecue, so we may as well wear Levi's."

When he left, Katie wandered around, mechanically picking up coffee cups, turning off the lamp, and undressing for bed.

She lay down, stared at the ceiling, and tried to absorb what had just happened. Ramon wanted her to marry him and go to Puerto Rico with him! It was impossible, absolutely out of the question, too soon to even contemplate such a thing.

Too soon to contemplate it? Even if Ramon gave her time, would she ever really contemplate it?

She turned her head into her pillow and could still feel his hands caressing her with such violent tenderness, his mouth hungry and urgent on hers. No man alive had ever made her body come to life like that, and she doubted that anyone else ever would. It wasn't just practiced sexual technique with Ramon, it was instinct. It was natural for him to make love with such demanding, dominating sensuality; he was, by birth and culture, a dominating male.

Funny, Katie thought, she had liked being dominated by him. She had even felt a surge of excitement earlier today at the way he had ordered her into his arms with his quiet, "Come here, Katie." And yet, he was so gentle.

Katie closed her eyes, trying to think. If Ramon gave her time, was it possible that she might marry him? *Absolutely not!* her mind sensibly replied. But her heart whispered, *maybe* . . .

Why, Katie wondered, why would she ever consider marrying him. The answer was in that strange feeling she sometimes got when they were laughing or talking—an inexplicable feeling that, emotionally, they were almost perfectly matched; a feeling that something deep within him was reaching out to her and finding an answering response within her; this strong magnetic pull that seemed to be slowly, inexorably, drawing them closer together.

At that thought, Katie's logical mind instantly went to battle with her emotions: If she was foolish enough to let herself marry Ramon, he would expect her to live on his income alone, yet she wasn't very happy living like an American princess the way she did now.

He was a Spanish male chauvinist; yet every instinct she possessed told her that he was a sensitive man, capable of great gentleness as well as strength. . . .

Katie almost moaned aloud at the predicament in which she found herself. She closed her eyes, and when she finally drifted into an exhausted slumber, neither logic nor emotion had won the battle.

5

Katie spent the following morning waiting for Ramon in a state of spiraling apprehension, too worried about appearing at her parents' party with him to even contemplate the greater problem of his proposal.

The possibilities for disaster at that party were almost limitless. It wasn't important to Katie that her family like Ramon, nor would she ever let their opinion of him influence her ultimate decision about going to Puerto Rico. She loved her family, but she was old enough to make her own decisions. What she did fear was that her family might say something to humiliate Ramon. Her sister, Maureen, was an outrageous snob who had conveniently forgotten that the Connellys hadn't always been wealthy. If she discovered Ramon was a farm laborer who drove a truck, Maureen was capable of snubbing him in front of a house full of people, as a way of emphasizing her own social superiority.

Her parents, Katie knew, would treat Ramon with the same courtesy they would show any guest in their home, regardless of what he did for a living . . . as long as they had no inkling that there was anything except casual friendship between Katie and him. If they so much as suspected that Ramon wanted to marry her, they were both capable of treating him with a freezing contempt that would reduce him to the level of a social-climbing parasite, and in front of all their guests. Ramon would be disqualified as a future son-in-law the instant they discovered that he couldn't possibly support Katie in style and comfort, and they wouldn't hesitate to make their position infinitely clear if they felt it was necessary.

At precisely three-thirty, Ramon arrived. Katie let him into her apartment and greeted him with her best, cheerfully optimistic smile, which deceived him for perhaps two seconds. Drawing her into his arms, Ramon tipped her chin up, gazed into her eyes and said with grave humor, "We are not going to face a firing squad, Katie. We are only going to face your family."

The kiss he gave her was gently reassuring and, somehow, when his arms released her, Katie felt infinitely more confident. The feeling was still with her thirty minutes later when their car swept through the stone gates of Forest Oaks Country Club and pulled up in front of her parents' house.

Set back from the private road on five acres of manicured lawn, the Connellys white-pillared colonial with its sweeping circular driveway was a very imposing structure. Katie watched for some reaction from Ramon, but he only glanced casually at the house as if he had seen thousands like it, and came around to help her out of the car.

He still hadn't said anything by the time they were halfway up the winding brick walk that led toward the massive front doors. Some devilish impulse made Katie slant a jaunty, sideways smile at him and ask, "Well, what do you think?" She jammed her hands into the back pockets of her designer jeans and took four more paces before she realized that not only had Ramon not answered, he had stopped walking entirely.

Turning, Katie found herself the object of his lazy, sweeping appraisal. With a spark of amusement in his eyes, his gaze traveled leisurely from the top of her bright head, lingered meaningfully on her lips and the thrusting fullness of her breasts, then faithfully followed the graceful curving lines of her waist, hips and thighs, drifted down her long shapely legs, stopped at her sandal-shod feet, then swept upward and returned to her face. "I think," he said with quiet solemnity, "that your smile could light the darkness, and when you laugh it is like music. I think your hair is like heavy silk shining in the sunlight."

Hypnotized by that deep voice, Katie simply stood there, warmth seeping through her system.

"I think that you have the bluest eyes I have ever seen, and I like the way they sparkle when you are happy, or darken with desire when you are in my arms." A wicked grin highlighted his lips as he glanced again at Katie's breasts, which were emphasized by her unconsciously provocative stance with her hands in her back pockets. "And I like the way you look in those pants you are wearing. But if you do not take your hands out of your pockets, I am going to take you back to the car so that I can put my hands in them too."

Katie slowly pulled her hands free, trying to surface from the sensuous spell he seemed able to cast over her with a few words. "I meant," she said in a husky voice, "What do you think of the house?"

He glanced up at it and wryly shook his head. "Right out of *Gone With the Wind.*"

Katie rang the doorbell, which she could hear pealing majestically above the raised voices and laughter coming from within.

"Katie, darling," her mother said, wrapping her in a quick hug, "come inside. Everyone else is already here." She smiled at Ramon, who was standing beside Katie, and graciously extended her hand to him as Katie performed the introductions. "We're very happy to have you here, Mr. Galverra," she said with perfect correctness.

Ramon replied with equal correctness that he was delighted to be here, and Katie, who had been inexplicably holding her breath, felt the tension drain out of her.

When her mother excused herself to check on the caterers, Katie led Ramon through the house and out onto the beautifully landscaped lawn where a bar had been set up for the use of the guests who were standing in small groups, laughing and talking.

What Katie had believed was to be a barbecue was, in reality, a cocktail party followed by a formal dinner for thirty people, and while it was immediately obvious that Ramon was the only man there wearing jeans, Katie thought he looked utterly fantastic. With laughing pride, she noticed that she wasn't the only woman who thought Ramon was gorgeous; several of her mother's friends were openly admiring the tall dark-haired man who stayed by her side as they wandered sociably from group to group.

Katie introduced him to those of her parents' friends and neighbors whom she knew, watching as Ramon conquered the females with his flashing smile and relaxed charm. That she had expected. What she hadn't expected was that he would interact so well with the men who were present, all of whom were prosperous local businessmen. Somewhere in the past, Ramon had obviously acquired a social polish and smooth urbanity that positively staggered Katie when she saw it. He was utterly at ease among this gathering of the martini set, perfectly able to converse on everything from sports to national and world politics. Particularly world politics, Katie couldn't help noticing.

"You're certainly well informed about world affairs," Katie observed when they were alone for a moment.

Ramon smiled obliquely. "I know how to read, Katie."

Chastened, Katie looked away, but as if he sensed her other question, Ramon added, "This party is not so different from any other. Whenever men gather they tend to discuss business if they are all in similar lines of work. If they are not, then they discuss sports or politics or world affairs. It is the same in any country."

Katie was not entirely satisfied with his answer, but she let the matter drop for the time being.

"I think I'm jealous!" she laughingly remarked a while later, when a forty-five-year-old matron with two grown daughters had monopolized Ramon's attention for a full ten minutes.

"Do not be jealous," Ramon said with bland amusement that made Katie think he must be accustomed to the fawning admiration of women. "They would all lose interest the moment they discovered I am only a farmer."

That, unfortunately, wasn't quite the truth, Katie discovered to her sublime discomfort two hours later. Everyone was seated in the elaborate dining room enjoying a gourmet meal, when Katie's sister inquired down the length of the long dining-room table, "What do you do, Mr. Galverra?"

Katie felt as if the clink of sterling silver flatware on English bone china stopped altogether, along with every other shred of conversation at the table. "He's in the trucking business—and groceries," Katie improvised madly before Ramon could respond.

"Trucking? In what way?" Maureen persisted.

"What possible way is there?" Katie hedged shortly, shooting a killing look at her sister.

"Groceries, did you say?" Mr. Connelly put in, his brows lifted in interest. "Wholesale or retail?"

"Wholesale," Katie interjected hastily, again cutting off Ramon's reply.

Beside her, Ramon leaned very close, smiled charmingly, and said in a low, savage voice. "Shut up, Katie, or he will think I do not know how to talk."

"Wholesale?" Mr. Connelly mused from his position at the head of the table. He was always eager to talk about the grocery business. "What end of it—distribution?"

"No, growing," Ramon answered smoothly, clasping Katie's icy hand under the table in silent apology for the way he had spoken to her.

"A corporation operation, I imagine?" her father said. "How large?"

Calmly slicing a tender piece of veal Oscar, Ramon said, "It is a small farm, barely self-supporting."

"Do you mean you're an ordinary farmer?" Maureen demanded in subdued outrage. "In Missouri?"

"No, in Puerto Rico." Katie's brother, Mark, leaped into the breach with all the finesse of a pole-vaulter with no pole. "I was talking to Jake Masters last week and he told me he once found a spider in a shipment of pineapples from Puerto Rico that was the size of a—"

One of the guests, who apparently wasn't interested in spiders, interrupted Mark's desperate monologue to say to Ramon, "Is Galverra a common Spanish name? I've read of a 'Galverra' but I can't recall his first name."

Beside her Katie sensed, rather than saw, Ramon tense. "It is not an uncommon name," Ramon replied. "And my first name is very common."

Katie, in the act of giving Ramon an apologetic, encouraging smile, intercepted a look from her mother that could only be described as displeased and she felt the knot in her stomach tighten.

By the time they could leave, Katie's stomach was positively churning. Her parents were polite as they said goodbye to Ramon in the entrance foyer, but Katie saw the narrowed speculation in her mother's eyes when she looked at Ramon, and without actually saying anything, she managed to convey to Katie, and undoubtedly to Ramon, that she did not approve of him or of his continued association with Katie.

To make everything worse, as Ramon and Katie were leaving, Maureen's seven-year-old son jerked on her skirt and loudly announced to one and all, "Mommie, that man talks weird!"

In the car Ramon drove in thoughtful, withdrawn silence. "I'm sorry I told you to wear jeans," Katie spoke finally as they neared her apartment complex. "I could have sworn my mother told me two weeks ago this was going to be a barbecue."

"It is of no importance," Ramon said. "What people wear does not change what they are."

Katie didn't know whether he meant that better clothes wouldn't have improved his image, or that he felt his image was adequate regardless of what he was wearing. "I'm sorry about the way Maureen acted," she tried again.

"Stop saying you are sorry, Katie. One person cannot apologize for another. It is ludicrous to try."

"I know, but my sister is such a pain in the neck, and my parents—"

"Love you very much," Ramon finished for her. "They want to see you happy, with a secure future and all the things money can buy. Unfortunately, like most parents, they believe that if your future is secure you will be happy. And if it is not, it follows that you will not be."

Katie was amazed by his defense of her parents. Inside her apartment she whirled on him, her gaze searching his dark, inscrutable face. "What sort of man are you?" she asked. "Who are you? You defend my parents, knowing that if I decided to go to Puerto Rico with you they would do everything to prevent it. If anything you were amused, not impressed, by the people you met tonight and the size of my parents' home. You speak English with an accent, but your vocabulary is better than most men I know who have college degrees. Who are you, anyway?"

Ramon put his hands on her tense shoulders and said quietly, "I am the man who wants to take you away from everything you know, and people who love you. I am the man who wants to take you to a strange country where you, not I, will have the handicap of language. I am the man who wants to take you to live in the cottage where he was born, a cottage with four rooms that are clean, but nothing more. I am the man who knows he is selfish to do these things, yet still I will try to do them."

"Why?" Katie whispered.

He bent his head and brushed his lips warmly against hers. "Because I believe that I can make you happier than you have ever dreamed of being."

Unbelievably affected by the merest touch of that mouth, Katie tried to follow his logic. "But how could I be happy living in a primitive cottage where I don't know anyone and couldn't speak to them if I tried?"

"I will tell you later." He grinned suddenly. "For now, I have brought my own swimming trunks."

"Y—you want to swim?" Katie stuttered in disbelief.

Ramon's smile was positively wolfish. "I want to see you with as little clothing as possible, and the safest place for that, for both of us, is down at your pool."

Relief won out over disappointment as Katie went into the bedroom and quickly stripped off her clothes, pulling on a shockingly bright yellow bikini.

She studied herself in the mirror with a faint smile. It was the scantiest suit she had ever owned; two extremely narrow strips of bright cloth that revealed every curving line of her body. She had never had the nerve to actually appear in it before, but today it seemed perfect. It was all well and good for Ramon to arbitrarily decide that he was going to keep his distance, but, perversely, she wanted to make it as difficult for him as possible. She brushed her hair until it was shining and emerged from her bedroom just as he came from the bathroom. He had changed into black briefs that hugged his body, displaying his magnificent physique in a way that made Katie's mouth go dry.

Ramon's response to her, however, was far less enthusiastic. His black eyes raked her all but naked body from head to toe. "Change it," he said in a hard tone that she had never heard before. Belatedly, he added, "Please."

"No," Katie said firmly. "I'm not going to change. Why should I?"

"Because I asked you to."

"You *ordered* me to, and I didn't like it."

"Now I am asking," Ramon persisted implacably. "Please change that suit."

Katie shot him a killing look. "I am wearing this suit down to that pool."

"Then I am not going with you."

Suddenly, Katie felt vulgarly naked, and she blamed Ramon for her humiliation. She went into her room, pulled off the suit and put on a green one.

"Thank you," Ramon said quietly when she walked into the living room.

Katie was too angry to speak. She shoved open the glass patio door, banged through the gate in the stockade fence, and marched down to the pool, which was nearly deserted. Most of the tenants were apparently spending Memorial Day with their families. Katie sank down gracefully on the chaise longue closest to the deep end of the pool, ignoring Ramon, who stood looking down at her with his hands on his hips.

"Are you going to swim?" he asked.

Katie shook her head, her teeth clenched together.

Sitting down on the chair across from her, Ramon lit one of those very thin cigars he seemed to like, and leaned forward, his forearms braced on his knees. "Katie, listen to me."

"I don't want to listen to you. I don't like a lot of the things you say."

"But you will listen anyway."

Katie's head swung toward him so swiftly that her long hair came spilling over her shoulder. "Ramon, that is the second time tonight that you have told me what I'm going to do and I don't like it. If I had actually been willing to marry you, which I never was, these past twenty minutes would have changed my mind." She came to her feet, enjoying the sensation of towering over him for a change. "For the sake of what's left of our evening, our *last* evening together, I will swim. Because I'm sure you're going to order me to do that next."

Three long angry strides, and Katie did a shallow racing dive into the pool. A few seconds later she felt the impact of Ramon's body hitting the water behind her. Katie swam for all she was worth but she was not really surprised when Ramon easily caught her, or even when he forcibly pulled her stiff, unyielding body against his. "There are four other people in this pool, Ramon. Now let go of me before I yell for help."

"Katie, will you shut up and let me—"

"That was strike three for you," Katie snapped furiously. "You're out!"

"Dammit!" he said savagely, plunging his hand into the hair at her nape and jerking her head back as his mouth possessed hers.

More incensed then ever. Katie twisted her head away and wiped the back of her hand across her mouth. "I didn't like it!" she spat.

"Neither did I," he answered. "Please listen to me."

"I can't see where I have any choice. My feet aren't even touching the bottom."

Ramon ignored that. "Katie, it was a beautiful suit and the sight of you in it took my breath away. If you will listen I will explain why I do not want you to wear it. Last night more than one of the men who live here asked me if I was getting anywhere with their 'vestal virgin.' They call you that."

"They what?" Katie hissed in outraged disgust.

"They call you that because they have all wanted you, and not one of them has had you."

"I'll bet that amazed you," Katie said bitterly. "No doubt you thought that anyone who'd wear such a vulgar bathing suit—"

"It made me very proud," he interrupted quietly.

Katie had had all she could stand. She shoved at his immovable chest. "Well, I hate to disappoint you—knowing how 'proud' you were—but I am not a virgin."

She saw the effect of her announcement in the hardening line of his jaw, but he made no comment on it. Instead he said, "Until now, they have treated you with respect, like a beautiful little sister. But if you appear out here in the littlest bits of string and cloth I have ever seen called a bathing suit—they will be after you like a pack of dogs after a bitch in heat."

"I don't give a blessed damn what they think! And," Katie warned darkly when he opened his mouth, "if you dare tell me not to swear, I will slap you so hard your head will fall off!"

His arms fell away and Katie swam to the ladder, climbed out of the pool, stopped at the chaise longue long enough to sweep up her towel and went back to her apartment alone. Once she was inside she would have locked the door but Ramon's clothes were still there, so she locked her bedroom door instead.

Thirty minutes later, when she had showered and climbed into bed, Ramon knocked at her door.

Katie knew better than to open the door and give Ramon the opportunity to take her in his arms. Where Ramon was concerned her body refused to listen to reason, and in two minutes he'd have her melting and pliant.

"Katie, stop sulking and open this door."

"I'm sure you can find your way out," Katie said coldly. "I am going to sleep." For emphasis she turned out the lamp on her nightstand.

"Katie, for God's sake, do not do this to us."

"There is no 'us.' There never was," Katie said. And then because it hurt somehow to have said the words aloud she added, "I don't know why you want to marry me but I do know all the reasons why I can't marry you. Talking about them isn't going to change anything. Please go away. I really think it's best for both of us this way."

There was an ominous quiet in the apartment after that. Katie waited, watching the clock until forty-five minutes had elapsed, then silently, cautiously, unlocked her door and peeked around the darkened apartment. Ramon had left, turning out all the lights and locking the door behind him. She went back to bed and crawled under the cool sheets, propping the pillows up behind her and turning on the bedside lamp.

What a narrow escape she'd had! Well, not that narrow—she had never actually considered marrying Ramon. In his arms she had been swept to the brink of sexual desperation, that was all. Fortunately no woman in this day and age had to marry just to assuage her sexual needs, including Katherine Connelly! She just happened to have wanted Ramon more than she had ever wanted anyone—even Rob.

That thought sent Katie's mind into chaos. Maybe she had been closer to capitulation than she'd realized. Her job wasn't all that rewarding; the men she knew seemed shallow and self-centered. And Ramon was the antithesis of them. He catered to her every whim. At the zoo he went wherever she wanted to go. If she looked tired he insisted that she sit down and rest. If she gave more than a passing glance at any refreshment stand he was quick to ask if she was hungry or thirsty. If she wanted to swim, he swam. If she wanted to dance, he danced—so long as he could hold her in his arms, she reminded herself crossly.

He wouldn't even let her carry a small bag of groceries or her overnight case. He didn't push open a door, walk past it, and let it come banging back into her face as many men did—then glance at her with a look that said, "Well, you women wanted equality; open your own doors."

Katie shook her head. What was the matter with her, thinking about marrying a man because he picked up a five-pound bag of groceries and opened doors for her? But there was more to Ramon than that. He was so supremely confident of his own masculinity that he had no fear of being gentle. He was self-assured and very proud, yet where she was concerned, he seemed strangely vulnerable.

Katie's thoughts reeled onto another path. How, if he really had lived in near-poverty, had he been so thoroughly familiar with the formalities observed at her parents' elaborately laid dining table? Not once had he shown the slightest uncertainty about which piece of silver to use with which course. Nor had he been the slightest bit uneasy around her parents' affluent friends.

Why did he want to marry her and not just go to bed with her? Last night on the sofa, he had known that she was long past the point of denying him anything. "Want me as much as I want you," he had insisted and implored. And when she did want him that much, he had pulled away, sat back, closed his eyes, and unemotionally asked her to marry him. Had he asked her to marry him instead of making love to her because he thought she was a virgin? Latins still prized virginity even in this day of sexual emancipation. Would he have wanted to marry her if he had realized she wasn't a virgin? Katie seriously doubted it and that made her feel humiliated and furiously indignant. Ramon Galverra had known exactly what to do to arouse her to a fever pitch of desire last night and he hadn't learned how from books! Who did he think he was, anyway? He was no virgin!

Turning out the light, Katie flopped back against the pillows. Thank heaven she'd come no closer to going to Puerto Rico with him! He would insist on being the unchallenged head of his household; he had practically said as much on their picnic. He would expect his wife to cook and clean and cater to him. He would, no doubt, keep her "barefoot and pregnant" too.

Why, no liberated American woman in her right mind would consider marrying such a classic male chauvinist . . . a male chauvinist who would be fiercely protective of his own . . . who would treat his wife as if she were made of fragile glass . . . who would probably work until he dropped to give her whatever she wanted . . . who could be so intensely passionate . . . and so gentle. . . .

6

Katie awoke the next morning to the insistent ringing of the telephone beside her bed. Groping dazedly she lifted the receiver from the cradle and pulled it across the pillow tucking it against her ear. Her mother's voice began before Katie could say hello. "Katie, darling, who on earth was that man?"

"Ramon Galverra," Katie, answered, her eyes still closed.

"I *know* his name, you told us that. What is he doing with you?"

"Doing with me?" Katie mumbled. "Nothing."

"Katie, don't be obtuse! The man obviously knows you have money—we have money—I have the feeling he's after something."

Katie groggily tried to defend Ramon. "He's not after money, he's after a wife."

The phone went silent. When her mother's voice sounded again, each word was iced with contempt. "That Puerto Rican farmer actually thinks he is going to *marry you?*"

"Spanish," Katie corrected, her mother's voice jarring her mind into focus.

"What?"

"I said he's Spanish, not Puerto Rican. Actually, he's American."

"Katherine," the voice demanded with terse impatience. "You are not, in your wildest imaginings, considering marrying that man, are you?"

Katie hesitated as she sat up and swung her legs over the side of the bed. "I don't think so."

"You don't *think so?* Katherine, stay there and don't let that man near you until we get there. Lord, this would kill your father. We'll be there right after breakfast."

"No, don't!" Katie said, finally coming out of her sleepy stupor altogether. "Mom, listen. You woke me up and I can hardly think straight, but there's nothing for you to worry about. I'm not going to marry Ramon; I doubt if I'll ever see him again."

"Katherine, are you sure? You aren't just saying that to pacify me?"

"No, really I'm not."

"All right, darling, but if he comes near you again just call us, and we'll be there in thirty minutes."

"Mom—"

"Call us, Katie. Your father and I love you and want to protect you. Don't be ashamed to admit you can't cope with that Spaniard, or Puerto Rican, or whatever he is."

Katie opened her mouth to protest that she didn't need to be "protected" from Ramon, then changed her mind. Her mother wouldn't believe her and Katie didn't want to argue with her. "Okay," she sighed. "If I need you, I'll call. Bye, Mom."

What was the matter with her parents, Katie wondered angrily a half hour later as she pulled on a pair of yellow velour slacks and a matching yellow top. Why would they think that Ramon would hurt her or do anything that would make her have to call them for help? Brushing her hair back off her forehead, she secured it with a tortoiseshell clip at the crown, then added a touch of coral to her lips and mascara to her lashes. She would go shopping for something frivolous and expensive to take her mind off Ramon and her parents, she decided.

The doorbell rang, as Katie had feared it might, as she was putting her coffee mug in the dishwasher. Her parents, of course. They had finished with their breakfast; now they had come over to finish with Ramon, figuratively speaking.

Resignedly, she went into the living room, pulled open the door, then stepped back in surprise from the tall lithe figure blocking the sunlight. "I—I was just going to leave," Katie said.

Ignoring her hint, Ramon stepped inside and firmly closed the door behind him. A grim smile touched his mouth. "Somehow, I thought that was what you would do."

Katie looked at his ruggedly handsome features, which were stamped with determination, and his powerful shoulders, which were squared with purpose. Confronted with six feet three inches of potent masculinity and iron resolve, Katie chose to make a strategic retreat in order to gather her scattered wits. Turning on her heel she said over her shoulder, "I'll get you a cup of coffee."

She was pouring it into a cup when Ramon's hands settled on her waist drawing her back against his chest. His breath lightly touched her hair as he said, "I do not want coffee, Katie."

"Some breakfast?"

"No."

"Then what do you want?"

"Turn around and I will show you."

Katie shook her head, grasping the edge of the Formica counter top so hard that her knuckles turned white.

"Katie, I did not tell you the main reason why I did not want you to wear that bathing suit, because I did not like admitting it to myself. And you are not going to like it, either. But there must always be honesty between us." He paused then said with a reluctant sigh, "The whole truth is that I was jealous—I do not want anyone but me to ever see so much of your beautiful body."

Katie swallowed, searching for her voice, afraid to turn around, shaken by the feel of his hard, muscular length against her back and legs. "I accept your explanation, and you're right—I don't like it. What I wear is my decision; no one else's. But none of this really matters anymore. I'm sorry for behaving so childishly last night; I should have come out to say goodbye to you. But I can't marry you, Ramon. It wouldn't work."

She expected him to accept that. She should have known better. His hands slid up her arms to her shoulders, tightening to gently but firmly turn her around to face him. Katie kept her eyes on the tanned column of his throat above the open collar of his blue shirt.

"Look at me, *querida.*"

That deep, husky voice calling her darling did it. She dragged her wide, apprehensive blue eyes up to his.

"You *can* marry me. And it *will* work. I will make it work."

"There's a cultural gap between us a million miles wide!" Katie cried. "How can you possibly think you can make it work?"

His eyes held hers steadily. "Because I will come home to you at night and make love to you until you cry out for me to stop. I will leave you in the morning with the taste of my kiss on your lips. I will live my life for you. I will fill your days with gladness, and if God sends us heartbreak, I will hold you in my arms until your tears have passed and then I will teach you how to laugh again."

Mesmerized, Katie stared at the firm sensual mouth slowly descending to hers. "We'd fight," she warned shakily.

He brushed his lips against hers. "Fighting is only an angry way of caring."

"We'd—we'd disagree about everything. You're tyrannical and I'm independent."

His lips clung to hers. "We will learn to compromise."

"One person can't do all the giving. What would you want in return?"

His arms enfolded her. "No more and no less than what I offer you—everything you have to give with nothing held back. Ever." His mouth covered hers, coaxing her lips to part for the gentle invasion of his tongue.

What began for Katie as a warm glow kindled into a fire, then burst into raging flames, racing through her in a quivering fury. She was leaning into him, returning his endless drugging kisses with helpless urgency, moaning softly as her breasts swelled to fill his caressing palms.

"We belong together," he whispered. "Tell me you know it," he ordered thickly, his hand forcing its way under her elastic waistband to cup her bare buttocks and move her tighter against the throbbing hardness of his aroused manhood. "Our bodies know it, Katie."

Caught between the wildly exciting feel of his hand against her bare skin and the proud evidence of his desire pressed boldly to her, Katie's weakened defenses crumbled completely. She wound her arms tightly around his neck, running her hands over his shoulders, smoothing his thick black hair, digging her nails into the bunched muscles of his back. And when he hoarsely commanded, "Tell me," she crushed her parted lips against his and almost sobbed. "We belong together."

The whispered words seemed to echo around the room, dousing Katie's passion with cold shock. She leaned back in his arms, staring at him.

Ramon's gaze took in the hectic color tinting the smooth curve of her cheeks, the panic widening the deep blue eyes beneath their luxurious lashes. Threading his hands through the sides of her hair, he cupped her face between them. "Do not be frightened, *querida*," he said gently. "I think you are not so much afraid of what is happening between us as you are of how quickly it is happening." His thumbs stroked her heated cheeks as he added, "I would do anything to be able to give you more time, but I cannot. We will have to leave for Puerto Rico on Sunday. That will still give you four full days to pack your clothing. I had intended to leave two days ago, I cannot delay my return beyond Sunday."

"But I—I have to go to work tomorrow," Katie protested distractedly.

"Yes. To tell them that you will be leaving for Puerto Rico and that this will be your last week here."

Of all the monumental obstacles to her actually marrying Ramon, Katie seized upon the lesser one of her job. "I can't just walk in there and resign with only four days' notice. I am required to give two weeks' notice, not four days. I can't."

"Yes, Katie," he said quietly. "You can."

"And then there's my parents—oh no! We have got to get out of here," she said with sudden urgency. "I forgot about them. All I need is for them to come over now and find you here. I've already had a 'Katherine' phone call from my mother this morning." In a flurry of motion, Katie broke free of his arms, hurried Ramon into the living room, grabbed her purse, and did not relax until they were in his car.

"What," Ramon asked, slanting her an amused, sideways look as he turned the key in the Buick's ignition, "is a 'Katherine' phone call?"

Katie watched the easy competence with which he drove, admiring his long masculine fingers on the steering wheel. "When my parents call me Katherine instead of Katie, that means the battle lines have been drawn, their artillery is being moved into position, and unless I wave a white flag quickly, they are going to start firing."

He grinned at her and Katie relaxed. When he turned up the expressway ramp onto eastbound Highway 40, Katie said idly, "Where are we going?"

"To the Arch. I have never had the time to really see it up close."

"Tourist!" Katie teased.

They spent the rest of the morning and well into the afternoon outwardly behaving exactly like tourists. They boarded one of the paddle wheelers for a short trip through the murky waters of the Mississippi River. Katie absently watched the passing scenery on the Illinois side of the river, her mind whirling with disjointed thoughts.

Ramon lounged against the railing—watching Katie. "When are you going to tell your parents?"

Katie's hands actually perspired at the thought. Wiping her damp palms against her yellow slacks, she shook her head. "I haven't decided," she answered, being deliberately obscure about what she hadn't decided.

They strolled along the old brick streets of Laclede's Landing near the riverfront and stopped at a wonderful little pub where the sandwiches were masterpieces. Katie ate very little and stared out the windows at the throngs of downtown office workers coming to the landing to eat.

Ramon leaned back in his chair, a cigar clamped between his teeth, his eyes narrowed against the smoke—watching Katie. "Do you want me to be there when you tell them?"

"I haven't thought about it."

They wandered along the parklike setting that was dominated by the soaring Gateway Arch. Katie lamely acted as tourist guide explaining that the arch is the tallest monument in the United States, rising to a height of 630 feet, then fell silent and stared blindly at the river flowing by in the foreground. With no particular destination in mind, she walked to the sweeping steps that led to the riverfront and sat down, thinking without really being able to think at all.

Ramon stood beside her, one foot propped near her thigh—watching Katie. "The longer you wait to tell them, the more nervous you will become and the harder it will be to do."

"Did you want to actually go up in the arch?" Katie evaded. "I don't know if the tram is running, but if it is, the view is supposed to be fantastic. I can't actually say from firsthand experience . . . I've always been too afraid of the height to open my eyes."

"Katie, there is not much time."

"I know."

They walked back to the car and as they drove down Market Street, Katie idly suggested that he might like to drive down Lindell Boulevard. Ramon automatically followed her directions. They were driving west down Lindell when Ramon said, "What is that?"

Katie looked up and to her right. "St. Louis Cathedral." She was amazed when he pulled up in front of the elaborate structure. "Why on earth are we stopping here?"

Ramon turned in his seat and put his arm around her shoulders. "There are only a few days before we leave, with many decisions to be made and much to be done. I will help you pack and do everything I can, but I cannot tell your parents for you, nor can I resign your job for you."

"No, I know."

His free hand touched her chin, gently lifting it, and the kiss he gave her was filled with persuasive tenderness.

"But why do you want to go into a church?" Katie asked when he came around and opened her door for her.

"Normally the finest skills the local craftsmen possessed at the time can be found in churches, no matter where in the world they are."

Katie didn't entirely believe that was his reason, and her nerves, already ragged and strained, were completely jangled by the time they had climbed the flight of shallow stone steps leading toward the domed cathedral. Ramon opened one of the massive carved doors and stepped aside for her to precede him into the vast cool interior. Instantly she was swamped with memories of burning candles and altar flowers.

Ramon placed his hand beneath her elbow, giving her no choice but to walk beside him down the center aisle. Katie kept her eyes moving over the endless rows of pews, scanning the distant vaulted ceilings with their spectacular mosaic scenes that glittered with gold, always avoiding the marble altar. Compulsively avoiding the altar. In the front pew she knelt beside Ramon, feeling like a fraud, an unwelcome intruder. She dragged her eyes toward the altar, then closed them against the dizziness assailing her. God didn't want her here—not like this—not with Ramon. It was too poignant being here with him. And too wrong. All she wanted was his body, not his life.

Ramon was kneeling beside her, and Katie had the terrifying feeling that he was praying. She was even quite certain what he was praying for. As if she could cancel out his private appeal, Katie began to pray, quickly, incoherently, the panic beginning to mount. *Please, please don't listen to him. Don't let this happen. Don't let him care for me so much. I can't do what he wants me to do. I know I can't. I don't want to. God*—Katie cried silently. *Are you listening to me? Do you ever listen to me?*

Katie jerked to her feet, tears blinding her as she turned and collided with Ramon's hard body. "Katie?" His low voice near her ear was filled with concern, his hands gentle on her arms.

"Let me go, Ramon. Please! I've got to get out of here."

"I—I don't know what came over me in there," Katie apologized, wiping her eyes with her fingertips. They were standing in the brilliant sunlight on the church steps. Katie watched the traffic gliding down Lindell Boulevard, still too distressed and embarrassed to even look at Ramon as she explained, "I haven't been to church since I was married."

She started down the steps, halting at the sound of Ramon's stunned voice. "You have been married before?"

Katie nodded without turning. "Yes. Two years ago when I was twenty-one, the same month I graduated from college. And divorced a year later."

It still hurt her to admit that to anyone. She had descended another two steps before she realized that Ramon wasn't following her. Turning, she found him regarding her through hard, narrowed eyes. "Were you married in the Catholic church?"

The harshness of his tone, as well as the seeming unimportance of the question, surprised her. Why was he more upset about whether she'd been married in the Catholic church than he was by the actual fact of her having been married? The answer hit Katie like a bucket of ice water, revitalizing, yet sharply painful. Ramon must be a Catholic. His religion would make it difficult to marry Katie if she had been married in the Catholic church and then divorced.

God had indeed answered her prayers, Katie thought with a mixture of gratitude and guilt for the pain she was about to cause Ramon with a lie. She had been divorced, but David had been killed six months later so there was no actual obstacle to Ramon's marrying her. On the other hand, he didn't know that and Katie was not going to tell him. "Yes, I was married in the Catholic church," she said quietly.

Katie was scarcely aware that they had gotten into the car and were driving toward the expressway. Her mind was drifting into the painful past. David. Ruggedly handsome David, who had needed a way to silence the gossip about his association with the wife of the law firm's senior partner, as well as several of the firm's female clients, and had done it by becoming engaged to

Katherine Connelly. She was lushly beautiful, delightfully intelligent and suitably naive. Those who had believed the gossip took one look at her and knew that they had been mistaken. After all, what man in his right mind would bother with all those other women when he had a woman like Katie?

David Caldwell would. He was an attorney, an ex–college football player. A sophisticated man of great personal charisma, and an ego that fed itself on women. Every woman he met was a challenge to him. Every sexual conquest he made proved he was better than other men. He was such a charming man . . . until he was angered. Angered, he was 195 pounds of brutal, violent male.

On the six-month anniversary of their marriage, Katie took the afternoon off from her job. She stopped at the market for some special items and drove to the apartment filled with excited plans to surprise David with a celebration. When she arrived, she discovered David was already "celebrating" with the attractive, middle-aged wife of the senior partner of his law firm. As long as she lived, Katie knew she would never forget the moment she had stood in the bedroom doorway and seen them. Even now the memory of it made her feel nauseated.

But the memory of the nightmare that followed was far more painful.

The physical bruises David inflicted on her that night had healed quickly; the emotional ones were scars now. They were healed, but they were still sensitive.

Katie remembered the phone calls that came in the middle of the night after she left him: David insisting that he would change, he loved her. David cursing her viciously and threatening her with brutal reprisals if she dared to tell anyone what he had done. Even Katie's hope for a dignified divorce had been dashed. The divorce itself was quiet, on the grounds of irreconcilable differences, but David himself was not quiet. In angry terror that Katie might tell his secret, he set to work maligning her character and even her family to anyone and everyone who would listen. The things he said were so vile, so vicious, that most of the people he talked to must have turned away in disgust or begun to question his sanity. But Katie was too humiliated and destroyed to consider that.

And then one day four months after the divorce, she dragged herself out of the pit of horror and misery where she had been dwelling, looked at herself in the mirror, and said, "Katherine Elizabeth Connelly, are you going to let David Caldwell ruin the rest of your life? Do you really want to give him that much satisfaction?"

With some of her old spirit and enthusiasm she set to the task of putting the pieces of her life back together. She changed jobs and moved out of her parents' house and into her own apartment. Her smile returned and then her laughter. She began to live again the life that fate had given her. And she lived it with a determinedly cheerful attitude. Except occasionally when it seemed so shallow. So terribly meaningless. So empty.

"Who?" Ramon snapped from beside her.

Katie leaned her head against the back of her seat and closed her eyes. "David Caldwell. An attorney. We were married for six months and divorced six months after that."

"Tell me about him," he said harshly.

"I hate talking about him. I hate thinking about him, as a matter of fact."

"Tell me," he gritted.

Haunted by the gruesome memories of her marriage to David that were swamping her now, and panicked by Ramon's relentless pressure to marry him, Katie grasped at the only escape she could think of at the moment: even though she despised her own cowardice, she chose to deceive Ramon into believing David was still alive in order to put an end to any more talk of her going to Puerto Rico and becoming his wife. Reminding herself to talk about David as if he were still living, she said, "There isn't a great deal to tell about him. He is thirty-two—tall, dark and very handsome. He reminds me of you, in fact."

"I want to know why you divorced him."

"I divorced him because I despised him and because I was afraid of him."

"He threatened you?"

"He didn't threaten."

"He struck you?" Ramon looked furious and revolted.

Katie was determined to sound offhand. "David called it teaching me manners."

"And I remind you of him?"

He sounded ready to explode and Katie hastily assured, "Only a little bit in looks. you're both olive-skinned, dark-haired and dark-eyed. David played football in college, and you . . ." She slid a covert glance at him, then recoiled in alarm from the blazing anger in his profile. "You look as if you should play tennis," she finished lamely.

As they were pulling into the parking space in front of her apartment, it dawned on Katie that this would undoubtedly be their last day together. If Ramon was as devout a Catholic as Spaniards were purported to be, he would not be able to consider marrying her.

The idea of never seeing him again was surprisingly painful, and Katie felt a little desolate and forlorn. She wanted to prolong the day, to be able to spend more time with him. But not alone—not where he could take her in his arms and in five minutes have her drowning in desire and confessing everything to him. Then she'd be right back where she was an hour ago. Trapped.

"Do you know what I'd love to do tonight?" she said as he walked her to the door. "That is, if you don't have to work."

"No, what?" he said through clenched teeth.

"I'd love to go someplace where we could listen to music and dance." Her simple statement made his face darken with rage. The hard line of his jaw tightened until a drumming pulse stood out in his cheek. He was furious, Katie thought with a jolt of fear. Quickly, apologetically, she said, "Ramon, I should have realized that you might be a Catholic and that my having been married before in the church would make it impossible for you to marry me. I'm sorry I didn't think to tell you before."

"You are so 'sorry' that you now wish to go out dancing," he said with scathing sarcasm. Then, making a visible effort to control his fury he asked tautly, "What time shall I come for you?"

Katie glanced at the afternoon sun. "In about four hours, at eight o'clock."

Katie chose a silky halter dress in royal blue that was the exact shade of her eyes and was striking against the contrast of red highlights in her hair. In the mirror, she scrutinized the slight amount of cleavage showing between her breasts to be certain Ramon wouldn't think the dress was too revealing. If this was going to be their last night together, she didn't want to spoil it with another argument about her clothing. She put gold hoops in her ears, a wide gold bracelet high on her arm, and stepped into dainty sandals that were the same blue as her dress. Giving her hair a quick toss to send it spilling back down her shoulders, she went into the living room to wait for Ramon.

Their last evening together. . . . Katie's spirits drooped alarmingly. She went into the kitchen and poured a tiny bit of brandy into a glass, then sat down on the corduroy sofa at a quarter to eight, slowly sipping the brandy and watching the clock on the opposite wall. When the doorbell rang at exactly eight, she jumped nervously, put her empty glass aside, and went to answer it.

Nothing in their brief acquaintance had prepared Katie for the Ramon Galverra who was standing there when she opened the door.

He looked breathtakingly elegant in a dark blue suit and vest that fit him to perfection and contrasted beautifully with his snowy-white shirt and conservative striped tie. "You look fantastic," Katie said with a beaming smile of admiration. "You look like the president of a bank," she added, stepping back to better admire his tall athletic frame.

Ramon's expression was sardonic. "As it happens, I do not like bankers. For the most part they are unimaginative men eager to reap the profit from risks, yet unwilling to take any risks themselves."

"Oh," Katie said, somewhat abashed. "Well, they're terrific dressers, anyway."

"How do you know?" Ramon replied. "Were you also married to a banker who you have forgotten to mention?"

Katie's hand froze as she reached for the silky printed shawl that coordinated with her dress. "No, of course not."

They went down to one of the riverboats and listened to Dixieland jazz, then back to Lacledes Landing, where they stopped in three more places for jazz and blues music. As the evening wore on, Ramon became increasingly cool and unapproachable, and the more aloof he became the more Katie drank and tried to be amusing.

By the time they had driven to a popular place out near the airport, Katie was slightly flushed, very nervous, and thoroughly miserable.

The place she had chosen was surprisingly crowded for a Tuesday night, but they were lucky enough to get a table beside the dance floor. There, however, Katie's luck ended. Ramon flatly refused to dance with her, and Katie did not know how much longer she could endure the glacial reserve that barely concealed his contempt. His hard eyes examined her with a detached, cynical interest that made Katie mentally squirm.

She looked around, more to avoid Ramon's cold eyes than because she was interested in her surroundings, and her gaze collided with that of a handsome man sitting at the bar watching her. He raised his brows, mouthed the word "Dance?" and Katie, in sheer desperation, nodded her head.

He approached the table, eyed Ramon's obvious height and lithe build with a certain wariness, and politely asked Katie to dance.

"Do you mind?" Katie asked Ramon, eager to get away.

"Not in the least," he replied with a disinterested shrug.

Katie loved to dance; she had a natural grace and a way of moving that was very eye-catching. Her partner, it became obvious, not only loved to dance, he was a positive exhibitionist about it. The colored lights flashed overhead, the music pulsed, and Katie moved with it, giving herself to the rhythm. "Hey, you're good," her partner said, forcing her with his own movements to do a much flashier kind of dancing than she preferred to do.

"You're showing off," Katie told him as the crowd on the dance floor began to move back and give them more room, then stopped dancing altogether. At the end of the disco number there was a loud round of encouraging, insistent applause from dancers and nondancers alike.

"They want us to dance some more," her partner said, tightening his hold on her arm when Katie would have started back toward the table. Simultaneously, another disco number started reverberating through the packed room, and Katie had no choice but to give in gracefully to what she privately felt was exhibitionism. As she danced, she stole a glance at Ramon, then quickly jerked her eyes away. He had angled his chair toward the dance floor, shoved his hands into his pockets, and was watching her with the dispassionate interest of a jaded conquistador observing a paid dancing girl.

As the music wound to a close there was a gratifying thunder of applause. Her partner tried to get her to stay with him for another dance, but this time Katie firmly refused.

She sat down at the table opposite Ramon and sipped from her drink, growing increasingly annoyed with the way they were behaving to each other. "Well?" she asked with a twinge of hostility, when he made no comment about her dancing.

One black brow rose sardonically. "Not bad."

Katie could have hit him. Another song began, this one slow and romantic. She looked around, saw two more would-be partners bearing down on their table and stiffened. Ramon, following her gaze, saw them and reluctantly stood up. Wordlessly he put his hand under Katie's elbow and led her onto the dance floor.

The love song, combined with the piercing sweetness of being in Ramon's arms again, was Katie's undoing. Moving close to him, she laid her cheek against the dark blue cloth of his suit coat. She wished his arms would tighten, that he would gather her against him and brush his lips against her temple as he had the last time they danced out by the pool. She wished . . . a lot of hazy, impossible things.

She was still wishing when they got back to her apartment. He walked her to the door and Katie practically had to beg him to come in for a nightcap. As soon as he had downed the brandy he stood up and without saying anything, simply started for the door.

"Ramon, please don't leave. Not like this," Katie pleaded.

He turned and looked at her, his face expressionless.

Katie started toward him, then stopped a few feet away, shaken by a surge of heartbreaking sadness and longing. "I don't want you to go," she heard herself say, and then her arms were around his neck as she pressed herself against his unyielding body, kissing him desperately. His lips were cool and unresponsive, his arms remained motionless at his sides.

Humiliated and hurt, Katie stepped back and raised blue eyes shimmering with tears to his. "Don't you even want to kiss me goodbye?" she asked with a catch in her voice.

His whole body seemed to stiffen into a taut, rigid pose of rejection, and then he jerked her into his arms. "Damn you!" he hissed furiously as his mouth came down hard, taking hers with a deliberate ruthless expertise that immediately had Katie clinging to him, responding wildly with helpless desire. His hands fondled her thoroughly, roughly molding her body to his. And then he abruptly pushed her away.

Trembling and breathless, Katie looked up at him, then backed away in alarm from the murderous rage blazing in his eyes.

"Is that the only thing you want from me, Katie?" he snapped.

"No!" Katie quickly denied. "I mean, I don't want anything. I—I just knew that you didn't have a very good time tonight and so—"

"And so," he interrupted in an insulting drawl, "You brought me in here to give me a much better time?"

"No!" Katie fumbled, "I—" Her voice choked as his black eyes raked her from head to toe. Just when Katie thought he was going to turn on his heel and leave, he turned in the other direction and strode over to the coffee table. He picked up the pencil she kept near the telephone and wrote something on the small pad beside it.

Striding back to the door, he turned with one hand on the knob. "I have written down a phone number where I can be reached until Thursday. If you want to talk, call me." His gaze lingered on her face and then he was gone, closing the door behind him.

Katie stood where he had left her, stunned and fragmented into jagged splinters of misery. That last glance before he left . . . it was as if he had been memorizing her face. He hated her, was furious with her, yet he had wanted to remember how she looked. Katie could not believe how shattered she was. Tears burned her eyes, and she had an aching lump in her throat.

She turned and slowly walked into her bedroom. What was the matter with her—this was the way she had wanted it, wasn't it? Well, not exactly. She wanted Ramon, she was ready to admit that to herself, but she wanted him *her* way: here in St. Louis, working at some decent job.

A determinedly cheerful Katie presented herself at her office the following morning, but the effects of her sleepless night were evident in the blue smudges under her eyes and the tightness of her normally spontaneous smile.

"Hi, Katie," her secretary greeted. "Did you enjoy your four-day weekend?"

"Very much," Katie said. She took the handful of messages her secretary handed her. "Thanks, Donna."

"Want some coffee?" Donna volunteered. "You look as though you haven't been to bed since Friday. Or," she finished with an irrepressible grin, "should I say you look as though you haven't been to *sleep* since then?"

Katie managed a wan smile in reply to Donna's banter. "I'd love some coffee." Glancing through the messages, she walked into her small office. She sat down in the chair behind her desk and looked around. Having a private office, no matter the size, was an important status symbol at Technical Dynamics, and Katie had always been proud of this external sign of her success. This morning it seemed trivial and meaningless.

How could it be that when she'd locked her desk on Friday she'd never heard of Ramon, and now the idea of never seeing him again was gnawing at her heart. Gnawing at her body not her heart, Katie corrected herself firmly. She looked up as Donna placed a white Styrofoam cup of steaming coffee on the desk.

"Miss Johnson would like to see you in her office at nine-fifteen," Donna said.

Virginia Johnson, Katie's immediate supervisor, was a brilliant, capable, attractive woman of forty, who had never married and who held the title of director of personnel. Of all the career women she knew, Katie admired Virginia more than anyone.

In contrast to Katie's small, functionally equipped office, Virginia's was spacious with lovely French-provincial furnishings and thick grass-green carpeting. Katie knew that Virginia was grooming her to take her place, that she intended Katie to be the next director of personnel.—the next occupant of this office. "Did you have a nice four-day holiday?" Virginia asked, smiling as Katie entered the room.

"Very nice," Katie said, sitting down in the chair across from Virginia's desk. "I'm not having such a good 'today' though; I can't seem to get back into the swing of things."

"Then I have some news that may fire your enthusiasm." Virginia paused meaningfully and slid a familiar-looking form across the desk toward Katie. "Your raise has been approved," she beamed.

"Oh, that's very nice. Thank you, Virginia," Katie said, scarcely glancing at the form which granted her a monumental 18-percent increase in salary. "Was there anything else you wanted to see me about?"

"Katie!" Virginia said with an impatient laugh. "I had to fight tooth and nail to get you that large an increase."

"I know," Katie said, trying to sound properly grateful. "You've always been terrific to me and I love the idea of the extra money."

"You're entitled to it and if you were a man you would have been making it before now, which is what I told our esteemed vice-president of operations."

Katie shifted in her chair. "Was there anything else you wanted to see me about? I have an interview scheduled now. The applicant is waiting."

"No, that's all."

Katie got up and started for the door, then stopped at the sound of Virginia's concerned voice. "Katie, what's wrong? Is it anything you could talk to me about?"

Katie hesitated. She needed to talk to someone, and Virginia Johnson was a sensible woman—in fact, the woman Katie most wanted to emulate. Walking over to the broad windows Katie gazed down seven stories below, watching the endless string of traffic. "Virginia, have you ever considered giving up your career to get married?" Turning abruptly, Katie found Virginia studying her with penetrating interest, her forehead creased into a frown.

"Katie, shall we be frank with each other? Are you considering marrying someone in particular or just looking toward the obscure future?"

"My future would definitely be obscure with him," Katie laughed, but she felt tense and depressed. Nervously smoothing her hand over her perfectly neat chignon Katie explained, "I met this man—very recently—and he wants me to marry him and leave Missouri. He isn't from here."

"How recently did you meet him?" Virginia asked perceptively.

Katie actually blushed. "Friday evening."

Virginia had a rich throaty laugh that was at variance with her diminutive size. "For a few minutes there you had me worried, but now I think I understand. Four days ago you met a splendid man, a man unlike any man you've ever known. You can't bear the idea of losing him. Am I getting the picture right? He's extremely handsome, of course. And charming. And he turns you on like no one else ever has. That's it, isn't it?"

"Just about," Katie admitted, mentally squirming.

"In that case, I happen to have the perfect cure: I recommend that you don't let him out of your sight unless you absolutely must. Eat with this marvelous man, sleep with him, live with him. Do *everything* together."

"Do you mean," Katie said in amazement, "that you think things could work out—that I ought to marry him?"

"Absolutely not! I'm suggesting a cure, not that you marry the ailment! What I'm prescribing is huge doses of the man taken around the clock—just like antibiotics. The cure is very effective and the only side effect will be a mild case of disillusionment. Believe me, I know. Live with him if you want to, Katie, but give up the idea of falling in love in four days, marrying him and living happily ever after. Which brings me to the question of why we always 'fall' in love. One falls down steps, off ladders, into rivers and down mountains. If love is so wonderful, why don't we soar in love, or climb in love, or. . . ." She broke off at the sound of Katie's infectious laughter. "Good, I'm glad to see you cheerful again." Taking an interoffice memo from the stack of correspondence on her desk, Virginia smiled widely and waved Katie to the door. "Now go interview your applicant and earn that raise of yours."

Watching the disgruntled young man leave her office twenty minutes later, Katie thought disgustedly that her secretary could have done a better job of interviewing him than herself. She had asked vague, general questions, not concise, pertinent ones, and then listened to his answers with total lack of interest. But her crowning achievement had come at the conclusion of the unfortunate interview. Standing up, she had shaken hands with him across her desk and regretfully advised him she couldn't be very encouraging about his chances for a position as an engineer with Technical Dynamics.

Rather huffily, the young man had replied, "I was applying for a job as an auditor."

"Well, not as an auditor, either," Katie had mumbled tactlessly.

Still hot with embarrassment over her blunder, Katie picked up her phone and dialed Karen's office number downtown. "How're things in the newspaper business?" she asked when Karen's secretary had put her through.

"Fine, Katie. How about you? How are things in the busy personnel office of mighty Technical Dynamics?" she teased.

"Awful! I practically told an applicant that he didn't have a prayer of getting a job with us in any capacity."

"What's wrong with that?"

Sighing, Katie said, "Personnel people are supposed to have more finesse than that. Normally we say we don't have anything available commensurate with their background and experience. It means the same thing but it sounds better, and it doesn't hurt anyone's feelings." Katie ran her hand around the nape of her neck, massaging her tense muscles. "Listen, the reason I was calling was because I wondered what you're doing tonight. I don't feel like spending the evening alone." *And thinking about Ramon*, Katie silently added.

"A few of us are going to the Purple Bottle," Karen said. "Why don't you meet us there? I might as well warn you, though, it's strictly singles. But they've got a good singer and the music isn't bad."

Katie's efficiency, if not her enthusiasm, improved after that. She spent her day solving the usual problems and settling the usual disputes. She listened to a supervisor complain loudly and at tedious length about a file clerk; then she listened to the file clerk's tearful complaints about the supervisor. At the conclusion, Katie ignored the supervisor's demands that the file clerk be terminated, and instead, she transferred the clerk to another department. After looking through the applications for employment she chose a file clerk who had impressed her during the interview as being extremely assertive and self-confident, and arranged for her to come in for an interview with the supervisor.

She calmed an irate accountant who was threatening to file a discrimination claim against the company because she had been passed over for promotion. She finished a survey on the company's compliance with governmental safety requirements.

Between all that and interviewing applicants, Katie's day flew by. At the end of it, she leaned back in her chair and somberly contemplated an entire life of days spent just like this one. This was "having a career." Virginia Johnson had devoted all her energy, her whole life, to "having a career." To this.

That restless, empty feeling that had been haunting her these past few months came over her again. Katie tried to ignore it and leaned forward to lock her desk.

Katie had the worst time of her life at the Purple Bottle. She stood around pretending to listen to the music, watching the men and women making their approaches. She was uncomfortably aware of three men who were sitting at a table directly on her right and looking her over—judging her assets, measuring her possible bed-worthiness against the effort required to approach her. Privately, Katie thought that all women who were considering divorcing their husbands should first be required to spend one night in a singles' bar. After that degrading and demoralizing experience, many of them would run flying back to their husbands.

She left at nine-thirty, one hour after she had arrived, and drove back to her apartment. In the car, thoughts of Ramon haunted her. She had a life to live here and he couldn't be part of it, while his life was too alien, too far away for her to even consider sharing it.

Katie went to bed at ten-thirty and after several hours, finally fell into a deep exhausted sleep.

*S*he slept so deeply that she didn't hear the alarm go off, had to dress in frantic haste, and still she was fifteen minutes late for work.

Thursday, June 3, her calendar boldly proclaimed as she unlocked her desk and reached for the cup of coffee Donna had brought her.

Thursday.

The last day she would ever be able to reach Ramon. How late would he be at that phone number? Until he finished working at five or six o'clock? Or would he be working late tonight? What difference did it make? If she called him she would have to be ready to leave and marry him. And that she just couldn't do.

June 3.

Katie smiled sadly as she sipped her steaming coffee. At the lightning speed with which Ramon swept her along, she probably would have been a June bride. Again.

Katie gave her head a hard shake and employed what was for her, a special talent she discovered she possessed during her divorce: By instantly forcing herself to think of something different the moment an unwanted subject entered her mind, she could totally repress the subject.

She was a positive whirlwind of productive activity all day. Not only did she handle all her scheduled interviews, she took three more applicants who had arrived without the required appointment.

She gave most of the clerical tests herself, repeating the instructions for how to type the sample copy as if it were the most interesting speech she'd ever made. She stared at the timer while they typed as if it were an absorbing masterpiece of complicated technology that utterly fascinated her.

She breezed into Virginia's office, thanked her profoundly for the marvelous raise and the wonderful advice, and then she slowly closed her office door and reluctantly went home.

It was not nearly as easy to practice her technique in the solitude of her apartment, particularly when the radio kept reminding her what time it was—"This is KMOX Radio and the time is six-forty," the announcer said.

And Ramon won't be at that number much longer, if he still is, the announcer in her mind added.

Angrily, Katie snapped off the radio and turned on the television, prowling around her apartment, unable to sit down. If she called Ramon, there could be no half-measures; she would have to tell him the truth. Even if she did, he might not want to marry her any longer. He had been furious to learn she'd been married before. Maybe the church wasn't the issue at all. Maybe he didn't want 'secondhand' goods. But if he wanted to be finished with her, why had he left her a number where she could call him?

The television screen flared to life. "It's seventy-eight degrees in St. Louis at six forty-five," the announcer intruded into her thoughts.

She couldn't call Ramon unless she was prepared to resign her job with one day's notice. That was all that was left. She would have to walk into Virginia Johnson's office and say to a woman who had been wonderful to her, "Sorry to be leaving you in the lurch, but that's the way it is."

And she hadn't even considered the problem of her parents. They would be angry, alarmed, heartbroken. They would miss her terribly if she went to Puerto Rico. Katie dialed her parents' number and was informed by their maid that Mr. and Mrs. Connelly had gone to the country club for dinner. *Damn it!* Katie thought. Why were they gone when she needed them? They should be at home, missing their little Katie, whom they only saw every few weeks. Would they miss her so much if they only saw her every few months?

Katie leaped to her feet, and in desperation to be doing something, changed into a bikini—the yellow bikini! Sitting at the dressing table in her spacious bedroom, she briskly brushed her hair.

How could she be thinking of giving all this up in exchange for the sort of home and life Ramon could offer her? She must be insane! Her own life was a modern American woman's dream. She had a rewarding career, a beautiful apartment, expensive clothes and no financial worries. She was young, attractive and independent.

She had everything. Absolutely everything.

That thought caused Katie's brush strokes to slow as she stared soberly into the mirror. Dear God, was this really *everything?* Her eyes darkened with despair as she again contemplated a future just like her present. There had to be more to life than this. Surely this wasn't everything. It just couldn't be.

Trying to shake off her dismal thoughts, Katie snatched up a towel and marched down to the pool. There were about thirty people swimming or relaxing at the umbrella tables. Don and Brad were with some other men drinking beer. Katie waved to them when they called to her to come and join them, but she shook her head no. Putting her towel down on the most isolated lounger she could find, Katie turned and walked over to the pool. She swam twenty laps, then climbed out and flopped down on the chair. Someone had a portable radio on. "It's seven-fifteen in St. Louis, the temperature a balmy seventy-eight degrees."

Katie closed her eyes, trying to shut her mind off, and suddenly she could almost feel Ramon's warm firm lips moving with gentle coaxing over hers, then deepening his kiss until it was wildly erotic and she was joyously surrendering to the searching hunger of his mouth and hands. His deep voice spoke quietly to her heart: "I will live my life for you . . . I will make love to you until you cry out for me to stop . . . I will fill your days with gladness."

Katie felt as if she were slowly suffocating. "We belong together," he had said, his voice thick with desire. "Tell me that you know it. Say it." She had said it. She had even known it as surely as she knew they *couldn't* be together.

He was so handsome, so masculine with his beautiful black hair and dazzling white smile. Katie thought of the slight cleft in his chin and the way his eyes—"Ouch!" Yelping with surprise she jackknifed into a sitting position as icy water ran down her thigh.

"Wake up, sleeping beauty," Don grinned, sitting down on the lounge. Katie squeezed over to make more room for him, watching him warily. His eyes were glassy, his face slightly flushed; he looked as though he'd been drinking all afternoon. "Katie," he said, his eyes delving into her deep cleavage exposed by the skimpy bikini top. "You really turn me on, do you know that?"

"I don't think that's very hard to do," Katie replied with a fixed smile, pushing his hand away when his fingers started to trace the trickle of water across her left thigh.

He laughed. "Be nice to me, Katie. I could be very nice to you."

"I'm not an old lady, and you're not a boy scout," Katie quipped, hiding her uneasiness behind flippancy.

"You have a clever little tongue, redhead. But there are better things to do with it than sniping at me. Let me show you an example." His mouth started descending toward hers and Katie pulled back, averting her head.

"Don," she almost pleaded, "I'm really trying not to make a scene but if you don't stop this I'm going to start screaming and we're both going to look very silly."

He jerked back and glared at her. "What the hell's the matter with you anyway?"

"Nothing!" Katie said. She didn't want to make an enemy of him, she just wanted him to go away. "What do you want?" she asked finally.

"Are you kidding? I want this woman I'm looking at—the one with the gorgeous face, a luscious body and a virginal little mind."

Katie looked him right in the eye. "Why?" she said baldly.

"Sweetheart," he teased, while his eyes made a thorough inspection of her body. "That is a stupid question. But I'll answer it the same way the man answered when they asked him why he wanted to climb the mountain. I want to climb you because you're here. Do you want me to be more blunt? I want to climb on you, or if you prefer to, you can——"

"Get away from me," Katie hissed. "You're disgusting and you're drunk."

"I'm not drunk!" he said, offended.

"Then you're just plain disgusting! Now go away."

He stood up and shrugged. "Okay. Shall I send Brad over? He's interested. Or how about Dean, he's——"

"I don't want any of you!" Katie said furiously.

Don was genuinely bewildered. "Why not? We're no worse than the next group of guys. In fact, we're better than most."

Katie was slowly straightening, staring at him as his words began sinking into her brain, pounding in her head. "What did you say?" she whispered.

"I said we're as good as the next group of guys, and better than most."

"You're right . . ." she breathed slowly. "You are absolutely right!"

"So what's the problem? What are you saving it for, anyway? Or, more importantly, who are you saving it for?"

And suddenly Katie knew. Oh God, she knew!

She almost stumbled over Don in her hurry to get around him. "It's not that damn Spaniard, is it?" he shouted after her.

But Katie couldn't take the time to answer, she was already running. Running down the path, bursting past the door in the stockade fence and breaking a fingernail in her urgent haste to pull open the sliding glass door.

Breathless with fear that she was already too late, she dialed the number Ramon had written on the pad beside the phone. She counted the rings, her hope dying with each one that went unanswered.

"Hello," a woman's voice said on the tenth ring when Katie was about to hang up.

"I—I'd like to speak to Ramon Galverra. Is he there?" Katie was so surprised to hear a woman's voice answering what was obviously a residential phone, that she nearly forgot to give the information the woman was obviously waiting for. "My name is Katherine Connelly."

"I'm sorry, Miss Connelly, Mr. Galverra isn't in. We expect him shortly, though. Shall I ask him to call you?"

"Yes, please," Katie said. "Would you be certain that he gets the message that I called, as soon as he arrives?"

"Of course. As soon as he arrives."

Katie hung up the phone and stared at it. Was Ramon really out, or had he asked that friendly-sounding woman to fend Katie off? He'd been furious when Katie told him she'd been married before . . . perhaps now that his passion had had two days to cool off, he was no longer interested in acquiring a "used" wife. What should she do if he didn't return her call? Should she assume that he didn't get her message and call him back? Or should she take the hint and realize that he didn't want to talk to her?

Twenty minutes later the phone rang. Katie snatched it up and breathlessly said, "Hello."

Ramon's voice sounded even deeper on the telephone. "Katie?"

She squeezed the receiver so tightly that her hand ached. "You said to call if I—I wanted to talk." She paused, hoping he would now say something to help her, but he remained silent. Drawing a long breath, Katie said, "I would like to talk . . . but I'd rather not do it on the telephone. Ramon, could you possibly come over?"

There was no emotion in his voice. All he said was "Yes."

But that was enough. Katie glanced down at the yellow bikini and flew into her room to change it. She debated over what to wear as if what she selected might make the difference between success and failure. Finally choosing a soft peach cowl-neck top and matching slacks, she dried and brushed her hair, added peach lipstick, some blusher, and then mascara. Her eyes were sparkling and her color was high as she looked in the mirror. "Wish me luck," she said to her reflection.

She went into the living room, started to sit down, then snapped her fingers. "Scotch," she said aloud. Ramon liked Scotch; she didn't have any. Leaving the front door slightly ajar, Katie raced next door and borrowed a bottle of J&B from the man who lived there.

She half-expected to find Ramon waiting for her in the apartment when she came back, but he wasn't. She went into the kitchen and fixed Ramon's Scotch the way he ordered it when they were out—on the rocks with a splash. Critically, she held the glass up to the light surveying the contents. Exactly how much was a splash, anyway? And why had she done such a stupid thing as to mix his drink so early that the ice would melt by the time he got here? She decided she would drink it. Wrinkling her nose at the taste, she carried the glass into the living room and sat down.

At a quarter to nine the shrill ring of the doorbell brought her leaping out of her chair.

Restraining herself at the last moment from flinging the door wide, she composed her features into a formal smile and opened it properly. In the mellow glow of the gaslight Ramon was framed in her doorway, looking very tall and devastatingly handsome in a light gray suit and maroon tie. His eyes looked directly into hers, his expression unreadable, neither warm nor cold.

"Thank you for coming," Katie said, stepping back and closing the door after him. She was so nervous she couldn't think where to begin. She decided to opt for a compromise. "Sit down and I'll fix you a drink."

"Thank you," he said. He walked into the living room and took off his suit jacket. Without even turning his head to glance in her direction, he tossed it carelessly over the back of a chair.

Katie was thoroughly abashed by his attitude, but at least if he was taking off his jacket he expected to stay for a little while. When she returned from the kitchen with his drink, he was standing with his back to her, his hands in his pockets, staring out her living-room window. He turned when he heard her and for the first time Katie saw the deeply etched lines of strain and fatigue at his eyes and mouth. Anxiously she scanned his features. "Ramon, you look exhausted."

He loosened the knot of his tie and took the glass Katie was holding out to him. "I have not come here to discuss the state of my health, Katie," he informed her brusquely.

"No, I know," Katie sighed. He was cold, remote and, Katie sensed, still extremely angry with her. "You aren't going to help me get this over with, are you?" she said, voicing her thought aloud.

His dark eyes were impassive. "That depends entirely upon what you have to say to me. As I told you before, there was little I could offer you if you married me, but one of the things I offered you was honesty between us. Always. I expect the same from you."

Nodding, Katie turned away from him, grasping the back of a chair for physical support since it was perfectly obvious she wasn't going to get any moral support from the man behind her. Drawing a shaky breath, Katie closed her eyes. "Ramon, at the church on Tuesday, I—I realized that you are probably a devout Catholic. And then I realized that if you are, you couldn't—wouldn't marry me if I had been married in the Catholic church and then divorced. That's why I told you I was divorced. It wasn't a lie, I *was* divorced, but David is dead now."

The voice behind her was coolly unemotional. "I know."

Katie gripped the back of the chair so hard her fingers went numb. "You know? How could you?"

"You had told me once before that I reminded you of someone else, someone whose death brought you great release. When you were telling me about your former husband, you again made the remark that I remind you of him. I assumed that you probably did not know two men who remind you of me. Besides, you are an extremely transparent liar."

His complete indifference tore at Katie's heart. "I see," she said, her throat constricting with tears. Apparently Ramon didn't want another man's wife, regardless of whether she was a divorcée or a widow. As if she had to further punish herself by actually having him tell her that in so many words, Katie whispered, "Would you mind explaining to me why you are still angry with me, even after what I've just told you? I know you are, only I'm not sure why you are, and—"

His hands gripped her arms and he spun her around, his fingers pressing into her flesh. "Because I love you!" he gritted tersely. "And for two days you have put me through a living hell." His voice sounded harsh, as if it were being gouged from his chest. "I love you, and for nearly forty-eight hours I have waited for you to call, dying inside with each hour that you did not."

With a teary smile Katie laid her hand against his cheek and jaw, trying to soothe away the tautness with her fingertips. "They've been terrible days for me too."

His arms closed around her with stunning force, his mouth opening over hers in a kiss that demanded she return the same stormy passion that he was offering her. His hands claimed her body, stroking her neck, her back, her breasts, then sweeping down, pulling her tightly to his rigidly aroused manhood. Instinctively Katie moved her hips against him. Ramon groaned with rampaging desire and plunged his hand into her hair, holding her mouth to his as his tongue began matching her inflaming movements.

He tore his mouth from hers and lavished scorching kisses on her face, her eyes, her neck. "You are going to drive me out of my mind, do you know that?" he murmured thickly. But Katie couldn't answer. His lips had already recaptured hers and she was drowning in an ocean of pleasure, willingly sinking beneath the waves of rapture that sent her deeper with each touch of his hungry, searching mouth and hands.

Katie slowly began to surface as the pressure of his lips against hers lessened, and then was gone. Feeling deprived and bereft, she laid her cheek against his chest, her heart racing like a trip-hammer and his own thundering in her ear.

His hand cupped her cheek and Katie lifted her gaze to his, melting at the new tenderness she saw in his expression. "Katie, I would have married you if you had married that animal in every church on earth and then divorced him in every court."

Katie hardly recognized the breathy whisper that was her own voice. "I thought the reason you were furious was because I'd let things come so far between us without telling you I had been married before."

He shook his head. "I was furious because I knew you were lying to me about your husband being alive so that you would have an excuse not to marry me; furious because I knew you were terrified of what you felt for me, and yet I could not remain here longer to overcome your fear."

Katie leaned up on her toes and pressed a kiss to his warmly responsive lips, but when his arms tightened around her she drew back. Stepping away from the temptation of his nearness, she said, "I think, before I lose my nerve and it gets any later, I had better tell my parents. After tonight there are only three days left for us to try to win them over before we leave."

Katie walked over to the coffee table, picked up the telephone and started to dial her parents' number, then looked up at Ramon. "I was going to tell them we were coming over there, but I think it would be better if I had them come here—" She gave him a nervous, rueful smile. "They can throw you out of their house but they can't very well throw you out of mine."

Waiting for her parents' phone to be answered, she raked her fingers through her rumpled hair, trying to think of how to begin. When her mother answered Katie's mind went completely blank. "Hi, mom," she said. "It's me."

"Katie, is anything wrong? It's nine-thirty."

"No, nothing's wrong." She paused. "I was hoping that, if it's not too late, you and dad might like to come over for drinks."

Her mother laughed. "I suppose we could. We just came back from dinner at the club. We'll be there right away."

Katie, searching madly for some way to keep her mother on the phone while she thought of a way to broach the subject at hand said, "By the way, better bring whatever you want to drink. All I have is Scotch."

"Okay, honey, we will. Want us to bring anything else?"

"Tranquilizers and smelling salts," Katie mumbled indistinctly.

"What, dear?"

"Nothing, Mom, there's something I have to tell you, but before I do, I want to ask you something. Do you remember when I was a little girl and you told me that no matter what I did, you and Dad would always love me? You said that no matter how terrible it was, you—"

"Katie," her mother interrupted sharply. "If you are trying to alarm me, you're succeeding very well."

"Not half as well as I'm about to," Katie sighed miserably. "Mom, Ramon is here. I'm going to leave with him on Sunday and marry him in Puerto Rico. We want to talk to you and dad about it tonight."

For a second the line went silent, then her mother said, "And we are going to want to talk to you, Katherine."

Katie hung up and looked at Ramon, who lifted his brows in inquiry. "I'm Katherine again." Despite her attempt at joking, Katie was unhappily aware of how devastated her parents were going to be by what she was doing.

She was going to stand by her decision to go to Puerto Rico, no matter what they said, but she loved them very much and she hated the unhappiness she was about to cause them.

She waited at the window with Ramon beside her, his arm comfortingly around her shoulders. She knew from the speed at which a pair of headlights made the sweeping turn into the entrance of her apartment complex that her parents had arrived.

Feeling sad and very apprehensive, Katie started to move toward the door but Ramon's voice stopped her. "Katie, if I could take the burden of what you are about to do from your shoulders and your heart, I would do it. I cannot—but I can promise you that for the next three days you will bear the only unhappiness I will ever intentionally cause you."

"Thank you," she whispered achingly, putting her hand in his outstretched palm, feeling strength in the reassuring firmness of his fingers gripping hers. "Have I ever told you how much I love the things you say to me?"

"No," he said with a faint grin. "But it is a good place to start."

There was no time for Katie to ponder his meaning because the doorbell was already ringing insistently.

Katie's father, who was famous for his charm and good manners, tore into the apartment like a whirlwind, accepted Ramon's outstretched hand and said, "Good to see you again, Galverra, enjoyed having you at the house the other day; you've got a goddamned nerve asking Katie to marry you and you're out of your goddamned mind if you think we'll permit it."

Katie's mother, renowned for her ability to maintain her composure even in times of extreme stress, stormed in right on his heels, holding the neck of a liquor bottle in each hand like a juggler. "We won't stand for this," she announced. "Mr. Galverra, we will have to ask you to leave," she said, one bottle pointing majestically to the door. "And you, Katherine, have lost your mind. Go to your room." The other bottle swept grandly toward the hall.

Katie, watching the unfolding scene with fascinated horror, finally recovered enough to say, "Dad, sit down. Mother, you too." When they both sank into chairs, Katie opened her mouth to speak, realized that her mother was holding both liquor bottles propped erectly on her knees, and pried them from her fingers. "Here, Mom, give me these before you hurt yourself."

Having relieved her mother of both weapons, Katie straightened, tried to think of how to begin, rubbed her palms against her peach-clad thighs, and cast a helpless look of appeal to Ramon.

Ramon put his arm around Katie's slim waist, ignoring her father's furious scowl at the gesture, and said calmly to him, "Katie has agreed to return to Puerto Rico with me on Sunday, where we will be married. I realize that this is difficult for you to accept, but it will mean a great deal to Katie to know that she has your support in what she is doing."

"Well, she sure as hell isn't going to get it!" her father snapped.

"In that case," Ramon said evenly, "you will be forcing her to choose between us, and we will both lose. She will still come with me, but she will hate me for causing a rift between the two of you—and she will hate you also, for not understanding and wishing her happiness. It is important to me that Katie be happy."

"It happens to be damned important to us too," Mr. Connelly grated. "Just exactly what kind of life can you give her, living on some two-bit farm in Puerto Rico?"

Katie saw Ramon pale, and she could have strangled her father for trampling on Ramon's pride like this. But when Ramon answered, his voice was composed. "She will have only a small cottage in which to live, but the roof does not leak. She will always have food to eat and clothing to wear. And I will give her children. Beyond that, I can promise Katie nothing—except that she will awaken every single day of her life knowing that she is loved."

Katie's mother's eyes filled with tears, the hostility was draining from her face as she stared at Ramon. "Oh my God . . ." she whispered.

Katie's father, however, was just warming up for battle. "So, Katie will be a drudge, a farm wife, is that it?"

"No, she will be my wife."

"And work like the wife of a farmer!" her father said contemptuously.

Ramon's jaw clenched and he turned even paler. "She will have some work to do, yes."

"Are you aware, Mr. Galverra, that Katie has been to a farm only once in her entire life? I happen to recall the event very vividly." His relentless gaze swerved to his startled daughter. "Do you want to tell him about it, Katherine, or shall I?"

"Dad, I was only twelve years old!"

"So were your three friends, Katherine. But they didn't scream when the farmer wrung the chicken's neck. They didn't call him a murderer at his own table and refuse to eat chicken for two years. They didn't find the horses 'smelly,' the process of milking a cow 'gross,' and a multimillion-dollar farm 'a great big stinking place filled with filthy animals.' "

"Well," Katie shot back mutinously, "they didn't happen to fall into a pile of manure, get bitten by a goose, or kicked by a blind horse, either!" Turning swiftly to Ramon to try to defend herself, Katie was amazed to find him looking down at her with a crooked grin.

"You're laughing now, Galverra," Mr. Connelly said angrily, "but you won't be laughing when you discover that Katie's idea of living within a strict budget is spending everything she makes and charging anything else she wants to my account. She can't cook anything that doesn't come in a bag, box or can; she doesn't know which end of a needle to thread; she——"

"Ryan, you are exaggerating!" Mrs. Connelly unexpectedly intervened. "Katie has lived on her own income since the day she graduated from college, and she does know how to sew."

Ryan Connelly looked ready to explode. "She does petitpoint or some damn thing like that. And not well! I still don't know whether that thing she did for us is supposed to be a fish or an owl, and neither do you!"

Katie's shoulders began to shake with helpless mirth. "It's a——a mushroom," she croaked, turning into Ramon's willing arms and dissolving with laughter. "I——I made it when I was fourteen." Wiping at her tears of hilarity, she leaned back in Ramon's embrace and raised her sparkling eyes to his. "Do you know——I thought they were going to think *you* weren't good enough for *me*."

"What we think," Ryan Connelly snapped, "is——"

"Is that Katie is ill-equipped for the kind of life she would have to lead with you, Mr. Galverra," Mrs. Connelly interrupted her husband's outburst. "Katie's 'working' experience has been at college and in her job, the sort of work that is done with the mind, not the hands and back. She graduated with high honors from college, and I know how hard she works at the job she has. But Katie has absolutely no experience with backbreaking physical labor."

"Nor will she have, being married to me," Ramon replied.

Ryan Connelly was evidently finished with trying to be reasonable. He jerked to his feet, took two long furious strides, then swung around glaring at Ramon with anger emanating from every pore. "I misjudged you the other day at our house, Galverra. I thought to myself that there was pride in you, and honor, but I was wrong."

Beside her, Katie felt Ramon go absolutely rigid as her father continued his blistering tirade. "Oh, I knew you were poor——you said as much, but still I gave you credit for having some decency. Yet you stand here and tell us that although you can offer her nothing, you are going to take our daughter from us, take her from everything she knows, take her from her family, her friends——I ask you, is this the action of a decent, honorable man? You answer me that, if you dare."

Katie, about to intercede, took one look at Ramon's murderous expression and stepped back. In a low, terrible voice, he drawled contemptuously, "I would take Katie away from my own brother! Is *that* answer enough for you?"

"Yes, by God, it's enough! It tells me what kind of——"

"Sit down, Ryan," Mrs. Connelly said sharply. "Katie, you and Ramon go into the kitchen and fix our drinks. I would like to speak to your father privately."

Shamelessly eavesdropping in the doorway while Ramon fixed the drinks, Katie watched her mother walk over to her father and put her hand on his arm. "We've lost the battle, Ryan, and you're antagonizing the victor. That man is trying very hard not to fight you, yet you're deliberately backing him into a corner until he has no choice but to retaliate."

"He's not the victor yet, dammit! Not till Katie gets on that plane with him. Until then, he's the enemy, but he's no victor."

Mrs. Connelly smiled gently. "He's no enemy of ours. At least, he's no enemy of mine. He hasn't been since the moment he looked at you and told you that Katie will live every day of her life knowing that she is loved."

"Words! Nothing but words!"

"Spoken to us, Ryan. Spoken sincerely and without embarrassment to Katie's parents—not whispered to her in some heated moment. I can't even think of a man who would say a thing like that to a girl's parents. He'll never let her be hurt. He won't be able to give her the material things, but he'll give her everything in life that really matters. I know he will. Now give in gracefully, or you'll lose even more." When her husband looked away from her, she touched his face, turning it toward her.

His deep blue eyes, so like Katie's, were suspiciously moist. "Ryan," she said softly, "it's not really the man himself that you object to, is it?"

He sighed, a deep ragged sigh. "No," he said in a hoarse voice. "It's not the man, not really. It's just that I—I don't want him to take my Katie away. She's always been my favorite, you know that, Rosemary. She was the only one of our children who ever gave a damn about *me;* the only one who ever saw me as something beside an open wallet; the only one who ever noticed when I was tired or worried and tried to cheer me up." He drew a long, labored breath. "Katie's been like a ray of sunlight in my life, and if he takes her away, I won't be able to see my Katie shine anymore."

Katie, unaware that Ramon had come to stand behind her, leaned her head against the doorframe, tears streaming unchecked down her cheeks.

Tipping up his wife's chin, Ryan took out his handkerchief and dabbed at the tears on her face. Mrs. Connelly managed a smile. "We should have expected this . . . it's exactly the sort of thing Katie would do. She was always so full of joy and love, so ready to give of herself. She always befriended the child no one would play with, and there was never a stray dog that Katie didn't fall in love with. Until now, I thought David had destroyed that beautiful, giving part of her, and I've hated him for it . . . but he didn't." Tears spilled over her lashes, glittering on her cheeks. "Oh, Ryan, don't you see—Katie's found another stray she loves."

"The last one bit her," Ryan chuckled sadly.

"This one won't," his wife said. "He'll protect her."

Holding his tearful wife in his arms, Ryan glanced across the room and saw that Katie was likewise crying in Ramon's arms, his handkerchief clutched in her hand. With a fleeting smile of conciliation at the tall man who held his daughter so protectively close, Ryan said, "Ramon, do you have a spare handkerchief?"

The brief flash of Ramon's smile accepted the truce. "For the women, or for us?"

When her parents left, Ramon asked to use the telephone and Katie went out to the patio so that he could have privacy to make his call. She wandered around, absently touching the plants growing in huge redwood containers, then perched a hip on the back of one of the lounge chairs, gazing up at the stars spilling like diamonds across the sky.

Ramon came to the open glass door and stopped, arrested by the sheer beauty of the picture she made. Lamplight from within the apartment silhouetted her against the black velvet night. With her hair falling in a loose, glorious tumble down her shoulders, there was a lush ripeness in her profile, combined with a quiet pride in the tilt of her chin that added to her allure, making her seem at once provocative and elusive.

Sensing his presence, Katie turned her head slightly. "Is something wrong?" she asked, thinking of his phone call.

"Yes," he said with tender gravity. "I am afraid that if I come any closer I will discover that you are only a dream."

A smile that was sweet yet sensual touched Katie's lips. "I'm very real."

"Angels are not real. No man can expect to reach out and take an angel in his arms."

Her smile widened delightfully. "When you kiss me, my thoughts are anything but angelic."

Stepping onto the patio he crossed to her, his eyes looking deeply into hers. "And what are your thoughts when you sit alone out here gazing up at the sky like a goddess worshiping the stars?"

Just the timbre of his deep quiet voice stirred Katie; yet now that she had committed herself to him she felt a peculiar shyness. "I was thinking how unbelievable it is that in just seven days my entire life has changed. No, not seven days, seven seconds. The moment you asked me for directions, my whole life veered onto a different course. I keep wondering what would have happened if I had walked down the hall five minutes later."

Ramon drew her gently to her feet. "Do you not believe in fate, Katie?"

"Only when things go wrong."

"And when they go beautifully?"

Katie's eyes danced. "Then, it's because of my clever planning and hard work."

"Thank you," he said with a boyish grin.

"For what?"

"For all of the times in the last seven days that you have made me smile." His lips covered hers in a warm, sweet kiss.

Katie realized that he had no intention of making love to her tonight, and she was grateful and touched by his restraint. She was emotionally spent and physically exhausted.

"What are your plans for tomorrow?" she asked a few minutes later, when he was leaving.

"My time is yours," Ramon said. "I had intended to leave for Puerto Rico tomorrow. Since we will not be leaving until Sunday, the only commitment I have here is to breakfast with your father in the morning."

"Would you like to take me to work tomorrow morning before you meet him?" Katie asked. "It will give us some time together and you could pick me up afterward."

Ramon's arms tightened around her. "Yes," he whispered.

Katie sat at her desk idly rolling her pen between her fingers. Virginia was attending the Friday morning operations meeting, which gave Katie until ten-thirty to make up her mind. An hour and a half to decide whether to resign her job or request two weeks' vacation and two additional weeks' leave of absence without pay.

She knew what Ramon wanted—no, expected—her to do. He expected her to resign, to make the break and sever all ties. If she merely requested a month off instead of resigning, he would feel that she was not committing herself wholeheartedly to him, that she was keeping an avenue of escape open to her.

Her mind drifted back to the way Ramon had looked at her this morning when he arrived to take her to work. His dark eyes had studied her face with piercing intensity. "Have you changed your mind?" he had asked, and when Katie replied that she hadn't, he had gathered her into his arms and kissed her with a mixture of violent sweetness and profound relief.

Each moment she spent with Ramon she grew closer to him emotionally. Her heart, for whatever reasons, kept telling her that he was right for her, that what she was doing was right. Her mind, however, was screaming warnings at her. It told her this was happening too fast, too soon, and worse, kept tormenting her that Ramon was not what he seemed to be, that he was hiding something from her.

Katie's blue eyes clouded. This morning he had arrived wearing a beautiful loose-sleeved gold golf sweater. Twice before he had worn well-tailored business suits. It seemed so peculiar that a farmer, particularly an impoverished one, would own such clothes that Katie had bluntly asked him about it.

Ramon had smilingly informed her that farmers owned suits and sweaters just like other men. Katie had tentatively accepted that answer, but when she tried to find out more about him, he had evaded her questions by saying, "Katie, you will have many questions about me and about your future, but the answers are all in Puerto Rico."

Leaning back in her chair, Katie somberly watched the controlled bustle of activity in the personnel reception area where applicants were filling out forms, taking tests and waiting to see Katie or one of her five male counterparts who all reported to Ginny.

Perhaps she was wrong to be uneasy about Ramon. Perhaps he wasn't being deliberately evasive. Perhaps this niggling, persistent fear was simply the result of her gruesome experience with marriage to David Caldwell.

Then again, maybe it wasn't. She would have to find out in Puerto Rico, but until all her fears were resolved, she could not risk resigning her job. If she did resign today she would be resigning without notice. If she resigned without notice, she would not be eligible for rehire at Technical Dynamics, nor would she get a good reference from them if she tried to go to work for another employer. Besides, Virginia would look like an absolute fool when she had to explain to the vice-president of operations, who had just approved Katie's enormous raise, that Katie, Virginia's own protégée, had resigned without notice—like the most irresponsible transient who swept the floors.

Katie stood up, absently ran a smoothing hand over her elegant chignon, and walked out into the reception area, past Donna and the two other secretaries who worked in personnel. Going into one of the cubicles where typing tests were given, she rolled a clean sheet of paper into the electric typewriter and stared at it, her hands poised indecisively over the keys.

Ramon was expecting her to resign. He had said he loved her. Equally as important, Katie sensed instinctively that he needed her; he needed her very much. She felt disloyal merely taking a month off. She considered lying to him about it, but honesty mattered very much to Ramon and it was something that mattered a great deal to Katie too. She didn't want to lie to him. On the other hand, after she had agreed last night to go to Puerto Rico and marry him, she couldn't imagine how to explain her doubts and misgivings this morning. She wasn't even certain it would be wise to tell him how she felt yet. If she had told David that she suspected some hidden side to his character, he would have gone out of his way to conceal it and convince her otherwise. It seemed far better to simply go to Puerto Rico and give herself time to know Ramon better. With time, her doubts would either be resolved or her suspicions would be confirmed.

Sighing, Katie tried to think of a better excuse to give Ramon for her decision not to resign. It came to her in a flash of inspiration. It was the truth; it relieved all her feelings of disloyalty to Ramon, and it was something she would be able to make him understand. It was so obvious that Katie was amazed she had even considered resigning without notice.

Quickly and efficiently she typed out a formal request to Virginia for two weeks' vacation beginning the next day, followed by two weeks' leave of absence without pay. Tonight she would simply explain to Ramon that she could not possibly have resigned without notice in order to get married. Men did not resign without notice to get married, and if Katie did it would reflect badly on all the other women who were struggling so desperately for an equal opportunity to obtain positions in management. One of the most frequent arguments against hiring a woman in a management position was that they quit to get married or to have babies or to follow their husband when he was transferred. The director of operations was a closet male chauvinist. If Katie resigned without notice to get married, he would never let poor Virginia forget it, and he'd find some legally acceptable reason to disqualify any other female candidate Virginia wanted to hire for Katie's job. If, on the other hand, Katie resigned while on vacation in Puerto Rico, the two weeks remaining to her as leave of absence would constitute two weeks' notice. That meant she would have only two weeks to resolve her fear about marrying Ramon.

Nevertheless, Katie felt tremendously relieved. Now that she'd thought about it rationally, she decided that when and if she did resign while in Puerto Rico, she would not say that she was doing so to get married. She would say what men always said: she was resigning "to accept a better position."

Having decided that, Katie wound another sheet of paper into the type-writer, and dating it two weeks hence, formally resigned in order to accept a better position.

It was nearly eleven-thirty before Katie was finished with the applicants she was scheduled to interview. Picking up her vacation request and her post-dated resignation, she walked into Virginia's office, then hesitated.

Virginia was engrossed in recording figures on a huge ledger sheet, her dark head of short-cropped hair bent over the task. She looked, as she always did, businesslike and feminine. *The Dainty Dynamo*, Katie thought with affection.

Straightening her navy blazer and smoothing the pleats of her red-and-blue-plaid skirt, Katie plunged in. "Ginny, can you spare me a few minutes?" she asked nervously, using the nickname she ordinarily used only after business hours.

"If it's not urgent, give me half an hour to finish this report first," Ginny replied without looking up.

With each second Katie's tension was mounting. She didn't think she could last another half hour. "It—it's rather important."

At the shakiness in Katie's voice, Ginny quickly raised her head. Very slowly, she laid her pen on the desk and watched Katie approach, her forehead creased with puzzled concern.

Now that the time had come, Katie couldn't think how to begin. She handed Virginia her vacation-leave-of-absence request.

Virginia scanned it, the vague alarm clearing from her forehead. "It's short notice to request a month off," Ginny said, laying the paper aside. "But you're entitled to the vacation, so I'll approve it. Why are you also requesting two weeks' leave of absence?"

Katie sank into the chair in front of Virginia's desk. "I want to go to Puerto Rico with Ramon. While I'm there I'll decide whether or not to marry him. In case I do decide to do that—here's my resignation. The two weeks' leave of absence can serve as my notice, that is, if you'll let me do it that way."

Virginia sank back in her chair and stared at Katie in astonishment. "Who?" she said.

"The man we talked about on Wednesday." When Virginia continued to stare at her incredulously, Katie explained, "Ramon has a small farm in Puerto Rico. He wants me to marry him and live there."

Virginia said "My God."

Katie, who had never seen Virginia like this, added helpfully, "He's Spanish, actually."

Virginia said "My God" again.

"Ginny!" Katie implored desperately. "I know this is sudden, but it's not that unbelievable. It's—"

"Insane," Virginia announced flatly, at last recovering her brisk composure. She shook her head as if to clear it. "Katie, when you mentioned this man two days ago I imagined him as not only handsome, but having a style and sophistication to match yours. Now you tell me that he's a Puerto Rican farmer, and you're going to be his wife?"

Katie nodded.

"I think you've lost your mind, but at least you have sense enough not to resign and burn all your bridges behind you. In four weeks, or much less, you'll regret this insanely romantic—and utterly absurd—impulse. You know I'm right or you wouldn't be asking for a leave, you'd be resigning."

"It isn't insane and it isn't an impulse," Katie said, her eyes pleading with Ginny to understand. "Ramon is different—"

"I'll bet he is!" Ginny agreed disdainfully. "Latin men are impossibly chauvinistic."

Katie ignored that because she already knew that Ramon was very Latin and very chauvinistic. "Ramon is special," she said, embarrassed at trying to put the way she felt about him into words, "He makes me feel special too. He isn't shallow or self-centered like most of the men I've known." Seeing that Ginny was no more convinced than she was before, Katie added, "Ginny, he loves me; I can feel that he does. And he needs me. I—"

"Of course he needs you!" Ginny scoffed. "He's a small-time farmer who can't afford to pay for a cook, housekeeper and bedmate. Therefore, he needs a wife, who for the mere cost of her room and board will be all three." Instantly, Ginny held up an apologetic hand. "I'm sorry, Katie, I shouldn't have said that. I shouldn't impose my own views of matrimony on you. It's just that I honestly feel you could never be content with that sort of life, not when you've had this."

"This isn't enough for me, Ginny," Katie said with quiet assurance. "Long before I met Ramon, I felt that way. I can't seem to be happy devoting all my time to me—my career, my next promotion, my future. It isn't that it's a lonely life, because I'm not lonely at all. It's an empty life; I feel useless and meaningless."

"Do you know how many women long for exactly what you have? Do you know how many women wish they had only themselves to think about?"

Katie nodded, uncomfortably aware that she was indirectly rejecting Ginny's way of life, as well as her own. "I know. Maybe it would be right for them. It isn't right for me."

Ginny glanced at her watch and regretfully stood up. "I've got to hurry, I'm due at a meeting downtown, and I won't be back until after you've left. don't worry about calling me within two weeks. Give yourself all four of those weeks. If you decide to resign, I'll simply put this in your file and say that you gave it to me in advance. It's bending company policy, but what are friends for?" She skimmed the letter and smiled at Katie's reason for resignation. " 'To accept a better position,' " she quoted. "Very nicely done."

Katie stood up too, her eyes aching with sentimental tears. "In that case, I guess this is goodbye."

"No, Katie," Ginny said with a laugh as she began shoving papers into her slim briefcase. "Two weeks from now you'll begin getting bored. Four weeks from now you'll miss the challenge of your career. You'll be back. In the meantime, have a nice vacation—that's all you really needed, anyway. you're just a little tired. I'll see you in a month—or sooner."

At 5:05 Katie plunged through the revolving glass doors and dashed across the pavement to where Ramon had pulled the car up at the curb to wait for her. She slid into the seat, bravely met his inquiring look and said, "I took a month's vacation instead of resigning."

His jaw tightened and Katie twisted in her seat to face him. "The reason I did was that—"

"Not now!" he snapped curtly. "We will discuss it when we get to your apartment."

They walked into her apartment together, neither of them having spoken a word during the thirty-five-minute ride home. Katie's frayed nerves stretched taut as she put her purse down, shrugged out of the navy blazer, and turned toward him. Aware of his smoldering anger, she asked cautiously, "Where do you want me to begin?"

His hands shot out, gripping her arms. "Begin with why," he ordered harshly, giving her a shake. "Tell me why!"

Katie managed to keep her fear-widened blue eyes on his. "Please don't look at me this way. I know you're hurt and you're angry, but you shouldn't be." Reaching out, she ran her hands up beneath the soft material of his gold golf sweater, her palms flattened against his muscular chest, trying somehow to soothe and gentle him.

The gesture backfired. Ramon jerked her hands away. "Do not try to distract me with your touch, it will not work. This is not a game we are playing!"

"I'm not playing games!" Katie shot back, pulling her hands from his grip with a strength that was fortified by her own simmering anger. "If I wanted to play games with you, I would have lied and told you that I had resigned." Stalking away from him to the center of the room, Katie stopped and whirled around. "I decided to request four weeks off so that I could resign from Puerto Rico for several very important reasons.

"In the first place, Virginia Johnson is not only my boss, she is someone whom I like and respect immensely. If I resign without notice, I'll make Ginny look like a complete fool."

Katie's chin lifted stubbornly as she continued her angry, impassioned speech. "And what about the men? If I quit without notice, it gives them all a perfect reason to feel vindicated and superior because *men* don't run off to get married. I absolutely refuse to be a traitor to my own sex! So . . . when I resign from Puerto Rico *with notice* I will say that I am leaving to 'accept a better position.' Which I happen to think being your wife is!" Katie finished defiantly.

"Thank you," Ramon said almost humbly. Smiling, he started walking toward her.

Katie, who had worked herself into a fine temper, began backing away. "I haven't finished yet," she said, her color gloriously high, her eyes stormy with hurt indignation. "You told me you wanted honesty from me at all times, and when I was honest you bullied and intimidated me. If I'm supposed to be completely truthful, I have to know that no matter how bad the truth is, you aren't going to get angry with me for telling it to you. You were unfair and unreasonable a few minutes ago, and I think you have an impossible temper!"

"Are you finished now?" Ramon asked her gently.

"No, I'm not!" Katie said, all but stamping her foot. "When I touched you, I was only trying to feel close to you. I wasn't playing games and I hated the way you treated me!" Having now exhausted her complaints, Katie glowered past his shoulder, refusing to meet his gaze.

Ramon's voice was coaxing and deep. "Would you like to touch me now?"

"Not in the least."

"Even if I say that I am very sorry, and that I want you to touch me?"

"No."

"You no longer wish to be close to me, Katie?"

"No, I don't."

"Look at me." Ramon's fingers touched her chin, turning her face up to his. "I hurt you, and now you have hurt me back, and we both ache. We can either strike out at each other in our pain until our anger is spent, or we can stop now and begin to teach each other how to heal our hurts. I do not know which way you want it."

Gazing up into his intent eyes Katie realized that he meant that literally; he wanted her to decide whether to turn their battle into a war that would last until their tempers were exhausted, or else tell him what to do or say to soothe her. Katie stared, the gracefully feminine curves of her face vulnerable and uncertain, her eyes deep blue with confusion. Finally she swallowed and bravely said, "I—I would like you to put your arms around me."

With aching gentleness, Ramon drew her into the circle of his arms.

"And I would like you to kiss me."

"How?" he breathed softly.

"With your lips," Katie answered, confused by the question.

His mouth brushed hers sensuously, his lips warm but not parted.

"And your tongue," she clarified breathlessly.

"Will you give me yours?" he asked, beginning to tell her how he wanted his hurt soothed.

Katie nodded, and his mouth opened hungrily over hers, their tongues tangling and caressing. His hands stroked restlessly over her shoulders and back, then down her spine, forcing her hips hard against his pulsing thighs. His mouth devoured hers as he pulled her down onto the sofa to lie across his lap, his fingers fumbling with the tiny buttons on her silk blouse. Impatient with the buttons, his hand returned to her breasts. "Unfasten them," he said in a low, urgent voice.

It seemed to take Katie forever to unbutton her blouse because her hands were trembling, and Ramon never stopped kissing her. When the last one was finally undone, he pulled his mouth from hers and whispered unsteadily, "I want you to take it off for me."

Katie's heart began hammering as she pulled her arms from the sleeves, letting the white silk slide through her shaking fingers. Ramon's gaze dipped to her lacy bra. "That too."

With fire racing through every nerve in her body, Katie unclipped her bra and slowly slid it down her arms. The ivory globes of her breasts swelled proudly beneath his possessive gaze, her nipples slowly hardening as if his fingers, rather than just his eyes, were touching them. Ramon watched them, his eyes burning with passion, his voice rough with it. "I want to see my baby at your breast."

Katie's embarrassment over her body's obvious response to him was eclipsed by the violent yearnings surging through her. Drawing a quivering breath, she said, "Right now, I would rather see you there."

"Give it to me, Katie."

An uncontrollable inner excitement shook her as she curved a hand around his nape, pulling his dark head down and simultaneously lifting her breast, offering her nipple to him. When Ramon began to suck on it, she almost screamed with the raw pleasure. By the time his lips released her, desire was running through her veins like molten steel. "Give me the other one," he ordered thickly.

Katie tremblingly cupped her other breast and lifted it to his mouth. The moment his lips covered it, flames shot through her. "Please stop," she cried softly. "I need you, I can't stand any more."

"You can't?" he breathed, swiftly lowering her to lie on the sofa, his mouth exquisitely exploring her ear, the curve of her neck and cheek, as he lay down beside her. Lost in a frenzy of rampaging desire, Katie felt his hands sliding up under her skirt, pulling the elastic lace band of her panties down from her hips to her lower thighs.

Ramon groaned softly as his fingers traced between her thighs. "You *want* me," he corrected. "You want me but you do not need me yet," he breathed, plundering her mouth with demanding insistence.

Katie was almost sobbing with desire for his possession, her hands feverishly rushing over the taut muscles of his back and shoulders. "I need you," she whispered fiercely, crushing her parted lips to his. "Please—"

Ramon raised his head and said almost gruffly, "You do not need me." Taking one of her hands from around his neck, he pressed it tightly against his rigid arousal. "*That* is need, Katie."

Opening her desire-glazed eyes, Katie focused on his strained face as he said, "You *want* me when I take you in my arms, but I *need* you every moment of every hour. It is an ache that never leaves me; a longing to make you mine that ties me into knots." Abruptly he asked, "Do you know what fear is?"

Bewildered by his sudden change of subject, Katie searched his handsome somber features, but did not attempt to reply.

"Fear is knowing that I have no right to want you, and knowing that I cannot stop myself. Fear is dreading the moment when you will see the small cottage where you will have to live and decide you do not want me enough to live there."

"Don't think that way," Katie pleaded, her fingers smoothing the short hair at his temple. "Please don't."

"Fear is lying awake at night, wondering if you will decide not to marry me, and wondering how I will bear the pain." Gently, he brushed away the tear that trickled from the corner of Katie's eye. "I am afraid of losing you, and if it makes me 'unreasonable' and bad-tempered, then I humbly apologize. It is only because I am afraid."

Melting with tenderness, Katie laid her hand against his jaw and gazed deeply into his dark eyes. "In my whole life," she whispered, "I have never known a man with enough courage to admit he's afraid."

"Katie. . . ." Her name was a hoarse groan that tore from his chest as his mouth came down hard and hungry on hers, his lips and hands fiercely urgent now, guiding her toward the peak of fulfillment, driving her as close to the edge as she was deliberately driving him. And then the doorbell rang.

"Don't answer it!" Katie implored when he immediately pulled out of her arms and sat up. "They'll go away."

Slanting her a rueful smile, Ramon combed his hand through the side of his thick hair, restoring it to order. "No, they will not. In the . . . excitement . . . I forgot to tell you that your parents were coming over to help us pack and then have dinner with us."

Katie jackknifed to her feet, scooping up her clothing as she dashed to the bedroom. "Hurry and let them in or they'll guess what we were doing," Katie told him when she saw that Ramon was merely standing near the sofa, his hands on his hips.

"Katie," he said with a wicked grin, "if I let them in too quickly, they will *see* what we were doing."

"What?" she asked, standing in the doorway to her room, her perplexed gaze sweeping over the sofa for incriminating evidence, then the floor, then over Ramon. "Oh!" she said, blushing like a schoolgirl.

Katie pulled off her clothes in mad haste, telling herself that she was being absolutely absurd. She was twenty-three years old, she had been married before, and she was going to marry Ramon. No doubt her parents assumed they had already made love many times. After all, her parents were modern, sensible people. Very modern and sensible—except where their children's behavior was concerned.

Exactly four minutes after the doorbell rang, Katie strolled out of her room wearing tan slacks and a soft cream jersey turtleneck, her hair brushed into a shining mantle around her shoulders. She managed to give her mother a cheery greeting, but her face was still slightly flushed, her eyes suspiciously languorous, and inwardly she was trembling with little aftershocks of desire.

She found Ramon, who appeared to be feeling none of her sensual sensitivity, fixing drinks for the four of them in the kitchen, laughing about something with her father. "I'll bring these drinks into the living room," Ryan Connelly said, picking up two glasses. Turning, he discovered his bemused daughter staring at her fiancé's profile. "Honey, you look radiant," he said, planting an affectionate kiss on Katie's forehead. "Ramon must be good for you."

Hot color ran up under Katie's cheeks as she smiled helplessly at her father. Waiting until he vanished into the living room, Katie turned to Ramon, who was putting ice into two more glasses. A smile tugged at the corner of his mouth. Without looking at her, he said, "You are blushing, *querida*. And you do look radiant."

"Thank you," Katie said in exasperated amusement. "I look as though I've been ravished, and you look as though you've been reading the newspaper! How can you be so calm?" She started to reach for the drink Ramon had just fixed her, but he put it on the counter beside his. Turning, he drew her tightly into his arms for a long, drugging kiss. "I am not calm, Katie," he whispered against her mouth, "I am starving for you."

"Katie?" her mother called from the living room, causing Katie to pull awkwardly out of Ramon's embrace. "Are you two coming in here, or should we wait out on the patio?"

"We're coming in there," Katie answered hastily. With a laughing look at Ramon, Katie said, "I once read a novel where every time the man and woman began to make love, the phone rang; someone came to the door; or something happened to stop them."

Ramon's grin was lazily amused. "It will not happen to us. I will not permit it."

10

Sunlight glinted on the big jet as it streaked southeastward, thirty thousand feet above the earth.

Careful not to disturb Katie, who was asleep, her shining head resting against his shoulder, Ramon reached across her and pulled the shade down over the window, shielding her beautiful face from the glare of the sun. The flight had been extraordinarily rough, and many of the passengers were showing distinct signs of alarm. But not Katie, Ramon thought with a tender smile at her sleeping form. Beneath her delightfully soft, feminine exterior, Ramon was discovering that she possessed tremendous courage, strength and determination.

Even yesterday and today, when her parents' obvious sadness over her impending departure had placed a terrible burden of guilt on Katie's slim shoulders, she had borne their unhappiness with calm understanding and smiling resolve, despite the emotional strain Ramon could see she was feeling.

On Friday night Katie's parents had volunteered to handle the subletting of her apartment and to pack the rest of her belongings for shipment to

Puerto Rico. Then they had insisted that she spend the weekend at their home instead of her apartment. Although he had also stayed there over the weekend, Ramon had not had either the opportunity or the excuse to be alone with her since Friday.

As the hours had passed, he had watched Katie's tension mounting, bracing himself for the time when she would weigh her uncertain future with him against the love and security her parents and job still offered, and tell him she had changed her mind about going to Puerto Rico. Selfishly, he had longed to get her back to her apartment and into his arms, where, with time and privacy, he knew he could make her passion overwhelm her mind. Yet, even without the physical stimulus of desire, Katie hadn't wavered in her brave resolve to leave with him.

Her long curly lashes made shadows on her creamy cheeks, and he pleasured himself with the sheer beauty of her profile. He was glad he had booked first-class seats for them, because they were roomier. Katie had mistakenly assumed that the reason they were "lucky enough" to fly first class was that the airline had oversold the coach seats and had automatically offered them vacant first-class seats for the same price, and Ramon had let her believe it.

Bitterness seeped through him, hardening his jaw, and Ramon turned his head to stare out the window across the aisle. A few months ago he could have taken Katie to Puerto Rico in Galverra International's private Boeing 727 jet, with its splendid bedroom, dining room and spacious living room, all furnished in magnificent antiques and carpeted in white. Katie would have enjoyed that, Ramon thought. But she would have been more thrilled with his own sleek Lear jet, which he had flown into St. Louis and which was now in a hangar at the St. Louis airport.

The Lear was his plane, not the corporation's, but like everything else he owned, including the houses, the island and the yacht, he had put the small jet up as collateral against loans the corporation had needed and now could not repay. What would have been the point of flying Katie to Puerto Rico in the Lear today, of giving her a taste of the luxurious life he could have offered her—when doing so would only make the life he was now able to afford appear even more drab and impoverished by comparison?

Wearily, he leaned his head against the back of his seat and closed his eyes. He had no right to ask Katie to share his exile, to take her from her fashionable apartment, her career, and ask her to live on a farm in a renovated cottage. It was selfish and wrong of him, but he couldn't bear to think of life without her. Once he could have given her everything, now he could give her nothing—not even honesty. Not yet.

Tomorrow he was scheduled for several meetings, one of which was with his accountant, and he was clinging to the slender hope that his personal financial situation might not be as disastrous as it now seemed. After the meeting he would know exactly where he stood, and then he would have to find some way to explain to Katie who he was and what he had been. He had insisted on honesty between them, and although he had not actually lied to her, he now owed her the truth—the whole truth. The thought of telling Katie that he was a failure twisted his insides into knots. He didn't care if the whole world thought of him that way, but it hurt unbearably to know he would be a failure in Katie's eyes.

It had been bad enough explaining the situation to Katie's father at breakfast Friday morning. Fondness for his future father-in-law softened Ramon's taut features as he recalled the unexpectedly hostile beginning of that meal.

When Ramon had walked into the private men's club where they had agreed to meet, Ryan Connelly had been waiting for him with suppressed anger radiating from his entire body. "What the hell kind of game are you playing, Galverra?" the older man had demanded in a low, furious voice as soon as Ramon sat down. "You're no more a small-time Puerto Rican farmer than I am. It's been driving me crazy why you looked so familiar to me. It wasn't just your name that seemed familiar, it was your face. Last night I remembered the article about you in *Time* magazine, and—"

As Ramon had explained to Katie's father about the impending collapse of Galverra International, Ryan Connelly's fury had given way first to amazement and then to compassionate understanding. Ramon had tried not to smile when Katie's father volunteered financial help. Ryan Connelly was a wealthy man, but as Ramon had explained to him, it would take one hundred investors like Ryan to shore up Galverra International. Otherwise it would still collapse beneath its own weight and take everyone who had invested in the corporation with it.

The big jet dropped sickeningly into a powerful downdraft, then soared upward with a stomach tightening lurch. "Are we landing?" Katie mumbled.

"No," Ramon said. He brushed his lips against her fragrant hair. "Go back to sleep. I will awaken you when we begin our final approach at Miami." Obediently, Katie closed her eyes and snuggled closer to him.

The cockpit door opened and the pilot started down the aisle toward the rest room. The passenger seated in front of Ramon stopped him with some questions and as the pilot bent down to reply, Ramon watched his eyes rove appreciatively over Katie's face, lingering there as he answered. Ramon felt a flash of annoyance that he immediately recognized as jealousy.

Jealousy—another new emotion with which he must learn to cope because of Katie. After bestowing a glacial look on the unfortunate pilot,

Ramon reached for Katie's hand and laced his fingers through hers. He sighed. At this rate, jealousy was going to be his constant companion.

Just walking through the airport with her and watching the men who turned to stare as she passed had set his teeth on edge. Dressed in a turquoise silk dress that showed off her long, shapely legs in their high heels, she looked like a model. No—the models he had known did not have Katie's lush curves or elegant perfection of features. They had glamour. Katie had beauty.

Katie flexed his fingers, and Ramon realized that he'd been possessively tightening his grip on her hand. Lightly, sensuously, he stroked his thumb against her palm. Even in her sleep Katie responded to his touch and moved closer against him. God, how he wanted her! Just having her nestled against his shoulder made him throb with desire and ache with tenderness.

Leaning his head back, Ramon closed his eyes and sighed with profound pleasure. He had done it! He had actually gotten Katie on this plane with him! She was coming to Puerto Rico. She was going to be his. He admired her independence and intelligence, and he adored the vulnerability and softness within her. She was the embodiment of everything he liked in women: she was feminine without being vapid or helpless; proud without being haughty; assertive without being aggressive. Sexually, she was liberated in her thinking but not her actions, which pleased him immensely. He knew he would have hated it if Katie had casually given her beautiful body to other men. She was infinitely more special, more precious to him because she had chosen not to indulge in casual sex. Which, he supposed, made him guilty of applying the double standard for men and women's morality, considering the number of women from St. Moritz to St. Croix he'd had in the last decade.

Ramon smiled inwardly, thinking of how irate Katie would be if she knew he felt this way about her morals. She would accuse him of being everything from outrageously old-fashioned to hopelessly Latin, which was rather humorous, because he suspected that the reason Katie was drawn to him was—

The brief pleasure he'd been feeling was promptly strangled by the same doubt that had been winding tighter and tighter within him for the past several days. He didn't know why Katie was drawn to him. He didn't know why she thought she should marry him, had no idea what reasons she was giving herself for doing so. The only valid reason would be that she loved him.

But she didn't.

Mentally, Ramon recoiled from that truth, yet he knew he had to face it and come to terms with it. Not once had Katie so much as mentioned the word *love*. Three nights ago, when he had told her that he loved her, the words had burst out of him, yet Katie had chosen to act as if she hadn't heard him.

How ironic that when, for the first time in his life, he told a woman he loved her, she hadn't even been able to say she loved him too.

Grimly, he wondered if this was fate's way of repaying him for all the times women had said they loved him and he had responded with silence, or a noncommittal smile, because he refused to claim an emotion he didn't feel.

If Katie didn't think she loved him, why was she on this plane? Sexually, she wanted him, he knew that. From the first moment he had taken her into his arms he had been forcing her to want him more, relentlessly fanning the flames of her body's desire for his. Apparently passion was the only thing she felt for him; desire her only reason for being on this plane.

No, dammit! That couldn't be true. Katie was too intelligent to consider marrying him solely for sexual gratification. She must feel something else for him. After all, there had always been a tremendous magnetic pull between them, and it was emotional as well as physical. If she didn't love him, could he possibly bind her to him with her body alone? Even if he was able to, could he bear to live with her, knowing his feelings for her were so much deeper than hers for him?

11

*R*eturning from the ladies' room in San Juan airport, Katie made her way toward the baggage claim area where the luggage was arriving from their Miami–San Juan flight.

A thrill of anticipation danced up her spine as she listened to the tide of incomprehensible rapid-fire Spanish interspersed with English, being spoken all around her. To her left, a group of distinguished, fair-haired men were speaking what Katie was certain must be Swedish. Behind her was a large cluster of tourists conversing in flowing French. Puerto Rico, she realized with surprised delight, must be a vacation place for more than just Americans.

She scanned the throngs of people and saw Ramon nod toward a porter who immediately changed direction, wheeled his trolley over to Ramon, and began loading Katie's six Gucci suitcases onto it. Katie smiled to herself because everyone else was waving frantically and calling to the busy porters, trying to attract their attention, but Ramon merely had to incline his head. And no wonder, she thought with pride. Dressed in a dark business suit and conservative tie, Ramon was the most impressive-looking man Katie had ever seen. There was an aura of implacable authority and calm purposefulness about him that even a porter couldn't miss. Looking at him, Katie thought he resembled an affluent business executive, not a struggling local farmer. She supposed the porter must have thought so too, and was probably expecting a handsome tip for his services. Uncomfortably, Katie wondered if Ramon realized that.

Why hadn't she suggested that they carry their own luggage? Between them, they could have managed in two or three trips since Ramon was traveling with only one large suitcase and a smaller one. She was going to have to learn to be thrifty, to remember that Ramon had very little money, that he even drove a truck to earn extra.

"Ready?" Ramon asked, placing his hand beneath Katie's elbow and guiding her through the crowded airport.

Taxis were lined up outside waiting for fares. The porter started for the first one at the head of the line with Katie following beside Ramon. "Is the weather always this beautiful?" she asked, lifting her face to the azure sky decorated with fluffy white clouds.

The pleasure in Ramon's smile told her how much he wanted her to like her future home. "Usually it is. The temperature generally remains in the upper seventies, and the easterly trade winds provide a breeze that—" Ramon glanced up to see how far ahead the porter was, and whatever he'd been about to say was left unfinished.

Following his angry gaze, Katie was shocked to see their luggage being loaded into a gleaming maroon Rolls-Royce, which was waiting at the curb ahead of the line of taxis. A chauffeur wearing an immaculate black uniform and visored cap was standing at attention beside the Rolls. As they neared the car he swept open the back door with a flourish, stepping aside for them to enter.

Katie stopped short and looked inquiringly at Ramon, who snapped questions at the chauffeur in Spanish. Whatever the man replied seemed to make Ramon positively furious. Wordlessly, he put his hand against the small of Katie's back and forced her off the curb and into the cool luxury of the Rolls' white leather interior.

"What is going on?" Katie asked as soon as Ramon slid in beside her. "Whose car is this?"

Ramon waited until the chauffeur had closed the passenger door before replying. His voice was tight with the strain of controlling his inexplicable anger. "The car belongs to a man who has a villa on the island, but is rarely here. Garcia, the chauffeur, is er, an old friend of my family. When he found out we were arriving today, he decided to meet us."

"What a thoughtful thing for him to do!" Katie said brightly.

"I specifically said I did not want him to do it."

"Oh," Katie faltered. "Well, I'm sure he meant well."

Turning his attention to the chauffeur, who was now seated behind the steering wheel looking expectantly into the rearview mirror, Ramon pressed a button that opened the glass partition separating the driver from his passengers. In a clipped Spanish voice he issued instructions, then the glass partition glided back into place and the Rolls slid smoothly away from the curb.

Katie had never been in a Rolls-Royce, and she was enchanted with the car. She ran her fingertips over the seat, luxuriating in the feel of unbelievably soft, white glove leather. "What's this?" she asked, leaning forward and pressing a button in the back of the driver's seat. She laughed as a small rosewood writing desk lifted electronically out of the seat and flipped down over her lap. Raising the top, she looked inside and found it equipped with thick parchment writing paper, gold pens and even a tiny gold stapler. "How do I put it back?" she asked, after trying unsuccessfully to push it into place.

"Press the same button again."

Katie did. With a faint mechanical whir the rosewood desk lifted off her lap, flipped up, and retracted into place as the concealing panel of white leather slid down to cover it. "What does that one do?" She smiled, nodding toward the button above Ramon's knees.

Ramon was watching her, his face completely expressionless. "It opens a liquor cabinet concealed in the seat in front of me."

"Where's the television set and stereo?" Katie joked.

"Between the desk and the liquor cabinet."

The delighted smile faded from her lips. Ramon, she realized, was not sharing her enjoyment of the luxury car's unique equipment. After an uncertain pause, she said hesitantly, "Whoever owns this car must be extraordinarily wealthy."

"He was."

"Was?" she repeated. "Is he dead?"

"Financially, he is dead." With that curt, inscrutable reply, Ramon turned his head away and stared out the window.

Bewildered and hurt by his coldness, Katie looked out her own window. Her dismal musings were interrupted as her hand, which was lying limply on the seat between them, was suddenly enclosed in Ramon's warm, firm grasp. With his head still averted, he said harshly, "I wish that I could give you a dozen cars like this one, Katie."

Comprehension dawned, and for a moment Katie was too stunned to speak. Relief washed over her, followed by unabashed amusement. "I wish you could afford to give me just *one* like it. After all, an expensive car is a guarantee of happiness, isn't it?" Ramon's sharp gaze veered toward her, and Katie widened her blue eyes with exaggerated innocence. "David gave me a Porsche for a wedding present, and look how happy my life was with him!"

The stern line of Ramon's mouth relaxed into a faint smile as she continued. "Now, if David had given me a Rolls-Royce, I would have been perfectly content with our marriage. Although," she said as Ramon's arm went around her shoulders, drawing her close to him, "the only thing that would have made my life absolutely ecstatic was—" Her sentence was smothered by the abrupt descent of Ramon's mouth as he covered her lips with his, kissing her deeply . . . kissing her, Katie realized, with gratitude.

When he finally lifted his head she basked in the tenderness of his smile. "What would have made your life absolutely ecstatic?" he teased huskily.

Katie's eyes danced as she snuggled closer to him. "A Ferrari!"

Ramon burst out laughing and Katie felt the tension leave his powerful body. Now things were in their proper perspective, out in the open where they could be laughed about, which was exactly what she had intended.

Puerto Rico took Katie completely by surprise. She had not expected a mountainous tropical paradise with lush green valleys and tranquil blue lakes sparkling in the sunlight. The Rolls climbed steadily along smooth, curving roads bordered with spectacular flowering trees, their branches covered thickly in pink and yellow blossoms.

They passed through picturesque villages nestled between the mountains; each village with its own town square in the center of which was the church with its spire pointing heavenward. Katie craned her neck, her eyes delighting in the vivid colors nature had splashed over hills and meadows, her voice happy as she exclaimed over everything from ferns to farmhouses. Throughout it all, she could feel Ramon's piercing eyes on her, watching her beneath their heavy lids, observing her every reaction. Twice she had turned abruptly to make some enthusiastic comment, and had glimpsed the anxiety in his expression before he could cover it with one of his bland smiles. He desperately wanted her to like his homeland, and for some reason, he seemed unable to believe that she really did.

Nearly an hour after they left the airport, the Rolls passed through another small village and turned off the paved road onto a dirt track, continuing to climb. Katie gasped in speechless wonder; it was as if they were driving through a red silk tunnel illuminated with gossamer sunbeams.

Blossoming royal poinciana trees marched along both sides of them, their laden branches meeting overhead, their fallen scarlet petals literally carpeting the road beneath the tires in deep red. "It's absolutely unbelievable," she breathed, turning to Ramon. "Are we getting close to your home?"

"About a mile and a half farther up this lane," he said, but the tension was back in his features, and his smile was nothing more than a slight curving of his tight lips. He was staring straight ahead as if he were as intent upon discovering what was at the end of the drive as she was.

Katie was about to ask him if the pretty flowers with the scarlet cups were a variety of tulip, when the Rolls emerged from the poinciana's two-mile-long red canopy and pulled into an ugly overgrown yard surrounding a run-down white brick cottage. Trying to hide her appalled disappointment, Katie turned to Ramon, who was staring at the house with an expression of such murderous fury that she unconsciously pressed back into the seat cushions.

Before the car had come to a complete stop in the yard, Ramon had flung open his door, lunged out of the vehicle, slammed the door violently behind him and was striding across the pitiful lawn with rage in every step.

The elderly chauffeur helped Katie out of the car, and they both turned in time to see Ramon rattle the cottage door, then throw his shoulder against it with so much explosive power that it flew off its hinges and crashed onto the floor of the cottage.

Katie stood frozen to the spot, looking at the gaping black hole where a door had been a moment before. Her gaze moved over the shutters hanging at drunken angles over the windows and the paint peeling off the wood trim.

In a flash, all of Katie's optimism and courage deserted her. She missed her beautiful apartment complex with its gas lamps and enclosed patios. She could never live in a place like this; she had been a fool to try to deny her own love of luxury, her own upbringing.

The breeze tugged a few silken strands of hair loose from her elegant chignon. Katie lifted her hand to brush them out of her eyes, trying at the same time to brush away the vision of herself standing in this overgrown weed patch, looking as shabby and unkempt as this awful hovel. In a year or two she would become as slovenly as her surroundings, because living like this would corrode anyone's personal pride until they just didn't care anymore.

Reluctantly she began picking her way along what was left of a brick walk leading to the door of the cottage. Red tiles had blown off the roof, shattering when they hit the walk, and Katie carefully avoided stepping on them with the thin soles of her expensive Italian sandals.

She walked hesitantly through the doorway, blinking her eyes to adjust to the gloom. Revulsion swelled in her throat. The inside of the empty cottage was covered in layers of dirt, filth and cobwebs. Where the sun streamed through the broken slats of the shutters dust floated in the air. How could Ramon live like this, she wondered in horror. He was always so immaculately well-groomed, she couldn't imagine him existing in this . . . this squalor.

With a supreme effort, Katie brought her frantic emotions under control and forced herself to think logically. In the first place, no one had been living here—the dirt hadn't been disturbed for years. Or the mice either, she thought with a shudder as scratching sounds emanated from the walls.

Ramon was standing in the middle of the room, his rigid back to her.

"Ramon?" Her voice was an apprehensive whisper.

"Get out of this place," he gritted in a low voice vibrating with fury. "The filth will cling to you, even if you do not touch anything."

There was nothing Katie wanted to do more than leave here—unless it was to leave for the airport, then home, then her beautiful modern apartment. She started to go, realized that Ramon wasn't following her, stopped and turned toward him again. He was still standing with his back to her, either unwilling—or unable—to turn around and face her. With a stab of compassion Katie realized how much he must have been dreading the moment when she would see this place. No wonder he had seemed so tense when they drove up the lane. Now he was angry because he was embarrassed and ashamed that this run-down cottage was the best he could offer her. She spoke to break the uneasy silence. "You—you said you were born here."

Ramon slowly turned and stared through her as if she didn't exist.

Braving his mood, Katie continued. "I assumed that you meant you had lived here since you were born, but no one has lived here for years, have they?"

"No," he snapped.

Katie winced at his tone. "Has it been long since you were here last?"

"Yes," he bit out.

"Places—houses that haven't been lived in for a while always seem dreary and ugly, even when they're really nice." She was trying desperately to console him, even though she knew he really ought to be consoling her. "It probably doesn't look the way you remember it."

"It looks exactly the way I remember it!"

His scathing sarcasm sliced into Katie's highly sensitized emotions like a razor blade, but still she tried. "If—if it looks exactly as you remember it, why, are you so furio . . . so upset," she amended hastily.

"Because," he said in a terrible voice, "I sent a telegram four days ago asking that as many men as necessary be sent to clean and make repairs to this place."

"Oh," Katie breathed in relieved surprise.

Her evident relief made Ramon's whole body go rigid. His eyes became twin black daggers that impaled her. "Do you have such a low opinion of me that you think I would bring you to live in this—this filthy shack? Now that you have seen it like this, I would not permit you to live here. You would never be able to forget the way it looks now."

Katie stared at him in anger and bewilderment. Only minutes ago she'd been certain of her future and that she was wanted, secure and loved. Now she was certain of nothing, and she was furious with Ramon for unfairly venting his frustration on her.

A dozen indignant rejoinders sprang to mind, only to lodge in her throat behind a lump of sympathetic tenderness that swelled unbearably as she regarded him. Standing there in the middle of the shabby empty house where he was born, Ramon seemed so utterly defeated, and so proudly determined not to show it, that her heart twisted. "I think you have a low opinion of me if you believe that," she said into the charged silence.

Turning away from his narrowed gaze, Katie walked to the two arched doorways leading off the right side of the living room and peeked inside— two bedrooms, one large one at the front of the house, and a smaller one at the rear. "There's a lovely view from both bedroom windows," she announced.

"Neither of which have glass in the frames," Ramon responded tersely.

Katie ignored him and went to another doorway. A bathroom, she surmised with a mental grimace at the rusted sink and tub. An unwelcome image of her parents' sunken marble bath paraded across Katie's mind, followed immediately by the memory of her own modern bathroom at the apartment. Bravely, she banished both from her mind and flipped on a light switch. "There's electricity right to the house," she enthused.

"Which is not turned on," Ramon snapped.

Katie knew she was sounding like a real-estate saleswoman trying to make a sale, but she couldn't help herself. "And this must be the kitchen," she said, walking over to an antiquated porcelain sink standing on steel legs. "Which has hot and cold running water." To prove it, she reached for the taps.

"Do not bother," Ramon said in a tight voice, watching her from the doorway. "They do not work."

Katie's chin lifted as she tried to summon the courage to turn around and face him. In the process she found herself staring out a wide grimy window above the sink. "Ramon," she breathed, "whoever built this house must have loved a view as much as I do." Verdant green hills spread out in a panorama in front of her, their slopes covered in blooming yellow and pink blossoms.

When she swung away from the sink there was genuine pleasure in her expression. "It's beautiful, absolutely beautiful! I would wash dishes for a living if I could look out at that while I washed them." Eagerly, her gaze moved over the large rectangular kitchen. At the opposite end, one entire wall of windows was joined at the corner with another large expanse of windows. Situated in front of them was a crude wooden table and chairs. "It would be like eating on a terrace—you can see for miles in two different directions," she announced, watching a slight uncertainty flicker across Ramon's frozen features. "Why, this kitchen could be made to look bright and spacious!"

Studiously avoiding looking at the peeling linoleum on the uneven floor, Katie turned and marched back into the living room. She walked over to the large panes of glass that extended across two walls and rubbed away a bit of the grime. Peering out through the patch she had cleared, she gazed at the view. "I can see the village!" she exclaimed in awe. "I can even pick out the church. From up here it's like a little white toy village with green hills all round it. Ramon, it's like looking at a—a picture postcard. These windows must have been placed so that no matter where you look there will always be something beautiful to see. Do you know what—?" Unaware that Ramon had walked up behind her, Katie whirled around and collided with his tall, powerful body. "This house has real possibilities!" She met his cynical expression with a bright smile. "All it needs is a fresh coat of paint and some new curtains."

"And an exterminator and an army of carpenters," Ramon replied acidly. "Or better yet, a competent arsonist."

"All right—fresh paint, new curtains, an exterminator and you with a hammer and nails." She bit her lip as a disquieting thought occurred to her. "You *do* know about carpentry, don't you?"

For the first time since they had arrived at the house, Katie saw a glimmer of humor touch his handsome face. "I imagine that I know as much about carpentry as you know about making curtains, Katie."

"Wonderful!" bluffed Katie, who hadn't the foggiest notion how to make a curtain. "Then you won't have any trouble fixing things here, will you?"

He seemed to waver, then he swept the shabby room with a contemptuous glance. His features hardened until his face seemed to be carved out of stone. Katie, realizing that he was about to refuse, put her hand on his arm. "This could be a cozy, cheerful home. I know you're embarrassed because I've seen it looking this way, but that will only make it more rewarding and exciting when it finally looks the way it should. I'll really enjoy helping you restore it—honestly I will. Ramon," she whispered beseechingly when he simply stared at her, "please, please don't spoil it for me like this."

"Spoil it for you?!" he exploded, raking his hand through the side of his hair. "Spoil it for you?" Without warning he reached for her, and Katie found herself crushed against him, his arms wrapped tightly around her. "I knew I should not have brought you to Puerto Rico, Katie," he said in an agonized whisper. "I knew it was selfish of me, but I did it anyway. Now that I have, I know I should send you back home, where you belong. I know it," he said, drawing a ragged breath. "But—God forgive me—I cannot bear to do it!"

Katie wound her arms around his waist and pressed her cheek against the solid hardness of his chest. "I don't want to go home; I want to stay here with you." And—at least for the moment—she was certain she did.

She heard his breath catch and felt the sudden tensing of his muscles. He drew back slightly and tenderly cradled her face between his hands. "Why?" he whispered, his black eyes intently searching hers. "Why do you want to stay here with me?"

A beaming smile lit Katie's features. "So that I can prove to you that this house can become the home of your dreams!"

Her answer caused an unexplainable sadness to shadow his eyes. It lingered there as Ramon slowly bent his head to her. "This is the real reason you want to stay with me, Katie." His lips brushed over hers, warm and tantalizing, while his hands drifted down her shoulders and over her back in an enticing, ever-changing caress.

Every nerve in Katie's body began to quiver in anticipation. It seemed like weeks, not days, since Ramon had kissed and caressed her with stormy passion. Now he was intentionally taking his time, making her wait, teasing her. Katie did not want to be teased and tantalized. Wrapping her arms around his neck, she pressed herself into his muscular body. She kissed him deeply, trying to break his iron control. Against her, she felt the rising hardness tightening his thighs, but as if to retaliate for her having deliberately aroused him, Ramon slid his lips from hers and began kissing the corner of her mouth, trailing his lips over her cheek, down the sensitive column of her neck, then up again to her ear, his tongue sensuously exploring each curve, each crevice.

"Don't!" Katie pleaded with a throbbing ache in her voice. "Don't tease me, Ramon. Not now." She half-expected him to ignore her. Instead, his mouth claimed hers with a fierce hunger and raw urgency that surpassed her own. His hands rushed over her, sliding up her nape and over her shoulders, possessively cupping her aching breasts, then sweeping low to press her tightly against his rigid, pulsing thighs.

Shuddering with pleasure, Katie dug her fingers into the bunched muscles of his shoulders and back, joyously fed the insatiable hunger of his mouth, willingly arched herself against the demanding, rhythmic thrusts of his hardened, aroused manhood.

An eternity later, the pressure of his lips lessened and then was gone as Ramon slowly raised his head. Even in her dazed state, Katie recognized the passion blazing in his eyes and knew he saw it in hers, too. Still shaking with quick, piercing stabs of desire, she watched his sultry gaze dip to her softly parted lips. His arms tightened convulsively as he started to bend his head to her, then hesitated, trying to fight the temptation. "Oh, God!" he groaned, and his mouth hungrily covered hers once more.

Time after time he began to pull away, only to change his mind and bury his lips in hers for another series of long drugging kisses.

When they finally stopped, Katie was shattered. Helplessly, mindlessly, joyously shattered by the combined force of their exchanged passion and pleasure. He rested his cheek against her bright head, his hands gently caressing her back, holding her close against the violent hammering of his heart, while Katie leaned weakly against him, her arms still around his neck.

Several minutes had passed when Katie thought she heard Ramon murmur something. She managed to lift her head, open her languorous blue eyes and look at him. Lost in her dreamy euphoria, she admired the masculine face looking back at her. He really was incredibly handsome, she thought; so utterly masculine with those hard, sculpted features. She liked his firm jawline, his determined chin with its attractive cleft, and the sensuality in the mold of his mouth. And he had the most compelling, riveting eyes—eyes that could melt her or freeze her. His hair was so thick and glossy black, beautifully styled and shaped to lie flat at the sides, yet just long enough for her to run her fingers through it at the nape.

Katie reached up and smoothed the hair at his temple, then rested her hand against his cheek, her thumb idly tracing the cleft in his chin.

Ramon's dark eyes had been watching her. They captured her gaze, holding it, while he turned his head and slid his lips back and forth against her sensitive palm. He spoke, and his deep voice was raw, hoarse with an intense emotion that wasn't passion. "You make me very happy, Katie."

Katie tried to smile, but the painful quality she heard in his voice made her eyes burn with tears. And after three days of emotional turmoil culminating in the last tumultuous hour, she was too weakened to stop them. "You make me happy too," she whispered, as two tears spilled over her lashes.

"Yes," Ramon said with solemn amusement as he watched the shimmering tears. "I can see that."

Katie gaped at him, feeling as if she were teetering on the brink of insanity. Ten seconds ago she could have sworn there were tears in his voice, but now *he* was smiling and *she* was crying. Except she wasn't crying, she was starting to laugh. "I—I always cry when I'm happy," she explained wiping away the two tears.

"Surely not!" he exclaimed in mock horror. "Do you then laugh when you are sad?"

"I probably will," Katie admitted, her face wreathed in a brilliant smile. "I've been all mixed-up ever since I met you." Impulsively, she reached up and pressed a kiss on his warmly responsive lips, then leaned back in his encircling arms. "Garcia will be wondering what we've been doing. I suppose we'd better go."

She sighed with such regret that Ramon grinned at her. "Garcia is a man of great dignity; he would never stoop to speculating about our activities." Nevertheless, Ramon obligingly released her. With his arm around her waist, they walked through the doorway into the sunlight.

Katie was about to ask when they could start working on the house, but Ramon's attention was riveted on a man about sixty years old who was walking into the yard.

When he saw Ramon, his tanned, leathery face broke into a slow smile. "Your telegram only arrived an hour ago—just before I saw the Rolls pass through the village. Do these old eyes of mine trick me, Ramon, or is it really you I see standing here?"

Grinning, Ramon held out his hand. "Your eyes are as sharp as the night you saw smoke coming through a window and caught me in the shed with a pack of cigarettes, Rafael."

"They were my cigarettes," the man named Rafael reminded him, simultaneously shaking Ramon's hand and affectionately clapping him on the arm.

Ramon winked at Katie. "Unfortunately, I had none of my own to smoke."

"Because he was only nine years old, and too young to buy them," Rafael explained, flashing a conspiratorial smile at Katie. "You should have seen him, *señorita*. He was lying on his back on a bale of hay with his hands behind his head, looking like a very important man who was enjoying his leisure. I made him eat three of the cigarettes."

"Did that cure you?" Katie laughed.

"It cured me of cigarettes," Ramon admitted. "I switched to cigars after that."

"And then to girls," Rafael said with humorous severity. He turned to Katie. "When Padre Gregorio read your banns at mass this morning, the *señoritas* all wept with disappointment, and Padre Gregorio sighed with relief. Praying for Ramon's immortal soul had been Padre Gregorio's most time-consuming task." Pausing in this good-natured monologue to enjoy Ramon's visible discomfort, he added, "But you are not to worry, *señorita*. Now that he is engaged to you, Ramon will no doubt mend his wicked ways and ignore those fast women who have been chasing him all these years."

Ramon shot a quelling look at the older man. "If you are through assassinating my character, Rafael, I will introduce you to my fiancée—assuming Katie is still willing to marry me after listening to you."

Katie was stunned that marriage banns—the formal proclamation of an intended marriage—were already being read in church here. How had Ramon accomplished that from St. Louis? Somehow, Katie managed a weak smile while Ramon introduced Rafael Villegas as the man who had been "like a second father" to him, but it was several minutes before she could pull herself together and pay attention to their conversation.

"When I saw the car heading in this direction," Rafael was saying, "I was glad that you are not ashamed to bring your *novia* here and show her where your roots are, even though you now—"

"Katie," Ramon interrupted abruptly. "You are not accustomed to this sun yet. Perhaps you would rather wait in the car where it is cool."

Surprised by this politely worded dismissal, Katie said goodbye to Rafael and obediently returned to the air-conditioned Rolls. Whatever Ramon was telling Señor Villegas had the man looking almost comically bewildered, then stunned, then extremely grim. She was relieved that when they finally shook hands and parted they were both smiling again.

"Forgive me for asking you to leave like that," Ramon said, sliding into the car. "Among other things, I needed to discuss some work I need done to the cottage, and it would embarrass Rafael if you were present when we talked about money." Pressing the button that opened the glass between the chauffeur and themselves, Ramon issued instructions in Spanish, then shrugged out of his suit jacket, pulled off his tie, loosened the top buttons of his cream-colored shirt, and stretched his legs out. He looked, Katie thought, like a man who had just been through an ordeal, but was relatively pleased with the outcome.

Questions tumbled over in her mind, and she started with the least important first. "Where are we going now?"

"We are going to the village where we will have a quiet meal." Ramon put his arm around her shoulders, his fingertips playing with the little turquoise stud in her earlobe. "While we are dining, Rafael will have his married daughter prepare her spare bedroom for you. I had intended for you to stay at the house but it is not habitable. Besides, I had not considered the need for a chaperon for you until Rafael reminded me."

"A chaperon! You can't mean it," Katie sputtered. "It's—it's—"

"Necessary," Ramon provided for her.

"I was going to say Victorian, archaic and silly."

"True. But in our case it is still necessary."

Katie's delicate brows rose. "Our case?"

"Katie, this village is like a small town where very little happens, so everyone watches what everyone else does, and they gossip about it. I am a bachelor, therefore, an object of interest."

"So I gathered from what Señor Villegas said," Katie retorted primly.

Ramon's lips twitched, but he made no comment. "As my fiancée, you too are an object of interest. What is more important, you are also an American, which makes you a target for criticism. There are many here who believe that American women all have loose morals."

Mutiny was written on Katie's beautiful face. Her high cheekbones were tinted with pink and her blue eyes were sparkling dangerously. Ramon, correctly interpreting the danger signals, swiftly pulled her close and pressed his lips to her temple. "By 'chaperon' I did not mean someone to follow you around, Katie. I only meant that you could not live alone. If you do, the moment I set foot through your door the gossips will say that you let me share your bed, and because you are an American, everyone else will believe it. You may think you do not care, but this is going to be your home. You will not like it if, even years from now, you cannot walk through the village without having people whisper about you."

"I still object to the idea, on principle," Katie said, but without much conviction because Ramon was sensuously exploring her ear.

His muffled laugh sent thrills racing down her spine. "I hoped you were objecting to the idea because you thought a chaperon would make it more difficult for us to . . . be alone together."

"That too," Katie admitted with breathless candor.

Ramon's chuckle was rich and deep. "I am going to stay with Rafael's family. Gabriella's house, where you will be staying, is only a mile away." Smoothing his hand from her silken cheek back to the coil of her chic chignon, he said huskily. "We will find the time, and the places, to share ourselves with each other."

Katie thought that was a beautiful way to describe making love; two people sharing their bodies with each other so that each could derive pleasure from the other. She smiled, wondering if she would ever understand him. He was such a unique combination of gentleness and strength; of raw, potent virility overlaid with smooth sexual expertise and tender restraint. No wonder she'd been confused since the day she met him. She'd never known anyone even remotely like him in her entire life!

At the edge of the village square Garcia pulled over and stopped. "I thought you might prefer to walk," Ramon explained, helping Katie to alight. "Garcia will deliver your things to Gabriella's house, then go back to Mayagüez, where he lives."

The sun was beginning its descent in a blaze of pink and gold against the blue sky as they strolled across the plaza in the center of which was a stately old Spanish church. "This is where we will be married," Ramon told her.

Katie's gaze roamed appreciatively over the church and the small buildings that surrounded it on all four sides, creating the village square. The Spanish influence was evident in the arched doorways and windows, and the black wrought-iron trim on the shops that sold everything from fresh bakery goods to small, intricately carved religious figurines. Flowers bloomed everywhere, hanging from balconies and windows, and in huge urns in front of the shops, adding their vibrant splashes of color to the picturesque little square. Tourists with cameras ambled across the plaza, stopping to peer into shop windows or sit at the little sidewalk café, sipping cool rum drinks as they watched the villagers.

Katie glanced at Ramon, who was walking beside her with his suit jacket hooked on a thumb over his shoulder. Despite his outwardly casual appearance, Katie could almost feel his anxiety as he waited for her first reaction to his village. "It's beautiful," she said honestly. "Very picturesque and charming."

The sideways look he slanted her was dubious. "But tiny, and not what you expected?"

"Prettier and more convenient than what I expected," Katie argued stubbornly. "It even has a general store. And," she added with a teasing glance, "it has two hotels! I'm very impressed."

Her joking succeeded where her sincere compliments had not. Grinning, he put his arm around her waist and drew her close against his side for a brief, tight hug. "The Casa Grande," he said, nodding toward a quaint three-story hotel with wrought-iron balconies, "boasts ten guest rooms. The other has only seven, but it has a small dining room and the food used to be good. We will dine there."

The restaurant had five tables, four of which were occupied with tourists who were laughing and talking. Katie and Ramon were given the remaining table. The waiter lit the candle in the center of the red-and-white-checked tablecloth and took their order. Ramon leaned back in his chair and smiled at Katie who was watching him with puzzled eyes. "What are you thinking about?" he asked.

"I was wondering where you lived before now, and what you've been doing. You couldn't have been working at your farm, or you wouldn't need to stay with Rafael."

Ramon answered slowly, almost cautiously. "I have lived near Mayagüez in the past, and until now I have been working for a company that is going out of business."

"Is the company in the farming business?" Katie asked.

Ramon hesitated and then he nodded. "Among other things, it is a canning operation. Instead of going to work for another company, I had already decided when I met you that I would prefer to work on my own farm rather than pay someone else to do work that I could be doing. During the next two weeks, I will still devote some time to the company; the rest I will spend working with the men who will be repairing our house."

Our house. The phrase made Katie's stomach clench. It sounded so strange. So final. Averting her eyes, she played with her glass, slowly turning it in her fingers.

"What frightens you about that, Katie?" he asked after a pause.

"Nothing. I—I was just wondering what I would be doing while you're gone."

"While I am working you can shop for things we will need for our house. Many items you will be able to buy in the villages. Furniture will have to be purchased in San Juan. Gabriella will take you to the shops and act as translator for you where one is needed."

"Furniture?" Katie stared. "Don't you have furniture in your place in Mayagüez?"

"I am going to sell it. It would not be appropriate for the cottage, anyway."

Katie, seeing the way his mouth tightened, assumed that his furniture would be an embarrassment to him, as the cottage had been, and that he didn't feel it was good enough for her. She knew perfectly well Ramon was having her stay with Rafael's daughter because he couldn't afford the expense of putting her in a hotel for three weeks; his explanation about wanting to forestall gossip didn't deceive her in the least. He couldn't afford a hotel, and he certainly couldn't afford a houseful of new furnishings, either. Yet he was going to buy them for her—to please her. Knowing that made her feel acutely uneasy.

What if something happened to convince her she shouldn't marry him after all? How could she possibly face him with an announcement like that, after she let him spend so much of his money trying to give her what he thought she wanted? She felt as if she were caught in a trap, a cage into which she had willingly placed herself, but as the doors began swinging closed on her, panic was setting in. Marriage in all its awesome finality suddenly loomed ahead of her, and Katie knew that somehow she had to feel free to leave if she changed her mind at any time during the next weeks.

"I want to pay for part of the furniture," Katie blurted suddenly.

Ramon waited for the man who was serving their meal to leave before replying. "No," he said succinctly.

"But—"

"I would not have suggested we buy it if I could not pay for it."

He meant that to end the discussion once and for all, but Katie was desperate. "That isn't the point!"

"No?" he asked. "Then exactly what is the point?"

"The point is that you're already spending a great deal of money renovating the cottage, and furniture is very expensive."

"Tomorrow I will give you three thousand dollars to spend on things for the house—"

"Three thousand dollars?" Katie interrupted, astonished. "How can you possibly afford to spend so much? Where will you get it?"

There was an imperceptible hesitation before Ramon answered. "The company that is going out of business owes me several months' back pay. I will get it from there."

"But—" Katie started to argue.

Ramon's jaw hardened into an uncompromising line. With cool finality he said, "As a man, it is my responsibility to provide a home for you and the furnishings for it. You will not pay for anything."

Katie's long lashes flickered down as she carefully concealed her rebellious blue eyes from his penetrating gaze. Ramon, she decided, was about to discover she was a brilliant bargain hunter. His furnishings were going to cost him exactly one-half of what they were worth—because she was going to pay for the other half!

"I meant that, Katie."

His authoritative tone froze her hand in the act of slicing her meat.

"I forbid you to use any of your money either now or after we are married. It is to remain untouched in your bank in St. Louis."

So determined was she to make her point that Katie forgot to be rankled by his use of the word "forbid." "You don't understand . . . I wouldn't even miss the money. Besides the money I saved from my job, I have a trust fund my father established for me years ago, and some sort of profit-sharing account from his business. Both of those have huge balances. I wouldn't have to touch the principal, I could just draw out some of the interest and—"

"No," he said implacably. "I am not destitute. Even if I were, I would not accept your money. You have known my feelings on that from the beginning, have you not?"

"Yes," Katie murmured.

He sighed, a harsh sound that was filled with an anger that Katie sensed was directed more at himself than her. "Katie, I have never tried to live on the income from the farm alone. I do not know yet how much money will be required to make the necessary improvements to the land so that every acre can become productive again. Once it is fully operational it will support us in reasonable comfort, but until then, whatever money I can spare must go into the land. That farm is the only security I can offer you; its needs must come before luxuries. It is humiliating for me to be explaining this to you now, after I have already brought you here. I thought you understood what sort of life I could offer you before you came."

"I did, and I'm not worried about doing without luxuries."

"Then what are you worried about?"

"Nothing," Katie lied, more determined than ever to use her money to help pay for the furnishings. Ramon was carrying the issue of pride too far! His attitude was unreasonable, unrealistic and positively antiquated—particularly if they were going to be married. But since he felt so deeply about the matter of her money, she simply would never tell him what she had done.

His expression gentled. "If you wish, you could put your money into trust for our children. I believe there are tax advantages to doing so."

Children? Katie thought with a quickening of her heart that was part pleasure, part panic. At the rate Ramon was rushing her, she would undoubtedly have a baby within a year. Why did everything have to be happening so quickly? She remembered Rafael's remark about hearing the banns read in church this morning, and her panic grew. She knew that banns had to be read on three consecutive Sundays before they could be married. By somehow arranging to have them begin today, Ramon had smoothly eliminated one week of the precious time Katie was counting on having before she had to make a final decision. She tried to concentrate on her meal, but she could hardly swallow. "Ramon, how did you manage to have the banns read here this morning, when we didn't arrive until this afternoon?"

Something in her voice seemed to alert him to her inner turmoil. He shifted his plate aside, no longer bothering to make even a pretense of eating. Watching her with an intent, speculating gaze that was utterly unnerving, he said, "On Friday, while you were at work, I phoned Padre Gregorio and told him that we wished to be married here as soon as possible. He has known me since I was born; he knows there is no obstacle to my being married in the church. I assured him that there was no obstacle for you, either.

"When I had breakfast with your father earlier that morning, he gave me the name of his pastor, who also knows you. I gave that information to Padre Gregorio so that he could assure himself, if he wished to do so. It was as simple as that."

Katie hastily looked away from his piercing stare, but not in time.

"Something about that displeases you," he concluded dispassionately. "What is it?"

After a tense silence, Katie shook her head. "Nothing, really. I'm just a little surprised that it was all handled without my knowing anything about it."

"It was not handled that way intentionally. I assumed your father had mentioned it, and he evidently assumed that you already knew."

Katie's hand trembled as she pushed her own plate aside. "Won't Padre Gregorio need to meet with me—us, I mean—before he agrees to marry us?" she asked.

"Yes."

Ramon lit a thin cigar, then leaned back in his chair, regarding her attentively.

Katie ran a nervous hand over her red gold hair, smoothing nonexistent strands into place. "Please stop staring at me like that," she whispered imploringly.

Turning to glance over his shoulder, Ramon nodded briefly at their waiter, signaling for the check. "It is difficult not to look at you, Katie. You are very beautiful. And very frightened."

He said it so coolly, so unemotionally, that it was a long moment before Katie was certain she'd heard him correctly. By then it was too late for her to react; Ramon was already tossing money on the table, standing up, and coming around to assist her out of her chair.

In silence they walked out into a black satin night studded with brilliant stars, and crossed the deserted square. After the warmth of the afternoon sun, the evening breeze was surprisingly chilly as it teased the silken folds of Katie's turquoise dress. She shivered, more from her bewildering emotions than from the cold. Ramon swung his jacket off his shoulder and draped it over her back.

As they passed the lovely old Spanish church, Ramon's words echoed in Katie's mind: "This is where we will be married."

Fourteen days from today, it was possible that she would be walking out of that church as a bride.

Once before she had emerged from a church as a bride . . . except it had been a huge gothic edifice with limousines lined up on the street blocking Saturday traffic while they waited for the bridal party. David had stood beside her on the steps in the sunlight while the photographers took pictures; he in his splendid tuxedo and she in her magnificent white gown and veil. Then they had dashed through the throngs of cheering well-wishers, laughing as they dodged the showers of rice. David had been so handsome, and she had loved him so much that day. She had loved him so damned much!

Lights twinkled from the windows of the houses they passed as Katie walked beside Ramon down the little country road, her mind suddenly haunted by memories she had thought were buried.

David.

During the six months of their marriage he had kept her in a state of bewildered humiliation, and later, fear. Even during their short engagement, Katie had occasionally noticed his speculative glances at other women, but the times were few, and she managed her painful jealousy by reminding herself that David was thirty; he would think she was being childishly possessive. Besides, he was only looking at them. He would never actually be unfaithful.

They had been married for two months before Katie finally criticized him, and then it was only because she was so hurt and embarrassed that she couldn't stop herself. They had been at a formal dinner-dance for the members of the Missouri Bar Association, where the attractive wife of a prominent Kansas City attorney captured David's interest. The flirtation began over predinner cocktails, gathered force when they sat together at dinner, and burst into full bloom on the dance floor. Shortly thereafter, they vanished for nearly an hour and a half, and Katie was left to endure not only the pity of the people she knew, but the glowering fury of the woman's own husband.

By the time David and she returned to their apartment, Katie's insides were churning with resentment. David listened to her tearfully indignant outpouring, his hand clenching and flexing, but it was another four months before Katie discovered what that convulsive flexing of his hand presaged.

When she was finished, she expected him to either deny that he had done anything wrong, or else apologize for his behavior. Instead he stood up, passed a look of withering contempt over her, and went to bed.

His retaliation began the next day. Her punishment was meted out with the refined cruelty of a man who, on the surface, seemed to be simply tolerating her unwanted presence in his life, but who was really succeeding in mentally torturing her.

No real or imagined flaw in her face, figure, posture or personality escaped his notice or went unremarked. "Pleated skirts make your hips look even broader," he observed impersonally. Katie protested that she didn't have broad hips, but she enrolled in an exercise class just to be sure. "If you cut your hair short, your chin wouldn't seem so prominent." Katie protested that her chin wasn't prominent, but she had her hair cut. "If you tightened up your knees, your rear end wouldn't wiggle so much when you walk." Katie tightened up her knees and wondered if she was still "wiggling."

His eyes were never still, they followed her everywhere until Katie became so self-conscious she could hardly cross the room without bumping into a table or banging into a chair. That too, did not escape his notice. Neither did the meal she burned, nor the clothes she forgot to take to the cleaners, nor the dust she overlooked on the bookshelf. "Some women can handle a career and run a house," David observed one night while she was polishing furniture. "Obviously you aren't one of them. you're going to have to give up your job."

Looking back, Katie could not believe how easily he had manipulated her. For two weeks, David "worked late at the office." When he was home, he shut her out completely. When he spoke to her at all, it was with cold ridicule or polite sarcasm. Katie tried repeatedly to patch their quarrel in every way she could think of, but David viewed her obvious efforts with freezing contempt. In two short weeks, he managed to reduce her to a piteous bundle of teary tension, and had her believing that she was clumsy, stupid and inept. But she had been only twenty-one then, and fresh out of college, while David was nine years older, very sophisticated and authoritative.

The thought of giving up her job broke her control. "But I love my job," she had said, tears streaking down her cheeks.

"I thought you 'loved' your husband," David had retorted coldly. He looked at her hands feverishly polishing the table. "I'm very fond of that Steuben bowl," he drawled insolently. "Move it, before you knock it over."

"I'm not going to knock it over," Katie burst out, rounding on him in a tearful fury and knocking the valuable glass bowl off the table. It hit the floor with a sickening crash and broke. Katie was as broken as the bowl. She flung herself into David's arms and burst into racking sobs. "I love you, David—I don't know what's wrong with me, lately. I'm so sorry. I'll give up my job, and I'll—"

David was avenged. All was forgiven. He patted her consolingly, told her that as long as she loved him that was all that mattered, and of course she didn't have to give up her job. The sun beamed down upon her marriage again, and David was his thoughtful, considerate, charming self once more.

Four months later, Katie left her office early intending to surprise David with a special dinner to celebrate their six-month anniversary. She surprised him. He was in bed with the wife of his law firm's senior partner, leaning back against the headboard casually smoking a cigarette, with the naked woman cradled in his free arm. Deadly calm washed over Katie, even though her stomach was twisting. "Since you've obviously finished," she said quietly in the doorway, "I'd appreciate it if you'd get out of here. Both of you."

She walked into the kitchen in a daze, took mushrooms out of the grocery bag and began slicing them for dinner. She sliced her finger twice without noticing the blood. Minutes later, David's low, savage voice hissed behind her, "You little bitch, before tonight is over you're going to learn some manners. Sylvia Conners' husband happens to be my boss. Now get out there and apologize to her."

"Go to hell," Katie said in a voice strangled with pain and humiliation.

His hands dug viciously into her hair, snapping her head back. "I'm warning you, do as I say or it will only go harder on you when she leaves."

Tears of tormented anguish filled Katie's eyes, but she met his glittering gaze without flinching. "No."

David let go of her and strolled into the living room. "Sylvia," she heard him say, "Katie is sorry that she upset you, and she'll apologize for her rudeness tomorrow. Come on, I'll walk you down to your car."

When they left the apartment, Katie walked woodenly into the bedroom she had shared with David and pulled her suitcases out of the closet. She was mechanically opening drawers and removing her clothing when she heard him return.

"You know, darling," David said in a soft, silky voice from the doorway, "four months ago, I thought you learned never to make me angry. I tried to teach you the easy way, but evidently it didn't work. I'm afraid this lesson will have to be a little more memorable."

Katie looked up from her mindless packing and saw him calmly unbuckling his belt and sliding it out of its loops. Even her vocal cords froze with stark terror. "If you dare to touch me," she said in a suffocated voice, "I'll have you arrested for assault."

David stalked her slowly across the bedroom, watching with malicious enjoyment as Katie backed away. "No you won't. you're going to cry very hard, and say you're sorry, and tell me that you love me."

He was right. Thirty minutes later, Katie was still screaming "I love you" into the pillow when the apartment door closed behind him.

She had no idea how much time passed before she dragged herself off the bed, pulled a coat on, picked up her purse and left the apartment. She had no recollection of driving to her parents' house that night, nor did she ever return to the apartment.

David called her day and night, alternately trying to cajole and threaten her into coming back. He was deeply sorry; he had been under tremendous tension at the office with his case load; it would never happen again.

The next time she saw him she was with her lawyer in divorce court.

Katie glanced up as Ramon turned into a narrow dirt driveway. Straight ahead in the distance she could see light glowing against the hillside. Gabriella's house, she assumed. She looked around at the surrounding hills, which were sprinkled with the twinkling lights from the other houses, some high, some low, some much farther away than others. It made the hills seem welcoming, like a safe harbor on a dark night. She tried to enjoy the sight, to concentrate on the present and the future, but the past refused to let go of her. It clutched at her, warning her. . . .

David Caldwell had not completely deceived her; she had *let* herself be deceived. Even at a naive, virginal twenty-one, she had sensed that he was not entirely the charming man he seemed to be. Subconsciously she had registered the controlled rage in his eyes when a waiter didn't scurry fast enough in a restaurant; she had seen the clenching of his hands on the steering wheel when another driver didn't move out of his way; she had even seen the veiled speculation in his eyes when he looked at another woman. She had suspected that he was not the man he wanted her to believe he was, but she had been in love and she had married him anyway.

Now she was on the verge of marrying Ramon, and she couldn't shake the creeping suspicion that he wasn't the man he wanted her to believe he was, either. He was like a puzzle whose pieces didn't quite fit together. And he seemed so hesitant, so uninformative when she asked questions about him and his past. If he had nothing to hide, why was he so reluctant to talk about himself?

That brought a storm of argument from Katie's heart. Just because Ramon didn't like to talk about himself didn't necessarily mean that he was concealing some sinister personality trait from her. David had loved talking about himself, so in that respect the two men were very different.

They were very different in every respect, Katie told herself firmly. Or were they?

She just needed some time to adjust to the idea of marrying again, she decided. Everything had happened so fast that she was panicking. In the next two weeks her irrational fear would leave her. Or would it?

Gabriella's house was clearly in sight when Ramon abruptly stepped in front of her, blocking her path. "Why?" he demanded in a terse, frustrated voice. "Why are you so frightened?"

"I—I'm not," Katie denied, startled.

"Yes," he said harshly, "You are."

Katie stared up at his moonlit face. Despite his harsh tone, there was gentleness in his eyes and calm strength in his features. David had been neither gentle nor strong. He had been a vicious coward. "I think it's because everything seems to be happening so quickly," she said with partial honestly.

His brows drew together into a frown. "Is it only the haste that worries you?"

Katie hesitated. She could not explain the source of her fear to him. She didn't entirely understand it herself, at least not yet. "There's so much to be done, and so little time to do it," she prevaricated.

He sighed with relief as his hands slid up her arms, drawing her close against his heart. "Katie, I always intended for us to be married two weeks from today. Your parents will be here for the ceremony, and I will handle all the necessary arrangements. All you have to do between now and then is meet with Padre Gregorio."

His velvety voice, his breath stirring her hair, the musky, masculine scent of his body, were all combining to work their magic on Katie. "Meet with

Padre Gregorio to discuss the ceremony, you mean?" she asked, leaning back to look at him as his arms encircled her.

"No, to convince him of your suitability to become my wife," Ramon corrected.

"Are you serious?" she breathed, her attention absorbed in the sensuous male lips slowly coming nearer and nearer to hers. Desire was beginning to course through Katie's veins, sweeping aside her doubts and fears.

"Serious about you? You know I am," he murmured, his mouth so close now that his warm breath mingled with hers.

"Serious about having to convince Padre Gregorio that I'd make a good wife for you?" she told his descending mouth.

"Yes," he whispered huskily. "Now convince me."

A hazy smile touched her lips as she curved a hand behind his head, bringing his mouth even closer to hers. "Are you going to be hard to convince?" she teased.

Ramon's voice was hoarse with burgeoning passion. "I am going to try."

Katie's other hand glided up his chest in a deliberately tantalizing caress that made his muscles tense and his breath catch. "How long do you think it will take me to convince you?" she whispered seductively.

"About three seconds," he murmured hotly.

12

*K*atie rolled over onto her back and opened her eyes, emerging from her deep, exhausted sleep with a queer sensation of unreality. The room in which she had slept was sunny and immaculately clean, spartanly furnished with an old maple dresser and nightstand that had been polished to a mirror shine.

"Good morning," Gabriella's soft voice spoke from the doorway. Katie's memory snapped into focus as Gabriella crossed the room and placed a steaming cup of coffee on the nightstand beside the bed. At twenty-four, Gabriella was strikingly lovely. Her high cheekbones and luminous brown eyes were a magazine photographer's dream. Last night, she had confided to Katie that she had been asked to pose by a famous photographer who had seen her one day in the village, but her husband, Eduardo, had refused to permit it. That, Katie thought irritably, was exactly what she would have expected from that taciturn, handsome man she had met last night. Katie thanked her for the coffee and Gabriella smiled. "Ramon came to see you this morning before he left, but when he learned you were sleeping, he said not to disturb you," Gabriella explained. "He asked me to tell you that he will see you this evening when he returns."

"From Mayagüez," Katie put in, merely to keep the conversation going.

"No, from San Juan," Gabriella corrected. A look of almost comic horror crossed her face. "Or perhaps it was Mayagüez. I am sorry I do not recall."

"It doesn't matter," Katie assured her, puzzled over her obvious distress.

Gabriella brightened with relief. "Ramon left much money for you. He said we should begin our shopping today if you feel ready for it."

Katie nodded and glanced at the plastic alarm clock beside her bed, surprised to see that it was already ten o'clock. Tomorrow she would be sure to be up when Ramon came to see her before he left for work at the failing farm in Mayagüez.

Silence hung like a pall over the seven men seated at the conference table in the boardroom at Galverra International's San Juan headquarters—a silence that was shattered as the baroque grandfather clock began ominously tolling the hour of ten—marking the final, gasping breaths of a dying corporation that had once been a thriving world conglomerate.

From his position at the head of the long table, Ramon's glance raked over the five men on his left who were Galverra International's board of directors. Each man had been carefully selected by his father, and each possessed the three qualities that Simon Galverra required of his board members: intelligence, greed and spinelessness. For twenty years, Simon had drawn on their intelligence, exploited their greed, and ruthlessly taken advantage of their inability to contradict his opinions or challenge his decisions.

"I asked," Ramon repeated in a cold clipped voice, "if any of you can suggest a viable alternative to filing corporate bankruptcy." Two directors nervously cleared their throats, another reached for the Waterford pitcher of ice water in the center of the table.

Their averted gazes and continued meek silence ignited the rage he was keeping under such tenuous control. "No suggestions?" he asked with silky menace. "Then perhaps one of you who is not incapable of speech altogether will explain to me why I was not informed of my father's disastrous decisions or his erratic behavior during the last ten months."

Running a finger between his shirt collar and his throat, one of the men said, "Your father said you were not to be bothered with matters here. He specifically said that to us, didn't he, Charles?" he asked, nodding for confirmation at the Frenchman seated beside him. "He told us all 'Ramon is going to be overseeing the operations in France and Belgium for six months, then he is addressing the World Business Conference in Switzerland. When he leaves there, he will be busy entering into negotiations with people in Cairo. He is not to be bothered with the little decisions we are making here.' That is exactly what he said, isn't it?" Five heads nodded in unison.

Ramon looked at them as he slowly rolled a pencil between his fingers. "So," he concluded in a dangerously soft voice, "not one of you 'bothered' me. Not even when he sold a fleet of oil tankers and an airline for half their worth . . . not even when he decided to donate our South American mining interests to the local government as a gift?"

"It—it was your money, and your father's, Ramon." The man on the end held up his hands in a gesture of helplessness. "All of us combined own only a small percentage of stock in the corporation. The rest of the stock is your family's. We knew what he was doing wasn't in the best interest of the corporation, but your family *owns* the corporation. And your father said he wanted the corporation to have some tax write-offs."

Fury boiled up inside of Ramon, pouring through his veins; the pencil in his hand snapped in two. "Tax write-offs?" he bit out savagely.

"Y-yes," another said. "You know—tax deductions for the corporation."

Ramon's hand crashed down on the table with the impact of an explosion as he surged to his feet. "Are you trying to tell me that you thought it was rational for him to give away the corporation's assets so we would not have to pay taxes on them?" A muscle rioted in his clenched jaw as he passed a final murderous look over them. "I am sure you will understand that the corporation will not be able to reimburse you for your travel expenses to attend this meeting." He paused, maliciously enjoying their stunned looks. "Nor will I approve the payment of your annual retainer fees for your services as 'directors' during this past year. This meeting is adjourned!"

Unwisely, one of them chose that moment to become assertive. "Er, Ramon, it is in the bylaws of the corporation that directors are paid the annual sum of—"

"Take me to court!" Ramon spat. Turning on his heel, he stalked through the doorway into his adjoining office, followed by the man who had been seated on his right, silently observing the proceedings.

"Fix yourself a drink, Miguel," Ramon gritted as he stripped off his suit coat. Jerking his tie loose, he walked over to the windows.

Miguel Villegas glanced at the elaborate drinks cabinet against the paneled wall, then quickly sat down in one of the four gold velvet armchairs facing the baronial desk. His brooding eyes were dark with suppressed sympathy as he looked at Ramon, who was standing at the windows with his back to him, one arm braced high against the frame, his hand clenched into a fist.

After several tense minutes, the hand unclenched and the arm came down. In a gesture of weary resignation, Ramon flexed his broad shoulders, then ran his hand around the back of his neck, massaging the taut muscles. "I thought I had accepted defeat weeks ago," he said on a bitter sigh as he turned. "Apparently I had not."

Moving over to the desk he sat down in the massive high-backed chair behind it and looked at Rafael Villegas's eldest son. With an expressionless face, he said, "I take it that your search turned up nothing encouraging?"

"Ramon," Miguel almost pleaded, "I am an accountant with a local practice; this was a job for your corporate auditors—you cannot rely on my findings."

Ramon was undeterred by Miguel's evasiveness. "My auditors are flying in from New York this morning, but I will not give them the access to my father's personal records that I gave you. What were your findings?"

"Exactly what you expected," Miguel sighed. "Your father sold off everything the corporation owned that was making a profit, and kept only those companies that are currently operating at a loss. When he couldn't find anything else to do with the proceeds from the sales, he donated millions to every charity imaginable." He took several ledger sheets out of his briefcase and reluctantly slid them across the huge desk to Ramon. "The item that is the most frustrating to me is the high-rise office towers you were building in Chicago and St. Louis. You have twenty million dollars invested in each one. If the banks would just loan you the rest of the money so you could finish them, you could sell them, get your investment back, and make a sizable profit besides."

"The banks will not cooperate," Ramon said tersely. "I have already met with them in Chicago and St. Louis."

"But why, dammit?" Miguel burst out, abandoning all pretense of being the impersonally professional accountant. His face was agonized as he looked at the coolly impassive features of the man he loved like a brother. "They loaned you part of the money to get them completed this far, why won't they loan you the rest to finish them?"

"Because they have lost faith in my judgment and my ability," Ramon said, looking at the figures on the ledger sheets. "They do not believe I can be relied upon to see that the buildings are finished and their loans repaid. From their point of view, while my father was alive they received their one-million-dollar interest payments every month. He died, I took control of the corporation, and suddenly we are almost four months delinquent in our payments."

"But it is your father's fault the corporation has no money coming in to make the payments!" Miguel gritted between his teeth.

"If you explain that to the banks, they reverse their original opinion and point out that while he was chairman of the board, I was still the president, and I should have taken steps to stop him from making these mistakes."

"Mistakes!" Miguel exploded. "They were not mistakes. He planned it this way so that you would have nothing left. He wanted everyone to think that when he died, the corporation fell apart without him."

Ramon's eyes turned hard and cold. "He had a brain tumor; he was not responsible for his actions."

Miguel Villegas stiffened in his chair, his dark, Spanish face glowering. "He was a miserable bastard, an egotistical petty tyrant, and you know it! Everybody knew it. He resented your success and he hated your fame. All that tumor did was make him finally lose control of his jealousy." Seeing the mounting anger in Ramon's expression, Miguel softened his voice. "I know you do not want to hear it, but it is the truth. You came into the corporation and in a few short years, you created a worldwide financial empire worth three hundred times what your father had made it. You did it, not him. You were the one the magazines and newspapers wrote about; you were the one they called one of the world's most dynamic entrepreneurs; you were the one who was asked to address the World Business Conference in Geneva. I was having lunch in a hotel at a table near your father's the day he found out about that. He was not proud, he was furious! He was trying to convince the men he was with that the conference had taken you as a second choice because he could not spare the time to go to Switzerland."

"Enough!" Ramon said sharply, his face white with angry pain. "He was still my father, and he is dead now. There was little love between us while he was alive; do not destroy what little feeling I have left for him." In grim silence, Ramon concentrated on the ledger sheets Miguel had given him. When his eyes swept over the last entry, he glanced up. "What is this three-million-dollar asset of mine you list at the end?"

"Not really an asset at all," Miguel said glumly. "I found the file among your father's private things at the house in Mayagüez. As far as I could tell, it is a loan you made to a Sidney Green in St. Louis, Missouri, nine years ago. He still owes you the money, but you cannot sue him or take any legal action to try to get it back now; under the law you have only seven years to file a lawsuit—that time has already elapsed.

"The loan was repaid," Ramon said with a shrug.

"Not according to the records I found."

"If you dig deeply enough you will discover it was repaid, but do not waste any more of your time looking through the files. You have enough to do." There was a brief knock on the door, followed immediately by the appearance of Simon Galverra's elegantly groomed secretary.

"The auditors from New York are here. Also, there are two local newspaper reporters asking to schedule interviews, and an urgent telephone call from Zurich."

"Send the auditors into the conference room, and tell the reporters I will give them an interview next month; that will keep them out of our way. I will return the Zurich call later." Nodding, she retreated, her skirt swirling around long shapely legs.

Miguel watched Elise leave, his brown eyes admiring. "At least your father had good taste in secretaries. Elise is beautiful," he observed in a tone of impersonal aesthetic appreciation.

Ramon unlocked the massive, carved desk and did not reply as he extracted three heavy files marked "Confidential."

"Speaking of beautiful women," Miguel went on with studied nonchalance as he gathered up his papers, preparing to leave. "When am I going to be able to meet the grocer's daughter?"

Reaching for the intercom on his right, Ramon pressed the button and issued instructions to Elise: "Have Davidson and Ramirez come up. When they arrive, send them into the conference room with the auditors." With his attention still on the files before him, Ramon said, "What grocer's daughter?"

Miguel rolled his eyes in amusement. "The one you brought back from the States. Eduardo says she is reasonably attractive. Knowing how he dislikes American women, that means she must be extraordinarily beautiful. He said she is a grocer's daughter."

"A grocer's——?" For a moment Ramon looked irritated and blank, then the uncompromising line of his jaw slowly relaxed. His eyes, which had been cold and harsh, kindled with warmth, and his stern mouth was touched by an unexplainable smile. "Katie," he breathed aloud. "He is talking about Katie." Leaning back in his chair, Ramon closed his eyes. "How could I possibly have forgotten I have Katie here?" Regarding Miguel through half-closed eyes, Ramon said with wry humor, "Katie is the daughter of a wealthy American who owns a large chain of supermarkets. I brought her back from the States with me yesterday. She is staying with Gabriella and Eduardo for two weeks until we are married."

While Ramon briefly explained that he was misleading Katie, and why, Miguel was slowly sinking back into the chair he had just vacated. He shook his head. "*Dios mio*, I thought she was going to be your mistress."

"Eduardo knows she is not. He mistrusts all American women, and he prefers to think I will change my mind about marrying her. When he learns to know Katie, he will like her. In the meantime, out of respect for me he will treat her as a guest in his home, and he will not discuss my past with her."

"But your return is undoubtedly the talk of the village. Your Katie will be bound to overhear some village gossip."

"I am certain she will, but she will not understand a word of it. Katie does not speak Spanish."

Heaving himself out of his chair, Miguel shot a worried look at Ramon. "What about the rest of my family—they all speak English—and the younger ones may inadvertently give you away."

"Only your parents and Gabriella and her husband remember their English," Ramon said dryly. "As of yesterday, your brothers and sisters know only Spanish."

"Ramon, after this, nothing you ever do or say will surprise me."

"I want you to be my best man."

Miguel smiled somberly. "That does not surprise me. I always expected to be your best man, just as you flew back from Athens to be mine." He put his hand out across the desk. "Congratulations, my friend." His firm handshake conveyed his pleasure as well as his unspoken regret for Ramon's staggering financial losses. "I will go back to work on your father's files."

The intercom buzzed, and the secretary's voice announced that the corporation's two attorneys, whom Ramon had instructed her to summon, were now in the conference room waiting with the auditors.

Still seated behind the desk, Ramon watched Miguel cross the broad expanse of thick gold carpet. When the door clicked shut behind him, Ramon let his gaze roam over his office as if he were seeing it for the last time, unconsciously memorizing it in all its quiet splendor.

The Renoir landscape he had purchased for an exorbitant sum from a private collector was framed beneath a portrait light, its colors a vibrant contrast to the rich, walnut-paneled walls. He had put all his personal possessions up as collateral to obtain loans for the corporation before he discovered the full extent of his father's destructiveness. Along with everything else he owned, the Renoir would soon be auctioned off to the highest bidder. He hoped whoever bought it would love it as much as he always had.

Leaning his head back against the chair, Ramon closed his eyes. In a minute he was going to walk into the conference room, turn the auditors loose on the records, and instruct the corporation's attorneys to file the legal documents that would announce to the courts and the business world that Galverra International was crippled. Broken.

For four months he had fought to save it, trying to transfuse it with his own money—doing anything just to keep it alive. He had failed. Now all he could do was make certain that it died swiftly and with dignity.

Night after night he had lain awake, dreading this moment. Yet now that it was finally here, he was facing it without the wrenching agony he would have felt two weeks ago.

Because now he had Katie.

He had given his life to the corporation. Now he was going to give the rest of it to Katie. Only to Katie.

For the first time in many years, Ramon felt deeply religious. It was as if God had decided to take away his family, his possessions, his status, and then, realizing that Ramon had absolutely nothing left, He had taken pity and given him Katie instead. And Katie made up for everything he had lost.

Katie brushed her lips with a tawny lipstick that matched the shiny polish on her long tapered fingernails. She checked her mascara, then combed her fingers through the sides of her hair, restoring the glossy mane to its windblown style. Satisfied, she turned away from the mirror above the dresser and glanced at the clock. At five-thirty it was still broad daylight, and Ramon had told Gabriella he would be here between five-thirty and six to take Katie to dinner at Rafael's.

On an impulse, Katie decided to walk out and meet him. After changing into a pair of white slacks and a jaunty navy silk shirt trimmed in white, she slipped out the front door, relieved to escape the rather oppressive presence of Gabriella's disapproving husband, Eduardo.

Overhead, the powder-blue sky was heaped with piles of whipped cream clouds. The hills rose around her, carpeted in emerald green and splashed with pink and red flowers. With a contented sigh, Katie lifted her face to the balmy breeze and started across the front yard toward the dirt driveway that led through the trees out to the main road.

She had felt a little lost being among strangers all day, and she had missed Ramon's reassuring presence. She hadn't seen him since he introduced her to Gabriella and her husband last night, then left an hour later to go back to Rafael's house.

"Katie!" The familiar voice stopped her in her tracks. Turning her head, Katie saw Ramon about fifty yards away on her left. He was cutting across the hillside from Rafael's house, and she had obviously just crossed directly in his path as she walked toward the road. He stopped, waiting for her to come to him. With a cheery wave, Katie turned and started up the hill.

Ramon forced himself to stay where he was, to luxuriate in the sheer pleasure of knowing she had come out to meet him. His gaze moved over her in a tender caress, watching the way her hair was blowing across her shoulders in a shining tumble of red gold. Her deep blue eyes were laughing up at him, and a welcoming smile was curving the inviting fullness of her lips. She moved with a natural, unaffected grace, her slim hips swaying just enough to be exquisitely provocative.

His heart pounded with the yearning to snatch her into his arms and crush her against him, to absorb her into himself. He wanted to cover her mouth with his and whisper over and over, I love you, I love you, I love you. He wanted to say that to her, but not enough to risk the possibility that Katie's response—or lack of it—would tell him that she did not love him. That he could not bear.

A few yards from him Katie stopped, immobilized by a strange combination of happiness and shyness. Ramon's dark blue shirt was open halfway to his waist, revealing an expanse of tanned chest covered with curling black hairs; his dark pants hugged his lean hips and hard thighs, faithfully following every line of his long legs. The raw, potent sexuality he was exuding made Katie feel strangely fragile and vulnerable. She swallowed, searching for something to say, and finally said with soft uncertainty, "Hello."

Ramon's arms opened wide to her. Huskily he replied, "Hello, *mi amor.*"

Katie hesitated, and then flung herself into his welcoming embrace. His arms closed around her, holding her to him as if he would never let her go.

"Did you miss me?" he whispered thickly, when his mouth at last released hers.

Katie pressed her lips to the base of his throat, inhaling the heady scent of warm, masculine skin and spicy after-shave. "Yes. Did you miss me?"

"No."

Leaning back, Katie looked up at him, her smile quizzical. "You didn't?"

"No," he said with quiet gravity. "Because since ten o'clock this morning I have kept you with me; I have not let you leave my side."

"Since ten o'clock—?" Katie started to ask, then something in his voice made her look at him more closely. Intuitively she recognized the ravaged emotions hidden in the depths of those onyx eyes. Reaching up, she took his chin between her thumb and forefinger, turning his surprised face first to the left, then the right. Keeping her expression bright, she asked teasingly, "How do the other men look?"

"What other men?"

"The ones who tried to beat you up."

"You mean I look as if I have been in a fight?" Ramon said.

Slowly, Katie nodded, her smile widening. "With at least six armed men and a demented bulldozer."

"That bad?" he grinned wryly.

Katie nodded again, then sobered. "It must be very hard, very depressing working for a company that you know is going out of business."

His stunned look told Katie that her conclusion was correct. "Do you know," he said with a bemused shake of his head, "I have been told by many men from many countries that I have a face that is absolutely unreadable when I wish it to be."

"And you wanted it to be unreadable tonight, with me?" Katie guessed. "Because you didn't want me to see that you're tired and depressed?"

"Yes."

"Did you have any of your own money invested in the company?"

"Virtually all of my money and most of my life," Ramon admitted smiling at her in amazement. "You are very perceptive. But there is no need for you to worry. After today it will be much easier, and I will not have to be there for so many hours each day. Tomorrow afternoon I can begin helping the men who are working on our home."

Dinner at Rafael's house was a relaxed affair with much joking and laughing around the table. Señora Villegas, Rafael's wife, was a stout, bustling woman who treated Ramon with the same solicitude she lavished on her husband and children—two boys in their early twenties and a girl of about fourteen. For Katie's benefit most of the conversation was in English, which the young members could not speak but apparently understood a little, because several times Katie saw them smile at something Rafael or Ramon said.

After dinner the men went into the lounge while the women cleared the table and did the dishes. When they were through, they joined the men for coffee. As if he had been watching for her, Ramon's gaze lifted and he held out a beckoning hand to her. Katie slid her hand into his firm grasp, and he exerted just enough pressure to pull her down beside him. She listened to Rafael Villegas talking to Ramon, making suggestions about the farm, but every moment she was vitally aware of Ramon's hard thigh pressing against hers. His arm was resting along the back of the sofa, his hand imperceptibly caressing her shoulder, his thumb moving idly against her nape beneath the cloak of her heavy hair. Except there was nothing idle about what he was doing—he was deliberately keeping her fully aware of his nearness. Or was he, Katie wondered suddenly. She thought about what he had said earlier about keeping her beside him, implying that he had needed her to get through his day. Was he keeping her physically close now, touching her this way because he needed her to get through the evening as well?

Katie stole a glance at his chiseled profile and, with a pang of sympathy, she recognized the preoccupation in his features.

Katie delicately faked a yawn behind her fingers, and Ramon's eyes were instantly on her. "Are you tired?"

"A little," Katie lied.

In three minutes, Ramon had seized on her comment, made their excuses to the Villegases, and whisked her out the front door. "Do you feel up to walking back, or would you rather I drove you?"

"I feel up to almost anything," Katie smiled softly, "but you looked tired and distracted, so I used that as a way of excusing you from being there."

Ramon didn't deny it. "Thank you," he said tenderly.

Gabriella and her husband had already gone to bed, but they had left the front door unlatched. Katie stopped to turn on a mellow lamp while Ramon walked over and sat down on the sofa. As she neared him, he reached out and captured her arms, starting to pull her down onto his lap. Firmly disentangling herself from his grip, Katie went around behind him.

Beneath her ministering hands his broad shoulders were taut as she began to massage the tenseness from his thick muscles. She felt so strange with him in this mood. There was a relaxed closeness between them that had never been present before; Ramon always seemed to have a leashed sexual energy that kept her senses in a state of trembling anticipation. Tonight that energy was a quiet magnetism. "How does that feel?" she asked, kneading the tendons at the base of the neck.

"Better than you can imagine," he said, bending his dark head forward to give her better access to his neck. "Where did you learn to do that?" he asked a few minutes later as Katie began quickly chopping the sides of her hands over his shoulders and back.

Katie's hands froze. "I don't remember," she lied.

Something in her voice made Ramon turn around sharply. He saw the haunted expression in her eyes, caught her arms and brought her around in front of him, pulling her down onto his lap. "Now I will make you feel better," he stated, his hands unfastening the buttons of her shirt, delving into the lacy cups of her bra, and pushing her breasts up and out of them.

Before Katie could gather her wits, his mouth was at her breasts, obliterating her thoughts, driving her into a state of hot need. With one arm around her shoulders and the other around her waist, he shifted her down onto the sofa, his body half covering hers. "He is dead," he reminded her fiercely. "And

I do not want his ghost between us." Despite the harshness of his tone, his kiss was filled with sweetness. "Bury him," he implored in a whisper. "Please."

Katie wrapped her arms around his shoulders, arching her lower body to his, and immediately forgot the world.

13

The next day, Miguel strode past the startled secretary, opened the door to Ramon's office, and shut it firmly behind him. "Tell me all about your good friend Sidney Green in St. Louis," Miguel said, with sarcastic emphasis on the word *friend*.

Ramon, who was leaning back in his chair, engrossed in some legal documents he was reading, glanced distractedly at Miguel. "He is not a friend of mine, he is merely a man who knew a friend of mine." Returning his attention to the documents, he said, "He approached me at a cocktail party at this friend's house nine years ago, and described a new formula for paint that he had worked out. He said that using his formula he could produce paint that would wear better and last longer than any other paint on the market. The next day he brought me an analysis of his paint, which was performed by an independent testing laboratory, and proved his claims.

"He needed three million dollars to begin to manufacture and market it, and I arranged for Galverra International to lend it to him. I also put him in touch with several of my friends who owned companies that bought paint for use on the products they manufacture. You will find the information in a closed file somewhere. It was as simple as that."

"Part of the information was in the file, I got the rest from the treasurer of the corporation this morning. It was not quite as simple as you think. Your father had Green investigated, found out he was a small-time chemist, and decided as such, he would never have the business acumen to market his product, and the three million would be wasted. Being the 'kind, loving father' that he was, your father decided to teach you a lesson. He instructed the treasurer to advance three million dollars into your personal account and make the loan from you personally to Green. One year later, when the loan was to be repaid, Green wrote and said he wanted an extension. According to the treasurer, you were in Japan at the time, and he took Green's letter to your father. Your father said to ignore the letter, and not to make any attempt to collect the loan; collecting it was your problem."

Ramon sighed irritably. "Nevertheless, the loan was repaid. I remember my father telling me that it had been."

"I don't give a damn what that devil told you—it wasn't. Sidney Green told me so himself."

Ramon's head snapped up, his jaw clenched in anger. "You called him?!"

"Well . . . yes . . . you told me not to waste any more time going through the files, Ramon," Miguel reminded him, flinching under Ramon's furious glance.

"Damn you! I gave you no authority to do that," Ramon exploded. Leaning back in his chair, he briefly closed his eyes, obviously struggling with his rampaging temper. When he spoke again his voice was controlled. "Even when I was in St. Louis, I did not call him. He knew I was in trouble; if he had wanted to help he would have contacted me there. He will interpret your phone call about an old loan as a pitiful ploy on my part to try to get money from him. He was an arrogant bastard nine years ago when he had nothing but the shirt on his back; I can imagine what he must be like now that he is successful."

"He is still an arrogant bastard," Miguel said, "And he never repaid one dime of the money. When I explained that I was trying to locate the records of the repayment of the money you loaned him, he said that you are too late to take him to court over it."

Ramon listened to this with cynical amusement. "He is right, of course. It was my responsibility to see that the money was repaid, and when it wasn't, to take appropriate legal action within the allowable time limit."

"For God's sake! You gave the man three million dollars and he is refusing to pay you after you made him rich! How can you just sit there like that?"

Ramon shrugged ironically. "I did not 'give' him the money, I loaned it to him. I did not do it out of kindness or charity, I did it because I felt there was a need for the superior product he could manufacture, and because I hoped to make a profit. It was a business investment, and it is the investor's responsibility to look after his money. Unfortunately, I did not realize that I was the investor, and I assumed the corporation's auditors would oversee it. To Green, his refusal to repay it now, when he does not have to, is nothing personal—he is merely looking out for his own interests. That is business."

"It is theft!" Miguel said bitterly.

"No, it is merely good business," Ramon said, regarding him with dry amusement. "I suppose that after telling you he would not repay the money, he sent me his regards and his 'deep regrets' for my sad state of affairs."

"Like hell he did! He told me to tell you that if you were half as smart as everyone always said you were, you would have demanded your money years ago. He said if you, or anyone else representing you, contacted him again to try to collect it, he would have his legal staff file suit against you for harassment. Then he hung up on me."

All of the amusement vanished from Ramon's expression. He put his pen down. "He what?" he asked with deadly softness.

"He—he said those things, and then he hung up on me."

"Now that was very bad business," Ramon said in a silky, ominous voice.

He leaned back and was thoughtfully silent, his mouth quirked in a faint, ironic smile. Abruptly, he reached over and punched the intercom button. When Elise answered his buzz, he gave her seven names and seven phone numbers to call in seven different cities all over the world.

"If I recall the terms of the loan correctly," Ramon said, "I loaned him three million at whatever interest rate was being charged on the day of repayment."

"Right," Miguel said. "If he had repaid the loan in one year, the interest rate then was eight percent, and he would have owed you about $3,240,000."

"Today the interest rate is seventeen percent, and he has owed it for nine years."

"Technically he owes you more than twelve million dollars," Miguel said, "but it does not matter. You cannot possibly collect it."

"I have no intention of trying," Ramon said affably. His gaze shifted to the telephone on the desk, waiting for the first of the transatlantic calls to go through.

"Then what are you going to do?"

Ramon's brow lifted with amusement. "I am going to teach our friend Green a lesson he should have learned long ago. It is a variation on an old saying."

"What old saying?"

"The saying that when you are climbing up the ladder of success, you should never deliberately step on anyone's hands, because you may need them to help you when you are on your way down."

"What variation are you going to teach him?" Miguel asked, his eyes beginning to gleam with delighted anticipation.

"Never make unnecessary enemies," Ramon answered. "And the lesson is going to cost him twelve million dollars."

When the calls came through, Ramon pressed a button on his telephone that activated a speaker system so that both sides of the conversation were clearly audible to Miguel. Several of the conversations took place in French and Miguel struggled desperately to follow them, hampered by his rudimentary knowledge of a language Ramon spoke fluently. After the first four calls, however, Miguel had gathered enough of what was taking place to be utterly staggered.

Each of the men Ramon talked to were major industrialists whose companies either used or had used paint manufactured by Green's company. Each man treated Ramon with warm friendliness and listened with amusement as he briefly explained what he was trying to do. When each call was completed, Miguel was a little surprised to hear everyone of them ask if there was anything they could do to help Ramon in his "difficult circumstances," and in every case Ramon politely declined.

"Ramon!" Miguel burst out when the fourth call was over at four-thirty in the afternoon. "Any one of those men could bail you out of this financial disaster you are in, and they all offered to help."

Ramon shook his head. "It is a polite formality, nothing more. They offer to help, and it is understood that I will decline their offer. That is good business. You see," he said with a shadow of a smile, "we have all already learned the lesson Mr. Green is being taught."

Miguel could not suppress a chuckle. "If I followed those calls correctly, tomorrow the Paris press is going to report that their major automobile manufacturer had a problem with Green's paint fading on their test car, and has decided to use something else."

Ramon went over to the liquor cabinet and poured drinks for himself and Miguel. "It is not quite as lethal to Green as it sounds to you. My friend in Paris had already told me he'd decided against using Green's paint because it was too expensive; I was the one who had put him in touch with Green nine years ago. The problem with the fading paint was because it was incorrectly applied by his factory personnel, but of course he has no intention of mentioning that to the press."

He carried the glasses over to Miguel and handed him his. "The farm-equipment manufacturer in Germany will wait one day after the Paris press announcement before calling Green and threatening to cancel his order because of what he saw in the Paris press."

Ramon shoved his hands in his pockets and grinned at Miguel, a cigar clamped between his white teeth. "Unfortunately for Green, his paint is no longer superior; other American manufacturers have since produced an equally good product. My friend in Tokyo will respond to the Paris press announcement by stating to the Tokyo press that they have never used Green's paint so they have no trouble with their automobiles' finish fading.

"On Thursday, Demetrios Vasiladis will call from Athens and cancel all orders for marine paint for all of his shipyards."

Ramon took a swallow of his drink, sat down behind his desk and began loading papers into his briefcase that he would go over tonight after he left Katie.

Intrigued, Miguel leaned forward on the edge of his chair. "And then what?"

Ramon glanced up as if the matter had lost its interest. "Then it is any-one's guess. I expect that the other American paint manufacturers who make an equally good product will take up the sword and do their best to demolish Green in the American press. Depending upon how effective they are, the adverse publicity will probably drive down the value of Green's stock on the stock exchange."

14

*E*arly Thursday morning, Miguel was going over the financial statement he had prepared with Ramon, when Elise entered Ramon's office without her customary knock.

"Excuse me," she said, her face pale and stony. "There is a man—a very rude man—on the telephone. I have told him twice that you cannot be inter-rupted, but as soon as I hang up the telephone he calls back and starts shout-ing at me again."

"What does he want?" Ramon said impatiently.

The secretary swallowed apprehensively. "He—he wants to talk to the dirty bastard who is trying to put some green paint down his drain. Do you—is that you?"

Ramon's lips twitched. "I believe so. Put him through."

Eagerly, Miguel leaned forward. Ramon flipped on the phone's external speaker, then relaxed back in his chair, picked up the financial statements he had been reading, and calmly continued to study them.

Sidney Green's voice exploded through the room. "Galverra, you bastard! you're wasting your time, do you hear me? No matter what you do, I'm not paying one dime of that three million. Have you got that? No matter what you do!" When there was no response, Green shouted, "Say something, damn you!"

"I admire your courage," Ramon drawled.

"Is that your way of telling me you plan more guerrilla tactics? Is it? Are you threatening me, Galverra?"

"I am certain I would never be so crude as to 'threaten' you, Sid," Ramon replied in a bland, preoccupied voice.

"Damn you, you are threatening me! Who the hell do you think you are?"

"I think I am the bastard who is going to cost you twelve million dollars," Ramon said and, with that, he reached out a hand and disconnected the call.

Kattie quickly signed her name to the charge slip for one-half the cost of the furniture she had just purchased, then paid for the rest with some of the money Ramon had left for her. The salesclerk gave her an odd look when she asked for two receipts, each for one-half the actual amount of the purchase. Katie firmly ignored it, but Gabriella blushed and looked away.

Outside, the temperature was deliciously warm, and tourists were strolling along the sun-drenched streets of Old San Juan. The car was parked at the curb; a battered but reliable old automobile that belonged to Gabriella's husband, and which he was allowing them to use for their shopping expeditions.

"We're doing great," Katie sighed, rolling down her window to let the breeze into the stuffy car. It was Thursday already, the fourth day of their frenetic, but successful shopping spree, and she was happily exhausted. "I wish I could get over this feeling that there's something I'm forgetting, though," she mused, glancing over her shoulder at the two lamps and an end table that were crammed into the backseat.

"There is." Gabriella's pretty face was concerned as she turned the key in the ignition and shot Katie a rueful smile. "You are forgetting to tell Ramon the truth about how much this is costing." She pulled into the stream of downtown San Juan traffic. "Katie, he will be very angry with you when he discovers what you have done."

"He isn't going to discover it," Katie announced cheerfully. "I'm not going to tell him and you promised you wouldn't."

"Of course I will not!" Gabriella said with a hurt look. "But Padre Gregorio has spoken many times on Sundays about the need for truth between a husband and—"

"Oh, no!" Katie moaned aloud. "That's what I forgot." She leaned her head back and closed her eyes. "Today is Thursday, and at two o'clock this afternoon I was to meet with Padre Gregorio. Ramon made the arrangements on Tuesday and reminded me this morning, but I completely forgot about it."

"Do you want to see the padre now?" Gabriella offered an hour later as their car rattled into the village. "It is only four o'clock. Padre Gregorio will not be having his evening meal yet."

Katie quickly shook her head. She had been thinking all day about the picnic she and Ramon were going to have up at the cottage tonight. She was to bring the food up there where he was working with the other men. When the men left, Katie and Ramon were going to have a few hours alone—their first in the four days since she had arrived.

When they reached Gabriella's house, Katie slid behind the steering wheel, waved goodbye to Gabriella, and turned the dilapidated old car back toward the village, where she could stop in the general store for food and a bottle of wine for the picnic.

These past four days had a strange, unreal quality for her. Ramon had been working at the farm in Mayagüez in the mornings, and at the cottage in the afternoons until it was dark, so she only saw him in the evenings. She spent her days shopping and planning and choosing color schemes for Ramon's house with only her idea of Ramon's tastes to guide her. She felt as if she were on a vacation, earning her way by redecorating his house—rather than planning for her own home. Perhaps it was because he was so busy and she saw so little of him, and when they were together there were always other people nearby.

Rafael and his sons were also working up at the cottage with Ramon, and at dinner every night the four men were cheerful, but plainly worn-out. Although Ramon lavished her with his attention in the evening, keeping her near him while they sat in the friendly atmosphere of Rafael's living room with the rest of his family, the "time and place to share ourselves with each other" so far had not presented itself.

Each evening, Ramon walked her back to Gabriella's darkened house, led her over to the sofa, and drew her down beside him.

By now, Katie could hardly pass that sofa in the daylight without feeling her face grow warm. For three nights in a row, Ramon had tenderly stripped her of most of her clothing, aroused her until she could hardly stand it, gently dressed her again, walked her back to the bedroom, and silently bade her good-night with a final, passionate kiss. And each night Katie crawled beneath the cool sheets of her temporary bed in a state of aching, unfulfilled desire, which she was beginning to think was precisely what Ramon intended her to feel. Yet there was no doubt in her mind that he was always more aroused then even she was, so it made no sense for him to put them both through this torture.

Last night, in a welter of confusion and desire, Katie had taken matters into her own hands and volunteered to get the blanket from her bed so that they could go outdoors where there would be privacy and no fear of interruption.

Ramon had gazed down at her with eyes like fiery black coals, his face hard and dark with passion. But he had reluctantly shaken his head. "The rain will interrupt us, Katie. It has been threatening for the last hour." Even as he spoke a flash of heat lightning cast an eerie glow through the room. But it had not rained.

Tonight, no doubt, was the "time and place" he had been waiting for, Katie decided, and she was charged with anticipation. Katie pulled the car over in front of the general store and climbed out. Pushing open the heavy door, she walked into the crowded interior of the ancient building, blinking her eyes to adjust to the light.

Besides doubling as the village post office, the general store stocked everything from flour and canned goods to bathing suits to inexpensive pieces of furniture. Stacks of merchandise covered the wooden floors with only a narrow aisle between them for customers to walk through. The counters were heaped with goods, as were the shelves high along all the walls. Without the assistance of someone who worked there, it would have taken Katie and Gabriella weeks to dig their way through everything.

The Spanish girl, to whom Gabriella had introduced Katie before as Ramon Galverra's *novia*, saw Katie, beamed a bright smile at her, and hurried over. With her help on Monday, Katie had discovered thick, fluffy towels in solid colors of red, white and black beneath a stack of men's work pants. Katie had bought all six of them and ordered a dozen more in assorted sizes. Evidently the girl thought Katie had come to see if the rest of the towels were here yet, for she picked up a towel, held it up, and regretfully shook her head, relying on pantomime since she spoke no English.

Katie grinned and pointed to the shelves of groceries interspersed with shovels and rakes, then went over to make her selections. Carrying the fresh fruit, bread and packaged meat she had selected over to the crowded counter, Katie dug in her purse for her money. When she glanced up, the little Spanish girl smilingly presented her with two bills, each for one-half the amount of her purchase. The girl was so proud of having remembered that Katie always asked for the bills in this way, that Katie didn't bother trying to explain that it wasn't necessary for groceries.

The scene that greeted Katie when the car bumped past the canopy of scarlet poinciana trees took her completely by surprise. The yard was filled with battered old trucks, two horses and another truck loaded with debris, which had obviously been removed from the house and was being hauled away. Two men were replacing tiles on the roof, and two more were stripping all the peeling paint from the wood trim. The shutters had been repaired and were open beside windows with crystal-clear panes of glass. This was the first time Katie had been here since Sunday, and she was eager to see what progress had been made inside. She took a quick look in the car's rearview mirror, freshened her lip gloss, and smoothed her hair back into place.

She climbed out of the car and brushed a piece of lint from her designer jeans, then tucked her plaid shirt into her waistband. The constant staccato sounds of hammering that had been coming from inside ceased abruptly. The men on the roof scampered down as Katie walked up the brick path, which was no longer missing bricks or strewn with broken tiles. She glanced at her watch: it was exactly six, and apparently the men were finished for the day.

The front door, which Ramon had broken on Sunday, had been rehung, and the peeling paint stripped down to smooth bare wood. Katie stepped aside as eight men came through the doorway carrying their wooden tool-boxes. Rafael and his two sons were behind them. There was an army working up here, Katie thought with amazement. "Ramon is in the kitchen with the plumber," Rafael said with one of his warm, fatherly smiles. His sons both grinned at her as they passed.

The living-room walls, which were made of grooved boards, had been sanded already, as had the planked floors. It took Katie a moment to understand why the house seemed so cheerful and sunny. Then she realized that all of the windows were sparkling clean, and some of them were open, letting the balmy breeze in to mingle with the pungent scent of fresh sawdust. An elderly man carrying a huge wrench in each hand shuffled out of the kitchen, tipped his hat politely to Katie, then vanished through the living room and outside. The plumber, Katie guessed.

With a last appreciative glance around her, Katie wandered into the kitchen. Like every other wooden surface, the kitchen cabinets had been stripped, and the ugly peeling linoleum had been taken up. The sharp clang of metal on metal drew her attention toward the sink. A pair of long, muscular legs were stretched out on the floor, the torso belonging to them hidden beneath the sink. Katie smiled, recognizing those long legs and slim hips even without seeing the head and shoulders that were blocked from view by the convoluted plumbing pipes.

Apparently Ramon didn't realize the plumber had left, because his familiar Spanish voice issued a muffled order in a sharp tone. Katie hesitated uncertainly, then, feeling like a child playing a trick on an adult, she picked up the wrench lying on the counter and passed it beneath the newly installed stainless steel sink to Ramon. She almost laughed aloud when the wrench was rudely shoved back at her, and the same order was irritably repeated, this time accompanied by an impatient bang on the bottom of the sink.

Making a calculated guess, she leaned forward and turned on both taps. The torrent of water brought a string of savage curses that erupted from below the sink at the same time Ramon did, with water streaming from his face, his hair and his bare chest. Snatching a towel from the floor, he came to his feet in one lithe, furious movement, drying his head and face while Katie frantically dived for the taps and turned them off. In appalled fascination she listened to the scathing Spanish remarks coming from behind the towel, then jumped when he flung it down and glared at her.

His expression turned to blank shock. "I—I wanted to surprise you," Katie explained, biting her lower lip to control her laughter. Water was dripping from his curling hair, his eyebrows and his eyelashes, and sparkling on the crisp hairs on his broad chest. Katie's shoulders began to shake.

A gleam entered Ramon's eyes. "I think one 'surprise' deserves another." His right hand shot out and turned on the cold water tap. Before Katie could do more than squeal a protest, her head was being forced down into the sink a bare inch from the rushing water.

"Don't you dare!" she shrieked, laughing. The water was turned up harder, and her head forced even closer to the spout. "Stop it!" she howled, her laughter echoing in the stainless-steel sink. "The water is running all over the floor!"

Ramon released her and turned off the tap. "The pipes leak," he remarked without concern. He arched an eyebrow at her and added ominously, "I will have to think of some better way to 'surprise' you."

Katie laughingly ignored the threat. "I thought you said you knew about carpentry," she teased, plunking her hands on her slim hips.

"I said," Ramon corrected dryly, "that I know as much about carpentry as you know about making curtains."

Katie choked back a giggle and managed to look comically indignant. "My curtains are progressing far better than your plumbing." *Because Gabriella and Señora Villegas are doing the sewing,* Katie added silently.

"Oh, is that right?" Ramon mocked. "Go into the bathroom."

Katie was surprised when he didn't follow her, but instead reached for the towel and the clean shirt hanging on a nail. Outside the bathroom door she paused, mentally bracing herself to face again the crawling insect population that had inhabited the rusty bathtub on Sunday. When she hesitantly opened the door her eyes widened.

Gone were the old bathroom fixtures. In their place was a modern vanity with a sink, and a large fiberglass shower stall with sliding glass doors. Experimentally, she pushed one of the doors aside, noting with approval that it slid smoothly on its track. The shower spout was dripping, however, and Katie shook her head in amusement at Ramon's lack of concern about leaking water. Cautiously, she stepped inside, avoiding the slippery puddle on the fiberglass floor, while reaching out for the tap to turn it off. Her mouth opened in a silent scream as a deluge of freezing water hit her in the face. Blinded, she turned to leap out of the shower and the leather sole of her shoe slid from beneath her, sending her sprawling on all fours beneath the icy downpour.

She crawled out of it on her hands and knees, her soaked clothing clinging to her skin, water streaming from her hair and face. Awkwardly, she struggled to her feet and lifted the hair out of her eyes. Ramon was standing in the doorway, visibly struggling to keep his face straight. "Don't you dare laugh," Katie warned darkly.

"Would you like some soap?" he offered solicitously. "A towel, perhaps?" he volunteered deadpan, handing her the towel he had been holding in his hand. He pulled the clean shirt he had just put on from his waistband and began unbuttoning it, continuing conversationally. "Would you allow me to offer you the shirt off my back, then?"

Katie, who was on the verge of laughing herself, was about to make some sheepish retort when Ramon added, "Strange, is it not, the way one 'surprise' can lead to another?"

Outrage burst within her at the realization that he had actually done this to her on purpose. Shivering, she snatched the shirt from his hand and slammed the door in his grinning face! He must have watched her step into the shower and then turned on the main valve, she thought furiously as she pulled off her freezing wet jeans. So this was how a Latin male retaliated for being made the recipient of an unintentional dousing! This was the sort of retribution their monstrous male egos demanded! She flung open the bathroom door, clad only in her wet underpants and Ramon's white shirt, and stalked out of the empty house.

Ramon was in the front yard, calmly spreading the blanket she had brought in the trunk of the car, beneath a tree. Of all the monumental arrogance . . . ! He actually believed she would meekly tolerate this sort of treatment. He truly expected her to stay here and have a cozy little picnic with him!

Ramon paused in his crouching position and looked up at her, his expression impassive. "Do not ever slam another door in my face," he said evenly. And then, as if that was supposed to conclude the entire episode, his expression warmed admiringly. Seething inwardly, Katie folded her arms beneath her breasts, leaned her shoulder against the doorframe, and crossed one trim ankle over the other, letting him look his fill. Because looking at her was all he was going to do. In another few seconds she was going to pick up that blanket, wrap it around her and drive back to Gabriella's!

Ramon's gaze moved from the cascade of reddish hair hanging in damp waves down her shoulders, over her thrusting breasts revealed by the clinging shirt, paused at the place where his shirt ended at mid-thigh, then continued down her long, shapely legs. "Have you seen enough?" she asked him, not bothering to hide her hostility. "Are you quite satisfied?"

His head lifted sharply, his eyes assessing her face as if he could not quite fathom her mood. "Is 'satisfying' me what you have in mind, Katie?"

Ignoring the sexual innuendo, Katie straightened and strolled over to the blanket where he was sitting back on his heels. "I'm leaving," she said, looking down at him with stony hauteur.

"There is no need to go for more clothes. Yours will dry, and in the meantime, I have already seen you wearing far less."

"I'm not going for more clothes. I have no intention of staying here for a picnic after you purposely soaked me to get even."

Ramon came slowly to his feet, towering over her, and Katie angrily kept her eyes on the bare expanse of his bronzed chest. "I need the blanket to put around me so that I can go back to Gabriella's, and you're standing on it."

"So I am," he said softly, stepping back.

Katie snatched it up, wrapped it around her toga-style and headed for the car, aware that Ramon was leaning casually against a tree, watching her every step. She slid behind the steering wheel and reached for the keys she had left in the ignition. They were gone. She didn't need to search the seat, she knew exactly who had them.

She glowered at him through the open car window, and he reached into his pocket, extracted the keys and held them out to her in his open palm. "You will need these."

Katie climbed out of the car and marched toward him with as much dignity as her trailing blanket would allow. Warily, she searched his face when she came within arm's reach. "Give them to me," she said, thrusting out her hand.

"Take them," he replied indifferently.

"Do you swear you won't touch me?"

"I would not dream of it," Ramon replied with infuriating calm. "But I see no reason why I should not make you touch me." In angry stupefaction Katie watched him shove the keys into the deep pocket of his Levi's, and cross his arms over his chest. "Go ahead and take them."

"Are you enjoying this?" Katie hissed furiously.

"I am planning to."

Katie was now so angry, she'd have knocked him down and wrestled him for the damned keys. She strode up to him, jammed her hand down into his side pocket, ignoring the intimacy, and jerked them out. "Thank you," she said snidely.

"Thank you," he replied suggestively.

She whirled around and took a step, only to have her blanket come loose and fall to the ground—with the aid of Ramon's booted foot, which was firmly planted on the end of it. With her fists clenched impotently at her sides, Katie swung around on her heel.

"How could you think I would deliberately do a thing like that to you?" he asked her quietly.

Katie scanned his handsome, composed face, and her anger evaporated, leaving her deflated. "Didn't you?"

"What do you think?"

Katie bit her lip, feeling utterly foolish and thoroughly obnoxious. "I—I don't think you did," she admitted, glancing at her bare feet in dejected shame.

His voice was tinged with amusement. "Now what are you going to do?"

Katie's blue eyes were warm with laughter and apology when she raised them to his. "I am going to show you how sorry I am by waiting on you hand and foot for the rest of the night!"

"I see," he said with an answering grin. "In that case, what should I do now?"

"Just stand there while I arrange the blanket, then I'll pour you some wine and fix you a sandwich." With amused satisfaction, Ramon allowed her to fix him three roast beef sandwiches, keep his wineglass filled, and provide him with slices of cheese whenever he requested one.

"A man could get used to this," he chuckled when Katie insisted on not only peeling his apple but cutting it into wedges and feeding it to him.

Katie looked at him in the deepening twilight, her senses alive to his nearness. He was stretched out on his back, his hands linked behind his head, looking like a lithe, powerful jungle cat who knows that his prey is within reach and not going to escape.

"Katie," he murmured in a sensuous voice. "Do you know what I want now?"

Katie's hand stilled as she lifted her glass of wine to her lips, her pulse quickening. "What?" she asked softly.

"One of your back rubs," he announced, rolling onto his stomach, presenting his back for his ministrations.

Katie put her glass aside and came up on her knees beside him. His broad, muscled shoulders and tapered back felt like bunched satin, smooth and warm beneath her stroking fingers. She continued kneading and rubbing his hard flesh until her hands tired, then she sat back down and picked up her wineglass.

"Katie?" he said again, turning his dark head away from her.

"Hmm?"

"I did it on purpose."

In one lightning movement, Katie dumped her wine on his bare back, scampered to her feet and sprinted toward the house. Ramon grabbed her by the waist when she was halfway across the dark living room, his whole body shaking with laughter as she kicked backward at him. "You beast!" she gasped, caught somewhere between hilarity and hostility. "You are the most treacherous, arrogant—"

"Innocent person you know," he chuckled. "I give you my word."

"I could murder you!" she laughed, wriggling and writhing ineffectually in his unbreakable hold.

Behind her, his deep voice suddenly became very husky. "If you continue to do that, *I* am going to need a cold shower."

Katie stilled, becoming aware of the stirring hardness pressing against her rounded bottom, while desire began to pour through her veins. His lips brushed her ear, then slid sensuously down the curve of her neck, tasting and exploring every inch of her exposed skin. His hands caressed her breasts with the same possessive mastery that always made her knees weak.

"Your nipples are hard," he told her in a low, throbbing voice, his thumbs brushing over the hardened, sensitized nubs. "And your breasts are swelling to fill my hands. Turn around, *querida*," he murmured hotly, "I want to feel them against my chest."

Shivering with anticipation, Katie turned in his arms. He stared at the cleft between her full, aching breasts, then lifted his burning gaze to hers. Mesmerized, Katie watched his mouth slowly descending, as his hand slid up her nape and his fingers sank into her heavy hair.

The moment his parted lips covered hers the kiss was out of control. His tongue plunged into her mouth with a driving hunger and naked urgency that made Katie burst into flames in his arms. His free hand swept down her spine, fusing her melting body to the scorching heat of his thighs, holding her there as he kissed her into absolute insensibility. He lifted his mouth from hers. "Come outside with me," he ordered hoarsely, and when Katie whispered "Yes," he groaned and buried his lips in the moist softness of hers for one more endless, shattering kiss.

A blinding flash of light exploded behind Katie's closed eyelids at the same instant a voice demanded, "May I ask who performed the wedding that precipitated this honeymoon, Ramon?"

Katie's eyes snapped open, her shocked gaze flew to the peculiarly garbed man who was standing in the now brightly lit room, then ricochetted to

Ramon, whose head was thrown back, his eyes tightly shut, his expression a combination of utter disbelief, irritation and amusement. Sighing, Ramon finally opened his eyes and looked over his left shoulder at the intruder. "Padre Gregorio, I—"

Katie's knees buckled.

Ramon's arms tightened, his gaze swerving from the priest to Katie's white face with its huge, stricken eyes. "Katie, are you all right?" he asked anxiously.

"I am certain that Señorita Connelly is not all right," the old priest snapped. "She would undoubtedly like to go and clothe herself."

Embarrassed antagonism brought bright flags of color to Katie's pale cheeks. "My clothes are soaking wet," she said. Unfortunately at that moment she became conscious that with Ramon's arms around her, his shirt was hiked up above the lace band at the leg of her underpants. Self-consciously she jerked the shirt down and pulled away from Ramon's supporting arms.

"Then perhaps you would like to put that blanket I saw outside, to the use for which it was intended, and cover yourself with it."

Ramon said something in sharp Spanish to the priest and reached out to stop Katie, but she sidestepped and stalked outside. She was humiliated, intimidated and furiously angry with herself for feeling like a naughty fifteen-year-old. That hateful, domineering old man was the priest whose approval she had to win before he would perform their marriage, she raged inwardly. Never, never in her life had she despised anyone more! In ten seconds he had made her feel dirty and cheap. She who was practically a virgin by today's standards!

Ramon was speaking to the priest in a calm voice when Katie entered the cottage wrapped in the blanket. He held his arm out to her and drew her comfortingly close to his side, but his first words were laced with reproof. "Why did you not keep your appointment with Padre Gregorio, Katie?"

Katie's chin lifted defensively as she looked at the priest. Bald at the crown, his head was circled with a wide rim of white hair. His bushy white eyebrows slanted up at the ends, giving him a satanic look, which Katie thought was entirely appropriate for an old devil! Nevertheless, her eyes wavered when they collided with his piercing blue ones. "I forgot it."

Katie could actually feel Ramon's narrowed gaze aimed at her head.

"In that case," Padre Gregorio said in a cool, uncompromising voice, "Perhaps you would care to make another—for four o'clock tomorrow afternoon."

Katie agreed to this command performance with an ungracious, "Very well."

"I will drive you back to the village, Padre," Ramon said.

Katie nearly dropped through the floor when, after nodding his acceptance, the priest directed a meaningful look at her over the rim of his wire spectacles. "I am certain that Señorita Connelly wants to return to Gabriella's now. It is growing late."

Without waiting for Ramon to reply, Katie turned abruptly and walked into the bathroom, closing the door. In a state of suffocating humiliation, she struggled into her damp clothing and combed her fingers through her hair.

Pulling open the door, she walked right into Ramon, who was standing in the doorway, his hands braced high against the frame on either side of her. The wry amusement in his expression chafed against her already lacerated emotions. "Katie, he thinks he is protecting your virtue from my lecherous intentions."

Katie, who was suddenly perilously close to tears, stared at the cleft in Ramon's chin. "He doesn't believe for one minute that I have any virtue! Now please let's go, I want to get out of here. I—I'm tired."

As Katie stalked toward Padre Gregorio who was standing at the car, her soaked canvas shoes made a loud, squishing noise and her denim Levi's slapped wetly against her legs. This indisputable proof that her clothes had truly been soaked brought a flickering smile of approval to the priest's lips, but Katie merely gave him a frosty look and slid into the car. On the way to the village, he made two attempts to converse with her, which Katie discouraged by replying in monosyllables.

After leaving the priest in the village, they pulled up at Gabriella's house. Fifteen minutes later, when Katie emerged from her bedroom in dry clothes, Ramon was standing in the living room, talking with Gabriella's husband, Eduardo. The moment he saw her, Ramon excused himself and invited Katie outside. Most of the ill effects from her encounter with Padre Gregorio had evaporated, but Katie was vaguely uneasy about Ramon's mood.

In heavy silence, they strolled through the neat little backyard. At the far end of it, Katie stopped and leaned her shoulders against a tree trunk. Ramon's hands came down on either side of her, imprisoning her. Katie saw the determination in his jaw and the cool speculation in his intent gaze. "Why did you not go to see Padre Gregorio this afternoon, Katie?"

Completely taken aback, Katie stammered. "I—I told you, I forget."

"I reminded you this morning when I came to see you, before I left for work. How could you forget it a few hours later?"

"I forgot it," she said defensively, "because I was busy doing what I've been doing for four days—trying to buy everything you need for your house."

"Why do you always refer to it as my house instead of our house?" he persisted relentlessly.

"Why are you suddenly asking me all these questions?" Katie burst out.

"Because when I ask myself the questions, I do not like the answers that occur to me." Moving back a step, he calmly extracted a thin cigar and lighter from his pocket. With his hands cupped over the flame he lit it, watching an uncomfortable Katie through the haze of aromatic smoke. "Padre Gregorio is the only possible obstacle to our getting married in ten days, is he not?"

Katie felt as if he were verbally stalking her, backing her into a corner. "I suppose so, yes."

"Tell me something," he said with casual curiosity. "Are you planning to keep your appointment with him tomorrow?"

Katie raked her hair off her forehead in an agitated gesture. "Yes, I'm going to keep it. But you may as well know right now that he doesn't like me, and I think he's nothing but a tyrannical busybody."

Ramon dismissed this with a noncommittal shrug. "I believe it is customary, even in the States, for a priest to assure himself that an engaged couple is reasonably suited to each other and has a good chance of making a successful marriage. That is all he wishes to do."

"He's not going to believe that about us! He's already decided the opposite."

"No, he has not," Ramon stated implacably. He moved closer and Katie unconsciously pressed back against the rough bark of the tree. His gaze roamed her face, calculating her answer to his next question before he even asked it. "Do you *want* him to decide we are not suited, Katie?"

"No!" Katie whispered.

"Tell me about your first marriage," he commanded abruptly.

"I will not!" Katie flung back, her whole body stiffening with anger. "Don't ever ask me to do that, because I won't. I try never to think about it."

"If you had truly recovered from it without scars," Ramon continued, "You should be able to talk about it without pain."

"Talk about it?!" Katie exploded in stunned rage. "Talk about it?" The violence of her own reaction momentarily shocked Katie into silence. Drawing a deep breath, she gained control of her stampeding emotions. With an apologetic smile at Ramon who was studying her like a specimen under a microscope, she said, "It's only that I don't want the ugliness of the past to spoil the present, and it would. Surely you can see that?"

The ghost of a reluctant smile touched Ramon's face as he gazed down at the smooth perfection of her glowing features. "I can see," he sighed softly. His hands slid up her arms in a gentle caress, tightening to draw her close against his heart. "I can see that you have a beautiful smile, and that you look tired."

Katie twined her arms around his neck. She knew he wasn't satisfied with her explanation, and she was grateful beyond words that he wasn't going to pursue it further. "I am a little tired. I think I'll go to bed."

"And when you are lying in bed, what do you think about?" he asked, his voice husky and teasing.

Katie's eyes held an answering sparkle. "A color scheme for the kitchen," she lied.

"Oh, is that right?" he breathed softly.

Katie nodded, a slow smile touching her lips. "What do you think about?"

"The wholesale price of pineapples."

"Liar," she whispered, her gaze on the sensual mouth that had moved tantalizingly close to hers.

"Yellow," he breathed against her lips.

"You mean the pineapples?" Katie murmured absently.

"I mean the kitchen."

"I thought green," she said, her heart pounding with anticipation.

Ramon drew back abruptly, his entire expression friendly and thoughtful. "Perhaps you are right. Green is a lively color, and one rarely becomes tired of it." He turned her and headed her toward the house with an affectionate pat on her derriere. "You think about it in bed tonight."

Katie took a few surprised steps, then turned to look at Ramon with puzzled disappointment.

His even white teeth flashed in a lazy grin as he quirked a brow at her. "Did you want something more? Something better to think about in bed, perhaps?"

Katie felt the sexual magnetism he was exuding as if it were some primitive force against which she had no resistance.

Even his velvet voice seemed to reach out and touch her. "Come here, Katie, and I will give it to you."

Katie's whole body felt flushed as she walked into his crushing embrace. The turmoil of the last hour, the wild fluctuations of mood from desire to humiliation to anger and now to teasing, had twisted Katie into a mass of raw emotion that exploded the instant Ramon's arms closed around her.

Driven by a desperate need to somehow reassure Ramon—and herself—that everything was going to be all right, she kissed him with an unleashed urgency, a deep passion that sent a tremor through his powerful frame and made his arms tighten convulsively.

Ramon pulled his lips from hers and kissed her face, her forehead, her eyes, her neck.

And just before his mouth sought hers for one last stormy kiss, she thought he whispered, "Katie, I love you."

15

*K*atie and Gabriella spent the morning and most of the afternoon combing through shops in two neighboring villages. Katie liked Gabriella immensely. Besides being a wonderful companion, she was a tireless shopper. At times she was more enthusiastic about what Katie was doing than Katie was. But then, endless shopping with hundreds of things to buy and no time to do it was not Katie's idea of pleasure.

Katie paid for the sheets and coverlet she had just bought, while Gabriella delicately removed herself from the procedure that involved Katie's requesting duplicate bills, each for one-half the amount of her purchase, then paying for it using equal parts of Ramon's money and her own.

"I think Ramon will like the colors I chose for the bedroom, don't you?" Katie asked gaily as they slid into the car.

"He should," Gabriella said, turning in the seat to look at Katie with a smile. Her thick black hair was beautifully windblown and her eyes were bright. "Everything you buy is to suit him and not yourself. I would have bought the coverlet with the ruffles."

Katie, who was driving, glanced in the rearview mirror before pulling into the slow traffic, then she fired a wry look at Gabriella.

"Somehow I can't quite see Ramon surrounded by dainty ruffles with pastel flowers."

"Eduardo is as manly as Ramon and he would not object if I chose to make our bedroom feminine."

Katie had to admit to herself that what Gabriella said was true; Eduardo would probably acquiesce to Gabriella's wishes with one of those faint, amused smiles he frequently gave her. In the last four days, Katie had revised her opinion of Eduardo. He didn't look at the world with stern, disapproving eyes—he only looked at Katie that way. He was always unfailingly courteous to her, but the moment she walked into the room the warmth left his expression.

It might not have been so uncomfortable for Katie if he were small and homely or big and slow-witted, but the truth of the matter was that Eduardo was a very impressive man, which immediately made Katie feel that she was somehow lacking. At thirty-five, he was extremely handsome in a darkly Spanish way. He was three inches shorter than Ramon, with a powerful build and an attitude of confident male supremacy that alternately annoyed and intrigued Katie. He was not Ramon's equal in either looks or polish, but when the two men were together there was an easy comradery between them that made Katie acutely aware that she, and only she, failed to meet some unknown standard of Eduardo's. He treated his wife with indulgent affection; Ramon with an odd combination of friendship and admiration . . . and Katie with nothing more than courtesy.

"Have I done something to offend Eduardo?" Katie asked aloud, half-expecting Gabriella to deny anything unusual in his attitude.

"You must not pay any attention to him," Gabriella said with amazing candor. "Eduardo mistrusts all American girls, especially wealthy ones such as you. He thinks they are spoiled and irresponsible, among other things."

Katie assumed that "other things" probably included promiscuous. "What makes him think I'm wealthy?" she asked cautiously.

Gabriella flashed an apologetic smile at her. "Your luggage. Eduardo used to work at the desk of a fancy hotel in San Juan while he was going to school. He says your luggage costs more than all the furniture in our living room."

Before Katie could recover, Gabriella turned grave. "Eduardo likes Ramon very much for many reasons, and he is afraid that you will not adjust to being a Spanish farmer's wife. Eduardo thinks, because you are a wealthy American woman, that you lack courage, that you will leave when you discover that your life here is sometimes hard; that when the crop is poor or prices are low you will flaunt your money in front of Ramon."

Katie flushed uncomfortably and Gabriella nodded sagely. "That is why Eduardo must never discover that you are paying for part of the furniture. He would condemn you for disobeying Ramon and he would think you are doing this because what Ramon could buy wasn't good enough for you. I do not know why you are paying for things, Katie, but I do not think it is because of that. Someday you can tell me if you wish to do so, but in the meantime Eduardo must not find out. He would tell Ramon immediately."

"Neither of them will find out unless you say something," Katie reassured with a smile.

"You know I will not." Gabriella glanced up at the sun. "Do you want to go to the auction at that house in Mayagüez? We are very close."

Katie readily agreed, and three hours later she was proud owner of a dining set for the kitchen, a sofa and two chairs. The house had been owned by a wealthy bachelor who, before his death, had obviously developed an appreciation for fine wood, excellent craftsmanship and solid comfort. The chairs were wing-backed, deeply tufted in a nubby cream cloth with rust threads. There were two ottomans to match. The sofa was rust with wide rolled arms and deep, thick cushions. "Ramon will love it," Katie said as she paid the auctioneer and arranged to have the furniture delivered to the cottage.

"Katie, will you love it?" Gabriella asked anxiously. "You are going to live there too, yet you have not bought one thing just because you want it."

"Of course I have," Katie said.

At ten minutes to four, Gabriella stopped the car in front of Padre Gregorio's little house. It was on the east side of the village square, directly across the street from the church, easily identified by its white paint and dark green shutters. Katie took her handbag off the seat, threw a nervous smile at Gabriella, and slid out of the car.

"Are you certain you don't want me to wait for you?" Gabriella asked.

"Positive," Katie said. "It isn't a long walk to your house from here, and I'll have plenty of time to change clothes afterward and go to see Ramon at the cottage."

Reluctantly Katie walked up to the front door. She paused to smooth the skirt of her pastel green cotton shirtwaist dress and run a shaky hand over her light red hair, which was caught into a soft chignon with tendrils at her ears. She looked, she hoped, very prim proper and composed. She felt like a nervous wreck.

An elderly housekeeper answered Katie's knock and admitted her into the house. Following her down the dim hall, Katie felt like a condemned prisoner walking the last steps to meet the executioner—though why she felt so upset was something that baffled her.

Padre Gregorio stood up when she entered his study. He was thinner and shorter than she had thought last night, which was absurdly reassuring considering that they weren't going to engage in physical combat. Katie took the seat he indicated across the desk from him, and he sat down.

For a moment they regarded each other with polite wariness, then he said, "Would you care for some coffee?"

"Thank you, no," Katie replied with a fixed, courteous smile. "I haven't a great deal of time to spare." That was the wrong thing to say, Katie realized as his bushy white brows snapped together over his nose.

"No doubt you have more important things to do," he said curtly.

"Not for myself," Katie hastily explained, by way of a truce. "For Ramon."

To her immense relief, Padre Gregorio accepted the truce offering. His tight lips relaxed into something that was almost a smile as he nodded his white head. "Ramon is in a great hurry to have everything finished, and he must be keeping you extremely busy." Reaching into his desk, he pulled out some forms and picked up his pen. "Let us begin by completing these forms. Your full name and age, please?"

Katie told him.

"Marital status?" Before Katie could answer, he glanced up and sadly said, "Ramon mentioned that your first husband died. How tragic for you to have been widowed in the first bloom of your marriage."

Hypocrisy had never been one of Katie's faults. Politely but firmly she said, "I was 'widowed' in the first bloom of our divorce, and if there was a tragedy, it was that we were ever married at all."

Behind the spectacles the blue eyes narrowed. "I beg your pardon?"

"I divorced him before he died."

"For what reason?"

"Irreconcilable differences."

"I did not ask you for the legal grounds, I asked you the reason."

His prying struck sparks of rebellion in Katie's breast, and she expelled a slow, calming breath. "I divorced him because I despised him."

"Why?"

"I would rather not discuss it."

"I see," Padre Gregorio said. He shoved the papers aside, laid down his pen, and Katie felt the fragile truce begin to crumble. "In that case, perhaps you would not object to discussing Ramon and yourself. How long have you known each other?"

"Only two weeks."

"What an unusual answer," he remarked. "Where did you meet?"

"In the States."

"Señorita Connelly," he said in a chilling tone, "would you consider it an invasion of your privacy if I asked you to be a little more specific?"

Katie's eyes flashed militantly. "Not at all, Padre. I met Ramon at a bar— a *cantina*, I think you call it here."

He looked stunned. "Ramon met you in a *cantina?*"

"Actually, it was outside."

"Pardon?"

"It was outside, in the parking lot. I was having some trouble and Ramon helped me."

Padre Gregorio relaxed in his chair and nodded his complete approval. "Of course. You were having automobile trouble, and Ramon assisted you."

As if she had taken an oath to tell the whole truth and nothing but, Katie corrected him. "Actually, I was having trouble with a man who was, ah, kissing me in the parking lot, and Ramon hit him. He was a little intoxicated, I think."

Behind his gold wire spectacles, the priest's eyes turned into icicles. "Señorita," he said with contempt, "are you trying to tell me that Ramon Galverra engaged in a drunken brawl in a public parking lot of a *cantina* over some woman he did not know—namely, you?"

"Of course not! Ramon hadn't been drinking, and I certainly wouldn't call it a brawl—he only hit Rob once, and that knocked him unconscious."

"And then what?" the priest demanded impatiently.

Unfortunately, Katie's wayward sense of humor chose that moment to assert itself. "Then we stuffed Rob in his car, and Ramon and I drove away in mine."

"Charming."

A genuine smile drifted across Katie's features. "Actually, it wasn't quite as terrible as it sounds."

"I find that hard to believe."

Katie's smile faded. Her eyes turned a deep, rebellious blue. "Believe whatever you wish, Padre."

"It is what *you* wish me to believe that astounds me, *señorita*," he snapped, rising from behind his desk. Katie stood up, her emotions so tangled by this unexpectedly abrupt conclusion to their interview that she scarcely knew whether she felt relieved or worried. "What do you mean by that?" she asked, puzzled.

"You think about it, and we will meet again on Monday morning at nine."

An hour later, Katie had changed into slacks and a white knit shirt. She felt angry, bewildered and guilty as she began the hike up the long hill from Gabriella's house to the cottage where Ramon was working.

On the first plateau, she turned to look out over the hills splashed with wild flowers. She could still pick out the roof of Gabriella's house, and Rafael's house, and of course, the village itself. Ramon's cottage was so much higher than the surrounding houses—two more plateaus up, in fact—that Katie decided to sit down and rest. Drawing her legs up against her chest, she wrapped her arms around them and perched her chin on her knees.

"It is what *you* wish me to believe that astounds me, *señorita*," the old priest had said. He actually made it seem as if she were *trying* to give him a bad impression, Katie thought angrily, when in actuality she had shopped all day in a shirtwaist and heels so that she would be appropriately and respectfully dressed when she kept her appointment!

She had merely told him the truth about how she and Ramon had met, and if that outraged his old-fashioned morality it was certainly not her fault. If he didn't want his questions answered, he shouldn't ask so many of them, Katie thought wrathfully.

The more she thought about it, the more blameless Katie felt for the hostile tone of her first meeting with Padre Gregorio. In fact, she was feeling quite justifiably indignant about the whole thing until Ramon's words floated through her mind. "How could you forget your appointment with Padre Gregorio only a few hours after I reminded you of it? . . . Padre Gregorio is the only possible obstacle to our getting married in ten days. . . . Do you *want* him to decide we are not suited, Katie?"

Uncertainty promptly cooled Katie's ire. How could she have forgotten that appointment? Her first wedding had required months of preparation and countless appointments with dressmakers, florists, caterers, photographers, printers and a half-dozen other people. Not once had she ever "forgotten" an appointment with any of them.

Had she subconsciously wanted to forget yesterday's appointment with Padre Gregorio, Katie wondered a little guiltily. Had she deliberately tried to make a bad impression on Padre Gregorio today? That question made Katie squirm inwardly. No, she hadn't tried to impress him either way—bad or good, she admitted to herself. But she *had* let him form a distorted and unflattering image of her meeting with Ramon at the Canyon Inn, without trying to correct it.

When he tried to probe into her divorce she had practically told him it was none of his business. With innate honesty, Katie conceded that it was very much his business. On the other hand, she felt she had a right to resent anyone—anyone at all—who tried to force her to discuss David. Still, she could have been less hostile about the subject. She could have simply told Padre Gregorio that her reason for divorcing David was adultery and physical brutality. Then, if he tried to delve further into the subject, she could have explained that the details were impossible for her to discuss and she would rather forget about it.

That's what she should have done. Instead she had been uncooperative, flippant and coldly defiant. In fact, she could not remember ever being so brazenly discourteous to anyone in her life. As a result, she had antagonized the only man who could stand in the way of her marrying Ramon in ten days. What a foolish, irrational thing for her to have done.

Katie picked up an African tulip that had fallen beside her and began idly stripping it of its scarlet petals. Unbidden, Gabriella's words came to mind. "You have not bought one thing just because *you* want it." At the time, Katie had disregarded that as being untrue. But now that she really thought about it, she realized that she had unconsciously avoided choosing one single item that would put the stamp of her femininity, or her personality, on Ramon's house. Because that would obligate her to marry him and live there.

The closer their wedding day came, the more alarmed and hesitant she was becoming. There was no point in denying it, but admitting it didn't help either. When she left St. Louis with Ramon she had been so certain that coming here was the right thing to do. Now, she was certain of nothing. She couldn't understand her fear or her uncertainty; she couldn't even understand some of the things she was doing! For someone who prided herself on her logical thinking, she was suddenly behaving like a complete neurotic. There was absolutely no excuse for her behavior, Katie thought angrily.

Or perhaps there was. The last time she had committed herself to a man, to marriage, her world had fallen apart. Few people knew better than she what an agonizing, humiliating experience a bad marriage could be. Perhaps marriage was not worth the risk. Perhaps she should never have considered remarrying and—no! Absolutely not!

She would not let the emotional scars David left her with ruin her life and destroy her chance to have a warm and happy marriage. She would not give David Caldwell that much satisfaction—dead or alive!

Katie jumped up and brushed off her slacks. On the second plateau, she turned again and looked down on the village. She smiled softly, thinking that it looked like a page from a travel brochure; tiny white toy buildings nestled in green hills, with the church in the center. The church where she would be married in ten days.

Her stomach instantly clenched into knots at the thought, and Katie could have wept in desperation. She felt as if she were being torn to pieces. Her mind pulled her one way and her heart tugged another. Fear coiled in her chest, desire pulsed through her veins, and her love for Ramon burned like a steady, glowing fire in the center of it all.

And she did love him. She loved him very much.

She had never actually admitted that to herself before, and the admission sent a fierce jolt of pleasure and panic through her. Now that she acknowledged her feelings, why couldn't she just accept her love for this beautiful, tender, passionate man, and follow wherever it led her?

Follow love wherever it led her, Katie thought with bitter despair. She had done that once before, and it had led her into a living nightmare. Biting her lip, Katie turned away and started up the hill again.

Why was she suddenly thinking of David and her first marriage all the time, she wondered miserably. The only similarity between David and

Ramon, other than their height and coloring, was that they were both intelligent. David had been an ambitious, talented attorney; a polished, worldly man. While Ramon. . . .

While Ramon was an enigma, a puzzle: a well-spoken, widely read, intelligent man with an intense interest in, and staggering grasp of, world affairs. A man who could mingle with effortless ease among her parents' sophisticated friends—a man who chose, nevertheless, to be a farmer. A man who chose to be a farmer, yet had no deep feeling, no real pride, in his land. He had never offered to take Katie into the fields, even though she had asked to see them, and when he discussed improving the farm with Rafael, Ramon spoke with resolute determination—but never any real enthusiasm.

Katie had been so surprised by his attitude that earlier this week she asked him if he had ever wanted to do something besides farm. Ramon had answered with an uninformative "Yes."

"Then why are you going to do it?" Katie had persisted.

"Because the farm is here," he had replied unanswerably. "Because it is ours. Because I have found more peace and joy being here with you than I have ever known."

Peace from what, Katie wondered desperately. And if he was really happy, he didn't always look it. In fact, there were many times this past week when Katie had glanced at him and glimpsed a grim tautness in his face, a ravaged harshness in his eyes. The instant he realized she was watching him, the expression would vanish. He would smile at her—one of his warmly intimate smiles.

What was he hiding from her? Some deep sadness? Or something much worse? A streak of viciousness like David's or—

Katie shook her head in denial. Ramon was nothing like David. Nothing like him. She stopped in her climb to break off a branch of a small flamboyant tree. It was covered with yellow blossoms and she raised the branch to her nose, trying to chase away the tormenting uncertainties that pursued her everywhere.

As she came to the top of the hill, Katie heard the sounds of hammers and saws coming from the cottage. Four painters were working on the outside applying a fresh coat of white paint to the bricks and wood trim, another was painting the shutters black.

Her spirits lifted when she compared the run-down hovel it had seemed to be on Sunday, with the way it looked now. In five days, with the help of an army of carpenters, Ramon was transforming it into the picturesque little house he must have remembered visiting in the days when his grandfather lived here.

"Flower boxes," Katie said aloud. She tipped her head to the side, trying to visualize the boxes blooming with flowers below the wide windows on either side of the front door. That was exactly what the cottage needed, she decided. That would make it a storybook cottage in a storybook setting on a storybook island. But would her life be a storybook life here?

She found Ramon stepping off a ladder on the far side of the house where he had also been painting. At the sound of her softly spoken "Hi" he turned in surprise; a slow, devastatingly attractive smile sweeping across his tanned features. He was so obviously pleased to see her that Katie felt suddenly, absurdly happy too.

"I brought you something," she joked, taking the blossom-covered branch from behind her back and thrusting it toward him like a bouquet.

"Flowers?" Ramon teased, accepting the branch with grave formality. "For me?"

Though his tone was light, Katie caught the warmth kindling in his expressive eyes. She nodded, a provocative smile curving her lips. "Tomorrow it will be candy."

"And the next day?"

"Oh, jewelry is customary. Something tastefully expensive, but small— nothing ostentatious that might alert you to my true intentions."

He grinned. "And the next day?"

"Lock your doors and guard your virtue, because that's collection day," she laughed.

His broad chest was bare, gleaming like oiled bronze, and he smelled like soap and sweat, a combination that Katie found strangely stimulating as he pulled her into his arms. "For you," he said as his hands moved lazily over her back and his mobile mouth came nearer to hers, "I will be an easy conquest: my virtue for the flowers alone."

"Shameless hussy!" Katie teased a little breathlessly.

His eyes darkened. "Kiss me, Katie."

✿16

Katie's head jerked up as Padre Gregorio said her name from the altar, followed by Ramon's. He was reading the banns, she realized. Everyone in the crowded church seemed to turn in unison toward the pew near the back where

Katie and Ramon were seated between Gabriella and her husband, and Rafael's family.

The villagers certainly knew who Ramon Galverra Vicente was, Katie thought, which wasn't surprising, since he had been born here. But what was surprising was their peculiar attitude toward him. From the moment he had walked into church at her side, they had been watching him with open curiosity. A few of the villagers nodded or smiled at him, but there was curiosity in their expressions too, mixed with uncertainty and even awe.

Of course, Ramon's demeanor before the service began had definitely discouraged anyone who might have wanted to make a friendly overture. With an aloof, coolly courteous smile, he had passed one glance over the inquisitive occupants of the church, sat down beside Katie, and completely ignored them.

Katie shifted uncomfortably in the hard pew, her expression one of rapt attention as she listened to Padre Gregorio's sermon, of which she understood not one word. She was beginning to wonder if the fates were all conspiring to prevent Ramon and her from being alone together for any appreciable length of time. In the last seven days there had been no occasion for the "sharing of each other" that Ramon had predicted there would be.

On Friday, while Katie was still wrapped in Ramon's arms joyously receiving his drugging kisses of gratitude for his "bouquet," a bank of dark clouds had rolled across the sky, blotting out the sun. What began as a sprinkle soon became a downpour. They spent a pleasant, if very unsatisfactory, evening playing cards with Gabriella and her husband.

Saturday it cleared, and the men worked all day at the cottage. Now that the electricity was on, Ramon was keeping them working inside when darkness fell, which eliminated the cottage as a trysting place. Early Saturday evening, Gabriella's husband, Eduardo, suggested to Ramon that Katie might enjoy a trip to Phosphorescent Bay.

Katie had been amazed that Eduardo, of all people, would suggest a romantic outing for them, as well as offer his car for the drive to the southwestern coast of the island. She couldn't imagine Eduardo in the role of Cupid, when she knew he heartily disapproved of her. The mystery was solved the moment Ramon consulted Katie and she eagerly agreed to the trip. "Then it is settled," Eduardo said. "Gabriella and I will be pleased to have you accompany us." That effectively prevented Ramon and her from being alone in the house while Eduardo took Gabriella to the bay. Beneath Ramon's expression of bland surprise, Katie could tell that he was very annoyed with his friend.

Despite that, the evening was an unexpected success. At the beginning of the fifty-mile drive over well-maintained island roads, Ramon was silent and thoughtful as he sat beside Katie in the backseat. Realizing that Eduardo was the cause, Katie put on her brightest smile and soon had Ramon grinning at her while he tried to answer her endless questions about the passing landscape.

Phosphorescent Bay was a magical experience for Katie. The same heavy clouds that had brought the rain and kept most of the tourists away from the Bay, also obliterated the moon. With Gabriella and Eduardo in the front of the rented motorboat and Katie and Ramon in the rear, Katie alternately turned her face up to Ramon's for a lingering stolen kiss, then twisted in her seat to watch the shimmering green lights that swelled in the wake of the boat. At Ramon's suggestion, she leaned over the side and dipped her arm into the water. When she lifted it, a veil of the same shimmering green lights clung to her arm. Even the fish that leaped from the water left a shower of light behind them.

For his part, Ramon relaxed in the boat, looking like an indulgently amused native who was humoring three tourists. If there was anything he enjoyed more than watching Katie enjoy herself, it was thwarting Eduardo's wish to have some romantic privacy with his wife in the back of the boat. Each time Eduardo suggested Ramon and Katie take the front seat, Ramon declined with a good-natured, "We are perfectly comfortable back here, Eduardo."

By the end of the evening, it was Eduardo who looked annoyed and Ramon who was grinning with satisfaction.

Thunder boomed, echoing through the dim church, followed by a triple flash of lightning that illuminated the splendid stained-glass windows. Katie smiled wryly, accepting what was apparently going to be another day when the weather drove them indoors, another day and evening when Ramon and she would not even be able to talk alone.

"We have a perfect day for shopping," Gabriella announced at eight-thirty the next morning as she carried her cup of coffee into Katie's bedroom. "The sun is out," she added gaily, sitting down on the bed. She sipped her coffee, watching Katie who was getting ready for her appointment with Padre Gregorio.

"Do I look demure enough, do you think?" Katie asked, straightening the gold chain at the waist of her mandarin-collared white dress.

"You look perfect," Gabriella smiled. "You look the way you always look—beautiful!"

Katie rolled her eyes, laughingly accepting the compliment as she left the house, and promised to come back for Gabriella as soon as she was finished with Padre Gregorio.

Fifteen minutes later, Katie was not laughing. She was pinned to her chair, flushing under Padre Gregorio's piercing scrutiny.

"I asked," he repeated ominously, "if Ramon knows that you are using your money, your credit cards, to pay for the furnishings for that house?"

"No," Katie admitted apprehensively. "How did you find out?"

"We will get to that in a minute," he said in a low, angry voice. "First I want to know if you are aware that Ramon is returning to this village after an absence of many years? That he left it long ago for something better?"

"Yes—to work for a business that failed."

Her admission made Padre Gregorio look even angrier. "Then you understood that Ramon has come back here to start over again, with nothing?"

Katie nodded, feeling as if the ax were about to fall, though she wasn't certain from which direction.

"Do you have any idea, *señorita*, how much strength and courage it takes for a man to return to his birthplace, not as a success, but as a failure? Do you realize what it does to his pride when he must face people who all believed he had left them and achieved success—and who will now see that he has come back defeated?"

"I don't think Ramon feels defeated or disgraced," Katie protested.

Padre Gregorio's hand hit the desk with a crash. "No, he was not disgraced—but he is going to be, thanks to you! Thanks to you, everyone in this village is going to be saying that his rich *novia* from the United States had to pay for the towels so he could wipe his hands!"

"No one knows that I've been paying for half of everything!" Katie burst out. "Except you, and—no one," she amended quickly, protecting Gabriella.

"No one, except you and I," he mocked scathingly. "And Gabriella Alverez, of course. And half the village who are this minute gossiping about it to the other half! Do I make myself clear?"

Miserably, Katie nodded.

"Gabriella has obviously kept it secret from Eduardo, or he would have told Ramon. You have forced her to deceive her own husband for you!"

Apprehensively, Katie watched him trying to get control of his temper. "Señorita Connelly, is there the remotest, the slightest possibility that you thought Ramon would not object to what you are doing?"

More than anything, Katie longed to snatch at this excuse, but her pride prevented her from cowering. "No, I had mentioned to Ramon that I wanted to share the cost of things, and he—he wasn't pleased with the idea." She saw the priest's eyes narrow. "All right, he was adamantly opposed to it."

"So," he said in an awful voice. "Ramon told you not to, but you did it anyway, only slyly, is that it? You disobeyed him."

Katie's temper flared. "Do not use the word *disobey* to me, Padre. I am not a trained dog. Secondly, I would like to remind you that I have been 'slyly' spending a great deal of *my* money for Ramon which I think comes under the heading of charity, and is hardly a crime.

"Charity!" he exploded furiously. "Is that what Ramon is to you—a charity case, an object of pity?"

"No! Of course not!" Katie's eyes were huge with genuine horror.

"If you are paying for half of everything, then you are spending twice what he can afford. Are you so spoiled that you must have exactly what you want right now, this minute?"

Compared to this, Katie thought the Spanish Inquisition must have been a breeze. She couldn't avoid his question, and she certainly couldn't tell him she'd paid for half of everything so she wouldn't feel obligated to marry Ramon.

"I am waiting for an answer."

"And I would like to give you one," miserably. "Only I can't. I didn't do it for any of the reasons you think. It's too hard to explain."

"It is even harder to understand. In fact, *señorita,* I do not understand *you.* Gabriella is your friend, yet you do not hesitate to involve her in your treachery. You are staying under Eduardo's roof, yet you feel no remorse for repaying his hospitality by forcing his wife to mislead him. You want to marry Ramon, yet you disobey him, deceive him and disgrace him. How can you do that to someone you love?"

The color began draining out of Katie's face and Padre Gregorio, noting her stricken expression, shook his head in frustration. When he spoke again his voice was strained, but gentler. "*Señorita,* despite everything, I cannot believe that you are either selfish or heartless. You must have had some good reason for doing what you have; tell me so that I can understand."

Speechless with misery, Katie could only look at him.

"Tell me!" he said, his face angry and bewildered. "Tell me that you love Ramon, and that you did not realize the village would gossip. I would believe that; I would even help you explain it to Ramon. Just say that, and we will finish making the arrangements for your marriage right now."

Katie's stomach was cramping painfully, but her pale face was composed. "I don't owe you any explanations, Padre. And I will not discuss my feelings about Ramon with you, either."

His bushy white eyebrows knitted together into a thunderous scowl. Leaning back in his chair, he subjected Katie to a long penetrating stare. "You will not speak of your feelings for Ramon, because you have no feelings for him. . . . Is that it?"

"I didn't say that!" Katie denied, but the convulsive clenching of her hands in her lap betrayed her inner turmoil.

"Can you say you love him?"

Katie felt as if she were being torn to pieces by raging emotions she could neither understand nor control. She tried to say the words he was waiting to hear, to give him the assurance he had a right to expect, but she could not. All she could do was look at him in frozen silence.

Padre Gregorio's shoulders drooped. When he spoke, the terrible despair in his voice made her feel like bursting into tears. "I see," he said quietly. "Feeling as you do, what kind of wife could you possibly be to Ramon?"

"A good one!" Katie whispered fiercely.

The intensity of her emotion seemed to stun him. He stared at her again, as if he were truly trying to understand her. His gaze moved over her pale face, searching her blue eyes and discovering something in their agonized depths that brought a puzzled gentleness to his voice. "Very well," he said softly. "I will accept that."

This astonishing announcement had an equally astonishing effect on Katie, who suddenly began to shake from head to toe with an unexplainable mixture of relief and alarm.

"If you tell me that you are prepared to fulfill your duties as Ramon's wife, I will believe you. Are you willing to put his needs before your own, to honor and respect his——"

"Authority?" Katie provided tersely. "Don't forget 'obey' him," she added mutinously as she stood up. "Isn't that what you were going to ask?"

Padre Gregorio also arose. "Suppose that I was?" he queried in a tone of cool curiosity. "What would you say?"

"Exactly what any other woman with a brain, a mouth and a backbone should say to such an outrageous insulting suggestion! I will not, *will not* promise obedience to any man. Animals and children obey, not women!"

"Are you quite through, *señorita?*"

Katie swallowed and nodded firmly.

"Then allow me to tell you that I was not going to mention the word 'obey.' I was about to ask you if you were willing to respect Ramon's wishes, not his authority. And for your information, I would have asked Ramon for exactly the same commitments I asked you to make."

Katie's lashes shadowed her pale cheeks, hiding her acute embarrassment. "I'm sorry," she said in a small voice. "I thought——"

"There is no need to apologize," Padre Gregorio sighed wearily. He turned and walked over to the window that looked out on the little square and the church. "And you will not need to come back here again," he added without looking at her. "I will let Ramon know what I have decided."

"Which is?" Katie managed.

His jaw was set as he shook his head. "I want to think about it quietly for a while before I decide anything."

Katie ran her hand through her hair. "Padre Gregorio, you can't prevent us from being married. If you don't marry us, someone else will."

His back stiffened. Turning slowly, he gave her a look that was both angry and amused. "Thank you for reminding me of my limitations, *señorita*. I would have been very disappointed in you if you had not found some new way to antagonize me just before you leave, so that I will have the worst possible opinion of you."

Katie looked at him in frustrated fury. "You are the most self-important, self-righteous—!" She drew a long, deliberate breath, trying to steady herself. "I don't happen to care what your opinion of me is."

Padre Gregorio inclined his head in an exaggerated bow. "Thank you again."

Katie pulled up a handful of grass and irritably flung it away. She was sitting on a large flat rock, her back supported against a tree, looking blindly out across three miles of gently rolling hills and valleys. The sun was setting in streaks of red and gold, but the view hadn't soothed her temper after this morning's meeting with Padre Gregorio. Neither had six hours of shopping with Gabriella. A hundred yards off to her right, the men working in the cottage were putting down their tools and leaving for dinner at their homes, after which they would return to finish their remaining tasks.

Idly, Katie wondered where Ramon had been all day, but she was too frustrated and annoyed with herself and that prying priest to give it much thought. How dare that man question her motives and emotions, she thought, glowering ferociously at the looming mountains.

"I hope," drawled a deep, amused voice, "that you are not thinking of me with that expression on your face."

Katie's head swung around in surprise, sending her glossy hair spilling over her right shoulder. Ramon was standing less than a yard from her, his tall, broad-shouldered frame blocking the golden sunset. He looked as if he had spent the day in the office of the cannery, and had merely removed his suit coat, unbuttoned the collar of his crisp white shirt, and turned the cuffs up on his tanned forearms. His black brows were lifted slightly in inquiry, his gaze unwavering on her face.

Katie gave him a plastic smile. "Actually, I was—"

"Plotting a murder?" Ramon suggested dryly.

"Something like that," Katie muttered.

"Is the intended victim anyone I know?"

"Padre Gregorio," she admitted as she came to her feet.

Gazing down at her from his daunting height, Ramon shoved his hands into his pants pockets. The action stretched his white shirt over his muscular chest and wide shoulders, and Katie felt her pulse give a little leap in answer to the sheer, powerful masculinity he emanated. However, his next words snapped her attention back to the issue at hand.

"I saw him in the village a few minutes ago, Katie. He does not want to marry us."

Katie was perversely crushed that Padre Gregorio's contempt for her actually went that deep. Her beautiful face flushed with indignation. "Did he tell you why?"

Unexpectedly, Ramon smiled; one of those sudden, devastating smiles that always took her breath away. "Padre Gregorio seems to think that you lack certain attributes that he feels are necessary to make me a good wife."

"Such as?" Katie demanded mutinously.

"Meekness, docility and a respect for authority."

Katie was torn between antagonism and guilt. "What did you say?"

"I told him that I wanted a wife, not a cocker spaniel."

"And?"

Ramon's black eyes glinted with laughter. "Padre Gregorio thinks I would be better off with a cocker spaniel."

"Oh, is that right!" Katie retorted heatedly. "Well if you ask me, that interfering old tyrant shows an unnatural concern for your welfare!"

"Actually, he is concerned about *your* welfare," Ramon said wryly. "He greatly fears that after we have been married a short time, I may be tempted to murder you."

Katie turned her back to him to hide her confusion and hurt. "Is what he thinks so important to you?"

Ramon's hands settled on her shoulders, gently but firmly drawing her back against him. "You know it is not. But any delay in our marriage is important to me. If Padre Gregorio will not change his mind, I will have to find a priest in San Juan to marry us, and the banns will probably have to be read again. I want to marry you on Sunday, Katie, and Padre Gregorio is the only one who can make that possible. You know that. Everything else is in readiness. Work in the cottage will be finished tonight, your parents already have plane reservations for Saturday, and I have reserved a suite for them at the Caribe Hilton."

Katie was vibrantly aware of his warm breath stirring her hair; of the intimate feeling of his hard, muscular body pressing against her back and legs as he continued: "Padre Gregorio has just left for Vieques Island. When he returns on Thursday I want you to talk to him and give him whatever reassurance he needs."

Katie's resistance began to crumble as he turned her into his arms and covered her mouth with his. "Will you do that for me?" he murmured huskily when he broke the contact.

Katie gazed at his strong, sensual mouth. She raised her eyes and looked into those dark compelling eyes of his, and the rest of her defenses disintegrated. He wanted her so badly, his thighs were already hardening against her. And she wanted him too—just as badly. "Yes," she whispered.

His arms tightened fiercely as he claimed her mouth in a hungry searching kiss. When her lips parted eagerly to admit his tongue, he groaned with pleasure, and the sound struck some primitive response in Katie. Unashamedly she met his passion with her own, wanting to give him the same pleasure he was giving her. She kissed him as erotically as he kissed her, her hands convulsively sliding over his back and shoulders, her body arching to his.

She gasped with dismay when he ended the kiss and raised his head. Still shuddering with aftershocks of desire, Katie opened her slumberous eyes. In the deepening dusk, his gaze held hers. "I love you," he said.

Katie opened her mouth to speak and couldn't. Her stomach churned wildly, then clenched into an agonizing knot. She tried to say "I love you" but the words she had screamed again and again to David on that hideous night long ago, stuck in her throat now, paralyzing her vocal cords. With a low, anguished moan, she wrapped her arms around his neck and began kissing him with frenzied desperation, while every muscle in his body was tensing to reject her.

Pain ripped through Ramon like a hot jagged knife. She didn't love him. God damn her! She didn't love him.

"I—I can't say it," she wept brokenly, clinging tightly to him, her body molded to his. "I can't say the words you want to hear. I just can't."

Ramon stared at her, hating her and hating himself for loving her. Reaching up, he started to pull her arms from around his neck, but Katie wildly shook her head, tightening her hold, pressing even closer to him. Tears rushed from her beautiful blue eyes, sparkling on her long lashes, wetting her smooth cheeks. "Don't stop loving me," she pleaded fiercely, "just because I can't say the words yet. Please don't!"

"Katie!" he said harshly. Her soft lips trembled at the cold rejection in his voice, and he gripped her shoulders. He intended to free himself from her arms, to push her firmly away.

Katie knew it. "Please don't," she whispered, and her voice broke.

So did Ramon's restraint. With a groan, he drew her into his passionate embrace and smothered her lips with his. She melted against him, the fire in her response igniting the flames deep within him. "Katie," he whispered achingly, tightening his arms as she kissed him with a blazing ardor beyond anything she had ever shown him before. "Katie . . . Katie . . . Katie."

She loved him, he knew it! He could feel it. She might not be able to say the words, but her body was telling him she loved him. No woman alive could give her body to a man the way Katie was giving him hers, unless she had already given her heart.

He moved her down into the grass, and even while he did, Katie's lips clung to his, her hands feverishly caressing him. She was setting him on fire, and Ramon unbuttoned his shirt and pulled it off, willing to let himself be burned to ashes, so long as Katie went up in flames with him.

His hands dispensed with her blouse and bra, then luxuriated in the feel of her naked breasts swelling eagerly against his palms. Bending over her, he captured her mouth, the driving rhythmic plunging of his tongue boldly telling her what he wanted to do to her. And Katie welcomed the possessive invasion.

His body felt like a furnace as he pulled her up to lie on top of him, his eyes devouring the sight of her pale breasts crushed against the dark hair on his chest. "I'm starving for you," he whispered thickly. "I want you so much that I ache for you."

He curved his hand around her nape, pulling her mouth down to his, and said thickly. "Make me ache more, Katie."

She did. She kissed him with all her heart and body, wringing a low, animal groan of pleasure from him as she moved sinuously against his rigid arousal. Ramon clutched her tighter to him, wanting to absorb her body into his, letting her drive him into agonies of desire before he finally rolled onto his side, taking her with him.

Katie's lashes flickered open. Ramon was breathing fast, his face hard and dark with passion. She lifted her lips to his, and he started to bend toward her, then checked himself. "Before this is over," he sighed hoarsely, "You are going to drive me out of my mind."

Katie expected him to finish what they had begun. Instead he lay back and stretched out beside her, cradling her head in the curve of his arm and shoulder, keeping her close against his side while he stared up at the night sky. Katie lay there, bewildered. She couldn't imagine why Ramon had suddenly stopped, unless he somehow thought it was what she wanted. But it wasn't what she wanted at all! How could he think that when her whole body was yearning for his, when she wanted more than anything to give him pleasure?

She rolled onto her side, fully intending to take matters into her own hands. "If I do drive you out of your mind, it's your own fault," Katie said, and before he could reply she began leisurely and seductively tracing the outline of his ear with her tongue.

His free hand crossed over to lightly grip her waist, caressing it. His hand gripped her tighter and he shuddered with pleasure when she put her tongue into the hollow crevice and sensuously explored it. "Katie, stop it," he warned in a throaty growl. "Or I am going to do that to you."

Undaunted, Katie continued her arousing exploration. "You already did," she breathed into his ear, "And I like it."

"I like it too, that is why I want you to stop."

Katie gathered all her courage together and leaned up on an elbow. For a moment she stared thoughtfully at the shining silver chain and medal lying in the dark mat of hair on his chest, then she lifted her wide, questioning eyes to his. "Ramon," she said, tracing her fingertips down the chain, oblivious to the stirring effect this was having on him. "Has it occurred to you that we don't have to stop?"

Ramon captured her wayward hand, holding it to prevent its further tantalizing descent. "It has occurred to me—" he murmured dryly, "—about two hundred times in the last ten minutes."

"Then why are we? Stopping, I mean?"

He turned his head and looked at the tiny stars twinkling shyly in the inky blue sky. "Because the men will soon be returning from their evening meal." It was the truth, of course, but it wasn't the reason he was holding back. If he could be absolutely certain Katie loved him, he would simply take her somewhere else where they could have privacy now. If he had been certain she loved him, he would have been making love to her every day since they arrived in Puerto Rico. If Katie loved him, then the physical union of their bodies would strengthen and deepen that love.

But if all she felt for him was intense physical desire, if that was the only reason she was willing to marry him, then satisfying that desire before they were actually wed would relieve the pressure that was driving her to the altar. And that he would not risk doing. Particularly not, he thought with bitter self-recrimination, when for nine days he had been deliberately arousing her passion to a fever pitch and keeping it there, without any intention of fulfilling her desire and giving her release. He was purposely feeding her sexual appetite without ever satisfying her hunger. For that, she would have to marry him first.

From the moment he had taken her into his arms in St. Louis, there had been a tremendous physical chemistry between them. He had recognized it then, and he had been exploiting it ever since. He was ashamed of what he was doing to her. Katie trusted him, and he was using her own desire as a weapon to force her to marry him. But the weapon was a double-edged sword, because he was physically torturing himself by kissing and caressing her until they were both wild, and then drawing back. Every time he held her it was sheer torment knowing that she was sweet and warm and willing to be taken, and then not taking her.

What sort of man was he to stoop to this sexual blackmail, Ramon wondered contemptuously. The answer was as humiliating as the question: He was the sort of man who deeply loved a woman who apparently did not love him. Fiercely, his mind rejected that. Katie loved him! He could taste it on her lips. By God, before they were married, she would admit it! He would make her tell him she did.

Or what?

Closing his eyes, Ramon drew a deep, ragged breath. Or he would have to let her go. His pride and self-respect would never let him live with her, loving her like this, knowing that she didn't love him. He couldn't bear the shame, or the pain, of an unrequited love.

Beside him, Katie snuggled closer, rousing him from his reverie. "It is time to leave," he told her, reluctantly sitting up. "Gabriella and Eduardo are expecting us for dinner. They will wonder where we are."

Katie flashed a wry smile at him as she pulled on her blouse and combed her fingers through her rumpled hair. "Gabriella knows where we are. Eduardo will automatically assume that I've dragged you off somewhere to try to seduce you. Where I'm concerned, Eduardo suspects the worst."

Ramon eyed her with glinting amusement. "Eduardo is not worried that you might steal my virginity, Katie. I lost it long ago—on the same night he lost his, as I recall."

Katie's pretty chin lifted in an attitude of well-bred disinterest, but her voice was tinged with jealousy, which delighted Ramon, who had hoped for just such a reaction. "How old were you then?"

"None of your business," he laughed.

17

T hank you again," Katie called gaily, two days later. She wiped a smudge off her cheek, then waved goodbye to Rafael, his wife and his sons, who had been helping her clean the cottage, arrange furniture and hang curtains all day yesterday and today. She watched Rafael's old truck clatter down the drive, then turned to Gabriella, who was tiredly pushing herself out of a chair.

They had been working since dawn and it was now late afternoon. "Do you think Ramon will be surprised?" Katie asked, her face wearing the same expression of happy exhaustion that she saw on Gabriella's.

"Will he be surprised?" Gabriella repeated, her dark eyes shining with merriment. "Two days ago, there were workmen in here and the place was bare. Tonight when he sees it, every piece of furniture is in place, the bed is made and there are even candles and linen placemats on the kitchen table. Ramon will not be able to believe his eyes!" Gabriella predicted.

"I hope you're right," Katie said with a touch of pride. "I told him this house could be pretty, but he wouldn't believe me."

"Pretty?" Gabriella said with a shake of her head as she picked up her purse and trailed to the front door. "It is beautiful. You have a great talent for decorating, Katie."

Looking at her, Katie thought of the endless miles they had driven together, the frenetic shopping expeditions, the exhausting hours of searching through shops. Through it all Gabriella had been cheerful and supportive. "Gaby," Katie said softly, shaken by a deep surge of affection and gratitude, "You have a great talent for being a friend."

A smile lit Gabriella's features. "Strange, is it not—this kinship between us? We have known each other for only eleven days, yet you are almost like a sister to me."

The two women, who had been sharing a bottle of wine while they worked, smiled sheepishly at each other, their faces flushed with drink and pleasure, then Gabriella turned and left.

Katie picked up Gabriella's wineglass, drained the last drops from her own, and glanced at her wristwatch; it was five o'clock. Last night she had made Ramon promise to come here straight from work, which meant he ought to be arriving any time during the next half hour. In the kitchen she washed both glasses and set them on the new white Formica counter top so they would be ready when Ramon came.

Humming, she opened a cupboard and took out the other bottle of red wine and the corkscrew. Actually, she had already had enough wine. *A little more than enough,* she thought wryly. She was feeling rather warm and overexhilarated. But, she reminded herself gaily, the completion of the house was a very good reason for celebration.

She glanced around the kitchen. Cheerful and inviting, just as she had told Ramon it could be, she decided proudly. Above the wainscoting, the walls were covered in a bright green-and-white wallpaper. One wall displayed a collection of native wicker and straw baskets of every size and shape, which Katie had purchased for a fraction of what their price would have been in the States. All the cupboards had been stripped and repainted white, with an inset of wallpaper that matched the green and white on the walls.

She left the kitchen and wandered from room to room. In the bedroom, she paused to needlessly smooth the handmade coverlet on the bed. It was sewn in large squares, each square a different pattern, but each incorporating the basic colors of gold, white and brown. Gold curtains hung at the wide windows, harmonizing and complementing the dark oak dresser and headboard, and the thick gold carpet that partially covered the polished oak floor. She straightened the folds of the curtains so that they hung gracefully on either side of the windows. The room was perfect, she decided.

And masculine.

Katie pushed the unwanted thought aside and sauntered into the living room. She had spent about three thousand dollars of her own money, but it was worth it, she thought proudly. The rust-colored sofa with its rolled arms and thick tufted back was positioned opposite two chairs upholstered in nubby cream and rust threads. A broad expanse of sculptured cream carpeting stretched between them on the polished floor. The huge coffee table with its burl-wood inlays and narrow brass trim had been her biggest extravagance, but when she had seen it she couldn't resist it, or the matching lamp table between the two chairs. Or was the antique hammered brass lamp her biggest extravagance? Katie couldn't recall, but it didn't matter anyway. The room, with its rough-textured cream curtains and long windows, was rich and inviting and perfect.

And masculine, a little voice whispered.

Katie studiously ignored it and went into the bathroom where she washed her face and brushed her hair. Her eyes were shining with expectation when she looked at herself in the mirror above the new vanity. Or were her eyes just glassy from too much wine? Katie shrugged and glanced around the bathroom. Had she gone too ultramodern here, she wondered apprehensively. Since the bathroom fixtures were white, she had carried the theme into the wallpaper, using a shiny white paper with bold reprints of newspapers printed on it. At the time she had thought herself clever; if Ramon got tired of the black and red towels he could substitute another color for the red and it would seem like a whole new bathroom. She dried her hands on a red hand towel, then carefully refolded it and placed it on the vanity atop the black one. The rest of the towels should have arrived at the store in the village by now. Tomorrow she would stop and pick them up after she saw Padre Gregorio.

She cast a last glance over the bathroom, her head tipped consideringly to the side. It might be a little too modernistic for the rest of the house, but it was certainly vivid.

And masculine.

Katie finally admitted it—but if it were true, then surely Ramon would be pleased. After all, he was very masculine. She went over to the coffee table in the living room and began rearranging the bright yellow and orange flowers in the center.

The maroon Rolls-Royce glided to a purring stop on the shoulder of the road a few feet beyond the dirt track that led up to the cottage. Ramon glanced impatiently at the long red canopy of blossoming flamboyant trees, deliberating over having Garcia drive him to the front door of the cottage. He was eager to see Katie, and he didn't want to take the time to walk the two miles up the track. On the other hand, if Katie realized the chauffeur took him to and from work in the Rolls every day, she would naturally ask further questions. Questions he would have to either refuse to answer, or answer with blatant lies. Out of necessity he had misled her, but he would not lie to her.

"Wait for me at the usual place tomorrow morning," he instructed Garcia. Ramon opened his door and climbed out of the car, without waiting for the chauffeur to reply. He knew that tomorrow morning at seven-thirty Garcia would be pulled over at the side of the road, waiting around a blind curve a half-mile from the village square. No questions asked, no explanations expected. Even though Garcia was no longer being paid, the old man still insisted on driving Ramon. "We have been together a long time, you and I," Garcia had told Ramon at the airport the day Katie had come to Puerto Rico. With somber dark eyes and great dignity he had added, "Until this car is sold, I will do for you what I have always done."

Walking up the track, Ramon thought of Garcia with mingled fondness and regret. If Ramon asked him to keep the motor running in front of a bank while he went in and robbed it, Garcia would do so without hesitation. His reward for twenty years of faithful service was going to be unemployment— and a letter of recommendation. Ramon wished he could give him more than that. He deserved more.

In the doorway of the cottage, Ramon stopped dead; the day's worries and problems slipping away, forgotten. Katie was here, in his house, waiting for him. Sunlight streamed in the window, bathing her in a golden halo of light as she bent over something in the living room, rearranging sprigs of vibrant wild flowers in an earthenware bowl.

A feeling of deep contentment seeped through him, spreading its warmth through his veins. How strange that he had supposedly been one of the "richest" men in the world, yet he had never had this to come home to, never experienced this feeling before. He had come home to mistresses and servants, in mansions, penthouse apartments and villas by the sea. But he had never found this exquisite feeling of peace waiting for him—because he had never really come "home" at all. Katie was home.

People had envied him before; now they would pity him because he had lost his wealth. How incredibly stupid! Now he had Katie, and Katie made him very rich. This beautiful angel with the red gold hair and laughing blue eyes was going to bear his children and share his days and nights. She was everything that had always been missing from his life. She was joy.

Very quietly and without emphasis, Ramon said, "I love you, Katie."

She whirled around, a smile lighting up her face. "Well?" she beamed at him. "What do you think?" Arms outstretched she turned in a circle, watching him expectantly over her shoulder.

Ramon knew she had heard him, and his heart sank at her lack of response, but he let it pass. "I think you are beautiful," he said running his appreciative glance over the bright green velour top that left her midriff bare, and the matching shorts that revealed her long, shapely legs.

Katie rolled her eyes. "Not about me! About the house, the furniture, everything. . . ."

For the first time, Ramon looked at something besides Katie. What he saw dumbfounded him. "How did you manage to buy all this with the money I gave you? I never meant for you to have to stretch it so far. I intended to give you more when you said you were ready to look for furniture."

Her face fell. "Don't you like it?"

"Like it?" he grinned. "I have not even looked at it yet. But how—"

"Stop thinking about the money. I happen to be a terrific bargain hunter," Katie said, linking her hand through his arm, and leading him from room to room.

Ramon's reaction puzzled Katie. She could tell that he liked what she had purchased, and that he was pleased. He was lavish with his praise and his praise was genuine, yet something was bothering him.

She did not have long to wait to discover what it was. The kitchen was the last room on her guided tour. When Ramon had finished inspecting it, he walked over to the counter top where she had put out the wine. Katie watched him, admiring the way his long, capable fingers dealt with the corkscrew, deftly uncorking the bottle. "Well?" she said expectantly. "Now that you've seen the whole house, what do you think?"

"I think it is extremely attractive," he said, pouring wine into both glasses. He handed one to her. "Are you planning to live here?"

The question stunned her into momentary silence, then she said, "Yes."

"For how long?" he asked dispassionately.

The wine she had drunk was making her feel foggy. "Why are you asking me these questions?"

"Because there are two bedrooms in this house," he said, watching her intently. "The second one, as I am sure you know, is meant for children. Yet you went to a great deal of trouble to furnish it with a handsome desk for me, bookcases and one overstuffed chair. Not two chairs. You intended that room to be used by me alone, not by both of us and not by our children. Your apartment was filled with plants, yet there is not one plant in this house. Your bedroom was extremely feminine, yet—"

"Plants?" Katie blinked at him, her emotions veering from alarm to mirth. "I didn't even think of plants! I'll give you plants for a wedding present!" she decided promptly.

"And will you give me children?" he asked, his face impassive.

"Not," Katie quipped, "for a wedding present. Think of the gossip!"

Ramon's gaze swerved from the faint flush on her high cheekbones to the empty wine bottle beside the one he had just opened. "How much of that bottle did you drink?"

"A little more than half," she declared rather proudly. "Gabriella drank the rest."

Ramon felt like shaking her. Instead, he walked over to the wide windows at the corner of the kitchen. Tipping his glass up, he drank deeply, then stared out at the panoramic view. "Why do you want to marry me, Katie?"

Katie saw the tension in his shoulders, the tautness in his profile, and desperately tried to keep things light. "Because you're tall dark and handsome!" she teased.

The brief, sidelong smile he sent her was without humor. "Why else do you want to marry me?"

"Oh, the usual reasons people get married these days," she joked. "We like the same movies, we—"

"Stop playing games with me!" he snapped. "I asked you why you want to marry me."

Panic jolted through Katie's entire nervous system; her heart began to race wildly. "I—" She tried to speak and couldn't. She knew Ramon wanted her to say she loved him, and that he wanted to hear her make a final, irrevocable commitment to marry him. Katie could do neither. Afraid not to speak, yet unable to say anything that would satisfy him, Katie could only look at him in mute misery.

In the electrified silence that crackled between them, she could feel Ramon mentally withdrawing from her, and when he finally spoke there was a harsh bitter finality in his words that thoroughly alarmed her: "We will not speak of it again," he said.

In heavy silence they walked back to Gabriella's. Katie tried to cloak herself in the comforting glow of the wine she had consumed, but she was feeling more apprehensive with every step. Instead of coming in for dinner, Ramon stopped at the front door, briefly touched his lips to her forehead, and said "Good night."

There was an ominous ring to that, Katie thought. It sounded more like goodbye than good night. "Are—are you coming over to see me before you leave for work in the morning?"

He turned on the step and looked at her, his face utterly unreadable. "I am not going to work tomorrow."

"Then will I see you after I meet with Padre Gregorio? I thought I'd go over to his house first thing in the morning. Then I was going to go up to the cottage to take care of some things that need to be done."

"I will find you," he said.

"Ramon," she said, afraid to let him leave in this mood, "I don't think you were very enthusiastic about—about the cottage. Didn't you like it?"

"I apologize," he said politely. "You did an excellent job. It suits me perfectly."

Although he'd put no emphasis on the word *me*, Katie noticed he avoided using the word *us*. She didn't know what to say to him in this distant, coolly courteous mood. She opened the door. "Well, good night."

Ramon stared at the door she had just closed, while bitterness and pain rose like bile in this throat. He walked aimlessly for hours thinking about the past two days. For two days he had waited for her to say she loved him. He had teased her and laughed with her and made her moan with passion in his arms, but not even in her most heated moment had she responded to his "I love you." She would kiss him or smile at him, placate him like an infatuated little boy, but she would not say it back.

The moon was high in the sky when he returned to his temporary room in Rafael's house. He stretched out on the bed and stared at the ceiling. He had asked her for honesty, and she was being honest. She was refusing to claim an emotion that she didn't feel. It was as simple as that.

God! How could she not love him, when he loved her so damned much.

Katie's image danced before him: Katie coming up the hill toward him with that graceful leggy walk of hers and the breeze teasing her glorious hair; Katie looking at him, her deep blue eyes sparkling with laughter or dark with concern because he looked tired.

Ramon closed his eyes, trying to postpone the moment when he would have to make a decision, but it was no use. The decision had already been made. He was going to have to send her home. He would send her home tomorrow. No, not tomorrow, the next day. He had to keep her with him one more day . . . and one more night. Just one more. One more day to watch her moving around the cottage, to memorize the way she looked in each room— so that he could remember her there when she was gone. One more night to make love to her in the bedroom she had decorated for him, to join his raven-ous body with hers and lose himself in her. He would lavish her senses with every exquisite pleasure a man could give a woman, make her moan with delight and cry out with rapture, and then bring her again and again to shud-dering ecstasy.

One day and one night to accumulate memories: memories that would bring him as much torment as they would pleasure, but it didn't matter. He had to have them.

And then he would send her home. She would be relieved, he knew that now. He had always known it. Whatever her reasons for agreeing to marry him had been, she was never entirely committed to the idea. If she were, she would not have decorated her future home as a handsome bachelor retreat without a trace of her own personality.

18

*P*adre Gregorio greeted Katie with polite reserve when the housekeeper showed her into his office the next morning. He waited for her to take a seat, then sat down behind his desk.

Katie tried to match his composed expression. "Ramon said that you feel I lack meekness, docility and respect for authority."

"I said that, yes." He leaned back in his chair. "Do you disagree?"

Katie slowly shook her head, a smile touching her lips. "Not at all. In fact, I consider it a great compliment." When his expression didn't alter, she hesitated, and then continued. "Obviously you don't see it that way. You told Ramon that was the reason you didn't want to marry us."

"Would you have preferred that I tell him the main reason—that the woman he loves does not love him?"

Katie's long, tapered fingernails dug into her palms. "I didn't say—"

"Señorita Connelly!" he interrupted in a low, controlled voice. "We are not going to waste any more time waltzing each other around in circles that more time waltzing each other around in circles that go nowhere. You are looking for a way to avoid this marriage, and I have given it to you."

Katie was stricken. "How can you possibly say a thing like that?"

"Because it is true. I sensed it from our first meeting. When I asked you how long you have known Ramon, you told me 'only' two weeks. You deliberately led me to think you are the sort of woman who frequents *cantinas* in the hope of meeting men, men whom you let publicly caress you in parking lots. You are nothing of the kind, *señorita*, and we both know it."

He held up an imperious hand to silence Katie's outburst. "It is too late for that now. There are other reasons I believe what I do: I told you that if you would simply say you love Ramon, we would finalize the marriage plans. If you really wanted to marry him, you would have said it whether it was true or not, so that I would agree to the ceremony.

"When I told you that, instead, I would accept your word that you intended to make Ramon a good wife, your face turned as white as a sheet. Ten seconds later you jumped up and accused me of trying to make you promise to respect his authority and obey him."

Katie's gaze dropped to her lap. She rubbed her moist palms against her knees. "There's nothing I can say to prove you're wrong, is there?"

"You do not want to prove I am wrong, *señorita*. In your heart, you want to avoid this marriage." He took off his glasses and wearily rubbed the bridge of his nose. "Perhaps you are afraid of commitment, of giving your love. I do not know. But I do know this—when Ramon realizes that you can give him only your body, and not your heart, he will not be satisfied. No man with any pride will let himself continue to care deeply for someone who does not care for him. Ramon's love for you will wither and die, because he will make certain that it does; he will kill it himself. When that happens, he must be free to find another, and to marry if he chooses. Knowing all of this, I cannot, I will not bind him to you for the rest of his life with the unbreakable ties of Holy Matrimony."

Katie's eyes were burning with tears she refused to shed, and there was a lump in her throat the size of a boulder as he finished: "It would be best for both of you if you went back to the States immediately. If you lack the courage and decency to do that, then live with him in sin or marry him in a civil ceremony. I cannot stop you. I have given you a way out of this, I expect you to give Ramon a way out too—do not bind him to you in the church."

Katie stood up stiffly. "And that's your final decision?"

It seemed to take Padre Gregorio forever to rise to his feet. "If you must phrase it that way, yes, it is my final decision. I will leave it to you to tell Ramon." His blue eyes turned almost sympathetic. "Do not feel guilty because you cannot love him, *señorita*. Ramon is the sort of man who is attractive to women. Many have loved him in the past; there will be many who will love him in the future, and be more than eager to be his wife."

Katie's head was proudly erect, but her eyes were swimming with tears. "I don't feel guilty, I feel furious!" Turning on her heel she walked to the door.

Padre Gregorio's voice sounded incredibly sad. *"Señorita . . ."*

Katie kept her face averted, unwilling to give him the satisfaction of seeing her cry. "Yes?"

"God bless you."

The tears clogging her throat prevented Katie from answering. She opened the door and walked out.

Katie drove up to the cottage, half-blinded with tears of humiliation and fear. Padre Gregorio was right. She had been looking for a way out—no, not a way out, a way to gain more time. "Damn you, David!" she whispered thickly. This awful mess she was making of her life was his fault. Even dead he was haunting her; literally haunting her. It was because of him that she couldn't overcome this slumbering panic that she might be making the same mistake twice.

Once before she had married a man who her own instinct had warned her wasn't what he appeared to be. Now she wanted to marry another man and she felt that way again. She couldn't shake that feeling.

She pulled up in front of the little storybook cottage and let herself inside, relieved that Ramon wasn't there. She didn't want to have to explain her ravaged face. How would she? How could she say, there is something about you that is scaring me, Ramon.

Katie wandered into the kitchen and methodically spooned coffee into the new percolator she had purchased. When it was made she poured it into a mug and carried it over to the kitchen table. With her hands wrapped around the hot mug, she gazed out at the terraced hills stretching in two directions, letting the magnificent view quiet her rioting emotions.

She thought back to the way she had felt about David before they were married. Some intuition, some instinct, had warned her that David Caldwell was not the man he wanted her to believe he was. She should have listened to herself.

And now she wanted to marry Ramon—and every instinct she possessed was telling her that he was not the man he wanted her to believe he was, either.

Katie rubbed her fingertips against her temples. Never had she felt so afraid and confused. There was no time left to stall. Either she was going to ignore her instinctive fears and marry Ramon, or she had to go back to the States.

The thought of leaving him made her almost physically ill. She adored him!

She loved his dark eyes and dazzling smile, the reassuring strength in his firmly chiseled features, and the quiet authority in the line of his jaw. He was six feet three inches of taut, powerful muscle, yet he was gentle and tender with her. In height, he dwarfed her own five feet six inches, yet being with him made her feel protected and cherished, not threatened and insignificant.

By nature, he was a dominating male, virile and self-assured, while she was stubborn and independent. She ought to resent him for wanting to confine her to the role of wife and mother, but she didn't. The idea of being his wife filled her with joy, and the thought of bearing his children thrilled her. She would gladly clean his house and cook his meals in return for being held in those strong arms of his at night.

He wanted her to accept a form of sexual bondage, commit her body and her life into his keeping. In return, he would be her lover, provider and father to her children. Katie shamefully admitted to herself that it was what she wanted too. It might be un-American and unemancipated, but it seemed so right, so fulfilling. At least for her.

Katie stared at her hands lying limply in her lap. Ramon was everything she could ever want: an intelligent, sensitive, sexy man who loved her.

Except he wasn't real.

He wasn't what he wanted her to believe he was. She didn't know why she felt that way, or what was wrong, but the feeling wouldn't leave her.

Ramon pulled Rafael's car to a stop in front of the general store and climbed out. Eduardo opened the passenger door. "I will go in with you. Gabriella asked me to buy some milk."

"What?" Ramon said absently.

"I said—" Eduardo shook his head in exasperation. "Never mind. You have not heard a word I have said all morning. Getting married is affecting your hearing, my friend."

"I am not getting married," Ramon said grimly, leaving Eduardo gaping at him as he shoved open the door and walked into the store. In contrast to the heat outside, the crowded little store was cool. Ignoring Eduardo's staggered look, as well as the ten customers who were all staring at him with avid curiosity, Ramon selected several cigars, then carried them over to the counter where two salesclerks were waiting on customers. Eduardo put the container of milk on the counter beside Ramon's cigars and said in a low voice. "Are you joking?"

Ramon glanced at him. "I am not joking."

A pretty little Puerto Rican girl waiting on a huge woman who was exchanging an apron, saw Ramon and her face brightened. She asked the other clerk, a middle-aged man, to take care of the refund and stepped over to the line that had formed behind Ramon and Eduardo. "Señor Galverra," she beamed, speaking in Spanish. "Do you remember me? I am Maria Ramirez. I used to have pigtails when I was little and you used to pull them and tell me that I was going to be pretty when I grew up."

"I was right," Ramon said with an effort at a smile.

"I am engaged to be married to Juan Vega now," she said, still smiling as she reached beneath the counter and pulled out a large package wrapped in white paper and tied with strings. "These are the towels Señorita Connelly ordered for you. Do you want to take them with you?"

"Fine," Ramon said with a curt nod. Reaching into the back pocket of his Levi's, he pulled out his wallet and glanced at the sales slip. "You only charged me for the cigars, Maria. How much are the towels?"

"Señorita Connelly has already paid for them with her credit card," she reassured him.

Ramon tried not to sound as impatient as he felt. "There must be some mistake."

"Mistake?" Maria repeated. "I do not think so, but I will look." She cut the string and tore open the white paper. A pile of thick, fluffy red and black towels spilled onto the counter. Behind him and beside him, Ramon felt the villagers pressing imperceptibly closer to get a better view of the contents of the package. "Here is the charge-account receipt and these are the sales tickets," Maria said as she pulled them from between two towels. "No, there is no mistake. Señorita Connelly paid for these towels with her charge account at the same time she paid for everything she took with her a week ago. See, it is all here on the sales slips, included in the five-hundred-dollar total. She paid for a toaster, percolator, dishes, pots and pans, glasses in several sizes, a blender, a rotary mixer, kitchen utensils and all these other items."

The old man beside Ramon poked him slyly in the ribs. "You are a lucky man, Ramon. Your *novia* wants you to have only the best. Not only is she beautiful, she is very generous too, eh?"

"Wrap up the towels," Ramon snapped at Maria in a low, savage voice.

Maria paled at the look on his face and began clumsily and hastily pulling the edges of the paper together. "Here—here are Señorita Connelly's duplicate bills, each for one-half the amount she spent," she stammered, her eyes recoiling from Ramon's murderous expression as she handed him the slips. "Señora Alverez," she glanced apprehensively at a furious Eduardo as she spoke his wife's name, "explained that I do not have to prepare duplicate bills this way, unless Señorita Connelly pays in cash, but I—I do it anyway."

She shoved the package toward Ramon as if it were hot, and her voice dropped to a panicked whisper. "That way, I never forget."

Ramon's tone was glacial. "I am certain that Señorita Connelly has appreciated your help, Maria." Everyone hastily backed out of his path as he strode out of the store with fury raging in every purposeful stride.

Eleven villagers watched the door slam behind Ramon and then Eduardo. In unison they turned to stare at each other, their faces reflecting a variety of reactions from alarm to satisfaction. Only one occupant of the store was oblivious to what had just taken place—an Englishman who did not understand Spanish. He cleared his throat politely and shifted the parcels in his arms, but he was ignored.

Maria was the first to speak. She looked around at the others, her soft brown eyes wide and stricken as she whispered, "What did I do wrong?"

The middle-aged man, who was the other salesclerk, regarded her dryly. "Maria, you have just given Señorita Connelly more 'help' than I think she wanted."

The old man who had gibed Ramon about his *novia*'s generosity slapped his thigh and cackled gleefully. "I told you Galverra didn't know what the girl was doing. I told you!" His weathered face creased into a satisfied grin as he looked at his neighbors. "Told you he'd never live off a woman even if he was starving." Smugly he added, "He ought to take a stick to her!"

"I will come back for the other apron," the enormous woman said as she headed for the door.

"Where are you going, Rosa?" her friend called after her.

"To offer up a prayer in church."

"For the American girl?" one of the ladies asked, laughing.

"No, for Gabriella Alverez."

"Ought to take a stick to her too," the old man announced.

When she heard Ramon come in, Katie stood up and made a great pretense of rearranging the straw place mats on the kitchen table. It was crazy how her spirits soared at the mere sound of his voice calling her name.

"Here are the rest of the towels you ordered," he said, dropping the package carelessly on the table. "The girl at the store said they had already been paid for. Is this coffee still fresh?" he asked as he went over and poured some into a mug.

Katie smiled at him over her shoulder and nodded as she pulled the bunched towels out of the wrapping and began refolding them.

"I still cannot imagine how you managed to buy all this with the money I gave you," he remarked.

"I told you," Katie said brightly. "I'm a fantastic bargain hunter."

"You are also a liar."

Katie spun around, feeling a prickling of fear that escalated to panic the moment she looked at him. In contrast to the deadly quiet of his voice, Ramon's face was a mask of savage fury.

"How much of your money have you spent?"

Katie's mouth went dry. "Very little. A—a hundred dollars."

His eyes slashed her like razors. "I asked you how much!" he repeated in a terrible voice.

"Two—two hundred."

"Lie to me just once more," he warned silkily, "and I will make your first husband seem like a saint."

The threat made Katie almost sick with fright. "About three thousand dollars."

The next question hit her like a whip. "Why?"

"Because I . . . didn't want to feel obligated to marry you."

Naked pain sliced across his features in the instant before his whole body went rigid, tensing against it. "Garcia will take you to the airport at two o'clock tomorrow afternoon. He will have a check with him to reimburse you for what you have spent. There is no need for you to make any explanations to Gabriella and Eduardo; they already know you are leaving."

Katie was breathing in shallow, suffocated breaths. "You're actually going to send me back just because I bought some things for the house?"

"Because I told you not to do it," he corrected her scathingly.

"And just—just for that? For—for disobeying you?" Katie felt as if she had been physically beaten. Her mind couldn't seem to absorb the shock. He must be insane; the man she had thought she knew could never, never do this. Not for such a small thing.

She started slowly toward the door on legs that felt wooden. As she passed Ramon, she glanced at him, her eyes dark with pain and disillusionment. "Just for that," she murmured and numbly shook her head. "Don't!" she cried out as his hands spun her around and brought her crashing into the wall of his chest.

His eyes glittered down at her from a face that was white with rage. "You are nothing but an eager body and an empty heart," he gritted viciously. "Did you think I was so desperate for your body that I would accept the temporary loan of it and call it a marriage?" He flung her away from him as if he couldn't bear to touch her, and strode to the doorway, where he turned, his voice murderous. "If you have not cashed the check Garcia gives you within fourteen days, I will have everything in this house carried outside and set on fire."

Katie snapped the locks shut on the last piece of her luggage and carried it to the open bedroom door, setting it down beside the other five pieces. There was nothing more to do tonight except sleep.

She sat down on her bed in Gabriella's spare bedroom and listlessly looked around. She had wanted time—now she had it. She had the rest of her life ahead of her to wonder whether she had thrown away her chance for glorious happiness, or escaped from another nightmare of a marriage. Katie glanced up at the mirror, and the grief-stricken face that looked back at her was a perfect reflection of her inner feelings.

Gabriella was asleep, and Eduardo had gone out immediately after dinner. Katie shuddered just remembering that ominous meal. Not one word had been spoken by anyone. Eduardo had eaten in furious silence and Gabriella, who was as pale as death, kept giving Katie pitiful little smiles of sympathy and reassurance in between muffled sniffling noises. Katie, who was incapable of swallowing past the lump in her throat, had carefully avoided Eduardo's thunderous gaze and looked with helpless apology at poor Gabriella. When the meal was over, Eduardo had shoved his chair back, stood up and glared wrathfully at Katie. "I congratulate you," he said between clenched teeth. "You have managed to destroy a very great man. Not even his own father succeeded when he tried, but you did." Then he turned on his heel and stalked out.

Katie glanced automatically at the plastic clock beside the bed when she heard the front door open and close. Eduardo's heavy footsteps were coming toward her bedroom. Hastily she swiped at her cheeks with her fingertips, then glanced up to see Eduardo looming in the doorway. Her chin came up in weak defiance as he stalked over to the bed where she was sitting.

Thrusting a large leather-bound photograph album at her, he said coldly, "This is the man whom you have reduced to the level of a beggar in the eyes of this village."

Numbly Katie took the album from him.

"Open it," he snapped. "It belongs to Rafael and his wife. They want you to see it before you leave."

Katie swallowed. "Is Ramon there with them?"

"No," Eduardo said curtly.

When he left, Katie opened the album. It was not filled with snapshots: it was filled with dozens and dozens of magazine and newspaper clippings. Her eyes riveted on the first one, and her hand began to tremble violently as she lifted the plastic-covered page. It was a newspaper photograph of Ramon standing in front of a dozen microphones as he addressed the World Business Conference in Geneva, Switzerland. "Oh, God," she whispered. "Oh, my God."

Snatches of copy flew out of her; pictures of Ramon in a hundred different poses assailed her senses. Ramon, his handsome face very grave as he spoke to a gathering of Arab oil sheikhs; Ramon, lounging back in his chair at a conference table with international business leaders; Ramon, with his briefcase in hand, boarding a jet airliner with the name "Galverra International" emblazoned on the side.

Katie tried to read the articles, but her whirling mind could absorb only phrases:

Noted for his genius as a negotiator, Galverra was responsible for the acquisitions that elevated Galverra International to the status of a financial empire . . . Fluent in Spanish, French, Italian, English and German . . . Graduate of Harvard University . . . Master's degree in business administration . . . Masterminded mergers all over the globe . . . An innately private man who resents the intrusion of the press into his personal life. . . .

There were shots of Ramon in a tuxedo, gambling at a casino in Monte Carlo while a dazzling blonde smiled adoringly at him, Ramon leaning against the railing of his huge oceangoing yacht, the breeze ruffling his hair.

Many of the other pictures testified to his reported refusal to admit the press into his personal life, for they were fuzzy and obviously taken from very far away with some sort of special lens.

It was all there, including the beginning of the end. There were pictures of half-completed skyscrapers in Chicago and St. Louis, along with stories about the corporation's suffering staggering financial losses in Iran.

Katie closed the album and wrapped her arms around it, clutching it protectively to her heart. She laid her cheek against the binding, and her body shook with harsh wracking sobs. "Oh, darling, why didn't you tell me?" she choked brokenly.

 19

Garcia carried the last two pieces of her luggage out to the Rolls, and Katie turned to Gabriella, who was hovering despondently in the living room. "I am so sorry," Gabriella whispered as Katie hugged her goodbye. "So very sorry."

Eduardo stepped forward and stiffly offered his hand. "Have a good flight," he said, his attitude more coldly aloof than it had ever been.

Garcia opened the door to the Rolls, and Katie got in. She looked at the sumptuous white leather interior with its gold-trimmed gadgetry that had once delighted her. This was Ramon's car, of course, Katie realized with a fresh stab of sorrow. No wonder he had looked so bleak when she had been enchanted with it—he was losing the car. He was losing everything—even her.

Realizing that Garcia hadn't closed the door yet, she glanced up at him. He reached into the pocket of his black uniform and extracted a bank draft. Katie stared at it in dumb misery. It was for thirty-five hundred dollars—five hundred dollars more than she had spent. Apparently Ramon hadn't even believed her when she was telling the truth.

Katie felt sick. Most of what she was being blamed for wasn't even her fault! If only Ramon hadn't tried to pass himself off to her as an ordinary farmer, she wouldn't have been so suspicious and afraid to marry him. She wouldn't have felt she had to pay for half of everything. None of this would have ever happened. But it had happened. She had shamed and humiliated him, and he was sending her away.

Sending her away, she thought as the car pulled down Gabriella's driveway. What was the matter with her, letting Ramon send her away like this! This wasn't the time to start being obedient. It wasn't the time to be frightened and intimidated, either, but she was. With a shiver of terror Katie remembered the raging fury in his expression yesterday, the murderous wrath in every carefully enunciated word he said to her. But most of all, she remembered his threat: "Lie to me one more time, and I will make your first husband look like a saint!" In that moment, he had looked enraged enough to do it.

Katie bit her lip, desperately trying to find enough courage to ask Garcia to take her to Ramon so that she could explain. She *had* to go to him. Frantically, she told herself that Ramon wouldn't do the things to her David had. Ramon didn't know what he was threatening her with when he said that. Anyway, she was not going to lie to him, so he would have no reason—

It was no use, Katie realized. She wanted to go to him, to explain, but she couldn't face his rage alone. Irrational or not, she was terrified of physical violence.

She needed someone to go with her to confront him. Katie's hands began to tremble with a combination of panic and determination. There was no one here to help her, and it was already too late. Ramon hated her for what she had done. No, he *loved* her. And if he did, he couldn't possibly stop loving her this easily.

He had to listen to her, Katie thought feverishly as the maroon Rolls glided through the village and stopped to allow a group of tourists to cross the street. Dear God, someone had to make him listen! Just then, Katie saw Padre Gregorio crossing the square from his little house to the church, his dark robes billowing in the gentle afternoon breeze. He glanced toward the car, saw her face through the window, and slowly turned away. Padre Gregorio would never help her. . . . Or would he?

The Rolls was already picking up speed. Katie couldn't find the button to open the communicating window. She knocked on it and called "Stop— ¡Parese!" but only the merest flicker of Garcia's eyes in the rearview mirror told her he had even heard her. Obviously, Ramon had instructed Garcia to put her on a plane, and he meant to do just that. She tried the door handle but it was electronically locked.

In inspired desperation, she covered her mouth with her hand and cried, "Please stop, I am going to be sick."

That got results! In a flash Garcia was out of the car, opening her door and helping her out.

Katie jerked her arm loose from the amazed old man, who thought he was helping her. "I'm better now," she called, running across the square toward the church, toward the one man who had once offered to help her explain to Ramon. She darted a glance over her shoulder, but Garcia was waiting beside the car, apparently under the impression that she was having some seizure of religious fervor.

At the top of the stone steps Katie hesitated, her stomach tightening with dread. Padre Gregorio had nothing but contempt for her now; he would never help her. He had told her flatly to go back to the States. She made herself push open the groaning oak door and step into the cool candlelit darkness.

She scanned the altar and the little decorative alcoves where candles flickered in small red glass holders, but the priest wasn't there. And then she saw him, not performing some task as she had expected, but sitting all alone at the front of the church in the second pew. His white head was bent, even his shoulders were bent, in a posture of abject despair, or devout prayer, Katie wasn't certain which.

Her footsteps faltered, and her meager reservoir of courage went dry. He would never help her. In his way, Padre Gregorio disliked her as much as Eduardo did, and for more and better reasons. Turning, Katie started back down the aisle.

"*Señorita!*" Padre Gregorio's sharp, imperative voice cracked out like a whip, making her whole body stiffen.

Slowly, Katie turned and faced him. He was standing in the center of the aisle now, looking more stern than she had ever seen him.

Katie swallowed past the raw ache in her throat, and tried to drag air through the thick ropes of tension in her chest. "Padre Gregorio," she said in a ragged, pleading voice. "I know what you must think of me, and I don't blame you, but I never understood until last night why it would be so humiliating for Ramon to have me paying for things, especially in the village. Yesterday, Ramon discovered what I have been doing, and he was furious. I—I've never seen anyone so furious in my life." Her voice dropped to a suffocated whisper. "He's sending me back home."

She searched his austere face, hoping for some sign of empathy or compassion, but he was staring at her with narrowed piercing eyes. "I—I don't want to go," she choked. She lifted her hand in a helpless, beseeching gesture, and to Katie's utter horror, tears flooded her eyes and began racing down her cheeks. Too humiliated to even look at him, Katie tried unsuccessfully to brush away the torrent of tears streaming down her face. "I want to stay here with him," she added fiercely.

The priest's voice was a gentle whisper. "Why, Katherine?"

Katie's head snapped up in amazement. He had never called her "Katherine" before, and she was almost as stunned by that as she was by the incredible tenderness in his voice. Through a haze of tears she stared at him. He was walking toward her, a smile slowly dawning across his features and illuminating his whole face.

He stopped in front of her and prodded gently, "Tell me why, Katherine."

The warmth and approval in his smile began to melt the icy misery in Katie's heart. "I want to stay because I want to marry Ramon—I don't want to avoid the marriage anymore," Katie admitted with childlike candor. Her voice gained strength as she continued, "I promise you I'll make him happy. I know I can. And he—he makes me very happy."

Padre Gregorio's smile positively beamed, and to Katie's profound joy and relief he began asking her the same questions he had tried to ask her on Monday. "Will you put Ramon's needs before your own?"

"Yes," Katie whispered.

"Will you commit yourself entirely to this marriage, putting its success ahead of all other priorities in your life?"

Katie nodded emphatically.

"Will you honor Ramon and respect his wishes?"

Katie nodded vigorously and added, "I'll be the most perfect wife you've ever seen."

Padre Gregorio's lips twitched. "Will you obey him, Katherine?"

Katie looked at him accusingly. "You said you weren't going to ask me to promise that."

"And if I did ask you?"

Katie briefly weighed the beliefs of a lifetime against her entire future. She looked right into Padre Gregorio's eyes and said, "I would promise."

His eyes lit with laughter. "Actually, I was only inquiring about that."

Katie breathed a sigh of relief. "Good, because I'd never have kept the promise." Imploringly she said, "Now will you marry us?"

"No."

He said it so kindly that for a moment Katie thought she had misunderstood him. "No?" she repeated. "Why—why not?"

"Because you have not yet told me the one thing I need to hear you say."

Katie's heart flung itself against her ribs with a sickening thud, and the color drained from her face. She closed her eyes, trying to shut out the memory of herself screaming those words, willing herself to say the words again now. "I—" Her voice broke. "I can't. I can't say it. I want to, but I—"

"Katherine!" Padre Gregorio said in bewildered alarm. "Here, sit down," he said quickly, gently pushing her into the nearest pew. He sat down beside her, his kindly face a study of anxiety and concern. "You do not have to say you love him, Katherine," he hastily reassured her. "I can see perfectly well that you do. But can you at least tell me why you find it so painful to admit, and so impossible to say?"

White-faced, Katie turned her head and looked at him in helpless consternation and shuddered. In a voice that was a raw whisper, she said, "I keep remembering the last time I said it."

"Child, whatever happened, you cannot carry it around inside of you like this. Have you never told anyone?"

"No," Katie said hoarsely. "No one. My father would have tried to kill David—my husband. By the time my parents came back from Europe the bruises were healed, and Anne, their maid, promised never to say how I looked the night I came back to their house."

"Can you try to tell me what happened?" he asked softly.

Katie looked at her hands lying limply in her lap. If talking about it would finally exorcise David from her mind, from her life, she was ready to try. She spoke haltingly at first, and then the horror came pouring out in a torrent of choked, anguished words.

When she was finished, Katie leaned against the back of the pew, emotionally exhausted, drained of everything—even, she realized with a jolt of surprise—the pain. Hearing herself talking about David out loud had made her realize that there was no similarity between Ramon and David; none at all. David had been a selfish, egotistical, sadistic monster, while Ramon wanted to love and protect and provide for her. And even when she had defied, humiliated and infuriated Ramon, he had not physically abused her. What had happened in the past belonged there.

Katie glanced at Padre Gregorio and realized that he seemed to have shouldered her whole burden. He looked positively shattered. "I feel much better," she said softly, hoping to cheer him up.

Padre Gregorio spoke for the first time since she had begun her story. "Is Ramon aware of what happened to you that night?"

"No. I couldn't talk about it. And anyway, I didn't really think it was bothering me anymore. I hardly ever think of David."

"It was bothering you," Padre Gregorio contradicted. "And you have been thinking of him, whether you realized it or not. Otherwise, you would have simply confronted Ramon with your suspicion that he was not entirely what he said he was. You did not confront him because in your heart you were afraid of what you might learn. Because of your terrible experience, you automatically assumed that whatever secret there was in Ramon would be as frightening as the secrets you discovered in this other man."

He was quietly thoughtful for several minutes, then he seemed to snap out of his pensive reverie. "I think it would be best if you confided in Ramon before your wedding night. There is always the possibility that because of your memories you will experience some understandable revulsion when you are again faced with the intimacy between a man and wife. Ramon should be prepared for that."

Katie smiled and confidently shook her head. "I won't feel any revulsion at all with Ramon, so there's no need to worry."

"You're probably right." Unexpectedly, Padre Gregorio's expression darkened to an irritated, thoughtful scowl. "Even if you do react to the marital intimacies with fright, I am certain that Ramon has enough experience with women to be able to handle any problems of that sort."

"I'm absolutely certain he can," Katie assured, laughing at Padre Gregorio's grumpy, censuring expression. The old priest's narrowed gaze swerved to Katie's laughing face. "Not *that* certain," she corrected hastily.

Approvingly, he nodded. "It is good that you have made him wait."

To her mortification, Katie felt her cheeks pinken. Padre Gregorio saw it, too. His bushy white brows lifted and he peered at her over the rim of his gold spectacles. "Or that Ramon has made *you* wait," he amended astutely.

They both glanced over their shoulders as some tourists entered the church. "Come, we can finish this discussion better outside," he said. They walked down the steps and stood on the plaza surrounding the church. "What are you going to do now?" he asked.

Katie bit her lip and glanced toward the general store. "I suppose," she said with obvious reluctance, "I could bring back the things I bought there and say in front of everyone that Ramon wouldn't . . . wouldn't . . ." she choked on the word, "*permit* me to keep them."

Padre Gregorio threw back his head and the plaza rang with his laughter. Across the street several villagers turned to stare as they emerged with parcels from the shops. "Permit and obey . . . that is most encouraging," he chuckled. Then he shook his head at her suggestion. "I do not think Ramon would want you to do that. He would not want to buy back his pride at the cost of your own. You might offer to do it, however. That would help convince him you are truly repentant."

Katie slanted him a jaunty, teasing look. "Do you still think I lack meekness, docility and a respect for authority?"

"I sincerely hope so," he said with a warm smile at her sparkling face. "As Ramon rather bluntly informed me, he has no desire to marry a cocker spaniel."

Katie's smile faded. "He has no desire to marry me, either, right now."

"Do you want me to come with you when you speak to him?"

Katie shook her head after a moment's thought. "When I came into the church, that was what I was going to ask you to do. I was terrified of his anger yesterday, and he actually threatened to make David seem like an saint."

"Did Ramon raise his hand to you?"

"No."

Padre Gregorio's lips twitched. "If he did not strike you with the provocation he had yesterday, I am certain he never will."

"I suppose I always knew that," Katie admitted. "It was probably just thinking about David that made me so afraid of Ramon yesterday and today."

Clasping his hands behind his back, Padre Gregorio beamed his general approval upon the mountains, the sky, the village and the villagers. "Life can be so good if you let it, Katherine. But you must trade with life. You give something and you get something, then you give something of yourself again and you receive something again. Life goes bad when people try to take from it without giving. Then they came away empty-handed, and they grab harder and more often, growing more disappointed and disillusioned each time." He grinned at her. "Since you are not afraid of Ramon doing physical violence to you, I assume you do not need me?"

"Actually I do," Katie said with a wry look at Garcia who was standing sentry beside the Rolls, his arms crossed over his chest, his eyes following her every move. "I think Ramon instructed Garcia to get me off this island, and if I've missed my plane that man will put me in a boat, a box or a bottle, but he'll do what Ramon told him to do. Do you think you could convince him to take me back to Gabriella's, and also tell him I want to surprise Ramon, so he shouldn't mention that I didn't leave?"

"I think I can handle that," he said, putting his hand under her elbow and walking with her toward the car. "A 'self-important, self-righteous' man such as myself ought to be able to intimidate one chauffeur."

"I'm terribly sorry about the things I said," Katie said contritely.

Padre Gregorio's blue eyes laughed at her. "One has a tendency to acquire those rather unattractive traits after wearing these robes for forty years. I confess that since you said that to me, I have done some serious soul-searching trying to discover if you were right."

"Is that what you were doing when I interrupted you in church a while ago?"

His face shadowed. "It was a moment of deepest sorrow, Katherine. I had seen you passing by the church in Ramon's car, and I knew you were leaving. I had hoped and prayed that before it came to that you would realize what was in your heart. Despite everything you said and did, I felt that you loved him. Now, shall I see if I can convince the loyal Garcia that it is in Ramon's best interest for him to disobey Ramon's instructions?"

When the Rolls pulled into Gabriella's yard, Katie debated about having Garcia take her up to the cottage instead. The problem was that Ramon might not come back to the cottage for days, and Katie had no idea how to find him. Gabriella would help her, so long as Eduardo could be kept from finding out.

She lifted her hand to knock on the door, but it was flung open. Instead of Gabriella, Eduardo was standing there, his face uncompromising and forbidding. "You are not leaving?"

"No, I—" Katie began pleadingly, but the rest of her sentence was cut off by Eduardo's crushing bear hug.

"Gabriella said I was wrong about you," he whispered gruffly. With an arm thrown around her shoulders, he drew her into the living room to face Gabriella's shining countenance. "She told me you had courage." He sobered abruptly. "You are going to need a great deal of it to face Ramon. . . . He will be twice as angry at being twice defied."

"Where do you think he'll go tonight?" Katie asked bravely.

Ramon sat with one hip perched on his desk, his weight braced on the opposite foot. His expression betrayed no emotion as he listened to Miguel and the four auditors who were seated on the luxuriously upholstered sofa at the far end of his office, discussing the bankruptcy papers that they were preparing to file.

Ramon's gaze was turned toward the windows of his high-rise San Juan office as he watched a jet climbing in a wide arc into the blue afternoon sky. Based on the time, he knew it was Katie's plane. His eyes followed it, clinging to it as it diminished to a silver speck on the horizon.

"As far as you personally are concerned, Ramon," Miguel spoke up, "there is no need to file bankruptcy. You have enough to cover your outstanding debts. The banks that loaned you the money, which you in turn loaned to the corporation, will foreclose on the island, houses, plane, yacht, art collection, etc., and recover their money by selling them to others. The only other personal debts you have are for the two office buildings you were constructing in Chicago and St. Louis."

Miguel reached across the large coffee table in front of him and picked up a sheet of paper from one of the stacks. "The banks that loaned you part of the construction money are preparing to sell the buildings to other investors. Naturally, those investors will make the profit when they finish the buildings and sell them. Unfortunately, they will also be able to keep most of the twenty million dollars of your own money that you put into each build-ing." He glanced apologetically at Ramon. "You probably knew this already?"

Ramon nodded impassively.

Behind him, the buzzer on his desk sounded and Elise's agitated voice burst over the intercom. "Mr. Sidney Green is calling from St. Louis again. He is very insistent about speaking with you, Señor Galverra. He is swearing at me," she added tersely. "And shouting."

"Tell him that I said to call me another time when he feels more com-posed, and then disconnect the call," Ramon said curtly.

Miguel smiled. "No doubt he is somewhat distressed about the rumors his competition is now spreading that his paint is defective. It is all over the *Wall Street Journal* and the business sections of the American papers."

One of the auditors glanced at Miguel with wry amusement for his naiveté. "I imagine he's a hell of a lot more upset about his stock. Green Paint and Chemical was selling for twenty-five dollars a share two weeks ago; it was down to thirteen dollars this morning. There seems to be something of a panic."

Miguel leaned back into the sofa and folded his arms complacently. "I wonder what could be wrong?" He straightened immediately at Ramon's sharp frown, however.

"Are you talking about Sidney Green from St. Louis?" The thin, bespec-tacled auditor on the right end of the sofa looked up for the first time from his ledger sheets. "That's the name of the man who heads the group who is planning to take over the office building you were constructing in St. Louis, Ramon. They've already made the bank an offer to buy it and finish it."

"That vulture!" Miguel hissed, and launched into a string of savage expletives.

Ramon didn't hear him. All of the roiling pain and fury he felt over los-ing Katie was exploding inside of him in a volcanic surge of pure rage that now had a target he could strike: Sidney Green. "He is also on the board of directors of that same bank, and it refused to extend my construction loan so that I could finish the building," he said in a low, threatening voice.

Behind him, the buzzer went off on his desk. Ramon answered it auto-matically while the auditors gathered up their papers, preparing to leave. "Señor Galverra," Elise said. "Mr. Green is on the line. He says he feels more composed now."

"Put him on," Ramon said softly.

Green's voice exploded over the speaker system. "Bastard!" he screamed. Ramon nodded a curt dismissal to the auditors, and flicked a look at Miguel that invited him to stay. "You dirty bastard, are you there?" Green shouted.

Ramon's voice was quiet, controlled and very dangerous. "Now that we have exhausted the topic of my legitimacy, shall we get down to business?"

"I don't have any business with you, you—"

"Sid," Ramon said in a silky voice, "you are annoying me, and I become very unreasonable when I am annoyed. You owe me twelve million dollars."

"I owe you three million!" Sid thundered.

"With interest it is now over twelve million. You have been drawing interest on my money for nine years; I want it back."

"Go to hell!" Sid hissed.

"I am in hell," Ramon replied with no expression in his voice. "And I want you with me. Beginning today, it is going to cost you one million dollars for each day the money remains unpaid."

"You can't do that, you don't have that much influence, you arrogant son of a—"

"Just watch me," Ramon bit out, then he broke the connection.

Miguel leaned forward eagerly, "Do you have that much influence, Ramon?"

"No."

"But if he believes you do—"

"If he believes it, he is a fool. If he is a fool, he will not want to risk 'losing' another million today, and he will call back within three hours so that he can get the money into my bank in St. Louis before it closes tonight."

Three hours and fifteen minutes later, Miguel was slumped morosely in his chair, his tie loose, his jacket open. Ramon glanced up from the papers he was signing and said, "I know you did not stop to have lunch. Now it is dinnertime. Call downstairs and order some food to be sent up from the restaurant. If we are going to work late, you should have something to eat."

Miguel paused with his hand on the phone. "Don't you want anything, Ramon?"

The question brought an image of Katie, and Ramon closed his eyes against the wrenching pain. "No."

Miguel called down to the restaurant and ordered sandwiches. When he hung up the phone, it rang again.

"Elise has gone home for the day," Ramon said, answering it himself. For a moment he was very still, then he reached out and pressed the speaker button.

Sidney Green's strangled voice filled the elegant office. ". . . need to know which bank."

"No bank," Ramon said curtly. "Deliver it to my St. Louis attorneys." He gave the name and address of the firm, then added, "Have them call me at this number when the check is in their hands."

Thirty minutes later, Ramon's attorney called. When Ramon replaced the phone he looked at Miguel, whose eyes were feverish with excitement. "How can you just sit there like that, Ramon? you've just made twelve million dollars."

Ramon's smile was ironic. "Actually, I have just made forty million. I will use the twelve million to buy stock in Green Paint and Chemical. Within two weeks I will be able to sell it for twenty million. I will take that twenty million and use it to finish the building in St. Louis. When I sell the building in six months, I will get back the twenty million I originally invested, plus this twenty million."

"Plus whatever profit you make on the building."

"Plus that," Ramon agreed flatly.

Miguel was eagerly pulling on his suit coat. "Let's go out and celebrate," he said, straightening his tie. "We'll call it a combination bachelor and success party."

Ramon's eyes turned enigmatic. "There is no need for a 'bachelor' party. I forgot to mention that I am not getting married on Sunday. Katie . . . changed her mind." Ramon pulled open the large file drawer on his right, carefully avoiding the astonished regret he knew he would see on his friend's face. "Go out and celebrate my 'success' for both of us. I want to look over the file on that building."

A short time later, Ramon glanced up to see a boy standing in front of his desk, holding two white paper sacks. "Someone phoned downstairs and ordered sandwiches, sir," he said, looking around in awe at the palatial office.

"Just leave them there," Ramon nodded toward the coffee table across the room and absently reached into the inside pocket of his suit coat. He took out his wallet and rifled through it looking for some one-dollar bills to give the boy as a tip.

The smallest he had was a five-dollar bill—Katie's five-dollar bill. He had never intended to part with it, and had folded it in half, then half again, to distinguish it from other money he would ever carry; a memento he'd treasured from a red-haired angel with laughing blue eyes.

Ramon felt as if he was shattering into a thousand pieces as he slowly pulled Katie's money out of his wallet. His fingers tightened convulsively around it, and then he forced himself to let it go. Just as he had forced himself to let Katie go. He opened his hand and gave the crumpled bill to the eager boy.

When the boy left, Ramon looked down at his wallet. Katie's money was gone. Katie was gone. He was an extremely wealthy man again. Bitter rage boiled up inside of him, and his hand clenched into a fist with the savage urge to smash something.

🌿20

*E*duardo ran his hand through his rumpled dark hair and glanced at Katie whose pale face was reflecting her mounting tension. "The security guard said he left the building three hours ago, at nine o'clock. Garcia picked him up in the Rolls, but neither Garcia nor Ramon returned to the villa in Mayagüez, nor is Ramon at his house in Old San Juan."

Katie bit her lip apprehensively. "Do you think Garcia might have told Ramon that I didn't leave, and Ramon is just refusing to answer the phone?"

Eduardo's look was filled with derisive scorn. "If Ramon knew you were still here, he would not be hiding from you—he would have descended on this house like forty devils, believe me."

"Eduardo," Gabriella said with an exasperated sigh, "You are petrifying Katie, and she is nervous enough without that."

Jamming his hands into his back pockets, Eduardo stopped pacing and stood looking down at Katie. "Katie, I do not know where he could be. He is not at either of his houses, nor is he staying with Rafael's family. I cannot think where else he would choose to spend the night."

Katie tried to ignore the painful stab of jealousy she felt at the possibility that Ramon might well have decided to spend the night in the arms of the beautiful woman he was often pictured with in the local magazine clippings. "I was so certain he would go to the cottage," she said. "You're positive he wasn't there?"

Eduardo was emphatic. "I told you, I went there. It was only ten-thirty, too early for him to go to sleep, but there were no lights on inside."

Katie bent her head abjectly, twisting her fingers in her lap. "If things had been reversed, I would have gone there—where I could feel closest to him."

"Katie," Gabriella said with sympathetic determination. "I know where you are thinking he is, but you are wrong. He would not turn to another woman tonight."

Katie was too preoccupied to see the dubious look Eduardo tossed at his wife. "You knocked when you went to the cottage, didn't you?" Katie said.

Eduardo's head swung to her. "Why should I knock on the door of a dark, empty house? Besides, Ramon would have seen the car lights coming up the driveway. He would have come out to see who was there."

Katie's smooth brow furrowed. "I think you should have knocked." She stood up more out of restlessness than anything else, and then said, "I think I'll go up to the cottage."

"Katie, he is not there, but if you insist on going, I will go with you."

"I'll be fine," Katie reassured.

"I do not want you to confront Ramon alone," Eduardo persisted. "I saw how furious he was yesterday, I was with him, and—"

"I was with him too," Katie reminded him gently. "And I'm positive I'll be fine. He can't be much angrier than he was yesterday."

Eduardo dug in his pocket and pulled out the car keys, handing them to her. "If I believed for a minute he is there now, I would come with you, but he is not. You are going to have to wait until tomorrow to talk to him."

"My parents are arriving tomorrow," Katie said desperately. She looked at the clock ticking ominously on the wall. "It's after midnight—technically this is Saturday morning. I'm getting married on Sunday—that's tomorrow."

Remembering what Eduardo had said about Ramon seeing the car lights coming up the driveway, Katie drove the last hundred yards without them. If Ramon was there, she thought it would be best to have the element of surprise on her side. Particularly because she didn't relish the idea of confronting a furious Ramon on the doorstep.

Up ahead a faint light was visible through the swaying branches of the trees and Katie's heart gave a wild leap of joy as she stopped the car. She walked up the moonlit brick path, her knees shaking harder with each step. The bedroom lamp was on!

She reached for the door handle, mumbling a disjointed prayer that it wouldn't be locked because she had no key, and breathed a sigh of relief when it opened easily. She closed it cautiously, then turned around. The living room was in shadow, but there was the mellow glow of lamplight streaming into it through the open doorway from the bedroom.

This was it. She pulled the sweater off her shoulders and dropped it on the floor. She ran shaky hands over the clingy cinnamon dress she had delib- erately chosen hours ago with the specific intention of tantalizing Ramon and hopefully weakening his resistance. It scooped very low in the front, exposing a glimpse of deep cleavage, had narrow shoulder straps, no sleeves and virtually no back. She combed her fingers through her long hair, then started walking very quietly.

In the bedroom doorway, Katie stopped to steady her rioting nerves—Ramon was lying on the bed, his hands clasped behind his head, staring at the ceiling. His white shirt was unbuttoned nearly to his waist, and he hadn't bothered to take off his shoes. His profile was so bitter and desolate that Katie's chest filled with remorse. She gazed at the dark, austere beauty of his face, the power and virility stamped in every line of his long body, and her pulse raced with a mixture of excitement and trepidation. Even lying down, Ramon seemed like a very formidable opponent.

She took one step into the room, throwing a shadow on the ceiling across his line of vision.

Ramon's head twisted toward her, and Katie froze.

He stared at her, his stark black eyes piercing through her as though he wasn't really seeing her at all.

"I didn't leave," Katie whispered inanely.

At the sound of her voice, Ramon shot up and off the bed in one lithe, terrifying lunge.

His granite features were an impenetrable mask, and Katie was too nervous to notice anything about his mood except that he was tensed, ready to spring at her. "I—I didn't want to go," she stammered. He stepped forward and Katie stepped back. "Padre Gregorio says he'll marry us," she told him quickly.

"Oh, is that right?" Ramon said in a low voice.

He started toward her and Katie started backing away. "I—I'll take back everything I paid for," she volunteered as he stalked her through the bedroom doorway and into the living room.

"Will you, now?" Ramon breathed softly.

Katie nodded vigorously, backing into the sofa and moving around it. "I—I saw Rafael's scrapbook," she explained breathlessly. "If you'd only told me who you really are, I would have understood why you didn't want me to pay for anything. I would have obey—" she choked on the word "—obeyed you."

"I see you have learned a new word," Ramon mocked.

Katie bumped into the lamp table and scooted sideways around it. "I'll fill the whole house with plants and ruffles and children," she promised desperately. The backs of her legs hit the chair, blocking any further retreat, and uncontrollable panic welled in Katie's throat. "You have to listen to me! I was afraid to marry you because I knew that you were hiding something from me, but I didn't know what it was, and David had—"

Ramon closed the distance and Katie put her hand out trying to fend him off. "Please listen to me," she cried out. "I love you!"

His hands gripped her shoulders pulling her against him with enough force to snap Katie's head back. For the first time she was close enough to see the expression in those smouldering eyes, and what she saw was not anger. It was love—a love so intense that she was humbled by it.

"You love me," he repeated in a strangely gruff voice. "And I suppose you thought that if you told me you love me, I would forget everything else and forgive you?"

"Yes," Katie whispered. "I thought you might. J—just this once."

"Just this once," he murmured in tender amusement, and his hand trembled as he laid it against her cheek, slowly running it back to smooth her hair. He made a sound that was half groan, half laugh as his fingers sank into her hair. "Just this once?" he repeated as if it were the greatest of understatements, and his other arm crushed her to him, his mouth capturing hers in a deep devouring kiss.

With joy and relief bursting like fireworks in her heart, Katie slid her hands up his hard chest, around his neck, and welcomed his tongue into her mouth. She arched herself against his rigid thighs, and Ramon shuddered with pleasure, his hands rushing over her shoulders and back, then lower, pulling her hips tighter to him.

He tore his mouth from hers and brushed scorching kisses over her temple, her forehead, her eyes and her cheek. "Say it again," he ordered hoarsely.

"I love you," Katie told him with a throbbing ache in her voice. "And I need you . . . and I want you . . . and I . . ."

Ramon's mouth opened ravenously over hers, silencing her words and sending her spinning off into a world where nothing existed but the fiery demands of his hands and mouth and body. He kissed her again and again, until Katie was moaning and moving against him, her body wracked with fierce, wild jolts of desire.

He took his mouth from hers, and gazed down into her glorious, sultry eyes. "Come to bed, *querida*," he murmured hotly.

Katie spread her flattened hands inside the open front of his shirt, her fingers moving over his hair-roughened chest, but to Ramon's frustrated disappointment, the beautiful woman in his arms said very softly, "No."

"Yes," he whispered, already bending his head with every intention of kissing away her objections, but this time she shook her head.

"No," she repeated. Smiling with wistful regret, she explained. "Eduardo didn't want me to confront you alone. The only reason he let me come was because he was positive you weren't here. I didn't come right back, so he's bound to have started up here on foot—to defend me from your wrath." Ramon's brows drew together in annoyance, and Katie smoothed her fingers over his heart, her smile widening. "And there are two other reasons why I'd like to wait. One is that we need to talk. You asked me for honesty, insisted on it, and then you deliberately misled me. I would like to understand why you did."

Ramon's arms loosened slightly, reluctantly. "What is the other reason?" he asked gently.

Katie ruefully looked away from him. "Tomorrow is our wedding day. We've waited this long already, and, well, Padre Gregorio—"

Ramon burst out laughing and swept her up into his arms. "When we were young, Eduardo, Miguel and I believed that if we did something wrong, Padre Gregorio would look into our eyes and he would know it." He carried her over to the sofa and settled her on his lap, his arm around her waist.

"Did it keep you from doing anything wrong?" Katie teased.

"No," Ramon admitted with a grin. "But it kept us from enjoying it."

In the dimly lit quiet of the living room she had decorated for him, Ramon explained to Katie why he had misled her and then, as simply as he could, he explained how the events of the day had drastically altered the prospects for their future. She listened to the story of Sidney Green, her face alight with laughter, her quick, intelligent mind easily comprehending the pressure Ramon had brought on Sidney Green and the havoc he had wrought on Green Paint and Chemical. Yet when he was finished, Katie's excited elation faded slightly.

"Katie, what is wrong?" he asked her softly.

Katie looked around at the cozy room where they sat. "Nothing, really. It's just that I'll miss this house; I could have been very happy here."

Ramon touched her chin, turning her face up to his. "You will like your other houses much better."

Katie frowned in puzzlement. "I thought you said the houses and the island were going to be taken away by the banks."

"It is still possible," Ramon said, "but it is not likely. Banks are like scavengers. When they scent a failure, they are quick to close in to ensure that they get their share of what is left. But if the 'failure' suddenly shows signs of recovery, they are just as quick to back away. They will wait and watch. They will consider how much more they have to gain if I should prosper, as I have in the past. My St. Louis lawyers tell me that Sidney Green has been crying to everyone from St. Louis to New York that I have been manipulating his stock and driving him out of business. The banks will hear that, and they will wonder if perhaps they have underestimated my influence. They will continue to circle, and to watch, but they will begin backing further away. When I resume construction of the St. Louis high-rise, the Chicago bank will scent a profit and they will decide to reconsider loaning me the money to finish the Chicago high-rise.

"So you see," he concluded, "you will have your houses and servants and—"

"—and nothing to do," Katie finished with a wan smile. "Because you think a woman's place is at home."

Ramon's eyes narrowed. "A moment ago, you said you could have been very happy here. Why can you not be happy in a more luxurious home?"

Katie, bracing for an argument, moved off his lap and walked over to the windows. She could feel Ramon's eyes on her back as she parted the curtains and stared out into the darkness, trying to think of a way to make him understand. "I said I could have been happy living here," she said quietly, "and I *could* have been—because we would have been working to build a life together. I would have felt useful and needed. I could still feel useful and needed, but you won't let me," she said.

Behind her, she heard Ramon get up and start toward her, and her voice gained determination. "You're going to begin rebuilding Galverra International, and my background is in personnel. I'm familiar with hiring practices and wage scales and government regulations and payroll procedures—I could help you, but you won't let me."

His hands settled on her shoulders, but Katie refused to turn as she continued. "I know how you feel about a woman working outside the home—you made that very clear the day of our picnic. You said that when a woman takes a job, it shows the world that what her husband can provide isn't good enough for her. You said that it hurts his pride and—"

Ramon's hands tightened on her shoulders. "Turn around and look at me," he interrupted gently.

Katie turned, half-expecting him to try to pacify her with a kiss. Instead he looked down at her with quiet gravity. "Katie, a man is always most sensitive about his pride when he knows in his heart that he has little of which to be proud." He tipped her chin up and gazed somberly into her eyes. "Telling a woman what her 'place' is, is a man's way of trying to make a woman settle for less than she has a right to expect. I was ashamed of how little I could offer you then, but I believed that I could make you feel happy and contented here, living simply as my wife. I was trying to convince you of the rightness of it, because that was the only argument, and the only future, I could offer. I would be very proud, and very pleased, to have you working with me now."

His head turned abruptly, and Katie followed his gaze. A small beam of light was tracing its way slowly up the long hill to the cottage. Eduardo, carrying a flashlight, was "coming to her rescue."

She glanced at Ramon, but instead of being irritated by Eduardo's impending arrival, he was grinning thoughtfully at her.

"What are you thinking about?" she asked him softly.

Ramon gazed down at her, his eyes dark with love. "I'm deciding what to give you for a wedding present."

Katie wrapped her arms tightly around his neck. *You are my wedding present,* she thought with aching tenderness. "What are my choices?" she twinkled.

"Either a baby or a Ferrari," he replied, grinning, and wrapped his arms around her. "You once said that a Ferrari would make your life 'absolutely ecstatic.'"

"I'd rather have a baby than a Ferrari," Katie laughed. Ramon laughed too, but he intended to give her both.

21

On a balmy June Sunday, Katherine Elizabeth Connelly walked slowly up the aisle of a stately old Spanish church, past the rows of shyly smiling villagers, to willingly and proudly meet her fate.

With sunlight streaming in rainbows through the stained-glass windows, she placed her hand in the hand of the tall, darkly handsome man who was waiting for her at the altar, and standing before a solemn priest with smiling blue eyes, she became Katherine de Galverra.

Ramon gazed down at the beautiful woman beside him, her shining hair entwined with flowers. He heard her saying her marriage vows, while other visions of her danced through his mind: Katie looking somberly beautiful and regally aloof in the singles' bar where they had met three weeks ago. . . .

Katie, handing him a five-dollar bill. "Please take it, Ramon. I'm sure you can use it."

Katie, her eyes glowing with merriment on their picnic as she accused him of being a male chauvinist. "It may surprise you to hear this, but not all women are born with a burning desire to chop onions and grate cheese."

Katie, dancing in his arms at the pool party, her lips still warm from their passionate kiss, her eyes dark and apprehensive. . . . "I think I am getting very scared."

And now, Katie, standing beside him in church. Katie, turning her face up to him: "I, Katherine, take you to be my lawfully wedded husband. . . .

Ramon looked down at her and joy exploded in his chest, pouring through his veins until it was almost past bearing.

Her glowing face was a picture he knew he would remember as long as he lived; her softly spoken words a benediction that lingered in his heart.

The memory was still vibrantly alive many hours later, when his wife finally came to him, the naked splendor of her body bathed in moonlight streaming through the bedroom window of the cottage. He watched her, aching to give her the world and everything in it, because she had already given him so much.

Love tightened his throat as her arms drew him to her, and he covered her body with his. Tenderness burst within him when she unashamedly welcomed him into her incredible warmth.

They moved together, two people making wild beautiful love to each other, until Katie finally cried out in shivering ecstasy; then he gathered her into his arms and, whispering her name, Ramon gave her the only gift that was his alone to give. He gave her himself.